Flowers In The Rain

The Untold Story of The Move

Jim McCarthy

WP
WYMER
PUBLISHING
Bedford, England

First published in 2024 by Wymer Publishing, Bedford, England
www.wymerpublishing.co.uk Tel: 01234 326691
Wymer Publishing is a trading name of Wymer (UK) Ltd.

Copyright © 2024 Jim McCarthy / Wymer Publishing.

Print edition (fully illustrated): **ISBN: 978-1-915246-59-2**
eBook formatting by Lin White at Coinlea Services.

Edited by Jerry Bloom.

The Author hereby asserts his rights to be identified
as the author of this work in accordance with sections
77 to 78 of the Copyright, Designs & Patents Act 1988.

All rights reserved. No part of this publication may be
reproduced or transmitted in any form or by any means,
electronic or mechanical, including photocopying, or any
information storage and retrieval system, without written
permission from the publisher.

This publication is sold subject to the condition that it shall not,
by way of trade or otherwise, be lent, re-sold, hired out or
otherwise circulated without the publisher's prior consent in any
form of binding or cover other than that in which it is published
and without a similar condition including this condition
being imposed on the subsequent purchaser.

A catalogue record for this book is available from the British Library.

Printed by CMP, Dorset, England

Typeset/Design by Andy Bishop / Tusseheia Creative.
Cover design: Jim McCarthy.
Original cover photos: © Robert Davidson (The Move in Hyde Park, London, 1966).
All inside photography: © Robert Davidson

"Without doubt, it was the Beatles, The Stones and The Move in that order, in England."
Tony Secunda, The Move manager

*"We hit the lights of London,
we took them by surprise.
Five hard kids from Birmingham,
with stardust in our eyes.
We played the game of hit-and-run,
we never did count the cost!"*
**Hit and Run, Trevor Burton.
(Original member of The Move)**

*"A cruise ship performer
surrounded by psyched-out hippies
and gone wrong Mods"*
John Cooper Clarke

Contents

Foreword by Paul Weller — 9

1. Psychedelic Anarchists — 11
2. In this profession people rush to cut you down to size — 19
3. Vote for Me! Sign across the line — 25
4. When I was a little boy my mama dropped me on my head — 27
5. Is there any truth in what they say? — 45
6. Please correct me if I seem to be making too much noise! — 49
7. So tomorrow won't be long…you're going to have to play it cool — 63
8. On a short vacation with my friends… — 71
9. Just about to flip your mind… — 81
10. Tear the world right off its hinges — 87
11. Ready Steady Go! — 103
12. I Can Hear The Grass Grow — 113
13. It seems that all my freaky clothes are turning into rags — 117
14. And this is where we came in, dear reader — 129
15. Come With Me — 141
16. "Psychedelic music is a load of shit…" — 153
17. Just about to trip your mind… — 159
18. I'm sure my brain, it had enough? — 163
19. I see rainbows in the evening… — 167
20. This crappy west coast hippie scene is becoming quite a drag — 173
21. The lights across the street, threw a rainbow in her hair — 177
22. Move! Move! Move! — 183
23. See the people all in line, what's making them look at me? — 199
24. Holiday in Reality — 209
25. She's sure good looking man, she's something else… — 215
26. Ever since, there's been a slight disturbance in my mind — 225
27. Hundreds of people – left out in the cold — 231
28. But can it last another day? — 235
29. Lying in wait for the moon to break… — 255
30. Is there something that you've wanted? More than anything? — 279

31.	"Go home to Birmingham and get yourself sorted out — or else you're going to die!"	**287**
32.	Let the wind blow you out of my memory, Let the rain wash you out of my eyes	**289**
33.	Lightning never strikes twice in the same place…	**293**
34.	Bound together by a legend - to protect us and defend…	**295**
35.	In this sad position where I lie, callous friends just pass me by…	**297**
36.	Why don't you turn around and look at me? I often wish I knew you…	**301**
	Chris 'Ace' Kefford	*301*
	Carl Wayne	*314*
	Roy Wood	*323*
	Trevor Burton	*336*
	Rick Price.	*338*
	Steve Gibbons	*339*
	Jeff Lynne	*340*
	Bev Bevan	*341*

Afterword by Glen Matlock **351**

Appendices:

Cancelled USA concerts: 1968-1969	*353*
Chelita Secunda (Salvatori)	*355*
Tony Secunda	*358*
Discography	*385*
TV and radio appearances performances: 1966-1971	*393*
Acknowledgements	*397*
About The Author	*399*

Jim respectfully dedicates
this deep dive with love and respect to:
Ronnie Doctrove (RIP), Danny Healy, Elaine Yeo,
Paulette/Lavinia McNulty-Harrison,
Orlando Gray, Piers Secunda, Michael Shrieve,
Tracy Young and Karl Hopper-Young,
Baz St. Leger, Dave Thompson
Rob Caiger and Tony Ware.
- and those powerhouse five young men -
Carl, Ace, Trevor, Roy and Bev.

Foreword

The Move came into my orbit in 1967 (a great year for music) after hearing, 'I Can Hear The Grass Grow' and later that year 'Flowers In The Rain'. Both were pop classics. Thereafter I heard that whole run of great singles. I saw them on TV for the first time with 'Fire Brigade' in 1968. They were going through the rocker look, rock 'n' roll had made a bit of a comeback in early 1968 and to me, they looked so cool. All of their sartorial looks they did well.

They had that "gang" look about them too. Tough and a certain menace about them. Very powerful stuff to see when you're 10 years old! Not quite Britain's Got Talent. Anyway, I was a fan for sure and all these years later, I'm still a fan.

Not only were they all great musicians, but they could also all sing (Roy and Ace's voices alone, are great and they're not even the lead vocalists!) They looked great and Roy Wood would be writing some of the era's greatest tunes too. Unique songs with his melodies and lyrics. So much talent in one band! One of the greatest things about YouTube is now we get to see so many great clips of stuff never seen before. The footage of The Move playing the *NME* Poll Winners concert in 1967 is just incredible! They are all playing so tight, so powerful, swapping the vocal parts.

Ace Kefford looking and moving so cool! Carl with his 'tache looking the bollocks. I just love that footage.

It's futile to compare The Move to any other of the 1960s groups. They all had such unique sounds and styles.

They were all pioneers! There was no one else like The Move – Carl, Roy, Bev, Ace and Trevor can be safe in that knowledge and us fans too! They are one of the great 60s bands and their music lives on…

P.S. Here's a little Move tale — in 1995 whilst shopping in West Byfleet. I bumped into Carl Wayne who lived nearby. He was great and he had very good energy. He said he wanted to get the original Move members back together to make an album and he wanted me to produce it! *Obviously, it never happened, but I still dream about how it might have sounded!*

Paul Weller, December 2023

The Move; mods, axes, gangsters, flowers, MI5 and the Prime Minister!

1.
Psychedelic Anarchists

Tony Visconti recollects the joy of hearing 'Flowers In The Rain' being played on the fledgling new Radio One station. "I let out an almighty whoop as I heard it. I was driving down Edgware Road in London. I thought it was a definite hit." Visconti was the newly-arrived-in-London-town-New York producer. He was brought in by The Move's manager Tony Secunda to shore up production duties, during the recording of 'Flowers In The Rain'. Aiding both Denny Cordell and engineer Gerald Chevin at Advision Studios.

Robert Davidson the Move's official photographer remembers it all very clearly. "The Move were on a roll, remarkably they had yet another hit with their third record, 'Flowers in the Rain'. It really didn't need any extra gimmicks to help it sell. Since it was the first ever single to be played on Radio One and it reached number two in the UK charts. But because of the madcap way Tony Secunda chose to promote it, it turned out incredibly disastrous for The Move. To put the story in some kind of context — there was a rumour going round concerning Harold Wilson — The then Prime Minister of the United Kingdom. Secunda had thought, "There's some mileage to be got out of this. I know — great idea! Let's produce a cartoon."

It appeared to be common knowledge, that PM Harold Wilson was allegedly having an affair with his secretary, Marcia Williams. Although nobody had mentioned it in the press. There were good reasons for this. Marcia Williams was later elevated to Lady Falkender and became known as the 'Lavender Lady' because of her scented notepaper. There was an equally scurrilous rumour, that she had also influenced Harold Wilson's Honours list. Tony Secunda had heard the rumours about the alleged affair. Election time was round the corner, so he thought, 'Wouldn't it be a good idea to help the Tories get back in power. We can get some publicity out of this, by having a salacious postcard drawn by a famous artist.' And this is what he did, unbeknown to the constantly gigging band. Apparently in an interview years later Roy Wood said, "Carl Wayne was the only band member to see it. He showed it to a lawyer and the lawyer said, 'Stay away from it!'" Of course, Tony Secunda, had the band's name printed on the card.

Davidson continues, "At the top of this postcard in wavy writing it read: *Disgusting, Depraved, Despicable.* Below this was a picture of Harold Wilson in bed, smoking a pipe and reading a newspaper. Beside him in a four-poster bed was his secretary in curlers. Mrs Wilson is seen having a look through the curtains to see what is going on. That was the cartoon, which has never been seen since. I've still got a copy of a copy of it however."

Flowers In The Rain - The Untold Story of The Move

Lady Falkender was famously litigious.[1] Underneath the cartoon it said, 'The Move have got a new record out called 'Flowers in the Rain.' The connection with Harold Wilson, apart from all the rumours was tenuous. Robert Davidson continues the intriguing and essentially foolhardy tale. "Robert, we've got to get this postcard out there," says Tony Secunda. "Yes... How are you going to do that?" says I. "Mr Michael Foot... says Tony."

"Michael Foot, fellow Labour politician wasn't getting on that well with Wilson. Mr Wilson was on the right of the left, but Mr Foot was to the left of the left. As the MP for Devonport, he also had a house in Hampstead. Tony of course, knew where he lived. He decided it might be a good idea to visit Mr Foot early one morning. So, armed with his trusty photographer (me) and carrying hundreds of copies of the postcard, we arrived outside Mr Foot's London abode. He used to take his dog for an early morning walk at half past seven. This too, Tony appeared to know. At half past seven on the dot, out comes Mr Foot with two barking dogs. Tony walked up to him and saying, 'Mr Foot.'

'Who are you? Press? Go away!'

Tony said, 'No, no, no. I want to make you an offer that I think may be to your advantage. It could be mutually advantageous.'

I went up to take a picture.

'You are the Press! Paparazzi!'

Tony disagreed, 'No, I promote popular musicians.'

He then turned on the charm offensive, for which he was famous. He was good looking in an Italian way and smiled flashing his big teeth. He told Michael Foot that the elections were coming up and maybe this cartoon would help pull the rug out from under Mr Wilson's feet. It could be to his advantage.

'Perhaps, Mr Foot might like to put one of these postcards, on every single seat in the House of Commons?'

'I can't do that,' he retorted.

'I don't see any reason why you shouldn't, responded Tony and gave him the whole bundle of postcards.

****

The Move are holed up at the Madison Hotel. The date is 2nd September 1967. The Move's lead singer Carl Wayne is suddenly jarred awake. He was being showered with that morning's newspapers. The agitated bassist of the Move, Ace Kefford threw them all over the bed. His face looking ashen and drawn. "We're in the fucking shit man — have a look at this?"

Potentially and soon to become stern reality — indeed they were in the shit. In fact, they were at war with the British Prime Minister, Harold Wilson. The most powerful man in British politics. Ace Kefford reiterated, "I'm gonna leave the fucking country! When Carl Wayne asked where he would go, Ace answered readily, "The Isle of Wight!" Hilarious...as back in those days, the Isle of Wight may have seemed

---

1 Marcia Williams aka Lady Falkender died on 6th February 2019.

further enough away to offer some refuge. However, they had to do a gig (as usual) that very night at the UFO Festival, Roundhouse, North London, appearing with Pink Floyd, The Soft Machine and Denny Laine. Yet another gig on the ferocious, hard-working circuit, they had been operating on, since early January 1966.

The night before on 1st September 1967, The Move were playing The Locarno Ballroom in Basildon. Trevor Burton remembers the sudden blast of publicity with clarity, "We came out of a gig down South, and it was like being Elizabeth Taylor or something. There must've been like a hundred photographers and flashbulbs going off and we didn't know why. And one of the guys said, 'Oh, you're being sued by the Prime Minister!' We all said: 'WHAT!'"

Drummer Bev Bevan recalls the headlines: "I spilled my cuppa all over the breakfast table." He told the *Birmingham Post & Mail*: "We were trying to look blasé about the whole thing. But deep down we were scared stiff," adding, with commendable understatement: "it was very, very heavy."

What was very heavy? It was the fact that The Move and their sensationalistic, Svengali manager Tony Secunda were being sued by the extant Prime Minister. Wilson was not amused by the 'Flowers In The Rain' publicity card, or its contents. That was the precise heaviness in point. Splashed all over the front pages on the strewn pile of papers, Chris "Ace" Kefford had scattered over the bed were some impending and awful stark facts staring the band in their collective faces.

The news was spreading worldwide and even the worthy *TIME* magazine in the USA featured the story. Newspaper headlines included 'The Move sued by Prime Minister', 'Move served with Interim injunction', 'False and malicious rumours', 'Wilson Gets High Court Ban On The Move' 'Postcard brings writ against psychedelic anarchists!' 'Hit disc deal may settle the Wilson libel case.' 'Court hears of warning over libels.' 'Psychedelic' and 'Wilsons Court move against group.'

Heady stuff indeed, even for this hard-nosed bunch of Brummies who had already created an industry sensation in their first year. With their white-hot live shows, stage smashing, setting off flares, auto destruction and all the associated rebellious publicity. Most of which was hustled up by the scheming and unpredictable Tony Secunda.

Tony Secunda was one of an elite corps of pop group managers, who galvanised the Swinging Sixties and helped shape the course of popular music. Among the top ranks were astute publicists and ravenous wheelers-dealers like Andrew Loog Oldham and Kit Lambert. The men behind the Rolling Stones and the Who respectively.

But Secunda was perhaps the wildest and toughest of them all. He was the driving force behind some of the biggest hit-makers of the era, including The Moody Blues, The Move, Marc Bolan, Marianne Faithfull, Steeleye Span etc. Although latter days, saw him dropping out of music into other areas, such as tree conservation, book editorial and agenting etc., Secunda, was a dark, brooding and somewhat menacing figure. He thrived on taking risks and was not afraid to indulge in the most basic scams and publicity stunts. He achieved results for his artists, taking some of the mores of the underground hippie scene, straight into the boardrooms of the staid music industry.

Secunda came from Epsom and was educated at public school. He first came to notice, when he was managing The Moody Blues, the Birmingham R&B group fronted by the vocalist Denny Laine. Apparently, Carl Wayne was in some way an instigator of the link between Secunda and The Moody Blues. They needed a London-based manager in their quest for success and Secunda secured them a recording deal with Decca. They had a number one hit with 'Go Now' in 1965. Secunda had then specifically gone up to Birmingham to see and hear the buzz on another promising Midlands group, The Move.

They brazenly set out to rival the Who with a wild stage act involving their own brand of "Auto Destruction". Plus, a take-no-prisoners vocal approach, underpinned by loud, dynamically tight rock and soul music. Encouraged by Secunda, the band adopted a violent gangster image, complete with Chicago-style suits, while their lead singer, Carl Wayne, indulged in smashing up television sets and effigies on stage with a very large axe. Secunda worked in partnership with the producer Denny Cordell.

Psychedelic anarchists indeed!

The Move travelled to London after hearing this sledgehammer news regarding Harold Wilson. They held a pow wow at Secunda's London apartment. The Move, comprising of Roy Wood, vocals, lead guitarist and chief songwriter, lead vocalist Carl Wayne, Chris "Ace" Kefford on bass and vocals, vocalist and rhythm guitarist Trevor Burton, plus drummer Bev Bevan, had spent an anxious night at The Madison Hotel, awaiting the morning's news headlines with growing trepidation.

The present year 1967 was to become the so-called 'Summer of Love' and is now seen as a cultural watershed. With all of its attendant upheaval and far-reaching cultural aspects. It was the year of anti-Vietnam demonstrations. The emergence of North Sea Oil, The Beatles and *Sgt Pepper's Lonely Hearts Club Band*.

The Monterey Pop Festival was staged in Los Angeles. Jimi Hendrix releases his incendiary debut album *Are You Experienced*. The world's first heart transplant is performed by Doctor Christian Barnard. Plus, so much more was instigated in this feted year of tumultuous social change. 1967 has with the passage of time, become a byword for massive societal transformation. During all this turmoil, The Move found their place in history both assured and also strangely overlooked. The Move's exciting, dynamic, chaotic and musically supercharged story needed to be examined. As an extremely unique and important place, in a corner of the UK's music history.

Bev further recalls, "We stayed overnight at The Madison and we felt like our every move was being watched. We were very careful what we said — in case our hotel rooms were being bugged by the Secret Service. When we went out, we'd check the street for signs of suspicious-looking characters and we'd watch each other's backs, to make sure we weren't being tailed."

The band already had a reputation for lurid publicity and a hard, cocky on-stage demeanour, allied to a superior stage show. Carl Wayne the group's outgoing and extrovert front man, rightly described The Move in an insightful moment, years later as, "The original anarchist band, we were the first punks. Wilson had secured an injunction preventing any further printing or distribution of the postcards, and we had to go to court on 6th September — that was for the first hearing."

More alarm was felt by the startled Bev Bevan: "We thought that we were going to lose all our savings, the little bit of money we'd been putting by for our futures. Here we were, five ordinary blokes, being taken to court by one of the world's political leaders. The next thing I knew, a writ arrived. The front of it read: "James Harold Wilson v Anthony Secunda and others." I had two thoughts — one was that I never knew Wilson's first name was James and the other that I was one of these sinister others. It was very heavy…"

****

Some onlookers maintained The Move were better before they even released any charting records. Carl Wayne agrees with this assessment, "We absolutely were, because it was a fresh, new energetic band in which there was no disharmony on a personal level. Before the singles, we were a good, solid four- and five-part harmony group. Playing first some great soul and R&B to a very high-level. Then playing a lot of West Coast stuff and rock 'n' roll. After the singles, we were then labelled as a "pop band" with a good image. And that psychologically took its toll — but we were always a formidable live act."

The band's controversial antics were a precursor to The Sex Pistols by a good ten years. The Pistols manager Malcolm McLaren owed a heavy debt to Tony Secunda, with his dark Svengali-like management style for The Move. McLaren copied some of the Move's choice of repertoire; like Sid Vicious covering 'Something Else' by Eddie Cochran in 1979. Their version reached Number Three in the UK charts. The exact same cover as Trevor Burton's earlier raucous take on the *Something Else from The Move* EP. Some of The Pistol's publicity stunts were suspiciously similar to Secunda's earlier barrage of artifice. The contract signing on a female model's naked back by Carl Wayne, Roy Wood, Denny Cordell and Secunda. This was aped in a close sense by the Buckingham Palace contract signing — as the Pistols drove up in (you guessed it) a Rolls Royce. To sign the necessary record label papers with A&M as the second signing label, after they were dropped by EMI mucho pronto.

Carl Wayne: "Oh! Tony Secunda was incredible. He gave us the leadership and guidance that we needed. In our case, if you took The Move without Secunda, then the creativity was from Roy Wood, and we would have just been a band playing its hits. With Secunda he dreamed up all the ideas, the stunts and the clothing. Creatively he was a genius and he saw the embers of a great band that he was able to fire up! In many ways he was able to bring out the best in everybody — by bringing out the worst!"

The Move would also be cited as having a notable impact on The Sex Pistols iconic and anti-establishment second single, 'God Save The Queen'. Glen Matlock, the first Sex Pistols bassist remembered, "I got chatting to Roy Wood in my local once. I said to him that 'Fire Brigade' was not unlike the Pistols, he said: 'I had noticed'. 'No Future', which became 'God Save The Queen' was my riff." One got the distinct feeling that Secunda had devised a "rock managers" template. A template that certainly Malcolm McLaren and The Sex Pistols followed closely.

Ace Kefford remembered the feelings of paranoia, "The Move became ultra paranoid that MI5 were hot on our heels. It was all very James Bondesque and as daft as it sounds, we knew he had a licence to kill." For the young band, the whole thing had gotten way out of hand and it wasn't a laughing matter. Was libelling the Prime Minister an act of treason? They knew people got shot in other countries for doing similar things.

Ace Kefford again: "The next step was for Wilson to sue us for libel. That meant we had to go to court again. First court appearance was the injunction and then a second appearance to face the libel charges."

Bevan adds, "Secunda thought that we should make an impression, so we turned up at the High Court in a red Rolls Royce. It was hired of course. Everyone assumed that it was ours — but we couldn't afford one. Despite the hype — and we were getting more headlines than ever before — we didn't like the way that things were going at all. We didn't mind smashing up TV sets and carrying H-bombs through the streets. But this was a whole new ball game. It wasn't funny anymore. There was a real danger that they'd try to make an example of us?"

The establishment had had their fingers burned by the Rolling Stones drug case and the ensuing public reaction. They'd shut down the pirate Radio stations and suffered the backlash. Now they had their chance to finally win one for a change — and The Move were in the dock. Bev Bevan reveals, "The court hearings were nerve-racking, although you wouldn't have thought it to see us. We were trying to look blasé about the whole thing, but deep down we were scared stiff."

The wording printed on the postcard, which was sent out to 500 different people through Tony Secunda read as follows:

DISGUSTING - DEPRAVED - DESPICABLE THOUGH HAROLD MAY BE - BEAUTIFUL IS THE ONLY WORD TO DESCRIBE

FLOWERS IN THE RAIN - THE MOVE

The Move letters are drawn in a facsimile of The Move "official" logo. Which Tony Secunda in later days told his son Piers he had named the "Pac-Man."
The night at The Locarno Ballroom, as the group left the gig, confronted by a horde of reporters and photographers, camera light bulbs were constantly popping as they hustled their way into the hall from the transit van. The band was initially completely mystified. They were already used to controversy in their short, but frantic career up to that date. But this was an entirely new slant. They quickly began to realise that something more controversial than usual was definitely occurring.
Ace Kefford explains, "We hadn't a clue about what had been done. We hadn't even seen the postcard, until we arrived at the gig, Then Tony Secunda arrived and hustled us into a dressing room and explained what had happened. He told us to let him do the talking, when we faced the press later on."
Exactly what Secunda had done was the latest in a long and effective range of

outlandish stunts that the manager had concocted. These stunts had given the young band, feverish news headlines and great publicity for their exciting, unparalleled live stage show. Plus, so far a string of three Top Ten hit singles. But Secunda was to incur the wrath of the full British political and judicial establishment. A good ten years before The Sex Pistols would cause a similar, rebellious anti-establishmentarian uproar and their subsequent banning from live shows with all the outrage they caused, Secunda had opened a political Pandora's Box that was to reverberate throughout the rest of these five young musicians' lives.

2.
In this profession people rush to cut you down to size

The stunt in question? Firstly some background. Gossip had been abounding in the Westminster rumour mill and beyond for some considerable time. Nothing unusual there! That the Labour Political Secretary Marcia Williams was carrying on a secret liaison, an extramarital affair, with a leading politician in the UK. It was claimed that Marcia Williams exerted an unrivalled degree of power throughout Wilson's two periods in office as Prime Minister, and his political career in general. She ran his office for a total of 27 years.

Williams was not afraid to resort to the law on a few occasions. She challenged claims made against her when in government, as a postscript to this earlier controversy.

In 2001 Joe Haines re-wrote his original book, *The Politics Of Power*, making other allegations about Williams. The BBC delayed the screening of a documentary-drama based on the book. After the television drama called *The Lavender List* marking the 30th anniversary of Wilson's resignation was aired on 1st March 2006. "The Lavender List" was the satirical name given to Harold Wilson's controversial 1976 resignation honours.

At the age of 74 in 2006 Lady Falkender sued the BBC successfully for libel. She was awarded £75,000, in respect of *The Lavender List*, with a further £200,000 in costs and the BBC undertook never to rebroadcast the programme.

Conversely, on the other side of this drama, and before Williams received her 'Ladyship', Secunda had used photo promo cards alongside the band's first two single releases. 'Night Of Fear' and 'I Can Hear The Grass Grow' respectively. These usually had some pithy and hip comments and a cool band shot taken by the Move's resident in-house photographer Robert "Bobby" Davidson.

For the third single release 'Flowers In The Rain' Secunda had the idea for a (in his words) "good political cartoon". This time around, the postcard in question, featured a caricature by London-based artist Neil Smith of the Prime Minister Harold Wilson. It had added references to "various false and malicious rumours" regarding "his personal character and integrity."

Secunda's "brainwave" was to show a scurrilous cartoon image. It depicted Wilson "in flagrante delicto" with Marcia Williams. Some say her influence on the Prime Minister included The Beatles, being put forward for the MBE awards at Buckingham Palace, as part of the 1965 Queen's Birthday Honours List.

Flowers In The Rain - The Untold Story of The Move

The notorious post card was a black and white illustration, measuring eight and a quarter inches by five and a quarter inches. Smith drew it in a '*faux*' Aubrey Beardsley style, in pen and ink. He mixed it in with touches of the current catchy psychedelic styles, with some etched ornateness. Harold Wilson is seen drawn, with a slightly Dan Dare, Mekon-like look.[2]

It shows Wilson naked on the bed like a distended, distorted, ugly homunculus. He sports an enlarged baby head, and he is totally stark bollock naked. He is perched on a large ornate bed. Two Royal Britannia figures adorn either side of the card, facing inwards towards the central tableau. Behind Wilson, Marcia Williams is seen fanning herself. She wears a plumed hat and a costume mask. Marcia Williams is seen naked, apart from a diaphanous nightgown. She wears a Marie Antoinette style, piled up white wig and eye mask and waves a fan coquettishly.

The fan has fairly hard to read wording as follows, 'Mrs Williams, Harold's *VERY* personal secretary.' Harold Wilson's wife (Mary) peers through the gap in the heavy velvet curtains. It is as if she is at a mystery ball. There is a typewriter and various papers strewn around the bed. And in the background, a large ornate mirror with two candles to the right. I don't know if this is some kind of concession, to attempt to obscure the meaning of the card. There is little doubt, that this salacious cartoon of Prime Minister, Harold Wilson, explicitly refers to this long-rumoured affair with his private secretary.

****

'Flowers In The Rain' was officially released on August 25th 1967 on the revamped Regal Zonophone record label. This label had not been in use for many years and originally was the Salvation Army's release label. It was started up in 1932 by merging both the Regal and the Zonophone labels. Over a 30-year period The Salvation Army recorded many of its fine bands and song brigades on this label.

Ken East, the MD of EMI remembered the reformation of the label: "Regal Zonophone; essentially, I formed a relationship with David Platz of Essex Music, because he had Denny Cordell. I thought 'We should get to know this bloke'. Procol Harum were with Decca and I talked to David Platz, about getting Denny to produce some records for us and also signing artists and Denny Cordell said, 'Only if I can have my own label'. In those days you didn't give people their own label and I said 'I'll tell you what I'll do (the Regal Zonophone label was moribund). I'll give you a label. But it'll have to be one of ours and it's called Regal Zonophone'. Denny said, 'As long as I can get my own identity, I'll be happy'. So, we resurrected Regal Zonophone. It had The Move, T. Rex, Procol Harum, Joe Cocker and that was a great time. The things that happened were just part of the every day ongoing business, that awful business of The Move and their cartoon of old Harold Wilson and Marcia Williams."

'Flowers In The Rain' was and is an immediate ear worm. An evocative and summery record and a vital, rousing part of that year's soundtrack. 'Flowers' fit the year 1967 perfectly like a velvet glove. Roy Wood's Fender Telecaster was double tracked on the dramatic opening. Following the loud burst of thunderstorm and

---

2 The Mekon was the main alien character that appeared in the popular *Dan Dare* comic strip in the *Eagle* comic.

the falling rain sounds. Which Gerald Chevin, the in-house engineer at Advision Studios in London, found lurking in the sound effects library. It had an immediate commerciality when released. It was backed with another incredibly commercial B-side (or 'flip' side) called '(Here We Go Round) The Lemon Tree'. Which was another instantly catchy Roy Wood song, this also received a lot of airplay.

It has stood as a supremely commercial song in its own right. However, the 'Flowers' single almost didn't get released at all. Firstly some background. Denny Cordell was now a close business compadre of Tony Secunda. They both ran their company New Movement out of Denmark Street. A short little street — you could dash from one end, to the other in about two minutes. With Ron Kingsnorth running Galaxy Entertainment a few doors nearby (later bought out by Don Arden). The Move were booked out of Galaxy Entertainment (usually by agent Sue Rose) as well. That kept everything nice and local. Denmark Street was is famous for its rehearsal studios, music business shops, publishers etc. It was known as Britain's 'Tin Pan Alley'. It is just off Tottenham Court Road, in the centre of the West End of London. Cordell was brought in as overall producer on this as he had been on the first two singles as well. Denny Cordell had also formed New Breed Publishing with David Platz. They had licensed the first two Move singles to Deram Records

Harold Wilson's Labour government had received a backlash from the younger, hip public opinion. For first outlawing and then banning the pirate radio stations. These had a cool, hip audience and were moored off the coast of the United Kingdom that year. Andrew Neil, cultural commentator, recently proffered the view in response to the film on the pirate radio stations *The Boat That Rocked*, released in 2009 and directed by Richard Curtis: "The pirate stations were not killed off by a Tory public-school prime minister (as in the film), but by a grammar schoolboy and Labour Prime Minister Harold Wilson. The destruction was not carried out by a Tory toff minister (as depicted by Curtis) but by a left-wing toff, Tony Wedgwood Benn (then Labour minister in charge of the airwaves)."

Yes! That's certainly how I remember the story; the pirate stations were shut — not by a stuffy Tory establishment but by a supposedly modernising Labour government. Fact really is stranger than fiction." Mick Jagger had opined, "Hello this is Mick Jagger here saying hello to Radio London, back again. You've given us a lot of good times."

A little earlier, on 22nd July, Carl Wayne, The Move's lead singer had chopped a full-size effigy of Harold Wilson to pieces with an axe during The Move's performance at the Free The Pirates benefit. They appeared along with The Pretty Things. This event was sponsored by Radio Caroline and held at Alexander Palace (aka Ally Pally). The benefit is in direct protest at the Wilson Government's attempts to silence and criminalise the so-called "pirate" radio stations with the Wireless Telegraphy Act, later renamed The Marine Broadcasting (Offences) Act 1967. Tony Secunda was one of the extant management for Radio Geronimo, the pirate radio station.

After this, the Labour government sanctioned the go-ahead for Radio One. Immediately becoming the mainstream replacement for the pirate stations. It launched on 30th September 1967 at 7:00am that morning. Some of the pirate DJs were gobbled up by the new BBC monolith. People like Tony Blackburn, John Peel and Kenny Everett among other DJs.

'Flowers In The Rain' was chosen as the first song to open the freshly minted BBC Corporation run Radio One. With Tony Blackburn presenting the first show. George Martin's specially commissioned 'Theme One' and Johnny Dankworth's 'Beefeaters' were the first tracks to be heard on the station. 'Beefeaters' was Tony Blackburn's theme tune for *Daily Disc Delivery* and so they were heard with 'Flowers In The Rain'.

Roy Wood remembers clearly that Tony Blackburn scrambled for a disc to play first, and it was 'Flowers In the Rain.' Tony Blackburn, said years afterwards, "It was just a mad panic on that morning, and I wasn't sure if all the records had been sorted out properly, and in the right order. The program came on and I just dived for the first record, I could lay my hands on, and it happened to be 'Flowers In The Rain'. "Many ears were primed to this new station (along with The Move, who had been avidly listening to the song, on the way to a photo-shoot.)

Years later, Glen Matlock heard the song. He was lying in bed and had copped off from his school with flu at ten years old. "It was great — so different to all the other pop pap!"

'Flowers In The Rain' was kept off the number one spot by Englebert Humperdinck, singing his awful dirge and housewife's favourite, 'The Last Waltz'. In early 1967 Humperdinck had also prevented The Beatles' 'Strawberry Fields Forever'/'Penny Lane' from attaining the top slot in the United Kingdom. Radio One now bridged a huge gap in the market.

Youth were crying out for a solid radio spot to fill the large gap left by the pirates' demise. Meanwhile Tony Visconti a young American hot-shot producer had hit London, just at the right time, to forge his initial recording career. After some work with Manfred Mann and Georgie Fame, Denny Cordell invited Visconti to Advision Studio to watch The Move work on a proposed single track, which Cordell was having quite some issues with.

Visconti helped shore up production duties on 'Flowers In The Rain'. He also added embellishments musically, along with Cordell and engineer Gerald Chevin. That helped make the song, The Move's third top five smash. (They had hit number two, number five and a number two in a row).

Tony Visconti was looking for breaks in London and he certainly found them. "I wrote a score for a small wind quartet for Denny Cordell's production of 'Flowers In The Rain'. It was a happy accident for all concerned. Denny was unhappy with the track and felt that his production didn't nail it. There was also a spot where the tempo lagged behind, almost imperceptibly. Denny was so upset, that he argued that the only solution was to trash the track — with no plan of re-recording it. I'm not sure what the reason for this was but it was likely down to budgetary constraints. Then again, he may have felt that The Move already had enough good material. I really argued for the song. And I said that I thought it was a definite hit and maybe if I wrote an arrangement for wind instruments, I could save it. Denny indulged me, but I couldn't just do the simple thing. Instead of the usual string section I chose a quartet of flute, oboe, clarinet and French Horn. My logic was simple — the song had a pastoral theme, albeit through the filter of magic mushrooms. I used instruments that Mendelssohn would've used, and I even paid homage to him by quoting the 'Spring Song' in the outro. I got Denny to record the quartet at half speed during the bridge to create a very special effect. As it happens, a wind quartet played back at double speed has the apparent sound of a harmonica — but who knew? This was the age of experimentation."

Tony Visconti spotted the special musicianship and songwriting in The Move pretty much immediately, "I recognised their talent straight away — it was a cutting-edge song. They were like the second Beatles to my young mind. Denny Cordell was a very temperamental and perfectionist producer and wanted to discard the song. Because of a slight dip in the tempo, as how Denny saw it. But I didn't see that. I wanted to work on it (as a co-producer) and "save" the song. I got Denny to agree to spend £60 extra."

In another very funny ad-lib, piece of freewheeling 1960s recording techniques, they wanted the song to open with a big cannonade of thunder and rain. The thunder effects were found, in the special effects library at Advision Studios by Gerald Chevin. However, it was felt that some extra rain and gushing water effects, were also needed. It fell upon the head of Allen 'Dumpy' Harris, who was The Move's steady, road manager. Denny Cordell instructed Harris to take a long lead and a microphone and to walk it out to the toilets. Allen maintains this was at least, a good 30 feet from the recording console approximately. "I think we tried it about three times, three takes! I held the mic over the loo and flushed the chain. We all had a laugh really, because nobody would have thought you would have used a mic down the loo like that." Keen listeners can hear this, after the initial thunder effects, in the beginning section. Just after, you can hear the tinkling 'toilet flush effects' courtesy of Allen Harris. 'Flowers In The Rain' reached number two in 1967 on the UK singles chart and number four in the Ireland charts.

Roy Wood's early songs, 'I Can Hear the Grass Grow', 'Disturbance', 'Night Of Fear' and the basis of 'Flowers In The Rain', had all derived from a book of fairy stories and early poems, which Wood had authored as an art student at Moseley College of Art. Later on Wood's paintings and pastel drawings, would adorn the covers of his early solo recorded work and album covers, such as *Mustard* and *Boulders*.

Robert Davidson remembers the group's early look. "The sixties were an exciting time, and we absolutely thought, we were going to change the world. Tony Secunda was very controlling, and the band was very young and very malleable. When I first met them, they were a great bunch of kids from Birmingham. I remember Roy Wood had a great big alarm clock, tied around his waist."

Secunda and The Move's trouble was inevitably exacerbated by other events earlier that heady year. With The Rolling Stones versus the establishment, specifically in concern to the much-publicised drug bust at Redlands — the West Sussex home of Keith Richards, earlier that February. At the trial in June at Chichester both Richards and Jagger were found guilty. Keith Richards was sentenced to a year in prison and fined £500. While Jagger received three months and a £200 fine. But a backlash was brewing. This was summed up in an editorial in *The Times* by the editor William (later Lord) Rees-Mogg. Under the headline "Who Breaks a Butterfly on a Wheel?" It questioned the severity of the sentence, noting that it was "as mild a drug case, as can ever have been brought before the courts".

The article added: "There must remain a suspicion in this case that Mr. Jagger received a more severe sentence than would have been thought proper for any purely anonymous young man." The establishment was outraged further the following month. When *The Times* carried a full-page advertisement headed: "The law against marijuana is immoral in principle and unworkable in practice." Sixty-five leading lights called for changes in the law, with signatories ranging from doctors, Nobel laureate scientists and MPs to Graham Greene, David Bailey, Jonathan Miller and all four Beatles. The ad caused an uproar when it appeared and was debated in the House of Commons in the week of publication. But the following week Richards' conviction was quashed on appeal and Jagger's prison sentence was reduced to a conditional discharge.

So, for Secunda and The Move their timing could not have been better (or worse) to be square in line, for a right, royal establishment bashing. The band claim they are completely unaware of the new promo card. (Possibly apart from Carl Wayne?) There is some ambiguity here, some people say the band knew about the card. The Move are continuously gigging, performing numerous concerts across the UK. While the band played gigs and blazed away onstage, explosively wowing the UK audiences the trouble was brewing…

Robert Davidson remembers, "Michael Foot took a little bit of persuading, but he took the cards and went off with them. Tony also sent them to anyone you can think of. Any journalist going! They were also sent to many TV people. He did this without The Move knowing what was going on at all. The band literally didn't have a clue."

It soon appeared that one of the postcards was dropped through the door of Number 10 Downing Street in Westminster, London. The official residence and office of the Prime Minister of the United Kingdom. In the days when you could walk right up to the entrance and door to 10 Downing Street. Not anymore.

3.
Vote for me!
Sign across the line

The very next day, newspaper headlines read: *"Pop Band Sued By Prime Minister for Libel."* A couple of days earlier on 31st August, a copy of the printed postcard, which was originally addressed to Mrs. Anne Valentine, fell into the hands of the Paymaster General (of His Majesty's Forces) Colonel George Wigg. Mr Wigg also doubled as the Government's security watchdog. He immediately informed the Prime Minister. Colonel Wigg had the ear of Harold Wilson. Wigg could be frequently found muttering all kinds of gossip and hearsay into Harold's shell-like.

When a copy of the postcard reportedly dropped through the door at Number Ten Downing Street Wilson saw it immediately as a potential libel suit. And he didn't wait long to act. The Prime Minister issued an immediate writ. Wilson was then granted an interim injunction on 1st September 1967. His first injunction ran until 6th September. The writ was against Secunda, Bev Bevan, Trevor Ireson (Burton's birth name), Christopher Kefford, Carl Wayne, and Roy Wood. Also, the designer of the drawing on the postcard, Neil Smith; C.C.S. Advertising Associates. Ltd., of Wardour Street, Soho, (who sub-contracted an order for 500 copies of the card) and Richard Moore and Leslie Ltd, of Great Chapel Street, Soho, who printed those 500 copies.

Ken East, the Managing Director at EMI in 1967 recalls, "Joe Lockwood came in one morning about 9:00am. 'Mr East, what's all this about?' He and Lord Goodman were friends. Lord Goodman was Harold Wilson's lawyer, and I had not as yet seen this thing. Ron White (EMI) is shitting himself — we all were. Ron White was eventually made the Deputy Managing Director. He was always the bridesmaid, never the bride. He was a good man. I was the Managing Director in Manchester Square; L.G. Wood was the Group Director of EMI Records on the top floor of Manchester Square, and we all had maintained a good relationship."

Eleven days after Radio One launched, The Move found themselves in the High Court (on 10th October 1967) facing Quintin Hogg Q.C, Conservative Member of Parliament for St. Marylebone. He also was the Shadow Minister for Home Affairs. The Move were defending a charge of a "violent and malicious personal attack" on the Prime Minister. Strangely enough, Quintin Hogg was largely responsible earlier for stoking the fires and innuendo, around the alleged affair between Harold Wilson and Marcia Williams. At least a couple of years before.

Later, Carl Wayne reiterated that the earlier, harder, five-piece Move line-up were indeed "The first punks." We smashed up televisions and instruments on stage and once incited an audience to riot and tear a Cadillac to pieces while girls danced and stripped off on the car roof." And can there be any greater anarchy than to be accused of maliciously libelling the most powerful man in Britain?"

Carl Wayne went on to describe Secunda's talents as a manager. "Tony Secunda was a very skilful businessman. He was also creative and had a very artistic mind. He was the best manager I ever knew, and he did his job extremely well. Not just for the money but he was the kind of guy, who let the band make their dreams come true. He tried to give The Move the same sort of reputation that The Rolling Stones had and not like The Beatles' safer image. He wanted a band with a dangerous image. Tony was a really rebellious guy, and he hated 'the Establishment' and all it stood for. It might be why he suggested the promotional ideas he did. Such as demolishing TV sets on stage. He also saw in me a performer that would do the stunts and promotional gimmicks he invented."

So it was that "five thickos from Birmingham", in Carl Wayne's words, with little day-to-day interest in flowers or any form of horticulture, became hippy poster children.

The live Move were the same tough, take-no-prisoners-outfit though! That certainly hadn't changed. For example, scaring the "hippies" at the UFO Club, when they resumed smashing up TVs with axes! And feeding the dopeheads present, some 'special' banana skin joints, which Secunda and Cordell hurled into the crowd. But as far as the Flower's record's publicity was concerned, Tony Secunda's job was done!

4.
When I was a little boy my mama dropped me on my head

Before this major publicity catastrophe, involving Harold Wilson had taken place. The Move had only been in situation, for about seventeen months. They were formed and shaped in another exciting and parallel, musical universe about 120 miles from London. They were founded in, but needed to escape from the exciting, busy, creative music scene. Existing in England's "second city" of Birmingham situated in the heart of England, known as the Midlands.

The Move were unquestionably one of the truly great bands to come out of the UK. The Move could be described as the most iconic band, you never knew existed. On one hand, a band with a slew of hit singles. All different and all unique! A band whose ferocious live show, was considered the very best! Especially by the people who saw, the original five-piece Move in all their primal, full-strut, gigging glory. Few bands wanted to follow The Move after one of their incendiary live sets. Tony Secunda was asked once, if anyone could follow The Move live. He simply said "No one!" They incorporated the hippest, pop and rock, plus Mod and soul influences. All in a tightly structured fashion. With an emphasis on fashionable image and uncliched cover versions. Yet, the lives and details of this enigmatic band are hardly known at all in the broader 1960s rock pantheon. Countless events, controversies and ructions, happened in their initial roller coaster ride.

During The Move's three-to-four-year reign of pandemonium and uproar, publicity driven furore, surrounded the band. Aided and abetted by the mysterious Machiavellian, dark enigma that was Tony Secunda. The Move's history is shrouded in fights, divisions, arguments over publishing money and obdurate egos. One guy in the group suddenly emerging into a supreme songwriter, further supplying them with hits. Keeping them in the charts for a glittering initial run. It also could be said that these incredible hits, capsized their initial, roots, rock and soulful vision? They became known as a 'pop' act. Instead of the soulful, rocked-out, towering live act, with a razor's edge that they were.

They were sued by the Prime Minister of Britain. Incomparably outrageous in the music world of 1967. If it could be compared to today's media saturated world, it could be akin to being sued by God and the Holy Trinity! (or the President of the United States himself).

They went through three different managements, in the space of the same years.

The fact that their first manager, Tony Secunda, had put them squarely and defiantly on the map. Using the band's street edge, to try and convey Secunda's "fuck you" attitudes. Taking them out of Birmingham and placing them directly into the heart of the London "happening" scene, with a well-regarded Thursday night residency at The Marquee Club in Central London. Immediately out-hipping, most of the top London bands.

The fact that the five young egos, eventually began to clash in so many dramatic ways. The fact that the elementally, charismatic bass player and singer Ace Kefford had to leave. Or was he pushed? Leaving a gaping hole in the band, that was never, ever filled. With the subsequent loss of the other "gone wrong Mod" in the group, rhythm / bass guitarist Trevor Burton. Who (along with Ace) was the wilder, renegade side and 'beating Mod heart' of The Move.

Then — finally the irrevocable loss of Carl Wayne — the charismatic, fearless vocalist and Move front man. The band staggered on inviting (the now world-famous) Jeff Lynne (then leading The Idle Race) to become part of The Move and releasing more hit singles. Before morphing into the much more successful and much less exciting Electric Light Orchestra.

Danny King, one of the singing "guvnors" on the Birmingham music scene, was in possession of a large and formidable record collection of which Carl Wayne, Ace Kefford and Trevor Burton, dipped into frequently to find musical treasure. What came to be known later as rare Northern Soul collectibles and other rare danceable grooves.

The Move formed, and like many other Brum bands, their early act comprised of impeccable covers of 'Too Many Fish In The Sea', the original by The Marvelettes. It was also covered by The Young Rascals in New York. 'Is It True' and 'Respectable' by the Isley Brothers (to me, The Move beat The Yardbirds' version of the latter into a cocked hat), 'I Can't Hear You No More' by Betty Everett. Betty also had the fantastic 'The Shoop Shoop Song (It's In His Kiss)' under her belt.

As time (swiftly) sped on into 1967, The Move grew more musically organic, spreading their musical wings again. Covering contemporary hip West Coast and UK sounds with particular respect shown to Love, The Byrds, The Nazz, Spooky Tooth, Tim Rose, The Beach Boys, Moby Grape and more.

The cover versions they chose. Whether it was the earlier R&B and soul-rock sounds. Or the more contemporary freakier beat sounds. Plus, (from the start of 1968 onwards) a rousing set of edgy, rock 'n' roll songs. These covers were all unified by The Move's skilful choices. They often baffled other Brum bands, who didn't quite know, where they were getting these fantastic new tunes they played. They were living and breathing this music.

As a young kid, it was always a big plus for me, that like the Beatles, The Move had a solid history in listening to and playing great black soul and R&B singles from the USA. Overlaid with The Move's ferocious edge, they did not go for immediately obvious songs. They had five well-attuned ears, to what people were going to react to in the audience. Songs that lent themselves to great vocals and harmonies. A heavy vocal delivery with good harmonies. Underpinned by very tight and aggressive rock playing.

The five musicians that eventually came to make up The Move, were all part of

When I was a little boy my mamma dropped me on my head

a tightly knit Birmingham scene. Birmingham had suffered greatly during the Second World War with the Nazis bombing the city often. If you thought the scene in London was happening, then Birmingham was just as big. Musicians such as Keith Smart, (the veteran drummer with The Rockin' Berries, Lemon Tree, Wizzard etc) described just how bustling and extraordinarily fertile, the music scene was in Birmingham in the 1960s: "There were bands everywhere — literally everywhere."

A small independent magazine (or paper really) called *Midland Beat*, (originally totalling about 8 to 10 pages for most issues) kept up with news, of the ever-changing bands being formed in the city. *Midland Beat* eventually changed into a new publication called *Brum Beat*.

Jim Simpson was responsible for taking the first batch of photographs of The Move. Looking incredibly young, they are all wearing long college type scarfs. Looking both preppy, the beginnings of a Mod style in appearance. "Yes, I knew them for those days," Jim Simpson recalls clearly, this one of his first photo shoots. The photo session took place in December 1965. "I famously shot the very first ever Move photos. Outside The Mackadown. (A famous pub and a big gig for all the Birmingham bands). It used to be the ultimate gig. It was in a place called Kitts Green. Like many other landmarks of the 1960s, The Mackadown was demolished in 2000, now housing yet another Lidl supermarket. This area was also the birthplace of Mr Roy Wood. "Well, they were wild — it was wild. They were very orchestrated, very contrived, and they set out to do outrageous things."

Jim's photography was very much part of the scene back then. Simpson was a man of several talents. He was a musician, and he went on to manage bands. Such as the popular local band Locomotive. In which Jim not only managed, but also blew trumpet. Locomotive also had the ambition, to get out of Birmingham. They played clubs in London, like the Bag 'O Nails and the Eel Pie Club. And for musical completists and deep divers, Locomotive actually had a hit, which charted at number 25, with a song called 'Rudy's In Love', written by Norman Haines and produced by the redoubtable Gus Dudgeon for Parlophone.

After dying a death, at one gig at the Cedar Club, they were probably trying to be too clever and "progressive." They pulled a winner out of the hat, by ending the set, playing a rough version of 'Rudy's In Love.' With the result, the whole place was jumping. Tony Hall, ex-promotions at Decca immediately wanted to record it. Like many others, Jim Simpson maintains. "From the musical point of view, we dwarfed Liverpool without any doubt. Birmingham was the rock 'n' roll capital of the UK. Lots of them never got heard outside of the region. Danny King was the best pop voice I have ever heard in this country."

As far back as early 1963, The Vikings, then comprising of singer Carl Wayne, Terry Wallace, Johnny Mann, Barry Harbour and also Dave Hollis (who worked with future Move roadie Allen Harris), were all toiling at those long gruelling stints at clubs in Stuttgart or Hamburg in Germany. As the years went by, this grotty German toilet circuit was made more famous by The Beatles, with their early, Preludin-paced, pissed up, countless sets, performed at the infamous khazi — the Star Club in Hamburg.

The Vikings also carried with them a second vocalist called Alan Waldridge. He was kept on hand, like a spare set of vocal parts, should anyone's larynx or vocal chords start to shred and collapse under the mighty demands of singing seven nights a week. And well over seven hours a night, Carl Wayne came to toil with his band. It gave him a great grounding in the business. As a part of his long and in terms of career, ultimately, fruitless sessions, it did give Carl and other members, the chance to get their act honed to a very high degree. Carl Wayne was one guy that realised, being stuck in this circular, fixed gig routine was not gonna last forever. Wayne saw beyond this dead-end street. He had eyes and ambition to strive further. There has got to be another stage forward.

Carl Wayne
Carl Wayne (his birth name was Colin Tooley) was born in Dudley Road Hospital, Birmingham on 18th August 1943 and came from Hodge Hill, Birmingham. He was an extrovert lad (a cheekie-chap type of personality) and generally a well-balanced kid.

Colin enjoyed helping in his dad's shop. His father ran a grocery and provisions shop. A local woman called Elsie would often come in and serve behind the till when business was bustling. Elsie would bring along her young son Roy. Roy was four years, Colin's junior. Colin was often caught teasing Roy and was regularly given a clip around the ear for tormenting the young and shy Roy.

Shooting pea contests between the two kids was a regular occurrence. Colin Tooley's first band was called The G-Men, who formed in the late 1950s. This was during the skiffle craze, and they arranged dances at the Curzon Coffee Bar and in various church halls. "I first started with groups at school — I attended Saltley Grammar School, Birmingham. I had a band called The G-Men with my best friend Chris Wheeler and his brother Ralph." Colin was always highly organised and collected the takings at the door. He remembered his pockets becoming so heavy with half-crowns he had difficulty keeping his trousers from falling down. He was singing and he could play some bass and guitar, although his ability to play the instrument(s) was apparently questionable!

Later, when you saw photographs of Carl and The Move. He was seen holding a guitar on *Top Of The Pops*. But live video of The Move doing The Byrds' 'Christian Life' on *Colour Me Pop* in 1969 shows Carl playing some solid, un-flashy bass guitar.

Colin Tooley turned professional when he joined Keith Powell and The Vikings in 1961. He was a "temporary" replacement singer when Keith Powell became ill and was unable to complete some bookings. For the role of front-man Colin Tooley changed his name to 'Carl Wayne.' A commercial and suitably 'showbiz' name. One part of the new surname, originated from the film star John Wayne. The other 'Carl' was an attempt to fit in with The Vikings moniker. The potentially Nordic sounding 'Carl' was supposed to fit into the Vikings' theme. Funnily enough there were some other Carl's in Birmingham groups in those days: Carl and The Cheetahs, Carl Fenn and The Mysteries. Upon their return to Birmingham, Carl Wayne and The Vikings, played Joe and Mary (Ma) Regan's circuit of ballrooms. Quickly establishing themselves as one of the city's top live acts.

A word is needed here about Ma Regan and her famous reign in Birmingham.

When I was a little boy my mamma dropped me on my head

She was one of the most influential figures of the early beat scene in the area. Ma Regan was an ex-schoolteacher. She was a shy but formidable woman. After the war, she opened tea shops in the Birmingham area and started tea dances. This then led onto the dance halls. They started out on a small scale and they had a lot of success. She managed many local groups, including The Redcaps. But she is mainly remembered for staging so many amazing shows at her set of venues. The venues in their tightly structured domain were The Plaza in Handsworth, The Plaza at Old Hill. The Ritz Ballroom at King's Heath and the smaller (or should I say tiny) Brum Beat Kavern Club (in an obvious name lift from the 'other' Cavern Club?) This venue was located in Small Heath.

She managed to get virtually every one of the major British beat groups, including The Beatles, and many American performers to play for her at some time during those years. She was a lady, who was truly a legend in her own lifetime!

Along with Mike Sheridan and The Nightriders and The Spencer Davis Group, Island Records founder Chris Blackwell actually went to Birmingham to see Carl Wayne and The Vikings, with the idea of signing the band to the Island label. Blackwell ended up signing the Spencer Davis Group instead! There was a pecking order, like there is an everything in the music scene in Brum. The three best vocalists were considered to be Danny King, Carl Wayne and Mike Sheridan. Eddie Fewtrell the owner of the Cedar for example, described Carl Wayne, "As the best male vocalist in a group, that I've ever heard. He was absolutely magnificent. Singers like Robert Plant, for example, are absolutely brilliant at what they do but you can't imagine him singing Sinatra. Whereas Carl could actually sing anything."

Not everybody agreed with Eddie Fewtrell's opinions of the vocalists. Jim Simpson thought that Roy Everett was the best singer in the city. Roy did not break out of the Birmingham city scene and was considered, more of a blues type vocalist.

While wearing a choice newly tailored pink suit on stage, Carl Wayne proved so popular with the audience, that when Keith Powell returned, Carl Wayne was allowed to stay and perform regularly in the group. His position was now as the second singer. With the band's name being changed to 'Keith Powell, Carl Wayne & The Vikings.' That year Carl Wayne took over as frontman. Due to the inevitable friction developing between Keith Powell and himself, Keith Powell left and with his father went on to form another group called The Valets.

In January 1963, Carl Wayne and The Vikings were sent over to Germany for a gruelling six-month booking. Carl fancied himself as an instrumentalist. "I started in the music business playing bass guitar, but I was never any good. I managed to persuade The Vikings, to let me play bass with them when they needed a bass player. My one and only performance with that group was truly forgettable. The bass player I recommended then suggested me as a good replacement to which the boys in the band said, 'I hope he can sing better than he plays bass!' My influences were Elvis, Cliff, Eddie Cochran and all the great American and British rock 'n' rollers."

Carl Wayne and the Vikings recorded back then too. They got signed to the Pye Records label in 1964 and recorded 'What's The Matter Baby' at Hollick & Taylor Studios in Handsworth for their first single. Soon after, bass guitarist Barry Harber left the band for a career in life insurance. He was replaced temporarily by Tony Lewis from Ronnie and The Senators. Carl remembers the emergence, of a visually dramatic and energetic young player: "It never worked out with Tony Lewis. We were playing at the Old Hill Plaza, along with our old singer Keith Powell and his Valets. In The Valets, was this blond-haired young lad. He was moving like a demon. He was singing like a bird and twanging his bass! Like we'd never heard before." Carl Wayne said straight away, 'He's for us!'"

This young kid, a startling bassist and vocalist, was a very early 'move' and an upgrade for The Vikings. Here a very important link was formed. Christopher "Ace" Kefford came in, adding punch, vocal dexterity and mucho dynamics to The Vikings. In time he was to do the very same in The Move. However, after seven years of toiling and slogging, Carl Wayne saw the writing on the wall. He let the Vikings know he was leaving. The band were chowing down at the Bombay Indian restaurant on Essex Street, before their evening performance at The Station pub.

Terry Wallace, the Vikings guitarist clearly remembers the bombshell: "Carl Wayne was always going to leave but he never did. I laughed at first, but he interrupted me quite sternly. 'Terry!'… he said it so forcibly, a hoarse silence fell over the rest of the company. 'This time it's for real! I'm leaving — I'm taking Bev and Ace with me… what you do, is up to you now, but for us it's over. Roy Wood and Trevor Burton are joining us — we're making a big move'." In fact, Carl Wayne and The Vikings played their final gig on Christmas Eve 1965. This was at Selly Oak's Station Pub, now called The Bristol Pear.

In one of the first interviews in the big London weeklies, *Melody Maker* dated 30th April of 1966, Carl Wayne says, "We thought we'd be a big feedback group based on The Who. We discovered quite by accident that vocal harmony was our greatest asset." Along with their unbelievably tight live, instrumental and rocking soul presence. They had just signed exclusively to Marquee Artists Management in London. "Anyway, we just did our usual things — Motown with a big beat."

At that time, Carl was going out with the delightful, eighteen-year-old Pauline Evans. She would go on to run the Midlands version of The Move Fan club. This was run out of her home in Erdington. Pauline was a beautiful young woman, and pictures exist of her winning a beauty title, in a monthly magazine called *SHE* (similar in style to *Vogue*). Pauline handled the day to day Move fan club business as directed and set up by Secunda. Letters would be sent out to fans on printed Move headed paper. Evans recalled, "I remember meeting Carl at the Carlton Club — it was a successful club back then. It became known as Mothers run by a guy called Big Phil Myatt. They used to do a lot of the clubs round Birmingham, Yardley and Small Heath. Carl was a bit older than the other guys. Carl managed the band internally if you like. He used to do all the wages and all that management type stuff. He was definitely the sensible one in the group back then. Carl completely grew into The Move. June Woods came in as my assistant for a while. (She was then known as June Hayton). There were also two ladies, down in London based in Denmark Street, called Sally Myers and Joan Robinson. They came in later, after I left the running of the fan club."

Chris Kefford aka 'Ace The Face'

Christopher "Ace" Kefford was born on 10th December 1946 and was originally from Sheldon and then the family moved to Yardley Wood. He grew up very hard. Chris Kefford lived in the older, back-to-back houses, with the toilets (two planks of wood over the hole) serving around fifty neighbours, "At least you had a warm seat," laughed Ace in a recent Martin Kinch interview. Chris went to a very rough school, learning to look after himself. Kefford, went to Yardley Wood Secondary Modern. "Because if you didn't, you'd get the shit kicked out of you."

In a 1995 interview with music journalist and musician Alan Clayson, he described the school as, "A dump, very rough, when I was there. I got into James Dean, the way he looked. My school uniform was cheap black jeans sewn up, as tight as I could get them. Black shirt, red waistcoat, I got off my grandad and greased back hair." Both he and Trevor Burton had grown-up rough. "We've been brought up tough at school and on the streets."

Ace remembered wearing cardboard in his shoes and changing it to 'newer' cardboard when he got to school. Ace remembered the gang at school then. "Real dead-end kids, who broke into shops and pinched cigarettes. The gang had names like Chunky, Spooky, Huker and Scratchy. That's the way it was, and the toughness carried on into The Move band eventually. The thing about it is later on we turned out to be flower children (Laughs). A screwup in the era of basic musical evenings. Especially amongst working class people. My mum and grandad both played the piano by ear. The style was with 'boxing glove' left hands. My dad bought me my first guitar, an acoustic with a pickup you could buy separately, plus an amplifier as big as a cornflakes box. My uncle Chris, my mum's brother, was only nine months older than me. Before, I had a tea chest with a broom stuck into it and a string stretched — I was playing the 'bass.' Cousin Chris had a guitar and a washboard. We were about thirteen. We were into all the instrumental groups. We used to go and see them at the Birmingham Town Hall: The Shadows, The Packabeats and The Hunters. We played down my grandad's social club. It was a rough, very working-class background. My grandad bought me my first bass. He was a big fan of The Shadows bass guitarist Jet Harris."

Chris joined his first band called Chris and The Shades. This was a line-up that was put together by his slightly older uncle Chris. Ace's other uncle Reg (Jones) joined. Ace told Alan Clayson, "Chris and I were both into all the instrumental groups that we went to see at Birmingham Town Hall. We used to sit in the house, playing guitars together. He had a Watkins Copycat. We got another guitarist, "Mugsy" Morgan. Apparently, a local legend and an extremely funny character. We had a new drummer, Barry Smith come in and joined us. Though Graeme Edge, later of The Moody Blues, was with us for a while. Then my dad took on the hire purchase for a pink Fender bass like Jet Harris had. I had the Jet Harris look too." Later, they became Steve Farron and The Chantelles, doing The Shadows numbers that Chris loved, "I loved Jet Harris' and his pink Fender bass." But they had disbanded by the end of 1963. Another Brummie and well-known musician and songwriter, Dave Scott-Morgan was part of the band for a little while.

Chris Kefford along with his uncle Chris, joined well-known Birmingham singer Danny King's backing group, who were sometimes known as 'The Jesters' for some gigs. (And sometimes known as 'The Royals'). To avoid constant name confusion with his uncle Chris. The youngest Kefford took the stage name of 'Ace the Bass' and / or 'Ace the Face' which soon stuck.

Ace Kefford had joined Keith Powell's Valets after a visit to Jones & Crossland music store, where he was told The Valets needed a bass player to fill in for a few gigs. Both Ace, his uncle Chris Jones and drummer and close friend Barry Smith (aka Baz St Leger) all hooked up with Danny King. Danny King was considered the best singer around in Birmingham at that time. Danny King clearly remembers, the young Chris Kefford. "There was this bloke following us around. Everything that Chris Kefford did, whether it was his playing or his flashy dance moves! This bloke hanging around would say, 'Yeah that's ace!' From then on Chris became known as Ace 'The Face' Kefford."

By now, Ace was also working in the fruit market up early in the mornings. Sometimes clocking out and then straight to gigs. "I used to get a lot of comments, especially when I started combing my hair, in The Beatles style. Roundabout then Chris and me wrote the song called, 'This Locket'."

Apparently, Danny King, although with no doubt a great singer, had a developing taste for domestic comfort. Believe it or not, in the days before video recording, Danny King had an extremely obsessive need, to catch every episode, of the extremely popular television soap opera *Coronation Street*. This duly meant that Danny was only available for gigs, later in the evening! Or on any nights that *Coronation Street* was not on. I kid you not! Also, apparently Danny was in the incredible, vicelike grip of a gambling addiction. He was extremely partial to the pull of (and the 'pulling on') pinball machines. Ace Kefford became quickly disillusioned with Danny King and The Jesters. Ace summarily left the band. He rolled up his sleeves and started to work as a builder's labourer on the construction of the Rotunda in the Birmingham Centre.

One lunch hour Ace was ambling along by the almost completed Small Brook Ringway Centre on Hinckley Street. He intended to browse around Jones and Crosslands Music Store. At the time, Ace was earning a steady wage, by shovelling cement on the newly erected Rotunda construction site. When asked about joining The Vikings, for the then considerable sum of twenty pounds a week, Ace Kefford recalled; "In one minute I was shovelling shit on the Rotunda. Then the next minute I'm in Carl Wayne and The Vikings, making £20-odd a week. I snapped it up! Carl and the Vikings were doing about twenty bookings a week. They were doing doubles and trebles. Getting £40 to £50 each. My old man was on £12 a week, as a plasterer. I was also getting crap money as a labourer."

Ace joined the band pronto, "Though I wasn't too happy about the shirts, ties and velvet collared suits they wore. Or their music, which was mainly Top 20 and smoochy ballads like 'My Prayer'. Even when they did a Chuck Berry number it was all very polished. I wore the Montague Burtons suit, and I managed to get some good input into the set with my Sam Cooke and The Impressions material. I was doing stuff like 'Jump Back' and 'Every Little Bit Hurts' by Brenda Holloway. We had a drummer for a while before Bev called Dave Hollis. Bev was in The Diplomats at the time."

Bev Bevan recalls the Vikings days, "We were in Carl Wayne and the Vikings together. The Vikings was virtually a cabaret band really. Suit and tie, sharp, plain, clothes and it wasn't a rock 'n' roll band at all. Johnny Mann was a lovely lead guitarist, but here again it was, a more cabaret style really. We played everything; rock 'n' roll, blues, making things up. With Carl, Johnny and me, sharing lead vocals, just to fill the time. To keep going, I popped a couple of pills then, but we were more into getting legless on German beer." Years later when the Electric Light Orchestra were selling millions Bev said that they were the happiest days of his life, "Living on cornflakes and wondering how we were going to get home."

Johnny Mann was a weird James Dean obsessive, with a bedroom full of Dean posters. He was a bit staggered when he first looked at Ace Kefford, as Ace was entering a Vikings rehearsals. Mann shouted out, loudly exclaiming, "Yeaaaaaaaaahhhhh! Knock out!" Then he walked off. Whether this was derision and / or jealousy, it's hard to make out. Either way, it was bloody funny. Especially the way Ace tells it. Despite all the trouble, Ace has had in his life, he's got a very sharp, photographic memory and a great sense of humour. Terry Wallace took Ace under his wing and helped ease the young musician into the group.

Ace remembered the almost habitual format of the 'beat bands' in Brum at the time. "All the bands… the majority of them, would go to the record store and buy the latest Beatles record. You practiced it on the afternoon and played it on the night like a human jukebox. You'd get good money for doing it — but there was no originality. Sometimes the fans were too much. It reminded me of my last assembly at school, when I had to go up to receive some sports certificate in my Teddy Boy clothes and all the girls screamed. I hated it in the end and so did Trevor Burton. We thought we had to do it then — we said, we're going to form a new band. Fuck it! We can all dress Mod smart and do what the hell we want!" Ace at 18 years old and Trevor Burton at 16 years old respectively — were very hungry young men.

Ace looked back then at the determined resistance to the changes they were going through. Ace remembered, "We were younger than a lot of the other guys in the Birmingham bands. They didn't understand what we were going on about. And on the other hand, we didn't understand what all the fuss was about. We wanted to be Mods, and we wanted to be part of what was really happening now. Trevor and I were just a couple of working-class kids. And there was always this incredible rivalry between us. I was a fucking nutter in them days. Trev said something to me at the first rehearsal, I got him down on the floor and started kicking him in the head. The band arrived at rehearsals, they said, 'This ain't a good way to start a band Chris, is it? What's the matter with ya?'"

"Carl Wayne had heard about The Move plan. He changed his image and everything and came with us. By then I had told Carl, I'd be leaving The Vikings. Next thing I knew, Carl was saying he wouldn't mind changing his image and joining us. He was in his twenties, and like an 'old man' to us then. So was Bev — but Carl could get work, was a good front man. It seemed totally logical to include him. Then Bev Bevan joined and of course, we had asked Roy before Carl and Bev."

Ace was best mates with John Bonham, the future Led Zeppelin drumming legend. Many Birmingham drummers quaked when Bonham walked into a gig. They hoped he wouldn't want to play a number on their kits. Most of the drum kits could not withstand the brutal hammering that John Bonham dealt out. His pulverising style was evident even back then. Leaving kits lying around in shards on the stage. Ace maintains that he and Bonham were besties. "We used to meet down the Cedar Club and other places. 'Bonzo' was unbelievably loud. He was playing like that already, when he was about 15 or 16. He was in the running to be the first drummer in The Move. Something happened, he didn't wanna do it."

"The first person they asked was Roy Wood," remembers Bev, speaking to Des Tong. "And then they asked me. I'm not sure exactly? It's a bit of a grey area? They might have asked John Bonham before me, I don't know. They won't admit that" Bevan recalls with a mischievous grin. "John Bonham was my best mate, anyway. We'd known each other for years,"

Ace Kefford reminisced in an interview with Martin Kinch; owner of the Cherry Blossom Clinic fan-site, "So, I went up and said 'John, we're doing this new thing. We've got me, Trevor and Roy Wood. Do you want to come with us on the drums? He turned us down. He didn't want to do it. He wanted to carry on with what he was in. He was with Robert Plant then."

Leaving Bonham and Plant to their own musical aspirations (which later on, created some very much larger noise, all by themselves), Bevan joined Ace, Trevor and Roy. Teaming up with the well-known Birmingham singer Carl Wayne. Carl came in as the last piece of the musical puzzle. He had a solid business head, and he also owned a PA system. Carl asserts, "We didn't wanna play all this crap anymore. We're here in the clubs until three in the morning, for drunks, pimps and whores. What for?"

It's said that Bonham didn't like Carl Wayne. Carl totally disagreed, "I've heard strange stories, which stated Bonham would not join the group, because I was the singer. But that's absolute bollocks, because he was a great friend of mine." Ace insists that, "That was before Bev joined — but I think he would've been the wrong drummer. He would have blown us off the bleeding stage."

An interesting couple of gigs happened for Ace after The Chantelle's but before Carl Wayne. These sparked his growing interest in black music even further. The next Carl Wayne and The Vikings single, produced by Alan A. Freeman and released by Pye Records was a song entitled 'This Is Love'. It was composed by Danny King who also duetted with Carl on the vocals. But like the first Vikings single it did not sell enough copies to make the charts.

As a last attempt, another Carl Wayne and The Vikings 45, a cover of Otis Redding's 'My Girl' was issued in the USA only but met with little interest there. Ace Kefford said; "We weren't particularly bothered about the singles not doing well. Nothing had happened with the singles. Yet we didn't care, because at least we had records out. Which meant we could say we were 'Pye Recording Stars' on the posters for our gigs and bookings." Two B-sides that Ace remembers with a juddering shudder, are 'Shimmy Shammy Jingle' and 'You Could Be Fun (At The End Of A Party)'.

They were both written by Carl Wayne's solicitor, an old guy from central Birmingham called Howard Wynschenk who thought he was a bit of a songwriter. He was a big mate of Alan A. Freeman at Pye Records. Carl recalls the solicitor's song writing efforts: "I used to demo a few of the songs at Edmund Studios. Stuff like 'He Got Oil', 'You Could Be Fun', 'Shimmy Shammy Jingle,' which were complete and utter drivel. But I liked him, he was a decent man, and he got me recording. He wrote these under the name of Robert Romaine and he stipulated that he wrote our B-sides. When I tell you his best effort for us was 'Shimmy Shammy Jingle', you'll follow my drift. He was a decent guy really and he did get us recording."

After the cancellation of their record contract Carl Wayne and The Vikings secured

When I was a little boy my mamma dropped me on my head

more German bookings in early 1965. But before they were to leave, drummer Dave Hollis left and was replaced by Bev Bevan for the last year of existence. Bevan had played in a well-known local group called The Diplomats. The band's full name was Denny Laine and The Diplomats. Bev was to become yet another important and essential link in The Move chain.

Bev Bevan
Beverley Bevan was born on 25th November 1944. "The Bevan family hailed from South Yardley in Birmingham. Beverley Bevan lost his virginity to a Rotherham miner's daughter and further to touring in Germany. He was so poor he slept on sheets covered in blood and semen." This is an extract from Bev's book, *The Electric Light Orchestra Story*. which includes some information on The Move but is mostly ELO based (Mushroom Books, 1980). Bev has kept a diary since 1962. You could say he was the Bill Wyman of The Move. Like any rock star life, you learn that life isn't always a hot bed of expensive limos, good wine and even better women.

With a name like Beverley, in a rough city like Birmingham, He made the right choice to shorten it to Bev Bevan. "My father, Charles Bevan used to play drums part time in a dance band. He was nicknamed 'Bev Bevan' and obviously I thought I ought to get the name on an official basis. I inherited a major thing from my father and that was working for myself. He hated working for other people and he would do anything to avoid it. Whether he was a coal merchant, setting up a mobile library, training boxers in a local gym. Racing motorbikes — anything to keep his independence."

Unfortunately, Bev's father died when Bev was just eleven years old. His mother Ada ran a small shop in a Victorian terraced row, situated along the busy Stratford Road, located in Sparkhill, Birmingham. Access to the goodies in the shop felt just like a child's paradise to Bev. He got a lot of encouragement from his mother to go into the music industry and play drums. He attended the Moseley Grammar School — a fairly buttoned up and strict place. Chalkboards and teachers with mortar boards — the entire shebang.

At the age of 14 he had a religious awakening, he first heard 'Jailhouse Rock' by Elvis Presley. He got suspended from the school for the first time. The sin was taking in his school grey trousers to make them into drainpipes. A pair of mock crocodile shoes were purchased to ape the winkle pickers that would become a major style object. After the short suspension Bev had a rousing welcome back by the younger kids watching his return as they saw him ton up to the school on his Dawes Dominator bike, painted a cool black and yellow. A young rebel and a Teddy Boy of sorts.

In preparation for being a rockstar, Bev practiced writing 'Bev Bevan' again and again, all over his school notebooks. Bev was close too throughout school, and sat next to a guy, called Bobby Davies from Acocks Green in Birmingham. Bobby Davies however, followed in a different career path but also attained success and stardom by becoming comedian 'Jasper Carrott.' With a massive following he has had several TV shows and TV series to his name.

"We decided to form a group at school, myself and four classmates — Ronnie Smith, Tony Lewis, Dave "Wongy" Weiland and Phil Ackrill (who would go on to be my lifelong best friend until his passing). We called ourselves Rocking Ronnie & the

Renegades, but we eventually became the Senators. For no apparent reason I opted to be the drummer. I found a new kit of Broadway silver sparkle drums at a music shop in Birmingham city centre. They were £32, a small fortune in the late 1950s. I asked my mum if she would lend me the money and was shocked when she immediately said yes. It was months later that she told me that my dad was a drummer and that she was delighted I had inherited his talent. Shortly after the Second World War he had a dance band called The Bev Bevan Trio. So not only did I inherit his drumming prowess, I inherited his name too."

Some very early influences on Bev's drumming style stood out, "I think that I was first influenced in that drumming style when I heard 'Lullaby Of The Leaves' by The Ventures in 1961 (my last year at Moseley Grammar School). I didn't know the drummer's name at the time (it was Howie Johnson). Also, shortly after that I was much influenced in a similar style by Brian Bennett's drumming on Cliff Richard and the Shadows tracks 'Do You Wanna Dance' and 'It'll Be Me'." The latter went on to be included in The Move's memorable *Something Else From The Move* EP. Bev brought in a lot of the rock 'n' roll elements to The Move. As for Bev Bevan's all-time influences on drums, he cites the following, "Hal Blaine (Phil Spector), Keith Moon (The Who), John Bonham (Led Zeppelin), Danny Seraphine (Chicago), Anton Fig (Joe Bonamassa) and his all-time favourite, being his fellow Brummie John Bonham."

Big Bev was a schoolboy rebel, and his feelings of musicality were growing stronger. With the drums set up at home, Bev looked at the sparkling drum kit and deep in thought, pondered, "Well now all I gotta do is learn how to play them." Two friends Tony Lewis and Ronnie Smith were hanging around: "We formed a band. We found it almost impossible to get gigs." Eventually providing their services for free at Hall Green Youth Club. "Even then we could only play during a break in the Square Dance." The beleaguered lads all played through a tiny amplifier. With Bev drowning out everybody on his brand spanking new kit.

Bev also realised this could be an important step forward. Girls started hanging around and two things were becoming super important. One — girls were talking to Bev and two — he was accepted as one of the lads at school. The guys eventually settled on a name and called themselves The Senators. The Hall Green Youth club eventual paid them £2 and 10 shillings. They wore a stage outfit of sorts. Black shoes with buckles, grey slacks, white shirts, red ties and a blue blazer with a red cardboard handkerchief. I hope they didn't look too much like a gaggle of holiday camp attendants. The Senators had a kind of residency in a Soho side street in Birmingham. They played in a place called the Las Vegas Coffee Bar. Playing the dimly lit dump, two or three times a week, until about two in the morning. Bev remembers, "The place was packed wall-to-wall with prostitutes, pimps, perverts and homosexuals. Not that we knew one from the other."

Bev managed to obtain two GCEs. These being O-levels in Art and English Literature. According to Bev, "This put me down immediately for The Beehive." This was one big, old ghastly store in the centre of Birmingham. It was designed for Victorian middle-class families to do their shopping at ease. The Beehive had dropped in ranking. A long way down since its Victorian heydays. The staff were still there but the customers had stayed well away. Jasper Carrott also arrived at The Beehive. Carrott had the same two GCE O-level exam results as Bev, putting him on

When I was a little boy my mamma dropped me on my head

the same level of potential as Bev, with the chance to mind numbingly become, after the requisite training — a Beehive Trainee Buyer.

One high point at the store was Jasper and Bev both got put together in Father Christmas' Grotto and with the thousands of displayed 'lucky dips' for kids, they did everything they could to dispel the soul-destroying boredom of working at The Beehive. However, a break was to occur, with a link to a trainee, in the television department at Rackham's. This was another department store in the city. His name was Bryan Frederick Hinds. Hinds would soon become internationally known. By then Hinds was sporting the new moniker of Denny Laine. He is primarily best known for his stint as lead singer with The Moody Blues and their massive hit 'Go Now!' He is also remembered for his long-time association with Paul McCartney in the post-Beatles band Wings.

Bev remembers Denny Laine as being extremely ambitious. Laine talked a good fight, but he also pursued his ambition beyond just talking. To make the transition to gigs they bought an old rusty Bedford van for £30. This also alleviated the need, to be seen on the Birmingham bus routes. Avoiding being gurned at constantly by old ladies and just about everyone else. The fascination being that each member had decided to peroxide their hair blond. In those times and as a young lad, this was a startlingly visual, bonding device, to be seen outside of a Bedford van or the stage.

As Denny Laine and The Diplomats, this cute blond look worked well in the posed band photographs. They also got a recording contract with EMI. This was being handled by a guy called John Birch. Birch had also produced the 'zany' Freddie and The Dreamers. None of The Diplomats recorded efforts, were either applauded or indeed released. The gruelling tedium and boredom of the travel to gigs and driving et al was alleviated one night when a guy approached the band. He asked them in a broad Black Country accent, "Hi! Our kid! Giss us a go with your group."

"He had some very big mates with him who looked very menacing," Bev remembered, "So we thought we had better give him a vocal slot." Bev remembers him clearly as absolutely brilliant. "He did Elvis Presley's 'One Night' and by the time he had finished, Denny Laine wanted him in the band. He was Nicky James from Tipton and he had four paternity suits taken out against him."

The group picked him up from Scunthorpe and they all piled into the Bedford. Bev remembers Nicky's speciality all too well. This was an anatomical one as Nicky was the possessor of a very enormous knob. Nicky would say to people, "It's like a baby's arm, holding an apple." They were now named Denny and The Diplomats - *featuring Nicky James*.

On the strength of Nicky's name and charisma, the band got a recording contract. They had to do an audition for Pye Records. Tony Hatch was a well-known producer, writer of many hit singles (including 'Sugar And Spice' for The Searchers) and he was an enthusiastic go-getter in the music industry. Hatch decided to give them a listen. He came up to the Springfield Ballroom in Birmingham to check them out. He came over to Bev at one point and said, "Is that all you can play?" Even though Hatch found Bev's drumming 'samey' that night he thought The Diplomats were good enough, to bring down to London and record some demos at Pye Studios.

Bev with The Diplomats managed to support The Beatles at one gig at The Old Hill Plaza, Birmingham. This was part of the legendary Ma Regan's gig circuit. Paul

Flowers In The Rain - The Untold Story of The Move

McCartney praised Bevan's drumming, after a rousing solo in 5/4 time. A very cool stroking of Bev's ego, from one of the biggest of the big boys. But by now Denny Laine's ego was starting to become even more inflatable and more insufferable. He was Denny Laine but he was also *the* Denny Laine. He dyed his hair black but in a token revenge, Bev and guitarist Phil Ackrill also dyed their hair black. When Danny Lane saw this, he had an apoplectic fit. "Why are you dyeing your' hair black, I'm Denny Laine, not you guys!"

He also turned on the hapless Steve Horton. Steve had remained blond in respect and deference to the domineering Laine. But Horton got very short shrift from Laine, "You're the only blond left! You're the real fucking prick Steve! Everybody's gonna think that you're Denny Laine!" Such was Laine's enormous and ever-growing corpulent ego that you couldn't win either way. And no good deed ever went unpunished!

Denny went off and joined another band called The Moody Blues. They would hook up with a fascinating character from London called Tony Secunda and go on to achieve stardom.

Bev had sadly gone back to working in the store. The Diplomats were no more, Phil Ackrill had got married. The hapless Steve Horton also had to go. He later hooked up with Danny King and The Valets. The fabulously engorged Nicky James had also been pushed out a little earlier.

The bulge in his specially tightened trousers and his terrific Elvis impressions did not quite overcome his unbelievably broad accent. Saying good night to the audiences with a surreal, "Ta very much, loik!" To the gagging band members, it was pure pantomime Salvador Dalí. To the audience, they probably couldn't give a shit. As long as Nicky's knackers and evident bulge was on clear display.

Bev was glum and not looking forward to the January sales and the distinct possibility of lesser stardom on the semi-pro circuit in Birmingham. However, a confident, gregarious chap walked into the store and provided the next rung on the ladder for Bev Bevan. An escape from becoming a locally known musician. From being a big fish in a small pond. This was Carl Wayne, still fronting The Vikings and now the city's top professional band. Carl said simply, "Are you looking for a gig? Our drummer is leaving." Bev was miffed at being asked to audition. Even though he was well known throughout Birmingham by now. He must've played well enough as Carl said, "You're in, you'll get £30 quid a week and your first set of dates will be in Germany, next week." At the age of 20, Bev Bevan was going to come into contact with another £30 since he had bought his first drum kit. Life on the road and in Hamburg with The Vikings followed on and Bev recalled it like this. "From 7:00pm, we did seven 45-minute spots with just 15-minute breaks, right up until 2 o'clock in the morning."

Each weekend there were three-hour matinees as well. The accommodation they had was the absolute shits. All areas were totally covered in rubbish. Rats roamed around as freely as they fancied. Lots of dried blood and semen stains were encrusted into the bed sheets. Both Carl and Bev quickly began to realise, that this was another dead end! They were going to hit a wall and hit it very soon.

The Vikings had already released two singles on Pye Records before Bev joined. They also had a secure residency at the Cedar Club in Birmingham. It was here that part of the initial seeds of The Move were born.

Trevor Burton

Trevor Burton was born on 9th March 1949. His family was based in the Aston area of Birmingham, a working-class area. His original family name was Ireson and like Carl Wayne, Trevor gave his surname a more stage-like and filmic touch, by changing it to Burton. Trevor described the area of Aston, "As being like a village within Birmingham, it had its own Manor house (Aston Hall), its own brewery, its own bakery, its own dairy. There were lots of little factories and little streets of factories around. It was a place on its own. Birmingham was brought together sometime later — the outlying little villages and towns. Birmingham was like the trading centre, and they brought it all together into the city of Birmingham." Aston apparently was the last place to become part of Birmingham. Trevor considered himself to be from Aston and not from Birmingham.

His father was working in the steel mill feeding coal into the furnaces. He was a hard worker and unfortunately for Trevor, his father died when Trevor was just sixteen years old. In fact, he died a couple of months after Trevor had joined The Move. So, Burton senior, missed his son's early glory years. His mother was a great, solid hard-working woman. Trevor found out later that she was very proud of what her son had achieved. But she would never tell Trevor. Both his parents were musical. They sang around the working men's clubs. Trevor's brothers were also musical. The oldest brother sang with a big band set up. His middle brother was in a skiffle band. Music ran in the (Ireson) family. "My oldest brother was about fourteen years older than me. My middle brother was about eleven years older. So, there was a big gap between the middle brother and me." Trevor laughed as he remembers, "My mother always used to say that my middle name was "mistake".

Young Trevor grabbed the music bug when he was about six or seven. Hearing on the radio songs like 'Singing The Blues', 'Hound Dog' and 'Blue Suede Shoes'. He was captured by music and then he heard Buddy Holly and that was it for him.

Trevor saw Johnny Ray when he was about nine or ten years old. He was fascinated by seeing girls screaming at somebody on stage. He also saw Lonnie Donnegan when he was ten and he found that a "phenomenal" experience also. At first Trevor was primarily interested in drums, "I was about six or seven when I started to play the drums. I would knock out a rhythm on anything at hand, anything I could hit. My uncle made me some drumsticks at work and so I had a makeshift drum kit with homemade drumsticks. A biscuit tin with lots of elastic bands wrapped around it for a snare and an old kettle turned upside down for a tom-tom. Then we found an old drum kit in a junk shop. It had a bass drum, a snare, a set of skulls, a wood block and two small cymbals and off I went and never looked back."

The young and precocious Trevor was a natural in his initial playing on the drums. No lessons, he just got on the kit and started to play and had a natural feel. Seeing Buddy Holly playing his Fender Stratocaster further propelled the young Trevor, "When I was 8 years old, I got my first guitar which my brother had brought back from Singapore and taught myself to play. I've loved guitars ever since."

He gives a feel of being a kid in Aston; "Back in the 1950s England was very austere. It was still bankrupt from the war. Everything was brown and grey. Food was still rationed when I was a little kid. I think up until I was about eight or nine actually. Then everything started to pick up. Just around the same time as rock 'n' roll is breaking through for us kids back then. It was the light in the darkness. Our light in the darkness."

Trevor's ability to play drums came in handy later in The Move's live set, when Bev Bevan came out front stage to sing 'Zing Went The Strings Of My Heart' and also at certain demo recordings. One version of 'A Certain Something' written by Dave Scott-Morgan has Trevor doing a shuffle on the kit. Trevor got into singing, primarily because he was an ice skater, "I met some guys at the ice rink. They were into the music. They were a bit older than me. One had a guitar; one had a drum kit. The drummer was Keith Smart (later of The Rocking Berries, Balls, The Ugly's, Wizzard and more). Keith and I were like brothers. We grew up together, Keith and me. I think my mum used to go out with his dad actually, when they were both young."

Trevor formed a band called Trevor Burton and The Everglades. "I was the front man and I used to sing. Eventually we found another ice skating guy, who became the bass player. In a strange, (almost pre-Sid Vicious-like stance), the bass player would just stand there and plug-in but not switch on! So it looked like we had a full band (laughs). We had two guitars, bass, drums and me singing out the front like Cliff Richard." At that time Trevor was just 13 years old. "I was still at school and gigging about four nights a week. And I was making more money than the teachers then. I was making about £15-£20 a week, which was a lot of money then in 1964. Particularly for a 13-year-old boy. I was earning twice as much as my dad was."

In a tip of the hat to the "real world", Trevor had one job which lasted just a week. "That was servicing cars — I was underneath the car one day, changing the oil. It all came out all over my head, I said, 'That's it, I quit!' I never went back. That's the only job I ever had! (Laughs)"

Danny King was ploughing his own rock 'n' roll furrow in Birmingham, even before The Beatles had gotten going. Danny went out to Germany two or three times as well. The young Trevor had joined his band. "He was well respected around the Midlands. He had a chance to be a big star. But he turned it down. People wanted to sign him up.

Norrie Paramor who was the head honcho at EMI Records wanted to sign him up. Danny was set up for some recording sessions, but he just didn't go. He didn't even turn up even. He said he didn't wanna be famous in that way — he just hated it. I was in his band for about just over a year. I was sixteen and a half when The Move formed after leaving Danny. Danny King was playing old-style straight-ahead rock 'n' roll and he was considered to be the foremost singer in Birmingham at that time."

Danny King was in possession of a phenomenal record collection. Shelves and shelves packed full of tasty imported 45rpm singles. They were all neatly stacked in alphabetical order, all pristine. They were all mostly American 45 imports.

Trevor laughingly remembers, "Danny used to cover up all his 45s with bits of tape. You couldn't see who it was recorded by. Or who wrote the song, or what the song was called? That was so none of the other bands, could steal the song and they would be unique to Danny King."

Trevor remembers trying to get to gigs, right out in the sticks with Danny King's band before motorways were built. "It was all 'B' roads everywhere and it used to take ages and hours, to get anywhere back then. In terms of musical influences, later, I really dug deeper and got into all the blues greats, too. Sonny Boy Williams, Howlin' Wolf, Muddy Waters, BB King, Freddie King, Screaming Jay Hawkins and many more. I saw all these blues artists when they played in Birmingham in the sixties and it got into my skin. I was hanging out with Ace Kefford, who was in The Vikings with Carl Wayne. We used to meet up for late night chats at Alex's Pie Stand and at the Cedar Club. There was a stage at the Cedar — not a very big stage — and a little dance area. There was a circular bar in the middle, and an eating area. There were a few tables you could sit and drink at and that was it really. Also, a little casino, a couple of card tables and the roulette wheel and some one-arm bandits. You would (very) often find Danny King in the Cedar as he was addicted to the fruit machines. It was a great little scene — they used to close about three in the morning. So, you could go there after gigs, get some food and a drink and meet up and chat."

Ace saw the changes coming. "Pye saw us as brand leaders of Brum Beat, as opposed to Merseybeat. The first single 'What's A Matter Baby' was a Timi Yuro cover. Danny King wrote the A-side of the second one. Trevor Burton was in his backing group, The Mayfair Set. Trevor and Danny sang it together, like The Everly Brothers. I remember them at The Carlton Club, playing 'This Is Love' to us in the dressing room. Carl was saying, 'Can we have that song, Danny, for our next single?' Trevor and Ace were both aware of what is going on in London. "You have to remember The Small Faces, had broken out about this time. The Who are coming through, you had The Kinks and these guys are all in the charts. The music world is changing, looking at all that. Ace and I said, 'Why don't we get the youngest, the best musicians, out of all the bands and put a new band together?'"

5.
Is there any truth in what they say?

Trevor and Ace forged ahead with the exciting plan to start a "superstar" band in Birmingham, towards the end of 1965. "The first guy was Roy Wood; he was playing the guitar with Mike Sheridan. He is a very talented guy, a great guitar player and a great singer. He looked good as well. He was about the same age. We pulled him into a little side room at the Cedar Club one night. We asked him if he was interested and he said, 'Yeah, count me in. But keep it secret!' (Laughs). Roy looked different, I have to say, he had terrible skin. I think that's why he grew that beard eventually. He used to always put his pancake make-up on his face before shows. Sometimes he looked like he had just put cement on his face — hahaha!" Trevor continues, "Ace may have told you this as well, but John Bonham was there and he was on the periphery of things. We were friends with John and Robert Plant. They were in The Band Of Joy and they all sang out of the Cedar Club as well. As I remember we didn't ask John Bonham to play. But he was always around then. Of course, Bev was playing with Ace in The Vikings. And Bev was quite a unique drummer for the time. He was a very heavy drummer and really, really loud! A bit Keith Moon-like, and a crazy style, a good bit crazy." Trevor had gone through an early, "full scale looning scene" already at his tender age. This didn't end any time soon.

Roy Wood
Roy Wood was born on 8th November 1946 in Kitts Green, a suburb of Birmingham. For some years the legend persisted that his real name was Ulysses Adrian Wood. Until it was eventually revealed that this was probably the result of somebody close to The Move in their early days, filling in such names on a 'lifelines' feature for the press as a joke. Roy started off playing harmonica (his dad bought him a chromatic harmonica at the tender age of 10) and drums. He was making the usual racket any kids learning these instruments would. His first 'gig' was playing the drums at his sister's wedding, at the age of six, along with the Sam Harris band. Sam played timpani for the Symphonic Orchestra.

At about the age of 12 he decided guitar was to be his next instrument and he was a quick learner. He began learning Chuck Berry and Little Richard style guitar riffs. Within a six months or so period he was in his first band called The Falcons. Wood had already boarded a bus bound for Birmingham Town Hall to see The Shadows with Cliff Richard. This spurred on his guitar playing enthusiasm even further. Roy remembers the sound of Hank Marvin's guitar when he first heard it live, "His guitar was so clean, it sounded like he'd been dipped in Dettol Antiseptic). Bruce Welch was playing a Fender Jaguar, and he was really tight. You could hear the strings stretching and squelching."

The Falcons were carted around Birmingham in an old Morris van by driver Mick Davis. They even gigged at the Lea Hall British Legion where Roy Wood's mum pulled the pints. Early on Roy's musical humour and eccentricity began to blossom. Roy had a party piece with The Falcons, he loved playing the 'Theme From the Dambusters.' In a very scaled-down version of the future Move light show, which Mick Davis, the intrepid driver recalls, "The barman there used to flash the lights, as if it was last orders. All the while, Roy feverishly plucked out the Dambusters tune." He left the Falcons in 1963 to join Gerry Levene and the Avengers. His flair for drawing led to his attending Moseley College of Art but he was expelled in 1964. I wonder if the young Roy, when dreaming ahead and creating artworks at Moseley Art School, realised the power and the longevity of those initial thoughts and written ideas? Another guy called Tony Withers (a member of Ronny and The Senators) attended Moseley's Art College at the same time as Roy.

Roy took over from Tony in The Senators and Tony literally gave Roy his coveted Binson 'Echorec' unit for nothing. A touching display of guitarist unity for once. The Binson was also used most famously by Hank Marvin.

Mike Sheridan And The Nightriders (the band that later became The Idle Race) had now obtained the guitar talents of Roy Wood who prior to this had only lasted with The Avengers for four months. He already had two of the qualifications before he even plucked a string. He answered an advertisement in the *Birmingham Post & Mail* that read:

WANTED
LEAD GUITARIST TO JOIN PRO GROUP
MUST HAVE FENDER GUITAR, VOX AMP AND BINSON ECHO

Roy also attracted attention with one of his early writing attempts. Norrie Paramor agreed to record and release one of Roy's songs with The Nightriders, 'Make Them Understand'. It was recorded at Ladbroke Studios, a small studio behind Vincent Ladbroke's shop in Bristol Street. Johnny Haines had done some early primitive recording sessions upstairs in the Ladbrokes organ showroom. This got Vincent Ladbroke infused and fired up. Vincent was a frustrated songwriter and was looking to strike upwards. He set up the recording studios at the rear. Mike Sheridan recalls, "It wasn't a bad song with a kind of a Tom Jones feel. I was in mind to give it a Tom Jones feel vocally. Tom Jones was massive at the time with 'It's Not Unusual'. But my recorded attempt to do a Tom thing at the recording, was a bit of a flop."

Dave Pritchard was at the recording and remembers the early songwriting attempt. "We didn't know Roy could write the kind of songs he did write eventually. 'Make Them Understand' was a very poppy, mid-tempo kind of thing, big pocket. Almost a Tom Jones thing, the rhythm that was going on."

Roy Wood remembers, "The early songs I wrote at school or college or when

Is there any truth in what they say?

I was in Mike Sheridan's lot were never really taken seriously. I didn't think people were interested in 'em. I was writing fairy stories for adults, things with a nasty twist. I didn't have a clue what do with them. So, I saved them up in folders, and then started producing them for lyrics, when I was encouraged to do so in The Move. It was quite useful," he says with typical self-effacement, "because they gave us a head start."

Changes were afoot and quickly, not only in the Birmingham music scene, but in the music scene in Great Britain, as a whole. Two young confident, stylish, whippersnapper Mod-looking boys went and saw Davy Jones and The Lower Third perform their Mod-styled set at the popular Cedar Club and the rest is music history. Particularly when they approached Roy Wood to play guitar in their new, fresh band. In which the best of the best in Birmingham, were to join and create a totally new sound, on a totally new level.

Ace Kefford recalled, "Trevor and I were there one night, and Davy Jones and The Lower Third were performing at the Cedar Club." Their vocalist Davy Jones (later better known as David Bowie) suggested to Trevor Burton and Ace Kefford that they should form their own group. Kefford also recalled that Davy Jones and The Lower Third "were like The Who, wearing target jumpers, hipster trousers, doing stuff like 'Heatwave' and 'Needle In A Haystack'. Chatting afterwards, David put the notion in our heads of forming our own band. We approached Roy Wood who was already singing that sort of stuff with The Nightriders. I had a similar spot in The Vikings doing 'Jump Back' and 'Every Little Bit Hurts', I was trying to copy Stevie Winwood — just like everyone else around then."

Davy Jones may have been tickled and was impressed with their desire to succeed. Jones (Bowie) urged the eager twosome to find the best players in town and make up a supergroup. Then to leverage their own strengths and talent. Bowie was thinking along the very same lines that they were. His resolve got them to focus their minds and start seriously getting on with the job. The Mod thing was to inform the mood, the Mod styles, their selective choice of cover versions and their attitude to life stage performance. "Because of the variety of our cover versions we would attract both Mods and rockers to our gigs. It could be a potentially, dangerous situation. We certainly had a problem with the Mods, who came and had a go at us, because they thought we were rockers," laughed Carl Wayne, we looked Mod and were into soul. But we also liked Eddie Cochran."

Mike Sheridan said, "We'd played almost everywhere in England supporting The Beatles, The Who, The Small Faces, Van Morrison's Them, Dave Dee etc, you name 'em. We'd come full circle. Times were changing and Roy was the first to see the light. For me Roy's departure signalled the end."

Roy recalls The Move first repertoire. "In The Move, we were playing Motown, (and US soul and R&B) but actually playing it more, with a rock aspect. Everybody sang and we did more harmonies. Earlier on we wanted to sound unique, but with a bottom end of musical tension like The Who and vocally similar to the Beach Boys. Whatever was good at that time. We were fed up, with being 'human jukeboxes' just playing chart material."

6.
Please correct me if I seem to be making too much noise!

The "Young Turks" as Carl called them, were ripe and ready to go. The Move played their 'unofficial' debut gig at the Belfry Hotel in Stourbridge on 23rd January 1966.

The crowd was young and enthusiastic, and they drew considerable applause from the appreciative audience. Later that same night, at about midnight, they drove up to the Cedar Club on Constitution Hill and played their second gig and this has always been seen as the "official" first Move gig. It was home from home in the sense that club owner Eddie Fewtrell was a great friend of Carl Wayne's and eventually the entire band.

Eddie Fewtrell knew them initially from Carl Wayne and the Vikings' regular gigs at the club. They were given the keys, and this enabled the band to rehearse anytime they wanted at the Cedar. That night was divided between the usual late night drinking scene and a lot of the musicians from bands in Birmingham. Many were extremely curious and expectant, to see what The Move (the crème de la crème) band from Birmingham, was going to deliver on stage.

They were not disappointed; the band came out all guns blazing. Delivering a tight hot show and winning over the expectant Midlands audience. Many of those present were aware of the melding of three popular local bands to form The Move. No doubt, Mike Sheridan and The Nightriders and Danny King's Mayfair Set were at first hand. The buzz around this new amalgamation of musicians was building fast locally around Birmingham. Jeff Lynne, who was in attendance at their first gig was totally knocked out by the band. As was singer-songwriter guitarist Dave Scott-Morgan. Carl Wayne remembers the early dynamic underpinning of the gigs. "The black soul songs we were doing in the very early days were very much from the influence of Trevor and Ace. You must never forget that, although people talk about Roy being the key influence on The Move. It's complete and utter gibberish."

Roger Spencer, future drummer with the Idle Race was there. "I was at that gig and they were magnificent. I just remember these guys coming on — they looked like stars. They looked the part. They sounded the part. All those great voices out the front, they were unbelievable!"

****

Alex's Pie Stand (aka The Snackerie) is now talked about in hallowed terms by many of these musicians. Alex's was a teeming central spot in Birmingham during the 1960s for band members to get a hot meal after their late-night gigs. Situated opposite the central Albany Hotel it was well populated, particularly on Saturday night after performances. The bands would park their vans along Smallbrook in Queensway. Groups met at Alex's and exchanged stories, discussed future plans, and caught up on the latest music news. Musicians could feast on piping hot cups of tea, hamburgers and hot dogs. So many Brummies will remember Alex's portions of his famous *Fleur de Lys* Steak & Kidney or Chicken & Mushroom meat pies. The Move line-up was partially negotiated by the hungry fivesome, meeting and chatting about ideas at Alex's Pie Stand.

Dave Scott-Morgan remembers the early scene, where every band member knew every other one and congregated late at night in Birmingham. "One night outside Alex's Pie Stand, (Alex was closed early) we looked out of our steamed-up car windows. Someone said I'm starving. Charlie (Carl) Wayne suggested, 'Let's go to the Cedar Club for a chip butty. Don't be daft, Charlie, you can't get a seat in there? You can't get a chip butty at a nightclub? Yes! You can, sit here', said Carl, 'Just watch me'. So that's what we did, we drove to the Cedar. We installed ourselves at one of the tables near the stage. In the dimly lit gully that passed for a restaurant, we watched with peals of laughter, as Carl Wayne ordered up the chip butties! A result! The waiter gingerly scribbled something on a pad and disappeared into the kitchen. The way he re-emerged with a tray was utterly hilarious. From which we were served, with totally exaggerated decorum and his broken English, 'There you are gentlemen… they are the good size and enjoy your meal'. Giant doorstep pieces of bread, cut into sandwich blocks. Spread thickly with butter and all in between the chips — absolutely glorious!"

Dave Scott-Morgan clearly remembers, "Carl Wayne had a much more, different take on glory to me. One of the most outrageous things he used to do, was smash up television sets on stage. The way 'Charlie' did it was akin to a religious experience. I know — I was part of the expectant congregation at The Belfry Club, a grand hotel in Wishaw near Sutton Coldfield, out in the countryside. Jeff Lynne was there; he was blown away by the band and Roy Wood's guitar playing. Carl Wayne was on stage with the recently formed "supergroup" The Move. The music had evaporated into a long solo. Roy Wood was studiously thrashing his Fender guitar and Trevor Burton on rhythm guitar, stood onstage like an angry sphinx. He strode around, lasering the audience with his steely glare. At the stage front, Carl was transfixed into a mean pose and lost in an apparent meditation. All the time stage lights were flashing. That was a new thing too, before the name 'Strobe' lights was ever invented. At the back Bev Bevan industriously flailed away at his drum kit. I do believe I saw the flicker of a grin pass over Bev's face. Then Carl brought out the axe…"

Steve Gibbons vividly recalls the first gig: "I thought it was the best thing I'd heard, from all the Birmingham bands. mainly because just from that particular period, there were probably around about a hundred bands in Birmingham and the majority were mediocre and some of them were quite good. So, the competition was pretty fierce when The Move kicked in, because they worked really hard on their harmonies. I've always loved harmonies in rock bands. The Move stood on top."

Please correct me if I seem to be making too much noise!

Trevor Burton also remembered, "In the same week, maybe we played at a place called The Elbow Room in Aston, Birmingham (3rd February). A lot more musicians came and saw us there. That was it! That's where it really kicked in! We were a force to be reckoned with, especially vocally. We were one of the best in the country — we must've been. It just all came together and gelled very easily."[3]

Eddie Fewtrell recalls in his book *King Of Clubs* (Fewtrell was a man that loved his music), "I then started out promoting bands, such as The Walker Brothers, through a guy in London called Barry Gibb. This guy Gibb kept asking me to put his wife on the stage. Because I was promoting bands like Carl Wayne, Denny Laine and The Diplomats and hundreds of other small groups in Birmingham at the time. Danny King was a celebrated voice in that Birmingham fraternity."

Danny King was another singer that Fewtrell liked a lot, "Danny was really good you know, and we also had people like Tom Jones playing here before he had a nose job."

Ron Gray was an ex-champion boxer, and he remembered, "The Cedar Club had atmosphere, it was always packed. The reason that Eddie was Number One in the city, was that every club you walked in through the door the atmosphere hit you — that's why his clubs are always full."

Bev Bevan remembers clearly that double header night. "After the Belfry club we drove down to the Cedar Club for our inaugural Move gig and that was the night I met Val. She was to become my wife, and we met, at the very first Move gig." Bev maintains at least initially, "I don't think The Move would've got off the ground at first if it wasn't for Eddie Fewtrell. All the rehearsals and all the gigs he gave us, just to get the band off the ground. Tony Secunda came down to see us at The Cedar Club. Just because we were there so often. By a year later, we had completely left the Birmingham scene."

The Move went into 1966 with a busy gig sheet. The roster was expanding, all the way through the year. Perfecting their stage moves, constantly changing the repertoire. Building up their inherent, dynamic power and gathering followers at every step. They hit the ground running that first year, with a united and firm resolve. The young band went into Ladbroke Sound Recording Studios[4] in January 1966 and recorded four demo songs. All were written by budding composer Roy Wood.

Ladbroke Studios was run by Johnny Haines, who recorded a good few live recordings of the early 5-piece band. Possibly including their debuts at the Belfry and Cedar Club. I know I, as well as many other Move "aficionados", would love to hear some of those early, electrifying live shows. As regards the four demos, you could say, that Roy hadn't found his feet as yet. But these four songs show versatility, some great, raw Mod-style, flamboyance and initial flashes of those scintillating vocals which would become heightened throughout 1966. They are finding their way, towards a definable Move sound.

The first cut, 'You're The One I Need'[5] is a complete and utter corker. With a great raw Ace Kefford vocal. It opens with Roy Wood jabbing out some guitar-stuttering, feedback which starts the crazy, uninhibited track. It's a swirling-tumbling-chaotic-Mod-vibing cut. The production with absolutely no inhibition whatsoever,

---

[3] The Elbow Room eventually closed down for good in 2012 following some shooting incidents.
[4] Later known as Zella Studios.
[5] Included as the first track on disc one of *The Move Anthology* released on Salvo in 2007.

dynamically swerves around the ear drums. It also sounds like a possible one take in the studio… with a feel of total spontaneity. Complete with a loud piercing whistle from Ace during the performance. Are The Move, the only band who actually used the 'human' whistle as a 'thing' on their recorded pieces? The strident whistles by Ace, appeared in a good few songs, particularly in their early career. The bass and drums appear to be skidding around chaotically, with Roy and Trevor's sweeps, up and down the guitar necks adding a further topsy-turvy trajectory to the sound.

It's a raw R&B Move track. Bev builds the drumming by pushing the rolls hard on the snare and toms, crashing right onto the cymbals. The song ends with sputtering, chiming, staccato feedback. I wonder if this feral beauty, ever saw the light of the day at very early gigs?

Apparently, the Birmingham press at that time reported this as being the first recorded Move single. Certainly, 'You're The One I Need' could've been a really hot blaster of a debut single. Being put out there as early as January 1966, but it wasn't to be. (Personally, I would've loved for The Move to have done three or four of this type of killer, along with the 'Grass Grow' stuff. Some full-on Mod style, music attack, to shake up the natives).

'Fugitive' is a tambourine-driven song with a Trevor Burton vocal and the feeling of an accordion in the background. It's mid-tempo and in a low-key mode. Again, some backing vocals, calling to "run, run, run, run." 'Winter Song' is a light, country tune with another Ace vocal. Airy backing vocals let the song breathe. A plaintive song, which heralds the coming of winter and the hardships it can cause in its wake. Another strident Ace whistle signals the beginning of the country-style guitar solo part. These whistles will become an idiosyncratic part of The Move's recorded history. The last demo they recorded and (as yet) not included on any Move anthology or album so far, is a fragrant tune, 'I Know Your Face.'

This features a softer Carl Wayne vocal. It has a lilting, Latin, almost bossa nova drumbeat. It's a wonderful song with chiming guitars and Bev using either a heavily amplified cymbal bell or triangle to emphasise the exotic Latin feel. Roy thought on these different styles, "I wish I could do that now, just write freely and not being so influenced by fashion. Which you do over the years, as you learn tricks and get influenced by all around." Peter Mew at Abbey Road Studios had to work extra carefully to salvage the material from this four track Move acetate as it had badly degraded over time. It needed extremely careful handling.

The Move were getting their ducks in a row. They did a live radio recording for broadcast. Apparently, The Move's dynamic loudness startled the engineers at the BBC Studios on Broad Street in January 1966. They were more used to recording 'sedate' artists in those days. The program was broadcast on 2nd February and was presented by a local broadcaster called Tom Coyne.

Supporting The Move that day were another new and unheard band called Williams Conquerors. The Conquerors had been signed to Pye Records and played their first release called 'She.' The entire taped session remained in the possession of guitarist Bob Adams who dutifully kept a copy.

Roy Wood's 'The Fugitive' recorded that month, on the initial four track acetate was played live on The Move's session. The rest of the material was some of the current hip R&B stuff they were covering at that time. Cool material like Betty

Please correct me if I seem to be making too much noise!

Everett's 'I Can't Hear You No More' (vocals Carl), Brenda Lee's 'Is It True', (vocals Carl), 'Respectable' (vocals Ace, with a very fine shuffle beat from Bev Bevan) from the first Isley Brothers album *Shout!*. Also recorded on the session was The Marvelettes 'Too Many Fish In The Sea' (vocals Roy), and 'Don't Hang Up' by The Orlans (vocals by Bev, Carl).

A band from London called Bluesology showed up early one evening for a performance in Birmingham, at the Cedar Club. One young man carefully watched them rehearsing intently. Fronted by the veteran vocalist Long John Baldry, their young organist named Reginald Dwight (of course now Sir Elton John), in his official biography said; "We snuck in and watched them. Not only did they sound absolutely amazing, but Roy Wood's songs also sounded even better, than the cover versions they played. I can remember watching The Move and having a kind of revelation. This is it isn't it? This is the way forward. This is what I should be doing!"

Both Trevor and Ace had earlier caught a performance at the same venue by the soul-influenced, raspy tenor voice of Jess Roden and the band he fronted, The Shakedown Sound. Jess Roden went onto vocals with the popular Alan Bown Set — another favourite at The Marquee with the Mod crowd and beyond. Roden had moderate solo artist success after signing with Island Records. Ace and Trevor were floored by this Roden and Shakedown Sound performance. Giving them just the impetus they needed to pursue their growing ambition. Ace remembers clearly that night's spectacle: "The performance was brilliant, it literally took our breath away. Jess did a particularly fantastic vocal on 'Leaving Here' — an Eddie Holland penned number that had the longest introduction in the history of a pop record. Plus, Jess and the band had a great, tight Mod image while we were still having to play in Montague Burton suits."

The two cheeky and nervously confident musicians actually went up to Jess Roden and invited him to become part of a "new and exciting project." Roden wasn't interested, but that didn't put our two intrepid scene makers off at all. At that time, although they were well known in the local scene and involved in the Mod scene where they could be found dancing to the hip new R&B records and checking out the latest USA imports, Trevor and Ace soon realised that to keep going as they were, was a sure-fire way to end up in a totally dead-end street, musically and career wise. To either learn a trade, an apprenticeship. Or shovel shit on The Rotunda or other building sites, for however long that lasted.

The sound of The Move was quite extraordinary, a really tough sounding, band musically. Overlaid with gorgeous lead and harmony vocals. The music The Move produced in the beginning was truly unique, intriguing and difficult to define. It was part pop, part rhythm and blues, part psychedelic freak-beat rock. Darkly edgy it also had a wry edge, absorbing Wood's whimsical, dark and humorous lyrics allied to confident, unhesitant ensemble playing. An overlay of three and four part layered harmonies added a gorgeous, warm vocal panoramic sheen over the music. All five guys in the band could sing with strong, distinctive voices. Bev Bevan (sometimes known as 'Bullfrog Bevan') had a very deep bass voice used to great effect, when the band needed some light relief and the audience some differing, cool vocals.

The Move got Bev to sing 'Zing Went The Strings Of My Heart'. "I liked the Coasters, and my voice resembles that of their bass vocalist Dub Jones. I suggested that we included it in our original stage set for a bit of light relief really," remembers Bev.

Trevor Burton had a tough rock and soul voice. Gritty and with a raw blues influence. Trevor liked to belt it out. But he was also capable of a more gentle and tender singing style. As on 'The Girl Outside' on the first Move album. Although he was suffering with a bad cold when that particular vocal went down on to tape in the studio. (Check out Trevor's vocal gyrations on 'Something Else'). For further direction towards his more raucous vocal side, 'Something Else' can now also be heard, in two different versions, due to the recent remasters.

Roy Wood had a higher and more nasal voice. His vocals worked particularly well on some of the more dreamlike lyrics that he was writing at that time. 'Fire Brigade', the fourth Move single to chart, is one song that particularly suited his voice. There is an earlier version with Carl singing. But to me, the Roy Wood vocal version is the great version. They also recorded another earlier version, which is known as the 'piano version' with Matthew Fisher of Procol Harum supplying keyboards.

Carl Wayne doubled with Roy at times and also sang the classic middle eight. Their combined voices brought the entire performance up many notches. Roy also sounded perfect on their cover of Neil Diamond's 'Cherry Cherry', replete with great harmony vocals by the four-man front line. This cover was played on the first Move radio session in 1966. They added clever little inferences to the cover versions, never merely aping them and always adding something extra.

Carl Wayne usually took the lead vocal and overall, he sang the majority at first. Carl was often described as a "fearless performer." His versatile voice was a potent projectile with The Move. Going from a smoky tenor that took on a prowling, raw growl in his voice. Allowing Carl's soul and rhythm and blues influences, to come to the fore. Carl learnt a lot in his Vikings band days about intonation and singing in more classic styles of song delivery. The Move allowed him to throw open his vocal range in a much more liberated fashion. Personally, I would've loved to have heard more of him singing in this raw style that Carl developed in the first years in The Move. Carl Wayne was considered one of the very best singers in the UK scene. Wayne was underrated but cherished by fans of the early Move (and great vocalists).

Ace Kefford in his earlier days would mimic Stevie Winwood's soul rasp. But Ace was another very versatile vocalist. He had a striking, soulful voice with some range and also a budding talent for songwriting, which was quelled, during the first two and a half years of The Move. Ace was also able to throw some very cool Mod dance shapes whilst simultaneously playing his white Fender Precision slab bass. As well as being a ladies' magnet and a favourite on stage, Ace was a striking visual magnet. Carl Wayne once said, "Ace had the black soul thing going on, and I was more the white soul thing."

The Move immediately raised the musical bar in Birmingham. People were taking elated and immediate notice back in those first weeks of 1966. The young, tall Norse-like, blond Robert Plant was in a band called Listen and he became a firm follower and admirer of the band. After bringing together the pick of Birmingham's musicians, The Move's gruelling, beat-group apprenticeship and further rehearsals began to whip them, into a super tight ensemble. They covered the same tunes as some bands in town. ('Our Love Is In The Pocket' and 'Open The Door To Your

Please correct me if I seem to be making too much noise!

Heart' were two R&B stompers by Darrell Banks). These really suited The Move's rocking, soul attack attitude, right down to the ground. They later added songs by The Byrds, Love, Tim Rose, Moby Grape and other blossoming West Coast acts. All were mixed into the heady gumbo. From the very start, The Move's multi-part harmonies were one of two things setting them apart. The other was their strong image.

Tony Secunda, a former merchant seaman, had strong ideas about their look. Their innate, visual charisma was intensified, through stylish clothes and ultra stylish cover versions; delivered at a very high velocity volume while strutting their collective stuff on stage. The Move looked like a band — not just a front man with four guys. All five had the look, the stance and the attitude.

The Cedar was *the* club, the place to showcase your band. The place to play and be seen. The Cedar hosted many of the big names of the day. "It was a social place, the place to be late night. So, we had two or three shows elsewhere and then we'd all meet up and congregate at the Cedar Club," remembered Wayne. Bev Bevan echoes Carl: "Eddie Fewtrell was great for The Move. He was a good friend of Carl's. He used to let us use The Cedar to rehearse during the day. We had a key to let ourselves in. You could smell the stale beer from the night before. Eddie let us play there, both gigs wise and whenever we wanted. It was a great place to play too with real atmosphere. People like Tom Jones and Ben E. King used to go whenever they were in the Birmingham area and get up and sing. The Cedar hosted lots of names like Jimi Hendrix, Rod Stewart, The Faces, Status Quo, and Cat Stevens."

Once the key players were in place. The decision for what to call this new group came about naturally. The band saw themselves, as part of a burgeoning and important social and musical movement. The original thoughts on the group's name was 'The Movement'. It was soon cut in half, and they became simply The Move. A much better, much catchier and punchier name. The Move, as the name signified, to what they were doing, and it had nice Mod and R&B ramifications. But it was also a name that could and would last, outside of just the passing Mod timeframe itself.

Trevor Burton remembers his take on how The Move's name came around. "I think it came from Mike Sheridan actually. Yeah! Roy came along and said, 'I've got this name for the band: The Move.' Mike came up with the name and we said, that'll do — that's great! Other people remember it differently but that's what I remember."

Tony Secunda said he christened his charges The Move because the name had a simple ring, like The Who. Others say Roy Wood came up with the name because the band members had all moved out of other groups. Roy himself opines, "When I thought of the name, I liked those short snappy names that were coming in — I called it 'Move.' I did some lettering on some cups and saucers and plates. But the promoters changed it to The Move. We all used to meet up after doing double gigs because the money was really crap back then. Two gigs in one night. We were all fed up with human jukeboxes."

The Birmingham Beat edition of the BBC's Rock Family Trees TV programme has Mike Sheridan reminiscing, about when he first heard The Move's name. His face is a funny mixture of consternation and sarcasm. "I said well, what's that called then? They said, 'The Move!' We all fell about laughing! We all thought, it was such a stupid name. Looking back of course, it was a big move for everyone concerned."

Importantly, Trevor remembers the sheer thrill of the beginning days, "I still remember the first rehearsal we had, and we all realised that we had something special. Taking it out and playing it live — that was 'something else', another great memory. We had our first hit in that first year we were together. It all went very, very fast. It felt different instantly, from the first rehearsals, we knew we had something special. We had done our apprenticeships, six nights a week, two gigs a night. We knew we were going to make it. We knocked the shit out of everybody in town, everybody knew! It was just a matter of time and how."

Bev Bevan recalls the first days of the band, "We rehearsed at Carl Wayne's house (in the back garage) also acoustically and then at a local village hall near Carl's house, where all the equipment was set up. Then after that we moved to the Cedar Club in Constitution Hill."

They rehearsed for about six weeks, solid rehearsals every day. They also did a couple of warm-ups at the Coleshill Youth Club. Roger Spencer remembers popping round Roy's house one afternoon that Christmas before 1966. "Mike Sheridan and me went round to Roy's. All the young dudes were there, Ace, Bev, and Trevor with Carl Wayne. It was obvious they had been rehearsing."

Trevor Burton remembers one aspect of the early rehearsals, "Carl and Ace came up with quite a lot of the early stuff. Ace had been building an incredible Chess Records collection. And what we did was, we focused on the vocals first of all, because that was the power. I think we only had like half a dozen rehearsals before our first gig. We were pretty fast at picking things up — we did like six weeks of rehearsing. The vocals were phenomenal with The Move. We were singing four-part harmony, which was incredible for the time."

Ace Kefford says, "The truth was we hated ourselves for being so secretive to blokes who were our mates. But we had to get out of the Birmingham scene, before it was too late. What's important is we were so inspirational to the Brum scene generally." Roger Spencer and Mike Sheridan went round to see the nascent band at Roy Wood's house. Roger was unaware of any undercurrents. "I didn't think anything. They said they were just listening to some of Roy's songs. When we went round there, they were just sitting around. There was sat The Move! No, no, I was completely naïve. Never even thought about it."

Bev echoes the other two original members, "Totally! The line-up worked absolutely perfectly. To this day and I have worked through ELO, Black Sabbath, ELO Part Two, Bev Bevan Band and currently with Quill, the original five-piece line-up of The Move, was the tightest band I ever worked with (just listen to all those live BBC recordings from 1966/1967). People might say it was John Bonham. But I was the loudest drummer in the Birmingham area. So, I think I really rocked up The Move. John Bonham used to come to watch me, and we became good pals. I think I helped influence him as well as him me. Song wise I think it was me (the "rocker" in the band) who suggested 'Something Else,' 'Weekend,' 'It'll Be Me,' 'So You Wanna Be A Rock & Roll Star,' 'Don't Make My Baby Blue' and 'Sunshine Help Me.' We basically, between us, were all throwing ideas about, which songs to play. Whereas almost every other band were playing The Beatles and the Stones and whatever, we came up with mainly USA songs and R&B. They were fantastic. Yeah, and the rest of the stuff we were doing, that was pretty unheard of."

Bev Bevan's drumming really fitted The Move. He and they were completely

Please correct me if I seem to be making too much noise!

made for each other. Bevan had a very unrestrained and dynamic attack on the kit. For example, his careening drum rolls on 'Rock And Roll Star' and 'I Can Hear The Grass Grow' live are fantastically exciting. There was a feeling that Bev could go careering right off the kit. That it could all fall apart at any second. Similar in some ways to the intuitive, untrained ADHD insanity of Keith Moon's fervent drumming. Keith had two drumming lessons with Carlo Little and then off he bolted. His rhythmic spark was ignited. Both Keith and Bev, had a cliff-hanging quality to their intense single and double-stroke drum rolls around the kit. But they always hit the spot right back on the one.

Bev was at that glorious early stage. Where he hadn't become too skilled as a drummer or too "learned" if you will! He was very spontaneous. His untrammelled drum rolls all around the kit, lasting for over two bars, were an absolute frantic blast within The Move's music. His drum introduction to their Byrds cover, 'Rock 'n' Roll Star', live at The Marquee is superb! He quite simply, plays and cuts right across the beat for the first bars... His flailing cymbals are ridden mercilessly. Creating further anarchic drum dissonance. This while playing right up and against The Move's two-guitar dynamo intro. It generates an additional music maelstrom, overlaid into the music. Bev cracks right down hard on the one, The Move are propelled forward — rocketing into that seriously tough groove. This takes (The Byrds) Roger McGuinn's softer folk-rock approach, from the original into a more galvanic, exhilarating soundscape. On a good night, it just blew The Marquee apart.

Bev Bevan had a really unusual drum grip for his left hand for the time. I had never seen any other drummer play with that grip. It was like he was playing with the drumstick lodged in between the first and second finger. Bev clarifies that stick position, "I'm proud to say, I haven't played like that now for about probably 30 years. That was The Move. When I started playing, I was still at school and I was quite a sportsman. I broke my wrist playing football and lost all grip with my left hand. Once the plaster was off there was no grip left. The only way I could grip the stick was by ramming it between my thumb and finger really. The skin down there was like an open wound sometimes after gigs."

There was a really raucous vibe to Bev's drumming, particularly in the early days. As well as his naturally, thunderously loud drumming style. This both excited and pushed The Move's front line hard. Allied to Ace's head-punching bass and their combined loud intensity, they were the perfect rhythmic dream team to push The Move machine into total overdrive. Bev clarified more, on that unique rhythm section, "I could hear Ace loud and clear. We just got the bass drum, particularly the bass drum and the bass pretty locked together really." Bev also recalls their elemental power, "I think very few bands got to go live with us. They couldn't follow us live. Nobody wanted to follow The Move. The best example probably was on The Move, Jimi Hendrix tour. Where we didn't want to follow Jimi. But he didn't want to follow us, either for that matter."

Carl Wayne liked some other bands, like The Artwoods very much. (They had future Deep Purpler Jon Lord on keys in the line-up, plus Keith "Keef" Hartley on drums). Bev says of The Action, "When we got to London we were impressed by them. They had the residency at The Marquee. They looked the part, they looked good. But we didn't think they had the songs. We got on well with The Tremeloes on the road."

The Tremeloes had a clean-cut pop image. But the Trems allegedly, were the shagging Beastly Boys, when it came to the ladies. Carl Wayne remembered humorously, "they would shag a horse if it moved." They definitely had a rep, behind-the-scenes about that... as well as a wealth of well-written commercial hits.

Trevor remembers at the very start of The Move; "We had a mixed following back then — lots of different kinds of kids. There were lots of Mods in the crowd as well. Yes, I liked the Mod look and some of the music. It was a good scene, and I had a lot of fun with it." Looking back Trevor has fondness for many of the Move songs. "It's hard to say, but I like 'I Can Hear The Grass Grow' and 'Cherry Blossom Clinic.' 'Useless Information' and 'The Girl Outside' are lesser known from the first album but are some of my favourites. Roy wrote 'The Girl Outside' for me to sing."

Ace Kefford and Trevor Burton went to the clubs and danced to the music. Giving them extra edge and style when it came to playing live and throwing shapes on stage with The Move. The band was booked initially by local agents in early 1966 and then at a gig at The Belfry Club. Here is where, manager-to-be Tony Secunda turned up.

Ace Kefford remembered, "Phil Myatt from Mothers Club told Secunda about us and he turned up to that show." Secunda loved The Move from the word off. Secunda recalled, "I had come back from South Africa to England in January 1966. I spent about three months searching all around the country. I saw something like 150 groups. I knew what I was looking for, and immediately when I saw The Move, I knew this is what I had been looking for! The guys themselves, knew what was happening — and they knew what they wanted, as well as me."

Carl Wayne: "We were all in because it was a new, fresh energetic band. In which there was no disharmony on a personal level. Before the single hits we were a good, solid five-part harmony group, playing a lot of West-Coast stuff. After the singles, we were then labelled as a pop band with a good image. And that psychologically took its toll! We were always, always a totally formidable live band."

Bev Bevan also remembers the sheer power of the band on stage, "It was amazing. I've been lucky to have worked with so many great bands over the years. But I think the original five-man Move line-up was just extraordinary. They were all so good. It was really entertaining for me, because I could watch it from my drum riser. I can really see the crowd reaction better than they could really. All the dance movements and stuff." There were many limitations back then, which increased the raw power of the band. And generally, they could hear what they were doing? "With Ace and me, as bass and drums — I mean, I think I could hear him loud and clear. Monitors came along later! I don't think I started using monitors as such until the ELO days."

****

Parts of Tony Secunda's history are a little hazy. He was apparently born in Epsom, Surrey. He had spells in the Merchant Navy. He was a wrestling promoter, as was mentioned by Robert Davidson, Secunda turned to pop and to the newly emerging 'tripped out' entrepreneurialism. He was very much about making money. Secunda

Please correct me if I seem to be making too much noise!

also inspired fear. He was a kind of surrogate Machiavellian, Fagan-like, father figure to the young Move band.

Carl's feeling was that "Secunda and later on Don Arden became surrogate fathers. To whom we would utterly capitulate. No wonder we were so fucked!" Then Carl underlines, "Secunda was determined we were 'going to be a hard band, not a namby-pamby band'."

Trevor Burton doesn't recall that much animosity about people being nicked from various Birmingham bands. "They may have been some animosity for a while, but once people saw the band, they couldn't deny how great it was. I never got any nastiness from anybody. Maybe Ace did sometimes. It was quite easy, not to like Ace at times. Coz' he could be quite arrogant (laughs). So could I as well! In our own ways we were both pretty arrogant I think."

Pauline Evans, Carl Wayne's longtime girlfriend and later fiancé (They were together for six years) had to negotiate for the newly set up Move Fan Club. Pauline went from working at Wilson Cycles for £5 per week. Pauline negotiated her 'Move' wages with Secunda in his car. He wanted to give her £7, but she didn't budge and negotiated and got £10. Pauline remembers that Carl was driving a Ford Anglia around then. In more successful days, he was driving around in a Jensen.

Pauline also remembered Don Arden and his entourage later visiting Birmingham where a meeting was held at The Albany Hotel. She also remembers a trip down to London. She did not take to Don Arden at all. Pauline's first impressions were soured. "I did not think a lot of Don Arden, not a lot at all! He had got a young girl in there; she was auditioning, and she was singing one of The Beatles numbers ('Yesterday') and she was having to undress. This was right in his office. (I believe that was at Galaxy Entertainment Agency) They were in Carnaby Street first, then they went to Denmark Street. That didn't go down at all with The Move. And it didn't go down at all well with me."

After the initial meeting with Tony Secunda things started to go up a few (hundred) gears. They signed up with Secunda to Marquee Artists Management in March 1966. This, based on their hot live shows, demonstrates they were gathering plenty of kudos. This had ensured that the legendary, London-based, Secunda was already taking keen note of the hubbub building around the group. He had already dipped his finger in the Birmingham scene with The Moody Blues and come up trumps. It was time to get a second helping of this lucrative Brum Beat pie.

At one particular Moody's gig at The Moat House Club, they were introduced to Tim Hudson who had connections in London. These 'connections' were keenly looking to manage a band. Enter Tony Secunda directly into The Moody Blues story. He then became a major player in the whole Brum Beat scene. Secunda secured The Moodies a regular slot, at the famous Marquee Club in Wardour Street, Soho, London. They had stepped in for Manfred Mann, when singer Paul Jones contracted laryngitis. Their track 'I'll Go Crazy' was well received by the regular crowd.

Ray Thomas, the Moodies vocalist, flautist and harmonica player said, "The chap who was training us (Secunda) made us knuckle under to the firmest discipline and eventually we all got pulling together. Now we trust and respect each other completely."

A big break came when Tony Secunda got the band, to perform a regular spot at London's famous Marquee Club. Ray Thomas recalled; "All the great bands had their own night at The Marquee. Manfred Mann had a regular spot, but Paul Jones had bad laryngitis and couldn't sing. At the last minute, we were called to fill-in for them. We went on and played our own type of rhythm and blues and we went down a storm! Things took off from there." The Marquee management offered The Moody blues a regular night to perform.

Denny Laine said, "The Marquee was an important step for us, and we played regularly but also backed visiting American musicians whilst they were in the UK." It wasn't long before Tony Secunda arranged a record deal with the Moody Blues signing to the prestigious Decca Records label. From this, The Moody Blues, seemed all set for stardom. They released their debut single 'Steal Your Heart Away', which didn't chart, but led them to appear on the ITV pop music show *Ready Steady Go!*. Their next single 'Go Now' set the apex and international standard. With Denny Laine's doleful vocal and the group's backing, the trademark Moody Blues sound was forged. The track became a worldwide hit and in late 1964 it went all the way to number one, in the UK charts. It went top ten in the US. Back then, The Marquee Club, although a small club, a 400-ish capacity (depending on the stage set up) was the main club in London. The Who, Jimi Hendrix and Cream were all "discovered" there. It was quoted by the *Melody Maker* as being "The most important venue in the history of pop music."

Many years later, on 22nd February 1995, an obituary for Tony Secunda appeared in *The Independent* newspaper based in London. Chris Welch, a longtime music journalist, described Secunda (with some insight) as follows: "Secunda, was a dark, brooding and somewhat menacing figure. He thrived on taking risks. And he was not afraid to indulge in the most basic scams and publicity stunts. But he achieved results for his artists and took the ethics of the underground hippie scene, right into the boardrooms of the music industry."

Tony Secunda has melted into the background mostly, unlike other managers of the time. This could be possibly due to his early death in 1995. He was in the same top vanguard as Andrew Loog Oldham, Don Arden and others. In fact, he inhabited a very unique space. Due to his eccentricity and his defined use of publicity stunts. The Move were definitely Secunda's plaything. Much more so than his previous act, the relatively straight forward Moody Blues. Secunda genuinely thought The Move had something special. The (then) 26-year-old public school-educated Secunda, was cut from similar cloth to Brian Epstein, Andrew Loog Oldham and Kit Lambert, the respective managers of The Beatles, The Rolling Stones and The Who! All except, that his tailor seemed to specialise in suits for self-styled hard nuts.

Secunda was sometimes a friendly genial chap. When he wasn't putting the frighteners on anyone who crossed his path, though not a tall man, at times when aggravated, Secunda employed the effective trick of 'nutting' people in the face — facilitating a swift trip down towards the carpet. These were social devices he had learnt as a former Merchant Navy man and wrestling promoter. It is also claimed that Secunda did some gaol time. Later that year and seeing they were firmly on the ascent, Secunda signed The Move to his New Movement management operation in November 1966. "Tony was powerful with an extraordinary presence, very focused.

Please correct me if I seem to be making too much noise!

He didn't give a shit, and he saw himself as like Napoleon Bonaparte. He was quite scary; God help you if you crossed him. In Tony's book, there was no such thing as bad publicity," recalls Robert Davidson.

Bev Bevan reflects on all the early different hairstyles. "He had us doing a gangster image to start with. We had all these beautiful suits made to measure in Savile Row. He also wanted us to have our hair, like, the hair going down over one eye. It was all very Chelsea set. We were like, (in a broad Brummie accent) 'What's he doing? We're just lads from Birmingham. Like — What's he doing?' (laughs)."

Trevor Burton was deeply intrigued by Secunda: "I always found it really exciting being around him. I think Malcolm McLaren was the 1970s version of Tony Secunda. It's like he read Secunda's book, with what he did with the Pistols. You never knew was going to happen with him. It could explode into madness at any time."

Carl Wayne also always maintained Secunda's credibility: "Oh, he was incredible! When you think about it, The Move were created by Tony Secunda. He gave us the leadership and guidance that we needed. Management can be on different levels. You can have those that will manage a successful band from a financial point of view and allow them to create what they are and their music. In our case, if you took The Move without Secunda then the creativity was from Roy Wood, and we would have just been a band playing its hits. With Secunda, he dreamed up all the ideas, the stunts and the clothing — sending Blackberry pies with bottles of champagne for 'Blackberry Way', doing a photo session at the fire station in Birmingham for 'Fire Brigade' — and of course the Harold Wilson affair! He also had the animals who would do what he wanted to do! In Trevor, Ace, and me — the fiery part of the stage act. I think Roy would obviously qualify this himself, but I believe he was slightly embarrassed by the image and the stunts — but the rest of us weren't."

Ace Kefford is totally firm about one thing, "Tony Secunda was brilliant. Without Secunda no one would've heard about The Move!"

7.
So tomorrow won't be long... you're going to have to play it cool

Birmingham is considered the United Kingdom's second city. The Birmingham Blitz was the description of the heavy bombing by the Nazi German Luftwaffe of the city of beginning on 9th August 1940 and ending on 23rd April 1943. Birmingham was an important industrial and manufacturing location. In total around 1,800 tons of bombs were dropped on Birmingham — making it the third most heavily bombed city in the United Kingdom in World War Two, only behind London and Liverpool. The Birmingham music scene in the early 1960s gravitated between two poles — bands that wanted to sound like Cliff Richard and The Shadows and those groups wanting to follow the innovative leads set by The Beatles.

The 1960s burgeoning beat scene had gestated earlier in the 1950s. It was to become affectionately known as 'Brum Beat'. Similar to what was happening in all the large UK conurbations. Liverpool was buzzing and to a lesser degree at that time, the city of Manchester. Obviously in London the music scene was on a large scale. Keith Smart (the noted drummer of Lemon Tree, The Rockin' Berries, Balls, Wizzard etc) told me the Birmingham music scene "was probably the biggest of them, in all the major English cities."

Keith Smart's comments are backed up by Barry Smith (drummer with The Chantelles). "At that time, it was easy to find out that Birmingham had a huge amount of bands. More than Liverpool, London, Manchester and Coventry etc. Many bands in the city simply used to register their names. It wasn't compulsory but a lot of them did it."

At the same time Birmingham became a breeding ground for some of the most well-regarded and famous bands in rock 'n' roll history. Just like anywhere else, they were young kids, seeking to escape the dark realities of a stark industrial existence. And in many cases, tough working-class backgrounds, with little money and little opportunities. Each of these bands in their own way, forever redefined and recharged the sound and meaning of modern popular music. Over time Birmingham fostered internationally successful acts, such as Black Sabbath, Judas Priest, Duran Duran, Steel Pulse, UB40 and tons more. These bands won popular acclaim and critical respect, amongst the Birmingham scene and the larger Black Country musical diaspora.

As Barry Smith also mentioned, the proliferation of music shops was further testimony to the amount of bands being formed and gigging in the city. All needing to buy musical equipment, back line, etc. Places like Music X, supposedly the biggest music shop in the world. Other places like Jones and Crossland made up a proliferation of music shops, catering to the large demand.

There was also a defined musical circuit, that many bands played in Birmingham, called the Ma (Mary) and Pa (Joe) Regan circuit. The (now) legendary Irish husband and wife team that played a big part in the Brum Beat scene.

The man who managed everything for them was Dennis Brown. Dennis used to ride around the ballrooms, and he would collect together all the sacks of half-crowns. He used to take them round to the Regan's house in Woodbourne Road in Edgbaston where they were tipped into, big, old tin baths.

On 23rd April 1966, The Move and The Steam Packet Show featuring Long John Baldry were a fantastic double bill who appeared on the Regan circuit, at The Plaza in Kings Heath.

Bev Bevan remembered instances when he had played the circuit with Denny Laine and The Diplomats. "Mary Regan and her husband Joe's original ballroom venue was the Gary Owen Club in Small Heath. Not far from Birmingham City's football ground, St Andrews. Then came a converted snooker hall in York Road, Kings Heath, which they re-named the Ritz Ballroom. Next came The Plaza in Handsworth, and finally The Plaza in Old Hill. The most memorable day in the short but eventful life, of Denny Laine and the Diplomats was on 5th July 1963 — we opened the show for The Beatles at the Old Hill Plaza on the Halesowen Road."

For Bev, this early peak experience of preceding The Beatles on stage was at the crazy beginnings of 'Beatlemania.' John, Paul, George and Ringo had already had massive hit records with 'Love Me Do' and 'Please Please Me' and had just registered their first number one with 'From Me To You'. They were currently topping the LP charts with their debut album *Please Please Me.*

"We were popular in the Black Country, so Joe Regan decided we were best suited for the unenviable task of being the group on stage — directly before the biggest pop phenomenon since Elvis Presley. There was a huge crowd that night — literally hanging from the rafters."

"Ma Regan took care of the business side of things. This left Joe to run the venues and act as compere. He was usually dressed in evening suit and black dickie bow. He would confidently announce the various bands, groups and singers in his lilting Irish brogue. The Handsworth Plaza was the biggest of the four venues. Joe Regan was not much of a bookkeeper. So a few times on a night off we would roll up at the Plaza. Then convince him that he definitely had booked us for the night. We'd slot in with all the other groups there and play a 30-minute set. We would pick up our £12 fee and drive to Alex's Pie Stand in Birmingham to celebrate our little 'con trick.'"

Bev Bevan feels a certain affinity with a particular thing that he thinks has made Birmingham's musical heritage so strong. Not the endless grinding and clanking of heavy metal presses in the factories or the city's remarkable multicultural mix. Bev reckons, right in the heart of Brum's musical heritage was a second-hand record stall on the Bull Ring markets. "When I was a kid in the late 1950s and early 60s. We all used to go down to the old Bull Ring market," he says. "There was a stall there.

So tomorrow won't be long...you're going to have to play it cool

Where you could pick up ten 45rpm singles for around a quid. They sold them in job lots. "We'd take them home and religiously play the 'A' sides and the 'B' sides. We'd listen intently to every word of the lyrics, every note of the music. Often, we'd try to copy the records and, let me tell you, there was a lot of weird stuff. What it meant was that the kids growing up to be musicians were exposed to a wide range of music from all round the world. It was a rock and pop education, and it was right there for the taking on the market on the Bull Ring."

****

The Move were greatly admired, and they garnered chart hits. They enjoyed a hazy admiration based on this slew of hits. Those lucky enough to have seen them back in the day were safe in the knowledge that they were among the best live British acts. Coupled with their onstage charisma and strength, The Move slipped through the cracks, in terms of any of their real history being explored. Their influential freakbeat music has never been looked at in any depth. They are a very important 'cult' band who were always hiding in plain sight? I asked the ailing Trevor Burton recently what his overview of The Move was now? Looking back Trevor immediately said:

"We were — and are — an important but overlooked band."

Some of the London snobbery that came as part of the music papers in those days, was evidently floating around. Sniffy, odious bastards, like DJ, wannabe pop artist and later on, convicted paedophile, Jonathan King.[6]

King often made barbs about The Move's music. The usual middle class, wanker piffle trotted out to get a rise out of his *Disc and Music Echo* readers. Stuff like, "Individually let's consider The Move. Appearance wise they hit a high level in advance mediocrity. Looking like a cross between The Four Pennies and are worse than an average Mod group. 'Night of Fear' is a weak record and inconceivable that it made the charts for the top five. The sideboards like Eric Clapton were months ago. Destroying on stage like The Who — years ago outmoded and non-original. I am judging them from records, press and TV appearances. I wanna see them live before I commit myself to this year's version of Los Bravos? Give me the Electric Prunes!"

One wonders with Carl Wayne's ego bristling and his penchant towards settling matters quickly, how close did King ever come, to getting his Charterhouse and Cambridge-educated teeth rattled severely? It was said that Carl slammed the idiot up against the wall once! But I haven't been able to verify. He deserved a lot more.

Keith Altham, who interviewed The Move reckoned, "Carl did not like the piss-taking DJ. King who had accused them of not being able to reproduce their sound on stage. They do! They will — and they have! Carl favoured the direct method of approach, when he (or the band) was insulted. He had quite recently offered to alter the shape of Jonathan King's (leering) lop-sided face at *Top Of The Pops*. King had

_{6 King was found guilty at the Old Bailey in 2001 of sex offences against five youngsters aged 14 and 15. Later charges against the former pop producer and DJ were thrown out in June 2018, over failure to disclose evidence. An independent review found mistakes in the police investigation of leadership, supervision and disclosure, and made 27 recommendations. King was acquitted of 23 serious sexual assault charges against teenage boys. The offences, which he had denied, were alleged to have taken place between 1970 and 1988.}

turned up and Tony Hall the promotion manager and Secunda forcibly asked him to leave. It soon dawned on the idiot that Carl Wayne might want to rearrange his face, following all the catty, depreciative remarks King had made about the group. It makes a change from the Love Generation anyway!"

The "Brummie beer monster bad boys" — who were not "real" heads... man! 1967 was the supposed year of rapid change. But the same kind of entrenched snobbery that existed in England had not disappeared. It certainly hung over the country like a stratified blanket. The snootiness and queasy loathing toward working class individuals still existed. (As it does today but in a different guise). The music industry was mostly controlled by the upper and middle classes (still is). And with a few 'good' crooks and other dodgy chancers thrown in for good measure. The Move's attitudes, looks and music, followed suit at a dizzying pace. Yet, The Move's rapid changes were nothing different to what The Beatles were doing in terms of styles and constant musical change.

Tony Visconti remarked in an online interview with Bob Lefsetz. "To me The Move were Birmingham's answer to The Beatles. 'Flowers In The Rain' was a very cutting-edge song in 1967."

"You're either on the bus or you're off the bus!" So sayeth Ken Kesey in the pages of *The Electric Kool-Aid Acid Test* (published a bit later in 1968). In those brain-stretched days, dope smoking hipsters loved that type of head-twisting balderdash. In some ways it meant nothing. In other ways, it could mean everything. Zen 'koans' for the Portobello Road brigade? Every time you looked around, The Beatles were already rocking a new and deviating vibe. New types of clothes, diverse eyewear and sunglasses and face fashion. Such as divergent moustaches, side whiskers and beards. Always changing, never static. The music was changing all the time. Keep up or be square!

Be here now! If you were one of the many hippies that fancied the Eastern Mysticism detour you could waltz right into Baba Ram Dass territory. As long as it wasn't your 'last waltz'. This Eastern mysticism wrinkle was in many ways, popularised by one of the mighty Fab Four.

George Harrison had vanguarded a lot of interest in this direction (thanks a lot George!) by his introduction into the rock sphere of the sitar and his studying with Ravi Shankar. He also produced the Radha-Krishna recordings with their debut release appearing on Apple Records in 1971. Even though George was described as being very spiritually minded, I personally found (some of) his songs, to be an incredibly dour listen. Stuff like 'Old Brown Shoe', 'Savoy Truffle', 'While My Guitar Gently Weeps' and others. Personally, I could've done without the five odd minutes dirge, of 'Within You, Without You' on *Sgt. Pepper's Lonely Hearts Club Band*. I'd have much preferred it if 'Penny Lane' and 'Strawberry Fields' were on there. That would've made it, a truly brilliant 'concept' record. I realise this might make old Beatles' fanatics, start retching over my inscribed voodoo doll. I just felt that truly great albums, were lessened by these tunes. Plus, the impact on the music of other fashionable, mind changing, music altering ingestions; heavily influencing the collective sound palettes. It is no wonder people were called 'heads' maaaaaaan!

The same musical freeways could be seen (and heard) in the path of The Small Faces. From their early Mod singles monsters, 'Sha La La La Lee' and 'All Or

Nothing' to 'Here Come The Nice' to 'My Minds Eye' (a much maligned single and apparently not finished off in the studio). Apparently, we all heard a demo released as a finished single. I remember loving it as a young kid — it was such a gorgeous song. I'm in the minority though and it's one of the shortest singles, I have ever heard. Brevity doesn't decrease it — in many ways it increases it. Leaving you wanting so much more. They evolved to 'Itchycoo Park' and Stevie Marriott's ear-goggles were now hearing the heavier 'Afterglow Of Your Love' and 'Wham Bam Thank You Mam'. Which were hinting at the harder rocking 1970s arena / stadium future to come.

Likewise, The Kinks with earlier Mod rock stylings like, 'You Really Got Me' to the famous Ray Davies London-esque diaries of 'Waterloo Sunset' and 'Autumn Almanac', plus, other great songs like 'Scattered' on their later *Phobia* record.

Many, many unique bands from that period arrived. They either collided with, or they came up through the Mod, pepped-up, live scene. Which just as quickly morphed, from a speeding, amphetamine charge into a more psychedelia, trippy, spaced-out period. This change caused a schism in some kids (with some like me) moving from the Mod styles of dress towards the similar, but more obvious 'skinhead' clothing styles. I was too young for Mod, but picked it up, in the skinhead styles.

When I was a kid, 'heads' were definitely considered to be absolute wankers. Tribalism in its most strident manner. Certainly, they were derided by the working-class kids I knew. 'Heads' had no real clue about broader music and were considered, to have absolutely no clue about style etc. My take on it is that so-called 'hippie' types, looked down their noses, at working class kids. They just didn't get it. They were too educated, but in the wrong ways. All head, but no heart or soul. There were many kids like me that used to go out to hear Ska plus Blue Beat and then some early reggae; James Brown's King label 45rpm singles and some happening chart hits (Motown for example — I loved the Norman Whitfield 'psychedelic' soul' Motown period etc).

But I would not think twice, about going to see Free, Osibisa, Santana, Love Sculpture and other freakier, guitar-based explorations. These were all going on then, a real musical gumbo. (I saw some of these acts, down at The Farx Blues Club in Southall — a very hip little venue). Although you probably kept it on the quiet down the pub, with the skinhead mates present. The sixties bands tapped into that natural flow — you could not avoid it. It seemed that large parts of the molecular structure of society were absorbing these fast musical changes and the culturally based influence, that some bands brought. Osibisa and their use of African cross rhythms, for example.

The Move's early music set lists were very much based on Mod listening favourites. Plus, obscure R&B cover versions, from Ace's (Chess Records collection) and Danny King's record collections. These were cuts that pretty much no one knew. Immediate and hard-hitting tunes. Soulful and sharply dressed up. Inviting you to dance. Echoing the aspirations, of working-class teenagers. To dress cool, to meet a lovely woman. To make some headway and some money. To try and avoid being mugged off — in a completely dead-end job. To go out and have a really good time.

A lot of this preening and posturing display was lost on the more middle-class 'head' scene. The aspirational aspect of it was not there. They were already enjoying a generally reasonable standard of living to begin with. Of course, this is a generalisation. But they had a decent entrance portal through life. Which could be said to be more assured, in those more stratified days. It's also based on how I saw the attitudes around me within the working-class fraternity, and the more educated grammar school types. To use two demarcations along class lines...

A lot of the 'heads' were fucking clueless. They indulged in so-called 'idiot' dancing. It was literally called 'idiot dancing.' I didn't just make that up. 'Idiot' in more ways than one. A very un-coordinated, deeply undignified and embarrassing type of flouncing and flopping about. Like they were having some kind of temporal, loose-limbed fit. Calling it dancing is a definite insult to cool moves. They wore Afghan coats, flared jeans, with a makeshift insertion at the bottoms. Using different forms of material to enlarge out the flared effect. Sometimes velvet, sometimes paisley and sometimes makeshift. There was a uniformly, pervasive stench of Patchouli oils. Not one of the best cologne types I've come across. Personally, I found some of the 'head' gear could be very artistic. The Lord Kitchener stuff, mixing old Army stuff and Chelsea Pensioner type clobber with nicely designed flares, Cuban (Suede) heel boots in black or dark tan, Paisley shirts and cool (Tootal) scarfs. Some bands pulled it off really well.

The Move and Small Faces for example. These two bands, went through all the various clobber changes, with style and elan and very little sweat. These two groups had come up through the Mod scene. They went on to wear the psychedelic clothing, with much more style and thought.

During 1966-1967 dress wise, The Move went from a US 'preppy' ivy-league college look — This 'look' was seen in the first photos taken by Jim Simpson in Ward End Park in Birmingham in late 1965. Then came the original dark 'gangster' double breasted suits, all tailored to an excellent fit. Bev Bevan remembers these suits being tailored in Savile Row. In one of the first photo shoots, (shot by Tony Gale) they were sporting the Mod suit look. Bev casually arranged his suit jacket to hang languidly over his shoulder. After the photoshoot, Secunda came up to Bev and snarled, "What the fuck are you doing? Are you trying to look like Michael Holliday?"[7]

He had another admonition for the band, this time when they went shopping in Carnaby Street. They came out wearing more standard Mod threads. Secunda retorted, "What the fuck do you wanna look like The Who for?" Those darker suits eventually changed, and all five guys started sporting, brightly coloured Mod style suits, cut in a tight Italian style, tight on the shoulders and waist and legs. They morphed from these 'pastel candy' coloured suits into their freakier 'psychedelic' clothing in 1967.

The Move smashed all their looks easily and they all looked great: As bespoke suited gangsters, leathered-up rockers, beads and kaftan hippies, sharp slick Mods and as 'casuals'. Bev Bevan hated wearing the hippie gear. On TV's *Rock Family Trees* he grimaced, as he remembered, "We were gangsters and then hippies with beads, Trevor and Ace Kefford were into it. I was a bit of a rocker, if anything! I don't wanna wear a bloody kaftan!"

Even when they were wearing the paisley gear and the new vibey, Granny Takes A Trip clobber. They still exuded an aura of menace. They looked like psychedelic gangsters while wearing the octagonal sunglasses or the square ones that Carl and

---

[7] A light-pop Bing Crosby style singer who had a few hits up to 1964 including 'Story Of My Life and 'Starry Eyed.'

Trevor favoured. Necks resplendent with tresses of wooden and glass beads, they just couldn't get rid of that 'street' working-class Birmingham attitude.

The Move soaked up the summery vibes couture and enjoyed themselves. But still giving off the aura of the sort of hippies who would happily give you a sturdy right hook. The attitude of "Our music is the best — follow us onstage, if you even dare" followed the band on and off stage. That heady patina and street attitude of threat remained at least for a good year or longer…

Nigel Waymouth was one third of (along with John Pearse and his girlfriend Sheila Cohen), Granny Takes A Trip. The store opened on King's Road, Chelsea in 1966. Nigel inputs some details on those beautiful original clothes. "Those brocade type jackets. They were no heavier than a wool jacket. They cost around five pounds. They are now as rare as hen's teeth, if you can get one. I think there's a jacket in the V&A. If one of those jackets came up in the market you could charge £10,000 or more because they are so iconic. George Harrison had one. He is in various photographs wearing one. John Lennon bought one. They used to come into the shop and buy things themselves."

Some background on the tiny but internationally famous Carnaby Street. It's a very short street indeed, maybe 200 yards in length. At that time clothes shops became known as boutiques. Sometimes you would also hear the word 'emporium' bandied about. Names such as Lord John, Lady Jane, John Stephen, Sir Harry, Pussy Galore, Biba (based in Kensington), Granny Takes a Trip, Hung On You, Apple, Mr. Fish, Quorum and I Was Lord Kitchener's Valet.

"We were young, rich and beautiful, and the tide — we thought — was turning in our favour. We were going to change everything of course. But mostly we were going to change the rules," so said the young, desirable Marianne Faithful, and they did. In these current, dowdy, drab, grey and black and blue tracksuit-wearing, Adidas trainers, overkill days, it's hard to believe the actual volume and avalanche of creativity exploding within those years — mutable and flowing constantly.

No such cruddy clobber for The Move or Roy Wood! Roy Wood had an early penchant for having some of his stage gear made for him. He might be doing a gig somewhere and see something he wanted to get specially tailored for himself. June Woods remembers one funny story from Roy; "I made myself a pair of red tartan trousers with braces and turned up to a Move gig wearing them. Roy was so enamoured with them he pestered me for weeks to make him a pair too! I eventually gave in, purchased the same material and arranged to meet Roy. I waited by the Navigation pub on Bromford Lane, Erdington. Roy duly turned up in an old cream and black van. He called it 'The Rocket' and it was a heap of junk — but at least it got there. He took me back to his place (where his mum and dad lived) in a flat on The Meadway in Birmingham. I said hello to his parents, who waited in the kitchen. I measured Roy for the tartan trousers and had to make sure 'the bum didn't hang too low' (laughs). I sewed them as quickly as I could. He was waiting impatiently for their delivery, and he wore them and was pictured in them for months afterwards! In fact, I don't think he ever paid me for the fabric! I still see them in old photos today."

Roy went over some of the gear that they wore. "I had some stuff made at Granny Takes A Trip. But they quickly realised, that there was money to be made from bands, so the prices kept going up and up. I used to go to Kensington Market. You could buy some proper second-hand Victorian clobber there, which was very good. This was in the day, when I was actually slim enough to be able to wear it. I didn't really follow the trend of the rest of the band, which slightly annoyed Tony Secunda... I think he felt that he was losing his grip on the band. There was a seamstress local to me in Birmingham (June Woods) who was very good. I could draw a picture of what I wanted. And she would make it... no problem. Two of the pics you sent... with me playing guitar in the white shirt and the blue jacket. She made the jacket. She also made the black and yellow outfit, on the front of that *Disc* cover, with the castellations at the bottom."

Speaking of The Meadway flats, one thing that was bound to get the band (and particularly Carl Wayne) into a parlous state of rage was picking Roy Wood up for gigs. He was up on the top of the block of flats. Tony Ware (a future member of a later Ace Kefford band) laughed at some early recollections of the band and the behind the scenes dramas: "Roadies John 'Upsy' Downing or Allen 'Dumpy' Harris would drive the van. Carl Wayne would get there to Roy's place. Then climb the stairs to Roy. 'Get up, you fucking bastard!' He'd be lying in bed with his clothes on. Upsy would have already been out for about an hour and a half or two hours. He was driving round, picking all the band members up. So they were all sitting in this white, double-wheel transit van and they'd turn up at The Meadway. Roy was on the top floor. I think it was about eight stories high. They used to dread it because somebody had to go and get Roy. They'd have a big argument about it. Who was gonna go up and knock the door. Upsy has been picking the band up and they're already waiting at the door, so they are all ready to jump in the van. Roy just used to stay up all night writing songs, he used to be flaked out in bed all day. Then of course, there's a gig to do. They would have to travel like 500 miles before they even set up the gear. I mean, there's a bad atmosphere, because they'd all been sitting in this tiny van for half hour. Waiting for Roy, to get out of bed." Ware also remembered them, rehearsing in a "village hall around the area in Solihull."

Allen 'Dumpy' Harris has a slightly different memory. He recalls being the only road manager for The Move, with Upsy Downing coming in later. "I was on my own at the very beginning. I think most of the way through for twelve months, through most of 1966. Things were getting bigger; we got more equipment. I just couldn't manage. So, Upsy came in, his girlfriend was the sister of The Applejacks bass player. We were all friends with The Applejacks. He was great, we used to get on really well. Keith Smart was a great guy, and he was one of his best friends. Upsy came in through Carl initially. He was also a friend of Carl's and I knew him before The Move."

Allen is firm in maintaining that The Move were the originators of some early, dramatic lighting effects. "Till then many bands just relied on the lights in the theatres. I don't know if Tony came up with the idea, but I put it together — I had all these lights made up. They were strobe lights — we had a box made up by an uncle of Carl's. It had four big dimmer control designs. It took two of us to pick it up. I could control all the lighting. We had two big boards, to the side of the stage on stands. With twelve Par bulbs — what they called Par 36 bulbs. Coloured bulbs, really big ones... I used to sit there, and I controlled the lights, according to the music. Nobody had ever done that before."

8.
On a short vacation with my friends...

Barry Smith had a long, long relationship with Chris Kefford. "I was living originally in Hobmoor Road, which is in the Yardley area. My mother remarried and we moved to Canon Hill Park, Edgbaston, just literally around the corner. My dad was just finishing a chalet in the garden, where I had to move all my stuff into. He was building this chalet as far away from the house as he could to escape all the noise. I responded to a music advert and there was a knock on my chalet door and in came The Chantelles — complete with the young Chris Kefford. He was about the same age as me, he was twelve! Chris is my second, oldest muso' mucker, from loads of gigging together, from about 13 years of age. Only proceeded by Dave Pegg who had asked to join me, in my first band a year before. That band with Dave Pegg was called The Connoisseurs."[8]

Barry Smith had started out with former Way of Life bass player/singer Danny King in his early 1960s band, Danny King & The Royals. "When we played with Danny King & The Royals, we actually headlined at Birmingham Town Hall. It was very rare for a band to headline the Town Hall back then. That was one of the biggest gigs in the Midlands. Danny King was a phenomenal performer and a great singer."

Barry Smith also played the drums, with brothers Chris and Reg Jones in The Chucks. Complete with his attempts at a crazy, flame blowing, routine onstage. One night at the Dudley Labour Club, Barry Smith stepped out from behind his drum kit. He put the spout of a bottle of petrol to his lips. He tilted it, filling his mouth with the highly flammable and dangerous liquid. The crowd were cowed, into a deep, possibly, preservation-based silence. Barry pulled out an *England's Glory* match from its box. Barry struck a flame. As he did so, he developed an uncontrollable bout of hiccups. He panicked and spat the petrol out, spurting from his lips. "Suddenly there were flames shooting everywhere," so sayeth Keith Williams, his bandmate and bassist in The Chucks. Keith was totally agog, along with all the goggling audience. Pandemonium ensued but no serious casualties were registered.

The sudden publicity went 'viral.' Which, in those days, meant articles in newspapers and plenty 'word of gob' on the street. The national publicity ignited The Chucks. For a hot minute, they were even hotter news than before. The Chucks were off to Germany after this. Firing on all fronts.

Later on Smith worked with Danny Burns & The Phantoms. He also joined The

---
[8] Dave Pegg ended up playing bass with both Fairport Convention and Jethro Tull for many years.

Way of Life in 1968. He had a good grounding in that fertile Birmingham scene. Barry also remembered that "Roy Wood asked me and Chris to join him in a band. We would have been about fourteen. Both Chris and I said, we weren't really interested. He looked very nerdy; he hadn't really done a lot as yet. Roy didn't look anything like he later ended out."

Barry Smith continues the history. "Chris and Reg Jones were Ace's uncles. Chris Jones was an absolutely phenomenal guitarist, and I mean phenomenal. I would put him up against Jimmy Page, no problem. Chris Kefford was the second singer to Chris Jones. Chris Kefford was really good at playing bass and singing. This at the really young age of twelve onwards. He kind of sounded like a black woman. The Chantelles was a band where everybody sang. I was a converted jazz drummer. I would say I was the only drummer in Birmingham that had proper full jazz training. The Chantelles would rehearse at The Warstock Pub in Yardley Wood and play there Friday nights. The Chantelles graduated from The Warstock and the Haven public houses, to the Wharf Hotel in Holt Fleet. But I was also playing rock 'n' roll. Back then, it wouldn't be unusual to be doing as much as thirty gigs a week. Chris developed the blues / soul voice. He would always tell me what he was doing and what he was working on. We spent so much time together, it's just not true. Every night and every week we would do, sometimes two or three clubs in one night. What happened at the end of The Chantelles was that the two Chris's (Ace and Chris Jones) and myself just quit."

Barry remembered that back in the day, he and Chris Kefford, in order to avoid looking dressed like the audience were always on the lookout for cool and unique clobber! Even then the young Kefford was a prime mover... "Chris was, excuse the pun, an ace performer, a number one. He was an incredibly stylish bloke. He looked as cool as hell. We would often go to the Bull Ring rag markets in Birmingham. Both the outdoor and indoor markets, trying to find interesting clothes that other people would not be wearing."

Birmingham was a very happening city back then. A large conurbation with a lively and bustling music scene. There was an urgent need to look sharp for these young aspiring working-class musicians. There was a popular menswear shop on the corner of Navigation Street and John Bright Street called Chetwyns. If you could afford it, they sold imported suits, jackets, shirts, ties etc directly from the United States. Plus, loose drape jackets and cutaway collar shirts etc. Then in the early sixties the fashions changed. Most young guys got their Italian style suits from Burtons or Colliers. Although Chetwyns did continue to survive with the imported American look. Above Chetwyns was the Whisky A Go Go[9], a club hosting live bands. Local bands like King Bee's, The Modonaires, Jugs O'Henry, Moody Blues, Denny Laine, Spencer Davis Group played there, as well as Motown and R&B bands from the USA. Greats like Sonny Boy Williamson and Ike and Tina Turner.

"The owners Chris & Steve Healey were two great guys who ran the welcome team — every night the Whisky was open. They both wore natty striped jackets and cool clobber. The original manager, and also I recall he was the DJ some nights, was Ronnie Whicheler, a great guy with thick red hair, a real 'dude'," recalls one

---

9 Before it was the Whisky A Go Go it was called Laura Dixon's Dance Studio. It was rock 'n' roll but with no booze and only soft drinks or tea or coffee.

of the regulars Bob Summers, who also remembers the fast, sweaty environment, "I remember Georgie Fame playing virtually all night. They couldn't get him off the small stage, until he collapsed with exhaustion — or further lack of stimulation."

The proliferation of bands was astounding in Birmingham. Everywhere you looked, there was a group or a new group forming. The G-Men, The John Bull Breed, Jerry Levene and The Avengers, The Beachcombers, The UK Bonds, The Hound Dogs, Mark Stuart and The Cresters, The Mountain Kings, Dave Lacey and The Corvettes, The Kavern Four, The Strangers, Danny King's Mayfair Set, The M&B Five, Denny and The Diplomats, The Dominators, The Concordes, The Strangers, The Shakers, The Renegades and so many others combos. Most of these bands never saw the light of day. Some of them were boring and unoriginal! But, boy, the city was alight with music and awash with bands everywhere.

****

Birmingham would definitely not be the place that it is today without Eddie Fewtrell who became known as 'King of Clubs'. Eddie Fewtrell was born one of ten children in the 1930s. He hailed from the backstreets of the rougher Aston area. Much of Eddie's childhood was spent keeping the house together and caring for his younger brothers.

An alcoholic father and an invalid mother had prevented him from attending school and leading a normal life. A scenario, a million light years away from his environment. As someone commented, "The influence that Eddie in particular had in Birmingham was enormous. It was best summed up by his great friend, the comedian Bernard Manning. The comic once said: "If Eddie Fewtrell says it's Christmas! Then everyone starts singing carols."

In the beginning it seemed like it was all just a big party in Birmingham. And at the centre of it all, the Cedar Club. The Fewtrell brothers, Eddie and Chris, led the largest local 'firm' in town. They were well enough established to beat back the Kray twins, Ronnie and Reggie when the Krays visited to have a sniff around, seeing if they could expand their East London based criminal empire into Birmingham.

The 1960s in Birmingham was a mecca for live Mod bands, especially at The Whisky A Go Go, right on the corner of John Bright Street and Hill Street.

The *TV Times* splashed this caption: "Liverpool today — Birmingham tomorrow. That beat business in rock music. Yes, the Brum Beat from the booming Merseyside market."

Before all these venues opened the nightlife in 1950s Birmingham was extremely austere. This was due to the fact that Lord Cadbury, was on the Birmingham Watch committee. He was a devout Quaker and did not believe in entertainment and booze for the masses. You won't find a pub situated around Bournville — the home of Cadburys. After he died, Birmingham started to become alive at night. In 1961, the Locarno Ballroom opened at the bottom end of Hill Street. Monday nights was rock 'n' roll night. They would play the records of the current top 20 artists.

By 1966 the night club scene was happening. Many clubs were now owned and ran by Eddie Fewtrell. Fewtrell and his brothers ran the local and the city wide 'firms' in that time. There was the Rum Runner, just off Broad Street, after you dipped down the alleyway. The Runner had a gambling casino on the left-hand side and a huge patronage. Entrance cost ten shillings. In those days a good night out would cost a 'fiver' or less. Affordable for a working-class person in those days. Further up Broad Street, down at the end of Gas Street, dwelt a nightclub called the Opposite Lock. Named after the motor racing language. The club attracted the motor racing fraternity.

It was an older clientele than those attracted to the Rum Runner. All these clubs had different scenes with different means. Then in the late 60s the Fewtrell brothers opened a couple of really large night club venues. Both clubs had girl's names. One, Rebeccas, was in Lower Severn Street. Just up from the Hippodrome and the other called Barbarella's, just off Broad Street, near the old Bingley Hall Centre. They were bigger clubs and attracted a large following from older teenagers up to their late 20s and into their early 30s. They would attract international stars mainly. Artists that were currently in the charts. Of course, suits and ties were the dress of the day. Although dress codes were getting more relaxed. Ties were mandatory but you could now get away with a leather jacket and trousers but no jeans of course.

The Move played into the first two to three months of 1966 and were working bookings steadily. Playing around Birmingham and the local Midlands area. Their early gigs at the Cedar Club were very popular. They had great support acts, such as Little Stevie Wonder, Doris Troy, Charles and Inñez Fox. Lots of local talent like The Shakedown Sound (with a singer called Jimmy Cliff, who went on to bigger things). The Sombreros (who featured Rick Price before they morphed into Sight and Sound).

The Matadors were on the same bill, a band out of Coventry that managed one Columbia single, 'A Man's Gotta Stand Tall' (released under the name of The Four Matadors). As far as tall men standing, 'Big Albert' Chapman who became a legendary doorman and runner of clubs in the Birmingham scene, became deeply embedded in the Brum Beat scene.

'Big Albert' started off on the Ma and John Regan circuit at their two Plaza venues in Birmingham. Albert talks about the fees the bands were getting: "About that time The Move were getting about £450 a night, which at that time was great money. The support act would get about £18 or £20 a night." Albert was school friends with Ozzy Osbourne and Tony Iommi, and he later worked with Black Sabbath. He also managed Quartz; renamed from Bandy Legs, who had a deal with Don Arden's Jet Records. They had soaked up Derek Oldham from the Lemon Tree and members from the Idle Race. Albert got involved with the re-opening of The Elbow Room: "The main punters at the clubs would be musicians or villains or car traders."

On the scene at the time was a young road manager called John Kirby. John was working with The Montanas. The Montana's had a big following in Wolverhampton. He was very good friends with Upsy Downing. Always on the lookout for fresh new import material Carl and Bev would visit John's place, to see if he had any new R&B stuff they could listen to. One song in particular Kirby thought would be a great fit for the nascent R&B loving band was a hot new cut called 'Secret Agents' by The Olympics.

John remembers the song caught their attention, "Carl and Bev really loved the tune. A few days later Carl called and said they were going to do the B-side 'We Go Together (Pretty Baby)'." Unfortunately, no recording of The Move's version exists. Kirby maintains it was superb live.

'We Go Together' is a driving bouncing song with more than a passing similarity to the 1963 stomper, 'Can I Get A Witness' from Marvin Gaye.[10] Actually both sides of this Olympics song were a perfect fit for The Move's driving harmonised sound.

Armed with these well-wrought and selectively picked cover songs. The Move started to pick up the pace in terms of gigs all throughout that February of early 1966. Their feet weren't touching the ground. The first gigs were mostly based in the Birmingham area. They played the Cedar Club several times, with warm welcome and the Whisky A Go Go. The Move started to gig solidly — gaining momentum throughout the year. A time in which Carl Wayne has often mentioned that The Move were at their very best. This was even before the first hit single in early 1967. There was very little personal disharmony and as yet nothing their outrageous manager Tony Secunda had cooked up (although crazy) was all within reason.

After Secunda stepped into the management breach, he took them down to London and quickly got them the Thursday night residency at the Marquee Club. That Thursday night slot had belonged to The Who just prior. Secunda had booked them in for two shows at the Marquee in April 1966. After this, he signed them to Marquee Management in May. The Move started playing the weekly slot as well as zigzagging up and down, the MI Motorway, back-and-forth to Birmingham. But later on that year the gigs in the South and around expanded and the gigs in Birmingham became less.

At the Marquee Club debut, they were supporting Gary Farr and the T-Bones. Ace Kefford says firmly that it was here at this gig that a large aspect of one of the beginning rifts within The Move was inflamed. A chance remark would be the spark that ignited and possibly fanned a growing, ego-driven resentment between the five young musicians. Or specifically; a resentment of the other four young men towards Ace. When Secunda sauntered into the club along with Ricky Farr, Farr opined very loudly in front of the group, "You are a great band, but you need somebody to be a focus here," and he pointed to the blond Kefford. "That's the guy — the one with blond hair! This guy stands out!"

Kefford believes that's when he was separated out from the four other egomaniacs in the group. Ace perceived that had begun to spread a bad taste in the band. Of course everybody wanted to be stars of the show; especially Carl Wayne. Carl of course had hired the young Ace into The Vikings, after seeing his spectacular singing, stage moves and bass playing, well before The Move's formation.

Kefford remembers, "This was the start of my paranoia in the group, and this was well before my overuse of drugs. It wasn't my fault, what could I do about it?" Barry Smith remembers a funny anecdote about Ace's 'Face' good looks and his placing in the band: "Ace was invited to a party. He knew Robert Plant was going to be there. Ace walks in and Plant goes to him, "Well, I thought, I was the best-looking bloke in the room, until you came in." Chris had the style. Chris always looked cool. He always looked super cool on stage. He performed his arse off."

Rikki Farr was also part of Marquee Management. He was managing The Action and was pretty close to Tony Secunda at that time. Farr also became more involved in producing shows. He is possibly best known for staging and 'hosting'

---

10 The mighty Marvin apparently just dusted that song off in one hot studio take, which amazed the happening Motown trio and songwriting team of Holland, Dozier and Holland.

the Isle of Wight Festival in August 1970 with a crowd of 600,000 people, bigger even than Woodstock in America the year before. Rikki went berserk berating some French "communists", who were at the event who wanted to get in for free. Even if things were slowly getting more corporate, the free-love and something-for-nothing brigade, were still out in full force.

Support act Gary Farr and the T-Bones had a Mod following and people rated them, especially Gary's voice. But they were never able to translate that into success via record sales. Gary Farr had a cool Mod face and blond hair and didn't look a million miles unlike Ace Kefford. They released three singles and an EP on Colombia. But they lacked something — really good songs!

They weren't going to give The Move any worries that night at the Marquee. Both the Farr boys were the sons of the famous Welsh heavyweight boxing champion 'Tommy' Thomas George Farr (12th March 1913-1st March 1986), hailed as one of the most famous Welsh and British boxers of all time.

Tony Ware, a future compadre of Ace Kefford reckons, "The Marquee Club was made to measure for The Move. The atmosphere and the power, the stage was just right — the right size of an audience. Just perfect!"

Secunda said some eventually fated words: "The Move's explosion onto the scene was very necessary. This is a group who are progressing very rapidly. They have a lot of talent and the only way we could make people realise that they were not just an insipid group, was to absolutely explode. Musically the Move will survive — they are one of the things of the future."

In a feature in the *Birmingham Weekly Mercury*, dated 1st May 1966, Secunda maintained The Move had signed a new contract deal, for a whopping £70,000. *(The figure seems very, very high for the time)*. "He is guaranteeing this amount for twelve months work. This high figure, is an indication of his belief that the group, can and will click. Secunda intends to spare no expense, to steer The Move to the very top. Another group The Action, under Secunda's wing are currently being recorded by George Martin, The Beatles A & R man, for EMI Records."

Bev Bevan was extremely tickled, when a "happening" number one charting band, came to see The Move at the Marquee Club. The Easybeats had a smash hit with 'Friday On My Mind'. The hit was produced and selected from a bunch of demos by Shel Talmy (who notably also produced The Kinks and The Who). It's a classic piece of bristling 1960s pop rock. A bonafide classic — a colossal hit, right out of the box. They flew in from Australia, they were over to do promotion and record some new demos in London. They were recording at IBC Studios. The first show they went to was at The Marquee and guess what? It was The Move. "They looked at each other, after our set. I think they were completely and utterly blown away," says Bevan. "And said, 'We should go home, guys. We can't follow this'. Well, they were good, but they weren't The Move. I think they said that themselves. So, we did get some great compliments actually. They did actually come up and talk to us, after our set."

An Italian TV report about the Mod suit style was broadcast on Rai Storia in December 1967. However, the TV video itself is date stamped '05 Dicembre 1966'. We see the band being fitted out for their individual pastel-coloured suits in Savile Row, London. 'Disturbance' (the B-side of 'Night Of Fear') plays as the soundtrack.

On a short vacation with my friends

The young Trevor Burton is trying on stuff and throws a few Mod dance shapes at the same time. Trevor talked the fashion, "Yeah! Originally, we had the trousers and the bouffant hair, like the early Mods, the scooter guys, all that period. Before they all became skinheads! (laughs). The early Mod thing was a much groovier thing."

The film then cuts to the band in Hyde Park, all wearing the self-same suits and cool white moccasins, miming to 'Disturbance.' The film has a wonderfully, agile 60s vibe to it. As the camera pans in around the tree, and the group in a nice circular sweep, a lithe blonde woman, runs through the park with her small galloping terrier dog. The whole thing has a feeling of expectancy in the air. London was *the* place, and the band were up-and-coming 'young Turks.' That same day Robert Davidson took photos of the band and this time they were miming in a different way. They were photographed as living, breathing, shop front art models. Positioned and posed, in the window of the famous furniture store Heals, in Central London.

Another early stunt was reported by the *Daily Mirror's* 'Inside Page' on June 17th 1966. The Move were photographed standing around in the middle of Manchester's Piccadilly area with an exact replica of a USA 50 Megaton 'H' bomb. The bomb itself was originally built for Granada TV. Secunda thought that it would make a very interesting prop for a photograph. The group drove up with the large prop, in a pantechnicon, right into the centre of Manchester and deposited the 'bomb' in the road.

Ace Kefford recalls, "The stunt with the fake H-bomb was very funny. We went stomping around through the streets of Manchester, hoping to get arrested. We were tramping up and down for two hours with this wretched bomb and nobody took a blind bit of notice. Eventually a copper told us to move on." Trevor Burton relives the day, "The police arrive, and they were talking to Carl Wayne. Tony Secunda, he's going, 'Carl, kick him! Hit him! Get arrested!'"

Ace adds, "A photographer took a picture, and the papers said we had been arrested making an anti-Vietnam protest. ('Situationism' right on the spot?) The police were loitering and looking unimpressed, Secunda went on with tongue pressed firmly in cheek. We didn't want any 'cheap publicity' so we did as we were told. They asked who is in charge of this thing and it all got a bit awkward." The bomb itself was eight and a half foot high and three feet wide. It is now lying in a props depository somewhere in Manchester.

Mr Bill King at the prop-making firm that made the "bomb" says, "It's not ours either, we don't want it, and it takes up too much room. We don't get too much call for H-bombs these days."[11]

In 1966 the new pop / rock festival scene had begun to start sprouting and The Move appeared at one very significant event that year. Named the Windsor Jazz and Blues Festival. The Move played on Saturday 30th July 1966. Saturday's line-up was a mixture of jazz, blues and pop. It included Chris Farlowe and The Thunderbirds, with a band that included the brilliant guitarist Albert Lee and Dave Greenslade on organ. Gary Farr and The T-Bones were also on an afternoon slot. They appeared before the estimable Jimmy James and The Vagabonds had got the evening underway. James was originally from Jamaica and like Geno Washington. Was another hugely

---

11 A photo taken of The Move by Bobby Davidson with the fake bomb appears on the cover of the sheet music for 'Night Of Fear', the Move's debut single on Deram Records.

Flowers In The Rain - The Untold Story of The Move

popular R&B and soul act on the 1960s club circuit. The Move were another of Saturday night's favourites and whilst their first hit, 'Night Of Fear' was five months away from release. They earned their place on the bill by the sheer merit of their outstanding live shows. They now had the coveted weekly residency at London's Marquee Club. The band were outstanding and getting better by the gig. The Move were also attracting attention, with one of the first, pre-psychedelic light shows.

Allen 'Dumpy' Harris provides a little more detail. "I remember the first night we played The Marquee. We had a sixteen-week contract, signed and agreed with them. The first night we played, we had a film projected onto a screen. Which was my mum's bedsheet, set up across the back of the stage. The projector was in the middle of the floor, and we projected flashing images, and on the back of those, things like ZAP and BOOM and lots of other stuff. It didn't last long because you couldn't set it up in the middle of the Marquee. That's when we did the lights! Then the next thing you know Pink Floyd, is doing the very same thing! We were as a group, starting all of those new innovations off!"

Allen Harris recalled, "Secunda's wife (Chelita) had something to do with a mental hospital and had got a big strobe light. It knocked a load of girls out, at the front of the stage. It was used as a psychiatric thing. It flashed in all different colours — A flash at a certain point that affects your brain. But it could induce an epileptic fit as well. We got banned from using this and then they were all banned from anywhere. We could use one which was a smaller one, which only went up to a certain frequency which was safe. So, we were using that with that lighting the other lighting. I used to quite like it, because I was always thinking of something else to improve the effects, with the music. I remember putting one of these explosives in the dust bin one night on the stage — I nearly went bloody deaf. Did the band enjoy all this stuff to? I don't think Roy was into it. I think the rest of the guys definitely did!"

Allen Harris carries on, "I used to do the sound as well. Ace was really loud, he's just gone up onstage and turned his bass all the way up! I had to sort of stop him from overpowering the others. They did get louder and louder. They used Fender gear at the beginning as Carl had built up some supplies and he had a PA system with The Vikings. The original Park Amplifiers, endorsed by the band, were a cooked-up marketing rivalry, on the part of Jim Marshall.

The large Birmingham music store on the ring road, Jones and Crossland, was run by Johnny Jones. He was a good pal of Jim Marshall. Jones served as a distributor towards the north of England. Meanwhile, Jones and Crossland was selling its own 'in-house brand' line of guitars, amps and other musical instruments. Named in honour of Jones' wife's maiden name, Park. They moved over to using the WEM stacks that were even louder.

American producer Joe Boyd had said, he used to see The Move at The Marquee. "They were so fucking loud." The 1000 x watt WEM PA comprised of ten x 100 watt slave amplifiers. All using the new RCA silicon transistors and circuitry driving 4x12" column speakers, with a smoother response. This was the set up used at the Windsor Jazz and Blues Festival in 1967. It was the world's first high clarity, high power touring PA system. The more image conscious groups like The Move and Pink Floyd were vying with each other to perform on stage with the highest amount of power.

On a short vacation with my friends

****

For Joe Boyd a young, agog American in this thriving music scene in London, everything was fresh and new. Boyd was completely blown away by seeing the live Move. He started attending their weekly Thursday night residency at The Marquee. "I must have seen them seven, eight times. I used to take people down when American musician friends would be in town, I'd say, 'You gotta hear this band' and we would go down and listen. For example, I took Mike Bloomfield from the Paul Butterfield Band down, who was just completely blown away by them. The same with John Sebastian from the Lovin' Spoonful. And Phil Ochs too. We're talking now about the summer of 1967. 'Rock' was a new American term that grew out of Bob Dylan at Newport. It was definitely not rock 'n' roll. It wasn't pop. It was roots-based. In America, everything was based on the blues, everything was based on American roots. It had so much to draw on in America. But these Brummie kids and the LSD revolution — They were a bunch of working-class kids from the Midlands... some are taking acid and are exploring new possibilities within the format of music. I think one of the biggest influences on The Move was Motown, they loved Motown and the R&B stuff."

"In a way, the group that was the closest, (aside from Moby Grape), who I never saw live... One group that I did see live, which to me was trying to do something like what The Move was doing, but not as well, was Vanilla Fudge. My feeling when I was standing there in The Marquee, watching them was 'Holy Shit! I think I need to get some Americans to see this. This is unbelievable. This would be a mind blower at the Fillmore.' I think if Secunda had taken The Move at the height of their powers, jumped on a plane, flown out and met with Bill Graham and said, 'Can we have The Move open for Jefferson Airplane or whatever?', The Move could have made an impact on the US and utterly transformed their lives."

"Mike Jeffries had this vision that really you had to seize the moment! He had toured with The Animals and then with Hendrix. Bill Graham had already booked Jimi at the Fillmore. Before he did Monterey Pop. They had the booking at the Fillmore before they left for Monterey — because Mike Jeffries commissioned a poster, which I still have on my wall. Hendrix wanted his own poster to commemorate his first Fillmore gig (20th June 1967) and asked Hapshash and the Coloured Coat to do this one (artists Nigel Waymouth and Michael English). Yeah, Jeffries knew that there was a whole culture of posters, in San Francisco by Mouse and all those people. He wanted to take an English psychedelic poster, advertising the Fillmore date with him to America. He paid us for 500 posters, we manufactured the silk screens. It's a wonderful poster, which Jimi liked, with a Native American vibe and stuff. So, he had them shipped to San Francisco. He distributed them around the city, leading up to the gig. Mike Jeffries understood that's where the money was — that's where the career was — in America."

Boyd pursued The Move connection. "I met Roy Wood once again, many years later. But we did have one meeting back then. I took Jac Holzman, the owner of Electra Records, because they were unsigned. Electra had just come out with The Doors and Love and Lord Buckley. So, I thought, this is where Electra is going. Why not! Let's get The Move in on it! We needed and very much wanted to sign The Move to Elektra."

Joe Boyd wasted no time, "Jac Holzman and I drove up to the Mecca Ballroom in Edgbaston and we saw them perform there. Jac was really impressed. We went into the dressing room and Tony Secunda was there too. But the reaction to us was just a culture chasm. I think they didn't know what, or who the fuck Electra was. Maybe a small label was considered just that — Too small. We were just playing a different game. Of course, nothing came of it. They very soon signed with Deram and Denny Cordell and Essex Music and all of that. Because Secunda — I think that was the sort of thing, he always had his eye on. Later I got to know Tony quite well. He's been a very interesting, engaging and fascinating character. I can't say I liked him particularly, but I was intrigued by him. I think he'd been in prison. He started out life in show business, as a promoter of wrestling matches or something, he was a kind of Fagan-like figure."

Regarding Secunda, Bev Bevan recalls that, "He had such incredible self-confidence. We were swept off our feet when we signed the management contract. We were green lads from Birmingham, and he took us shopping in Carnaby Street and immediately changed our image."

Trevor Burton laughs remembering, "Secunda was a bit scary, because you never knew what he was going to do next. Volatile I think the word is. One night we were in a really nice Indian restaurant in London's Fulham Road. At the time it was quite an 'in' place. An Indian band, sitars, people sitting on cushions on the floor, really upmarket. We were with this guy from Chess Records. We had this incredible meal. Then it came time to pay the bill and Tony says, 'Right! We're gonna do a runner! When we get to the door upstairs — we'll run and get out of here!' Tony gets to the top of the stairs, and he just ran away! He ran up the road. Ace and I are still inside the restaurant, we are locked in. Suddenly the door bursts open again! Tony had come back in. He said R U N! And we all ran up the road. The guys at the restaurant are throwing bottles at us, as we are running up the road. There's these two guys sitting in a car. Tony pulls open the door — jumped in the back of the car and said to us, 'Get in!' He said to this guy in the car, 'Drive up the road — Now!' And the guy did! (Laughs). That's what it was like with Tony Secunda."

9.
Just about to flip your mind...

Robert Davidson was getting slowly pissed off with the lack of payment for photography. It would take a while longer before a horrific event totally convinced him to get out of this scene and situation. "I guess I stayed so long because it was so exciting. You never knew where you would be going next. One day I found myself flying off to Paris with The Moody Blues, who were playing at L'Olympia; They had a number one in England and were a huge success in France. After the show, we went to the trendiest nightclub in Paris with the band. Brigitte Bardot wasn't there apparently, but her sister Mimi was. I never realised that Brigitte Bardot had a sister. But this woman purporting to be Brigitte Bardot's sister came over. We were all being fêted, and we could have had anything in the room we wanted. Mimi, who was very attractive, goes up to Tony and said in her very French/English, 'Ello, I am Mimi. I am Brigitte Bardot's sister'. 'Yeah?', Tony Secunda says, 'I'd rather meet your sister'."

It was Secunda who pushed Roy Wood into writing original songs for the band to record. Although Roy's only previously published composition was a single B-side by The Nightriders, called 'Make Them Understand', the A-side of 'Take My Hand.' Wood came up with the inventive 'Night Of Fear' for The Move's first record release — in the shops by the end of 1966. It clambered all the way to number two in the UK charts by early 1967.

That riff came out of left field and showed a band with a tight and powerful sonic bandwidth. But surrounded by an unusual, zany and tongue-in-cheek approach. A deft lightness of touch — tempered with an aggressive musical fire. Unlike most pop songs the up-beat melody for 'Night Of Fear' contrasted strongly with Roy Wood's dark lyrics. A magazine article at the time proclaimed; "Meet the pioneers of the psychedelic sound." Rumours spread that "psychedelic" must mean LSD drug-use and strange "happenings." Years later, Bev Bevan recalled; "Nobody believed that Roy wasn't out of his head on drugs — but he wasn't. It was all fairy stories rooted in childhood."

"Tony's idea was not to sign us to a label until we'd built up a reputation and got our name in the papers," said Ace. "Tony became our sole manager, via his Straight Ahead Productions company with Denny Cordell and some others. They had lease control over the master tapes which I believe we had to pay for, from our royalties. We were as green as salad."

On 3rd September 1966, the *Melody Maker* ran a story, "The Move to sign with Tamla?" "Negotiations are taking place for Birmingham's Move group to sign with

America's Tamla Motown label. If the group are signed by Tamla boss Berry Gordy their first release will be out next month, and they will be the label's first British signing. The group will not attempt a 'Tamla style' but will stick to their own." They were recommended to Tamla when visiting Americans heard The Move playing in Birmingham. (Most probably on a bill at The Cedar Club, with a support American act). This could have been due to the influential Barney Ales, the powerful head A&R man at Motown. Ales also had the ear of Berry Gordy.

The Move also had a residency at The Birdcage in Portsmouth. The first Birdcage Club opened its doors in late February 1965 at Kimbell's Ballroom, Osborne Road, Southsea. It reflected the mid-1960s shift from blues and R&B to soul and dance music. It was opened by Rikki Farr, whose brother's band The T-Bones were the club's first act. DJ Pete Brady played all the latest soul records to Pompey's growing Mod audience.

The club had one famous night 'away' at the Savoy in July 1965 starring The Who and local favourites The Crow. A month later it moved to its own premises at Eastney by which time regular favourites included Jimmy James & the Vagabonds, The Action, Chris Farlowe & The Thunderbirds and Rod Stewart — usually with Steam Packet, Long John Baldry, Julie Driscoll and Brian Auger. While visiting American acts included Wilson Pickett, Ike & Tina Turner, Major Lance, Ben E. King and Inez & Charlie Fox.

In 1966 the club introduced all-night sessions, then closed during June for a revamp. When it re-opened the newer music was not always based on American soul and Tamla Motown. The Move and groups like The Hollies, The Small Faces and the In-Crowd (to become known as Tomorrow) appeared alongside a new DJ "Mad King" Jerry.

Chris Welch from *Melody Maker* was taking notice of the Move gigs, on another tidy package in late October, "The Fairfield Hall, Croydon, blew up with a wild pop package show featuring The Move, Jimmy James, The VIPS, The Herd and Spencer Davis on Friday last week."

It was a Marquee show, and the ravers were out in full force. Wynder K. Frogg opened the show. "A good organist, his band have a lot to learn about volume control. The audience looked like a good crowd of listeners for Steve Winwood's set at the end of the show. In the meantime, The Move had fun letting off thunder flashes and clouds of smoke, inducing the crowd into a frenzy. By the time the Spencers came on with a tightly knit, well-played set, there was screaming uproar. Stevie in a green shirt and black boots, sang viciously against the noise, and he was great on 'Nobody Loves You', 'Mean Woman Blues', and the new one 'Gimme Some Loving'."

Another journalist from *Melody Maker* was following the new band and wrote on them often. Nick Jones reviewed the Speakeasy Show, from 24th December 1966. Robert Davidson took some great shots of Carl taking an axe to TVs, with the audience very close to the band. The photos record a sweaty, smoky club gig. "Amidst a smog of smoke bombs, smashed TV sets, smashed people, and the psychedelic decor — well, who would settle for anything else? London's in and out crowds spewed forth from the opening of the new Speakeasy Club in Margaret Street last Thursday. The premises were big. The bar was well stocked, and humanity oozed from every nook and cranny like wasps round a jam-pot. It was The Move who proved to be the jam

Just about to flip your mind...

pot. Everybody looked. Heads turned as they flowed through their act. Once again, they're hard core, full of professionalism and confidence. They have proved to be way too overwhelming to stay unnoticed. Even the miniskirts became obsolete. Finally came 'Watch Your Step'. It was not quite how Bobby Parker used to play it. And again, up went the tension, up went the volume, and up swung the axe. Singer Carl Wayne demolished the TV set, with the picture of Adolf Hitler on the front, in several foul blows. The smoke bombs went off and the transfixed audience coughed and spluttered into life and made for the outdoor air. Everybody freaked out!"

As 1966 turned to 1967, record nights often featured blue beat and ska (the earlier forms of the evolution of reggae music from Jamaica. All these cuts were all available on multifarious imports and on British home-grown labels). While bands like Cream and Pink Floyd brought the new sounds of what became the 'Summer of Love' to The Birdcage. Tastes changed, hair grew longer and bigger and the Mod/soul/amphetamine world of The Birdcage and the Pompey Mods was supplanted gradually by the new psychedelic vibes, of weed and hash and of course LSD.

LSD will run through this story, with jagged and sometimes devastating effects. Regular Birdcage club visitors The Paramounts had gone to Number One, under their new name of Procol Harum. The club however did not survive the rapidly cycling 'freakier' transition and closed finally in August 1967. Music was entering a new transition — albeit one that threw shadows over the industry and culture for years to come. RIP - The Birdcage, Pompey.

The Move played one club at 79 Oxford Street which evaporated scene-wise, before long. Before it was the Tiles Club, it was called Beat City. Which was run by the legendary Alexis Korner. In 1964, Korner had the Stones playing their last ever club date at the venue. The Move played there with support The Gods on Friday 3rd February 1967. By now The Move's gig diary was packed for the opening month of that year. They are playing as far up as Scotland in Glasgow and Edinburgh. Then all the way down to the South Coast of England and many points in between. You certainly couldn't ever miss The Move in London.

In terms of some canny 'guerilla' advertising, one young Londoner Ron Eve recalls, "I remember that The Move stickers were absolutely *all* over the London Underground." In fact, Secunda had people posting Move stickers everywhere, on lamp posts around the centre of London. Don Arden's son David often wondered, "Who or what is this 'Move' thing that's going on?"

Another bonkers publicity stunt, very typical of Tony Secunda's attitudes, started 1967 with a suitably piss-taking, anti-establishment side to it. Harold Wilson called a snap General Election in 1966. During this time the group had posed with a MOVE WITH THE TORIES - VOTE CONSERVATIVE poster. (As the band were mostly very working class; this will have been a Secunda ploy)

On 4th February 1967 they invited Tory leader Edward Heath to "guest" with them on organ, for a gig in aid of Conservative Party funds. The starchy reply was "owing to his extremely busy program,' the Right Honourable MP was "unable to accept your kind invitation." In a *Melody Maker* report, The Move were to appear on a televised church service from Birmingham Cathedral, with Ernie Wise and the Three Monarchs.

When the producer Barry Edge asked The Move to appear, they said; "Sure...

but ask if it's alright, to chop up an effigy of the devil, during the televised program." The Bishop of Aston gave them short shrift, telling them no thanks and The Move declined to appear. Around the same time Secunda let loose yet another wind-up rumour, that he had asked top star and film actor Marlon Brando to come and record with The Move. The wind ups just never stopped happening. The same report stated that The Move were finishing off a documentary called *Colour Supplement 1966*, a Peter Whitehead film on 'Swinging London', which was being filmed at the Tiles Club in Oxford Street, London.

The Action were also getting good press. They started to make waves. Just before the time The Move debuted, around mid-1966. They were London boys and from the same Mod club scene. They were touted for strong live shows and were regulars at The Marquee. Like The Move, they had a great Mod name. They released 'I'll Keep Holding On', which made the UK chart top 50 during April of that year. But they or manager Rikki Farr didn't seem to have the necessary punch-through to make it all happen. Of course, Rikki Farr made plenty of noise, but he may not have been the manager that Tony Secunda was at that stage. George Martin had produced all their singles. Somehow though, The Action's music didn't translate to singles. The material didn't seem strong enough and they appeared to vanish around that year.

They also had no album released. It's felt that maybe with a Denny Cordell production, they could've broken through. But we'll never know. However, one of the members Alan King broke through later with the band called Ace. They had a hit in 1975 with the catchy tune 'How Long'. The rest of the band also moved into more acid-psych, heavy rock and became the group Mighty Baby, releasing two albums.

In April 1967, the ensuing notoriety from the Cathedral stunt, The 'H Bomb' in Manchester and the ongoing press barbs, jibes, lies and barrage of semi-demented wind ups and other stunts (including the attempts to get arrested) had all helped to gain The Move recognition nationwide.

Deram Records was the newly formed subsidiary of Decca Records. Publicity-seeking Tony Secunda made sure beforehand that newspaper reporters were present when the band signed the contract on the back of a topless model, Liz Wilson in Soho! Bobby Davidson remembered the assembled hoop-la and was on hand to ensure the signing was photographed and documented. Secunda was like, "Got a topless model coming. You shoot it Bobby, I'll come over with the boys! We'll do it, bang! bang! and just get it printed, as soon as you can, like ten minutes later. Rush it round and we'll go down the *Daily Mirror* and get it into the paper." Hard, fast paced-and no messing around.

Robert was a groomed, good looking young man. "Katie Manning wanted to make me into a male model. That's why she changed my name from Robert to Bobby Davidson. She was one of my girlfriends. She was an outrageous girl, but that's another fucking novel story."

Katie was one of the Doctor Who assistants During the John Pertwee era. Miss Manning puts it in her own words, "I'm a very private person. I've been secretive since childhood. There are too many people involved I don't really need to talk about. And I've been a naughty girl. Naughty girls don't write books! I think I've been about as naughty as you can get."

Denny Cordell, Tony Secunda, Roy Wood and Carl Wayne were all present (chomping on fat cigars) to make sure the Move's 'New Deal' signing in Soho, was finished off with the band's signatures. Another McLarenesque, pre-punk, up yours gesture, but a good ten years before the Sex Pistols. Ace Kefford remarked saying, "Johnny Rotten did a write up and said, "We ain't done nothing different, from what The Move was doing in 1967."

10.
Tear the world right off its hinges

The Move began life as a super charged Mod-soul cover band. In fact, this remained part of their set well up and into early 1967. It also garnered complaints from members of (the whining Hurray Henry boys) The Pink Floyd. They would often share the same bill (one of the Floyd's members, was quoted in the music press, as disliking playing with The Move, because they "brought too many Mods with them" who came to see their 'soul covers' and "syncopated stage moves"). Stuff that the band members of Pink Floyd couldn't attempt, even if they had wanted to. Floyd would've resembled four one-legged men at an arse kicking contest if they tried anything outside their droning, moribund sound. Living is easy with ears closed. To me, the music of early Pink Floyd, always denoted half-assed playing, sleepy drumming, allied to pretentious lyrics. Middle-class University student music. Similar to 'wokesters' these days... people generally full of themselves but without any un-preprogrammed clue.

Floyd didn't allow themselves, to aspire to the music of black America, whereas it was a big part of where young Mod kids were coming from. In terms of the style and sound and attitude, the Floyd had a snooty demeanour, with an aura of superiority. They certainly seemed to look down at The Move and the 'Mod audience' as well. One look, listen and learn at their naff clothing. Safe wardrobe and music were enough to convince one otherwise, of their ingrained superiority.

"The Move from Birmingham are a stark, loud, flashy, hard punch — whose music smashes you right in the guts. At London's Marquee Club last Thursday, they crashed home with anything from Edwin Starr's 'Stop Her On Sight' to an Indian-Chinese sounding piece, on which guitarist Roy Wood plays some frightening sound effects. They swing, sway and swirl on the stage like hip clowns! If the reaction they received on Thursday is anything to go by, The Move are a new group to certainly be reckoned with."

So proclaimed Nick Jones from the *Melody Maker*. The weekly inkies became slowly aware of this new power in UK music. One early English pop writer Nik Cohn, characterised Ace Kefford as "the singing skull itself." Perhaps, if Ace and Trevor were speeding during the gigs, then the wired, chewing of gum, could and would become incessant, throughout the frenetic performances.

On 15th April 1967, The Move threw down another set at The Cadillac Club in Brighton. People were moaning because they weren't seeing TVs being axed to dust. "We feel it's time for audiences to enjoy the sound," say the Move. Also, the stage thrashing had Top Rank ballrooms banning them right off their circuit. This had already stopped them doing the support on The Walker Brothers tour. Perhaps this was lucky for the Walker Brothers. I don't know how the Walker Brothers could've possibly followed The Move.

It was noted, "The transition from gimmickry to music. May have left the more, immature fans wailing at the box office. But for those who persevered comes the realisation of the Move's presence. A presence only achieved by an exceptionally good and ultra-exciting group. The front line: Trevor Burton, Roy Wood, Carl Wayne and Chris Kefford all sing like lead singers. While drummer Bev Bevan cooks away behind, with an impressive approach. Numbers like 'Love Is In The Pocket', 'Stop', 'You've Been Cheating', and 'I Can Hear The Grass Grow' demonstrate the Move's tight, beautifully rehearsed wall of sound. Their harmonies stab out, like 'soul' Beach Boys. Yet somehow each singer retains a distinctive individuality, which adds to the power of The Move, rather than confusing the issue. They are a hard-working, unaffected, polished and professional act. With that vital "added ingredient" that something (or these days the X Factor), which is going to give the Move a lot of success."

One cool song they covered was, Tim Rose's 'Morning Dew'. Sung by Ace Kefford, Spooky Tooth did a version of this, and they sounded quite similar in delivery to Ace. Later live they did 'Cherry Blossom Clinic', as well as live 'Useless Information' which was great, showing The Move's repertoire, changing throughout that year, up to the first album release in 1968. Then a further change to harder, newer and old rock 'n' roll favourites.

Ace Kefford was a big fan of Tim Rose. The Band Of Joy (with Ace's uncles) was dying on its feet, when John Bonham resisted blandishments from Denny Cordell to join a new outfit called The Grease Band. These men were to be back up for Joe Cocker who had a middling hit into the UK top fifty with his self-written 1968 song 'Marjorine'. An unusual song with a haunting melody and chorus, he was to achieve much greater things by appearing at the Woodstock festival and ravaging his tonsils with a raw feral version of The Beatles' 'With A Little Help From My Friends.'

Bonham didn't want to become a full-time Grease Band member, so he briefly joined singer-songwriter Tim Rose, whose version of 'Hey Joe' had been re-arranged by The Jimi Hendrix Experience. In the set too, was Rose's equally famous 'Morning Dew' and also his 'Foggy Mountain Breakdown.' This being the title theme for the 1967 film about the infamous 1930s bank robbers / murderers, Bonnie And Clyde who ended up completely riddled with bullets. This bluegrass instrumental by banjo-pickin' Lester Flatt and Earl Scruggs had been re-arranged to accommodate a tasty Bonham drum solo.

"I was a big fan of Tim," related Ace Kefford, "I had all his albums. He was supposed to have written 'Hey Joe' and John Bonzo was in the backing band. When I saw Tim one night in Birmingham I was over the moon! There, on stage, my best mate was drumming for Tim Rose! I couldn't't believe it!"

At a Tim Rose recital at the newly opened Factory, once a warehouse, in the middle of Birmingham, Robert Plant brought Jimmy Page along to check out John Bonham's drumming power.

The Move appeared live on a multi-bill show in Germany on 21st March 1967. The programme was recorded in Offenbach, near Frankfurt, for Hessischer Rundfunk, a German regional TV station. The tracks were recorded live with an audience and many top-line bands, played the show. The three tracks recorded feature strong performances, with plenty of in-your-face attitude, with Trevor and Ace throwing some cool shapes. Ace is particularly charismatic, doing an 'on the spot moonwalk' as he effortlessly pumps his Fender Precision slab bass during 'I Can Hear The Grass Grow'. Ace is also exhorting us to, "Get a hold of yourself now baby, See I need you to help now baby, Get a hold of yourself now baby."

Carl Wayne is on fine vocal fettle, even though he was suffering with a bad sore throat during the performance. You can hear Carl's voice crack occasionally as he forces his voice towards a growl. Roy Wood brings wonderful, cutting, chiming guitar from his Fender Jaguar set up. It appears the band is going through those cool German Kempt Echolette amplifiers. Here Roy is wearing a 'Liberty' style, brocaded Granny Takes A Trip jacket. The band prowl backwards and forwards on stage. Trevor plays his guitar propped up and out from his stomach. He is slapping it as if he is cuffing a recalcitrant, unruly child. Ace throws some utterly cool shapes and scans over the top of his shades while singing. These dance shapes include an on the spot, tip-toed, moonwalking Mod set of steps.

The first two singles, 'Night Of Fear' and 'I Can Hear the Grass Grow', sound great in this live context. As does the *Move* debut album cut, and the 'Flowers' B-side, 'Walk Upon The Water.' With its hypnotic, bass-pulsing, thumping rhythm the band is really on form here. Good quality video of these three songs were incorporated into the 2017 Esoteric release. A CD and DVD combo pack, titled, *Magnetic Waves of Sound - The Best Of The Move* which has most of The Move filmed performances (live and mimed). The hour-long DVD features 21 appearances on BBC TV and German television and a promotional film, all shot between 1967 and 1970. The CD has all the hits from 1967 to 1970.

It includes the classic Move *Top Of The Pops* appearance doing a superb, 'Fire Brigade,' shortly before Ace Kefford quit. Roy looks super cool as his Mod looking hairstyle is growing out. Looking like a crossover styling 'Musketeer D'Artagnan Crusader' wearing, singer and guitarist. Soon, his barnet will make a re-appearance and subsequent hair up-grade. Roy's facial features would afterwards slowly disappear. Under his ever-growing beards and hair. Never to be seen again.

Apparently, a lot of BBC TV stuff has been wiped. No one realising back then the importance of the legacy of what was going on in 1967. Apparently, there is one clip somewhere, from BBC Two from 1968, possibly from a *Late Night Lineup* appearance. This is purported to be a colour film featuring Carl Wayne smashing and axing a TV set. One wonders what other filmed gems have been lost through massive amounts of tape wiping?

That June at The Marquee, The Move had introduced front projection, throwing slides and various visuals onto the band and venue as they played. They were often using cut outs from comic book panels like *Zap, Blam, Pow* etc. As you would expect this stuff was influenced by the New York based artist Andy Warhol and the pop art movement that was gaining momentum at that time. Warhol made bright, graphic representations of everyday things. Campbell's Tomato Soup tins, Elvis, Marilyn Monroe, Chairman Mao, Coca Cola bottles, all became utterly re-imagined. Warhol made the ordinary, extraordinary, using silkscreen designs and painted pieces. His catalogue now is worth millions.[12]

They were also, no doubt, influenced by the extremely popular *Batman* TV series from the USA. This camp, funny series started out in 1966 and went all the way through to 1968. The immensely popular DC comics superhero series also took advantage of using corny but funny visual expositions. Adam West as Bruce Wayne and Burt Ward as Robin were a great team and the whole thing worked wonderfully. The Move were proof you could write 'psychedelic' songs without overtones of peace and love and with a lightness of touch. You could dress sharp, even if you were wearing beads and kaftan styles. It was all in how you wore it. How you carried it off. You could enjoy all those vibes and have a lot of fun with them. But you didn't have to be an "earth child" or a tediously pretentious West Coast hippie. This was hilariously dealt with in song form. Notably appearing with the topical, sarcastic and funny lyrics to 'Vote For Me.' This was the unreleased A or B side of the mooted third single, to be released later on in that summery year.

The Move were not joiners, they were alpha males and leaders of the pack. They perfectly melded, Mod attitude and psych-beat fashion and sounds together. With added, warm overlaid, Beach Boys intensity harmonies. There was also an aggression and chill in their music. The backline supplying big thunder with Bev Bevan's rocking, heavy drumming and Ace Kefford's chest-punching bass lines. Ace Kefford played magnificent bass and with his 'dive bombing' technique on bass, adding mucho gusto to the music. You can hear it on many live cuts ('Why' live in Sweden) and 'I Can Hear The Grass Grow' and more.

Even though the recording is not great The Move are pumping fire during the live set at Konserthuset, Stockholm in 1967 broadcasted on Swedish Radio. Ace removed the bridge pickup cover of his Fender Precision (see the *Beat Beat Beat* performances). He soon would remove the pickup cover as well. (The 'Fire Brigade' *Top Of The Pops* performance). Ace had performed numerous shows with the Fender Precision. A brief note on the Precision Fender slab. It said that about only 25 of these basses were made around that time. The music was a meld of proto punk, overlaid with caprice. It had a feeling of playfulness, interloped with these strange, original songs and lyrics. All mixed with some of the heaviest (and loudest) music ever played aloud onstage before punk or metal.

Joe Boyd recalls during his regular visits to catch the band. "One thing about going to see them at The Marquee was, all I can say is, that they were very, very loud! It's not that The Marquee is that big a room either, so the volume was overwhelming. Hendrix did that too — a year later and volume was, I guess, becoming a growing thing. I think The Move were one of the first groups to really make volume a central pivot. A big thing was The Move totally overwhelmed you with the sound. I think also it was part of the essential balance, because Bev Bevan was such a powerful drummer that you had to crank up the amps just to stay level with him and with Ace Kefford's bass sound."

Young drummer Will Birch attended the Windsor Jazz and Blues Festival the previous year. Birch was to later provide the beats (and many lyrics) for The Kursaal Flyers and later still the cult band The Records. He remembers a surprise

---

12 The highest price ever paid for a Warhol painting was achieved in May 2022 when *Shot Sage Blue Marilyn (1964)* sold for a staggering US$195,040,000 at Christie's New York. This sale set a record, making it the most expensive piece of 20th-century art ever sold.

performance, "The festival was held on 30th July 1966, the same day as the famous World Cup Final day. Headliners that evening were The Who. They did an okay performance as I recall, and they were my then favourite group. Immediately down the bill to The Who were to be the Yardbirds but MC John Gee walked on stage and announced, 'We are sorry that The Yardbirds can't be with us tonight. But here now to entertain you are... The Move!'"

Will Birch was amazed: "The Move took the stage wearing individually colourful two-piece suits, a presentation that looked a little quaint at the time. Also, the group's on-stage set-up, with the drummer centre back with four across the front; guitar, guitar, lead singer, bass was somewhat retro. They had a highly choreographed routine or so it seemed. Always moving backwards and forwards to come up to their mics, but never side to side. A bit like a beat group from earlier that decade."

Birch further details the performance: "Song by song they took it in turns to take the lead vocal. I don't remember any original songs at that point. It was all covers of recent R&B and soul songs; some were fairly obscure. Midway through the set guitarist Roy Wood sat down centre-stage to perform an extended sitar-like solo. (An early appearance of Roy's 'banjar'. Anyone wanting to hear an approximation of what Will Birch heard that day, is immediately directed to listen to 'Fields Of People' on the remastered *Shazam* CD version Where Roy plays a 'raga-thon' on his banjar). I didn't think they were in any way pre-punk. Not really!"

Roy Wood recollects the crazy magic; "In 1966, we started playing The Marquee, we took over from The Who. We used to get the same audience every week. So, we couldn't repeat the same show, and we learnt a lot. I had a spot during the middle of the set. The other guys would walk off and leave me alone. That's where I started inventing instruments, to amuse myself really. I came up with the riff for 'I Can Hear The Grass Grow' during that solo slot. I put together a five-string guitar, with bass strings and sitar strings. I then fed it through a pedal (and through my trusty Binson Echorec). This was before Jimmy Page and Pink Floyd were doing that stuff. I also invented the 'banjar' — a banjo/sitar, with the skin taken off the front. I was listening to a lot of Chinese music then. I was also the first person to play a guitar with a violin bow. Jimmy Page came along one night and he saw me doing that."[13]

Trevor Burton had pointed out the earlier Elbow Room gig as being a high point for The Move. Roy Wood points out another gig, that was yet another ascent up the mountain, "We had a well regimented set at The Birdcage and when we played at the Jazz and Blues Festival on the night of the England World Cup. In Windsor, yeah! So, it's a memorable date. We were on, playing instead of The Yardbirds, they cancelled, and we were put on instead. I think that was when —- that was the night we made it! We were still pretty much unknown when we were announced. They wouldn't have known who we were. But we got an amazing reception. And the music press gave us incredible reviews. That was a gig, where we actually looked at each other and said, "Wow, we are really going to make it.""

Will Birch resumes his clear memories. "They were disciplined and slick, which was quite refreshing compared with say, The Pretty Things. I didn't think they came across as menacing, although facially they may have looked a little hard nut. They

---

13 Eddie Phillips, guitarist with The Creation is generally cited as the first guitarist to use a violin bow with a guitar, a technique he experimented with while in his first band the Mark Four and later committing the sound to vinyl on the Creation's only UK chart hits, 'Making Time' and 'Painter Man', both released in 1966.

didn't smile much but they seemed to want to please. It was almost like cabaret but balanced against a hip repertoire of these US covers. Stuff that they can only have discovered on US import 45s. Or maybe by having listened to DJ Mike Raven on Radio 390. There was very little verbal in-between songs. There was no messing about, tuning guitars and playing with amp settings. The Move were slick, smart, and confident. I also saw them do the West Coast hip stuff. And then the more out and out rock 'n' roll. But that all came later around mid-1967. I never did meet the original band personally, but I did meet Roy Wood in 1977 when he came to a Kursaal Flyers show at the Lafayette Club in Wolverhampton. We had a chat backstage."

Will Birch adds, "From the moment I first saw them, I couldn't see how they could possibly fail, as long as they had some original material. It was all cover versions at that point. Then came 'Night Of Fear' a few months later, followed by all of Roy's subsequent hit songs." The next day on Sunday 22nd, Tony Secunda's other managed act The Action were sandwiched between power trio Cream and Georgie Fame. The Action roared through 'Harlem Shuffle' and 'Land Of A Thousand Dances'.

The Move's on-stage passionate performances soon attracted the attention of the pop and rock crowds. Elton John once stated that if The Move were anywhere within driving distance of where he was at that moment, he would never miss one of their shows. They were his favourite live band of the era! Later on in both of their careers Bev confirmed this about Elton… "I went to see Elton John at the NEC Arena in Birmingham, many, many years ago. And his opening line was 'Good Evening Birmingham — the home of my favourite group, The Move'."

The Move were the subject of extensive and intensive photo-shoots. These being mostly directed by the talented young Bobby Davidson. "Never smile — that was Tony's instruction," remembers Davidson. "Always look into the camera". That was me. "I hate people looking off camera. If they look down the lens, the picture has a lot more impact."

Of the first major photo session in London's Hyde Park with Robert Davidson, Bev Bevan thought the results, "made us look aggressive and ugly. Of course we thought it was better to look pretty in pictures, just like The Beatles. But this was much more dramatic."

Bev Bevan puts the Move's and Secunda's attitude in a nutshell, "We went to London with the express aim of becoming famous and doing whatever it took to do that. I suppose you could say we jumped on several bandwagons. I guess the psychedelic flower power thing was one of them. But we didn't believe in all that. We thought of it as a laugh. Along with a lot of good clothes and looks, we were working class boys from Birmingham, not university students from London."

The Move were building their reputation up, not just with a white-hot stage act, but with Carl Wayne's antics. At one notable event at The Roundhouse. An actual Chevrolet was driven into the venue and towards the stage. All this to the backdrop of Ace Kefford vocalising and the band performing Bobby Parker's 'Watch Your Step.'

Will Birch was amazed at the sheer chutzpah of the nascent fiery group, "After the Windsor Jazz Festival, me and some mates started going to see The Move at the Marquee Club. This was at their Thursday night residency. By now they were wearing slightly more colourful suits. Their act became even slicker, as further US soul covers had crept into their set. I remember that these were maybe their four opening numbers around that time: 'Cherry Cherry' given an intriguing workout (composed by Neil Diamond) with Roy Wood on lead vocal. 'Stop And Get A Hold Of Myself' (from Gladys Knight & The Pips) featuring a Trevor Burton lead vocal. 'One Night' (Elvis Presley) with Carl Wayne on lead vocal. 'Open The Door To Your Heart' (Darrell Banks) with a sensational Ace Kefford lead vocal. Then Bev Bevan came up front of stage, to sing lead on 'Zing! Went The Strings Of My Heart' (The Coasters) while Trevor Burton took over on drums.

Birch recalls "we saw them at their Marquee show on 17th November 1966. That night, for the second of two 45-minute sets there was a TV set placed on stage. Right in front of Bev Bevan's bass drum. MC John Gee announced, 'Tonight we're going to watch *The Frost Report* (Hosted by David Frost the well-known UK TV reporter/presenter) on TV.' I don't think Gee had any idea of what was about to occur." During the final song – Bobby Parker's 'Watch Your Step' sung by Ace, Carl produced from out of nowhere an axe. He started laying into the TV and axing the stage itself, while John Gee — weeping, by all accounts — begged him to stop. Instead, Wayne poured lighter fuel on the boards. As the flames licked, Gee ran on stage, Wayne ripped the distraught manager's wig off and chucked it on the smoking pyre. We were seated in the second or third row. We were fearing that broken glass might land on us. Then, without warning, the fireworks were lit by a couple of guys (Allen 'Dumpy' Harris and John 'Upsy' Downing) at the back of the stage and rockets started hitting the club's low ceiling, only to fall onto the audience. The room immediately filled with smoke. It was outrageous, frightening but highly entertaining."

Dumpy Harris added to all the mayhem by setting off a whole stack of smoke bombs. At the end of their set, the interior of the club, resembled the aftermath of a RAF bombing mission. Beside himself with joy, the irrepressible Secunda hot footed it, to a local phone box, immediately phoning the Fire Brigade and the Police force. MC John Gee the head honcho at The Marquee was apoplectic, "They went way too far," blubbed the visibly upset Marquee manager. But he forgot to tell reporters, that when he tried to stop Carl Wayne, setting light to the stage. The lead singer summarily tore his toupee off and threw it into the burning television sets. The next week on 24th November, The Move's eight-month association with The Marquee came to a jarring and abrupt halt! Whether John Gee pressed for compensation for his toupee, along with all the damage to The Marquee stage and the interior surroundings, appears to remain off record.

Will Birch remembers the pandemonium afterwards. "The set ended, and John Gee was outside the dressing room door on the stage right, shouting, 'Where's Tony Secunda?' As we left the Marquee, three fire engines were outside, blocking Wardour Street. It had been a most dramatic evening."

The audience rioted, the police were called, and Wardour Street was cordoned off. The Move, had by now made their getaway. The amazed and shaken Birch escaped unscathed and clearly all these years later, vividly remembers this amazing night of rock 'n' roll theatre.

"The Move at the Marquee Club, in that summer of 1966. I heard many in the audience that night, talking about The Move's outrageous behaviour in concert. This was totally new to me. But before the band came on, there was an announcement saying, that the band would not be engaging in any theatrics that night. This under threat of the termination of their residency contract. I was still curious about what that all meant. It was only a few weeks later that I got someone to explain it to me," explains an initially baffled, young American in London, Chris Dolmetsch. "I saw the Move at the Marquee Club in June 1966 at the insistence of some colleagues, in the Discurio Record Shop. I was working there as a stock clerk for the summer. I got a Marquee Club membership and went around to check out this then-unknown-to me group. I was "gobsmacked!" (a word 'new' to this Yank at that time). I returned for two more performances and then I returned to the States."

"We were a pretty wild band," admitted Carl Wayne to Spencer Leigh, "We smashed up TVs and we had a bogus H-bomb in Manchester, but it worked against us. We had to live up to the myth, that we were aggressive louts." Roy Wood added, "This did work against us, we'd smash up TVs on stage. Then the promoters would ring up the agent and say, that we had smashed up the dressing room. So, they didn't have (or want) to pay us?"

****

'Night Of Fear' was released on 9th December 1966 and reached Number Two in the UK Singles Chart on 26th January 1967. The jangling, catchy tune (all two minutes and 12 seconds) stayed for a long ten weeks in the charts. The song was a wry, funny pastiche of Tchaikovsky's '1812 Overture'.

Roy had mentioned some years on, "Personally I didn't think it was good enough. But when it succeeded, it did give me the incentive to carry on." Looked at from a druggy 1967 point of view, this song could be seen as an insight into a bad lysergic acid trip or something equally freaky. But it is another fantasy Roy Wood 'story', who as far as I know never took a tab of acid in his life. Ace Kefford sings the memorable interjection, "Just about to flip your mind, just about to trip your mind." All the vocalists have a hand in singing with Carl Wayne on lead vocals, Trevor Burton, Roy Wood and Ace on harmony vocals. Carl Wayne gives his opinion, on the first single "So what if we've used bits of Tchaikovsky's '1812 Overture' in it, which is regarded as controversial. Well, it's because Roy Wood, our lead guitarist and composer, regards it as being the all-time classical rave up. It's always being played on the radio — so what if some people think we're mad that's fine."

Like many others who rated The Move highly, this is not my favourite Move single. It is very catchy and has a great central idea from Roy Wood (who was introduced to classical music at home by his parents) for the intro. By attaching the Tchaikovsky overture aspect to it, it ensured the debut song had a totally unique flavour. The harrowing lyrics and rhythm being attached to a reassuring, favourite classical piece. Which was firmly lodged it in the collective consciousness. It could also be inferred that The Move's general love of soul and R&B from that time may have subconsciously led Roy to possibly 'lift' the idea from a 45rpm single released in 1966 by Ike & Tina Turner. 'Tell Her I'm Not Home' on Loma Records featured a wonderfully raw Tina vocal. This particular record also featured a bastardisation of Tchaikovsky's war-like theme.

With Secunda at the helm, The Move had created more short-term controversy, than any of their contemporaries, bar The Rolling Stones. One article read "Meet the pioneers of the psychedelic sound" and as a result of its trippy sound. Rumours started circulating that the word 'psychedelic' was a synonym for LSD! And that The Move were using it copiously. Later on that year — two of the members were!

Bev Bevan restates; "'Night Of Fear' was from one of a series of concurrent fairy tale figments of Roy Wood's imagination." Particularly in that earlier batch of songs and especially being coupled with that particular B-side. A little-known fact is that the flip side was firstly known as 'The Disturbance.' This raucous, boisterous, punky blow-out was considered for the A-side for a time. (Apparently Roy fancied its chances as the A-side). I wonder what the public would've made of that as a release. The full-on version with Secunda and Cordell, screaming their heads off towards the end would certainly have raised some ripples or maybe hackles? This is also one of the songs that Roy wrote around the time he spent at Moseley Art College.

'Disturbance' is a song about a mental hospital charity. Featured on 'Disturbance' were the funny, precocious lyrics of Roy Wood with genuinely funny couplets, like this one, also sung by Roy: "At the age of seven, I just couldn't read my ABC. But I gave my teacher tips, on how the cavemen used to be." Apparently 'Disturbance' was banned in New Zealand. The authorities said the record is offensive, as it deals with insanity. Tony Secunda told *Disc*, "It just proves they are four years behind the times."

There was talk of The Move topping the bill at the Olympia Theatre in Paris, later on in June. This was to follow their successful appearance supporting The Rolling Stones.

Bevan, meanwhile, was delighted that his work formed an integral part of the early Move sound. "The drums were very important, which was great for me, and 'Night Of Fear' is a very percussive song. But honestly, I was never particularly happy with the drum sound on the single. I thought it sounded weak. I was much happier with 'I Can Hear The Grass Grow' which has a much better drum sound. People say there are elements of Keith Moon on this song, and I definitely liked what 'Moonie' did. I got to know him a little bit as well and he was a total maniac but a good guy. The snare has always been my favourite drum. So, there was naturally, a lot of snare in those Move records. I'd listened to a lot of American drummers — great session players like Hal Blaine. I also remember 'Cathy's Clown' being a big influence on me, with its big snare drum sound. I remember thinking that was just brilliant; those drum rolls, played by Buddy Harman, which had a military feel about them. You can hear the influence of those drummers on songs like 'Fire Brigade' and 'Flowers In The Rain.'

The band, led by Carl Wayne, did a short two-minute advert for Radio Caroline. Introducing themselves and the new record: "We hope all of you enjoy listening to our first disc 'Night Of Fear'." A fun promo video was shot in Simon's Boutique in the Kings Road in Chelsea, London. It shows the band messing about at the beginning, as a 'reporter' is trying to locate The Move. Carl appears as the dimwit reporter wearing a long plastic coat with a hat pulled down firmly, over his head, so his ears are sticking right out. Carl is asking the band members one by one, "Who are you?" in a simpleton style voice. Firstly Trevor, then Roy, who does his Phantom of the Opera style push-my-nose-up routine. Then comes a one–shoe-wearing Bev Bevan. Then Ace appears and it cuts to the band, dotted round the boutique, miming to the song. It's a funny and affectionate look at the early band.

'Night Of Fear' was the first of a series of top five singles in the UK, from the unique penmanship of Roy Wood. The B-side, the startling, hilariously high camp histrionics of 'Disturbance' starts with Bev's loud staccato, flam drops on the snare drum. A technique of drum punctuation used in a song to highlight or give dramatic pause. This was a very punchy style and much favoured by Bevan. He used this form of drum language, very often at the beginning of his career. He drove the song with furiously rapid rolls around the kit. Plus, sharp press rolls, to punctuate the song's high drama. Denny Cordell and Tony Secunda, shrieking their heads off at the end added the requisite Hammer House of Horror hysterics. There is an earlier version minus the Cordell and Secunda coda which also builds to the abrupt tape cut at the end. Hysterics or not!

The Move soon found out that Tony Secunda was not someone to be taken lightly. Bev Bevan said, "Shortly after he'd taken us on, he arranged a day of press for us in London. We strolled in about half an hour late and didn't think anything of it. He literally screamed at us. He gave us such a severe bollocking! I mean, screaming and shouting and pushing us around. We'd never experienced anything like that before. From then on, we were frightened of him. "How dare you — don't you know, who the fuck I am? These people are important, and you come down here…"

Bev recalled the shock effect; "I had walked in just laughing and smiling. But we did gain instant respect for him, and we weren't ever late again. Even Carl, the tough guy in the band. We were all shitting a bit. Carl had had a career, where he was the leader of the band and a tough guy. And nobody told Carl what to do."

It appears that Roy Wood, was never a big fan of Tony Secunda. Roy's introverted timidity and Secunda's almost lunatic fearlessness, were not exactly a match. Wood believes, "The failure of the Move in America was down to bad management — we didn't get the breaks. It was all madness with Secunda, I tried to distance myself from it as far as I could. If I could've been more background that would've suited me. I was in the business mostly, as I wanted to get my songs heard."

On the other hand, it gave them continuous, wild publicity. The Move were never out of the papers. They were described as "the arsonists of pop." Some of the blurb about The Move around then "The destroyers (literally) of beat, the X-Men of the scene. They are destructive and totally unrepentant." It's a deliberate policy — and here is manager Tony Secunda to talk about it: "The Move have already proved their point, in terms of hit records and a stack of bookings from management who previously wouldn't trust the boys within a mile of their halls. We don't respect property. We feel our job is to put on a show… Do an exciting production, which matches the mood of the music." Carl Wayne added, "Don't start calling it psychedelic. It's not, it's a show — we chop up television sets on stage! As a group gesture, against the one-eyed monster, which has the adult population glued to their chairs, hour after boring hour. We already put the fear into the *Ready Steady Go!* people, when we dressed up a midget. He exploded from the bass drum. They called in legal experts and frowned and panicked. But he got us talked about and that's all that matters."

Dumpy Harris recalls the attempts to constantly up the ante with the evolving stage effects. "We used carefully timed, thunder flashes, to accentuate different parts of the music. A new development was sticking on Brillo Pads, in time with the flashes. Then we would get an amazingly symbolic spray of sparks everywhere — it looked really fantastic."

Carl was intense in his take no prisoners viewpoint. "We've chopped up stages, done some feral damage! It's alright if management gets stroppy. We just tell them; we will send them some planks of wood through the post to do the repairs. The Move take it further, we reflect violence in our music, by physical violence on stage."

Tony Ware saw the band twice in their early days. He was incredibly impressed by their power. "They had a wildness about them. Bev Bevan did in his drumming. There was something really wild about them. Not too many bands have got that. You've either got it or you haven't really. That was the power - right down to the bone, kick ass! Just blow the fucking face to pieces. That was their attitude, you know." *(Author note: The only comparisons I can make in the bigger music picture with (The Move) are Moby Grape and MC5. In terms of sheer feral rock and soul force. With Moby Grape's, eccentric songwriting and mixture of personalities).*

****

Melody Maker stated that: "Decca Records are launching a new label, described as a 'hip label for groovy people." Deram hit it straight out of the ballpark, enjoying strong chart success, with hits from Cat Stevens for one. Deram scored a massive bullseye with its first and only number one single: Procol Harum's classic, the haunting, 'A Whiter Shade Of Pale'. (This was allied to a distribution deal with Denny Cordell's production company Essex/Straight Ahead Music).

In its first year, Deram had hit the ground running. Both sides of the debut 'Night Of Fear' Move single were recorded at Advision Studios (which at that time was located in the Fitzrovia manor of Central London at 83 Bond Street). Denny Cordell was the producer and Gerald Chevin was the in-house engineer. The Move's manager and Denny Cordell were also partners.

Denny Cordell had also previously run an Island Records offshoot, Aladdin. Here he had picked up some production skills. He'd gone on to work with Georgie Fame and the original Moody Blues. From late 1966, Cordell been working as an independent producer with The Move. Cordell was based in the offices of Essex Music. Cordell's production company New Breed signed The Move and subsequently they signed with Deram, the Decca subsidiary label set up at the suggestion of their bellicose, sharp talking, forward-thinking promotions man Tony Hall. Decca were perceived as being a deadly-dull, straight boring label. Deram, this label-within-a-label was now intending to release exciting music, by the same new breed of "underground artists". Essex Music's owner David Platz was someone else, whose livelihood depended upon being hip to such sudden market shifts. Platz saw the writing on the wall. Publishers needed to develop new artists who were writing their own songs. Other Essex artists already signed to Deram, included Cat Stevens and David Bowie.

Procol Harum were faring well. By 15th July '67 'A Whiter Shade Of Pale' was lodged at a sturdy number 10 in the US charts. It was announced that guitarist Ray Royer and drummer Bobby Harrison had left Procol Harum. Plus, Jonathan Weston, was no longer the band's manager. It was easy to note, that new band recruits, guitarist Robin Trower and drummer BJ Wilson had both been former members of lead band member Gary Brooker's old band The Paramounts. Jonathan Weston's replacement was Tony Secunda. According to Matthew Fisher, "Weston was ousted because, instead of waiting to see how 'A Whiter Shade Of Pale' fared, he had asked an agency to book the band on a lengthy tour of small British venues. The result was that a few weeks later. We were Number One in the charts, and we were playing for £60 per night instead of £500 or more."

The behind-the-scenes triumvirate of Cordell, Hall and Platz could hear other, much bigger opportunities knocking and fast. The sudden success of his artists on Deram made David Platz realise that he was missing a big trick. Decca were reaping too much of the benefits. He negotiated control of his own label Regal Zonophone with Decca's old rivals EMI. He funded Cordell's independent production / management company in order to start supplying the raw materials. New Breed underwent a name change and was registered as Straight Ahead Productions on 3rd July 1967. Platz also provided funding for the irrepressible Tony Hall to leave Deram/Decca and set up as the independent Tony Hall Enterprises, to specifically promote the new Regal Zonophone releases. Some Essex acts were nailed down tightly at Deram/Decca.

However, The Move and Procol Harum recordings had been 'leased' to Deram, via the New Breed / Straight Ahead Productions company. They were now to be released on Regal Zonophone. Procol for example were complicit in much of this. Happy enough to go along with what (possibly quite little) part of it, they fully understood at the time. There were positives: control was wrested away from the major labels directly! Without losing the benefits of their pressing and distribution facilities. They had a streamlined, smart and forward-thinking team around them. But what about the conflict of interests? Procol Harum now found themselves essentially working for a flexible, multi-headed, many-named, but ultimately self-interested organisation. That controlled and made income from their recording label, the publishing company, the management, the production and promotion. Sounding a lot like the 360° recording deals that were being developed, not so long ago in the music business. Where the 'suits' own parts, of all aspects of a band. The merchandise (usually a very strong source of revenue for gigging bands), royalties, future payments and so much more.

Although announced in August 1967, Regal Zonophone wasn't ready to roll until 2nd September, nearly four months after the release of 'A Whiter Shade Of Pale'. The first release on Regal Zonophone, was The Move with 'Flowers In The Rain'. Procol Harum had to wait until September 30th before (their second 45 release) 'Homburg' — the new label's third release.

On the same day as the high-profile launch of the new Radio One, a Denny Cordell production for Regal Zonophone was chosen to be the first record played, 'Flowers In The Rain', which climbed to number 2 in the UK charts. 'Homburg' reached number 6 in the UK and sold a million copies. Somehow, it still felt like a let-down. Even more so when the single stalled at number 34 in the USA charts. The delay hadn't helped matters, but in truth Cordell's choice of follow-up was somewhat misguided.

'A Whiter Shade Of Pale' was big, stately and intriguing. 'Homburg' was melancholy and almost wilfully obscure. There is a slight similarity between both songs in terms of timbre and the melancholy feel. The band had other, more commercial songs in the can. But Cordell wasn't hanging around, he was moving on and moving Stateside. He had bigger plans, plans that saw him setting up a new label in the USA. He set up shop in Los Angeles and formed Shelter Records. Other than issuing a few reggae singles in the States for (good mate) Chris Blackwell of Island Records (The Maytals, The Wailers etc), Denny dramatically changed course in a musical sense. He was now producing and releasing — firstly Joe Cocker and The Grease Band.

Cordell's roster now became more Americanised with Phoebe Snow, JJ Cale, Mudcrutch, Leon Russell and others. As soon as he got involved with Joe Cocker in 1968, Denny Cordell abandoned any pretence of being interested in developing Procol Harum. He fobbed them off on his new deputy, Tony Visconti and then left them to their own devices. Meanwhile, The Move, Joe Cocker and Tyrannosaurus Rex, all had hits for Regal Zonophone.

After various disagreements with David Platz at Essex, Cordell departed for America. But Platz had kept on diversifying, and he was establishing, similar arrangements with several other independent producers. Platz also launched a new label through Pye Records called Fly. Here he shunted over his choice bands, including The Move and the truncated T. Rex. But not Procol Harum.

The Move's failure to conquer America early on was a major, wasted opportunity in the opinion, prominently and poignantly shared by Joe Boyd. Boyd was fortunate enough to see the original five-piece band, in their full-on gunning glory. Taking in their incendiary sets, most weeks at the Thursday night, London Marquee residency.

Jac Holzman head honcho and owner of Electra Records asked Joe Boyd, who was to be relocated to London, "What is our presence like in England?" Boyd immediately told him. 'It's crap — your albums cost a pound more than anybody else's. There I have no promotion, your artists never come here. Frankly it's a joke!' Three weeks later, I got a call from Paul Rothchild, the hot Electra label producer saying, 'Come and see me and Jac at the office'. They took me in and said, 'How would you like to go to London and open an office up there for Elektra?'"

Joe Boyd was summarily hired by Elektra Records in Los Angeles (the LA based, hipster label home of Love, The Doors, MC5 and The Paul Butterfield Blues Band) to talent scout talent over the pond in London. "I had shot my mouth off, and I got myself a job. They had a distributor at 7 Poland Street. They distributed Electra and also the jazz label Blue Note. They gave me a little desk out the back there. We started to manufacture the key Elektra releases. Phil Ochs, Judy Collins, we had a big hit that later that year with The Baroque Beatles book."

Boyd remembers a ritual that he had firmly installed at that time in the summer of 1966. First of all he would take clients, visitors and friends to Chinatown. For a chow-down dinner at Lee Ho Fook (Yes I know — *Holy Fook*?). Then a pretty short saunter a few hundred yards up the narrow, hallowed Wardour Street towards The Marquee Club for the weekly Thursday night residency of The Move. Lucky and privileged were those who got to see the original five piece Move in their prime. Some lucky visiting musicians were Paul Butterfield, Mike Bloomfield, Phil Ochs, John Sebastian and Jack Holzman. Joe Boyd further described it; "They were privileged to see The Move in their fiery prime. This was a phenomenon that few Americans had the real privilege of seeing."

Boyd quickly realised these weren't hippy-drippy, middle-class kids. They were working-class street kids from Birmingham, and they wanted to make it. And on their own terms. An apt quote from Joe Boyd's *White Bicycles* book describes, "Ace Kefford went straight for the most powerful, nail-your-chakras-to-the-seat-of-your-pants bass lines." Boyd maintains, "They made a far more superior fist of deconstructing soul tunes than did Vanilla Fudge a year later. Everything was always moving, faster and faster, with more and more dazzling harmonies, arrangements and power. The confidence was overwhelming."

Joe Boyd puts his initial amazement into words, "I was just stunned by The Move and how they would end the set. It was really unbelievable. This is the kind of thing that no American group would ever do. Because the thing about it was in Britain, there was still people dropping acid and doing all this new, really progressive music. And also charting some new course into the future of youth culture and all this kind of thing. There was still part of a tradition of pure show business. It was a show. The Move were very conscious of how they looked. How they kept the audience on their toes! How they performed. And then they did this thing, at the end of the second set. I can't remember the song that it was. But it would end with a long instrumental." *(Watch Your Step - Bobby Parker).*

Boyd describes the scene as follows:

It would end with a long instrumental passage.
Then, one by one, they would leave the stage.
Carl, then Trevor and then Roy and then Ace.
They put down their instruments and left them leaning against their amps, all feeding back.
So, there's this roar of controlled feeding noise.
It wasn't out of control feedback that would make everybody run for the exit.

It was just a roar of sound. Bev Bevan was pounding away. Doing a frenzied drum solo, all against the roar of feedback — He was the only person left on stage…

Bev would finish his drum solo, and he would lean down.

I spotted this the second time I went. Then I saw it for the first time. I didn't even notice that he had leaned down
and that he did something, behind the bass drum.

Then he got up and left.

So, you're confronted with this empty stage —
roaring out with feedback

And then Bev's cherry bomb goes off.
In a small club…

I mean it was a huge firecracker and it was just ear splittingly *l o u d !!*
and as it goes off.
BAAAAAANNNGGGG!!!!

The backstage guy - pulls the plug on the main switch
and
everything
goes
deafeningly
silent.

Wow!!
That was really incredible!!!

11.
Ready Steady Go!

The Move did their first TV appearance on 9th December 1966. On the very popular program called *Ready Steady Go!* (aka RSG) hosted by the happening personality girl Cathy McGowan (now married for many years to singer Michael Ball). Cathy McGowan was similar in looks to Davina McCall. Same ultra-glossy hair and energetic personality. McGowan was presented as "an ordinary girl" with "a Cleopatra look" wearing Mary Quant and Barbara Hulanicki. She was as much a face of the Sixties as Twiggy. She also had the hip sobriquet of 'Queen of the Mods'. The show was co-hosted with Keith Fordyce. (He was terribly old — he must've been in his late thirties. I'm not sure if that was an actual sin against youth in those days.) Fordyce was its first presenter, "a lovely man but very ancient." Wearing collar and tie, looking like a news reader. He was an affable and quaint square.

The Move's first appearance was notable again for a startling publicity stunt. Bev Bevan was just as startled as everybody else. "This was The Move's first UK TV appearance. We were doing 'Night Of Fear' and of course, it was Tony Secunda's idea. A midget burst right out of my bass drum. He was toting and then blazing away with a (fake) Tommy Gun. The midget was dressed up as a gangster. You know, with a pinstriped, big lapelled suit, brimmed hat, jumping right out of the bass drum! Firing a replica Tommy Gun, he was blazing away at the audience. We were wearing gangster suits then. We just had them made in Savile Row. Were we shocked? Oh yeah! Absolutely! Secunda wanted to try and catch the sheer sensationalism of it. Yeah, we didn't even know about it. It was really set up well and definitely the camera men didn't know it was going to happen either. It ended and happened so quickly. I was playing the drums, and the guy must have been battered around inside. That's what makes me wonder if we were miming that show. I wouldn't be actually hitting the bass drum, would I? Well, we were still coming to terms with… we were all learning what Tony Secunda was about. And the crazy things that he was capable of doing."

In the 1980s, the rights to tapes of the series were acquired by pop artist-turned-entrepreneur, Dave Clark. Many editions were lost or erased. Of the original total of 178 episodes, 170 episodes are missing and a further 3 are incomplete. This, most likely putting paid to the chance of ever seeing the episode with The Move.

****

The beginning of 1967, the so-called 'Summer of Love', as 1966 swiftly faded, started up with another 'happening' gig in London. Which has had much hype and mystery attached to it over the years. The gig had the name of (a pretty big mouthful) *PSYCHEDELICAMANIA*. It was held on New Years Eve 1966 finishing on 1st January 1967. Featuring The Who, Pink Floyd and The Move.

Two and a half months after opening The Roundhouse in London's Chalk Farm this gig was held in the cavernous space, labelled a "Giant Freak-Out All Night Rave" to celebrate New Year's Eve of 1966. The 10pm until dawn event, featured some of the biggest psychedelic rock acts of the time. The review below describes Pink Floyd's "groovy picture slides" (seen just months before at the venue's opening party). Allen Harris maintains the Pink Floyd stole these initial ideas from The Move.

Nick Jones reported in the *Melody Maker*, January 7th 1967, "The Who were smashing the sound barriers, topless audience members and freezing temperatures or swirled around The Move. The Roundhouse (a former railway engine shed) at Chalk Farm was once called "a derelict barn" it was a freezing enormous building. On the Saturday it saw in the New Year. None of its lack of creature comforts did it much in the elevation of its stature. However, despite the lack of facilities "the participants", meaning the paying guests adjusted as they always do, they blasphemed at the groups. Got it 'together' in the corners, and kept 'looning' about, to keep the blood circulation on 'the move."

"'Emancipated from our national social slavery' as the ads shrieked, are supposed to 'realise as a group,' whatever potential they possess for free expression. Either there was no potential among these liberated souls, or somewhere the organisation went wrong. If to get high, expand the conscience, freak-out, have the senses bombarded with kinetics and sound! You first have to suffer frostbite, malnutrition and nausea!"

"The Who got on to the stage after a good hour wait, during which participants were treated to 'See-Saw', by Don Covay. The Who almost succeeded in winning over the show with an immediate flurry of smoke bombs and sound barrier smashing. But somebody pulled out the plug and the Who suddenly fell as quiet as a graveyard. The trouble re-occurred, and it cut short two more numbers."

"After playing most of their new album tracks rather half-heartedly, Pete Townshend wheeled upon a fine pair of speakers and ground them with his shattered guitar, into the stage. It was fair comment. The group had thrice been switched off as well as being constantly plunged into darkness by a team of lighting men. None of whom seemed to know where, in fact, the stage or the Who were positioned. The proceeds of the 'happening' went to Centre 42 which ultimately, hopes to raise money for a brand-new amphitheatre at the Roundhouse. Whether they will continue to put on pop shows when the theatre is built remains to be seen. They owe it to the pop scene to do so."

The Move were much more successful that cold night. Technically they had no hitches and their act came smoothly, to a very stage-shaking climax. On this freezing night Dumpy Harris and the group tried out a new and startling massive backdrop. A barrage of blinding white light, epileptic fit inducing, strobe lights. These were obtained somehow through Chelita Secunda. With husband Tony borrowing them from a nearby mental institution. TV sets were stuffed with inserted Hitler and Rhodesian Prime Minister Ian Smith dummies. These were summarily swiped with iron bars and Carl attending to their destruction, with the mighty, dreaded axe. This started a furore in the crowd, as well as The Move's high-octane loud set. From behind and from the rear of the freezing auditorium, a hulking and very unusual sight was unfolding. A 1956 Chevrolet (bought for £75 according to Robert Davidson) was driven up slowly and deliberately towards the stage.

Carl Wayne now used the large ceremonial axe to start chopping up the vehicle in no uncertain manner. Carl Wayne was now 'Chevrolet Finder General', with the axe poised to full effect. Bobby Davidson's candid pictures clearly show the American car being chopped to bits. Shattered windscreen glass lies scattered everywhere. With dents and big slices and gouges, rupturing the bodywork of the big American car.

Trevor Burton is seen elatedly jumping around on the stage in the background! Trevor is looking completely off his tits, minus his guitar, with his trousers undone. In front of him, one of the strippers, is languidly dancing away. As if totally lost, in her own stoned world. In the photo Trevor is probably caught here in a fabulous Mod groove-out dance. The look of sheer elation on his young, high, excited face, is fantastic. It catches the elemental power of music and the euphoria of being in a red-hot band live, all at once. The two girls dancing at the front were both, either entranced and/or stoned enough to strip to the waist.

It seems that the audience forgot about the two strippers, who were gyrating semi-naked. There was an icy atmosphere of both menace and anarchy (in the UK) throughout the crowd. The remaining, shivering crowds, surged menacingly towards the stage, the demolished car and the two 'birds.'

Ace Kefford remembers the stage was invaded. "I think it was an hour before The Who could get on. Christ only knows, what happened to those strippers." The two women were ignored mostly, as Carl Wayne started to demolish the Chevrolet and the televisions. It was said that the car got turned over completely. Towards the end of the raging, carnage-filled set, feedback buzzed onstage, surrounding, a stripped-down arrangement of Bobby Parker's, 'Watch Your Step'. Ace and the band chant… 'Watch Your Step, Watch Your Step…'

All the while smoke is creeping around the band on the stage. The lights specially commissioned for The Move, buzz and flicker in time to the R&B classic. A current YouTube video named *The Move Interview - Crazy Live Footage 1966! 360* shows the young band clowning and messing about in a rare on-the-road interview. It is notable further for some very rare live footage of the band with Ace and the band intoning "Watch Your Step', you better watch out child". A television begins to burn. Smoke clouds billow up on the stage. Ace repeats the hypnotic, ostinato bass line. Trevor and Roy supply brief flurries of arpeggiated guitar. Throughout the ongoing guitar feedback and musical miasma, the flames are licking higher and more thick pluming smoke is seen. The outgoing Carl Wayne is prowling around the stage and gets to work and performs a serious work-out with the axe on stage. The TV and whatever else he can see, gets it through the murk of smoke. All are chopped away at, in the enthralling climax of The Move's set.

Coincidentally, in a current but very relevant aside, my good mate Karl Hopper-Young and I were in Brighton, watching a Sex Pistols 'tribute' band. We met Charlie Harper, the longtime leader of UK Subs. Who I believe is a sprightly 80 now. Charlie is a long time groover on the music scene. Karl introduced us. Charlie asked about my book. I told him, "I'm writing a book on The Move." He immediately said this —

which was really great. I repeat my and his first sentence:
"Yeah - I saw them!"
"Charlie, you saw The Move? Where did you see them?"
From over the span of years, Charlie exclaimed, "I saw them at The Roundhouse on New Year's Eve 1967. When they smashed all the TVs up. Well,
it was one of the most amazing shows I have ever seen! Seriously I mean it. Yeah, it was like The Who used to smash everything up! But The Move took it all much further than The Who."

All in all — a ritualistic, hypnotic and riveting slice (sic) of 'rock theatre' or 'auto destruction.' Just like all great rock music should be. This would've come after 45 minutes of The Move pumping the audience and priming them for this moment. The Move admit they got carried away, "a bit too much" reported the *Disc and Music Echo*. "To date they have chopped 17 holes in various stages and one night the whole stage collapsed, taking the Move and the equipment with it."

Pete Townshend had started smashing up stuff on stage — his guitars mostly, before The Move started the determined trashing of TVs, stuffed with effigies. The "one eyed monster" as Bev put it and parts of the stages. Townshend was the art student in The Who. He attended and went to the same Ealing Art School in West London. As had Ronnie Wood, Freddie Mercury and your author. It gave Townshend a great buzz, to stomp all over his smashed-up guitars. After first wedging them through his Marshall amplifiers (Jim Marshall's music shop was also in West Ealing) and generally pounding them to splinters.

Gustav Metzger was a German artist who specialised and performed art pieces. These were conceptually known as 'auto destruction.' These art works related to the (Japanese) Gutai Associations and Metzger became a big fan of The Who's 'auto' trashing onstage. He asked them to perform at Ealing School of Art. I'm not sure how much Tony Secunda was personally ensconced in the volatile art world coming from his wrestling background. Probably very little, but he was surrounded by other people who were. Movers and shakers like Denny Cordell and others. Certainly, his wife Chelita Secunda was very aware of and linked deeply into the current art scene in general. It's here I think that The Move's links to the arts are very interesting. There was the 'auto destruction' aspect which didn't last much longer than nine months. Had it continued they would not have been allowed to play at any venues in the UK at all. There is the 'situationist' art style coming into play. There was Secunda's use of Nigel Waymouth and Michael English. They designed as the 'Pop Art' graphic artists that wonderful 'Op-Art' Move poster.

This superb 'Op Art' poster was used for the 11th July gig at The Marquee prior in 1966. A true visual classic of its time. The Move also had a comic strip, running in *Rave* magazine for a few months, drawn by Michael English. Although it wasn't a strong piece of comic artwork, it showed that Secunda and The Move were using all kinds of visual devices and avenues to explore publicity in those halcyon days of experimentation. Malcolm McLaren similarly voiced later that The Sex Pistols were creating chaos or as Malcolm would put it, "Cash Out Of Chaos." They too had a strong link to Art schools with Jamie Reid's blackmail style lettering: The ripped and torn punk ethos, sewn and stitched together graphics. A wonderful subversion of visual devices, used in (for then) a startling manner.

This whole link with English Art schools and rock lineage in the UK is a long and very important one. But it is beyond the remit and scope of this book to expand on this. Suffice it to say, they had the requisite (albeit short-lived as he got expelled from Moseley School of Art) art student in Roy Wood. And certainly, two fashionably, formative members in Ace and Trevor who were definite, snappy-dressing, style hounds. More of this later.

It's a little-known fact that Tony Secunda tried to muscle in on the Sex Pistols management later on and take the Pistols on board. Quite frankly, Secunda and The Sex Pistols could've been a marriage made both in heaven and hell. Instead of all the guff McLaren came out with, a lot of which was reactive to some of the overdriven Pistols' publicity. But uncannily similar to The Move in many ways. I'm sure Secunda would've combatted and railed against the "establishment" much further. Possibly made even further inroads into the Sex Pistols. Creating 'situationism' with their music and Jamie Reid's art.

The *Move* album was said to have ten songs, all written by Roy Wood ready for release in early 1967. It's believed that Secunda wanted to pile on the pressure with more and more publicity stunts. Keeping the band in the public eye constantly and to delay the record for a while. This delay actually turned into an entire year — it did not get released until April 1968. This turned out to be one of the worst aspects of Tony Secunda's management.

The over-insistence on endless publicity stunts and bad boy-isms was great but this was the time, in which albums were starting to attain their almost newly mystical quality. The Beatles for example in their first year released two albums, five singles and three EPs. Secunda had The Move gigging all the time through 1966. They got a deal — they recorded the first single at the end of the 1966 after being signed, charting in the beginning of 1967. However, they needed to have done at least one album that year. Or certainly an EP; with one original Roy and three covers perhaps? They needed to have more chart presence, as well as their uncanny ability to light up stages around the country.

Trevor Burton remembered, "We would be in the studio recording a single in four or five hours. This was all on four track machines — all pretty primitive. I enjoyed recording a lot, it was very hard work! Doing all the overdubs, all the vocal stuff was fantastic. To do all the harmonies, the 'oohs' and the 'aahs' and all that. But we didn't stop; we were six nights a week, all year long. If we had two weeks a year off, that was about it. We made all our money through gigging. I never got any royalties. I got about £1,000 I think at the end of it, for everything. Denny Cordell and Secunda had the rest, I think. God bless 'em! Rob Caiger, the remastering honcho of The Move catalogue said he had gotten a quote about Denny Cordell. Someone had asked Denny what happened to all the money, and he said, 'Well morally, it might have been wrong, but it was legal. (laughs)'."

David Platz the quietly spoken, well-mannered chairman and owner of Essex Music Publishing had a big roster of music musical stars, including The Move. In 1967 he also set up his own publishing company, Bucks Music. He founded the record labels Fly, later relaunched as Cube. Platz passed away in 1994. Leaving behind a long legacy of hits now run by his son Simon. Platz also had an American arm to the London based company. In the USA it was named TRO Essex. This was an umbrella company, which now owns over fifty different publishing companies. He also set up a deal with A&M Records in Los Angeles to release and distribute The Move's music, in the States. In 1967 the cutting edge of the British music business was as small as it was sharp. Involving much socialising and show-and-tell.

Platz was someone else whose livelihood depended upon being hip to such sudden market shifts. Particularly if matching songwriters to artists was becoming a thankless task. (Due in most part, to The Beatles and their revolution in innovating the songwriting process in bands). Publishers now and pronto needed to develop artists that wrote and recorded their own material.

Denny Cordell was one of the many people, to whom an excited Guy Stevens, had played the 'A Whiter Shade Of Pale' demo. Cordell had also run the Island offshoot, Aladdin. Where he had picked up some basic production skills.

"We used to try and copy the Stax sound. Particularly at the time on 'A Whiter Shade Of Pale'. We were trying to copy 'When A Man Loves A Woman' by Percy Sledge," confessed Denny Cordell.

If anything, Cordell came a little too close to achieving his objective. Sledge's song had made number four in Britain in May 1966, and stayed on the charts for 17 weeks. Consequently, it had been as much in the air when Brooker wrote 'A Whiter Shade Of Pale' as had been the Hamlet cigar ad. Cordell's production just made a fairly obvious debt, very obvious indeed. The subsequent focus on borrowings from Bach in Procol Harum interviews was so much magicianly misdirection. Dead classical composers are much less litigious than living popular ones. Percy Sledge was no fool though. He covered 'A Whiter Shade Of Pale' almost immediately following its release, as a Stax single no less. (Although, it was mysteriously deleted soon afterwards).

In his live shows it still provides an opportunity for him to effectively perform his greatest hit twice. "It was if you like, looked at from one aspect — it was a soul ballad," as Brooker admitted in 2002. So far that makes the 'A Whiter Shade Of Pale' songwriting credit read something like; Reid / Stevens / Dylan / Carroll / Brooker / Bach / Loussier /Sledge / Fisher… though Cordell might also have staked a claim for a piece of the action for his other significant contribution during recording.

The song was still running at six to seven minutes. This by the prevailing laws of radio airtime was way too long for a successful single. Cordell excised the second and clumsiest verse and faded the song out abruptly. Just at the start of a chorus repeat, thus halving the song as originally written. In terms of maintaining narrative progression, Cordell's edit was an act of artistic destruction. But in terms of honing the song into an enigmatic four-minute gem of radio playable length, it was truly inspired.

Cordell loved the song, but still couldn't make up his mind whether it was commercial enough. Cordell was super picky sometimes. He would find it difficult to come to a final mix conclusion. Are the cymbals too splashy, which of the several mixes, he'd created was best. There was much prevarication before he finally played a noticeably worn acetate to Deram's Tony Hall. Hall had no such doubts. He passed it on to Alan Keen, programme director for offshore pirate station Radio London, so Cordell could hear what it sounded like over the airwaves.

DJ Mark Roman played the acetate at around 4.00pm. Monday 17th April being the likeliest date. He remarked that it sounded like a hit to him. And invited listeners to ring the station's Curzon Street office if they agreed. The office was inundated with calls. Cordell had all the market research he needed, plus invaluable pre-release publicity. The losses and legal expenses would ultimately be shouldered by the band. The behind-the-scenes triumvirate of Cordell, Hall and Platz could hear other, much bigger opportunities knocking. The success of his artists on Deram made Platz realise that he was missing a trick. Decca were reaping way too much of the benefit, so he negotiated control of his own label Regal Zonophone with EMI.

****

Digging through magazines I gleaned reports that claimed The Move were planning to go to Vietnam to entertain American troops in October '67. At London's Marquee Club they are said to have taped a special 40-minute show for the American Forces Network, titled 'The Move In London.' Whether this is another bit of Secunda publicity frippery I don't know. Nobody I know has come across or indeed ever mentioned this film, which would be brilliant as a well recorded, broadcast quality document of the original Move at their London home in The Marquee.

The Mothers of Invention were purported to come to Britain in an exchange deal with The Move. The Move were to go to the United States around 2nd September. They were to attend a promotional visit, to include a concert at New York Town Hall on 30th September. While over there, they were going to record another album and further material for singles. Denny Cordell was to fly out to the States and handle these Move sessions. None of these dates were finalised for The Mothers over here in the UK, doing mainly radio and television work. No Mothers live gigs were mentioned at all.

Yet another possibility mooted, was "The Move were joining the 'committee' of the American Environmental Pop Festival to be staged in New York in May and June. This involved sharing a bill with The Beach Boys and composer Leonard Bernstein. Also, it was purported The Move will be designing their own show with 'environmental involvement'." Another forerunner in The Move history — the climate change agenda in 1966/67? Not only that, but "The Move would help pick the acts for the show. They will also be redesigning their entire act." The event was to be dubbed "The First Memorial To The 20th Century Environmental Pop Festival." This was alleged to have some $500,000 in cash backing from the *Pepsi-Cola* company. Plus, the possibility of being relayed visually to other countries via the satellite Telstar.

The Move did eventually do a very short tour in America in 1969. This was nowhere near any of the spectacular publicity just covered. Indeed, The Move's 1969 tour was a ramshackle, threadbare affair, without any seeming interest from their American record company A&M Records (founded by Herb Alpert and Jerry Moss). A&M Records didn't even bother to send a representative to meet the band at the airport. Anything that could go wrong, did go wrong. This has got nothing to do with the actual performances they did. Bill Graham, the redoubtable and the most reliable promoter in the States made sure the gigs would go okay. The organisation and planning generally and the whole event was real fag end stuff. The grotty tour (in terms of record company support the band literally did mostly everything themselves) heralded the end of the original group falling apart. (By original, I mean with the gregarious front man and stunningly powerful lead singer Carl Wayne, leaving in early 1970. This was the third and final blow. After losing Ace Kefford and then Trevor Burton). To say this tour was at the opposite end of all these mooted big USA events, would be a colossal understatement. More later, detailing that fated tour, as it happened in 1969.

Another American tour-based news item reported: "As The Move have switched record labels, from Deram to Regal Zonophone they are now issuing their third single on 25th August 1967. This means the band will not now be leaving, or going to America as planned. It will be postponed, until the January or February of 1968. They have signed with General Artist Corporation, a big American agency for a three-year agreement."

The short article also noted that 'Here We Go Round The Lemon Tree' was also being issued in the United States on 25th August by The Idle Race on the Liberty Records label. It also said A&M Records did a good job of promoting The Move's last two singles in the US. It's interesting to note that ELO's later success was based on something The Move didn't do at the time: Constantly touring the USA, acknowledged as the key to ELO breaking big in America. If the Move had toured hard in the USA, it could / would have been a different story. Alas we'll never know. 1967 was also the year, in which the staging of festivals gathered momentum, and The Move appeared at plenty of these varied events.

****

Granada TV were talking up a new TV show, to be hosted by The Move. A half an hour program, said to be a proposed replacement for the popular, but defunct *Ready Steady Go!* On 6th March 1967, The Move and Pink Floyd were featured on Granada's *The Rave* programme. This was a pilot to test out the new show. But more groovy Move mayhem ensued. The Move performed 'Night Of Fear' and 'Watch Your Step' and Pink Floyd performed 'Arnold Layne'. Apparently, Granada hoped that the show would be shown across all the ITV network, but this never happened. The *Rave* broadcast doesn't appear in many TV listings, with most sources saying it was never broadcast.

However, the following letter in the *NME* (18th March 1967) suggests it was shown in the Granada Television region of Manchester (as well as Yorkshire TV): "I've just watched The Move and the Pink Floyd on TV and the show was great! Because both these groups produce the most fantastic freak-out music!" gushed Susan Broadfield of Yorkshire.

There was also this, "Granada should be congratulated for showing the daring experiment, combining things which are already in existence. Free pop music, satire, psychedelic visuals and the kind of condensed philosophy which made Bob Dylan and now the 'LSD people' notorious — something greater than any of these was created — something teeming with imagination — something which only TV can put over." This was another young writer (Tim Horrocks from Lancashire) who was obviously bowled over by what he saw.

In his second book, Laurie Hornsby's superior and highly recommended, verbal history on Brum Beat, *Brum Rocked On*, Laurie has some relevant information. It was the very same evening The Move had been lugging the imitation H-Bomb around Manchester city centre that this pilot show was broadcasted. Laurie ascertained that it was only broadcast live, throughout the North-West of England, before it was unceremoniously yanked while live on the air. Laurie shares my opinion of Pink Floyd. "Also on the show were the 'Hooray Henry's' of psychedelic pop. At the rehearsal the show's producer, Pip Carter sternly instructed The Move to forget any ideas of performing the smashing-up routine on the air. On overhearing the producers lecture the 'Hooray Henry's' began to rib The Move, as being "egotistical common hooligans." "They were probably right", commented Ace Kefford. "Ribbing us was the worst thing, they could've done."

Tony Secunda sensed yet another headline and smuggled the notorious, trusty Move axe into the studio. Secunda hid it behind the amplifiers. Winking at Carl Wayne as he did so. Live on air The Move could be well described as loose cannons. The second song they had chosen to perform, Bobby Parker's 'Watch Your Step' was appropriately named. Roy broke into a squalling, wah-wah pedal infused guitar solo. Carl Wayne suddenly produces the axe and begins to furiously lay into the stack of television sets that had been piled up on the stage set purely for visual effects. After 15 seconds of total mayhem with Ace Kefford and Trevor Burton hopping around, literally trying to watch their step, and to avoid Carl's chopping and splintering, through the pile of TVs, the 'big girls blouse' producer pulled the plug and the whole Granada network audience found itself suddenly staring at their blank TV screens.

The voice of announcer Trevor Lucas apologised profusely. He informed the viewers that normal service would be resumed as soon as possible. "In the meantime, some light music for your pleasure," he said. "And Pink Floyd never got on the TV screen," laughed Ace.

This 'pilot' show on Granada Television, resulted in the switchboards being blocked for well over an hour. The absolute and utter outrage! Well I never ever, EVER!

Flowers In The Rain - The Untold Story of The Move

12.
I Can Hear The Grass Grow

Around this time, The Move made a three and a half minute, colour 'telefilm' based around 'I Can Hear The Grass Grow' for release in America. This was on the back of the success of the 'Night Of Fear' film. They were also approached by the BBC to appear in a 30-minute pilot show for a new 'pop programme', still in the planning stages.

Special Move days were also being planned in major stores throughout Britain. The first at Swan and Edgar in London's Piccadilly on 31st March 1967 — The release day of their second single on Deram Records, 'I Can Hear The Grass Grow', also written by Roy Wood. This was a complete, aural dynamo. Upping the ante from 'Night Of Fear' and featuring many elements which stamped out the inherent Move sound with an ultra-confident delivery from Carl Wayne. It reached number 5 in the UK singles chart on 10th May 1967. It had a welcome stay for a good ten weeks. It was coupled with 'Wave Your Flag and Stop The Train.'

Both sides were recorded at Advision Studios. The songs were recorded quickly, between gigs and photo shoots on 5th January. Engineer Gerald Chevin and Denny Cordell were behind the console. As well as The Move promo card, the single also had another Robert Davidson photo featuring a bald, weird, looking gentleman in a tight black catsuit. He is holding an air-horn towards the ground. It was captioned "Mr Trippington certainly can hear the grass grow."

'I Can Hear The Grass Grow' had some wonderful backing vocals, (especially those high "yipping" accents on 'I Can Hear etc'). A wonderfully, propulsive drum and bass section by Ace and Bev that hits the ground running. Excellent jagged guitars from Trevor and Roy, with nice little Roy flourishes to hone the melody. It's a Move classic. The 'B' side was 'Wave Your Flag And Stop The Train.' Said to be a straight - on tribute to The Monkees success.

Another effortless and excellent 'B' side. It's a mid-tempo chugger, with super strong, double tracked vocals from Carl Wayne. It features a wonderful, harmonised confusion of vocals between 1:39 to 1:50 seconds. This, where the band build the voices up into a mini orchestral piece and is absolutely wonderful: "I can't figure out what's with her mind, I can't figure that she's out of time." With a nice, emphasised, train-like chugging beat, taking us back into the next verse.

The original band were intuitive maestros in putting together these parts. Featuring those little vocal gymnastics, based on Roy's writing direction. The Move hit the ball right out of the park here. Brimming with confidence, an excellent studio performance with a 'live' feel for 'I Can Hear The Grass Grow'. It captures the idiosyncrasies of Roy Wood's songwriting. Another song that was partly formed in his Moseley School of Art notebooks.

Robert Davidson maintains he came up with the original title for the pulsating A-side. The song title was said to have been derived from a Health and Efficiency nudist mag *(Robert - I say!)*. Robert had read an individual letter within. The author of the letter was heard complaining, "I listen to pop music on the radio. Because where I live it's so bloody quiet that I can hear the grass grow." Robert told the story to Roy Wood who went away and who no doubt, being further inspired by the phrase, wrote the rousing song. Roy expanded about the song further in the April 1967 edition of *Beat Instrumental*, where he said the song is "about a mentally ill person." With the song's allusions to psychedelia and losing one's mind, journalists were obviously thinking it referenced the use of mind-altering chemicals. It has a great Mod, freak-beat sound. A driving, pounding from the rhythm section and those two coruscating guitars.

Roy Wood remembered the structuring of the song: "When we did a lot of the Motown stuff, there were four of us on the front line. When we started the evening, we started from one end of the band, and we would just go through along that line. The lead singer would change all the time. That's the first time I managed to put it into a record."

Strangely enough, the song didn't do as well in chart terms as 'Night Of Fear' but it was the song that really established the early Move sound in their single releases, although the sound changes from single to single. Another track, simply titled 'Move', with a great Mod R&B feel to it and with excellent intro harmony vocals, was to be the B-side. However, technical problems during the mixdown, caused distortion on the mono master on 30th January 1967. So, it was shelved, not to be heard again until the reels were discovered years later by Rob Caiger and subsequently newly mixed to stereo forty years later. Instead 'Wave your Flag and Stop The Train' was substituted as the B-side. It has been described as a straight-on tribute to The Monkees' success.

The Monkees was an incredibly successful TV show from the USA. A direct attempt to create a cuddlier (and Americanised) Beatles. *The Monkees* show led on to an absolute slew of hits internationally. Plus, a run of at least five to six decent albums, packed with an absolute plethora of gorgeous hit singles penned by many of LA's finest songwriters such as Gerry Goffin and Carole King, Neil Sedaka, Neil Diamond, Tommy Boyce and Bobby Hart, as well as the four Monkees themselves. Davy Jones, Peter Tork, Micky Dolenz and Mike Nesmith all contributed strongly to the overall superb catalogue.

There was a grumpy and pedantic review of 'I Can Hear the Grass Grow' by Alan Price in the *Melody Maker's* 'Blind Date' section. "It's that Hollies thing — 'Stop, Stop, Stop.' Too similar and they're trying to sound like The Beatles. Is it The Move? They made 'Night Of Fear?' Is it a Denny Cordell production? I suppose it will be a hit but I'm not particularly impressed. What do the lyrics mean?"

****

The Move ran afoul of lazy promoters, who didn't advertise gigs properly. Allen Harris remembers one gritty situation: "They bowled up to one gig in Welwyn Garden

City, there was about ten people in the audience. In typical unscrupulous fashion the two promoters, who were two brothers, decided that due to the small crowd (due to the fact they hadn't bothered to advertise the gig), they weren't going to pay the band. A call was made to Ron King at Galaxy Entertainment in Denmark Street. Ron said he was sending a couple of operatives along, to deal with the situation. I said to him, 'Ron, they won't pay us. They are giving us some stick.' I started to get the stuff back into the van. I'm going down this passageway and next thing I know, there's a chap at the one end and the other one at the other end behind me. I panicked and I threw the guitar case at him. Unfortunately, a gun dropped out of the case. It was a starting pistol that we had. I can't remember why we had it now. I managed to get out of the building, and I phoned Ron up again. I said 'Ron, they've got our gun — they won't let me check our stuff out.' Ron says, 'I'll send some boys down. Lock yourself in the van'."

Allen continues, "I clearly remember when the Galaxy Agency guys arrived, I went back into the hall with them. The kids that were left in the hall — these guys from Galaxy, they took everybody out. Then, there was just the two brothers left. I can picture these two Galaxy guys now. I clearly remember them, putting these leather gloves on. They gave the two brothers a really good hiding. What happened after that was, they had got the starting pistol. They had pulled the police in and I'm in trouble over that. The two promoters both finished up in hospital. It was around that Easter time."

Being locked in the van and driving The Move to gigs, at times, some fun was needed in an attempt to alleviate travel boredom. One particular practice not often spoken of in more polite company and not entirely uncommon was known by various titles, such as 'invoking the blue Angel' or 'Pyro-flatulence'. It certainly could lead to some hilarious mini situations. At one time either Ace or Carl was sitting in the front. With their legs and feet up on the dashboard. It was decided to treat everybody, to a close-to-home explosive display. He pulled out a cigarette lighter. In short order, he let off a ripping fart. The vile gas would then be gingerly lit by the cigarette lighter. This would immediately cause the inevitable methane and carbon dioxide explosion. Flames would burst and explode forward, from between the farter's legs. Allen Harris said it was "fucking horrible". Allen, as usual was driving, whilst trying to breathe through his nose. "All these flames flying around and that. Yeah, we'll be left stuck... I had to stop driving — I couldn't stop fucking laughing." That is utterly amazing man, in a very grotesque way!

The public school-educated Robert Davidson was also sitting in the van. Bobby was utterly horrified by this vile display of aromatic flame throwing. He was clutching his throat — gagging! While simultaneously trying to avoid his blond, bouffant, stylish hair becoming incinerated. "I do remember travelling in the wagon, this was one of their party tricks. I forget who. Probably Carl would light a fart. I'd never ever seen that done before. The methane coming out. He would get a match lit up or do a fucking, great big fart and set light to it. There would be this blue flame. It was through the trousers and just lighting a bloody fire, never seen that before. I was staggered."

13.
It seems that all my freaky clothes, are turning into rags

Carl kept his head firmly on his shoulders. But he did try out a tab of acid while the promo filming of 'I Can Hear The Grass Grow' was going on. An amusing black and white film with a central 'Mad Hatters tea party', plus some rabid lady stalker fans chasing the group around a park theme. Carl hated it (the tab of acid that is) and was not inclined to ever repeat the experience. Carl would come out with anything from, "We're not psychedelic, we're showmen", to "Young people love violence. We're waiting for the new Mod Presley."

The Move kept their heads on their shoulders — well certainly three of them did! Trevor and Ace definitely took their noggins on a full scale, psychedelically flavoured, joyride during that crazy year. Although Carl did try LSD and smoke a couple of joints. It was definitely not his thing.

Asked once at a London party if he fancied a joint, Wayne came out with, "No! I've already eaten." Showing both the witty and straight side of him. Nigel Waymouth remembered how everybody was incredibly snotty-nosed about the use of pot. In terms of — "pot was the real thing". Even wine was off limits. And definitely not beer! And a bit later on, definitely not coke and heroin.

This unseen promo footage for 'I Can Hear The Grass Grow' was eventually released on *Magnetic Waves Of Sound* on Esoteric Records in 2017. This release also includes the entirety of The Move's January 1969 appearance on the BBC 2 show *Colour Me Pop* with the four-piece band captured in bold colour and mostly playing live. 'Beautiful Daughter', 'Wild Tiger Woman' and 'Something' were mimed, 'Blackberry Way' and all the other songs were done live. You can even see Carl Wayne playing competent bass guitar on 'The Christian Life', another Byrds cover with the lead vocal taken by Trevor Burton. The sound and visual quality of the clips is by and large excellent. 'Blackberry Way' from the German show *Beat Club* is an abridged excerpt (perhaps it's all that survives?), we could've done with the entire thing. The transfer to widescreen from the original aspect ratio has resulted in a slightly distorted image, a squashed look. A flaw which is more noticeable during full line-up shots, through the *Colour Me Pop* material. As with the other remasters, *Move*, *Shazam*, *Best Of The Move*, and the 40th Anniversary *Anthology 1966-1972*. This compilation is accompanied by a cool essay from Mark Paytress. There is an insert, featuring a Move poster on one side. Clippings from music papers and promo shots, adorn the other side.

The 14-hour Technicolor Dream held at Alexandra Palace on 29th April 1967 was one of the seminal events of the counterculture revolution in 1960s London. This event was organised as a fundraiser for the paper, the *International Times*. The multi-media, multi-arts event featured poets, artists and musicians of many hues. It was headlined by Pink Floyd. Yoko Ono performed, watched by John Lennon, while other acts included The Crazy World of Arthur Brown, Soft Machine, The Move, Tomorrow, The Pretty Things, Jimmy Powell & The Five Dimensions and Pete Townshend, among others. Heralded as the dawn of the 'Summer of Love' — London's answer to the American Merry Pranksters inspired Acid Tests in the mid-60s.

Not that there weren't any other gatherings in the UK capital, where people were turned on to hallucinogens. Or conversely, where a combination of music, lights and mixed media attempted to create an atmosphere conducive to psychedelic space travellers. Middle Earth and other hippie hangouts were doing this for most of the late 60s. But this was the biggest event to contain all of the above — and more. It was a bloody nightmare of a venue, with the acoustics of a boomy aircraft hangar but it had a certain charm.

Roy Wood having just done a soundcheck, was walking off stage when he bumped into a familiar face. "I was strolling down the big hall, making my way back to the dressing rooms," Wood recalls. "The place was virtually empty, when who should be coming towards me but John Lennon with another bloke. John was wearing his short Afghan coat with the little badges on it. I thought, bloody hell, this is unreal. I'd never met him, never come across any of The Beatles at that stage, but he was one of my favourite people. As he approached me, he suddenly stopped and, like a soldier, he saluted me. So, I saluted him back and he walks on. Then he turns around and says: 'Nice one, man'. 'Cheers, John. Ta very much'. I was delighted that he knew who I was."

Lennon, accompanied by Indica Gallery owner John Dunbar, had arrived to see an obscure Japanese performance artist called Yoko Ono (not yet his girlfriend). Fresh from a session for the song 'Magical Mystery Tour', Lennon had dropped a tab of acid that very morning. Roy Wood didn't touch LSD. He certainly had other things to occupy his mind. The Move's third single, the glorious, psychedelically tinged 'Flowers In The Rain' was about to establish the Birmingham band nationally, give further credence to the brand, that became known as the 'Summer of Love', and also ignite a nationwide furore!

Around this time Ace's wife Jenny permed Ace and Trevor's hair into tight bubble Afro-style cuts. In part a tribute to Jimi Hendrix and his influence across the music world that year. It was around then that Bev Bevan noticed a growing increase in drug use, in these two former Mod boys who brought so much fire and energy and stance to the band. They became more insular, sharing the private joys and 'in' jokes, of being the band's perpetual stoners. They also became much harder to communicate with.

"Ace's wife was a hairdresser," Burton recalls. "It was just a mad moment. I kept the perm for a year and then my hair started falling out in large chunks."

The guys in the band couldn't stop laughing, when they first clapped eyes on the

It seems that all my freaky clothes, are turning into rags

two newly, permed-up, Afro-haired, "gone wrong Mods" as John Cooper Clarke later described them. The two babies in the band, also got heavily into the newly arrived LSD.

"It was still legal then," Trevor Burton says. "We'd get it in a dropper bottle and put it on sugar lumps. You never knew what the dosage was. I think Ace and I were some of the first people in England to do acid back then — although I'm sure other people would disagree.[14] It didn't do Ace any good though. He was 'crazy' anyway and that triggered his (as then undiagnosed) bi-polar disorder and he went off the rails."

Bev remembers, "Ace was such a cool looking guy. I felt he lost some of his direct cool. By getting the Afro perm, then starting to wear granny glasses, along with the hair look."

Trevor was definite and truthful about the path into drug taking: "It was only Ace and me that took drugs in The Move. We were like kids in the sweet shop. Our other thing was amphetamines. When you're gigging six nights a week you don't mind a little help."

These two reckless Move 'bambinos' were absolutely not above throwing each other the bottle of liquid Amyl Nitrate. Especially when they were doing their groovy live version of The Byrds' 'Eight Miles High', which the band covered with their usual musical elan. Perhaps the nitrate, speed, weed and acid high, as they hurtled upwards, into the multi drug-o-sphere entirely matched the swirling version of The Byrds tune they were playing?

Trevor Burton remembers Ron King was the one who had introduced him and Ace to Amyl Nitrate at first. He gave them a box to try out. "Well, we tried it and we fell about laughing, it was such good fun. We did it for a couple of months, until they were all gone. We used to have them under the strings, at the end of our guitars. We were working six nights a week and with all the travelling. We were young. You can do it at that age. You just don't give a fuck!"

Allen Harris recalls one rough and ready presence at Galaxy. "I remember the first time that I went to the office. Ron King's secretary was a biggish girl. She was on the phone! It would be all 'fuck this' and 'fuck that' and it shocked us. When we were in the office, she would be drinking a pint. The first time I've ever seen a girl with a pint glass."

The Move appeared for the first time on Hastings Pier in May 1967. Colin Bell was fresh out of school: "I saw the five-piece and I stayed in contact with Carl Wayne right up to his death. I was fifteen and a half. In the school holidays, a friend of mine told me about all the major bands appearing on Hastings Pier. The Stones, Hendrix, everyone. I went down on that summer holiday. The very first band I saw was The Move piling out of the van. Roy was a little bit shy. Carl was the chattiest. Followed by Bev, who was sort of taciturn that day. I actually felt quite intimidated by Ace and Trevor. They didn't look very happy. They had out 'Night Of Fear' and 'I Can Hear The Grass Grow', which they played that night, obviously. I was working backstage and chatting to them all. I was genuinely approaching Trevor and Ace, with a bit of trepidation, particularly Ace. I mean, he used to knock people out occasionally

---

14 *It has been documented many times that The Beatles first dropped acid with some dentist and other people in late 1966. They subsequently drove into Central London in a Mini where they were driving at about 3 miles per hour.*

and that. They weren't unfriendly. I think it was… I just felt there was some tension there. It was the first name band that I've ever met. I saw The Move, Dave Dee, and became a lifelong friend. I saw The Tremeloes, The Herd, just about every band you can name, appeared on the pier. Carl gave me his address at the time. He said, 'If you're up north, you've got to come up see me.' This is just my impression but the vibe between Carl and Roy was a little strange too, I seem to recall."

Bell felt undercurrents percolating though the group: "I remember talking to Carl, and I think even in those early days, I felt his vision of where they were going, wasn't the same as Roy's. I also knew Tony Secunda. One of my oldest friends, and my inspiration for getting into the business was Denny Laine. A slight tangent, but basically I heard, 'Say You Don't Mind'. Johnnie Walker played it on the radio, six times on the trot! Which I don't think had ever been done before. Denny, sadly, passed away December 2023. We were mates and in fact Denny was sleeping on Tony Secunda's couch in Tony's office, because he was totally broke! When Paul McCartney rang up — which of course was Wings, he was trying to form a band."

Colin forged a strong bond with Denny. "Later on, I helped Denny out financially. Denny wanted money basically to get over to the States. He had been offered a place, in something called the 'World Classic Rockers', which was basically 'names' from big bands. So, he got the money to go there and he never, ever came back! Denny was always grateful for Tony Secunda's help."

Another "moving" story with another hilarious twist: Tony Secunda had The Move booked into a ten-week residency. Every Sunday at the Great Yarmouth Aquarium in Norfolk. The first appearance (and others) was with Billy Fury and supports The Nashville Teens on 25th June 1967. The residency was to run until 27th August. It only lasted for two weeks, before The Move were ceremoniously ousted by impresario Larry Parnes.

Parnes was Billy Fury's manager and had set up these shows. The first show comprised The Move headlining the opening part of the show. That portion of the show featured Tomorrow (before this, they were Unit 4+2 and The In Crowd), Amen Corner, two slots by Peter Kaye, and The Move. Billy Fury topped the second bill; supports were The Nashville Teens and The Plainsmen. The Move were known for their intensely loud (in terms of volume and performance) stage act. They hadn't gotten any quieter by then either. The Move appeared the first week at the end of the bill. As usual, they were playing very loudly. Rattling countless dentures and causing a right old commotion amongst the old dears in the audience. Carl Wayne and his trusty axe were also said to have rent a rather large slice through the main stage curtain. Complaints were inevitably made.

The Move were told, at the following week's show. The levels had to be kept down to a "reasonable" volume. The second week, of course they played as raucously and loudly as ever! Needless to say, they were canned. John Rooney of The Plainsmen was tickled: "The Move played twice as loud as they did the week before. You could've heard them in Lowestoft." That was the end of their ten-week residency in Great Yarmouth.

I doubt (apart from the loss of money) The Move or Secunda could have given a flying, backwards toss! According to Keith West, Tomorrow's vocalist. He laughed as he remembers the ridiculous billing. "God knows who booked that. It was a real end-of-the-pier-type scene with Billy Fury, attracting a considerably older age group than the other acts. West's outfit decided they would get themselves out of the situation, the best possible way. They played so loud during the first set that Parnes warned them that if they did not turn the volume down in the second set they would be thrown off. "So, we played even louder and got thrown off!"

The Move went along with it as well and also got thrown off, on the beginning Sunday. The police had already warned The Move about the 'drug songs.' Directly asking them to take 'Eight Miles High' out of the set. I bet they took full heed of that — Not!

Due to their overwhelming popularity, The Move were reinstated back at The Marquee in Soho. Following the infamous fireworks event the year before and the subsequent Marquee ban. Will Birch follows up on this great performance, "On 11th July 1967 they returned to the Marquee. Having since enjoyed two hit singles. I queued from late morning. Their uniform appearance in colourful suits was gone. They were now wearing kaftans and beads. The songs they covered had moved on from soul and R&B in favour of US West Coast rock and early psychedelia, The Byrds, Love, Moby Grape, that sort of thing. They were still ultra tight and ultra convincing on stage."

Funnily enough, even though he could be considered the "straight man" of the band, Carl Wayne brought in most of the superb West Coast "psychedelic stuff." "He brought in these songs as he really wanted to sing them — like 'Stephanie Knows Who' the brilliant Love tune for example." Bev recalls, "Carl used to frequent a fabulous record place in central Birmingham called The Diskery. Carl was listening too and picking a lot of this new stuff up there. I think it's amazing how Carl had been in the Vikings and then he really turned himself around really well. He also sang these songs so brilliantly." The Diskery has been open for business 67 years now and is still going strong.

The Move had a very balanced, equal opportunities, attitude to upsetting everybody: Managers, promoters and even some of the more strait-laced fans. Smoke bombs, facsimile H-Bombs, attempted fires, flares, riots and more. All of this had made them the most talked about band in ages. Numbered among the guests in the audience, were the Metropolitan Police and the London Fire Brigade. The Fire Brigade attending was said to have made copious notes. Watching as mayhem and smoke billowed around them.

The Move purely saw this as a gimmick and were egged on insistently by Tony Secunda. They didn't give the stunts much deep meaning. Certainly, not any intended Eastern mystical nonsense. This was sheer unadulterated and aggressive show business. (The business of show). All the bands indulged in it, but in 1967, some shrouded this in a kind of airy-fairy, melange of mystical bullshit: The prevalent and ever-growing, type of wet-brained hippy stuff, usually brought on by the large amounts of Moroccan hashish, Red Lebanese or the lethal Tibetan Temple Balls (sometimes laced with Opium, which could give the smoker, a truly mind boggling buzz).

I know, I smoked some of this unbelievably, paralysing shit once. It took me about two minutes to get up from the sitting position — never again! These exotic "delights" were being ingested, at any time, or even most of the time. Either smoked in joints or crumbled into, then cooked, hash cookies (an even more intense high). Or smoked through a bong, a bottle with an attached pipe affair. The cooling water would take away any smoke harshness and heat from the back of the smoker's throat. Therefore, keeping the 'buzz' mellow and in good shape.

This is not to say that The Move were complete strangers to the all-encroaching drug scene. But definitely Bev Bevan, Roy Wood and Carl Wayne, could variously be described as major/minor beer monsters at various times. Ace Kefford and Trevor Burton definitely had the taste, for all the other sweets in the pharmaceutical pantry. Uppers, speed pills and various jazz cigarettes. Unfortunately, for one of these two young, charismatic musicians and singers it was to be a taste too far, which led to an incisive and shattering personal calamity.

This was a further predilection for an overindulgence LSD. A drug which is (or should) be taken in minute, pin drop doses. But one that has had powerful and potentially significant effects on some of the most creative movers and shakers in the music industry. As it did for one of the five charismatic members of the original Move.

Likewise, Peter Green and Danny Kirwan of Fleetwood Mac. Both were damaged badly by the effects of this relatively unstudied drug. The Beatles seemed to manage okay and went on to write about the effects of acid (LSD) and put songs together under the influence of same. Although it could be said that John Lennon's excessive use of LSD at that time had also had a very serious effect on his mentation. Further to this, his use of heroin, which coincided at the beginning of his relationship with Yoko Ono, all seemed to add up to a lack of ambition, a possible falling off of his talent, an inability to write as much as he did and other interpersonal matters.

Syd Barrett of Pink Floyd was not so fortunate. Barrett had occasioned a full-on mental breakdown, perhaps hastened and pushed to an extreme edge by LSD and other substances. Barrett's dreamy torpors gradually appeared to wend their way further and further into psychic collapse.

Syd was becoming hollowed out and slowly slipped into the mind's pre-abyss anteroom. With schizophrenia developing or pre-existing; riding alongside to bind him to his final destination for the rest of his life. Fellow artist Duggie Fields, who shared an apartment with Barrett in central London around then described LSD as "the last key to unlocking Syd's door."

Barrett's transformation, from a happy extrovert to a depressed introvert was progressive. Although there does appear to have been one major tipping point. With many friends, such as former Pink Floyd bandmate Richard Wright, telling stories of how Syd became "a completely different person" after a drug-fuelled long weekend away. While no one remembers the exact date of this particular weekend for sure, people have since referred to it as the 'lost weekend.'

It sounds similar in effect to the weird weekender, when Peter Green, Danny Kirwan and Dennis Keane, the road crew manager of Fleetwood Mac were taken to some mansion in a forest area in Munich, Germany. Hosted by a particularly weird hippie couple, young, entitled hip and dark of vibe. Green made some pretty unearthly music jamming that night, from what historic folk lore has told. Unfortunately Peter Green is said to have come back inalienably altered by the use of LSD (or perhaps a much too large dose of the drug that he had been given to ingest by these creepy 'hippies').

Although John Altman, who writes, about this Munich / Green incident, in his autobiography *Hidden Man* has a much different slant on Peter Green's state of mind during that period. John states he played with Green throughout 1970 for about eight months.

Altman disputes this Munich 'evil-drug-hippie' story that has grown up around Peter Green. He states that Peter Green was okay when he played and jammed with him repeatedly at that time in 1970. Altman says Peter was really on the ball. It was later on, that his further use of LSD caused his inner collapse and his mental health issues to develop apace. Green, along with his younger and equally impressionable guitar colleague in the band Danny Kirwan were both affected.

"Peter Green and Danny Kirwan both went together to that house in Munich," their one-time manager Clifford Davis recalls. "Both of them took acid as I understand. Both of them as of that day, became seriously mentally ill. It would be too much of a coincidence, for it to be anything other than taking drugs, as of that day."[15]

Sadly, the other great, guitar savant Danny Kirwan, especially after such early promise, spent the rest of his days mostly living in sheltered accommodation. He was reported at one stage to be living in St Mungo's Shelter in Covent Garden, London. Down and out and an essentially homeless alcoholic. Four years on, Kirwan was located, at a Los Angeles hostel for the homeless. He was living on social security and a small trickle of Fleetwood Mac royalties. To my mind, there's something daemonic about these tragic incidents. With the subsequent destructive effects on the supra talented Peter Green and the younger Danny Kirwan.

Syd parted ways with Pink Floyd in April 1968. Or certainly his departure was announced that month. Much closer to home Ace Kefford parted ways with The Move, in that very same fated month. Leaving the band that he and Trevor Burton had excitedly talked about and put together, with verve and passion.

The Syd Barrett episode parallels in a similar eerie and strange fashion, Ace Kefford's self-administered "overdose" of acid in liquid form. Taking in to account the comments before, about people taking acid, as a "micro dose" or in a "micro-dot". In other words, a very small amount. Ace had (over) used a bottle of home-made LSD. He had bought the phial from some Birmingham student, idiot, chemist, acid-dabblers. This led to a catastrophic mental and physical collapse at the age of just 22, which was described in the papers at the time as Ace having a "nervous breakdown."

Syd Barrett had become more and more reclusive. He finally gave away nearly everything he owned and walked back to his mother's home in Cambridge, a good fifty miles from London. He reverted to his real forename Roger. He rarely interacted with anyone, and he simply painted. He died in Cambridge of pancreatic cancer in 2006. Syd was aged 60.

Peter Lorrimer Whitehead was a happening, experimental filmmaker and captured The Move at one UFO Roundhouse gig. Fragments of The Move can be seen here. You can make out Trevor Burton and Ace Kefford, in the very beginning of the film. But they are "psychedelicised" into the overall "trippiness" of the woozy opening shots. They are on screen for mere seconds. 'Yesterday's Papers' (a really

---

15 Some sources claim that Kirwan was not present at the Munich commune. Fleetwood Mac roadie Stuart 'Dinky' Dawson recalled that only two of the Fleetwood Mac contingent went to the party: Green and Keane.

well-done series of mostly 1960s based videos) on YouTube has about four or five good clips of The Move. They are highly recommended to watch. Particularly *The Move Get Sued By The British Prime Minister Harold Wilson* That is an excellent video, tightly edited and lots of deeper information. Featuring the urbane voice of Robert Davidson, talking through some of the trickier points of Tony Secunda's management history at that time. *Tonight Let's Make Love In London* filmed in 1967, unfortunately focuses on the Pink Floyd. Unfortunately there is no trace of The Move live in this. This could simply be that Secunda and Whitehead, did not come to terms and agreements for the filming and music licensing.

Whitehead had earlier interviewed The Move during a visit to Central London. On the roof of New Movements place in Denmark Street. There is an endearingly funny opening. With the band twirling round in a circle — kicking each other up the arses. You can hear how green, young, full of enthusiasm, and in love with early exposure to London life they all are. Before all the later drug and ego rift problems started. With Ace, Carl and Roy having a really good laugh. Whitehead asks Ace, "what's your name?" and he spells it out, "A - C - E." Carl interrupts and says laughing, "It originally had an R in it?" A really funny little moment, it's a sweet snapshot of the band. Before fissures, jealousies and cracks, began to ripple through the group. Whitehead is known for the film *Charlie Is My Darling* shot in 1965, while the Rolling Stones were touring in Ireland.

Mainly through these two early efforts, Peter Whitehead is considered one of the first people to be involved, in what became pop video promotion, in the pre-MTV era. *Charlie Is My Darling* captures the energy and rawness of the young, vital Stones at their raucous, charming, early pop star peak. A dispute between Andrew Loog-Oldham and Alan Klein (the American who Oldham went into partnership with to manage the Stones) meant that the film, never received an official release until 2012. Whitehead did further work with the Stones, including the promo film for the singles 'Have You Seen Your Mother, Baby, Standing In The Shadow?' and the audacious clip for 'We Love You.'

It was reported that "The Move group will finish working on *Colour Supplement 1966*, part of the Peter Whitehead film on Swinging London." This being filmed at Tiles Club on Oxford Street. To my knowledge this film or clips, has not been circulated. There is silent Kino film footage of the five-piece Move in 1966. Wearing their pin-striped gangster suits, throwing shapes and performing in a club in which the striped awning, looks very much like The Marquee.

In a contemporary aside, Bev and his wife Joy spent a weekend with Robert Plant and his wife, and they went to a Wolverhampton Wanderers football game. Plant told Bev how much The Move had meant to him and John "Bonzo" Bonham back in the day when they were playing in The Band of Joy. Plant and Bonham were massive fans of The Move. Back then, Robert's favourite singer, was Jess Roden. As previously mentioned Roden was approached early on in regards The Move, lead singing role. Right back in the beginning days by Ace and Trevor.

****

The Move went into Advision Studios on 6th July 1967 and recorded one of the

It seems that all my freaky clothes, are turning into rags

'Summer of Love' classic songs in just two (initial) takes. Denny Cordell and Gerald Chevin were both in attendance. As stated before, Cordell was unhappy with what he heard. Cordell maintained there was slight slump in the performance.

Enter the soon to be stellar, the fresh, ambitious and energised Tony Visconti: "I met Denny Cordell in my music publisher's offices, The Richmond Organisation in April 1967. I was the house record producer; Denny and I met by chance by the water cooler. He said he was the house producer for the sister company back in London, Essex Music. I helped Denny produce a Georgie Fame session in New York, (Fame wasn't there) by writing out a simple chord sheet and some trumpet parts. Denny was impressed and I got a call two weeks later from him offering me a job as his assistant/deputy producer. I don't recall any rehearsals. Denny just took the band into the studio and asked The Move, 'What do you have for me?' We spent long hours getting a new song recorded. That would both be the rehearsal and final master take, although mixing would be on another day. Denny was very persuasive and wouldn't stop the band from recording until he had the best take possible. I never saw a band driven so hard in the studio."

Cordell and Tony Visconti gelled almost immediately. Cordell enduringly calling him, "Ah! My American cousin!" "This gave me a pure frisson of delight, a feeling that doors were opening in a good way." This posh, distinguished looking, tall Englishman was indeed to become integral to Visconti's early musical journey.

Two weeks later Cordell was to call Visconti and ask him, "how soon can you get over here from New York?" As Visconti remembers clearly, "I arrived in London on 27th April 1967, and I stayed for 22 years."

Joe Boyd outlines some of Denny Cordell's personality: "He was a very nice guy. He was not like Tony Secunda. He was a nice, upper middle-class boy. Denny Laverack-Cordell. Horse racing and the whole lot! He had this slightly patrician air to him. But he was very friendly to me, he was very cool. He spoke like a posh boy, but he would cut his accent down a little bit to try and fit in. He was a puzzle to me, because he was very laid back and very calm and very unaggressive. Yet, he ended up sitting there, in the side office of Essex Music with Procol Harum, The Move, and Joe Cocker. It was an entire music stable — which was amazing. I was in touch with him, but I was never as close to him, after he moved to America. I did see him occasionally, because I moved to LA at some point. The way he started up Shelter Records (with Leon Russell), he built another empire and then evidently... I don't know all the details, but Shelter Records went under."

Visconti was not hanging out much. "I rarely saw a member of The Move outside the studio. I met them in the studio for the very first time. They seemed very competent to me. I was very impressed with how tight they were when they played together. Denny drove Bev very hard and one day he made Bev play the kick drum for hours. Until he and Gerald Chevin, got the best sound possible. It literally drove Bev to tears. Same thing happened with Ace Kefford's bass sound etc. Everyone then was all about 'Eleanor Rigby' and string sections. I thought we needed to get off the strings and use some other classical instruments. So, I wrote something pastoral, in the vein of Mendelssohn. It was kind of a wacky arrangement, but it eventually reached number two."

"The band was a little wary of me. There weren't many Americans in London at that time, so I was kind of exotic. I had a problem understanding their English and Birmingham accents. There were words like "chuffed" and "knackered" which were unknown to me. But we were at least around the same age and we soon got on very well. I thought they were a great band. I heard someone describe them back then, as "the poor man's Beatles." I thought they were just as unique. Roy and I got on really well. I got on with Carl Wayne really well too. He was the 'gentleman' of the group. I could see that Roy was the leader. I got on with Trevor and Ace too, we were all friendly together. I adored the young group! Unfortunately, they seemed to have gotten the nickname of "The Poor Man's Beatles" unfairly. *(Author note: Another example, of the stupid snobbery, casually thrown about by middle-class, hack journalists, as I evidence throughout this book)*. Denny and Tony Secunda were friends, because they both cut their teeth in the music business, by working for a Beatles merchandising company together called Seltaeb.[16] Which is Beatles spelled backwards. They were public schoolboys and spoke with posh accents, Denny more so. (Oddly I could understand posh accents better, because we saw many British film actors in US films). I met Secunda prior to working with the Move. I always felt uncomfortable around him. He seemed inauthentic, not really into the music. But more into the business of making money. I'm with Gerald Chevin on this. As a non-musician and a non-engineer, Secunda would drop irrelevant non-sequiturs, to appear to be in the know, but he was just an irritant."

Olav Wyper was the creative director at Essex Music, working with David Platz. He felt that although Secunda was a great sensationalistic manager, he did not have the all-important management links in America. This would've taken The Move to the next, conquering international level. He states quite readily, "When I was at CBS in particular, I came across (particularly in America), bands that were average. But that had huge successes and long careers. I also came across bands, that were hugely talented and had very short careers. The difference was — who was managing them! Who was planning their careers! Who was deciding what they should do! And, more importantly, what they shouldn't do! That's the key to management. I think if Charlie (Carl) and The Move had stayed together and been with the right people, they would have been a world-class and a world-dominating band. That must have been a real sadness for all of them."

'Flowers In The Rain' was not a smooth run at first and Visconti recalls, "The sessions were typical. Rehearsing the song, then recording many, many takes of it. The atmosphere was workmanlike, no party. I don't remember any drugs, not even beer or hashish being there. They were very professional."

'Flowers In The Rain' was going to be discarded until Visconti suggested a remedial arrangement. "Yes, it's true. The tempo slowed down somewhere in the middle and Denny was going to discard the song because of that. Cordell felt that the band had gone 'out of time' during the middle eight and he wanted to scrap the song. Not even re-record it."

Tony Visconti thought the track could be saved and beat The Beatles at their own (George Martin) game. I stood up for the group and said it was a great song and if he let me bring in some orchestral instruments, I could write a cool arrangement

---

16 Seltaeb was the Beatles company set up in 1963 by Nicky Byrne to exclusively look after the merchandising interests on behalf of Brian Epstein, who managed NEMS Enterprises and The Beatles.

It seems that all my freaky clothes, are turning into rags

that would distract the listener that it had slowed down. Denny graciously said to go ahead."

Further to this Visconti had the wind instruments recorded at half speed, to cover up any slight falling out of time on the middle eight. Played back at normal time, they sounded like pixies and covered over any slight defect. Fortunately, the experiment worked wonderfully, and the song was a big hit.

****

The relentless Move gig roster and workload continued unabated. Another festival, The Barbecue 1967 Tulip Bulb Auction was held at Spalding in Lincolnshire on May 29th 1967. The bill attracted some great names: Hendrix, Cream, Geno Washington, Pink Floyd, Zoot Money, Sounds Force Five and The Move. Admission price was £1. Sounds Force Five, a popular local covers band, opened the festival, doing songs like Joe Tex's 'Show Me' and other soul and R&B numbers. Apparently, they went down well. For some reason the event has largely faded into history, although being considered by some to have been the first UK rock festival. Covered accommodation came in the form of the Spalding Town F.C. stand right next door. It was the largest building in the area that could hold a large crowd.

In addition, Zoot Money's Big Roll Band were booked along with local covers outfit, Sounds Force 5, booked to ensure a decent turnout. Sounds Force 5 performed during changeovers between each band from the side of the stage. Advertising was national and massively underestimated, with thousands making their way to the market town. The usual British 'parochial panic' happened, causing national radio to warn travellers to turn back. Attendance numbers have been estimated with a venue capacity of 6,000 and twice as many unable to gain entry. Estimates vary wildly but some reckon tens of thousands of ticketless fans arrived and the town braced itself for trouble and disorder. Mods and rockers fresh from their recent seaside fracas joined music fans from all over the country.

The Spring Bank Holiday was a hot and gloriously sunny weekend. Which could've been trying (or frying) for the large crowd just laying around inside a metal shed. The event appeared to be unorganised, and the sound was terrible. Whilst the venue at the start for Pink Floyd was bare, it quickly filled up with fans being trapped underneath the stage. Jimi Hendrix had many issues, including tuning problems; was late on stage and he only did a half-hour set, and finished by throwing his guitar into his speaker stack (the same red Stratocaster he would burn at Monterey the following month). It was widely agreed that Clapton out-played Hendrix that day. And that Geno Washington put on a great show.

John Thorne, then a cub reporter with the *Spalding Guardian*, remembers the event and the trepidation felt by the town. "It was just a job for me to cover. (Yeah right!) I wasn't particularly a fan of Jimi Hendrix, but I had seen Geno Washington before and was a fan of his." The trouble never materialised but Spalding would never do anything like it again.

It's quaint to think of The Hendrix Experience, staying in The Red Lion Hotel in Market Place the night before. No thought had been given as to how busy the town would be on the day itself and how his band would get to the venue. This event was chaotic and shows the lack of experience the promoters had. Geno Washington wraps it all up by saying, "There were thousands and thousands of people there — Mods, rockers, hippies. People were hanging from the ceiling. The atmosphere was electric. Anyone who was there that day will never forget it."

One concert goer re-lived the day, "The Move were an excellent band. They were using Orange Amps, the heads wider than the cabinets, so it all looked a bit ungainly. They'd had two hits by then 'Night Of Fear' and 'I Can Hear The Grass Grow'. Carl Wayne did a few disgusting impressions; gyrating and rubbing up on the microphone, while curling his bottom lip but the set was a real highlight. Pink Floyd were the first big band to start and were "pop artists" at that time. Impossible to believe almost, but they had had two recent hits and were thought of as a psychedelic pop band. They were really terrible. The light show was truly pathetic! I think The Move came on next, they were one of the best bands on the bill for impact and sound. They got a bit of life into the audience and impressed me more than I expected."

The Tulip Bulb Auction Hall was a cattle auction shed. It was a gig put together by the all-too-common rip-off promoter. The venue was not suitable for such a purpose and the number of tickets had been massively oversold. It was packed, hot, stuffy and very tense. The tension between the bands and the audience is quite clear. Equipment problems were rife including a faulty or, at the very least inadequate PA system. The combination of circumstances, unsurprisingly, produced a hesitant and distracted performance.

The Move during this period were the quintessential British rock band. They appeared live at Stadthalle Offenbach, Germany on 26th June 1967. There they recorded for *Beat! Beat! Beat!* They did great versions of 'Walk Upon The Water', 'Night Of Fear' and 'I Can Hear The Grass Grow.' The 1967 hippy-garbed Move blow through their paces. Their performance gives ample evidence that they were just as engaging live, as they were in a studio setting. More so!

Free The Pirates also organised a "Free Radio Ball of the Year" at Alexandra Palace in London on 22nd July 1967. This was just before the Marine Broadcasting (Offences) Bill was passed in Parliament. About 3,000 people attended the event which starred The Move, The Pretty Things and Tomorrow as well as other groups, The event was hosted by Radio Caroline DJs Johnnie Walker and Robbie Dale. Also, Jeff Dexter was another DJ, and there was a lot of talk about the psychedelic effects of smoking banana skins!

14.
And this is where we came in, dear reader

'Flowers In The Rain' was officially released on 25th August 1967. Immediately after the release of this anticipated third single, The Move went on to play the Festival of the Flower Children at Woburn Abbey. This jaunt was set up on the grounds owned by the Duke of Bedford. The festival was spread over the 26th to 28th August. It also featured a truly, horribly drawn poster. Possibly drawn and designed by someone taking bad acid in suppository form? The headline acts were the Small Faces, the newly formed Jeff Beck Group and Eric Burdon and the Animals. All of whom, were making great music at the time. Other acts included the Bee Gees, Alan Price and more.

The Move were visually morphing, into their temporary hippie stage and still looking cool. Ace is playing a Harmony H22 bass guitar (a strangely, semi acoustic, looking bass). Ace does not seem to have used this bass that often before he started toting the white Fender Precision slab style bass. This chunky looking bass was also favoured by John Entwistle (aka The Ox) from The Who.

Some soppy jokers apparently started throwing sparklers up above the stage during The Move's set which was apparently curtailed by the stage canopy catching fire after the lit sparklers were thrown.

Another Brummie Denny Laine had formed his 'Electric String Band', and they played. It's said, Denny headed back to London the morning after. He called Brian Epstein, however, there was no response, as Epstein had unfortunately died some hours beforehand.

In the 'Summer of Love', festivals in the UK were very different to those happening in California and other parts of the USA. They aspired to the same vibes but somehow looked more British and even parochial. The psychedelic buses were smaller, and people brought umbrellas, just in case it rained. Drugs were not seemingly available; tea was much more so.

The Duke of Bedford's stately English home was an elegant venue, and the promoters really pushed the whole 'beautiful people' and 'love in' angle. 25,000 concert goers paid £1 per head (30 shillings for the whole weekend). Flowers were in evidence, paper ones that is — selling at 5 shillings each, and bells galore at 10 shillings a tinkle from hawkers who stood on the outskirts crying, "Come on, buy a bell, and go to hell. "There was no booze sold on site, but ice cream vans were present, and tea was sold. All very British, I say dear boy!

The weather held good for the whole weekend and a lovely time was had by all. The Duke of Bedford trousered his £5,000 — that was his percentage of the gate money. The Syn played, as did Tomorrow with the talented Keith West ('My White Bicycle' was their current hit). Other acts included Tintern Abbey an English freak-beat band, who made one single called, 'Vacuum Cleaner', now a very collectible item. Dantalian's Chariot featured cool guitarist Andy Summers, (later of The Police and earlier with Zoot Money). They had another long lost, but now rare psychedelic single at the time 'Madman Running Through the Fields'/'Sun Came Bursting Through My Cloud.' The Marmalade also diversified the bill. They were a little time away from the chart toppers they became with a run of hits.

Immediately afterwards, The Move topped the bill at the Blues Festival at Pynkney Hall near Fakenham, Norfolk. This was staged from 6pm to midnight on August 28th. Also on the bill were Clifford Bennett and The Rebel Rousers, The Alan Bown Set, The Family and The Workshop from Bristol. All the groups were playing in a marquee holding 2,000 fans, but it was hoped that over 10,000 people would attend the festival.

The Move were already becoming *persona non grata* following the 'Free The Pirates' benefit at the Alexandra Palace.

'Flowers In The Rain' was played everywhere along with its wonderfully and commercially eccentric B-side, 'Here We Go Round The Lemon Tree'. I recently asked Tony Visconti, how working with The Move compared to other artists. "They were a great bunch to work with. They sounded great, They sounded every bit as good, as The Stones and The Beatles. I think Tony Secunda was more of an impediment to their success. The Harold Wilson cartoon was his idea. And that was the beginning of the end. In this particular case — there was such a thing as bad publicity. The band just went along with it, and it nearly destroyed them."

"It was a nightmare," says Wood. "We were hauled into the Old Bailey and an injunction was passed. Three of us —Ace and Trevor and I were all still under 21. So, we were classified as 'infants.'"

Tony Secunda was summoned to Quintin Hogg's chambers and given "a right fucking roasting", but he was still unrepentant. Since the band were on all the front pages of newspapers in Britain, Europe and America.

A second injunction is then granted to Wilson...
The afternoon prior to The Move's Locarno gig, the Prime Minister has complained of an alleged libel on The Move's promotional postcard. Mr. Quintin Hogg, Q.C. is given the brief to represent Labour Prime Minister Harold Wilson by solicitors Goodman, Derrick and Co. This company was headed by Lord Goodman, the chairman of the Arts Council, a Labour Life peer and personal friend of Mr. Wilson. In true two-faced, political, back-stabbing etiquette. It was alleged to be Quintin Hogg who had dug in and actually started all the sexually charged innuendos around the Wilson and Marcia Williams (Falkender) affair. Mr. Justice O'Connor in the High Court of Justice, Queen's Bench Division grants an interim injunction against "Anthony Secunda and others" until 6th September.

A statement is issued by solicitors Goodman, Derrick and Co: "In the Vacation

Court this afternoon, Mr. Quintin Hogg, Q.C., applied ex-parte on behalf of the Prime Minister. For an injunction to restrain Anthony Secunda, Bev Bevan, Trevor Burton, Christopher Kefford, Carl Wayne and Roy Wood from printing, publishing, circulating or distributing a card, alleged to be libellous of the Prime Minister. The injunction was granted until 6th September, when a further hearing will take place."

Over in Denmark Street life continued apace. Peter Watts, in his concise 2023 book on the "hallowed" Denmark Street, pointed out, "as the old-school publishers departed, it wasn't just music shops filling up the now vacant spaces. A band booking agency Galaxy Entertainment moved in at number seven." Run by Ron Kingsnorth, who was nicknamed 'Ron the Pom' and often referred to simply as Ron King, he'd had dealings with the notorious Krays before he moved into the music business.

Val Weedon (now an MBE) who had previously helped run the Small Faces Fan Club for another rock heavyweight Don Arden, worked for Galaxy Entertainments. She remembers The Move and Amen Corner coming in to discuss bookings. But they weren't always there for business. "Ron also rented the top of the building" says Weedon. "Where he had a small flat. They used to have parties up there. They had this two-way mirror that looked into the bedroom. It was rented by a DJ who would entertain young ladies while the bands would go up and watch. It was all a bit seedy."

Denmark Street has always had a shady side. Maybe it's the shadow of the Rookery. But the tinge of criminality, hung around the street, long after the slums were cleared out. There were figures, like the previously mentioned Ron King who was from the East End and had gravitated from minor crime to club ownership. Then he moved into the music business through Don Arden. Kingsnorth was now managing bands and booking tours.

Galaxy employee Val Weedon recalls that, "People were always coming after Ron for owed money. A few times we were sent over the road to a coffee bar (The Giaconda?) until we got the all clear. After somebody had threatened to come down with a shooter."

King soon gave up the music business, moving to New Zealand where, among other things, he allegedly ran brothels. The exact reasons he sold up to Don Arden and moved on very sharpish are beyond the scope of this book.

Val Weedon was a junior assistant at Galaxy Entertainment at the time of the 'Flowers In The Rain' debacle. Val had to go over to The Move's bookings agency. Val was fielding the phone calls, with people trying to get hold of the management or the band.

"I was just told to take messages and tell anyone, that no one was there in the offices, which they weren't. It was just me, answering the phones. There was a funny incident one lunch time. I met up with Pauline Corcoran, who ran the Small Faces Fan Club. We had worked together; she was my best friend. We met up for lunch and I was telling her about answering the phones in The Move's management office. Two women on the next table looked over when I said the name The Move and I thought they were impressed. So, I started boasting and talked louder. I was showing off (well I was young)! When I got back to Galaxy, Ron called me into his office. He was not happy with me; he said the wife of the Move's manager had phoned him to complain about me spouting my mouth off! Ooops! Fortunately, Ron was really nice about it, he was a great boss — much better than Don Arden."

According to Val Weedon, King was not especially fond of Tony Secunda. Ron King had also joined the anti-Secunda camp. Until I mentioned it to Val Weedon, King had never really posited his stance on Secunda to her. He says, "When I was booking them — they begged me to pay them on the night. So, one night I did. He (Secunda) then cancelled the other booking we had. I then phoned him and of course you would know, what I said to the bastard. I thought he was nasty, but he could put on a "nice guy" act."

Tony's office politics were under duress too. Sally Myers and Joan Robinson had set up and run the Move fan club in London. There was a sudden decision that Pauline Evans, (Wayne's fiancée) was going to run it from Birmingham. This pissed off Joan no doubt as she put a lot of work into setting it up. Sally walked away from the set up — her reasons are not fully known. Joan Robinson was instrumental in getting the documentary made by Pathe News (she worked for it) and they filmed inside Tony's and Chelita's London flat.

One person wishing to remain incognito says, "Looking back is often done with rose tinted glasses. I still don't believe that they (The Move) didn't know, what Tony was doing publicity wise. They certainly knew about the 'Flowers' postcard before it all went pear-shaped. Tony was a man of many moods — mainly drug related. I don't remember him being a drinker. Deep down he was an incredibly creative man. He led that late 1960s music scene! It went downhill in the 1970s. But a lot of the new things had already been done. They had already been put in place. I think most of the bands got shafted back then! I never ever thought Denny Cordell was innocent for example. I found it very bizarre that they dumped Tony and then went on to Don Arden. Who as you know, was also in Denmark Street. Tony was never personally physically violent to the band. He certainly didn't keep a gun on display on his desk (yes, I saw that). I have to say the original band were, very good live. Certainly, all through their Marquee residency and through the gigs around the Southeast, from '66 through to 1968."

The 'Flowers In The Rain' court case loomed ever nearer. The three "infants" are treated in exactly the same manner as the adults... So, The Move and Tony Secunda are summoned to the High Court in London to defend themselves against these charges. From this, the first, large crack in the structure of this crazy, mercurial, volatile group begins to appear. Unfortunately, this court case would instigate the beginning of their end. Fissures would start to appear. Eventually causing the band to sunder and disintegrate and slowly sowing the seeds, for what was to become ELO. In my opinion - a much less interesting and more middle-of-the-road band.

Over the prior, nearly two years, before any of this happened of course, the group had already caused a sensation and uproar around Britain. With a solid-edged, four-part harmony-led show, allied to a loud, tight rocking band sound. Divided between hip West Coast covers, rock 'n' roll standards, Soul and R & B tunes and the roster of three already impressive hit singles, all penned by their enigmatic, redoubtable songwriter Roy Wood. Their stage show had also incurred the wrath of promoters and stage managers around the UK. Mainly, because of the use of fireworks and distress flares and the stage trashing and axe chopping by Carl Wayne. Receiving the axe were old, knackered televisions adorned by stuffed together effigies of Ian Smith, (then Southern Rhodesian Prime Minister and seen as an all-round apartheid baddie),

And this is where we came in, dear reader

Adolf Hitler and Harold Wilson amongst other stuffed and cobbled together effigies.

They were prepared to do Secunda's mastermind bidding. Certainly, with Carl Wayne, Kefford and Burton. These three had no problems when it came to argy-bargy and the use of fists to sort matters out promptly.

Many of the London 1960s bands were fairly effete, middle-class boys or upper-class university types like Pink Floyd. But The Move had a true authentic edge. This aspect wasn't just merely plugging on the part of Secunda's endless publicity tropes or the media hungry for hype. This street attitude was reinforced with the band, glowering out defiantly at the camera during their photo shoots. They had a good way with the practised five-ways scowl under the firm suggestion of Secunda.

Other hip artists like Brian Jones of The Rolling Stones said, "I'd really like to see The Move, they really are an extension of our idea of smashing the conventions. Those kinds of smash ups they have, like destroying TVs, cars and all that, are all part of this dissatisfaction with convention."

Paul McCartney also name checked them while reviewing the singles for *Melody Maker*. Amongst them was 'I Can Hear the Grass Grow.' McCartney reviewed them, saying, "They sound really cool, and this is a really nice single. I haven't seen them live yet but the reports are really good. Their smashing up of TVs and all that — it's really great. This is a great record — It will be a hit. It just depends on how they are handled and how they look after themselves."

Pete Townshend was also aware of them and said, "I think they've got the same sort of following that we used to have in the old Marquee Club days. That's the kind of fans that they deserve. The best type of fans. Faithful."

Tony Secunda hired a red Rolls Royce and both he and the band trundled their way down the M1 motorway from Birmingham to London's High Court. The Rolls Royce broke down on the way which resulted in them arriving late for the proceedings on 12th October 1967. In fact, they missed most of the proceedings brought against them by the so-called pop-loving Prime Minister of Great Britain. In the annals of rock rebellion and anti-establishment posturing, it certainly was an outstanding first! Never before or since repeated. The Sex Pistols short reign of infamy crashed and burned even quicker than The Move's notorious exploits were to last.

But nevertheless, they appeared in high spirits. That day, The Move were dressed in impressive "flower-power" garb with top notch paisley and brocaded jackets. Ace Kefford and Trevor Burton were both sporting the highly visual Afro-bubble tight perm hair styles. Trevor said the other members of the band fell about laughing, when they saw the new 'Brum Fro' perms.

This Afro style big hair look was being adopted amongst the hippest of the rock world's cognoscenti. Eric Clapton during his Cream phase, MC5's singer Rob Tyner also sported a seriously massive Afro fuzz. The Jimi Hendrix Experience amongst others. Big hair was the order of the day. Allied to the evolving explosion in black culture and fashion. Which saw many African Americans wearing amazing, courtly Afros, both men and women.

A High Court usher described their clothes as, "The gayest attire ever seen here." Trevor Burton was described as wearing "green trousers, lace shirt and velvet jacket. Roy Wood was adorned in "white boots, flower jacket and blue pinstripe trousers." Bev Bevan was more "soberly attired in a dark grey suit."

I think the usher is actually getting Tony Secunda mixed up with Bev. Bev was actually wearing a red corduroy jean jacket (Bev must have liked this jacket because it showed up again on the back cover of the *Something Else From The Move* EP. The jean jacket had white fur trim. He also wore dark trousers and a dark psychedelic shirt with beads and appliqué on it. Carl Wayne "a flowered jacket, blue pinstripe trousers and bright green moccasins" and Christopher Kefford, "a black and gold flowered jacket, a lace shirt and sandals."

Ace's permed Afro hair was also commented upon (although not Trevor's). Chris Kefford aged 20, "has a wild Harpo Marx (sic) blond hair style." Much of their current trendy clobber was selected from Granny Takes A Trip. Manager Secunda was more soberly attired, wearing a dark double-breasted suit style. The group arrived in central London and immediately walked into a waiting phalange of reporters and the BBC TV cameras and crew... BBC reporters caught the late arrival on camera.

Mr Justice Melrose Stevenson the presiding judge, listened as Quintin Hogg QC represented Harold Wilson. Hogg described the postcard promoting 'Flowers In The Rain' and the record as "a song and dance number which had nothing to do with public affairs." Hogg went on to describe the card as libellous to the Prime Minister which warranted the criminal proceedings. Hogg further added that Tony Secunda had commissioned the designer, the advertising agency and the printers to produce what amounted to a "violent and malicious personal attack on the Prime Minister."

Back then, a group of young upstarts daring to sully the image of the UK's Prime Minister by mailing out and hand delivering an illustrated potentially libellous postcard, even managing to pop one copy right through the door of Number 10 Downing Street: This jolly jape, all to advertise that infamous third single in that sparkly year, was definitely a bridge too far — Harold Wilson was absolutely not going to take it sitting down.

Hogg did not fully expand on the rumours surrounding Harold Wilson and Marcia Williams. He also did not describe in detail the contents of the postcard. However, court reports described that Mr Wilson was drawn in the nude on the card. The woman in the card was described with typical legalese understatement as, "a woman that was not his wife."

Tony Secunda justified the action in "producing, distributing and sending the card through open post." Outside to reporters and caught on film, Secunda stressed, "If the record is a hit, that could come to about £10,000. It's impossible to say at this stage how much it will cost, but we won't see the money, so we won't miss it. It wasn't a publicity stunt; how can anybody say that? Wilson started legal proceedings, we did it as a cartoon, remember that! It wasn't intended to be anything but that." Further in Hogg's statement, he emphasised Secunda's "inconsistent pleas — that it was meant as a joke and that it was inspired by Secunda's dislike of the Prime Minister."

The rumours around Wilson and Marcia Williams had been circulating for some time in the political rumour mill. Quintin Hogg had confirmed that Wilson had been aware of malicious rumours about his personal character integrity, and he had up to now ignored them. Although Hogg Q.C. acted for Wilson in a typically cringe inducing hypocritical Parliamentary backstabbing fashion with Hogg having alluded to this matter in Parliament some three years earlier. Quintin Hogg also criticised the decision to send the postcard to journalists, television producers and music publishers.

On the day of the court case, Robert Davidson snuck a camera into the High Court. "I was sitting in court observing his Hogg's ears, which stuck out in an elephantine sort of way. The case was being held 'in camera.' Marvellous! I thought. I'll go along and take some pictures. In camera' actually means 'in secret.' I wonder, was I naive or I just didn't want to understand? Whichever it was, I had taken my trusty camera into the High Court. Tony and the band were supposed to be there as well, but they had not arrived yet and I was in the court waiting for them. The sun is streaming through a huge picture window behind Quintin Hogg. He is standing there in front of this massive window, with his large, protruding ears, all red and glowing. I am thinking 'Wow! Great picture!' So I walk up to him, go 'click' with my camera and take a picture. Immediately, he bellows out, "Arrest that man!" Before I know what is happening, these gorillas — enormous gentlemen, appear from nowhere. I was carried with my little feet hardly touching the ground and swept down into the bowels of the earth. I thought that this was going to be it."

"'You've been very naughty,' they say."

"You know cameras aren't allowed here."

"Really?"

"You know you can't take pictures in here, thinking that that's going to be your next best-selling poster, or any such nonsense." Then they pulled the film out of my camera, and I responded, 'Please don't hit me,' putting my hands over my face and fearing the worst. 'Now, just make sure you just don't do it again,' they said and put me outside the back door of the courthouse. Just at this time, Tony and the band were arriving. Secunda greets me with, 'Hello Robert, how's it going?' I replied, as if all in a day's work, 'Well, I've just been kicked out of the High Court by Quintin Hogg'."

The BBC clips are funny, showing a cameraman pointing his camera up towards Trevor Burton. Burton stands twirling an umbrella above his Afro permed hair. Looking down at the camera, Trevor's usual sneery, punk attitude comes through wonderfully, "Well we were late getting here, so it was all over by the time we arrived. We got there about twenty-five to eleven." The BBC reporter responds, "So you missed Mr Quintin Hogg? Trevor Burton, with a pronounced sneer responds, "Yeah! Thank God!"

Asked about their political standpoint singer Carl Wayne (holding a copy of Timothy Leary's book *Tune In, Turn On, Drop Out*) joked: "We've no faith in any political sides at all. We vote for people like Frank Zappa, Jimi Hendrix, you know? Anybody!"

Underneath all the bravado, drummer Bev Bevan recalls, "Remember we were only kids, we really were, and we were terrified. James Bond movies were really big at the time, and we would swear the Secret Service guys were after us. And we even thought they'd be like, you know, we could be shot? Picked off by a sniper or something. We were kids from Birmingham, down in London and suddenly we were being pursued by all the paparazzi. We were being sued by one of the most powerful men in the world. We were like lambs to the slaughter. We really didn't know what was going on at all."

Trevor Burton echoes Bevan here, "That really scared us, when you fuck with the Prime Minister, you've got to watch your step (sic). MI5 was parked outside

Tony's place, and we are being followed by god knows who. It was like being in a James Bond movie."

The newspapers reported The Move pop group have made an apology in the High Court to the Prime Minister for a "violent and malicious personal attack." Quintin Hogg QC described the publication as making use of "malicious rumours" concerning his character and integrity. As part of the libel settlement, the band and their manager Tony Secunda, have agreed to devote all royalties from their record to charities of the Prime Minister's choice. The defendants also included the card's artist, the advertising agency and printers. All have apologised for their involvement and have agreed to pay the costs of the proceedings estimated at £3,000.

Mr Hogg labelled the card "scurrilous" and criticised the decision to send it to journalists, television producers and music publishers. He further opined, "But in the present instance, the scurrility of the card, coupled with the extent of the circulation and threatened circulation left him with no alternative but to assert his legal rights and thereby to make plain his determination to establish the complete falsities of these rumours. The defendants have now realised the unacceptable nature of the conduct and it is fair to say you have never any time suggested there was a word of truth in any of the suggestions contained in the libel."

Representing the group's manager, members and the artist, Richard Hartley said his clients wished to express their "profound regret" for what had happened.

Secunda denied the publication was a publicity stunt, suggesting the resultant libel action had created that impression. Secunda was also interviewed on camera outside the courtroom. Sitting in the Rolls Royce, the manager stated, "Wilson started legal proceedings. We did it as a cartoon, remember that. It wasn't intended to be anything but that."

Roy Wood recalls the cloying paranoia of those days. "Apart from being hounded by the press, we suddenly noticed we were being followed by a big black car with the windows blacked out. Two very heavy blokes from MI5 visited Secunda, scared the shit out of him. I wasn't aware of phone bugging or physical threats myself, but they did enough. We'd be loading up our van after a gig and their car would be parked opposite. They made it quite plain they were watching us. That went on for several weeks."

Carl Wayne admitted that they "were very scared. We just did what we were told. This was the Prime Minister we were dealing with, and we were very naughty boys."

The satirical UK weekly magazine *Private Eye* (Issue 150) took PM Wilson to the cleaners — producing a front cover with the banner heading: "Exclusive - The card Wilson wants to BAN!" Showing a 'spoof' cartoon by premier UK illustrator Gerald Scarfe. It depicts the Prime Minister in bed with George Wigg, the Postmaster General. With Mrs Wilson peering out through a curtain. Editor of *Private Eye*, Richard Ingrams also put in a good word, "Why then has 'WillSundra' (the magazine's pet name for the Prime Minister Wilson) used the mighty sledgehammer of the law to crack such a tiny nut? The fact is, since Profumo, he has been hysterically frightened of the slightest, possible hint of trouble on the sex front."

Mr Wilson nominated the Spastics Society and the Amenity Funds of Stoke Mandeville Hospital for the benefit of paraplegic patients to receive the royalties.

Stoke Mandeville at the same time was where the execrable 'Sir' Jimmy Savile (now thankfully deceased and finally stopped from his serial sex and other abusing) was operating and also raising money. Of course, Saville is now utterly disgraced for his egregious, historical sexual abuse crimes. Saville was operating even back then in plain sight.

Mr Hogg concluded Harold Wilson had never intended to be "harsh or vindictive" and he warned that in any future incident, Mr Wilson might not be so lenient. Mr Hogg said Mr Wilson agreed terms of settlement, which might be thought "extremely generous. "Any other postcards lying around, plus the glass negative plates etc were to be handed over. Richard Moore and Leslie Ltd also paid their agreed damages.

Hogg continued, "In view however of the widespread dissemination of the postcard, he wishes me to make it quite clear that he would not necessarily take the same lenient view of any subsequent occasion. Indeed, in the opinion of his advisers, the character of the libel was such as to warrant criminal proceedings."

In addition to the agreed payments, all the defendants were required to submit to a perpetual injunction. Meaning the royalties were to be paid in perpetuity — meaning forever. The monies from 'Flowers In The Rain' and 'Here We Go Round The Lemon Tree' and the damages were going to put into a trust. The money shared equally between the two charities named by Mr Wilson. Twenty years after the event Roy Wood complained that he was losing hundreds of thousands of pounds.

Wood was, and remains, incensed. "To this day I don't get a penny for that song — forty-three years later! We've been getting the crap longer than the Great Train Robbers. I was, to say the least, pissed off at Secunda. I'm hoping for the day when I might as well be open about it again and get the publicity going. When I hang up my boots, I wanted to leave something for my daughter Holly. Because why shouldn't she have it rather than that lot? When Carl was alive, he tried to reopen the case. Rick Wakeman's manager tried as well. They told him to get on his bike. Wilson's representatives are still at it. You have to tread carefully, or you could wake up with a crowd round yer."

At a very rough estimate, including inflation over the years, £10,000 in 1967 would be worth approximately £180,000 in 2023. But of course, that's not adding in world royalties, mechanicals and other royalty streaming sources. It's been said that Roy Wood lost well over one million in royalties over the years and in other forms of income stream.

After Harold Wilson's death in 1995, Wood tried to reverse this ruling and get the money back. But he didn't succeed — forever means forever, apparently. The charities who benefitted were by now changed to ones chosen by Lady Falkender. Roy Wood said that it was worse than a sentence for murder. When *Private Eye* bid a 'So, Farewell Then to Lady Falkender in 2019', they highlighted the hypocrisy of the whole affair. Falkender didn't sue Joe Haines for his revelations in *The Politics Of Power* (1977) or his later memoir, *Glimmers Of Twilight* (2003). But the BBC buckled at the first whiff of a court case.

The BBC emphasised that Wilson denied any affair with his secretary. Yet in his memoirs, Joe Haines, Wilson's press secretary revealed that Wilson had told him about the day that Marcia, in a fit of temper said to Mary Wilson, "I went to bed with your husband six times in 1965 and it wasn't satisfactory." According to Haines,

Wilson further added: "Marcia has dropped her atomic bomb at last."

If true, this could have exonerated Tony Secunda etc for libel. The Move and more precisely, songwriter Roy Wood, who would have been thousands of pounds better off. Or would they? Would the catchy single have climbed so high in the charts without this publicity?

Bernard Donoughue, a senior policy adviser to Wilson, suggests in his diaries that Marcia, "With eyes like a hawk and teeth like a hare", had some sort of weird hold over Harold. The Prime Minister "often indulged her wildest whims, almost like a daughter... and equally feared her, like a fierce mother... She was adept at mobilising his demons, stimulating nightmares and evoking his alleged enemies."

Donoughue suggests a day-to-day portrait of Marcia as singularly vindictive and paranoid. He joked that over lunch, "She gets upset that the whitebait on her plate are looking at her. She was also convinced that her mother was the illegitimate daughter of King Edward VII, and thus she was his granddaughter. This, she thought, was why the Queen had never invited her to Buckingham Palace."

Tony Secunda made an attempt to do some basic mathematics on the finer points of money made from the 'Flowers' recording. As to overall financial views, he said, "I can't disclose that because I have partners, and it wouldn't be ethical. Every record has a different breakdown when it comes to royalties for the composer and artist. The structure is sometimes more complicated when the artist is also the composer. There is roughly six shillings and three pennies to be split up on the average "single" costing seven shillings and four and a half pennies; the purchase tax takes one shilling and one and a half pence. At the moment I could say that the royalties would be around the £7,500 mark. In America, the royalties could amount to about £10,000. We get roughly a two pence royalty on every record. But there are a lot of other kinds of royalties each time the record is played. And for how long and over how wide an area, that kind of thing, it's all very complicated."

In fact, no thanks to Lady Falkender, over the years beneficiaries from the songs accruing royalties have been expanded. These now include The Friends of D'Oyly Carte, University of Huddersfield, A Soviet Poster Exhibition (huh?) Liverpool Tate, Variety Club, The Jewish National Fund for Israel, British Film Institute, British Screen Advisory Council, The Attlee Foundation, Oxford University, Joyce Butler Memorial Trust, 33 Signals Unit, Central Lads Club, Ratlingate Scout Appeal, Whitehall Choir, Victor Brusa Memorial Appeal, St Mary's Ladies' Lifeboat Guild, Oxford Operatic Society, Lloyd George Parliamentary Centenary Appeal, Bolton Lads Club, Tring Lane Workshops... Whew!

That was in 1967 and now, more than fifty years later, The Move have not seen a bent penny. But was Harold Wilson telling the truth about the 'false and malicious rumours?

Everyone involved in the production of the record, was placed under a permanent legal injunction to not discuss the details of this notorious case. In the 1990s, newspapers reported that The Move (Roy Wood) had lost out to the tune of £250,000 due to Tony Secunda's insane stunt. This is a pretty conservative figure. This caused a growing animosity between Secunda and the band. Despite Secunda's attempts to link them with the Tory party the year before. Which was bizarre as Tony Secunda was so anti–establishment. Ace Kefford complained about this stunt. Having come from a very working-class family. His grandfather was a lifelong member of the Labour Party. They were not tickled pink by the postcard and the resulting publicity. Also, ill feelings were still rankling within the band, outside of this huge, publicised event, although this further aggravated the issues.

Ace was beginning to feel sidelined. Without a doubt, the 'ace face' of the band was moody and uncommunicative. But Ace's role had been reduced somewhat. His contribution's songwriting wise were being ignored and certainly not encouraged. It's said that his song, 'William Chalker's Time Machine' was rejected. I'm not sure why, as it became a brilliant single for The Lemon Tree.

Obviously if Roy started to realise that big revenue streams were coming in on publishing, apart from the band's relentless calendar of live concerts, perhaps this expectant money pie was not wanting to be sliced up? However, Ace, and perhaps Trevor, writing B-sides and / or album tracks, would've actually freed Roy up a lot. Encouraging him to write more and be even more productive.

Bev says the ongoing personality issues were the main focus, "Out of the five of us, I think Ace was probably the least popular one amongst the group internally. He was very moody. He was like an angry young man."

Allan Harris had said, "That the moodiness and all the bullshit, I thought it had developed. But it was all happening from the beginning. I thought it was difficult. It really just was." Bev picks up from here. "I think Ace had mental problems. But we and I'd be part of that; I'm really sorry to say he wasn't. Ace didn't have a very good education, and we would take the 'mickey' out of him. Because he couldn't spell very well. So, I think he ended up basically not saying anything. And we were pretty hard-nosed Brummies."

Roy Wood had written 'Here We Go Round The Lemon Tree' and he let The Idle Race record the song. Former Nightrider Roy Wood had remained friendly with the group. Through Roy, contacts were established, allowing The Idle Race to record during off-hours at Advision Studios in London. To my ears, this version lacks the dynamic bass punch of The Move's B-side version. It was produced by Gerald Chevin and Eddie Offord. Both were adventurous engineers. The Idle Race, perhaps not wanting to be seen as a Move cover band, pulled 'Lemon Tree' at the last minute. They released something called 'Imposters of Life's Magazine.' A rather long and clunky mouthful to pronounce. In my opinion, a must less commercial cut than Roy Wood's song. 'Lemon Tree' was also extremely popular here in the UK. It got a good deal of radio play and was a very commercial B-side. I think it could have been a hit as an A-side release. The Idle Race went on to release 'Lemon Tree' in America on Liberty Records. This was to be their first single.

15.
Come with me

Roger Spencer was the drummer with The Idle Race, formed in 1966. "We were all single guys. We grafted, just worked and worked and built up a fan base pretty cleverly. My father was a drummer and after the war he got a dance band. I used to get his kit out and play in the bathroom and I joined a band. A little bit of gigging around, just pubs and clubs. I joined a band when I was 15 called Johnny Neal and the Hound Dogs, which lasted about four months. Then I did a gig with Dave Pritchard, and we worked with a fella called Mike Hurd at the Water Board in Birmingham and we did 'Dare Christmas 2.' We just played a couple of Shadows songs. Dave Pritchard was in a band called Biddie King and The Nightriders. They moved Biddie King out and he became the manager. Mike Sheridan came in. They needed a drummer, and I joined what was the formation of Mike Sheridan and the Nightriders and there were two guitarists when Roy Wood joined."

"We became the recording Nightriders, which did the EMI sessions and that was the Nightriders everybody remembers. Dave Pritchard, Roger Spencer, Greg Masters, Big Al Johnson and Mike Sheridan out the front. Big Al left, he didn't think he fitted. We auditioned and Roy Wood joined and then we did the EMI sessions at the alley. I was always a big Creek Moon fan, John Bonham fan. And of course, the King, our leader, the one and only Mr. Ringo Starr. I always had good dynamics as a young drummer."

"Jeff Lynne never wanted to join The Move. But in the end, he was dying from all the pats on the back. What a great band, love the records. We used to blow everybody off as The Idle Race, we worked with everybody. It was a great show. Roy kept coming back and coming back and coming back. In the end Jeff joined Roy. My father loved Roy and he used to call Roy 'the golden boy' when he was in the Nightriders. 'Look after him, he's the golden boy'. He saw the mark of excellence and talent there and of course the magic voice. We were top of the bill, it's the Swindon, Locarno. Second on the bill was a band called Tony Rivers and The Castaways. Tony Rivers spotted Roy and asked him to join his band, so he was being noticed. Jeff found it a bit difficult because he's not a frontman really. He's just an unbelievable talent."

Dave Pritchard was the rhythm guitarist with The Idle Race. "I remember we did one gig with The Moody Blues where they struggled hard to hold the stage after our performance. We were very good live."

Ray Williams was an A & R man and also at Liberty Records (Williams discovered Elton John). Williams was something of a polymath. He has been a major operator in the music and film industry ever since. Working as a press agent, A&R head, artist manager, film music producer, and publisher. Williams started his career by working with *Ready Steady Go!* presenter Cathy McGowan.

Dave resumes, "Well, he was working for Liberty and then he started managing us. Then he was just doing the management. Through Roy Wood, contacts were established allowing The Idle Race to record during down time at Advision Studios. That was great as we were working with Eddy Offord and Gerald Chevin. Ray Williams was looking for a band to sign to Liberty. The Birmingham scene was so incestuous in a way — but in a healthy way! Even though there was competition, it wasn't dog eat dog."

Andrew Lauder worked his way through various positions from the bottom up. He ended up within Liberty Records. Arriving at work one Monday morning, he found that the singularly, non-comital production manager Alan Whaley was gone. Andrew simply took over the vacated desk and started opening all the singles and the albums, currently being released in the USA. Shortly afterwards Bob Reisdorff walked past him and said, "You seem to have started this job, so you better carry on, and there'll be a pay rise too."

Lauder had arrived just around the time the first single by The Idle Race was released. Liberty were releasing an eclectic batch of vinyl. The Band of the Coldstream Guards was one such. There was also a slew of easy listening titles. Vicki Carr had a Number Two hit with, 'It Must Be Him' which did over one million units. The Johnny Mann Singers also had another Top Ten hit.

Liberty did have other jewels in their portfolio: Songwriter Jimmy Webb and The Fifth Dimension group — who cut such effervescent, happy (and slightly freaky) singles. The Dimension were having big hits, written by such great writers as the remarkable Laura Nyro. The unique, New York based chantress Laura provided such gleaming gems as 'Wedding Bell Blues', 'Time And Love', 'Save The Country', 'Sweet Blindness' and 'Stone Soul Picnic'. All infused with her bitter-sweet 1960s undertow and a wistful optimism… She managed to sound both sad and happy at the same time.

However, Andrew wanted to get his teeth into something echoing the UK/USA temperament. He was checking out the first two Beau Brummel records. Liberty had an arrangement with City Lights bookshop in North Beach, San Francisco. They imported those wonderful, dazzling freak-psychy posters, being made, printed and handcrafted by San Francisco artists. Both the posters and the bands intrigued Andrew Lauder. Liberty had signed Hour Glass with the young Gregg and Duane Allman. Their song 'The Power Of Love' single was a real touch of vocalised loving soul. The Idle Race were the first UK signing to Liberty. They also had a management deal with the label.

As many Brum Beat specialists will know, The Idle Race had evolved out of Jeff Lynne replacing Mike Sheridan. They were all contemporaries of The Move, they knew each other well. The first single release was 'Imposters Of Life's Magazine'. The record was expressly taken to John Peel at Radio One. He was then known as the 'fave underground scene' DJ.

The Idle Race became favourites through Lauder's ministrations and Peel's admiration. Kenny Everett was also a big fan, describing the band "second after the

Beatles". Just as Visconti had. Like The Move, The Idle Race did a lot of BBC live sessions. They followed up the first single with three more in 1968. 'The Skeleton And The Roundabout', 'The End Of The Road' and 'I Like My Toys'. All singles were well received but unfortunately didn't tickle the charts.

For a band that had not sold that well, Ray Williams at Liberty spent a good bit of money on the first album sleeve. *The Birthday Party* was awarded a tasty, gatefold sleeve (with a photo that resembled a birthday party in a large school refectory). Different heads were placed on the bodies, in an irreverent, Brummie, humorous manner.

****

In November 1968; the 'flowers postcard' printers, C.C.S. Advertising Associates Ltd of Wardour Street, London, headed up by director Alan Smith and Tony Secunda are now having some further legal contretemps. C.C.S. were now seeking £3,600 from 28-year-old Anthony Secunda of Ovington Square, London. Alan Smith, although he wasn't sure whether Secunda still managed The Move, remembered Secunda saying he had thought up the postcard idea himself. When Smith saw it, "he said it was a bit extreme." He also called it a "cruel joke." Smith went on to say that Secunda gave him a "verbal indemnity", in case there was any trouble.

Secunda told the court: "I did not agree to indemnify him at any time. After the injunction by the Prime Minister and prior to the court action in late September he came up with a printer and started shouting at me. He said he should be covered in some way. Because now he was part of the action. I said: 'Please don't worry about all this, get your solicitor to talk to my solicitor. He asked for an indemnity, and I declined.'

Mr Leon Brittan, *(yes - that one!)* acting for C.C.S, said it was part of the terms of the settlement with the Prime Minister. It was approved that some copies of the postcard should be handed over to Mr Wilson. It was also agreed that nothing should be said anywhere, anytime, to disclose what was on this postcard. Indeed, no reference to the contents of the postcard was made in court.

But things didn't go Alan Smith's way. The judge refused the claim and granted costs to Tony Secunda. Judge J.R. Herbert, said in his summing up, "In August last year, Mr Secunda, in an evil hour, devised what he thought would be a good advertisement for his pop group. It contained a picture with an accompanying caption. It was the most disgusting, baseless, gross libel, about which it is difficult to say anything."

Herbert continued, "No doubt after Mr Smith had seen the card and considered it, "near the knuckle" Mr Secunda had given a verbal promise to him. "However, it is quite impossible for anybody even in a nursery, on reading this, to not know that it was attacking brutally, the reputation of an eminent statesman and the Prime Minister of the country, as well as others. Anybody could see at a glance that this was dynamite. Mr Smith knew it best, that it was the most unpleasant slur on the character of this very famous man. It seems very hard on Mr Smith that he should not be able to recover anything from the defendant. But that is the result of an Act of Parliament."

Before 'Flowers In The Rain' was chosen as the proposed third single, another

Flowers In The Rain - The Untold Story of The Move

clever song — with an equally thrilling B-side was written by Roy Wood. This is a bonafide Move classic called 'Cherry Blossom Clinic.' This also appeared in a different re-arranged version, on The Move's second album *Shazam* (More of that later).

This potential third single is a thrilling piece of work. Ending up on their debut record, finally released after being recorded over a 14-month period. It features a definite seam of hitherto explored lyrical dimensions. Replete with (yet more) mental asylum-based lyrics. Both distinctive and evocative in nature by Wood. Trippy, psychedelic lyrics that made Roy Wood appear on the surface, to be a definable, utter 'space cadet'. Although Roy could have a very dreamy nature there was definitely nothing 'druggy' about him at all. The addition was a truly amazing piece of musical arranging. Tony Visconti directed the astounding string section. It is a truly remarkable piece of embellishment. Visconti was enabled to go full on with the added players for this special arrangement.

Visconti details, "The string session was one of the largest I conducted up to that point, maybe around sixteen players. I carefully arranged at my flat in Maida Vale. I don't play piano well, but I am a trained classical guitarist. And a big fan of Beethoven, Mozart, Mahler. They were always my inspirations. The session went very smoothly because of the preparation. I came out with this wacky arrangement. Denny was impressed and gave me many more opportunities to write for classical instruments."

Before his early unfortunate death (in June 2023) engineer Gerald Chevin told me how they achieved the magnificent and deep pumping bass sound on the A and B sides. On both 'Flowers In The Rain' and 'Lemon Tree' they had plugged Ace's bass guitar directly into the board. Not micing from the bass guitar amp, as usually would happen. Compare the bass sound on this single to any other 45rpm singles for that time. Kefford's driving bass on both sides of the single is a masterclass in propulsive, bottom end simplicity.

Tony Visconti adds some detail here of how the recording techniques were changing: "D.I. or Direct Injection for bass guitar, was just starting to become a standard way to record the bass. It created a more immediate sound, lower end and much more definition than simply going through the bass amp. As it was only 4-track recording there was no luxury of recording the D.I. and the amp on separate tracks. So, the D.I. got the preference. Unless the bass player knew how to get a great amp sound, which wasn't the case with Ace. Shared credit must go to Denny Cordell who was a low-end fiend. In a time when pop was rather tinny, on purpose. To make the mix jump out of small radiograms of the day. Denny loved American R&B for that low end sound. The fuller mixes that Denny produced have stood the test of time." Agreed — The 'Flowers In The Rain' production is expansive, has clarity and a wide screen depth to its sound. Especially in the Salvo remasters, mono and stereo.

Rob Caiger, producer for the 40th anniversary Move reissues and remastering supervisor inputs the following: "The Move's first album is very short, even adding two single A and B sides, which wasn't usual for the time. It was also mixed to mono at a time when LPs were also being mixed to stereo. Would the album have been improved with a few more Roy Wood songs or some inspired covers? Of course! Would the album have sounded better in stereo? The Move tracks that were originally released in "sixties-stereo" with instruments and vocals separated left and right rather than mixed properly, suggests not. But when I found the multitrack for 'Flowers In The Rain' and heard the palette of sounds it contained, it was clear this brilliant song deserved to be heard in stereo, mixed as the band sounded in the studio. Even though there were only 4-tracks, all the takes were on the reel. This enabled sound engineer Rob Keyloch to go back through the takes, separating each track before they were reduced to one track and a new take added. It's similar to what Giles Martin is now doing with his remixes of Beatles songs. I think we separated 16-tracks from the original 4-track reel, which gave us clarity of every instrument and all the vocals, revealing sounds that were not mixed in or heard within the original mono mix. The new stereo mix of those 16-tracks gives the song an almost cinematic soundscape. The sound of the new version of 'Flowers In The Rain' was even more magnificent than the original. And I was able to separate Tony Visconti's session with the wind quartet and send it to him."

There was also a rumour of a Move live show, recorded in the very early days in Birmingham by Johnny Haines. Caiger responds, "Well, to have that would be nice but the show that was taped was before their recording contract so strictly speaking, the tapes would be owned by the band, not the catalogue owners, Bucks Music. The tapes were with Johnny Haines or his family and I could never get them off him. I know Bev and Carl spoke to Johnny about getting the tapes but he would only release the tapes if Roy approved, which is absolutely correct. Bev and Carl would always take their lead from Roy as musical director of The Move, even when he was young at the start of the band. Roy always knew quality and how the music should sound, so if the tapes are still with Johnny, there's probably a good reason. I've not actually heard the live tapes so I can't comment on the quality or the songs the band played — but it would be fascinating to hear, whatever the quality."

It's a real shame that the technology at the time didn't allow for high-quality soundboard or multitrack recordings of The Move performances, especially of the early Marquee shows. Even the *Something Else From The Move* EP recorded on 4-track suffered from technical issues that rendered many of the songs and most of the live vocals unusable, only restored many years later.

In that period 1966 through to 1967 and into 1968, they were untouchable. The 'Flowers In The Rain' release itself was a perfect single and fit for that fabled 'Summer of Love' year.

"The year 1967 seems rather golden," Sir Paul McCartney later reflected. "It always seemed to be sunny and we wore far-out clothes and far-out sunglasses. Maybe calling it the 'Summer of Love' was a bit too easy. But it was a golden summer."

The cooling thunder burst, and rain intro provides a wash of cool, aural breeze before the deftly picked and double tracked guitar arpeggios. Followed by a wonderful surge on the bass. Taking us out of the "rain" effects and into the dynamic song. As Ace and Bev come in on the first rhythmic bar, the melody kicks in straight away. Followed by the uplifting song — cleverly composed by Roy Wood. A strong middle eight holds it together with the glorious chorus. A strong tenor, double-tracked lead vocal from Carl Wayne brings the song home. And the wonderful added woodwind by Tony Visconti is the final cherry on the cake.

Visconti also worked on charts for 'Cherry Blossom Clinic', which was included as a track on the eponymous first album. Before its release, the awaited long player was being mooted with the name of *Move Mass*. Visconti also worked on arrangements for the track 'Beautiful Daughter', which was included on the first side of *Shazam*.

It seems The Move weren't "allowed" to experiment and/or cover a wider range of musical styles in the way that The Beatles were. I'm talking about media perception, which although seemingly hip, is often quite narrow and follows the herd in many ways. Let's say the music press perhaps more than the public didn't allow them the leeway that the Beatles had.

Tony Visconti had his opinion on this: "I'm not sure how to answer this. They were allowed to experiment, but Denny had the last word. He was very good for them and treated them respectfully. But the Move were not quite as good as The Beatles. The Move had two lead singers, but The Beatles had four and four writers. George Martin was a musical genius; Denny Cordell was not!"

Keith West guest reviewed 'Flowers In The Rain': "Wow! It's the Move! A Roy Wood song. Very good. I like that big marching sound they always get. I think it should do between eight and five in the charts. It's not a particularly good record for their image. Because they changed a bit from all that "auto destruction" scene. They've got the best vocal sound in England. It's bloody huge. Oh yeah — that's what Roy Wood sounds like — Lou Christie!"

The first recorded rendition of 'Cherry Blossom Clinic' which was recorded that day, didn't live up to their (Cordell) standards and it was subsequently discarded.

'Vote For Me' was recorded in two feisty versions. Featuring fantastic, stabbing wah-wah guitar on the intro of one version. Which is my personal favourite version — that one, just jumps out of the speakers. The other version is minus the wah-wah guitar. Both takes are carried by a rocking Trevor Burton vocal and the lyrics are amazing. Showing a wry side to The Move's look at "hippie life" back then. They could actually take the piss and poke fun at hippie culture as they saw it. With an objectivity I think, missing in a lot of cases in 1967. The group would not touch back upon the 'Cherry Blossom Clinic' composition, for another three months.

****

Bobby Davidson remembered Tony Secunda's background: "He had been involved in promoting wrestling matches and he had come up from there. For Tony it was all about 'bums on seats', he would do anything to get a crowd in. So, every time we went out to do some pictures he would come up with some extraordinary idea. Usually verging on the illegal, immoral or downright dangerous."

As Ace Kefford put it in an interview, "I loved Tony — but he was as bent as a nine-bob note." Ace also remembered when he and Tony Secunda, went to pick up the slew of newspapers after Harold Wilson's response had broken publicly in the news. And with The Move, plastered all over the front of them all, "Secunda was dancing all over the pavement and he threw all the papers into the car, all over me." Ace arrived back to the Madison Hotel in Sussex Gardens, Paddington. Here as stated before, he threw the papers all over Carl Wayne and began to pack his bags.

Instead of 'Flowers In The Rain', we could've been treated to the abstract, invaluable and completely off the wall combination of 'Cherry Blossom Clinic' as an A-side and 'Vote For Me' as the B-side. It is said that Secunda and The Move felt that the two songs that dealt with mental illness and direct sarcastic, political digs at the "establishment" — plus the scruffy west coast hippie scene, which was becoming quite a drag, would've been a tremendously "out there" release. But it was felt that they (and Secunda) had already pushed it too far! And so the summery 'Flowers In The Rain' became the classic single, representing that fabled (in hindsight) summer in that much since, discussed year.

In the immediate aftermath of the court case, Bobby Davidson remembers Tony Secunda receiving a visit from two possible MI5 operatives. The facts were not made plain to Secunda — but the threats were. There are two versions of this story. Firstly, we will relay Bobby Davidson's take on this sinister event: "Before the court case, a few days after the story had broken, Tony heard a knock at his door, about 9 o'clock in the morning. Two ordinary looking men with homburg hats, both carrying briefcases, stood outside his flat in Earls Court. 'Are you Tony Secunda?' 'Yes', he answered, not sure whether to acknowledge or not, 'What do you want?' On hearing that he was Tony Secunda, they moved like greased lightning. Barging in through the door, they picked him up and held him against the door, lifting his feet up off the ground. They were still holding their briefcases and umbrellas and had their hats on. One of them grabbed hold of his balls and began twisting them round. Tony told me afterwards that he'd never experienced such agony or been so frightened in his life. Then these two terribly respectable gentlemen said, 'You've behaved badly. You've been very naughty; you've upset the Prime Minister Harold Wilson. If this continues...' Their tone was ominous. 'But it won't, will it, Sir...?' Grabbing him by the balls and gripping him extremely tightly, they threatened Tony and said: 'Listen, don't ever do that again!' Then they put him down gently and walked away. Tony rang me later and said: 'Robert; they frightened me, and I think this one's going to get a bit bigger.' At that moment Tony knew that he'd overstepped the mark. Once you start messing with the establishment, he warned me, look out! The two gentlemen disappeared just as quickly as they'd appeared. They never said who they were. They didn't come back — maybe because Tony, wisely, decided not to take on any more politicians."

Piers Secunda's memory bank holds the story in a different aspect, which we will get to after a bit of background. Piers is one of two of Tony Secunda's sons. Piers is from Secunda's second marriage to Patricia McRoberts. Patricia was also dating photographer Bobby Davidson before Secunda edged into the picture. Piers Secunda was reunited with his father in later years. Although this took a certain amount of subterfuge at first. His mother Patricia did not want him consorting with Tony at all. Piers and Tony worked out a way to communicate over the phone. Piers details the phone calls, "At least twice a week from the UK to the United States. I had a special drill worked out." Secunda senior would go back to the public pay phones in the USA and call in to the UK. Piers spoke to and heard from his father regularly in those later years.

By this time Tony Secunda was domiciled in San Anselmo. This small, picturesque town is situated over the Golden Gate Bridge outside San Francisco. It's about a 30-minute drive from San Francisco. To resume; Piers' version of the MI5 story goes more like this! Tony Secunda has gone back to his hotel at this stage (Why is he returning to a hotel? It is presumed he has accommodation and lived in the local Earls Court area. This is explained by the constant press attention at the time. This Secunda subterfuge was acted out, to give the press a slip).

"He was being followed constantly around then, as was the band, by unknown cars and unknown men. It was rumoured to be MI5. It could've been press and paparazzi. And of course it could have been general nutters. When he entered the reception and the seated area of said hotel, he sat down in the lobby to unwind. A man dressed soberly, walks in carrying an umbrella. He enters the hotel and briskly walked up to Tony. He then pinned him by the shoulder, against the back of his seat. He was using the tip of the umbrella, extremely forcibly. He then told him in no uncertain terms, to curtail his activities surrounding PM Harold Wilson and any further claims of impropriety on PM Wilson's part. Tony got the message immediately. The man left as if he'd never been there. He (or they in Robert Davidson's description) were never heard of or seen again."

Unfortunately, after this, this marriage between the Machiavellian, scheming and brilliant manager Secunda and his equally brilliant young Move proteges, began to sunder. The band were experiencing tremors of fear, which started to rend them apart. This signalled the start of the process of the band, ridding themselves of Secunda. He was an unpredictable man. Disliked by many, at times frightening, but a completely unique manager. Secunda fitted into those times as if he was made for them. The Move's inherent wildness and Secunda's anti-establishment attitudes and roiling imagination all made for a very exciting coupling.

Robert Davidson recalls with total clarity, "Tony was a total liability and a seriously dangerous gentleman. The Move said that he was costing them more than they earned. They had lost a huge amount of money with 'Flowers In The Rain'. But if you wanted to reach number one, you went with Tony and you took the risk. He would get the publicity. He was fearless. I became one of his slaves, which was an intolerable position to find myself in. And yet every time he won me over with his charm and charisma. He always reassured me, 'Of course I'll pay you. Don't worry about it Bobby'. With Tony, if he wasn't getting anywhere with his negotiations, he would headbutt people. He'd just go and headbutt them and they'd fall over. I saw him do it a couple of times and thought, 'How do you do that? Why don't you hurt your own head?' He called it 'nutting'. He'd say, 'I think I'm going to have to nut this person'. And I'd think, 'I'd rather you didn't'. Then he'd go bang! And over they'd fall. He gained a certain reputation in the business, 'Don't upset Tony, 'cos he'll nut you'. You were never quite sure, when he was going to do it. Perhaps that's why people like him are called 'nutters.' They just go boing! You'd fall over and think, 'Did I say something wrong? To reinforce this point, when I went to him to ask, 'What about paying me? I'm owed money.' 'Yeah', he'd say, 'Go and ask Laura.' She was his secretary. Laura, however, would say, 'He's told me not to give you more than a tenner.' That was nowhere near what I was owed."

Bobby Davidson continues, recalling his disgruntlement: "I was taking pictures and printing hundreds of photographs and handouts for him. The band suddenly had a number one hit and ostensibly, they were making loads of money. But the more money they made, the less came my way. It became very tricky maintaining my lifestyle."

Looking back over the years and perhaps not getting down and dirty with Secunda's plans and following through could have been a terrible mistake on The Move's part. One from which they never really recovered. (along with Ace Kefford's departure). In fact, by not zeroing in and cementing this flagrant publicity and indeed, by potentially capitalising on it further, raising its profile to a much greater degree. It was probably one of the biggest (if not the biggest) publicity blasts, any rising band could've got at the time. Particularly at that time and in that banqueted year of upheaval and change.

Perhaps, following this on with a truly inaugural USA tour, The Move gradually became rudderless, and they lost their compelling, rising momentum. The foundations that were built solidly but rapidly in 1966 began to quake. The onward propulsion that their career momentum was gathering through 1966 and into 1967 started to crumble. Internal doubts, fear and inter-band bickering all added towards the increased paranoid tension.

It was Joe Boyd's fervent opinion, "The Move at The Monterey Pop Festival, would've completely blown the hippies away. In the same way Jimi Hendrix and others did." Then they should have started to work the huge USA market steadily. With the flare and zeal, with which they had captured the UK. Who knows how much more popularity, fame and records would have been sold if those steps could've been achieved. It's easy in hindsight to make pithy assumptions. But a good set of lawyers (these days) would find a way to dramatise this publicity. Bringing it to the audience and general public in a very favourable manner and benefitting the band. A good set of lawyers, would no doubt, be able to contest the whole Harold Wilson thing. Particularly the fact that Roy Wood and members of the band were underage minors. And that Secunda (now unfortunately deceased) did not make the band privy to his intended publicity action. They knew about as much as anybody else.

"I do believe that when Tony Secunda went — and we got rid of Secunda because we got scared — that was the end of it. We dug our own graves because I think ultimately, Secunda could have got us through."

Carl Wayne

Around this time Tony Secunda was in New York and he told *Record World* he had hired Arthur. H. Gorson Inc to represent himself and The Move in the United States for management. *Record World* went on to report, "The group which is scoring with their latest single, 'I Can Hear the Grass Grow' is expected to arrive in America in September with said Secunda, 'a Town Hall engagement, if all goes well'. Promotion of the band in the US is to be handled by TRO, The Move's US publisher. In England their material is handled by TRO — The Essex Music Group. Secunda feels that the visual appeal of The Move in person can start a big Move movement among USA record buyers. He said the group was the first in England to use creative lighting, smoke bombs, flash powder, etc. in their act. They typically climax their onstage antics with the destruction of 'effigies of people who we don't like — like Adolf Hitler,' explained Secunda. Right now, Secunda (who stopped by with Denny

Cordell, producer of The Move and also of the very hot Procol Harum, with Deram's 'A Whiter Shade Of Pale') manages only The Move. 'It's a full-time job,' Secunda says."

In 1967 the Move toured this mayhem in Europe, then returned for a college tour during which they took apart the London School of Economics. There was previously a gig at the Slade School of Art where Adolf Hitler was again taken out, to be sliced, spliced and diced! A report stated, "The Move's Tony Secunda, received a threatening telephone call after the group had smashed an effigy of Hitler. During a session at London's Slade School of Art on Friday."

This article was reported in the *Melody Maker* on 24th December 1966. It went on to say the caller purported to be a member of the fascist British National Party. Secunda told the *Melody Maker*, "Some guy phoned me and said he was from the BNP, whatever that is. He said that if we chopped up Hitler they were gonna chop me up. Anyway, I've been in touch with the police and we're going to continue chopping up Hitler!"

Over the years, Carl Wayne has commented that they could and should have weathered this shite-storm which surrounded the release of 'Flowers In The Rain' and the subsequent court case. This definitely wasn't a (shit)storm in a teacup though. If only the young band had held their collective nerve and stayed with Tony Secunda as sole management, then broken into the USA, toured strongly and kept on building. Taking the American cities and hinterlands, with their already extant R&B and soul vibes. Intertwining these with these great classic freak-beat singles. Giving the Americans a revved-up taste of their own psychedelic rock. They could've created a big following in America. America would have lapped them up. Rob Caiger and I agreed. They needed a personal manager on the road and very regular meetings. This, also to soothe their young combustible egos. Things needed calming over and overviewing. With assurance by the management team and fairly regularly, they could and should have been a massive international act. By 1967 the templates for management and the new 'Rock Industry' were being improvised but being put in place. Tony Secunda was almost 'situationist' in his preferred style of creating chaos.

Carl Wayne offered in retrospect, "The 1967 court case was the beginning of the end. We were suddenly thrown into the High Court of Justice, and we were defenceless. We had no one to represent us or listen to whether we were involved. Had we been sensible, we'd have taken counsel and listened to what we should have said. Instead, we admitted to something that we didn't actually do. All because we thought it was good fun to do. When you think about it, it was completely and utterly fucking stupid — because we hooked ourselves onto something that we would later regret. It was really Secunda's bag, and we should have quickly stepped away from it. It was a stunt too far, but by then of course, we couldn't."

Carl Wayne however changed his mind years later. He realised that Secunda and The Move were a perfect fit in many ways. In fact, few people know that Secunda's contract only ended later on and after the release of 'Blackberry Way.' This was The Move's sixth single; released in late November 1968. Becoming The Move's first number one in the UK singles chart. Secunda was still peripherally involved because he dreamt up some stunts that went with the release of 'Blackberry Way'.

'Blackberry Way' was recorded on 29th November 1968 and was produced by

Jimmy Miller. He was riding high as the extant Rolling Stones producer of *Beggars Banquet*. 'Blackberry Way' had a sonorous, emotional flavour. It has a specific, strong Beatles influence. It nevertheless became the band's most successful single. Carl Wayne refused to sing lead, so Wood handled the lead vocal.

Wood said in a 1994 interview that 'Blackberry Way' is his favourite Move song of all time, further commenting that it could have been performed in any era and still worked. He commented that, "It has a timeless quality." The Move had also publicly added, "If the next single doesn't make it, we're finished!"

'Blackberry Way' has some similarities with 'Penny Lane', only with much less optimistic lyrics and a deeper, melancholic feel. The bridge appears to be a similar lift from the intro of Harry Nilsson's 'Good Old Desk.' When it was put to him in an interview, Roy Wood admits the influence of 'Penny Lane' on this song. He said, "I suppose it could have been. We were all very influenced by what The Beatles were doing because they were the best songwriters around."

Robert Davidson was also aware of a creeping change in the overall dynamics: "They were this brilliant band and up to then they were on an accelerating rise. But slowly bit by bit, chunks started to fall off. Tony Secunda left, the producer (Denny Cordell) fell away... Ace Kefford, who was a paranoid person at the best of times. Ace was a wonderful musician, a fantastic icon. But he crumbled under the strain of the fallout around the court case. The blond, beautiful bassist, the weak link in the chain is the one who becomes the sacrificial lamb. And poor old Ace, he was the one who fell in the spring of 1968 and ended up in a mental hospital."

16.
"Psychedelic music is a load of shit..."

How psychedelic is your pop? This is the question prompted by and asked to many of the groups in 1967. Carl Wayne in one of his many extrovert and effusive moments said, "Psychedelic music is a load of shit — we get quite nasty to anybody who calls us psychedelic." Carl added, "I'm instructed to say it's all about LSD. But to tell you the truth, I haven't a bloody clue what it's all about." This must have addled the more middle-class hippie bands. Who probably looked down their noses askance at The Move's attitude.

The Move weren't playing the hipster (aka hippie) game. Even though they were playing ultra-hip music. Even though they were playing a selection of the hippest cover versions. Both from the Afro-American side and the newer psychedelic freak-beat bands out of the USA and the UK. The Move looked hipper and could play musical circles around most of these bands. I'm talking Pink Floyd upwards or downwards. Whichever way you look at it.

Like many of the truly greatest acts, the seeds of destruction may have been gestating and simmering from day one. A super abundance of energy and talent was spread across, five charismatic young men. They were an edgy, combustible, combination of personalities. At first, the band buoyed by their own brilliance at this stage, hit the ground running. Nothing could touch them in 1966, vanquishing concert halls one by one, throughout the country. On stage and playing in a high velocity band like this, they were a massive cut above the average. Perhaps this could give them all a feeling of invincibility. A massive pride in self. A take no prisoners' approach. Excitement built and all five egos swelled some. But any ruptures in the band's united exterior were not entirely noticeable at first.

The ill-judged remark by Ricki Farr regarding Ace looking like the "front man" definitely pointed towards the first real (ego) fracture in 'The Move' game plan. It was with the arrival of the Afro-hair perms, heralding to Bev Bevan, that Ace and Trevor were downing drugs at a much higher rate than before. More certainly as 1967 progressed and with the advent of LSD available, the drug use would have united these two youngest. Becoming a trippy unit within themselves. As drug users can be wont to do. Altering their reality to the point, where they may have thought Roy, Bev and Carl were really "squares."

Chemistry is a very delicate thing. Anything dividing this mighty machine, was unnecessary and certainly it needed urgent management monitoring. Secunda or an assistant, should've been on this straight away. Easily said; considering this type of music situation was in its infancy. Although drugs and music were no strangers. With heroin, coke and speed having been round the music scene before. The introduction of manifold drugs to the industry in 1967 had a wholly different flavour. This was a broader, societal combination and something affecting communities and culture and the music scene as a whole.

Tony Secunda, although brilliant as a strategist and publicity instigator, could have handled and perhaps soothed the group's egos and temperaments with much more elan. Perhaps with more, much needed emphasis, placed on the psychology of the five young guys, who were very young. And as Carl Wayne pointed out several times throughout the years after, all the band members were missing fathers and father figures, all had died (or were estranged) by this time. Although Secunda could be seen as a 'strong father' figure he would have needed to zero in on the group's personal details.

In terms of egos, backbiting and the personal jealousies which began to erupt more regularly, Secunda's management style was described as "whimsical" by another scenester, The Rolling Stones manager, Andrew Loog Oldham. Oldham was himself no stranger to controversy and his endless, speed-propelled badinage. Oldham stylishly, entreatingly and entertainingly, spewed his verbal out to the press. In his role as the notorious first manager of The Rolling Stones he was the co-founder of the ultra-hip Immediate Records label. Oldham's speed spattered brain and tongue, could and would addle the assembled listeners and consumers before him. With his illustrious, fine turn in hustled banter. Remembering the finest old adage that... "Bullshit baffles brains."

The Walker Brothers package tour is one example of a less than favourable situation, although it could be argued, was potentially beneficial. Carl Wayne throws some light: "We had umpteen offers, including The Walker Brothers last tour. We turned that down because they refused to let us smash TV sets on stage, a big part of our act at the time."

Instead, Jimi Hendrix took their place. The Top Rank Organisation deemed The Move "not suitable." As if Jimi Hendrix was! Jimi Hendrix had been shunted into an ill-judged package tour organised by Tito Burns that placed him alongside The Walker Brothers, Engelbert Humperdinck and Cat Stevens — exposing Hendrix to exactly the wrong audience. A series of patchy, regional club gigs followed but Hendrix was yet to achieve the widespread fame to come.

Also, in April 1967 the *NME* reported that The Move had offered a £200 reward for the recovery of the master tapes of ten songs intended for their debut album potentially called 'Movement' or 'Move Mass'. (Or 'Lawnmower' — another Secunda / band wind-up).

The tapes were "stolen" from their agent's car by a construction worker called Fred Higgins when it was parked in Denmark Street. A popular dive in Denmark Street was La Giocondo — a cafe/bar where The Move and other faces around the nascent R&B scene visited. David Bowie was said to practically live there. The Move and Secunda took photos of builder Fred Higgins and the band hanging about. The tapes were "found" in a skip shortly afterwards. The damage caused to the reels meant that new mixes and masters would have to be made. Fred Higgins had apparently

"Psychedelic music is a load of shit..."

"found the stolen materials and returned them." This was the reason the album wasn't released until March 1968.

Denny Cordell also managed to switch the band from Deram Records, over to the newly formed Regal Zonophone Records. It's been long alleged that the "theft" was a hoax, another delaying scam, cooked up by Secunda to allow him to negotiate the band away from Decca/Deram to a label who would be willing to pay more *dinero* for the subsequent album release, as they tried to find time to finish off the record. It was another one of Tony Secunda's sensationalist, publicity tropes. Photos were then set up by Robert Davidson, of the band with Tony Secunda and a builder called Fred Higgins. They show the band having coffee with Higgins and all smiles, wandering about Carnaby Street. The band were constantly on the go. They were mostly recording tracks in a piecemeal fashion. Days here and days there. Between requests for band photo shoots from Bobby Davidson and constant driving / gigging up and down the country and also gigging in France and Sweden. Secunda was definitely very fond of publicity photographs — The Move did hundreds.

In another link to the art world, Secunda came in contact with a student called David Osborne-Dowle. David had moved from Cambridge to London and worked as a technician at the Shaftesbury Theatre in London's West End. He became friendly with Syd Barrett and knew him from Cambridge. David did tech for Jimi Hendrix and described this part of his life as "being in the right place at the right time." David got a place at the London Film School in 1967. He lived in a large, shared house on Ladbroke Grove, which belonged to "the record label" (possibly Transatlantic). Dowle shot two music videos at the time. Shooting in 16mm film stock, on a large BBC style camera — very possibly a Bolex.

One was for Procol Harum's 'Whiter Shade Of Pale' (which is now believed to be lost) and the other was for 'Flowers In the Rain'. David told his daughter Shauna about making The Move video, "That it was a beautiful day, spent with beautiful people on Hampstead Heath." David also remembered it as, "One of the best days of my life. It was all improvised and it wasn't planned. We knew that we were making a film, but we didn't know what we wanted it to be like. Music video was a totally brand-new concept back then."

Shauna remembers in the early 1980s, finding her father David sitting in front of the television, watching a live broadcast of *Top Of The Pops*. "He was waiting for something to come on. It wasn't like him — a large part of the charm of *Top Of The Pops* was the not knowing what you were going to get. I was about 11 or 12 years old at the time. This was the first time I saw the 'Flowers In The Rain' music video being broadcast. He explained that he'd been asked for it by the band. He sent the only copy that he had, because it was on film. It hadn't been used for a long time. I remember him describing Roy Wood as a 'gentle genius' remembering that he always worked hard behind the scenes."

In a wistful family moment, Shauna revealed, that David died just a few months before I contacted them. "He would have loved to talk about that day with you personally. As it meant so much to him." It was a moment of poignancy, during this writing to remember David. I'm really glad to have been able to include him and this sweet memory in the book.

In a little-known nod to pre-video sales, at the time of the 'Flowers In The Rain' single release, The Move had an 8mm film that people could buy. The adverts stated, "Write today to Style Film Productions. Get your own copy of a superb film of The Move for home viewing. £1.76 will get you a Black and White reel. £3.15 will get you a Colour reel. For the princely sum of £4 — you will get Super Colour (whatever that was)." Maybe it was the 'HD Ultra 4K' of the day?

On 21st June, The Move appeared at Burton Constable Hall in Skirlaugh for Midsummer Night's Dream which also featured sets by Angel Pavement, Elmer Gantry's Velvet Opera, Marmalade, Tramline, and Savoy Brown. Two weeks later, The Move appeared at the Royal Albert Hall for Sounds '68, a multi-bill engagement with the Alan Bown Set, Bonzo Dog Band, The Easybeats, and Joe Cocker. They also appeared at the Torquay Beat and Blues Festival held at the Town Hall in Torquay on Tuesday 1st August. The newspaper printed it as (ahem) "Flower Powder." The Move were supported by The Alby, The Jigsaw and The Package Deal. The shows also saw Simon Dupree appearing, on the third day it was The Artwoods.

On 2nd September, The Move played the Bank Holiday Bluesology Festival held on the Chateau Impney Grounds, Droitwich. With sets by Breakthru', Chris Farlowe, Family, Fleetwood Mac, and Skip Bifferty. The event was hosted by BBC Radio One DJ John Peel.

Later that month, The Move played the Starlight Room in Boston, England, with a fledgling band called Yes in support. On 1st November they played King's College in London. Support was the pop-psych band The Lemon Tree. Lemon Tree issued two 1968 singles on Parlophone Records, both co-produced by Andy Fairweather Low and Trevor Burton. Ace Kefford wrote The Lemon Tree's first A-side, 'William Chalker's Time Machine.' Although not doing well in the charts, it was a really good record. It's considered a freak beat classic from that time.

Bev recalls one important billing gig at The Paris Olympia supporting The Rolling Stones in the cavernous hall on 11th April 1967. "We were in awe of being on and sharing the bill with The Stones. They were incredibly friendly, except for Brian Jones. He just totally ignored us! I think we were a bit nervous. I think we spoke to Mick before we went on and they helped us relax. Everybody else in the band were fabulous, all of them, Mick and Keith and Bill. Of course, me and Charlie, as drummers do, were chatting away like drummers always do! As a drummer, I got on really well with Charlie Watts, who was really friendly too. Yes, there's photos of Ace and Trevor and Dumpy Harris talking to Charlie Watts. There's a really good one of Upsy Downing and Mick Jagger. I never rated The Stones particularly as great players. But Jagger was some frontman. I mean, he really was something special. They were second only to the Beatles, by then."

This was The Stones' third year in a row at the Olympia and the French audience favoured the band immensely. Bill Wyman remarked that "Paris was always a stronghold for us... The band's playing is spot on too."

The Move also found time to record on French television. This was for a mini show called *Age Tendre et Tête de Bois* (roughly translated as 'young age and wooden heads'). They tear through dynamic live versions of 'Night Of Fear' and 'I Can Hear The Grass Grow.' The early band looked fantastic. Roy and Bev at the back, Ace and Trevor bunched together to the left and Carl to the right, pulling some seriously bizarre moves. A mixture of Tom Jones, Mick Jagger and 60s go-go dancing. UK pop stars like Petula Clark would appear and French favourites like Johnny Hallyday and Claude Francois would often be seen performing. The show ran from 1961 to 1967 and featured world-renowned artists including The Beatles, Elvis, Stevie Wonder and Isaac Hayes. The show was compared in influence, to the *Ed Sullivan Show*.

The gig at The Olympia goes very well, with the French crowd loving the band. They were invited back, and it was reported that The Move were to appear in an hour-long colour movie being shot in Tangiers and in Cannes in May. Unfortunately like a lot of Move sizzle, this was another thing that didn't happen. Or if it did, it's never surfaced archive wise. There must be good film of the original band but it's very thin on the ground. A good record of the original band — an original set or something would show them knocking audiences out with all the energy and stage moves etc. Offers for the band were now streaming in from the USA, Germany, all around Scandinavia and South Africa. It was also briefly reported that Roy Wood was hurt when a smoke bomb used by the group exploded on stage at the Tiles Club London. It said Roy was deafened for 24 hours and rushed to a Harley Street specialist but recovered.

Bev grimaces at the travel strictures around the time. "Yeah, we always flew out of Heathrow. And often from Birmingham. There were so many flights in those days, and they were really dirt cheap. We also flew out of, back in those days, the Elmdon Airport in Birmingham. Trying to get around Britain back then, before the motorways were built was insane, on all the small and incredibly slow B roads."

17.
Just about to trip your mind...

London's UFO Club was a short-lived counterculture, hipster club established by Joe Boyd and John "Hopi" Hopkins. It featured light shows, poetry readings, well-known rock acts such as Jimi Hendrix, avant-garde art by Yoko Ono, as well as local house bands such as Pink Floyd and Soft Machine. The club operated in total for nine months from December 1966 to August 1967. It operated for another seven months at 31 Tottenham Court Road in Fitzrovia, then a further two months at The Roundhouse in Chalk Farm. The Move appeared on 26th May. Joe Boyd wanted to get them gigging at the club. This was up against the wishes, of some of the others like John Hopkins. Boyd remembered the incendiary shows at the Marquee. However, Boyd felt The Move didn't quite catch fire at the UFO club.

One feature writer commented, "The Move played to the largest crowd that UFO ever held" and although they were very exciting, he felt disappointed. They did two 45-minute spots, the first featured two Byrds numbers and 'I Can Hear The Grass Grow.' The second set featured just one number The Byrds' 'Eight Miles High.' In this case it was more electronic than musical using oscillators and what sounded like a super amplified harmonica. The Move were obviously trying to expand their appeal to the "flower power people" crowd at this gig.

Joe Boyd felt they were a bit dwarfed by the gig — not connecting with the mostly stoned-out "hippie" crowd. They were supported by The Nack. On one occasion at the UFO, the hippies supposedly booed the band, possibly for their choice of more 'Mod' music. Maybe The Move's full-on amphetamine charge didn't go down too well with the half-asleep stoners? In actual fact after interviewing Joe Boyd, the hippies booing Move syndrome was actually exaggerated. In his book called *Hippie* Barry Miles continues 'the booing offstage of The Move' story.

In a recent email, Barry Miles was much more succinct: "The Move were seen by the UFO audience as too commercial, too slick, too loud, and as having nothing in common with the UFO audience. It was the aggression in The Move's act that they didn't like. Honestly, beyond thinking they were trying to muscle into the "underground" scene, it was no big deal."

But Joe Boyd remembers it differently: "Now that's the May. That's the first gig where they were booed, wasn't it, apparently? Well, I don't remember them being booed wholesale, I have to say."

26th May 1967: The Move, The Crazy World Of Arthur Brown, Dave Tomlin, The People Show. Keith West was part of that scene, "They either loved you or hated you. Some bands that played there were hated, The Move, for example. They thought were too slick."

Ace Kefford recalls the UFO crowd's snobby hostility: "It really wasn't our scene. We still lived up north, so we were Northern lads coming down to London. I remember we resurrected our stage act of smashing up some TVs which we'd pretty much given up doing otherwise."

Trevor Burton laughingly remembers, "There was a rumour that you could get stoned by smoking banana skins. Tony Secunda and Denny Cordell skinned up 200 banana skin joints and then threw them into the crowd. So, all these hippies went madly scrambling for them. They did nothing at all, except give you a blinding headache."

"Well, there were a few people who were sort of involved with UFO, who were against The Move," recalls Boyd. "I had been from the beginning and once we got going and was successful. I had always said, "We've got to have The Move here. And a lot of people around Hopi, (John Hopkins) people from the *International Times* would say, 'No, no, no, what are you talking about. You can't have them at UFO.' (The encrusted snobbery I mentioned before, in action. Notice how the American Joe Boyd, is unaware of, or ignores this attitude. Focusing mainly on the bands powerhouse performance). I said, 'No, it's going to work great.' Then I think I had a double bill with the Floyd. Well, there was one gig on 26th May and then there was a two-day festival."

This was on the 1st and 2nd September. This second event was called the UFO Festival. It featured the following, Arthur Brown, Pink Floyd, Soft Machine, The Move, Tomorrow and Denny Laine. "That was after we'd moved to The Roundhouse," says Boyd. "And they went down better that night. The first UFO gig was in The Blarney Club, which is a really tiny play with a really small stage. That was just the way it was. It was part of the deal. It was an Irish dance hall and stuff, so we used to get our own Friday nights. There was very little room on the stage. There was very little room behind the stage, very little room at the sides of the stage. I think The Move were a little bit intimidated by the London psychedelic scene."

Joe Boyd kept the faith: "I was welcoming and told them how great it was that they were here and all that kind of stuff. I think it was a bit like that Judas cry of Dylan and the march to Free Trade Hall. It's like a few people may have booed. The audience didn't respond against them. My impression was that they were nervous. They used to love prancing around the stage. Carl Wayne coming up to the front and singing and stepping back and backing singers lurching to the microphones. All that kind of physical movement on the stage. It wasn't possible to do that on this stage. So, I think they felt a little cowed, both by the hippie audience, which wasn't their normal crowd. Plus, the size of the stage, the fact that they were on with the Floyd, you know. They were a little intimidated by the situation. I thought they were okay. But compared to gigs that I'd seen at The Marquee and I'm talking here about the 26th May gig. It wasn't a disaster, but they just didn't kill. Yeah, it wasn't one of their killer shows." Now that's cool, so they kind of redeemed themselves somewhat at the second gig.

Just about to trip your mind...

"We got kicked out of the Blarney Club because of the *News Of The World* article.[17] We moved to The Roundhouse and I ended up on Bank Holiday weekend, the beginning of September, putting on the so-called UFO Festival. We booked the Floyd, we booked The Move, we booked the Soft Machine, Arthur Brown. It was unfortunately, the death knell of UFO, because we didn't really bring enough people in. It's a bit of a blur that weekend. I spent my whole time, biting my nails and counting the box office."

Joe Boyd had links to Nigel Waymouth who produced posters for UFO and also a really superb poster for The Move at The Marquee. "In 1967 the people who ran the UFO Club on Tottenham Court Road asked me to team up with the late artist Michael English to produce a poster for their psychedelic night. As 'Hapshash and the Coloured Coat' we designed posters for musicians like Jimi Hendrix. We even recorded an avant-garde album. Around 50 of my friends turned up to the studio, tooting horns and making all sorts of noises, while I read out *Marvel* comic books to make them sound like epic poetry. After a while, the whole '60s atmosphere of "peace and love" morphed into something more aggressive and political. Michael English and I designed that poster particularly. We'd done something similar for the big UFO, which was semi-abstract and using stripes. Anyway, that was done to promote The Move. It was inspired from my days at UCL where I was studying Economic History. One department at UCL was the Slade School of Art. Ben O' Kern was the Professor of Painting there, he did these kind of swearing things. A lot of them are in the collection of the Victoria and Albert. They get pulled up from time to time. After the UFO poster, we did The Move soon after and decided to do the stripes again. We liked The Move; they were instrumental in using a lot of feedback and things like that in their music."

17 After a sordid article published in the *News Of The World* on 30th July the landlord told Joe Boyd the UFO could not continue at the Blarney. Brian Epstein offered the Champagne Lounge at his Saville Theatre, but Boyd decided on the larger Roundhouse venue. In October 1967, the UFO Club at the Roundhouse folded.

Flowers In The Rain - The Untold Story of The Move

18.
I'm sure my brain, it had enough?

An amusing incident happened on the way back from a Move gig. As they traversed their way back to Birmingham from the Skyline Ballroom in Hull. A ritual that frankly used to get on Allen Harris' nerves. Nine times out of ten according to Allen, and it didn't matter where they were, they all seemed to want to go back to the enticing womb of Birmingham. Farnsfield in Nottinghamshire looks to be a good three-hour drive back to Birmingham. Maybe more back then, traversing along the slow, windy 'B' roads. Allen Harris also remembers he thought Secunda was responsible for digging up the old and ancient British law. The law in which two ducks (I shit thee not!) can be used to pay court fines. Doubtless; this is more redoubtable, head-fuckery from Mr Secunda. I have to say I love this story. All these old fuddy-duddy squares... being mightily head-fucked around by these young brightly-dressed, noisy upstarts.

The *Guardian Journal* from Nottingham printed the story on Saturday 1st July 1967. In fact, the old charter discovered by Secunda, supposedly read; "you could pay the court fine, with a sack of grain, or a pig or a couple of ducks..."

The story starts with "Pop group guitarist Trevor Burton went to court yesterday wearing a peacock blue jacket and carrying two ducks. For Burton, 18-year-old member of The Move group, he took the ducks along, to pay any fine imposed on him by Southwell Magistrates. But the magistrates bound Trevor Burton of Aston, Birmingham over in the sum of £25 to keep the peace for a year. Burton, who along with three others connected with the group, admitted causing a breach of the peace, took the two ducks home with him."

The *Evening Post* on Friday 30th June 1967 added in the feature that Trevor Burton had brought along two ducks on a lead. Which he said afterwards, he would've offered in kind, towards paying any fine arising out of the charge. Which came under an act from 1361. Burton described as a musician of Wainright Street, Aston, pleaded guilty.

Mr P. A. Foster prosecuting said, "That at 2:15am on February the 17th Mrs Hilda Bartlett was serving at the all-night cafe, when the six youths came in. (Presumably the five members of the group and Allen Harris). Trevor Burton with the others in tow, eventually ended up in court and being bound over for a breach of the peace. On this particular nocturnal romp, they all descended on a night café in a place called Farnsfield. That night Mrs Hilda Bartlett of Abbotts Crescent, Farnsfield was the serving night manageress."

The *Guardian Journal* stated that "six youths came into the café. The first one ordered tea and also ordered a beverage which Mrs Bartlett said they did not serve. And Trevor Burton came up and asked for the same beverage. He then passed an obscene remark to the first youth."

Apparently Dumpy had nicked Trevor's mug of tea and they were just larking about with some added colourful swearing. Mrs Bartlett told him she would not stand for that language. She then ordered him to get out! Burton said: "Who do you think you are, the Sergeant Major?" A police officer, who was back in the kitchen, came out him and said: "Let's have you outside." Then Burton replied, "I don't have to leave."

The officer then took him by the arm to lead him out and Burton started throwing his arms about. They both fell to the ground struggling. Eventually the group went away. Mr. Jeremy Connor, acting for Burton said the men were travelling back from Hull. They were in high spirits and perhaps inclined to go too far. Connor also added there were degrees of bad behaviour, and he suggested that the incident they just heard about, was well down the list. In addition to being bound over, Burton was ordered to pay court costs of £6 and 17 shillings.

For Dumpy and Upsy, the incessant driving and The Move's constant need to return back to Birmingham, was creating very basic problems.

"I went out with Upsy in the van somewhere. On our way back, we were going to his house to drop him off. I needed the van the next day for something. But Upsy crashed the van. He narrowly missed a traffic island, and we went right over the pub wall on the Chester Road in Birmingham. There was this wall about this high, all round the pub. We finished up, right on top of the wall. No front wheels afterwards. The spare wheel on the roof, flew off and went right through the pub window. It was really early morning."

The Move's modes of transportation gradually improved. The first vehicle was a knackered old Ford Thames van. It was held together, with sticking plasters, smoke and mirrors. They eventually got rid of that, and they got a new dark green Ford Transit. They had that one for quite a while. Dumpy did the finance on that vehicle.

After that Tony Secunda obtained a used Commer bus. They took all the seats out. Making room to transport all the equipment to gigs and back. By then the band were travelling in a separate motor, an Austin Princess car, which was later followed by a Rover 3 litre, which whisked them off to gigs in much more comfort.

1967 was a rollercoaster year for the band and just about any other happening members of the UK music industry scene. As that symbolic year picked up, The Move's career and success ramped up. Trevor and Ace found both an invigorating and numbing solace. As Sly and The Family Stone used to sing, "Different strokes for different folks."

By using many drugs to get through the different strains and excitements. Uppers (amphetamines) were always a good choice for keeping the energy levels up during gigs. Of course, good old alcohol was also a great livener, a good social leveller and a liquid libation. However, it was Ace's and Trevor's use of LSD that had a markedly noticeable effect on these two young guys. Trevor Burton overall, didn't seem to incur too much damage. (I'm talking about during this 'first drug' stage. But later on during the Balls and following period, Trevor got into trouble with 'Class A' drugs). He didn't appear to lose any of his need to play hard and tough. And he gave good performances. He was able to carry off the gigs and continue on unscathed. Although his behaviour was becoming more erratic too.

Trevor was sullen, moody and aggressive. Which suited the overall vibe, of the other three front-line guys. Roy was (at that time) very shy, much more circumspect. Behind the front line at some gigs. But also, in the front-line at others. Bev was more stable, confident and consistently dynamic. Seemingly with no need to have to bolster his ego. Bevan's thunderous, aggressive drums did that for him.

19.
I see rainbows in the evening...

In November 1967, The Move were added to a sixteen-date tour and undertook this novel UK package tour that included The Jimi Hendrix Experience, The Nice, The Pink Floyd and Amen Corner. Pink Floyd were bottom of the bill. Although they had been banned by the Rank Organisation in 1966, which had led to their further banning from the Walker Brothers tour, The Move were to co-headline the tour with the Jimi Hendrix Experience and others with the package taking in cities like London (Royal Albert Hall), Birmingham, Manchester, Newcastle and eight other dates. Tony Secunda opined, "The Move haven't been smashing up stages or equipment now for six months. So, I'm hoping we're going to be able to sort out the situation with Rank Organisation very soon."

They were playing two shows each night with Hendrix topping the bill. Pink Floyd barely had time for one of their extended numbers, having been allocated a maximum of twenty minutes on stage. According to Bev Bevan, "It was a mellow tour, due to the fact that most people were smoking copious amounts of weed."

But there were problems, they lost equipment, there were variable audience reactions. Hendrix one night thrust his guitar into his speaker cabinet where it became lodged. Pink Floyd's Syd Barrett was already showing signs of the problems that would blight his life, disappearing and even missing gigs.

"Everyone used to hang out with everybody else," stated Noel Redding. "We (The Experience) were really close with The Move. Trevor Burton used to travel with us and if I was running late, I'd travel with The Move. So, after the show, we'd all go to pubs, get pissed, then attempt to get on the coach at the time. We would miss the coach and have to get buses and…"

According to Tony Secunda however, Floyd's managers had a reason for taking the package tour. "Basically, they were worried about Syd Barrett but needed to keep the band's name out there. But nobody knew if Barrett was up to it. The general feeling was that he was not."

Syd was departing for another, much farther away touring destination. Although he was on the tour, he wasn't really there. Syd sat with a vacant, hollow look and didn't talk to anyone. Kefford agrees. "Syd never spoke to anyone. He hardly moved sometimes. He was on another planet."

One audience member at the show in Belfast commented, "It was one of the loudest concerts I had ever heard in my life. It was so loud you could literally feel your insides resonating — along with your chair."

At times the bands received cool receptions, with Noel Redding mentioning how terrible the audiences were at times. At the Theatre Royal in Nottingham, Phil Ellis was delighted to see his hero Jimi Hendrix. "I have a number of very strong memories from the night, Stuff like Keith Emerson of The Nice throwing his old Hammond organ around, Trevor Burton walking out and kicking over an amp. Syd Barrett failing to show and The Nice's Davey O'List standing in for him. Andy Fairweather Low in a white suit, going down on his knees to sing 'Gin House' with the totally-out-of-place teenybopper band Amen Corner."

"It was probably the strangest and maybe the best tour I've ever been on," Bev Bevan recalled fondly. "I think we'd stopped smashing up the TVs by then — it wasn't the right venues for that really. We were fans of Hendrix, and Trevor particularly got to know Hendrix very well and went on to share a flat with Noel Redding. I got to know Mitch Mitchell. They were the most extraordinary trio to watch on stage. We used to watch them every night and say, 'You wouldn't want to follow that!'"

"Hendrix was a lovely guy," Bevan said. "On stage he was this absolute animal. But off stage he was very soft-spoken, and whenever a woman would walk into the room, he would stand up and offer his chair. He had lovely manners, and not what you'd expect at all."

Ace and Jimi got on really well: "He come up to me and rough up my Afro hair about and says 'Ace! What's happening man?'. I'd say 'Jimi, I haven't got a fucking clue'. I tried to talk to Syd Barrett, Trevor Burton had the time of his life. "It was insane! Insanity! There was a band coach, but The Move and Jimi Hendrix had their own transport. I travelled mostly with Jimi on that tour because The Move used to go home every night wherever they were because they all had girlfriends. I didn't, so I travelled with Jimi most of the time. It was great. Pretty stoned!" Chris Welch from the *Melody Maker* stated on 25th November 1967, "The Hendrix-Move tour thundered off on its trip round Britain with a deafening start... The Floyd gave one of their colourful and deafening displays of musical pyrotechnics and indeed all the groups were painfully loud... The Eire Apparent practically damaged my hearing system for life; The Nice, my favourite group, blew their cool; the Amen Corner raved like a show band and The Move thundered along in a shower of 'Flowers in the Rain'."

Nick Logan, a writer on the other weekly inkie, the *New Musical Express*, offered this on 18th November 1967: "Hail Jimi Hendrix, the personality, the contortionist, the wise cracker, the exhibitionist. Hail Noel Redding, and Mitch Mitchell, his traumatic Experience. How they were needed to close the package which opened at London's Albert Hall... The bill seemed as if it would never get off the ground. Thank goodness for Hendrix, the untamed and the unchained, swinging down from the trees through Knightsbridge and Kensington. To set the masses on fire in an ectoplasm of sound... Most of all it was Hendrix the showman, the king-size personality. And that was just what the rest of the group tour of first timers lacked — personality... A worthwhile tour for Hendrix fans but let's hope the rest improves a little as it progresses. Between times Jimi Hendrix had managed to get over to the Monterey Pop Festival."

As the concert poster shows, Jimi Hendrix and the Experience and The Move shared top billing, followed by The Pink Floyd, Nice, Amen Corner, and Eire Apparent. On stage, Hendrix got precisely 40 minutes. The Move, who preceded Hendrix, had 30 minutes. This followed by Pink Floyd with only 15 to 20 minutes, which was tight for a band known for their lengthy songs. Tickets cost between 17/6 and 5 shillings.

Pink Floyd's set was made up of one "song", a full-on version of 'Interstellar Overdrive'. Davy O'List thought, "Syd was an amazing guitarist. He really was, as much as Hendrix was in his own right."

Hendrix had three top 10 singles in Britain: 'Hey Joe', 'Purple Haze', and 'The Wind Cries Mary'. The Move also had three hits: 'Night Of Fear', 'I Can Hear The Grass Grow', and 'Flowers In the Rain'. Pink Floyd went top 10 with their single, 'See Emily Play'. Amen Corner scored their biggest hit, 'Bend Me, Shape Me'. Hendrix got most of the attention in the press, but in 1967 all the groups were popular in the UK. Many consider this package, one of the best ever to tour the UK.

Here are the venues played:

14th November	Royal Albert Hall, London
15th November	Winter Gardens, Bournemouth
17th November	City (Oval) Hall, Sheffield
18th November	Empire Theatre, Liverpool
19th November	Coventry Theatre, Coventry
22nd November	Portsmouth Guildhall
23rd November	Sophia Gardens Pavilion, Cardiff
24th November	Colston Hall, Bristol
25th November	Opera House, Blackpool
26th November	Palace Theatre, Manchester
27th November	Whitla Hall, Queen's College, Belfast
1st December	Central Hall, Chatham
2nd December	The Dome, Brighton
3rd December	Theatre Royal, Nottingham
4th December	City Hall, Newcastle
5th December	Green's Playhouse, Glasgow

The logistics of the tour were hampered by Britain's still archaic road systems "This was before they'd finished building most of the motorways as well," Secunda continued. "So, you'd be crawling along two-lane roads, one lane north, one lane south. It was really exhausting."

The show was comprised of two halves with an interval. Newcomers The Outer Limits and Eire Apparent opened with just eight minutes apiece. "But eight minutes was enough," Secunda shrugged. "If you were a new band, and you couldn't prove yourselves in eight minutes, you might as well give up there and then."

The short sets didn't give the bands much time to prove themselves, but it was good promotion, as Secunda later recalled: "The idea was to cram as many bands on to the bill as possible, not simply because it made financial sense, but also because it gave massive exposure to bands who might never get out there."

"The whole thing was that time of 'peace, love and brown rice, man' and all that stuff," recalled Bev Bevan. "A lot of the guys were getting stoned. It was a very peaceful tour."

"Everybody was mucking about," recalled The Nice's Keith Emerson. "It was like a huge school trip." A "school trip" with knife-throwing, instrument smashing and acid-related breakdowns, that is.

Compering the shows and artists was BBC Radio One DJ Pete Drummond. Like many of the 'pop' DJs of the time, he enjoyed a secondary income from playing records and introducing artists at festivals, all-nighters and tours such as this. With so many changeovers, Drummond was left to fill-in between bands. "I had to stand there and say: 'It'll be a few minutes before the next band... And being here in Glasgow reminds me of the Scotsman who...' and just go into some joke. Nine times out of ten they'd just shout out 'fuck off.' It was no ego boost for me. Hendrix used to say: 'Did you hear me tonight? I was out the back yelling 'fuck off' early on! 'Yeah, I heard you, Jimi'."

"It was a showcase for bands riding on Jimi Hendrix," Drummond said. "I think he got half the gate and everybody else was on fixed fees. I think Noel Redding and Mitch Mitchell were salaried. I was on £25 a night and apart from Hendrix, I had more money than anybody. Even though The Floyd were second headliners on this tour they weren't earning money. I had to buy food for bands, like curry and chips for the Amen Corner when we hit Cardiff. I think the Floyd earned about £20 between them per day, so they weren't that badly off."

A young fan remembered the excitement: "A whole crowd of us went there by train. The Move were sensational — it was during the EP *Something Else From The Move* period. I don't remember what Amen Corner or Eire Apparent were like. Hendrix blew them all away. He was very charismatic, and kept giggling and pointing at Noel Redding, saying, 'look at his hair.' It was the only time I ever saw him. It was ear-splittingly loud, and I was near the front."

It would have been difficult not to have been aware of The Move back in the autumn of 1967. Secunda made damn sure The Move were in the news at every possible opportunity. The Move's troubles were being compounded by the fact that they had their own version of Syd Barrett in the band in the shape of Ace Kefford. His increasing spates of crippling depression, aided by his LSD intake began to blight his life, and he never fully recovered. It was like Ace, Trevor and the ongoing great, acid test... As Ace frankly put it, "My head had gone..."

That aside, there was much at stake. A friendly rivalry co-existed between the Jimi Hendrix Experience and The Move, and it's hard to say who was most likely to upstage who at this point in the billing. Hendrix had the passion, but The Move had scored three top 10 hits up against Hendrix's three. This often resulted in the usual practical jokes that touring bands are prone to playing on each other, partly to relieve the boredom of touring.

"I remember The Move playing once, and I rode a bicycle across the stage," Noel Redding recalled. "Another time we put stink bombs in Bev Bevan's bass drum pedal."

"The Move were very funny," Dave Robinson, Eire Apparent's road manager recalled. "I remember a situation at soundcheck and overhearing Carl Wayne. He'd turned up late to the soundcheck because he'd been having his venereal warts removed!"

The Move found a spiritual home on that legendary package tour of 1967. They also had one other trick up their sleeve: the anarchistic stage antics of Carl Wayne. At one particularly memorable show at the end of the previous year, they shared the

I see rainbows in the evening...

billing with Pink Floyd and The Who.

In later years, with both Jimi and Barrett long since absent from the scene, British journalists pondered the thought of how these two geniuses of the guitar might have related to one another. In a 1974 edition of the *New Musical Express*, journalist Nick Kent asked Floyd's manager Peter Jenner, "Surely the two uncrowned kings of rock, Hendrix and Barrett, must have socialised in some manner? "Not really," replied Jenner. "Syd didn't talk to anyone."

"The Floyd didn't mix at all, with anybody," agreed Trevor Burton. "They were all like arty student types and we were fucking hardened rockers, you know, and they kept themselves to themselves. Noel and me quite often would go into their dressing rooms and try and communicate, but it didn't work very often."

"They weren't inclined to socialise," confirmed Keith Emerson. "I do recall one moment on the tour of overhearing Roger Waters ask the rest of the band: 'Well, when is it your turn in the studio?' And I asked Roger: 'What? You don't all go in the studio together?' And he said: "Oh, no, no, no! If we go in separately, it avoids all the arguments." Syd Barrett's time in Pink Floyd was all but over by the conclusion of the tour. He was replaced by David Gilmour in early 1968.

By November of course, it was difficult to say whose act was the most outrageous, and as the tour wound on, most observers agree that the two bands emerging with honours came out an even top number! In terms of straightforward crowd pleasers, The Move might have inched just ahead: short, sharp and to the point. A travelling white-hot jukebox, blasting out the hits. It was difficult to argue with any live set which included 'Night Of Fear', 'I Can Hear The Grass Grow', 'Cherry Blossom Clinic' and 'Flowers In The Rain'. But for sheer pyrotechnic elan, The Experience were unstoppable.

Tony Secunda remembered some of the weirder aspects of 1967 and the 'Flowers In The Rain' case, "Around when the lawsuit got started, the government put all these guys in shades, driving big black limousines on our case. We'd come out of a show and there would be this big limo parked across the road. It'd follow us to the greasy spoon to the next gig, wherever we went. Hendrix was doing his nut, because he thought it was the FBI or the CIA or someone, coming after him. It was really bizarre, we'd say, 'Jimi, why would they be after you?' We were thinking maybe they wanted to send him to Vietnam, maybe this, maybe that, and he'd just go, 'No, you don't understand, they're spooks, it's the secret service, they want to know what I know,' like there was some huge conspiracy he was involved in — UFOs and alien earwigs in the White House. So, he spun this out for hours, and then he finally cracked up, 'Hahahaha!! Man, you guys are so gullible'."

Two nights later, bands and media alike, descended upon the Belfast venue to join in with Jimi's 25th birthday celebrations. Everywhere this musical travelling circus went, the local press turned out in force, to catch "the wildman of rock" in full, fiery swing. Jimi seldom disappointed them.

"The thing about Hendrix on that tour," Tony Secunda recalled, "was that he hadn't bought into his own legend yet. He still felt he had something to prove. Later, he could complain, that it didn't matter what he did. Or how badly he screwed up, the audience would always applaud. And that got to him, of course it did. But when he toured with us, he knew he had to pull out all the stops and that there wasn't any room for mistakes. The Move would have eaten him alive otherwise."

Plus, Bev's view as well, "we didn't want to follow Jimi. But he didn't want to follow us either, for that matter. So, we got round that by… We closed the first half, gave the audience time in the interval, to get over seeing our set. And then Jimi closed the second half."

Roy Wood has a treasured memory of the two bands' friendship: "The best thing I ever heard was Jimi Hendrix play 'I Can Hear The Grass Grow' after a rehearsal once."

The master's rendition of The Move's second hit single, Wood averred, "was brilliant." 'You Got Me Floatin'' opens with swirling backwards guitar solo. It opens the second side of the second album release by Hendrix, *Axis: Bold As Love*. Roy Wood and Trevor Burton supplied backing vocals.

According to Roy Wood, "Me and Trevor Burton were in the studio next door while the song was being recorded. Noel Redding came by and asked us if we would like to sing on it."

Trevor Burton: "Noel and Mitch weren't cutting the background vocals too good. So, we asked Jimi, 'Do you want us to have a go?' He said, 'Yeah!' I think we did it in just two takes. Jimi was pleased with it. He sang his lead vocals live at the same time, while we put down the background vocals."

20.
This crappy west coast hippie scene is becoming quite a drag

The Move also had time to fly over to Sweden to play at the Konserthuset in Stockholm, Sweden on 15th December 1967. Apart from the live official EP and album (*Something Else From The Move* and *Live At The Fillmore 1969*), there is not a lot else, even in relation to bootlegs. Although there are a fair amount of live versions out now due to the remastered CDs. One bootleg that has done the rounds for a few years is this Swedish gig at the end of 1967.

The first song, 'Watch Your Step' was actually the set's closer, used as a vehicle in which they initiate some torrid axing and fire play. The recording starts mid-song, and it fades out before the song ends. It actually originates from an undated 1966 concert in the Netherlands, partially shown on TV there. The audio of the band is untrammelled. The video is allied to some nutty earlier interview footage, and it is all sublime.

Carl axes a TV onstage and sets part of the stage on fire! As already noted, this was just a normal night in a Move show. The next three songs come from the German TV show *Beat! Beat! Beat!*. This is well known live footage and with reasonable sound. After, and from the fourth song onwards, these are taken from the Konserthuset gig with some muffled Carl Wayne speech between numbers. One is specifically about "Harold Wilson; our beloved Prime Minister." It features a tantalising cover of 'Why' by The Byrds that the band never recorded or dropped to tape at the BBC. Unfortunately, some bleed and muffle spoil yet another great cover version by the band. That is one live Move version that I would like to hear in a good clear remaster.

A big pre-Christmas 'Christmas On Earth' pop party was planned for 22nd December 1967 at the Olympia Exhibition Hall in London. An all day and night event with The Jimi Hendrix Experience, The Move plus The Who, Keith West, Pink Floyd, Traffic, Soft Machine, Tomorrow and Eric Burdon & The New Animals. DJ John Paul was on hand to compere. The entire thing was professionally filmed, and the film footage is thought to be lost or buried deep underground somewhere. It was one of Syd Barrett's last gigs with Pink Floyd. The Move, as usual played an absolute blinder! Trouble was it was held at Olympia which is a huge, cold exhibition hall. Not conducive to good vibes at all. Many people have never ever heard of this gig, even though the absolute cream of British rock was in attendance. That's because it was badly publicised, combined with the freezing cold weather — meant few turned up!

Top Of The Pops was a one hour BBC Radio music program hosted weekly by Brian Matthew. It featured copious selections from recording sessions at the BBC Studios, assembled for syndication/export outside the UK. Rounding out 1967, The Move appeared on the show on an episode recorded on 29th December. They performed a cooking cover of the Moby Grape song 'Hey Grandma'.

Chris Dolmetsch, a young American in London, was enjoying his young life in the city: "I really enjoyed their music but while I was enthusiastic. I was aware at the time there were many, many groups — all competing for attention in a very crowded field. The last show I saw had Bluesology as the opening act for The Move. They had a young Reg Dwight (later Elton John) on keyboards and my recollection was that he looked awfully young, and his glasses somehow reminded me of Manfred Mann, who also wore glasses at the keyboard. The one Move original I do remember hearing at one of the gigs was 'Walk Upon the Water' which ended with a rousing cheer from the audience. For some reason, it led me to believe The Move specialised in humour and craziness in their performances. One song they sang was 'Too Many Fish In The Sea' (A rousing cover from The Marvelettes on Tamla Motown). I never thought at that time, that 60 years later, I would be trying to recall shows that I took for just regular club performances back then."

Ace's position in the group was to hit another rocky spot: "I was going to be chucked out of the group, six months ago, which nobody knew about. We patched it up and there was a better atmosphere, and everything was great. Then it came back again." Was this caused by the mixture of petty jealousies and rivalries towards Ace, and amongst themselves, Roy and Carl arguing, sometimes Trevor and Ace and later between Trevor and Bev? Or indeed Ace's overuse of most drugs, including the pretty much unknown and uncharted regions incurred by using LSD on a regular basis?

Ace also commented on his diminishing role: "Two years ago, we were doing Tamla-type music. I used to sing the majority of the numbers. In the last few weeks together, I wasn't singing anything. I had one number and even that has got cut out, which I wasn't too pleased about."

Bev adds, "We weren't sympathetic towards Ace really. Trevor and Ace had changed with all the drugs, and we'd lost them then really. They were almost like… they always seemed to be together. They were always getting stoned together. So, they kind of looked… I actually told them once, that they had a real arrogance against me. With all of the stupid stoned smiles." The two former Mods in the band. But now definitely gone wrong — way, way out wrong!

Bev also sensed that "Carl could feel like an outsider too. But in a different way to Ace and Trevor. He always looked at the business side of things. But he seemed to be always looking for other opportunities to feather his personal nest. I've got on well with Carl and I particularly got on well with Roy. I struggled a bit with Ace and Trevor mainly because they got so out of it. I think they looked down on us. Because we didn't do drugs and it was like, we've seen magic things man and you haven't."

As one ill-informed and flaky American critic observed, Ace has been described as "only there for visual purposes." Ace and Trevor, were The Move's beating Mod heart. They were its dynamic front line, along with Carl Wayne. Ace has been described as "only there for visual purposes." He seems to have been given short

This crappy west coast hippie scene is becoming quite a drag

shrift over the years. As if the only talent he had was ice blond hair and a distinctive, good looking, sculpted face. Sure; he had good looks in abundance. Possible jealousy on the part of the critic? It isn't a bad thing to be a frontline face in a charting band. After Ace, with his funky dance moves, onstage chemistry and huge, loudly effective bass lines, plus his unique voice, had left The Move, they never recovered.

The loss of Tony Secunda too, allowed a season of career floundering to follow! Essentially, The Move became a showcase for Roy Wood songs, some of which are absolutely brilliant. In the music business, money talks and bullshit walks, as we all know.

However, the pure, elemental rock and soul, unique energy The Move had did not come from Roy Wood. It came from Ace, Trevor, Bev, Carl and Roy. If you take one piece of the jigsaw puzzle out this unique chemistry will start to fall apart. They never again captured, the intense sweep and immense, hard groove they had. Maybe Ace was a simpler musician and Trevor Burton had more technique on bass. But so, what. Is that what music is all about? Music is not just about musical "chops." It is not just about how good you can play technically. Or, about how good you are. Or how many notes you can play. That is what led to the horrendous excesses, of some so-called progressive rock like Yes and Genesis (more public school, musically overblown wash). Lots of overly clever, musical chops, tons of 'Bill Brufordy' time signatures and all the rest of it. I am in no way knocking Bill Bruford, a fine, extremely accomplished drummer!

There is room for people who have a very high technical ability and skill set. I read Bill's book and even Bill appeared to suggest that he could not attain the musical heights he wanted to. But isn't enjoying your craft and skill, the very main thing? One funny line in Bill's book is one that many artists and musicians will relate to. From time to time at polite dinner parties, someone will ask Bill what he does. He replies that he is a musician. "Yes, but what do you really do?" retorts the silly bollocks enquirer.

This incomparably, utterly feckless, bullshit response has been uttered by multitudes of truly square individuals. It has been heard by musicians and artists the world over throughout the years. From plum heads who think listening to Queen is akin to listening to avant-garde jazz. This whole area of self-indulgent, ego-driven, 'prog' pomposity can also be applied to the later 'jazz fusion' stuff, which swiftly managed to disappear up its own, over sodden arse — with a gigantic, musical notes, saturated sweep. Go faster, play more and more, especially more lightning solos! Make it all utterly, oleaginous, precious and eventually totally unlistenable. I tried to listen to some Mahavishnu Orchestra again recently. Although, you can marvel at the lightning speed of Billy Cobham and John McLaughlin etc. My brain and soul didn't connect to it — it's incredibly intense. My brain was thinking, 'I need some space between the notes.' It was all far too clever for its own good.

There were two or three times prior, that Ace was going to leave. Tony Secunda said, "You can't leave, Ace, because the band will fall apart… If I take one element out now, it's all going to fall apart."

Secunda was uttering, some very fateful words. He must have known that genuinely unique, inter-band chemistry is very few and far between. Rarely is there a time when this chemistry can be in any way replicated just by simply adding a "competent" vocalist and / or musician.

Ace remembers some of the lack of interest, when trying to introduce some of his material to the group. "I remember once. I wanted to play them a song on acoustic guitar, in the dressing room. We were somewhere in Scotland. I'm playing the song (it might have been 'William Chalkers') and when I looked up they had all fucked off! (laughs)."

21.
The lights across the street, threw a rainbow in her hair

The *Melody Maker* reported on the alleged myriad complaints about The Move's highly controversial stage act. In fact, and more definably, Carl Wayne and his microphone stand aspect, of the stage act. As Carl responded to questions aimed at him, he reacted. "Is our stage act sexy? It's disgusting! There's no doubt about it, it's vulgar and obscene! If I was a father, I wouldn't let my daughter see it. The sexy bit comes from the positioning of the mic stand," explained the culprit: "It causes scenes among the kids in the front rows and that's why I do it. They're almost obsessed with it. If fathers and mothers are concerned, they should take their daughters away, because I don't give a fuck about them."

Despite universal dislike of the group by the older generation, including parents, churchmen, and a considerable number of politicians, The Move proved 'bad taste' is a good commercial position. They kept on making excellent, entertaining hits like 'Fire Brigade'. "We're knocked out with the record," said Carl, "extremely pleased with the way it has gone. It's sold 30,000 already. It's the most commercial number we've written. We're very self-critical and haven't got much faith in ourselves as a group. But the song is great and I'm pleased for Roy Wood's sake, because he wrote it. I firmly believe 1968 is going to be Roy's year. We have our first LP out in two weeks' time. But we're a very happy group now. We've never seen eye to eye with each other — because there are five singers in the group and that causes arguments about what to sing and what not to. As a matter of fact, for a change Roy sings lead on 'Fire Brigade'. We would like Bev Bevan to sing on our next single — he's got a voice like Paul Robeson."

'Fire Brigade' was released as the group's fourth single in Britain in February 1968. It reached number three in the UK singles chart. A cover version was recorded by The Fortunes and released as a single in the US but did not chart. According to Wood, he wrote the song in a single overnight session. This, after Secunda told the band, who had just finished playing a concert, that he had a studio session lined up for the next morning. He needed them to record a single straight away. Since Wood did not have any songs ready, or ones he thought of as immediate singles, the rest of the band left him alone that night at The Madison Hotel in London to write one.

Roy Wood: "Tony Secunda was always full of surprises. We'd played a gig in London, and we went back to the hotel and Carl Wayne came up to me and said,

'We've just been told that we're in the studio tomorrow and we've got to record a single! Have you got one? (laughs)'. I said, 'Well not on me. Not at the moment'."

Specifically, Carl Wayne gave him a bottle of whisky, grabbed Roy and got him into the hotel room with the explicit instructions to write a hit record for the morning. Can you imagine this scenario? Talk about not being under the most, intense pressure!

"Carl produced the bottle of Scotch out of his pocket. He gave me the key to one of the hotel rooms. In those days we used to always double up. We used to share, because we couldn't really afford single rooms. It was the first time I had ever had my own room in a hotel. He produced the key and the bottle of Scotch and said, 'Get on with it' (laughs). The other guys went out for a drink, before the pubs closed. It must have been about 11 o'clock at night. I stayed there in the hotel, and I just wrote all the way through the night. Then at about 8:30 in the morning the band came in and I played it to them. That was 'Fire Brigade' and they just sang along with it and said, 'Great, let's go and do it' (laughs). They had to sort of hold me upright, to do the session."

Wood would not only manage to write a supremely worthy successor to 'Flowers In the Rain', itself a glorious pop song by anybody standards, but he came up with an immediately commercial, semi-pastiche of rock 'n' roll, with an entirely unique and different edge. The subject matter, although centering around an unnamed girl, is softer, more surreal and sly. But allied to a tightly wrought band, musical performance. The song rocks along for two minutes and 20 seconds of perfect power pop. It's a truly well rounded, beautiful piece of pop music with Roy's penchant for lyrics that were both whimsical and childlike.

A superb middle eight features a sultry vocal from Carl Wayne. The massed harmony vocals from the band, give this song an aural feeling of warmth. Behind Roy's lead vocal and Carl's main vocal on the middle eight, plus the defined, pronounced 'oooh!' from Carl Wayne, just give the song a little bit of sex! In those days in 1968, Carl Wayne's punctuated 'oooh!' sounded seaside postcard cheeky but also deliberately sexual.

By the time 'Fire Brigade' was released, the charismatic Ace "The Face" Christopher Kefford was gone. *Move* became the only album by the group to chart, reaching the UK album charts to number 15.

The album was the only release to feature the charismatic, fated bassist. Ace left (and was simultaneously pushed) the group in late March 1968. After the preceding package tour with Jimi Hendrix Experience etc. There is a famous and iconic *Top Of The Pop*s appearance of 'Fire Brigade', which still survives. Apparently the BBC's library stock of back tapes have seen many wiped. But this one thankfully survives.

The original five-piece Move in black-and-white look absolutely fantastic. After DJ Dave Cash's intro they storm through the record. Ace's last appearance on *Top of the Pops*. Nothing appears amiss in the TV appearance, with both Ace and Trevor throwing shapes. They are laughing, smiling and the entire band, seems to have a ball, playing that brilliant single. Ace regretted doing drugs, stating "Me and Trevor Burton did loads of acid... But it screwed up my life man. Devastated me completely."

'Flowers In The Rain' had been a commercial success. 'Fire Brigade' similarly jumped out of the speakers of your transistor radio. Another fabulous 45rpm ear

The lights across the street, threw a rainbow in her hair

worm from the pen of Roy Wood. The twanging intro sounding like big Duane Eddy style, 1950s open-bodied guitars that were double tracked. Followed by a mighty Bev Bevan echoed 'flam' on the drums. Ace and Bev supply a superbly fat bass and drums backing. All through this joyous slice of pop history. 'Fire Brigade' was an immediate smash.

Sessions for 'Fire Brigade' began on 16th November 1967 at Olympic Studios in Barnes, London. The 4CD *Anthology 1966-1972* has both the single version plus an early, previously unreleased version, with Matthew Fisher (from Procol Harum) on piano.

An earlier retrospective release, the 3CD *Movements 30th Anniversary Anthology* from 1997 also had two slightly different recordings — the final version and an un-dubbed version, before the backing vocals were added and the tambourine and opening 'fire engine' sound effects were added.

There is also another demo version where Carl Wayne takes the lead vocal. But the actual release was the one! This song really suited the higher register in Roy's voice. These A and B sides were recorded at De Lane Lea Studios in London in December 1967. It was the second Move single released on the Regal Zonophone label through EMI. The record shipped out to retailers on 26th January 1968. The B-side 'Walk Upon The Water', another Roy Wood composition, was sung mostly by Trevor and Carl. This was another great composition from Wood and like The Beatles, The Move's B-sides are at the very least, really interesting. And at the best, they could vie for top billing on the A-side. This has a slightly woozy feel and is an admonition to avoid mixing drinking and driving. It sounds like Trevor is holding his nose, as he sings the middle eight. *"Three small bodies swept up by the morning tide, Now their souls are washed up, Faith destroyed their minds."*

It's probably a clever phasing effect used by Cordell and Chevin in the studio. Roy comes in with another one of his clever two liners, *"Better get the life inspector. Bring along his mind erector."* Followed by one of Bev Bevan's amazingly raucous rolls around the drum kit. Roy Wood supposedly had written 'Walk Upon The Water' as a follow-up single.

I don't think it is anywhere near as commercial as 'Fire Brigade'. Neither did Denny Cordell or Tony Secunda. Roy Wood remembers writing the song: "I think I wrote that as a follow-up to 'I Can Hear The Grass Grow'. I think it would have been a good one. But they decided not to use it and put it on the B-side of 'Fire Brigade'. I thought it would have made a good single but obviously they didn't."

I think level heads prevailed, in this instance, Roy. (Although Roy's earlier suggestion to release 'Disturbance' as the first Move A-side is, all at once, intriguing, alarming and downright hilarious). I would've loved to have seen the public reaction to 'Disturbance' if and when that was released. Mucho hysterical I would imagine — it is a true aural shocker.

As I've been listening through all The Move remasters, I remember getting a lump in my throat. On listening to the 'Fire Brigade' *(instrumental)* version on the 'Flowers In The Rain' CD single, released through Fly / Salvo in 2007, this remixed stereo version omits the lead vocals by Roy and Carl Wayne. But retains the beautiful, warm harmony sound of the four-man vocal team. With the added four-man harmonised attempt at a fire engine alarm system and the big Duane Eddy, open-bodied guitar sound, tight unison bass and drums. It's completely original, eccentric — it rocks along with the added pop power of The Move's unique harmony vocals. The song is a homage to, but a very Move-esque tribute to retro-rock. The *NME* reported at the time that 'Fire Brigade' had been banned in some Australian and American cities as "too suggestive".

Carl Wayne said he "didn't wanna sing it" although the fact that the axing performances had been curtailed may have prompted the extrovert, out-going front man to begin feeling somewhat bereft and under used.

Bev Bevan noticed the often-outrageous remarks made by Carl Wayne. His remarks had a tendency to change from interview to interview. It could be around this time that the schism bubbling between Roy Wood and Carl started to become more obvious and apparent, certainly in interview terms. With Carl coming out with various comments about Roy's appearance and his writing ability.

George Best, the fabulous footballer, still on top of his game, loved 'Fire Brigade': "I think this is the best single to date, but make no mistake, they will become better still. They are going to last a long time. Right now, I'm patiently waiting for the next LP."

Yet another delay was reported in the *Melody Maker* in late February 1968 concerning the debut album. It had been put back by two weeks because of technical problems, involving a five-colour process for the album cover. The short feature also reported, "They will record a 'live' EP at London's Marquee Club on 27th February and are appearing on BBC TV's *Top Of The Pops* today (Thursday) and *The Simon Dee Show* (Saturday)."

Bev commented, "Carl would often say that Roy was a brilliant songwriter and the best writer there is. Then in another interview say that Roy couldn't write a song to save his life." Bev opined that Carl had the most amazing voice, but Roy was not writing songs for that voice. Or indeed, songs that showcased or projected Carl's voice. Resentment began to fizz and rankle again in The Move.

The fact that Carl and Roy's relationship went right back to that Birmingham corner shop: it gave them both a familiarity and a continuity. But also, a complex differing of personalities. Offstage Roy tended to be very shy and dreamlike. "At times I'm not always organised." Whereas Carl Wayne was incredibly controlling and always had to organise things of a business nature, to an almost obsessive degree at times.

Bev appreciated Carl's strong input, "You see, Carl was very much the businessperson in the band as well. He wasn't the leader musically. But he was very good at balancing the books and all that. When Carl left the band, it was basically just me and Roy (and) Jeff by then. And Rick Price! Yeah, and he was called a newcomer. None of them, particularly Roy or Jeff, were remotely capable, or even interested in doing the books and stuff."

There was one aspect of Carl's organised behaviour, when it came to light, that pissed the band off. Bev says, "We didn't see the band accountant Alan Thompson. Carl said, 'I'm going to take over this day-to-day expenses and costs stuff'. And we said, 'Oh yeah okay that's fine.' We thought he was taking 2%. But Carl was taking 5% off the top, for doing the accounts."

In terms of getting another musician into the now four-man Move, it went like this: "Knowing us, because really, we were quite tight-fisted Brummies really, it didn't take us long to figure out that splitting the money four ways was a lot better than dividing it up into five ways. I think that's the main reason, that we didn't actually replace Ace for a fifth player."

Flowers In The Rain - The Untold Story of The Move

22.
Move! Move! Move!

The Move's much anticipated debut album was finally released on 1st April 1968. Another wind-up from Tony Secunda was a spoken introduction from Marlon Brando over a Roy Wood instrumental. Unfortunately, it never happened. It was reported in the press that Secunda and The Move had asked Brando to appear on their new LP.

The *Move* LP was put together over a period of fourteen months from October 1966 to February 1968. A long span of time in pop music, but it was an eternity in the mid-60s. Styles and sounds were changing monthly. The Move had released (four brilliant) singles during this time. So, they weren't absent from the scene. They appeared to be set upon a course of cutting singles, quickly and concisely. But this when their peers were crafting album-length epics. Was this something that separated them from the pack? Maybe giving them a 'pop band' sheen — good for publicity, but very confining for a band with this amount of power and versatility. Certain tracks on the EP would capture the other side of The Move that record buyers were not hearing. There was some snobbery, about singles versus albums. Although it didn't occur to the 'snotty' hippies, that singles are a very good way to promote your record and increase and boost album sales.

Over that fourteen-month period, apart from doing tons of photo shoots, magazine inserts and gigging furiously around the country, they managed to record enough material for this album. It's been said that the record is a patchwork. Some people thought because there were four singers on the record, that was somehow confusing. I don't agree. The Beatles also had four singers, although one of them (Ringo) was used once, on one song on each album and that was never a problem.

Comments were levelled that there were too many different styles on the record. 'Zing Went The Strings Of My Heart' could be considered an odd musical interloper. But not, if seen in the context of its affectionate inclusion in The Move's live set. Getting Bev upfront onstage, to flex his deep sonorous vocals. Again, it was an unusual and non-cliqued cover (from The Coasters) which they did very well. These were needed to bolster the lack of material from Roy, but were also genuinely viable, due to their easy skill, in reworking great cover versions.

And so, to the album and to some of its mixed reactions. The Move debut album sounded unique and still sounds unusual, in a most unusual year. Ping-ponging between punchy, tight, restless, kaleidoscopic pop and funky nods to early rock 'n' roll. Punctuated by the occasional forays into a pastoral English countryside idyll, with these two tunes, 'Kilroy Was Here' and 'Mist On A Monday Morning'.

Flowers In The Rain - The Untold Story of The Move

The album's closer on side two was 'Cherry Blossom Clinic' the proposed fourth single. With lyrics that could be ascribed to Roy Wood and his presumed dropping of acid, *"Suddenly from flowered skies, Twenty thousand butterflies... Glorify my bed in deep maroon, Turn from hot to very cool, Though it seems incredible, I could ride a bike around the moon."* Another of Roy's lyrical examinations of a mind, falling out of kilter and having to be confined, "owing to my state of mind."

Roy adds some details about the song's formation: "'Cherry Blossom Clinic' was about a nuthouse, basically, but a nice one. That was one of my early songs. When I left art-school it was one of my ambitions to write a children's book for adults. Fairy stories with strange twists in them. I had a lot of ideas written down and I used them in my songs."

'Cherry Blossom Clinic' tells the story of a man slipping into madness and hallucinating in his clinic room. It possibly refers to some form of ill treatment towards our protagonist in this psychiatric hospital, that the narrator is restrained to his bed. Roy weaves in a reference to Lewis Carroll's *Alice in Wonderland*. One line, *"Up above the sun is high - Like a tea tray in the sky,"* is a direct reference to / from the book.

Move divulged a lot of styles. A collection sounding just as eccentric and distinctive on the aforementioned oldies covers, (for example their version of Moby Grape's 'Hey Grandma') as they do on the offbeat originals. Roy Wood's originals ranging from the melancholy 'Kilroy Was Here' to the potty young lady. Who is so charmingly described in the freaky beat of '(Here We Go Round) The Lemon Tree' with lyrics such as, *"There's a girl next door to me, who's round the bend. But she wonders, why she can't make any friends."*

On 'Mist On A Monday Morning', these sweet and insightful words, describe a sozzled, travelling gentleman traversing the roads. He is looking back at his life, through a personal haze of bittersweet, alcohol-tinged memories: *"Drink and drink all day, till my memory melts away. I need a friend like Mist on a Monday morning."* They add a poignant but effulgent respite with its sweeping strings also arranged here by Tony Visconti. The glorious punchy, power pop chart busters 'Fire Brigade' and 'Flowers In The Rain', firming up a record, that gives *Move* its heady rush of melody and tangible sonic textures.

This is vivid, imaginative music — there are so many ideas in evidence here. I personally would've loved to have seen another record or EP — expanding some of the unique tunes, penned by the rapidly developing Roy, intertwined with the super competent, execution of this band. Unceasingly honed, on the road by relentless gigging. Nevertheless, this art-pop album is brimming with ideas.

It's peppered with other influences: The burgeoning UK psychedelia, soul, pop and rock elements. First, there's that lead singer conundrum. Such ever-changing leads can lend excitement. But it can also lead to confusion. Especially when the group enthusiastically mixes up Who-inspired art pop with three-chord rock 'n' roll oldies and some unique, whimsical British eccentricity.

Was the hype and the wait worth it? The Move's first and only studio recording of the original five-piece group apart from the *Something Else From The Move* EP, released to show the unrestrained, feral fire of the band. This was the other side of The Move that record buyers were not hearing. Only the lucky people that attended

Move! Move! Move!

their gigs.

Roy Wood's songs made good use of the four front men vocally. At any given time, people come in, doubled with each other or laying down four-part layers. Roy developed a style of an almost 'madrigal' type harmony singing, which would become much more evident on the second album *Shazam* and on singles like 'Omnibus'. A kind of mediaeval-sounding close harmony. On the first album, unison harmony vocal parts, are also used to great effect.

The opener is the rollicking 'Yellow Rainbow'. It starts with a glorious phasing effect, introducing the listener to this up-tempo stormer. Featuring thundering rolls, played on the tom toms (which sound detuned — slackened off on the drumheads, to give a more metallic, machine-like feel) from Bevan.

Led by a rousing lead vocal by Ace Kefford who sits back on the vocals here, using a more inflected, deliberation like, *"Fear our hope's about to be, Buried in 'obsurrrrrity"* but avoiding any vocal overkill. The harmonising is incredibly film-theme like. 'Yellow Rainbow' has a glorious phasing effect — introducing the listener to an up-tempo stormer. The production adds a sense of atmospheric heightened space to this sci-fi tale of impending nuclear doom for this world. *'Serpent's tongue from blackened cloud — Sometimes seems to speak out loud — Icy brew of winds prevailing — From the cauldrons of the storm"*

The middle eight has a sensational and heightened vocal feel. Roy's higher vocal joins Ace and the others in surprising unison. Three and four harmony vocal parts are used to great effect, *"I can take the atmosphere and chase it down... Overactive mind, works like an underground."* A totally original sound which boosts the frenetic song even more. The whole song is punctuated by *Danger Man / James Bond* style guitar patterns. Jagged edged, played in unison by lead rhythm and bass. All, creating an anxious, thematic feeling underpinning the piece. A refreshing and unique album opener.

Bev Bevan recalled the work rate, "The thing is, Roy wrote really great songs, but he wrote extremely slowly too. He was always working on the next single and invariably he would get it pretty much spot on! But he was not prolific by any means."

Their ability to rework great cover versions helped with the slower songwriting progress. The album has two other great covers on it. A rousing 'Hey Grandma' by the ill-fated and fabled Moby Grape and a bopping 'Weekend' from Eddie Cochran. The production on 'Weekend' is a little muffled and gives it a slightly sugary feel. If compared with the live version of the *Something Else From The Move* EP that was to come. Particularly 'Something Else' by Eddie Cochran, which showed Trevor Burton and his raw vocals in full anarchic effect.

In contrast there was 'The Girl Outside', another Trevor Burton vocal. Trevor was rife with a cold, and he needed a bottle of brandy to get through the (two) recorded takes of this delicate, pretty song. 'Mist On A Monday Morning' is elegiac, mournful, with a deft arrangement by Tony Visconti. Both the *Move* remastered CDs feature the unreleased 'Vote For Me' song. It's impossible to imagine how infuriatingly snobby, these middle-class hippies were. Forerunners of the current social justice warriors that everyone has to deal with at present. Back then it was overblown, university students with their dodgy, macrobiotic, brown rice ideas. These essentially 'square" (but thinking that they are hip) "hippie heads" are dealt with lyrically and firmly in the proposed B-side follow-up for 'Flowers In The Rain.'

'Vote For Me' is an electrifying full-on rant about hippies, coupled with an exhilarating performance. Featuring the immortally funny Roy Wood penned lines, *"This crappy West Coast hippie scene, is becoming quite a drag. It seems that all my freaky clothes, are turning into rags."* This song was recorded in two different studio takes. One with Roy's dynamic, stabbing wah-wah guitar intro and the other without. They're both adorned, with a raucous and fittingly raw Trevor Burton vocal.

The Move debut sounds unique, and the 1968 album still sounds unusual. Ranging between punchy, tight restless kaleidoscopic pop and funky nods to early rock 'n' roll. It is punctuated by forays into a more bucolic, pastoral world of English countryside. Songs such as 'Kilroy Was Here' and 'Mist On A Monday Morning.' "We were a lot wilder before Roy started to write the songs" is Trevor Burton's opinion. 'Kilroy Was Here' was described by Wood as, "an electronic opera, in the ninth dimension" to DJ Alan Freeman in the middle of 1967.

The album closer was the climactic 'Cherry Blossom Clinic', the proposed fourth single after 'Flowers In The Rain'. However, Kefford made a contrasting statement, saying that 'Cherry Blossom Clinic' was a cancelled single release. Due to Roy Wood coming up with 'Fire Brigade' which the band thought was a superior single. 'Cherry Blossom Clinic' had lyrics that could be (again) ascribed to Roy Wood's use of psychedelics. Another of Roy's lyrical examinations of a mind, falling out of kilter and having to be confined, *"Owing to my state of mind."*

Tony Visconti's arrangement supplies glorious, surreal, shimmering strings. Swooping and plucking. Just after *"helicopter lands upon my bed"* they stab in a unison attack that is just utterly thrilling. To my ears, as brilliant as anything George Martin had arranged with The Beatles. At the end the strings just sound like they're taking off (or indeed possibly landing) just like a colossal, vertiginous helicopter. You could possibly describe 'Cherry Blossom Clinic' as in the mood of 'A Day In The Life'. Tony Visconti's exuberant and thrilling strings, certainly adding a grandiose, climatic flourish to the tune.

Visconti also added strings to 'Mist On A Monday Morning' and 'The Girl Outside' and they ended up sounding like mini pop-overtures. Visconti was now friendly with and admired by the group, particularly Roy Wood. "After I proved myself with 'Flowers In The Rain', it became a '*thing*' to associate The Move with a bit of orchestral arrangements. In other words, I got the job. They were mini overtures. I wrote them on a small dining room table in my cold flat in Maida Vale. It was so exciting to conduct them — my first big arrangements since I arrived in London with lots of trained musicians and with The Move looking on. I gained lots of trust from Roy as a result. Roy thought I was a pianist and offered me the job as his keyboard player in his (later band) Wizzard. I had to turn it down, because I arranged on classical guitar at the time. Until this day I can't play piano well."

Right from the bat, the '1812' theme in 'Night Of Fear' demonstrated the classical influences in Roy's tunes. Later on, Roy insisted, "There were tracks on the first Move album, like 'Cherry Blossom Clinic,' that I felt needed more than just the guitars and drums. I used to discuss what I wanted with Tony Visconti and he'd write all the orchestra parts out. When I heard them played, I thought. Brilliant! This is what I want to do — even though the orchestra musicians were all a bit stuffed shirt about it."

Tony Visconti also had room to experiment in those more freewheeling days. There were rules but they could be broken. They could be stretched, to try out new techniques in the studio. Or at least, Visconti persuaded Cordell that they could. "Denny didn't know how to arrange things [although] he was a good vocal coach. He was a good band coach, and he was charming. The first strings I wrote for him was for The Move."

The Move album presented lots of different styles. A collective of songs, sounding just as off-kilter and distinctive with the added, aforementioned covers, as they do on their original songs. Roy Wood's originals, ranging from the melancholy 'Kilroy Was Here' to the gloriously potty young lady, so charmingly described in the frenetic, freak-beat of '(Here We Go Round) The Lemon Tree' with lyrics such as, *"There's a girl next door to me who's round the bend — But she wonders why she can't make any friends."* Roy on the song 'Lemon Tree': "That song was all about a nut case bird."

It's a wonderful recording — super tight with a three-note bass and drums. It has a wonderful middle-eight, with another excellent string section. Bolstering and climaxing with superb, sawing violins, just after the lyrics. *"I crept up to the window, In the hope that I might see her, Could the deadly shade of night, still bring her there?"* The song also features, a wonderful vari-speeded piano, tinkling away towards the end. Giving the production, a dislocated, eerie feel. Mass harmony vocals, produced with a wonderful, reverb overlay intoned, *"Mister can you hear me. Mister don't come near me."* As well as the band singing a great surreal chant, as the song fades out... *"Shaddup - Shaddup - Shaddup - Shaddup! (Boom) - Shaddup - Shaddup - Shaddup - Shaddup (Boom)..."*

Starting with Tony Visconti's double-tracked recorders, replete with a lovely harpsichord introduction, 'Mist On A Monday Morning' contains these sweet and insightful words. Describing an intoxicated, travelling gentleman on the road. Looking back at his life, through the personal haze (and daze) of bittersweet, alcohol-tinged memories. *"Drink and drink all day, till my memory melts away. I need a friend like mist on a Monday morning."*

They add a poignant respite to 'Mist on a Monday Morning' with its thoughtful and sweeping strings. *"Where is my wife, has she gone? I hear misty mornings call."* This is a track with depth and shows a maturity in Roy's very early writing. Almost an early sophistication on a view of a social underbelly. Visconti adds depth and weight to this song with these creative, rich, sonorous string charts. These punctuate this moving song with a sense of pathos. Coming to a sombre but sublime coda. With the recorder and strings, wonderfully balanced in the mix.

The two glorious, power pop, chart busters, 'Fire Brigade' and 'Flowers In The Rain' add fully to the album ballast. Giving *Move* its heady rush of melody and tangible sonic textures. This is vivid, imaginative music. There are many ideas all at once, but it holds together as a complete recording.

Nevertheless, "art-pop" albums are better when they are teeming with so many ideas, instead of too few! The Move were one of the first groups, to prove that axiom true. So many ideas and so many styles! There is a sense after a year and a half, that they didn't have one particular sound. Although the dichotomy is they definitely had an overall 'Move' sound. The Beatles had many styles and managed various genres they could inhabit — say on 'The White Album' for example. The Move with their many changes of sound. Their completely different sounding singles plus the (much delayed) length of time in releasing this first record, somehow confused the public.

Not getting out to America; with perhaps an inherent 'parochialism,' in terms of a cloying, closeness to Birmingham. With Tony Secunda's management style dealing with fun, uproarious and newspaper-worthy publicity stunts. But taking the important eye, off the big American picture, like Monterey Pop, impresario Bill Graham and his Fillmore venues, both East and West etc.

Visconti worked later with The Move on 'Beautiful Daughter' and 'Something'. One track that was placed on the *Shazam* album. And one, that became the future ultra strong B-side (of 'Blackberry Way'). "I was very involved with both 'Beautiful Daughter' and 'Something'. I don't think the band were very different. I can't remember much about the new line-up. I just remember doing my parts. My favourite arrangement was writing for 'Something'. The recorder was starting to be a thing in that year. I am a recorder player. Denny went for it, and I asked him for my fee. This was to give me money to buy two upscale recorders which I played on that recording. I also played the same recorders on 'Mist On A Monday Morning'."

Rob Caiger looks at The Move's development at this stage: "The point was, it was done as an album. But it was based really around their stage set that they were now getting into and that was in a different direction. So that album bears no relation to what The Move were at that moment! If you think about it. If you had stronger business management and Roy was saying. 'I can't write, it's too much'. It would be quite a legitimate answer that would have been fair enough that a strong manager would have been able to say, 'Right, we're going to have some of Ace's songs, we're going to have some of Dave Morgan's, we're going to have some of whatever, and we're going to do cover versions that you were going to do'. The killer presentations of the covers. Because everyone loved The Move's cover versions, the five part harmonies and the unique way they updated them."

Caiger continues, "So, if you were a strong manager, rather than fucking blowing up stages and axes! And I thought the stunts were brilliant. But no one is looking after business. No one is saying, 'Right, yeah, now! Let's stop fucking about. We've got to have the album out in four months.' So, all the things that are great. Like coming up with the story that the tapes are stolen. Let's just get the fucking thing finished'."

One is reminded again here, of Andrew Loog Oldham's comments about Tony Secunda having a "whimsical" management style. Remembering as Rob Caiger and most people do, that hindsight is a great thing. People were generally doing deals they thought were the best at the time.

The *Move* remastered Salvo 2007 release was newly presented as 2CDs. CD One is the original mono recording remastered, with five bonus tracks. CD Two features 'New Movement' sequenced by Rob Caiger. Starting out with 'Move Intro' Which is 25 seconds of unique, Move harmony vocals. Leading into 'Move', a Mod / Who inspired cut, with glorious, tumbling drums from Bevan and a strong tenor vocal from Carl Wayne. Underpinned again by those glorious, three and four-part harmonies throughout. Nice slicing, guitar thematics from Roy give this song an uplifting soul and R&B feel. This was recorded at Maximum Sound Studios by the team of Denny Cordell and engineer Dave Hadfield on 20th February 1968. Later on, the LP production master was compiled at EMI Abbey Road Studios on 7th March 1968 by engineer Ron Pender.

The Move's songs got covered during 1968 by The Fortunes with 'Fire Brigade.' Jason Crest covered, 'Here We Go Round The Lemon Tree', and Australian freakoid-psychsters The Leather Sandwich had a run at 'Kilroy Was Here'. American garage rockers The Blues Magoos versioned up 'I Can Hear the Grass Grow'. This was released as a single, from their third album *Basic Blues Magoos*.

The album got Pop LP of the month in the *Melody Maker*. The article was titled A VERY HAPPY MOVE. Some of the tidbits were, "There isn't one poor track", "Establishes Roy Wood as one of the major pop writers of the day", "The Move's fans will be surprised, at the wide range of musical experience", "Tony Visconti's writing particularly for strings is really excellent," and "All done with equal conviction". All in all, a glowing review.

The "psychedelic" cover of the *Move* album is very much of that year. In the sense of the artistic zeitgeist. It was painted by a very popular artist group The Fool. Their artwork being extremely colourful and a very eye catching, brand of rainbow-hued psychedelia. They were a really hot property for about two or three years. Described as a Dutch art collective; the artists Marijke Koger and Simon Posthuma went from happening in a hippie enclave on Ibiza in 1966, to happening in London.

The Fool had a shop off of London's Montague Square where John Lennon was one famous early visitor. In the Granada TV documentary, *It Was Twenty Years Ago Today*, The Fool commented, "He walked into our place, and saw our stuff, all the furniture and posters, as well as the clothes and he said, 'This is where I want to live'." This totally established The Fool. They did concert posters for Brian Epstein's Saville Theatre. They decorated Lennon's piano, guitar and his Rolls Royce (including the original paper inner sleeve for Sergeant Pepper, with flowing red edged graphics).

Marijke Koger and Josje Leeger designed clothes for people like Patti Boyd Harrison. They flourished at the height of "flower power" and their striking images helped define that time. They most famously painted the external Apple mural at the famous shop, opened by The Beatles in Baker Street. Which quickly went bust and closed. Marijke Koger says the name The Fool arrived from meeting the Aleister Crowley-obsessed, blues singer Graham Bond who introduced them to the Tarot deck and its artworks. Bond was obsessed with the occult, believing he was the son of the occultist Aleister Crowley.[18]

The *Move* cover has the central main design of three drop shadows in different colours. With the main lettering ranging rightwards. The front top left cover has the Shirley Scott-Jones Move logo. This logo was later tightened up for adverts and single releases. According to Piers Secunda, Tony Secunda came to call this logo 'the Pacman'.

The Fool during their short reign, also managed to design covers for the Hollies (*Evolution*) and The Incredible String Band. Plus, designs for Procol Harum, and they appeared in the George Harrison produced *Wonderwall* movie and designed some artwork for that film. They designed the clothes for The Beatles 'All You Need

---

18 Graham Bond was into some weird occult stuff. He eventually magicked himself under the wheels of an incoming Tube train on 8th May 1974 at Finsbury Park station, London. He was dead at the age of 36.

Is Love' historic, worldwide, television broadcast.

Whilst working with The Hollies on *Evolution* they collaborated with singer Graham Nash. And on some other sessions, for an album called *The Fool* in 1968. The album is reportedly a mix of string band (icy psychedelic affects, rippling pianos, banjos and deep organs) with bagpipes! They probably had a lot of help from the already musically and studio seasoned Nash. By 1969 The Fool were no more. They had split up with Koger relocating onwards to California.

Rob Caiger: "If Jac Holzman had listened to Joe Boyd, a visionary, and signed them directly to an artist-focused label as his Elektra Records was, I believe things would have been very different, especially concerning releases, especially in America where The Move needed to be. And Elektra was an American record label. But Jac Holzman never got The Move. But Joe Boyd did! God bless, Joe Boyd, he always championed The Move. But The Move were signed to a record label through their publishing company — so you've got a clash of interests. Your publisher is focused on individual songs but also controls your recordings. Records aren't their expertise. Singles and albums are all a label is focused on and they definitely know how to sell records and importantly, what should be released and when it should be released."

Joe Boyd wanted Elektra to sign up-and-coming British rock acts, like The Move, who had little relation to the folk and blues that were Elektra's pre-Doors strong suits. That led to a parting of ways not long afterward since, as Boyd said in a 2000 interview, "I think Holzman was nervous about a young, inexperienced person 3,000 miles from home, acting like a loose-cannon A&R man." It's funny how it took a USA guy, young and bright, to see The Move's brilliant appeal. Where it seemed to be lost on many other so-called 'hipster heads.' It has to be said though, another American, Joe Boyd's mate, John Hopkins, really didn't like them at all.

The Move needed no help in seeming eccentric. In a year filled with bizarre and emergent originals, The Move may have been the most unusual of all. Tony Visconti was of the opinion, that The Beatles were "allowed to do" what they wanted. But somehow, The Move were not "allowed" to be as open or as flexible. I am talking in terms of perception and media. All four Move singles to date, were different and the album was different. They were updating and changing their material constantly live on stage in three different eras — from 1966 into 1967 and 1968. They had evolved from hard rocking, Motown and R&B. Into more freaky West Coast psychedelia. They delved further on, into straight ahead Move-style unique rock 'n' roll. This was all coloured with their own, unique Roy Wood eccentric but commercial songwriting. Not quite fitting into any particular scene or sound. They rivalled (I'd say surpassed) The Who in their elemental, violent power.

The use of 'Mod' styles came at the very beginning, as it did with The Who. This was almost dropped by the time the first and second singles were released. From 'Flowers In The Rain' onwards, the singles became slightly more whimsical, (apart from 'Wild Tiger Woman') but they drew upon the times closely. The Move were also as defiantly British as The Kinks. During 1967 and 1968, they were more closely tied to psychedelia than the Davies brothers.

One commentator made the glaring and under researched comment that, "Indeed, the Move were arguably at the forefront of the second wave of the British Invasion. Building upon the bright exuberant sound of 1964 and 1965 and "lacking any rooting in the jazz and blues that fuelled the Rolling Stones, The Animals, and Manfred Mann, among countless others."

This of course, is absolute bollocks and also not true. One only has to look at those brilliantly executed cover versions that had made up the majority of The Move's set. Particularly the very early sets from the Cedar Club rehearsal days and through 1966 onwards, to see that they were firmly rooted in USA soul, Motown and R&B. Just as much as any of those other named current UK bands. With the added advantage of a four-man harmony vocal section. As well as four potential lead singers, which none of the other bands had. (Apart from The Beatles).

The schism slowly bubbling between Roy Wood and Carl started to become more obvious and apparent, with Carl coming out with various comments about Roy's appearance and his song writing ability. Carl once said at a cabaret gig that Roy's hair was like an "explosion in a bird's nest." Although it was used as a staged joke, one could imagine Carl saying it at times with gritted teeth. It emphasised Roy's freakier appearance.

But also, a complex differing of personalities. Offstage, Roy tended to be other-worldly at times and not at all well organised. Wayne used to have to kick Roy up the arse frequently.

Bevan opines: "What happened between those two childhood friends? Because they had hung around together before The Move, you know. Carl was a good three years older than him. That's a lot of time, when you're young, isn't it? Roy could be frustrating, because we knew just how good he was. And we were like, (and Tony Secunda was the same), it was almost like we were bullying him. That was hard on Roy."

Whereas Carl Wayne was very controlling and always had to organise things. Sometimes to an almost obsessive degree. No doubt that Carl was the businessman of the group. He kept them on the straight rails, organising gigs, making sure they were being paid etc. Also Dumpy Harris used to get driven insane by the band's demands. He said, "They used to fucking drive me mad. We'd be somewhere and they'd always want to be driven back to Birmingham. They had this kind of umbilical cord to their mums and Birmingham."

Bev remembers a near miss one night. "We might've been in Portsmouth, somewhere. Allen had been working really hard as usual. We'd expect him to drive us all back home. I remember, he literally fell asleep on the motorway, so I literally grabbed the steering wheel and averted a collision. I said, 'You just fell asleep', and he said, 'No, No, I'm just resting my eyes'."

By this time, Robert Davidson, supposedly "on the payroll" decided he'd had enough. As the appointed Secunda official photographer, Robert also photographed The Rolling Stones, The Action, The Moody Blues, David Bowie and the fiery Arthur Brown.

Strands of his young life were converging into an ongoing, amalgamating stressful situation. He was sick and tired of Tony Secunda's promises. To pay (and to back pay) him for all the pictures, he had taken throughout 1966 and 1967, right bang up to date. "I liked The Move — the exciting live shows — the day-to-day excitement generally. But I was sick to death of Tony." Tony apparently was not fond of paying his office bills either. He was quite often on the move, to escape said payment of accruing bills.

As Rob Caiger mentioned, he didn't really have a solid fixed base. Flitting around from office to office. From New Movement to Essex Publishing etc. Robert Davidson's relationship with the beautiful Patricia McRoberts, the young Shell heiress had now hit a bad patch, after four years or so together. It looked like they were heading for a split. Robert (being of a very dreamlike nature and certainly not a realist) wanted Patricia to give all her money away.

Robert supposed this would put them both on a more even keel financially. Robert at this time also became keenly aware that Secunda was lurking around the background. In relation to Patricia, Robert felt strongly, Secunda was looking to zero in on her substantial money reserves. Davidson also felt they were so completely dissimilar and that McRoberts would get badly treated and bullied, and in no time at all. By this stage Secunda had split out of his hot-house marriage with Chelita. At the time they were seen as one of London's happening *'It'* couples.

Secunda was the '*au courant*' pop manager. He was where all the action was at! With his then Chelita also being a very creative firebrand. She was vivacious and very well liked. Robert remembers her, "I liked Chelita a lot, she was fun and outrageous! She invented make ups nobody had ever seen! She started by using them on herself first. Later on, with Marc Bolan and T. Rex. She had already worked with society photographer Norman Parkinson in the Caribbean."

A Pathe News reel from the time (in which Carl Wayne and Trevor Burton are seen visiting) show a laughing, very attractive, gamine, slender and stylish young woman. I cannot imagine how she felt being around the volatile Secunda — particularly after he smashed up their Knightsbridge flat. Perhaps, it was not the interior makeover she had in mind? Chelita Secunda was something of a Sixties 'It' girl. Her family were rich and exotic. She knew The Beatles and The Stones. She did PR work for top designer Ossie Clark and she was married to Secunda. Chelita encouraged Bolan to wear glittery make-up. She put glitter under Marc Bolan's eyes before he went on *Top of the Pops* later in 1971.

As legend has it, in the process, inventing so-called 'Glam Rock!' But as John Lennon so drolly remarked, 'glam' was "just rock 'n' roll with some lipstick on."

Chelita came from a wealthy Sardinian Italian family. She had a lot of class. She briefly worked for Bolan. They first met when Chelita was his personal cocaine dealer. Allegedly both Tony and Chelita were heavily involved in the London coke scene around that time. Unfortunately, Chelita also succumbed to the unhealthy, cocaine lifestyle. This was now swiftly infiltrating the music scene. Easily enough done too! As at first coke gives you some immense energy. Coke also gives the illusions of invincibility. It makes users feel that they are making truly brilliant, inspired music. However, it can often lead to the wearing out of reel-to-reel tapes. As take after take is made and after a while any real energy is completely coked out of the recordings. It brings feelings of immortality, power, confidence and a new, illusory sparkly creativity.

Cocaine powder and the rock world would become as common as milk with cornflakes. Indeed, one has heard stories of people using cocaine on cornflakes… true nose candy enthusiasts like Ike Turner. Ike once claimed to have spent more than $100,000 on coke in a two-month period in 1989 (he says friends stole much of it).

Cocaine has helped destroy many a band. My first book on Santana and the Latin Rock scene (*Voices of Latin Rock*, Hal Leonard) showed how the band's popularity blew up into the stratosphere after Woodstock, and their first inspired recordings and live shows. With pure Peruvian ("pink flake") cocaine and other strains, flooding the West Coast music scene. Santana became big users. With the result that the band imploded from within, in just under three years. This also coincided with three, massively selling, classic albums. But their relationships deteriorated fast. By the time they realised, they had built an unseen "cocaine wall." The original group, initially a street wise fast band of brothers had fallen apart!

As the 1970s and 1980s wore on cocaine became more entrenched in the music scene. Tony Visconti relived some moments, "I was an on and off coke user back then. But I still maintained a healthy lifestyle in spite of it. For your information I stopped using all drugs in 1984, including cigarettes. Chelita was always pleasant to speak with. She was educated and had a lot to say. Once I saw her and her facial skin was beginning to erode. She had sores all over her face. I sent her to a great acupuncturist, who tried to help her! But her addiction was too far gone and all the rest you know..."

Visconti was not a fan of Secunda: "Tony Secunda was a kind of grifter. He was with Seltaeb. Secunda was the close pal of Denny Cordell; two public school boys who bonded during the time they worked together for the Beatles merchandising business. He had lots of swagger and Americans were in awe of anyone with an English accent. They could sound like they were powerful, but hard work was not his thing. He could get a deal done with his swagger. But that's where his job ended. He really didn't do well as a manager. I think the last time I dealt with him was when he tried to get me to produce Ace Kefford as a solo artiste, which didn't go well at all. Ace had a bruised psyche from what I know. Whereas I adored Denny Cordell for everything he did for me. To get me kick-started as a record producer. I had very little to do with Secunda, as I always felt I was talking to a big phoney."

Eventually Tony Secunda was divorced by his second wife Patricia McRoberts. On the day he was ordered by a London Divorce Court judge to get out of their Kensington home by 6:00pm, Judge Phelan had banned him from going within 100 yards of the seventeen room Georgian house at Campden Hill Square. Again, Tony is alleged to have smashed up the place and caused great personal distress to Patricia.

It is alleged by a person wishing to remain anonymous that by this time, Tony had gotten heavily into cocaine dealing, supplying many people in the London "scene." Ossie Clark the go-to fashion guru at that time had mentioned this also. This may strongly explain the erratic, destructive behaviour in Secunda which became even more erratic and with the added, triggered outbursts of violence. Excessive cocaine use often leads to bouts of mental intrigue. Causing extreme jealousy, rampant paranoia and a distorted ability to make the right decisions.

The constant, heavy user is usually found, bouncing off a "cocaine wall." By which they are invisibly "surrounded." In America this condition is colloquially known, as being "snow blind." Since those earlier, more innocent, but inevitably destructive days, it is now said that London is the Numero Uno city for cocaine usage in the world. Coke has also affected Ireland (Dublin, and other cities) greatly, which is where my parents and ancestry originate.

Flowers In The Rain - The Untold Story of The Move

One person wishing to remain anonymous made the following comments: "I lost touch with Tony around about 1970. Apart from supplying most of the coke in London in the late 1960s Tony was a lovely guy, who had really good intentions. But they just kept going pear shaped! The Move slagged off Tony! Yet in my opinion, they would have been nowhere without him! They were five guys from Birmingham — no different to many other groups of the day. Even The Idle Race were around — but they didn't have a 'Tony' in their lives."

I do think The Move were definitely one of the (if not the very top) superior bands to come out of Birmingham (and the entire UK). This was allied to a disciplined, defined, hustling attitude to success. In fairness to Secunda — Roy did not like him personally, but Carl, Trevor and Ace supported him most strongly. Trevor Burton was particularly enamoured of his anarchic style. Secunda was at odds with Roy's earlier timidity. Certainly, around the area of the shock publicity affects with which Secunda was so effective in dreaming up. Wood's animus was obviously deepened by the lifelong loss of royalty payments, from both sides of 'Flowers In The Rain'.

Bobby Davidson encountered yet another shocking and symbolic event. This definitely changed his mind about working in that highly charged and intense world. When Robert first told me the reasons for getting out of the increasingly claustrophobic Soho scene, he mentioned a significant and shocking event. It was an aside, but a very bizarre one. Upon hearing about the event, I thought at first Robert was talking about a little-known news story from late in 1968. Joseph de Havilland was a Hungarian painter who was reported in the news. But the de Haviland event was another weird occurrence, and it happened after Robert's gruesome encounter. Havilland was found "crucified" on Hampstead Heath, North London. His motives are not known. Notoriety or financial gain in some bizarre manner.

Joseph de Havilland said he left a message at Lambeth Palace: "I would like to inform the Archbishop, Head of the English Church, that a testament will take place, whereby a young man will be crucified. With real nails and on a real cross, to fulfil the first stage of a prophecy, to act on the will of God."

However, "interior decorator" de Havilland lived, and he didn't crucify himself. Three other men were identified as the ones who crucified him. Erich Leach, another interior decorator, and two other men, Desmond Pollydore and David Conklin, were charged and prosecuted with causing grievous bodily harm. The story remains shrouded in showbiz smoke and mirrors.

The case is still referenced as setting a precedent in English law. It is particularly interesting from a legal perspective. As the accused were not allowed to use the fact Joseph de Havilland had asked to be nailed-up as a defence. Beyond that, very little about this affair has ever been publicly revealed. Its primary impact at the time concerned the legalities — most particularly, whether de Havilland's consent rendered the "crucifixion" act legal under British law.

The showbiz mystery factor came from the involvement of celebrity solicitor David Jacobs (Brian Epstein, The Move etc). Jacobs is famous for securing enormous libel damages for Liberace after a newspaper had the temerity to suggest, that Liberace might be homosexual.

Jacobs represented the three defendants. It wasn't the kind of case you'd normally expect to be taken on by someone with such glamorous and famous clientèle. Police actually questioned David Jacobs himself, as part of their investigation into the crucifixion. Bizarrely and very soon after the trial. Jacobs was admitted to a mental health care facility, The Priory. Jacobs was openly gay and an extremely flamboyant character. He frequently represented clients who wished to keep their sexuality secret.

In 1968, "male homosexual acts" had only been legal in the UK for one year. Only months after the peculiar 'Hampstead crucifixion' case, David Jacobs had taken his own life, leaving behind some almost indecipherable, scribbled notes. These were found in his pockets. Notes which led to the police questioning several gentlemen, including some well-known public figures. They were questioned about parties, which had taken place at country estates and flats across England. This story (and the Robert Davidson 'gangsters in Soho' one) all remain an enigma... It's been suggested that it could have been a very extreme, gay sex game that went wrong or possibly even went exactly to plan?

Robert goes on to explain the decisive (deciding?) factor: "I think the incident was something to do with the ongoing Soho gang warfare and Mike Berkofsky and it was very near his studio. Mike was the photographer who had taken an iconic picture of Jimi Hendrix. Anyway, I used to work for Mike. So, this was in Mike Berkofsky's studio in Smith Square, which is right in the middle of Soho. There was a little cul-de-sac opposite where the Windmill Theatre is, or was? It's no longer there. And so, it was a week before my problem started. One of Mike Berkofsky's assistants came in early in the morning to open up the studio. She was horrified to discover this person (a man) had been crucified; literally nailed onto one of the garage doors. A turf war had been raging between the Krays; the brothers Ronnie and Reggie. They covered the East End, while the Richardsons, "looked after" the West End. The unlucky victim had obviously been caught in the middle of something nasty. "When she found him the next morning, he was in a very bloody mess and almost dead. I felt this was definitely a warning to me. People didn't write letters, they arrived with menaces and without the correct response, they could get violent."

Let me provide some back story to this Robert-related event. Possibly the most famous of Robert's photos is of Frank Zappa that arguably propelled Zappa to iconic status, leading him to say, later on in 1983, 'I'm probably more famous for sitting on the toilet than for anything else."

On Saturday 19th August 1967, the 19-year-old Davidson was at the Royal Garden Hotel with Secunda. They were doing a press call for Frank Zappa's upcoming show at the Royal Albert Hall. Robert scouted around for a suitable location inside the hotel to take some cool pictures. He heard Zappa speaking on the phone in the bathroom. Robert asked him, through the ajar toilet door if he could take his picture. "Some limey wants to take my picture on the john," Zappa told his wife, who was on the other end of the line. "Sure, whatever turns him on." This set of photos became known, as the 'Zappa Krappa' pictures.

Zappa's management, incorrectly thinking Davidson was benefiting exclusively from the increasingly popular images sent "representatives" to his studio forcing Robert to part with his original negatives. Zappa thought he was being totally ripped off and that Davidson was profiting from a poster version, universally known as the 'Toilet Poster', or 'The Zappa Krappa'.

"I signed myself out of the studio for a week and went into hiding. I said to

Mike's secretary Angie, 'Look out and take care of yourself. Something's about to kick off. I'm sure they won't hurt you, but they'll probably come looking for me.' This was in, I would say 1967. A man was discovered nailed onto the garage doors and only just alive. I think the person lived, but I'm not sure. It was thought something to do with local warfare. I think the *Daily Mirror* covered it. They also reckoned, a few months later, that it was something to do with some homosexual goings on."

"Why did these guys come to see me? Because Frank Zappa had done a deal with me down the telephone — saying that he wanted 20% of the poster. So, these three heavies came around to the office. First of all, there's two little ones and another massive one. In other words, he was built like a brick shithouse! He was cleaning his nails with a flick knife. The brick shithouse uttered, 'where's Robert?' Angie said, 'He just went out.' When I came back, I just said, 'Look out, there could be trouble here.' I had a really bad feeling about the whole thing."

"Anyway, this enormous geezer said, 'We want negatives, plus a large sum of money, and the printing plates and any existing posters by tonight and delivered to The Royal Garden Hotel.' Angie also had said to the massive goon, 'What happens if he doesn't give the negatives and the money?' The bloke cleaning his nails with the flick knife, immediately made a chopping motion. To his left and right hand, saying, 'Is Robert right or left-handed?' It was going to be chop-chop time and I was going to lose a hand. So, when she told me, I went, 'Holy shit, how much? I forget how much it was, but it was the equivalent of thousands now. I hadn't got it on me either. I had to quickly go and borrow the cash, get the original photo negatives and take them to the Royal Garden Hotel, which I did that evening. I was so frightened. I took all my stuff directly to Herb Cohen, who was staying with The Mothers at the Royal Garden Hotel, and they were flying over to Paris the following day. I took everything they wanted. I didn't even keep any copy-negatives, prints or posters. I don't know what I did, but I just thought, I want to keep my hand(s), and she just said, 'These guys are serious.' London was like open gang warfare then. I left everything at reception. And that was that. I hoped. It was serious — the Sixties were really crazy and scary. There was another very dark side, from the peace, love and pot vibes Maaan!"

Robert managed to survive this little row, and he lived to tell the tale. "The general climate of fear in Soho at that time meant that I couldn't go to the police. I was petrified! These debt collectors already knew where my studio was located. There was no way I could completely run to ground. They hadn't found me this time, but one day there'd be a tap on my shoulder. "You Robert Davidson?" "Yes." The possible consequences terrified me. I could easily imagine the scenario. However, I'd rather have my hands than a million quid, thank you very much. It was a no brainer. Taking the photograph of Frank Zappa and then losing all the negatives had a major impact on my life. I turned away from photography and I began to see my part in this story as a truly poisoned chalice."

Robert ruefully recalls losing some big monies; "The photographer who took it made a poster and sold it for his own profit! Then that poster was bootlegged all over Europe and eventually went into the United States and millions of 'em were sold,"

Robert was again ripped off. "I couldn't stop them from doing that." Even measures by his management proved useless. Due to the vast amount of pirated copying that had already taken place. In the end, neither Davidson nor Zappa received any royalties from the image. Davidson would go on to spend the better part of half a century searching for his lost negatives.

In an unusual and sweet twist. Robert lucked in, in 2010. He learnt that his negatives were about to be sold online by a Los Angeles memorabilia company, Rockaway Records. They had bought them from the estate of Herb Cohen, Zappa's manager. Davidson contacted Rockaway Records to tell the true story. Rockaway gallantly agreed to give him the 10 surviving negatives for a token sum. Rockaway's Mark Steckler stated: "We are just glad that Robert Davidson could get them back."

In 2017 the main Zappa photograph, appeared in the V&A's definitive exhibition on the 1960s 'You Say You Want a Revolution.' Whitebank Fine Art exhibited the photos in July 2017. They are also set to be featured, on the National Portrait Gallery's official website. I believe one of Roy Wood, in his 1967 'Granny Takes A Trip' finery and allied to the 'Flowers In The Rain' publicity, was on exhibition also.

During the 1970s, Robert became a follower of the Indian guru Bhagwan Shree Rajneesh, later known as 'Osho'. He is the father of Holly Davidson, a British actress, and he is stepfather to the actress Sadie Frost. Robert is a gentle soul, one of life's dreamers and a very cool, eccentric gentleman. He has managed to get through the 1960s with all the associated drug intakes and the mad relationships, while brushing up against the crazy Secunda / Move operation. His life is relatively peaceful these days. Robert is a gentle, peaceful dandy - *but not in aspic.*

23.
See the people all in line - What's making them look at me?

Ace Kefford has occupied one of those cult-like spaces in the music business archives. Every now and then in the music press over the years, you would read a suitably vague new piece. However, Alan Clayson's 1994 piece in *Record Collector* revealed the turmoil and the chaos that he had still experienced, before coming to land in rehab and to live for a while in Bradford. In some ways Ace has been lumped in with Pink Floyd's Syd Barrett and the Rolling Stone's Brian Jones and also poor Peter Green etc. Features that held that type of "loner madness" flavour.

Since his departure from The Move, Kefford has become easily the most enigmatic of the Brum Beat performers from that era. Ace's story is much different to theirs. In the fact that he has somehow, come through all the suffering and anguish, if not all in one piece, certainly with the semblance of some peace of mind and balance. Ace learnt to cope with his mental conditions and managed to survive mental collapse, addiction and a serious mental condition. Which nowadays is recognised correctly and can be treated effectively with medications.

He is still alive and in touch with his family in a meaningful way. Ace has lived a tough life at times. However, there seems to be a 'helping hand' looking after him, through many years of intense difficulties. Ace paid a price that would devastate his mental health for years to come.

By the early part of 1968, Ace Kefford's brain was extremely frazzled. He was increasingly inhabiting a very frail place. The Harold Wilson 'Flowers In the Rain' court case had increased his already deepening state of paranoia. He was still living on a weekly wage (as were all the members of The Move) and not pulling in any serious money. Obviously, they generated money from their relentless procession of gigs, but they were paid a wage, and the money was not paid to them from the proceeds of the gigs. Many other things were coming to a head between Ace and the other four members of The Move.

There was increasing friction in the group. Ace's (and Trevor's) arrogance and aggression was at a high level at that time. The entire band had increasing egos and an over-entitled attitude. Not unusual in most bands who are making it. Ace (rightly) felt that the band were ignoring his songwriting contributions — and they were! He had collapsed in the studio having a blackout or a breakdown of some description when they were recording 'Fire Brigade'. He also became more paranoid about frenzied fans chasing him around. Trying to pull his hair out, he once got stabbed in the face, near the eye with a pair of scissors. Was that an assassination attempt or somebody trying to get a lock of his blond hair?

It was six of one and half a dozen of the other. Ace could definitely have developed further, in the same way that Roy did. The fact that he had consumed large and constant quantities of LSD during the last few months also aggravated matters severely. This was making him much more unstable and with much less grasp on reality. Also, the taking of amphetamines (speed, uppers), over a period of time can have a very debilitating effect on mental health in terms of very erratic sleep patterns.

Plus living at a very "high" rate of pumped up, mental and physical perturbation, day by day. In those less enlightened days of the 1960s it was still pretty much a time of asylums, strait jackets, men in white coats. The use of heavily sedating drugs like Thorazine, Largactil (aka liquid cosh) and the use of (ECT) electric shock treatment.

Mental health issues were generally swept under the carpets. Along with many other evil societal abusive trends. Like the seemingly huge, hidden (and ever growing) areas of child abuse etc. Whilst reading Simon Spence's Stevie Marriott *All Or Nothing* book, it seemed to me, the very same symptoms and reactions, were happening to Andrew Loog Oldman (who at that time, had left the Stones management and was focused on managing The Small Faces) and very severely later on, with Steve Marriott himself.

Ace was trying to self-medicate the pressure and problems of fame, success and non-stop work with drugs. To aid either issues with ADHD (attention deficit hyperactivity disorder), possible stage fright or good old general overwhelm. Coupled with the relentless supply of energy needed to keep performing, not many people can possibly understand what this sort of pressure is like. All this was furthering Ace's precarious mental state. Making him harder to communicate with. The other band members really began to do a number on him. In terms of sending him to Coventry. This behaviour often takes the form of pretending that the shunned person, although conspicuously present, cannot be seen or heard. For Ace in his incredibly vulnerable state, which was not helped by the constant added mixture of acid and other drugs in his system, these actions against him by the other four, would have mightily added to his increasing paranoia. Why the Move members, enacted out this cruel farrago towards him, one can only guess. It was certainly a deeply, hothouse affair: The psychology of five testosterone-filled young men, all packed into the group van, playing their arses off at a very high level every night.

In those days, absolutely no-one had the benefit, of an accrued rock culture history with hindsight from fifty years on perspective. Nobody knew how long it was all gonna last. It was put out a single or album, get out on the road and work it hard. Everybody was at their wits end after the Harold Wilson affair.

They appeared to be very jealous of the fact, Ace got solo photo ops. He had incredible charisma and good looks. And he was very popular with the ladies. But the real tipping point was that Ace ingested a lot of home-made acid in Birmingham and all at once!

"At that time, I and another person, had bought a phial of acid. Afterwards, we went to my apartment and drank it. Of course, we did not know exactly how much we took, as it was in a bottle. In short, I went too far without knowing it. We both ended going to the Club Cedar. I was not understanding what was happening."

Prior, Ace had gone to some students' house in Birmingham. These stupid dopes were (think about cut-rate Oswald Owsley types) manufacturing bathtub drugs in Birmingham. They were making their own liquid LSD and Ace bought a phial from these clowns. Ace ended up necking a sizeable amount all at once. This was tantamount to a full-on mind-fuck session of psychedelic Russian Roulette. Ace and Trevor went on to The Cedar Club that night. (Remember LSD was something to be taken in microscopic pin prick doses. Or on a blotter, a sugar cube or similar. Essentially, it was to be taken in very minute doses). Ace began to experience a lot of anxiety as the trip came on. Kefford saw people dressed up as pirates (it was a fancy-dress thing going on that night).

Trevor Burton adds some detail to this troubling series of events. "Ace flipped halfway through the evening, so I put him in a cab and sent him home. He was never the same again." The driver was instructed to drive him back to his place in Chester Road, Wylde Green, Erdington. As the trip came on and developed Ace was having to face, what was known back then, as "the horrors" or as a "bad trip." Ace started to 'see' these little goblins. Little men with pointed heads all around him. This was the swirling, visual hallucinations aspect of taking LSD. These little creatures were clambering over him and talking to him.

Ace shudders, "Apparently, because in my childhood, I had a small problem with my psyche, overdosing on acid finally demolished my mental stability. No one understood any of this. If a panic attack happens on the road. Or if they happened during the transmission of *Top Of The Pops*, I was wanting to get out of there immediately. I did not understand, what was going on myself. I spent my later life in asylums for the insane, rehabilitation centres and other institutions — just to come back to where I am here and now."

(Author note: I personally took LSD about three times. The first time was okay and I felt "at one" and "communed with nature" in a local London park. But the second two times I got bored by the actual hours' length of "the trip". I discovered what I needed from acid. But I'm mighty glad, I didn't suffer any adverse effects. Those came later — primarily through alcohol and other drugs).

Collectively all of this was leading towards a resentful, seething musical and social situation within The Move. Which would finally burst its banks, with Ace being The Move's first casualty. Or as Robert Davidson put it, "The blond beautiful Chris "Ace" Kefford, who fell and became the group's scapegoat."

At his last rehearsal, Ace made his feelings known using some direct action. He flung his Fender Precision slab bass against the wall. Summarily, Ace left the rehearsal and quit The Move. Effectively, it was the last time the original five-piece played together. Sadly, this was the beginning of an eroding and twisting ending for The Move.

Ace details that last, grim day for the five-piece: "We were rehearsing in Birmingham at this village hall, and I couldn't take any more. It wasn't just the group. It was going out and being seen in public. How can you do *Top Of The Pops* If you can't even go into a supermarket and buy something? I hadn't thought, I was gonna leave the band before the rehearsal. The atmosphere was so bad, and I just couldn't take it anymore. The atmosphere stunk. The band were all still fucked up about the

Harold Wilson thing. But nobody was saying anything. So, I just took my bass off, smashed it against the wall and walked out. There'd been a lot of tension. I do blame people, but I was also very hard to put up with. It's all right having great charisma and being really groovy and photogenic, but if you're threatening everyone and they're too scared to question you; whether my bass is in tune in case they get the fucking bass, around the head... I was mad... I phoned my missus up and said, 'Can you take me home?' When we got back, I pushed her out, bolted everything up. Put settees and chairs in front of the door. I got some razor blades and slashed my wrists! I ended up in hospital. I'd had enough, I didn't wanna live any more. I'd been like that for months, hoping I was gonna feel better. But it never did get any better. It all started the night I took too much acid, man! I'd dropped loads of acid before. But I'd never swigged a bottle out like that? Screwed my life up, man. Devastated me, completely."

John Kirkby, the road manager with The Montana's, recalls The Move having a meeting at the Rum Runner on Broad Street, Birmingham to discuss the growing concern and disharmony about the ongoing Ace situation. There was a meeting between the band and Secunda at the offices. Apparently, this meeting did not go very swimmingly.

But from Ace's perspective, "Everyone was carrying on acting tough! But I think everybody was shitting themselves. A couple of weeks before that, I've been in the recording studios, doing the next single 'Fire Brigade'. I just blacked out, right during the session. I woke up on the floor and everybody was picking me up and taking me out to get fresh air. When they all went back into the studio to continue with the session, I just fucked off — got on the train and I went home. Pull down all the screens in the passenger department, my paranoia was so heavy. Luckily, I had done all my bass parts before. Again, I had just dropped some acid. Even after overdosing on the bottle of acid just before, I still hadn't learned my lesson."

Ace also recorded in an interview with *Ugly Things*, Issue 22, published in 2004. "That was the day when I started fucking losing it. The night when I dropped all that bloody acid. I was never right after that. I was always cocky and I was very sure of myself and everything before that. The night I dropped that lot, I sat in this flat I had." Ace recalls or recoils, "There were all these figures sitting around me, all through the night, keeping me company. Absolutely fucking mad, man. My missus finally got me into the bed and then she jumped out of the bed and shoooom — she shrunk down to the size of a little fucking thing. To about the size of a rabbit. I knew I had done something dangerous. When I saw all the stuff that was going on. That's what damaged me really. I just couldn't carry on with the band anymore, I had to leave."

The Move's history and Ace's last rehearsal was remembered in a well-presented BBC Television production called *Rock Family Trees* in 1995. This 45-minute documentary was based on Pete Frame's popular *Rock Family Trees* books. Laid out in a similar fashion as in generic family historical trees. Trevor Burton remembers the incident. "Ace went very strange for a while. He went very paranoid. It was a two-way thing. He would get in the car and go all the way to a gig. He would start talking to himself, saying 'They're not talking to me today.' Everyone would be saying, 'He's going barmy.' It was all the pressure, and one day at rehearsals, he threw his guitar at the wall and walked out. He went home and slashed his wrists and that's how he left the band."

Ace remembers this fraught time, from his point of view: "We're driving to a gig 200 miles away and 200 miles back. And none of the other members of The Move spoke to me at all."

It was probably shared responsibility. Ace (and Trevor it must be said) was arrogant, bad tempered, and inclined to explode a lot. It put the group on their back foot all the time. They hatched a plot to ostracise him within the group and they effectively forced him out. There was quite a bit of jealousy too. In fact, Tony Secunda in later years, opined to writer Dave Thompson, "Ace was definitely the star in The Move."

Ace had also appeared to have one incisive nervous breakdown following the intense package tour with The Jimi Hendrix Experience and Pink Floyd, which took the form of a severe panic attack. Carl Wayne believed strongly that the start of The Move's downfall was in Ace Kefford's departure. I totally agree. The band developed a hole that was never filled.

Carl opined, "Because it placed Trevor into the vulnerable position of having to play more instruments." It was said, the band could (possibly) have survived, if they had recruited a keyboard player to replace Kefford.

Roy Wood recalled of Kefford, "Ace left because he couldn't handle it. Ever since the day we formed, none of us really got on very well with him. He was a very strange person. He was very aggressive, and Ace and Trevor used to have a lot of fights all the time."

Although in a recent interview with Trevor, he told me, "Generally, me and Ace got on very well and I thought his bass playing was great." The rankling resentments and widening cracks were starting to show after 'Fire Brigade'.

"As a five-piece, The Move was just a magnificent band," says Bevan. "but once Ace left The Move were never as good again to be honest. In those early years. I'm talking 1966, '67 and '68 — The Move were brilliant. The vocal harmonies were fantastic, and we worked really hard. We were also incredibly ambitious, and we deserved what we achieved. In many ways I think we were underrated. We stayed permanently in the shadow of The Beatles and The Stones. We made the mistake, and it was a big mistake! Of just being a singles band when we should have been concentrating on albums! That was the way it was going at the time. We just kept churning out hit singles which was all well and good. But we never made a decent album really, which is a real shame."

Carl Wayne was pragmatic: "We made hit records and the good thing about The Move hits was that they were all individually different. If you think how different 'Night Of Fear' is to 'Blackberry Way'. They were all very different, I don't find any of them, in any way embarrassing. They are all still playable. It would have been interesting to have seen how The Move would have played those gigs had it been Trevor, Ace and myself doing them. (Carl is referring to Roy doing ELO and possibly writing for the Move still.) Certainly, Trevor and Ace had more of a blues influence! Ace and I had more of a soul influence. Ace more "black" soul to my "white" soul."

"I think it would have been interesting to see how The Move would have developed. Had we all stayed together and carried the burden — and I mean that in a kind way, of those hits. Because we would have had to compete on the same level with Hendrix, Cream, Floyd! We would have had to do the big arenas! We couldn't have done those as a pop band. We could have developed those songs, to play them in the big arenas. My feeling is that we probably could but who knows? Roy was restricted by what the radio stations at the time would play. If it was over 2:59, you'd be off and the next record on! In some of the other songs that we did, like 'Fields Of People' and 'Cherry Blossom Clinic', you can see how Roy was trying to move away from the singles sound. It was probably indicative of his insecurity, about where he stood as a writer at the time. Maybe he was trying to develop more of a different style."

Carl continues on the song writing theme: "I couldn't write. I never wanted to write, purely because I had the pleasure of working with Roy Wood. who was an outstanding writer. It's great to have confidence in someone and with Roy it was always 'Roy, write a hit song' and out it came! Roy also had previous writing experience with The Nightriders, so he wasn't new to it, and it was the obvious area to develop. What you would have developed, out of Ace and Trevor wouldn't have been as commercial. The songs would have been more blues-based, so it was quite clear to us that Roy Wood was the writer."

BBC Television was said to have commissioned Roy to write the theme music for one of the *Wednesday Play* series, coming up that autumn. Prior to this Secunda had poo-poohed suggestions Ace Kefford was quitting: "Chris is not appearing at present because he is in a serious nervous condition and under the strictest medical care. The pressures of the pop scene have done him in temporarily. He's got an ulcer and he's a very sick boy. As far as the stories of his quitting are concerned, it's a load of nonsense."

However, the *Birmingham Evening Mail* dated 13th March 1968 had the following short feature... POP GROUP MAN TREATED FOR INJURIES. The brief news piece went as follows: "Chris Kefford, 21-year-old member of the Birmingham-based pop group The Move, returned to London today after being treated at Good Hope General Hospital, Sutton Coldfield for wrist injuries. He had been staying at a house in Chester Road, Sutton Coldfield. Police called at the house after receiving an emergency call. And he was later taken to hospital by ambulance."

Ace's mental confusion is harrowing to hear. The triggered young man recalls the disturbing details, "I went back to my flat in Erdington. I was on my own and there were all these little men, sitting around me on the chairs. All around on the arms of the chair. I wrote a song about it afterwards, 'The Stick Men Will Get You'. I barricaded myself in and slashed my wrists. The walls were covered in blood, man. It was a cry for help, really. My wife called the ambulance and carted me off to Good Hope Hospital. Next thing I knew Carl Wayne turned up, all sympathy."

In *Record Collector* No. 179, July 1994, Ace remembers in more detail the events around the end of The Move period: "Officially it was me who left them! But they chucked me out indirectly with their behaviour. Trevor went soon afterwards, and The Move just ate itself away."

Ace became the scapegoat. His history of bad temper, arrogance and causing unnecessary friction, also burnt bridges in his wake. It's true, his lead vocal contributions to the group had lessened and he was singing one number — if that — towards the end! It has to be said this was not the best behaviour, from the other four guys at all. Further proof that this band, with this amount of talent should've had some daily personal management. To help with all this interpersonal pressure, to possibly prevent it being exacerbated further. They were probably all responsible. Ace was moody with an impending (or already pre-existing) case of bipolar disorder.

This would have been completely unknown then. Bipolar disorder in that era was referred to as manic depression. Similar in effect to Spike Milligan, who often referenced this state in his writings and TV appearances. With the condition incurring both associated incredible highs and then deep lows and slumps in between. Milligan's comedy (*The Goons* most famously) his crazy, funny, irreverent TV appearances and interviews, all exhibited his manic and sometimes richly, genius way of performing.

It is highly likely in the macho (albeit tinged with a touch of hippiness) world of the 1960s, and with little or no knowledge around any kind of mental health issues, Ace was probably unable to explain anything to the other four guys. He will certainly not have received the kind of comfort or open discussion he would have required. Ace would not have known how to describe his situation to them anyway. He will have been as baffled as they were. His heavy and indiscriminate use of LSD will not have helped though. His condition had not been diagnosed as yet. This can be a method of medical trial and error, occurring over a long period of time. Back then the information and knowledge on mental health and medications were nowhere near what they are now. In fact, I would say the issues around mental health then were decidedly just above primitive.

As one fifth of this charismatic band he contributed incredibly to the visual image. He had a great stage presence. He could dance (so could Trevor Burton). It was very unusual to see young white guys in a band that could actually dance. I'm not talking about completely choreographed moves. I am talking street-level club stuff. Ace threw some great onstage shapes. You can't imagine for example, Pink Floyd throwing any good moves onstage. Pink Floyd went down really badly supporting The Move at Mod type gigs. They couldn't play any soul or R&B vibes, even if they wanted to. I think like The Move, the Mods saw them as soppy college boys. They just stood stock still, like tailors' dummies. There was snobbery about things like 'Mod' dancing, with the 'heads.' Not that they could do it. They thought it was somehow uncool. It was so much cooler than they could've ever imagined. Certainly, they couldn't dance like it either.

It appears that Roy (and the band) didn't want Ace writing. Rob Caiger (The Move's main archivist and remastering head honcho) maintains this, and it has been reiterated by Carl Wayne: The psychology of the band was very delicate in many ways. They were five young, charismatic guys without fathers. Tony Secunda seemed incapable or oblivious to a degree. He needed to step up to the plate and start soothing the ruffled feathers. To use some psychology — to develop a better interpersonal and working situation between the band members. Try and expand the songwriting base. Secunda certainly had to deal with plenty of griping and moaning from the band members. Each having digs and issues with the other band members constantly — as time and success mounted. Apart from Secunda, they had the reliable and solid Dumpy Harris. But they needed an 'on the road' serviceable, individual, like a practiced therapist or soothsayer.

Ace was not helping himself either, his increasingly fragile psyche was being further disturbed and distorted by the use and abuse of these (unknown back then) new, volatile drugs. Ace clearly remembers his large daily ingestions. Particularly as the so-called 'Summer of Love' and the pressure on the band mounted. "I was having a gradual nervous breakdown. I was dropping acid every day. I always took anything, opium, coke, acid, speed. I was cracking up — just like Syd Barrett was. Syd could hardly move sometimes. He was on another planet. I was too, but at least I always delivered the show. They wanted me out of the band and Trevor to go over onto bass. They were saying I couldn't even tune the bass, let alone play it. At the time they were right. Admittedly, I was arrogant, and I had a temper. But another big part of the trouble, was this pretty-pretty boy look, as 'Ace The Face.'"

Ace remembered it had started before, "Earlier on at dates for example outside hotels in Scotland for some reason. They would be chanting 'Ace! Ace! Ace!' Tony was getting requests from *FAB 208* for photo sessions. The magazine just wanted me on my own. Tony explained to the others, it was for the overall good of the band. But they still didn't like it. After one of the photo sessions, I rushed back to a rehearsal in a taxi. I walked in and they all turned away. They sent me to Coventry. Also, I was being cold-shouldered in the van. 200 miles there, do the gig, 200 miles back and not a word! It was very frustrating for Tony, just like dealing with a bunch of schoolgirls."

Ace adds that in a in a recent conversation with Trevor Burton, "Trevor said to me, there's been something that's been bugging me for years, Ace. All that no talking in the van and stuff. Trevor told me that it was all planned: 'We all discussed it and said if we don't talk to him, he will eventually be forced to leave'. You have to remember; I was very ill. Sad in those days as nobody understood things."

"Ace kinda did himself in. He went from being really photogenic and good looking. Then he had that dreadful perm. He started wearing those granny glasses," Bev surmised after Ace leaving. "I mean, the drugs really affected him badly. Trevor took just exactly the same amounts, but he made it through more evenly. It seemed Trevor could handle the drugs better. In the middle of the 60s. It was way before people had heard of any mental illness. We didn't know what it was. It's kind of weird that there wasn't a father figure for any of us. If any one of us had had a dad. Like an intelligent dad, giving us some sound advice, that might have really helped us out."

Bev declared, "We should definitely have spent more time in the studio. Been given a lot more studio time, maybe the rest of us could have started contributing things. Instead of recording things on the hoof, every here and there. I wish that Ace and Trevor hadn't hit the drugs so hard! They just got so out of it. That's when the personalities became so different for us. Ace at one time didn't make it for a gig at all. So, they were beginning to mess up."

After the time Ace left The Move and according to John Pearson in his book on Wilf Pine, "Ace Kefford was increasingly at odds with the rest of the band, who wished to sack him! But they were frightened by the fact that Ace had two supposedly aggressive brothers, who they worried might cause trouble. Wilf Pine was a friend of Carl's and had connections in Birmingham. Don Arden asked if he would go up there, as soon as possible and sort matters out. So, he turned for help to his best friend in Birmingham, 'Big Al', the doorman extraordinaire, based at the Rum Runner (and at The Elbow Room) and he proved to be all important. Wilf explained to him how worried Carl and The Move were becoming. All they wanted was to get on with their music. Without any threat from Ace and his two brothers. Albert promised to find out what was happening and sort out a swift solution. Albert came back with some info.

Although Ace's brothers were said to be "a little lively", they were nothing to worry about."

John Pearson's facts in his otherwise excellent book are totally incorrect. Nicola Hancox, the daughter of Reg Jones, confirmed my suspicions: "Ace only has one brother. I'm sure you're right that Pearson was referring to Reg and Chris Jones (Ace's uncles). Although they were known as hard men, they really weren't. Apparently, they were known back then, as 'The Jones Brothers'. Pine's solution to the problem, was in in the shape of Mickey and Bluey, a pair of very tough twins he knew. Pine described them as 'an unbelievable fighting force' whenever they worked together. Albert spoke to them on Wilf's behalf and explained the situation. The following evening, when Big Albert saw Wilf at the Cedar Club, Wilf was told, that Albert had had a little chat with the twins. They promised him they'd help out if needed. Big Albert said to Wilf, 'Give Carl my telephone number and the number of the twins. If they get any bother from the characters we talked about, all they need to do is call us, and we'll deal with it for you at once'."

****

On 30th May 1968 at Zurich Kloten Airport, a motley looking assortment of passengers disembarked the chartered plane from London. Some forty young men in outstandingly colourful garb, sporting floppy hats, odd hairdos, jewellery and scarves, descended down the steps. They were met immediately by baffled customs officials and taken to the improvised customs area: A bus located at the end of the tarmac, some two kilometres away from the official desks. The gregarious, stoned gaudy lot, kept giggling and joking. And with good reason. They were part of the celebrated British music scene and had come to Zurich to play two concerts at the Hallenstadion.

A convoy of limousines rented from Welti-Furrer AG was parked beside the mobile customs to take the merry musos out through a back exit out of the airport, to the Hotel Stoller in the centre of Zurich. A contingent of policemen and water-cannons were also in place as The Move played the packed-out Hallenstadion for two nights in a row.

On both nights (30th and 31st May), organised by promoter Hans-Ruedi Jaggi, The Move played along with Eric Burdon (The New Animals), Traffic, John Mayall and Jimi Hendrix. The Zurich show was presented as a package tour, but consisted of just these two dates. Many drugs and other things were being smoked and drunk on the flight by a lot of the musicians aboard.

They were warned during the flight that they would undoubtedly be searched on landing at Zurich. Pockets and bags were hurriedly emptied of all drugs. Which were consumed, flushed, in readiness. Hendrix was particularly taken aside and intentionally searched. With one zealous security guard, running his fingers through Jimi's Afro hair.

The two-day event was apparently very chaotic. It became a stand-off between the autocratic Swiss police and a local band of raucous, drugged up Hells Angels. These tattooed road warriors, climbed into the orchestra pit. Keith Altham, (noted journalist from the *New Musical Express*) found Hendrix to be very self-indulgent.

With everybody hanging on every mad extravagant note that he played. "Jimi was soloing like crazy, but I felt what he was doing, was just practising, self-indulgent jamming."

Trevor Burton cast his mind back to that session with Hendrix: "I'll never forget it because I played drums. Zurich is where the Zildjian cymbals come from. At that time, they were the newest thing on the scene. So, all the drummers were taken to the Zildjian factory to have anything they wanted. Any cymbal they liked; they could take away. So, the rest of us decided to go down and have a jam. It was onstage at the gig, but it was before the show. It was just literally jamming. You'd start something up and everybody would join in — have a break and a joint and start again. Chris Wood (of Traffic) played flute and sax — apparently, he would never miss a jam."

It all began with a long version of the traditional air, 'Danny Boy'. Keith Altham witnessed one session, involving Jimi, Chris Wood on flute and fellow Traffic member Dave Mason on bass. This was so loud, that the police burst in to quell the disturbance, with truncheons drawn and at the ready. Later, Roy Wood, found himself playing bass, at yet another jam session, alongside Jimi, Chris and Steve Winwood with Jim Capaldi on drums.

It's said that Chris Wood recorded the jam on his portable tape recorder. Previously on 22nd December 1967, over a few drinks with managers and musicians at the London Speakeasy club, Jaggi had provisionally bought the top-class rock multi-pack all for the ridiculously low amount of £15,000.

But Jaggi had to find some financial sponsors back in Zurich. He would not get any government subsidies for this grand event, dubbed Pop-Montserkonzert.

Each night kicked off with a fashion show by the local boutique Bernie's. Once the fashions were displayed, a series of bands took to the stage, including: Anselmo Trend, Sauterelles, Hardy Hepp and The Koobas. The promoter had previously brought the Rolling Stones to the Hallenstadion, much to the disapproval of the Zurich officials. The Stones were notorious for having left a trail of broken concert hall furniture on their tours. In Zurich too, they had lived up to their bad-boys reputation. Jaggi became known after the Stones gig, as the 'Pope Of Beat'. He posed for photographs in front of his Bentley, with long hair, polo-neck sweater, velvet jacket, pointed boots, and surrounded by very blonde, very young girls.

The local constabulary had to support an event of this size. They discussed security with the arrogant young Jaggi, whom they considered a brazen upstart. Werner Wollenberger, the chief-editor of the *Zürcher Woche* had demanded a ban on such events. Particularly, after the fans at a Stones gig had transformed some thousand folding chairs into firewood.

This new music era tied in with an accompanying period of societal turbulence. Titled by the media as the 'Restlessness Of Youth', the phenomenon was spreading like a nappy rash, across Europe and overseas. It was all connected with the new 'beat' music. Students occupied universities and prevented professors from holding lecture. In Rome, Berlin, Paris and elsewhere, barricades were erected, (hence The Stones' 'Street Fighting Man') street fights with the police took place. In some ways similar to the current social warrior tactics. Cars were trashed and burnt and left smouldering in the streets. Bearing this in mind, the heavily moneyed, very conservative, Zurich authorities were determined to prevent the upheaval from spreading into Zurich.

A very early photo. Left to Right: Roy Wood, Bev Bevan, Chris 'Ace' Kefford, Carl Wayne, Trevor Burton.

Trevor Burton: "The Move were a force to be reckoned with, especially vocally. We were one of the best in the country - we must've been."

Before stardom hit hard - styling some Mod clothes in 1966. That year was spent gigging relentlessly nationwide, getting noticed and making their mark!

Tony Secunda had them outfitted in 'gangster' double breasted suits. They were styled in Saville Row, London. Simple, elegant and with more than a hint of menace. This shot taken in Hyde Park, London.

On tour in 1966, in The Gorbals... the rough tenement area of Glasgow, Scotland. Serious Young men, making serious, soulful rocking music.

Signing their contract on the back of model Liz Jones in Soho, London. Left to right: Carl Wayne, Denny Cordell, Liz Jones, Tony Secunda and Roy Wood.

Trevor Burton raves onstage at The Roundhouse. The two strippers almost went unnoticed as Carl Wayne took an axe to both the stage and a 1956 Chevrolet.

Roy Wood, seen here in 1967. Initially, the introverted one, he was encouraged by Tony Secunda, and blossomed as a unique songwriter, hitmaker, vocalist and guitarist.

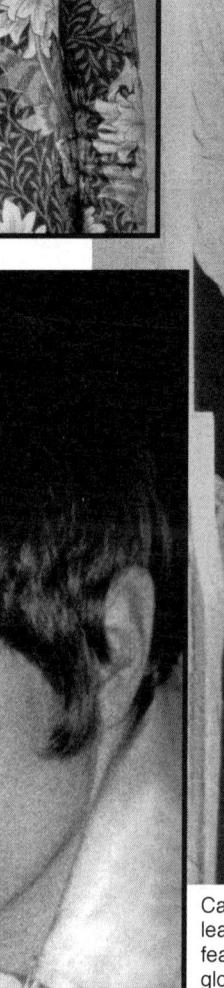

Carl Wayne in 1967. The Move's superb lead vocalist, he was charismatic and fearless onstage. He led The Move's glorious, four-man, vocal and harmony team. RIP Carl.

Bev Bevan in 1966. The "loudest drummer in Birmingham." His dynamic drumming was a perfect fit for the young band. Both in the studio and onstage.

1966. Chris 'Ace the Face' Kefford brought charisma, great vocals, and a massive bass sound to the group.

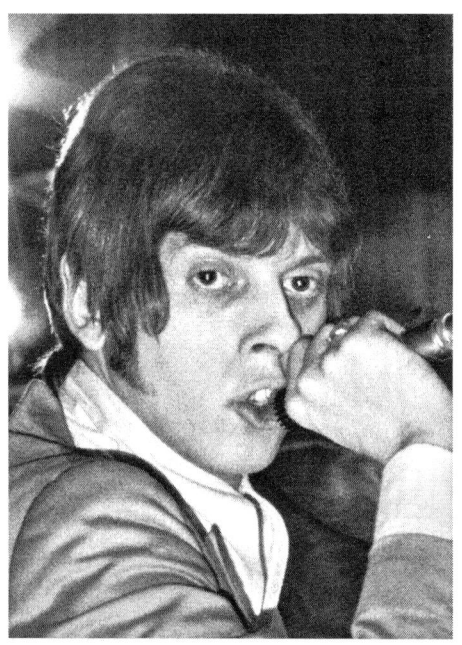

Trevor Burton in 1966. Responsible with Ace for starting the band. Great raw vocals with dynamic rebel cool and a strong live presence.

Pictured at Stamford Bridge, Chelsea Football Stadium, London.

Ace Kefford, styling the 'Summer of Love' beads and paisley finery during the 'Flowers In The Rain' era.

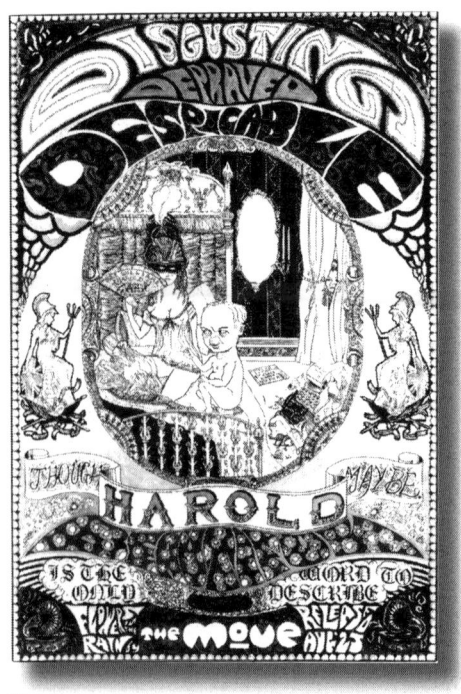

The Secunda originated postcard that caused all the trouble, with Prime Minister Harold Wilson suing the band and manager at the High Courts in London, October, 1967.

Bev Bevan rocking the 1967 'Summer of Love', kaftan look, which he absolutely hated.

Roy Wood and Tony Secunda on the way to the High Court, London, October 1967.

The Move as "living art" models in the Heals department store front window, London, 1966.

Carl Wayne wrecking TVs and seen here destroying effigies of Adolf Hitler and the apartheid, Rhodesian Prime Minister Ian Smith at the newly opened London nightclub, The Speakeasy in 1966.

Another shot from The Speakeasy, September, 1966. The shows became notorious for their wild and ritualistic stage antics, regularly smashing or setting fire to television sets, and on one occasion The Marquee Club itself.

Carl Wayne, ever the gentlemen jester. Asking a Parisien gendarme, for a light for this rolled joint?

Carl Wayne and Trevor Burton, two young Mods, sightseeing in Paris, during their gig supporting The Rolling Stones at L'Olympia, Paris, April, 1966.

Bev Bevan and Trevor Burton, stylish sightseers, look for postcards in Paris, April, 1966.

24.
Holiday in Reality

Ace Kefford was out of The Move and he now badly needed some money: "I was totally skint at the time. So, I signed a publishing deal for these songs (for the solo recordings in London to be done with Tony Visconti) that I was supposed to be composing. With the publishing advance I rented a place near Whittington, a village in Staffordshire. There were no other houses for miles. That's how I wanted it. I could not go outside. As I was acid flashing all the time (also commonly known as flash backs). I built some kind of shrine, and I tried to get into transcendental meditation. But I was still cracking up mentally. One day, I took all these tranquillisers and went into a coma. My wife and this Birmingham musician, John Fox, got me to the hospital to be stomach pumped. The next thing I knew was, they had used electro-convulsive therapy on me. And for a while it worked. I forgot what I was supposed to be worrying about. During that time, I saved a little girl from drowning. That made me feel quite good about myself and life in general."

During Rob Caiger's excavations for The Move's master tapes, one mostly long forgotten about and extremely rare tape reel also came to light. Rob's keen nose for detail made his detective work extremely precise. These were the 'lost' recording reels from Ace Kefford's aborted solo 1968 record. These attempted recordings were conducted during May, June and July 1968. The recording dates included 17th May 1968 at Olympic Studios. Further sessions were held at Trident Studios from 31st May to 15th July 1968. There were only nine tracks in total for the proposed album. (It's said there are possibly two tracks missing that Rob Caiger could not locate).

In order to put together an entire CD, Rob added six further tracks from the Ace Kefford Stand output and two tracks from Rockstar, another band that Ace formed and recorded with up to 1977. Included were the A and B side of a very David Bowie influenced single ('Mummy' and 'Over The Hill' released as an MCA single — more of this later). Strong writing and original, perhaps autobiographically, flavoured songs from Ace. Ace's songs could be very commercial, he certainly was showing considerable potential as a songwriter. And many could have fitted snugly into The Move's singles/albums discography. One song was written for and recorded by the Lemon Tree.

'I Can See A Rainbow', The B-side of 'William Chalker's Time Machine' is an example of Derek Arnold's (Lemon Tree bassist who also played with Bandy Legs and Quartz among others) songwriting. Again, this is a decent song, fitting snugly into that psychedelically-tinged era. It was released on Parlophone Records through EMI on 1st March 1968. Production was overseen by Trevor Burton, and

Flowers In The Rain - The Untold Story of The Move

Andy Fairweather Low of Amen Corner.

Regarding the A-side, Ace tells explains: "'William Chalker's Time Machine' is acid. I mean, lemon trees and mystic mist on a mountain high (laughs). I think I can remember playing this to The Move in the dressing room before a show. It's said that The Move recorded it in a live session for radio, but I haven't come across it."

The Lemon Tree were a short-lived but very interesting band. They could've developed a career of their own, with the right breaks. "'William Chalker's Time Machine' was played an awful lot on Luxembourg — we got a lot of power play type things and all the rest of it. It did good in the Midlands, the kind of regional charts and stuff. Alan Freeman and the Tony Blackburn show, we did both of those."

Fiery guitarist Bob Sawyer saw them early on. "I saw The Lemon Tree at The Woolsey Hall, Cheshunt Park in early '68. The club there was called The Beat Scene." Bob Sawyer was really impressed. After that gig in Cheshunt he said. "The lead guitarist played a black telecaster, had a fuzzbox and wore a brown suede fringe jacket. Derek Arnold played a Hofner violin bass. The drummer was breaking sticks at a rate of knots. He was that bloody powerful. (Derek Arnold — "That would have been Keith Smart. He was a heavy drummer back then"). He was a great drummer!" Bob Sawyer concludes, saying, "apart from their sheer attack! They fucking meant it."

Derek Arnold casts an eye over their attempts to break out: "Yeah, we were with Ron King at Galaxy Entertainment. We signed to Ron King along with Amen Corner. Mainly gigs with people like the Nashville Teens and people like that, cause King had got them under his belt. We did *Top Of The Pops* in 1968. We did three television shows, all within ten days in London. We used to stay in a place called the Madison Hotel. It was the 'pound a night' hotel. That was in Sussex Gardens. They had a bar there, and we're going out to have a drink in the bar. We didn't know anybody in London. Roger Daltrey was there, he was with three Danish birds that night. He said, 'Where are you going now lads?' We said, 'We don't know anybody. We're going back to the hotel.' Roger says, 'You can't do that! Hang on, I'll sort you out.' So, we followed him in his car, and he took us to The Speakeasy. He introduced us to the dancers. He says now you can spend a better night, celebrating doing *Top Of The Pops*'."

Despite the short-lived duration of The Lemon Tree Derek Arnold had a bit of success later on. "When we were first with Bandy Legs. We were signed to Don Arden's Jet Records. We backed Jimmy Helms, (A great R&B-soul-rock and numerous sessions singer) originally from the USA, possibly best known for his big hit 'I've Been Thinking About You.' A huge smash hit written by Helms. This produced his highest-ever charting success. It reached number 2 on the UK singles chart in September 1990. Incredibly, it hit number 1 on the US Billboard Hot 100 in February 1991. It stayed on the chart for nearly five months. It must be said, it's an evergreen, an absolutely glorious, anthemic single. "We did about twelve months, we did all the cabaret places and everything. That was the time when Jimmy had, 'Gonna Make You An Offer, You Can't Refuse'. When he had that, I think that was number one."

And so back to the Ace Kefford solo recording. Rob Caiger discovered this forgotten musical archive history in 2003 along with other great Move rarities. At the time Tony Visconti had produced the Ace tracks, Ace was still gripped by addiction and needing to self-medicate on a daily basis. "Unfortunately, I could not stop taking drugs and was still involved in narcotics twenty-four-seven. Tony Visconti was brought into produce and arrange. Jimmy Page came in and played guitar on one of the tracks. Nothing came of it as my head was gone completely, with all the drugs I was still taking. I just vanished, packed it in. I never went back. I just wanted to hide myself away."

Tony Secunda had thought he could wring some juice out of the 'Ace The Face' situation, as any good hustling manager would. He was however, overlooking Ace's precarious mental state and interested in pursuing the potential cash cow.

Secunda was always alert to potential business opportunities. That part of his personality was ingrained and very steely. He could quite easily overlook certain matters in the quest for fabulous publicity and increasing cash flow. He still saw potential in the ailing Ace Kefford. He was looking for a way to work the 'Ace the Face' thing. Secunda thought he could work this angle and get Ace's budding songwriting going. Secunda wanted to get him out there as a solo act. Put a good band together around him and record it.

Tony Visconti remembers how the project came about: "Tony Secunda had bypassed Denny Cordell and asked me specifically to produce Ace Kefford's music. Secunda said that because of Ace's good looks it was a no-brainer. Ace would become a star in his own right. Initially I believe this was a demo project, to see if an album or singles could be done. When it was apparent it couldn't, it was abandoned."

Visconti had a strong hands-on role. "I put the session musicians together for Ace. The sessions were booked in at Trident Studios. We recorded onto four and eight track tape. I booked the studio; I listened to Ace's demos and picked the songs I wanted to do with him."

One session Visconti booked for 12th July 1968 was with the following musicians: Clem Cattini on drums, Clive Hicks on guitar, Brian Brocklehurst on bass and Alan Wale on keyboards. All these musicians were paid the session fee of nine pounds and ten pence. The sessions ran from 7:00 to 10:00. A separate cheque was made out to Jimmy Page for playing guitar. He again got paid the same fee of £9.10. Plus, a 'doubling' fee of £1:00 was added. Cheques were billed from Tony's Orchestral Management for a total of £44 and were sent to Straight Ahead Productions, who were then located at Dumbarton House in Oxford Street. Tony felt almost instantly, "I soon learned that Ace would be difficult to work with. He had a temper, and he seemed to be irrational There were outbursts — he acted awkwardly. Honestly, I was glad when he walked out."

"My wife Jenny and I drove down to London," recalled Ace, who felt and was aware of his agitated and admittedly paranoid state. "I was fucking loopy wasn't I?"

The musicians had done the backing tracks. So, it was just Ace and Tony Visconti who would be in the studio. Ace says, "If anybody came into the studio... I'd be in the control booth, staring out, looking to see who the fuck is that. I was just completely paranoid."

Ace was still reeling from the intense and sudden success and climactic ending of being caught up in The Move's immense rollercoaster ride. Imagine New Year's Eve every day and multiply that several times. That's what it was like and then some.

But with the added pressure of Ace's increasing mental instability. Mix in with this, the pressure of using amphetamines for two years non-stop; travelling, smoking weed and then comes the completely unknown compound, known as LSD.

The opening song 'Oh Girl' sees Ace pressing into the earlier use of his Winwood-esque voice. This was seen as a possible A-side single. As an interesting aside, Ace recalls, "Spencer Davis asked me to cover for Muff Winwood one night at The Whisky A Go Go. I was 16, Stevie was 15. What an experience! My whole view of music changed. I started buying albums by Sam Cooke, Curtis Mayfield. The sound of Black America. It all came from standing next to the guv'nor really, Stevie!"

Ace looks back to the sessions, "I was one of the very first people that Tony Visconti ever produced. He was known as a string arranger back then. Tony brought in some specific songs and then I think Tony would've liked to add my songs as the B-sides. Tony brought in 'Oh Girl' and that Simon & Garfunkel cover 'Save The Life Of My Child' and 'Lay Your Head Upon My Shoulder'. 'Infanta Marina' is another unique song, Ace here pushes his voice, towards a semi-R&B vibe. The cut features layered chiming guitars. He remembered, "Chuck Berry used to write about young girls — songs like 'Sweet Little Sixteen.' Not too young though." Ace supplies nice stuttering, punky guitar on 'Trouble In The Air'. The only track I think, in which he played and added an electric instrument? A very atmospheric song with perhaps a touch of a 'mutant' Vince Taylor or an Everly Brothers vibe?

An early protest song about racial unrest — possibly in Birmingham — was included with 'White Mask'. Ace sings this in a very appealing manner. A slightly inflected stutter in his vocal and strong rhyming couplets could've made this into a very strong finished song. In fact, 'White Mask' when Rob Caiger and Ace came to listen to it again, had a full band performance. Ace felt it was better to take those layers out and just leave it with the acoustic barebones backing. Ace shows a lot of vocal versatility on these cuts, appearing to move his voice around to suit the material. Rather than singing a song in exactly the same vocal timbre. 'Lay Your Head Upon My Shoulder' is the song that triggered Ace into suffering a breakdown and walking out on the project completely. This final track recording, Ace felt was very (way too much) like 'Concrete And Clay' by Unit 4+2: "I didn't like it, that was the song, I walked out on — It was just total pop!"

This is no reflection on Tony Visconti, as Ace was suffering with acid flashbacks, panic attacks and experiencing encroaching bouts of severe depression. He totally overreacted to the possible inclusion of this track. Quite simply, it could've been dropped from the sessions and something else put in to replace it. The ending song was 'Happy Hour' and it sounds like an old style, piano led, public house, piss up. In fact, Ace said in an interview that, "I was pretty drunk recording it and everybody playing live was just having fun and fucking around."

In addition to the nine Tony Visconti sessions from 1968, when it was finally released on CD in 2003 all the Ace Kefford Stand studio recordings were added. Nobody seemed to like their single, 'For Your Love'. I don't know why they did this particular song. This was an over-covered song already. In my opinion, the demo version (also included here) is much better, than the muffled, stuffy studio version. Which came out as the first Atlantic single. 'Born To Be Wild' is covered here also, a good choice in terms of audience reaction. A sturdy version of the Mod favourite,

Sharon Tandy's 'Daughter Of The Sun' is a hip selection with a great vocal and some pumping bass from Denny Ball. Starting with shrill piercing feedback, 'Gravy Booby Jamm' is the B-side of the 'For Your Love' single. Again, with a better and less muffled production this freaky, snarling jam could've been elevated further.

As Ace intones, "I lost my head again — Yeah." A phrase anybody who has been around AA recovery or 12-Step rooms will be well familiar with.

These Stand sessions are rounded out by a second Atlantic released single. By then, the group minus Ace had morphed into Bedlam, detailed elsewhere in this book. With a decent Ace vocal, 'This World Is An Apple' concluded the obligation contractually, for two Ace Kefford Stand singles for Atlantic Records.

Ace remembers how fast the music industry was moving. The media was now intent on imparting Peter Frampton (then of The Herd — another emerging pop singles act) with the 'Face of 1968' appellation. "I was the same as Peter Green and Syd Barrett. If I hadn't been so much in the spotlight I might have gotten through it."

As 1967 gave way to 1968, Peter Frampton was experiencing similar trepidations. But without the collapse and all the overload of drugs that Ace was experiencing.

The Small Faces encountered some of the same problems as The Move. Both bands in common were booked by Galaxy Entertainments. Steve Marriott wanted to escape the "pop" perception of the group and the stranglehold. As he/they saw it, that had befallen The Small Faces. That they were considered a pop singles band with releases like 'Sha La La La Lee', 'My Minds Eye', leading up to what they thought was the "jokey" release of 'Lazy Sunday' from the impending *Ogdens' Nut Gone Flake* album with its wonderfully laid out, circular album cover, released on Immediate Records. A gorgeous example of the free-wheeling album graphics redolent of the time. The song was however, a huge public favourite and just about everybody loved 'Lazy Sunday'.

Unfortunately, Stevie Marriott began to lose much of his innate lightness of touch that came so naturally to him as a 'Small Face'. Was this due to the increased effects of all the cocaine that was starting to permeate the industry? Was it the buildup in the nervous system of this (at first magical) powder which appears to sooner or later, turn people into brutish, numb, verbal-spewing clowns with their personal and humorous elements being hacked off in increments? Then the rapid fall down the personality charts. That effervescent, easy, people's touch that Steve Marriott and Ronnie "Plonk" Lane enjoyed. That Lennon and McCartney and some others had. An abundance of the light — coupled with an ability to strike the common nerve. To catch the truth, standing on a street corner.

Both The Move and the Small Faces were generally perceived, as pop 'Mod' bands. Marriott's songwriting, however, was developing towards a heavier sound. On newer studio cuts, like 'Wham Bam, Thank You Mam' and 'Afterglow Of Your Love'. Similar things could be said to have happened to Roy Wood's later writing. In fact, although Marriott did write some other rocking classics later on, he also never lost his raw, big vocality and his guitar playing was incredible. Cocaine made him into a very brutish person. A caricature of the rock 'n' roll, black, soul guy that he saw himself as? Or as Melvyn: his Dr Jekyll-like wrestling alter-ego?

25.
She's sure good looking man, she's something else...

The *Move* album was followed on 21st June 1968 by another unique and tremendous release, *Something Else From The Move*. An EP recorded live at the Marquee, containing the first five-piece Move, slamming their way through some fantastic cover versions. For many years the master tapes were said to have been mislaid, before the songs resurfaced on a Castle Communications 2LP/CD set, *The Move Collection* in 1987.

The Move Official Fan Club newsletter collated by club secretary Pauline Evans alerted fans to a big event with the following missive: "Wanna make a record with The Move? It will be possible on 27th February at the Marquee Club, Wardour Street, London. Because that's when the boys will be making the live E.P. We mentioned it to you in the last newsletter. We will be all very glad to see all you Movers who can make it, screaming and cheering The Move and helping them make a fantastic 'live' E.P with loads of atmosphere."

That said, when released, the E.P included two tracks recorded on 5th May with Kefford having exited and Burton moving over to bass, it also captures the four-piece Move in full blast, sweeping through a brace of their favourite covers.

Bev Bevan: "The *Something Else From The Move* EP caught us as we really sounded. I don't think Denny Cordell ever grasped the wild energy of The Move. In the studio, Denny took all the toughness out."

Trevor Burton reinforces Bev's point. "We were natural rock 'n' rollers. By this time, we added a psychedelic edge to what we were doing. With those West Coast covers and Roy going wild with his wah-wah pedal."

This time the band were kicking it hard — with mostly UK and USA rock 'n' roll. And some newer "psych" rock. One observer stated it as a memento, a souvenir, of how bands truly sounded before PA systems. It precedes the currency of auto-tune and all the tricks that can make the most average singer and band seem fuller (and more in tune) than they are.

Although the band are on fiery full blast, throwing it down hard in front of The Marquee audience, the *Something Else From The Move* EP failed to chart. It was the first UK 7-inch by The Move to fail to do so. Something that for a stressful period became all too common. The Move had hit a brick wall in terms of sales and in seemingly making all the right moves.

Flowers In The Rain - The Untold Story of The Move

The remastered CD release with extra tracks starts with a short instrumental piece called 'Move Bolero' which had actually opened their set. But the original release really works because it literally explodes with their insanely dynamic version of The Byrds' 'So You Want To Be Rock 'n' Roll Star'. This is probably one of the best things I have ever heard live. In which a band performing a cover version really take it to another (higher) place.

It has an unbelievably dynamic energy. It's a torrid vortex. A blitzkrieg of power, attacking the audience with superb flailing drumming from Bev Bevan and a hypnotic, revolving bass line from Kefford. In fact, for the first bars, Bev Bevan plays against the beat. Creating an intense feeling of dislocation momentarily before coming down on the one and propelling this superb version into the stratosphere. The two corrugated, entangled tight guitars interact, casting off tons of attitude and threat from Roy Wood (using swathes of rich wah-wah pedal) and Trevor Burton, scything away behind him on rhythm guitar. Both ride the rhythm hard. Topped by a supremely celebratory and confident lead vocal from the irrepressible Carl Wayne. All making this, an exultant snapshot of just how powerful this band was live in its first incarnation. Gram Parsons of The Byrds opined, "Their version was much better than ours."

Carl recalled The Byrds covers they loved playing: "We really liked the Byrds' 'Rock 'n' Roll Star' and 'Eight Miles High'. We used to do all of those. Not only was it the harmonies that attracted us, because we were adept at doing four-part harmonies; there were things that were of great interest to Roy. Because he was an experimentalist with his instruments, as all good guitarists are. He loved the twelve-string stuff — which gave him another avenue to explore."

Bob Sawyer, previously with Praying Mantis, Iron Maiden and others also attested to The Move's elemental raw power: "Their live version of the Byrds' 'So You Want To Be Rock 'n' Roll Star' is — I can only describe it as... a gorgeously, menacing onslaught! Their live version is unbelievable. It's a sonic blast of sound. With great vocals, great drumming and the propulsive circular bass from Ace is superb."

Here is some prescribed rock 'n' roll medication for you right here, right now! If you can, put it on your CD or record player or stream and turn it up very loud and marvel. I completely agree with Bob Sawyers's assessment. I have not heard many bands smash a song so hard like this, live. They are knocking it straight out of the ballpark. The cut has a pre-punk energy but allied to more soulful playing.

This EP was an unusual release at the time. In fact, Secunda marketed it as a 'mini-LP'. A five-track effort lasting approximately 18 minutes. With the aforementioned track just erupting out of the speakers as the EP opener. Closely followed by Love's 'Stephanie Knows Who', a 3/4 time waltz which again has a storming rhythm section, with Carl's feral, open-throated vocals, displaying more than a taste of raw, free-flowing attitude.

Side one of the EP closes with a great classic version of Eddie Cochran's 'Something Else', one of the two tracks from the May recording. Trevor Burton supplies another raw, wild vocal. Trevor had a great rock 'n' roll voice and could turn on the rawness when it was needed. He comes up trumps here. The song is powerful and full of dynamic staccato breaks. With Bev Bevan displaying his simple

She's sure good looking man, she's something else...

but cracking, dynamic flam technique on the snare drum. Bev Bevan loved to use this snare technique. Very simple but extremely effective.

Around this time in interviews, The Move were righteously trumpeting the value of good old rock 'n' roll. Their straight-ahead, belting rock 'n' roll numbers went down fantastically on stage. Particularly as transmuted through The Move's eviscerating, onstage dynamic aggression.

Call Wayne announced, in a throwback to his "psychedelia is a load of shit' comments, "We are tired of airy-fairy lyrics. Remember the days of rock and round the clock! How the cinema seats were ripped up night after night and they danced in the aisles?"

Trevor Burton interjects, "We do a couple of real raves on stage and they're going down best of all. All it needs is a switch hundred percent and the whole rock era would return at once."

Bev exclaims, "There's loads of Teddy boys all over the country, they still have their winkle pickers and suits. They are dying for it to come back."

Ace Kefford exclaimed, "Yeah, I heard Wee Willie Harris went down an absolute bomb at The Cromwellian the other day!"

Trevor wound up some mild-mannered reader in the *Record Mirror* when he stated: "I personally really enjoy violence. I'm looking forward to a revival of gang warfare, on the scale of the Hells Angels in America." What an absolute bunch of wind-ups they all were (and Tony Secunda). Anything to wind-up the reading audience, right up to the max.

Punctuating the fiery dynamism inherent in The Move's music, 'It'll Be Me' (a Jack Clement composition) from the electric Jerry Lee Lewis, starts the second vinyl side and again bursts out of the speakers with an unrestrained self-confidence. The Move here reference the 1962 Cliff Richard version. This is slower than the Jerry Lee Lewis original. The Move really rock it up. A huge unison group sound breaks out and they beef up the breaks. With further great drum flams and cracks from Bev Bevan. A joyous, swooping Carl Wayne vocal brings out the full power of the rocker. *"If you hear somebody knocking on your dooo-ooor."* Carl opens the piece with a great uninhibited vocal. The close harmony vocals are as tight as always. *"Aaaah wahhh - waaaah!"*

On the original vinyl release, Spooky Tooth's 'Sunshine Help Me' closes the second side, the second track recorded at the May gig. It's another wah-wah led excursion. With Roy supplying plenty of scorching guitar fretwork. This is from the second recorded Marquee show. Which was taped a bit later in the year, after Ace had left. It's a tasty, measured, extremely exciting, and intense guitar solo by Roy. The barraging interplay from Trevor Burton's Fender bass guitar, intertwining and creating even further musical tension. It resolves perfectly towards the last bars as the guitar solo climaxes with Carl Wayne's impassioned roar, bringing it all back home! It shows the more progressive, distinctive bass style of Trevor. Although, it loses Ace's more primal pumped-up energy. This is probably one of the best live guitar solos that I've heard in terms of creating excitement, building tension and coming around and resolving the solo, with a superb, last guitar line flourish. It must be a solo that Roy would be proud of. Or any other guitarist or listener who enjoys unique, stylish, impassioned playing. Reissues features Carl's onstage banter, introducing 'Sunshine

Flowers In The Rain - The Untold Story of The Move

Help Me' as "featuring the brilliant talents of Roy on guitar and tap dancing".

Another remastered release of the *Something Else From The Move* EP by Esoteric Recordings' compiler Mark Powell has combined the EP's tunes with all the twelve songs recorded at The Marquee gigs in a newer stereo mix. I feel in some ways these stereo mixes have 'flattened out' the sound somewhat.

In reference to the first Salvo remasters these were originally remastered in 2007 by Nick Robbins and Rob Keyloch at Sound Mastering Ltd. A total collection of 17 tracks, containing 56 minutes of high-octane Mod and West Coast space rock. The only song in which the vocals and backing recording could not be salvaged (it's still on the shelf) is their version of Moby Grape's 'Hey Grandma'. Luckily Move completists will have the studio version on the debut album and as a BBC live broadcast.

The set list of *Something Else From The Move* is a wonderful mix of Roy Wood originals and cover versions of hit songs of the day from Spooky Tooth, The Byrds, Love, Janis Joplin and Jackie Wilson among others. The blend is perfect. The inclusion of the EP's five original tracks as "bonus material" is novel. The opportunity to compare the stereo mixes with the EP's original mono mixes, remastered by Ben Wiseman at Broadlake Studios all works very well.

New to the remastered CD is 'Too Much In Love', a mid-tempo Denny Laine R&B styled number. 'Too Much In Love' uses the dynamic intro trick. Where the rhythm guitars and drums come in together. Thickly churning up the rhythmic sludge. Ace holds back before he comes in fully on bass after the first intro bars. After throwing a bass dive bomb, Ace then gives the song the huge bass undertow that Kefford was known for. Gorgeous harmony vocals complement Wayne's lead vocals as Wood's guitar once again dominates. The first album cut (from the *Move* album) featured is 'Flowers In The Rain' with a big wah-wah guitar intro by Roy Wood and Bevan's drums pushing the beat on this psychedelic pop classic. With the live vocal variation on the ending they unison voice, *"watching flowers - in the rainaaaa-aaaaiiiannn"* in super tight, close harmony. Ending the tune, with some bass buzz and as a definite audience favourite.

Next up is another single/album cut 'Fire Brigade' with another chiming big guitar intro. Followed by the insistent big beat drumming of Bevan and more incredible guitar by Wood. Covering The Byrds became a Move favourite (later on with 'Goin' Back' and 'The Christian Life').

The Everly Brothers wrote 'The Price Of Love' but The Move make it their own — the deafening cacophony of Kefford and Bevan, giving way to Burton's chunky rhythm and Wood's understated lead guitar work. This is one, that even with the remastering, still sounds somewhat blurry. Jerry Ragavoy and Bert Bern's chestnut, 'Piece Of My Heart' was a hit for Janis Joplin and Big Brother. The Move give it a rolling and tumbling vibe, with Bev's drums. Carl Wayne injects a higher register of soul here. Jackie Wilson's '(Your Love Keeps Lifting Me) Higher And Higher' again leans on its R&B roots. With Wayne's vocals dominating, until Wood's guitar inevitably takes centre stage. Jackie Wilson is said to have angrily exclaimed, "What the fuck have they done to my song?".

The set closes with a cover of Spooky Tooth's debut single, the Gary Wright penned 'Sunshine Help Me'. The band showing off its vocal harmonies, picks up its

She's sure good looking man, she's something else…

paces and sweeps, swampily, down and dirty, through the classic tune. Carl Wayne's vocals waste no time here in getting raw and dirty. With the emphasis on pumping the soulful aspects of the vocal. It's great to hear Carl let off the leash and showing off his truly magnificent rock 'n' roll vocal pipes. Roy Wood proves he is more than equal to the challenge of matching Luther Grosvenor's guitar work on the original recording. Wood plays incredible lead guitar lines and a masterful solo.

Bob Sawyer inputs some seasoned guitar player comments and descriptions on Roy's stellar playing on 'Sunshine Help Me'. "The Woody guitar solo is just great and his finger tremolo is great on this solo. It sounds like he's kicked on the fuzzbox, on a 'low' setting. He has added more gain, judging by the way the sound of his Fender changes. He is using the pinched octave and using the fingers. I love the way his wah-wah sounds when he goes into the 'Eastern' style, droning notes, up against the top 'E' string. It is very 'experimental' and at around the 5 minutes mark he goes into 'Strangers In The Night' which was a trick Hendrix used also. Jimi quoted 'The Bond Theme' at a show… All of this, just goes to show, just what a great guitarist Roy is."

An unedited version of this performance, with a longer guitar solo closes this collection. This re-release of *Something Else From The Move* is accompanied by a 16 x page, colour booklet with an essay by reissue series compiler Mark Powell. The original EP is a classic and this edition's inclusion of the stereo mixes. Makes it the go-to buy. As with the Esoteric single CD release, I found the stereo sound, flattened out and somehow lacking in bass dynamism and such.

Denny Cordell was stationed at The Marquee on 27th February 1967 to try to capture the ambience and the feral dynamism of The Move on stage. This EP release was to showcase their formidable live act if many people knew them purely as a pop act, with very catchy, charting singles. This release set out to prove that they were also purveyors of well-wrought cover versions. With a solid glimpse of the very hip, versatile selection of styles that comprised their dynamic and ever-changing live act. The Marquee set is varied and pure fire.

However, after the first concert, which still included Ace it was agreed that the recorded live vocals, in terms of volume and frequencies, had been obscured at some stages of the show. The band went and re-recorded more live vocals at Marquee Studios. These studios were connected to the Marquee Club at 90 Wardour Street, London. They were situated around the back of the club. With the entrance at 10 Richmond Mews. The studio was founded in 1964 and closed up in 1988. Three of the songs on the original *Something Else From The Move* EP were salvageable and the rest were shelved back then. They never saw the light of day, until the Salvo re-releases in 2007. When it was released, the EP played at 33 1/3 rpm, rather than the normal 45rpm. No doubt to get more sound levels and songs onto the vinyl. Plus, to maintain a reasonable standard of dynamism and fidelity on the recording.

At the time the *New Musical Express* was touting the story that Carl Wayne is "definitely to remain with The Move." Tony Secunda added his own unique description for the EP, calling it a "revolutionary mini album."

All of the tracks from the original UK EP release, as well as all of the 5th February 1968 Marquee gig, plus some of the cuts from the "stitched" 5th May 1968 show, have been painstakingly restored. They were issued as part of the Fly/Salvo essential 4 CD *Anthology 1966-1972* box set. This is an all-round very good-looking package.

In keeping with the band's constant sense of style The Move get presented in a stylish black and white case, enhanced with cool red graphics. There is a strong, tight essay from Mark Paytress. All housed in a wonderfully designed 72-page book. With plenty of descriptives of the repertoire, which adds even more needed detail. It is jam packed with rare photos. Both black and white and full colour, from the very early days to the end of it all. A fitting and essential box set, at long last! For one of the great but overlooked bands. It also has a touching dedication to Carl Wayne. It is a must-have collectors' item for any Move fan. Get one while you can.

Christopher Dolmetsch had some eyewitness insights into the early Marquee shows and the live set. Plus, some stage announcements that he didn't understand at first: "The first time I saw the Move, there was a brief pre-show announcement that there would be no wrecking of the stage or of The Marquee allowed. At the time I had no idea what that meant. I was told about the group's on-stage antics later. But the set came off without a hitch. Carl Wayne did most of the song intros, including getting a rousing audience reaction when he introduced "Bullfrog Bevan" who came to the mic to sing 'Zing Went The Strings Of My Heart'. The crowd roared and found it all ultra-amusing. I also heard them do some standard R&B songs from Stateside groups including The Isley Brothers and The Impressions. Roy's songs were introduced as being by "our leading tunesmith" by Carl. It appeared that Roy would tend to look slightly embarrassed or annoyed or both. My first show was on Thursday 23rd June 1966. I attended subsequent shows on 7th July and 14th July 1966. This was their regular Thursday Marquee Club residency. They were well dressed, not yet in the highly colourful clothes associated with the 1967-1968 era. Roy wore a dark suit mostly and Trevor and Ace were somewhat more colourful. The audience was mainly made up of Move fans. They had an emerging fan club, and I recall at one time, seeing a table off to the side with postcards for autographs."

The Move never gave up on their seriously packed diary of gigs. Chris Charlesworth then a local news hound saw them and recalled, "I did see The Move perform at Bradford University in 1968. I worked for the *Telegraph & Argus*; the evening newspaper published in Bradford. Once a week I contributed to a music column called The Swing Scene. I reviewed the show for the paper and went backstage to try and talk to them. But they weren't into being interviewed by someone like me. Two years later, as News Editor of *Melody Maker* I am sure their attitude would have been very different. That said, I thought they were fantastic. A really tight band, playing what I would call 'power pop'. Very colourful, very professional, very sharp, great songs and arrangements. Pretty damn loud too as I recall. I played in a band myself in those days called Sandra & The Montanas and when I watched real pros like The Move (and The Hollies & Marmalade, also at Bradford Uni and of course The Who, twice the following year), I remember thinking I should hang up my guitar pronto, as the bands I played in weren't a patch on them."

In May 1968 The Move appeared at the Primo Festival Internazionale In Europa Di Musica Pop, a shambolic four-day event initially held at the 30,000-capacity Palazzo Dello Sport in Rome. It was arranged amidst campus occupation by students at the University of Rome. Riots were breaking out because students were stopped

She's sure good looking man, she's something else...

from marching on the US Embassy in protest of the Vietnam War.

The band were up to their usual tricks as they decided to let the Italian audience feel the presence of The Move in a spectacular manner. Other acts on the bill included Captain Beefheart & His Magic Band, Donovan, Family, Grapefruit, Samurai, and Ten Years After. The Move played on day three (the 6th) along with The Association, The Nice, Pink Floyd, and the Italian act I Giganti. On the third day, The Move, set fire to the stage with their pyrotechnics and were arrested by the police. The festival had been scheduled to last a week, but after that performance the Palazzetto Dello Sport was shut down by the authorities and the festival was over.

In a YouTube clip from the concert, the crowd are tumultuous and baying. There is a very electric atmosphere all around. Carl Wayne is interviewed and, in his extrovert, but laconic manner, explained what was going on. A pyrotechnic display had blown up on the stage and some of the equipment was also damaged.

The voiceover at the beginning comments, "And it was the British group The Move that effectively closed the festival on the third night." We see second Upsy Downing throwing a 'V' sign to the audience as he walks towards the stage edge. Bev throws his sticks in the air and as Trevor walks off to backstage, he kicks a policeman in the leg! The local police are seen on the stage as Bev's drum kit is being loaded off.

Enter Carl Wayne, talking with a knowing, laughing expression, "We had a slight technical hitch, some of the equipment shorted. Unfortunately, this caused rather a large bang. Which disturbed the very brave Italian police! We wish we could do it again, but we've got to go back home tomorrow. One of us has got arrested (Dumpy)." Allen was soon released and caught the flight home.

The footage cuts to an English sounding guy, "One of the road managers, threw two bombs and he got arrested." Back to Carl Wayne, "It was a good idea, but it was very badly organised." Hold on! "Before the gig we were gonna have a little excitement. We were going to blow all that up. (he points up to the side of stage) right up there. So, don't go up there, whatever you do? It's all still wired up! Don't go up on the stage, because you might get killed." Carl says this all with a knowing grin. The Move were still creating chaos, if not in the UK, then certainly in Italy and elsewhere.

Dumpy Harris has some keen detail on this event: "Yeah, I did that. There was a lot of people, 30,000-odd people, I think. We were told not to do what we were going to do. It was all set up, because I always had a little switchboard. All I had to do was flick the switches and everything. We were told not to do it. Tony was there, he was adding his usual pressure. He said do it! The next thing I know, the whole place is up in smoke. Everything's happening and the next thing I know I'm being carted off by these enormous policemen with guns. They had a lock-up underneath the stadium. I was marched down there, and I can picture it today. It was just me who was arrested because I'd pressed all the buttons. I remember sitting there and it was a room about twenty foot square and there's a bench all the way around the three sides of it. All these military policemen were there! I can picture myself sitting there now. I'm looking down and I'm thinking, 'Crikey, that's the biggest pair and the shiniest boots whoever's playing'. I was in there about an hour and a half. Secunda got me out. He fetched the British Consulate, and he squared it all up. But we had to leave the next day!"

Roy Wood gave some further insights into behind-the-scenes with The Move at the time. He didn't betray any of the current uneasiness the band was facing around releases and singles. Plus, the upheavals in the management. He was asked why The Move got into so much trouble. "We always seem to get mixed up in things! We never know what's going to happen next. Still, there's never a dull moment, I can tell you." Roy informed the interviewer, "A new Move album is to be recorded, with Jimmy Miller in September. I think Jimmy wants to invite a crowd into the recording studio. And then record a sort of live show. They want to release the album over in America first."

Earlier in their career Tony Secunda had been talking to technicians about a fabulous new advanced light show. This was to be another first in The Move's career of innovation. Roy says, "This light show is being built by an atomic scientist *(Surely not another H-bomb?)*. It works from an organ keyboard, which will control the projection of lights onto a black screen with ultraviolet paintings. It should give a tremendous atmosphere. Who cares if we're going against all the trends?"

In August 1968, The Move released their fifth single, 'Wild Tiger Woman', a Jimi Hendrix flavoured (or inspired) rocker. They had cut this at Olympic Studios on 20th May 1968. Because Denny Cordell was in and out of the country, the recording dragged on until 21st August. It was originally called 'Wild Tiger Woman Blues'. Trevor loved the tune, though Wood preferred the more whimsical, melodic B-side 'Omnibus.' The Move were tiring of their perceived 'pop band' perception and Burton particularly, was looking to play harder, louder edgier music. Bridging the chasm between the perceived 'pop' singles and their ferocious, take no prisoners live act.

Trevor broached some ideas with the band. The result was Roy Wood penning 'Wild Tiger Woman'. Featuring the slimmed four-piece Move with Trevor on bass and vocals and guest Nicky Hopkins on piano. 'Wild Tiger Woman' is not a million miles away from 'Fire Brigade' but with a much sexier, sleazier edge. This wild woman was, *"tied to the bed, she's waiting to be fed."* which led to the single being banned from Radio One. She also, *"Must have been, a former beauty queen, now she's a naughty girl."*

Burton got his vocal part in the song too. Trevor sang it, while appearing on *Beat Club* TV, with his trademark scowling sneer. Every inch the rocker who didn't give an open fuck. According to Burton, "It had the heavier rock 'n' roll sound we should have been playing all along. I really thought it was on its way to the very top."

Wood was less enthusiastic. "The song's all right, but I wouldn't choose to sing it now."

The song has cool Roy guitar flourishes towards the end. Bob Sawyer picked out a few flourishes at the end of the songs fade. Bob examines some of Roy's guitar techniques here, "There is a little bit of Elmore James in there at 2:35, towards the end and some very nice picking. Including bending the strings, towards a deliberate out of tune effect."

Either way, the song didn't tickle the top forty. Apparently, the version of the song released was rushed and poorly mixed. The single's mono mix was muffled compared to prior Move singles. A recent first-time stereo mix shows that the tune was nicely recorded. It was just an initially poor rough mix.

The song was a blast — a rocking dervish, with plucky and unique Roy Wood

She's sure good looking man, she's something else...

guitar playing. With great backing vocals and a tight group performance. It wasn't as immediately commercial as 'Fire Brigade'. Written by anybody else, it would be considered to be a potential charter. The B-side however, 'Omnibus' could have quite easily been the A-side. It is an immediately commercial track. Against its whimsical, childlike Roy Wood vibe there are other fanciful sexual undertones, whilst riding on this 'Omnibus'. The song is couched in pre-war transport terms, using the decryption 'Omnibus' rather than simply 'bus', this tied in with the prevalence of the current, psychedelic reveries and surrealistic looks backwards at the quainter mores and eccentricities of the British way of life. The customs, the taking of tea, the social manners and modes of transport like this. Roy is the naughty Omnibus driver — a sort of reversed Dick Turpin. *"Come and take a ride on my omnibus. We could take you right to the terminus."*

It also has an extravagant Roy middle eight, with Carl singing in full gusto. (again, like on the first album's cut 'Yellow Rainbow') It has a heightened sense of exaggeration in the production. Conveying over-excited states, almost of delirium. *"Sweet silver meadows. Protect us from the rain. Rains never break, take us to the stars again."* Meanwhile our omnibus driver is wondering if he can manage to make this ride, worthwhile for more than one lady? *"Save the girls upstairs for later. Now you wonder if I can manage them all?"* The end is a glorious extended coda. With pumping, beautiful, prominent bass playing from Trevor Burton. Roy does a nice extended Eastern chiming 'Banjar' style guitar solo which ends up with Trevor playing single bass notes. Trevor is holding the musical tension down behind Roy's solo, with crisp Bev Bevan five stroke snare rolls adding to the fire. Trevor Burton relieves the rhyming tension by resuming the revolving bass part and the song slowly fades out, in a glorious haze of Roy Wood's wah-wah pedal.

The 'Wild Tiger Woman' single release coincided with The Move's appearance at the inaugural Isle of Wight Festival, a two-day event (31st August and 1st September). This jaunt was held in Hell Field, Ford Farm, near Godsell on the Isle of Wight. According to the promotors, this was going to be the "greatest pop festival ever held in the country" and it was to be compered by John Peel, the ever popular and ever monotonously mumbling Disc Jockey. The bill included the Aynsley Dunbar Retaliation, Fairport Convention, Jefferson Airplane, Plastic Penny, The Pretty Things and Tyrannosaurus Rex. It was perhaps better known as the 'The Great South Coast Bank Holiday Pop Festivity' and cost 25 shillings to get in. Dumpy was not at all impressed. Harris settled for the brief descriptive: "It was a great louse-up!"

The group blew out nine speakers during their appearance on a cobbled together, ramshackle stage, made up of just two trailers covered by makeshift scaffolding and canvas. One concertgoer reckoned, "The most fun band that night was The Move, who played with reckless abandon: especially Roy Wood. Not like all the other 'moody' bands, who stared at their feet and sucked at their beards."

Both Carl Wayne and Bev Bevan were hesitant about releasing 'Wild Tiger Woman'. It ended up with the heavier sound that Trevor Burton wanted. 'Tiger Woman' flopped outright; the BBC ban clearly not helping. The band now went through yet another inner crisis. This, after the EP had also failed to achieve any great chart position. Losing Ace Kefford and now both Burton and Carl were at odds in relation to the direction of the band. Carl and Roy were also at odds, due to

Carl's diminishing vocal role within the group. They wanted to get rid of the "tinny" productions by Denny Cordell, and present singles with the substantive, heavier, fuller live sound The Move had.

There was media talk that if the next single flopped, The Move would split up. They hadn't lost their edge in securing news headlines. Roy, by this stage, was developing ears towards another project. Directly influenced by the string work on 'Flowers' and other songs embellished by Tony Visconti. Roy drew out sketches of what the band could look like and was secretly plotting ahead, with Carl on tympani for example. The other guys didn't fully realise that Roy Wood was getting bored of The Move. They were also thinking that his ideas were pretty daft!

They were specially filmed by Southern TV's Mike Mansfield at the Esso Refinery in Southampton. The group also appeared on *Time For Blackburn* before going to Holland and Germany for three days TV on 6th April.

In 1968 the Bilzen Jazz Festival was dedicated to peace. It inspired reporter Eric Dillens, in some weird manner, to try and do a survey on milk. In answer to the inane questions by the interviewer, Carl Wayne starts burbling about, "I love mother's milk, milk straight from the mother's breast." The Move along with the Idle Race (with Jeff Lynne) performed at the Bilzen Jazz Festival Belgium in 1968. Black-and-white film clips of the band show Carl in good voice. He is also threatening the cameraman with the rather large axe he has in his grasp. They perform 'Flowers' and a truncated clip of 'Sunshine Help Me.'

Rob Caiger looks at the management structure of The Move at that interim stage. "Strong management is only strong if their earnings were protected, and they had a framework for business. Maybe they could have stopped blowing up some of the stages and stuff like that. Causing all the outrage and actually spent time in the studio. So, when they did get around to blowing up stages it would have benefited the album. And the album would have been continually selling. Secunda should have been the marketing manager. The business manager should have been someone else. It's why Andrew Oldham never let the Small Faces out in America. Because they would or could get poached. They needed to go out there with someone a bit strong or hook up with a promoter like Bill Graham who was adamant artists needed to be protected, promoted and paid properly. If you're keeping bands on a tight leash, drip feeding them wages instead of royalties, they're going to be in the frame of mind to be poached. Look at what Peter Grant did with Led Zeppelin. Strong, shrewd and powerful management for his artists and making sure by fair means or foul, his act got all the money they were due. Then look at The Beatles and The Stones for releases, worldwide 7-inch singles, albums, and EPs, all well promoted with tours and TV appearances. The Move did some of that but never in a joined-up fashion that covered the biggest market in the world, America. The Move did one album, a few singles and one EP in what — three years?"

26.
Ever since, there's been a slight disturbance in my mind

"John Bonham, my best mate at the time and I, were the most feared musicians in Birmingham. In 1967, Ozzy Osbourne was in a bus queue. This old Rover pulled up. I got out in a frock coat, skin-tight trousers and white hair. I was like a skeleton with sunken cheeks. I jumped into a yellow Mini with Jen — my girlfriend, who had long blonde hair — and sped off. Ozzy was thinking, 'What an image!' — and I became his idol."

Ace Kefford

The quote above from the Alan Clayson book, *Led Zeppelin: Origin Of The Species, Part 2* shows the impact that Ace had on his Birmingham generation of peers. Guitarist Dave Ball clearly recalls, "It reminds me of the occasion when Ace turned up at our house in Sutton. He arrived in his little yellow Mini. He asked us to join up with him. This seemed like a good opportunity. Ace had been a big star in The Move and they had become notorious when Quintin Hogg sued them for libel on behalf of Harold Wilson. We figured that Ace would still be a name. He would be still able to draw crowds. So, we jumped at the chance of joining with him. We were doing some Cream tunes and some John Mayall and The Bluesbreakers stuff. Anyway, since Ace had left the Move, we decided to approach him directly and suggest that we form a band around him. He agreed and that was that. Simple, really."

Ace had run away from the 'Ace The Face' recording sessions in London. Leaving the unfinished tape reels at the studio. And everyone else scratching their heads on his disappearance. Letters and phone calls were made but all were unanswered. Ace was still hiding out in the countryside. The desperation at times of not making music and being creative really got to him and he did attempt another overdose. Thankfully he recovered again in hospital. But Ace was not down and out yet. He attempted yet another entree into the music business.

"Denny Ball called me and asked if I would team up with him and his guitar playing brother Dave. They've been playing in The Sorcerers with drummer Cozy Powell, he had moved up from Cirencester to work with them. "Did you know Cozy was brought to Birmingham by the Balls?" Asked Ace. "Oh? Keith Smart has already done that one, has he?" He wasn't called Cozy Powell in his youth, he was Colin Flooks. One of his pals thought he'd be better off, if they nicknamed him Cozy. Cozy

Flooks didn't quite have a ring to it, so he changed it to Cozy Powell."

Dave Ball traces the history of Ace Kefford's first post-Move musical ensemble attempt: "Even though we were playing in different bands, Denny, Cozy and I had been jamming a lot at the family home. Something (of a loud nature) just clicked between us, to the extent that we had done one live BBC Radio session, calling ourselves Ideal Milk. Dave Ball remembers with a mixture of happiness and possible regret, "Ace was trying to sort out a management deal. There were some meetings with Don Arden down in London. Don had Black Sabbath and the Small Faces at the time, but that didn't happen. It might be that Ace's reputation got in the way. He had a bit of a name, as being difficult to handle (being a bit nuts I mean). Having said that, Don had Ozzy on his books so go figure. Maybe one fruitcake was enough."

Ace was free to form a band. He (and Cozy) also, "admired John Bonham, still my best mate at the time. Cozy was thrilled to be mixing with us socially, and the whole new band — The Ace Kefford Stand — moved into the cottages to 'get it together in the country.' The Stand was a covers band really — 'Born To Be Wild', 'Spoonful', that sort of stuff. Cozy used to do a solo. He was incredible even then. Later, we did 'Communication Breakdown'. I was taken to London and Polydor Records by John Parsons. He used to run The Belfry in Wisham, where The Move did their first gig."

Ace received an introduction to Frank Fenter, the head of Atlantic Records. "I was to be the second white act to be signed after Led Zeppelin. It was such a thrill to be on the same label that Otis Redding had been on. I signed the contracts without reading them — same as I did with The Move. I split the advance, between the guys four ways — not a vast amount but okay! And that was the initial money gone. A mistake that has cost innumerable musicians, very dearly!

Dave Ball takes up the tale: "So we ended up with a totally useless manager from the Midlands. This guy had managed a few local bands. He also ran a very good gig at The Belfry (Golf Club). But really, he was a child, up against the wide-boy sharks in London. Also, he had no real connections outside of the Midlands."

Ace sheds some light on what the band were trying to do, "We wanted to do covers that sounded like Vanilla Fudge. I guess, that comes over on the first single. Slowed down with the heavy attack. We did play The Star Club in Hamburg in late 1968."

The band did four 45-minute sets. That was onerous but nowhere as insane as the gruelling, seven-to-ten-hour slots he had performed previously with Carl Wayne and The Vikings. We did one show in Frankfurt, maybe at the Zoom Club. Jim Simpson, who was the (then) manager of Black Sabbath, arranged the AKS German gigs."

Dave wryly recalls the ongoing lack of band direction, "the manager had nothing to say about what the band were doing, or where we were headed. I cannot remember a single meeting, where anybody asked what we were trying to say with the music. Or what image we were trying to create. Our choice of material was woeful. Ace liked The Band (well, we all did?) but that meant playing stuff from the album *Music From Big Pink*, things like that. Totally wrong for a heavy, three-piece band. Sadly, we weren't writing anything either. So, we became a sort of heavy covers band. Actually Denny (Ball) did throw out a couple of originals, but that was all. Somehow (Lord knows how!) we got a prestigious record deal with Atlantic Records. We were the

Ever since, there's been a slight disturbance in my mind

very first band, to go out on the actual Atlantic Label, outside of the USA. Guess who the second band was to sign with them? Go on, have a guess? Well, it was a combo called Led Zeppelin!"

Ace was the front man. He was the lead singer of the band, and he was appearing without his former bass guitar. His original Fender Precision apparently had been painted black for some reason that only Ace would know. The bass was still broken as a result of being thrown up against the wall.

Dave recollected, "The Ace Kefford Stand was a very good idea. That got executed very, very badly. Ace was then living in a cottage, outside of a village called Whittington, near Litchfield. It was part of old stables with a large mansion house at the rear."

Dave remembers the locale well: "Cozy Powell, Denny and myself managed to secure a flat in the house. We were so bored that sometimes at night for amusement. We would switch on the living room lights, then open the curtains on the windows and play cricket with the enormous moths flying into the room. Many were to fly straight back out when we scored a six! I managed to secure a bedsit inside the stables as it were, with the name of Fernando's Hideout. We were so broke then that we were living on cabbage leaves like a bunch of rabbits. Basically, we were on a rabbit food diet. We were so poor the church mice would come up the village and share their cheese with us."

Aside from the Star Club gig, Dave also remembered the possibility of a string of gigs. "We were to have been booked on a long Spooky Tooth bill and with one or two other British bands. We had a righteous old time there. On the two successive nights following, I get to the club and Cream and then Jimi Hendrix were on the bills. This was a great time to be alive. The Ace Kefford Stand gigs were a resounding success. There was a lot of swallowing of chemicals in general and lots more insane behaviour. This, along with Luther Grosvenor of the Spooky Tooth and others. I have some slides somewhere of me and Ace wearing the stupidest grins and sporting our foot-length joints — they were happy days indeed. Polydor Records used to release Atlantic's entire catalogue outside of the US. Led Zeppelin had a strong management team, and we just had Ace. We all knew Robert Plant and "Bonzo" from endless jam sessions at the Elbow Room Club in Birmingham. They also used to come and visit us at the cottages where we all used to go out for large drinking sessions at the local, The Bell Inn."

Other gigs were mooted abroad (a US tour was mentioned), there was talk of a gig at the Zoom Club in Frankfurt. They did a good few gigs in the UK from later 1968 and into 1969. Appearing with The UK Bonds on 8th November 1968, they played at the refurbed Punch Bowl in Birmingham. The band were advertised as playing "prior to their American tour." This again, at The Belfry in Wishaw on 15th March 1969. The South Bank Renaissance in Grimsby had an appearance on 9th May 1969. They supported Geno Washington and The Ram Jam band at The Dorothy in Cambridge on 16th May 1969. The Coventry Telegraph had them advertised for a late May gig at The Swan in Yardley. They were booked at The Rhodes Centre on 13th June 1969. They appeared at The Magic Village, Manchester on 21st June,1969. They did The Tin Hat in Kettering on Saturday 19th July 1969.

The Rainbow Suite in Birmingham hosted the group on 2nd August 1969. Along with the sojourns to Germany, they kept busy. Cozy Powell was asked about Ace and his mental and physical condition. Was Ace as drugged out as the press would have us believe? Cozy Powell cast his mind back: "He was having some treatment; I don't know what was medically wrong with him. He was generally okay but sometimes went a bit weird. He had some shock treatment, which is a shame. When I was with him, he was fine. It was afterwards, that he went a lot worse. Working with him, he was pretty good. We did a few shows, he was pretty big in the Birmingham area. Good looking bloke, long blond hair, we did okay gig-wise."

Dave Ball got some good gear in line for the debut gig. "Our first gig was at The Belfry in Wishaw on 21st September 1968. This drew a bit of a crowd, this being Ace's first gig since leaving the Move. I had borrowed two of Jimi Hendrix's guitars for the show. Cozy Powell blagged an extra bass drum from Mitch Mitchell, so we did put out a pretty powerful show that night. (For all the guitar nerds; the guitars were a Black Les Paul Custom and a White 3 pick- up Les Paul Custom (SG shape). Upsy Downing restrung them for me."

The Ace Kefford Stand made a strong initial appearance at this gig. Impressed by the content and the bands tight presentation, the promoter John Parsons made an approach on the band's behalf to Phil Carson. Carson was the head of A&R at Atlantic Records in the UK. Although Ace's brain was still befuddled and still reeling from over two years of non-stop pressured craziness with The Move. They were signed up, along with Raymond Froggatt, with Gazette Entertainment Agency, who were based in Corporation Street Birmingham.

Dave Ball thought the debut single was an absolute disaster. "We managed to put out one of the worst ever singles on Atlantic Records, as Ace Kefford Stand. Then one contractual obligation single, which went out as Big Bertha with Ace Kefford. They released a version of Graham Goldman's song, 'For Your Love'. The Yardbirds had already taken this song into the top ten in the spring of 1965. Unfortunately, the Ace Kefford Stand's version did not generate any great sales. However, they did create enough interest to be able to tour Germany as a "name" outfit. When we got home from Germany, Phil Carson found us a song by one of Atlantic's contracted house writers. That was, 'This World's An Apple' and then we just waited and waited. We had really broken up anyway by this point. We left Ace and we carried on as Big Bertha, adding brother Pete on Hammond Organ and a new singer. I believe Ace did try again with some new version of the Stand, before finally fading away."

Not quite, there is much more to Ace's musical story. After the Ace Kefford Stand. He was involved with a band called Rockin' Chair from Wolverhampton. But that was mainly a good few pub gigs. At that time, he started to feel a return of the paranoia and the mental health. Probably brought on by the stress of no real rest after The Move, the attempt to record the Visconti produced solo record, then going straight into the Kefford Stand. It was another year and a half of trying to "make it" and it just became too much again.

Dave Ball believes, "I still think that we squandered a great chance there. Ah well, that's rock 'n' roll, eh! There were numerous issues, If I had to blame our lack of success on one single component it would have to be direction (the lack of I mean). We had no leadership, Ace was the de-facto leader, because of his name of course! But he was not really equipped for this mentally. He had a terrific stage presence

Ever since, there's been a slight disturbance in my mind

and a fantastic voice. Particularly when we/he was doing the right material. I reckon that with good leadership (and for that read good management) we could have done something special. However, it wasn't to be."

Dave Ball hated the 'For Your Love' single that the Ace Kefford Stand released. They slowed the Yardbirds original song down in tempo. It had a grinding-quasi Vanilla Fudge flavour. Heavier in tone than the Yardbirds version. It had Madeline Bell and Sue and Sunny on backing vocals, Dave Ball on guitars and Denny Ball on bass. And some nice tom-tom work by Cozy Powell. *(Author: I prefer the demo version myself)*. This came out on Atlantic Records in 1968. It was coupled with an improvised studio jam. Led by some piercing guitar feedback, called 'Gravy Booby Jam'.

As Ace humorously puts it, the title was a verbal piss-take of the phrase 'Groovy Baby'). With Ace intoning, "Yeah, yeah, I've lost my head again." This was indeed a portent of things to come, that would plague the charismatic singer, bassist and songwriter for years.

Dave also recalled, "We went back to playing at the Belfry Club. Our fees went down from £100 and then down to £50. Ace wasn't really a businessman, and we had no real manager. We went from bad to worse, until the band had nowhere else to go! So, we broke up. It was a sad affair, leaving us to go back to Sutton. Cozy and I and Denny left and moved on. Dave Ball left and ended up in Procol Harum. Cozy Powell moved on and joined forces with Jeff Beck."

Cozy went onto a stellar career until his unfortunate car crash near Bristol, England, which killed him on 5th April 1998 at the age of just fifty. Cozy was driving his Saab 9000 over 160km on a wet, rainy day. His girlfriend had called him, asking him to get to her house as soon as possible. While driving to her house, she phoned him asking where he was. He replied, I'm on the way but then she allegedly heard him say: "Oh shit!" followed by a very loud bang. The musician wasn't wearing a seat belt and died instantly. His vehicle crashed into the central reservation barriers of the M4 motorway. The car rolled several times before stopping on a grass verge. A traveller told the BBC at the time that he saw Powell's car "cartwheeling" before it landed on its roof.

As a postscript to the Ace Kefford Stand saga, minus Ace, the renamed Big Bertha added a member in new singer John "Cuell" MacTavish, previously with Tintern Abbey. Tintern Abbey were around for just two years in 1967 and 1968. The Tintern Abbey band have an apparently collectible 45rpm single, which people on the obscure edges of psychedelia will hunt around for a copy of. However, for the less strict collector, it's also around on a lot of compilations. It's called 'Vacuum Cleaner/ Beeside'.

Big Bertha's 'The World's An Apple' was written by John Bromley. Bromley also played piano on the cut. It was produced by Frank Fenton and Paul Clay. The single came out on Atlantic Records in October 1969. However, the song is not that strong. The chorus needed to be worked up more than it was. It probably could have also done with a stronger production. The hazy, delirious and improvised 'Gravy Booby Jam' popped up again as the B-side. This fulfilled the Atlantic Records contract for the delivery of two single releases. Another disc made of plastic, joining the millions of obscure but somehow collectable releases throughout the rocking of ages.

Rob Caiger again mentions the need for great management not the local, parochial managers. "You know what, some of that stuff? Like the Ace Kefford Stand, Rockstar, there was some good stuff there. Ace needed but never got proper management with the Stand, with Gritt, with all these other little bands."

A further postscript and a signalling towards Ace's evident visual and musical charisma, both on and off stage, was that both Ozzy Osbourne and Jeff Beck came up to Birmingham looking for him. Both presumably had thought through the possibilities of Ace playing bass and/or singing or both, potentially adding his unique talent and visual charisma with either one of these established acts. By 1979 Ozzy Osbourne was in the process of leaving Black Sabbath. Ozzy came and visited Ace at the cottage. After this visit, Ozzy had left Sabbath the next day.

Ace: "I got a call to see, if I wanted to go to rehearsal for Blizzard of Oz. I said I'd think about it, but I thought if I join up with Ozzy, I'm going to die because he's crackers! Or his image was! I was already an alcoholic then. Also, I don't really like heavy metal music. But the main reason was I hadn't got the guts."

Ace expands the story further: "When I was living in Ullenhall, Cozy Powell phoned up to say that he was Jeff Beck's drummer now and Jeff wanted me as the singer. I said okay but I didn't have much confidence then. I went to a couple of London rehearsals with a bloke from Van Der Graaf Generator on bass. When Jeff dropped me off at the station, he said, 'After you left The Move, I came looking for you all over Birmingham. Not as a singer but as a bass player.' Thanks to The Move, I'd got this complex that I was crap on bass. Something I no longer believe by the way. Jeff Beck said Jimi Hendrix had rated me and had recommended me to him. What further proof do you need that you're a good bass player?"

27.
Hundreds of people – left out in the cold

Wilf Pine was an intense lover of the music industry. Funnily enough, Wilf picked up the live music bug by experiencing live — guess who? Yup! Pine saw The Move blazing away. Clive Meddick (an Isle of Wight-based promoter) had started importing bigger acts to the island. The Isle of Wight's top band at that time was The Cherokees. Meddick had been putting on 'Big Night Out' shows, featuring local bands. They were very formidable line-ups, with The Cherokees, Meteors, Midnight Creepers, Escorts, Tomrons and the Johnny Marshall Trio all on the bills. But times changed and bigger acts were needed. He first brought The Move, Amen Corner, Jimmy James and the Vagabonds, Overlanders, Simon Dupree and the Big Sound and Bluesology.

Meddick, according to Wilf, possessed "the Midas touch" when picking his performers. Meddick kicked off his new set of concerts at The Royal York Hotel with The Move. The noisiest, wildest, most sensational, rock band in the country. From the first hypnotic blasts of their opening number 'Night Of Fear' Wilf was truly hooked. For the first time in his life, Wilf was hearing a real live concert by a big-time band, and he has never forgotten the experience. All the group's five members were great showmen. As the most uninhibited rebels of British rock 'n' roll, after their startling opening number, they continued with 'Fire Brigade'. The evening climaxed with Carl Wayne's TV smashing antics before an all but hysterical, largely teenage audience. For possibly cathartic reasons, the youngsters loved it. And so did Wilf.

With The Move that night heavy rock exploded like a landmine in the middle of the Royal York Hotel. Queen Victoria's favourite island was never quite the same again and nor was Wilf! He got to know many bands and his reputation preceded him. By 1970 Pine was a producer and music mogul working for Don Arden and got Cherokee a record deal with Parlophone Records. Another band had the same name, out on the mainland, so they recorded under the appropriate name of Wilfred. Wilf had been running a regular set of gigs. The season at The Seagull Ballroom had concluded with something of a triumph.

Sue Rose at Galaxy had arranged for Procol Harum, one of the biggest international groups of the day, to appear at the ballroom on that last Saturday night. With such a draw, the show could have been sold out many times over. While they were performing a final encore of their greatest hit, 'A Whiter Shade Of Pale', Wilf was summoned to the telephone. Someone called David Arden was on the line and wished to speak to him. As Wilf knew exactly who he was, he immediately took the call.

"My father needs to speak to you as soon as possible," David Arden said. "Can you manage Monday afternoon at his office in Denmark Street?" "Yes," said Wilf without hesitating. Tell your father I'll be there."

Will wasted no time in grilling an island resident, a music biz agent called Bunny, about Arden. He quickly found out that Arden had just bought Galaxy Entertainment. Wilf had a friend in Galaxy already, with booker Sue Rose who had worked with The Move for him and other great acts. Wilf also met David Arden who was roughly the same age as himself. He was almost feeling settled in, before he met Don Arden himself. Don and Wilf had lunch at Bianchi's and he explained his buying of Galaxy Entertainment.

As Wilf himself said, "Bands like people who get results. Bands always like to get their money." Sometimes they experienced cases where promoters vanished. It was hard to find them without extensive networks, which the average Joe doing gigs didn't have. Wilf's network of contacts, dating right back to his earliest days at Blyth, would pay off again.

Wilf would look at the name, "Say, for instance, the promoter was known to have been working around the Birmingham area. All it needed was a swift phone call to one of my oldest friends, "Big" Albert Chapman."

Big Al, who knew everybody and those beyond, would quickly suss out where the moody promoter was hiding. He would relay the details to Wilf. A further phone call would be made. Usually, the reluctant promoter would shell out the owed cash. Without anybody having to visit him and impress upon him forcibly and physically the imperative to part with his money pronto, or else. In fact, Bev Bevan remembered after one gig. They had to make the call. The gig promoter got short arms, long pockets and developed a very short memory. Money was owed for services rendered. This was in relation to Don Arden and his firm.

Bev recalled, "Don didn't want you just to have a hit record. No — he wanted you to be number one and he wanted you to fill football stadiums. He wanted things to be huge."

TV presenter Fred Dinenage did a mini biography on Wilf Pine. With the title of *The Most Influential Gang Gangster Ever.* Wilf was indeed a celebrated member of the criminal fraternity. It seemed that he was well liked — he was even loved. He was feared by many gangsters in this country and also in the US Mafia. His fame reached across the pond. It is stated that the American Mafia, also admired Wilf. Dinenage states also that Wilf never ever went to prison in his life.

John Pearson was the writer, of the best-selling, famous book, *Profession Of Violence*, about the infamous Kray twins, Ronnie and Reggie. Pearson must have had complete, mad respect for Wilf, as he wrote another excellent book called *One Of The Family - The Englishman And The Mafia*. Complete with a very nice cover design, depicting a white Rolls Royce driving down an American street. It also has inserts and comments relating to Wilf Pine and his relationship with The Move and Carl Wayne. He was well known to The Krays obviously and including Charlie Kray, who became his great friend. He was born in Newcastle, in the Northeast of England.

Wilf had a terrible childhood, with an abusive father. He became a dustman. Wilf was a big, imposing guy with tattoos aplenty. He moved his operation over to the Isle of Wight. It was there where he became involved in music, putting on and promoting shows becoming even more enthralled in his love for music thanks to that experience of seeing The Move tearing it up at the Royal York Hotel gig in 1968.

28.
But can it last another day?

The next single was going to be The Move's make and break! After the 'Wild Tiger Woman' recording process and then immediately afterwards, Trevor Burton was feeling restless. He was by then still only 19 years old. "What Jimi was playing was very heavy, and I started discovering more about that music, about the blues and going down that road. We did a few shows with him, and I got to know him very well. He was a very gentle guy, very courteous, and always stoned out of his brains... we all were! Jimi was quite shy really. He hated his own voice and always wanted it buried in the track. But the engineer would always bring it up again."

These new influences led Burton to leave The Move's sphere and hang out with other more *outre* musicians. Trevor was jamming with Jimi, he was spending a lot of time at Steve Winwood's country house, with the band Traffic and playing the blues.

"I suppose the Move were a psychedelic pop band, then they went heavy. But then they started to do pop again and wearing warpaint," said Trevor, referring to the makeup the band members started to wear. "Well, thankfully, I left before the warpaint came along. I just got into this other music, and I felt I didn't want to go back to doing 'Flowers In The Rain'. I didn't want to do pop music anymore. After spending time with Traffic and these people, I just couldn't go back and do 'Flowers In The Rain' and 'Blackberry Way.' I aspired to something more and I didn't want to be a pop star."

Burton's abrupt leaving forced the cancellation of The Move's scheduled American tour. *Disc and Music Echo* reported on 1st February 1969 that Trevor Burton has quit and was out of The Move. The *New Musical Express* reported The Move were to appear, on the prestigious Johnny Carson Show.

****

Carl Wayne was a benevolent man on a good day. His garage was full of musical equipment, amplifiers and speakers etc., given to The Move as inducements and offers to endorse their products. Richard Tandy had joined a new band called Stacks. Stacks had just received the dreaded news: All their equipment had been stolen from their van. Derry Ryan made a call to Carl Wayne. Wayne handled it with his usual calm business head on. Stacks had some gear now to go out and play. That November Stacks were playing the popular Rum Runner in Birmingham. They were using The Move's equipment. That night The Move popped in for a late-night snifter. Eventually they took to the stage and they played 'Blackberry Way' for the first time to an audience of about thirty people.

There was also another Move explosion onstage. Causing even more personal fallout in the group. Just before this second original version of The Move personnel splintered, personal differences had been percolating. Nothing unusual about that in this troubled, ego-driven story. This suddenly flared up into a brawl between Trevor Burton and Bev Bevan, in full view of the audience, during a live date in Stockholm, Sweden.

According to Trevor, "Bev lost his timing. I threw me bass guitar at him! He threw his hi-hats back at me." Bev exclaimed 'When are you fucking leaving then?' I said, 'I just fucking did!'"

Bev remembers the resentment growing, "Trevor was grimacing and snarling throughout the gig and muttering while he was playing. He turns round to me and said, 'You're fucking playing it wrong!' I went '*WHAT!*'"

Trevor beats his way offstage, Burton was raging. "I kicked over the amps and as I was going offstage — Bev's hi-hats were whistling, as they flew past my head." Carl Wayne raced off the stage, to separate the guys.

Bev remembered, "I was literally throttling Trevor, and we were on the ground and I was literally choking him. It took the very fit Carl Wayne and our giant roadie Upsy to drag me off him."

Carl Wayne had turned round in mid-set to see two Move members in full-on, physical fracas mode. The audience was treated to a solitary Roy Wood playing solo. Yet another eventful crazy gig in The Move's turbulent history.

The pressure was constantly on top of these guys since the beginning and had never really abated. The next day Trevor Burton was on the plane back to the UK. Burton was out of The Move. However, just before finally physically departing for good Burton had managed another *Top Of The Pops* appearance (for 'Blackberry Way'). With Roy, Carl and Bev positioned on one podium and with Trevor on bass stationed on the other. You couldn't make this stuff up. Trevor also played at the prior-booked gig at the Streatham Ice Rink on 3rd February. The Move always had a strong edge of professionalism before they got (yet) another bass man in.

Trevor started working as a studio musician in London. He moved into an apartment with Noel Redding. They wanted to start their own band as well. But for some reason that didn't work out.

Hank Marvin, the respected guitar supremo from The Shadows was approached. Could you imagine Hank Marvin in The Move? Hank Marvin replied tactfully in the press, "I was very flattered, but I have no financial reason to join any group at the moment and I am enjoying being solo." Hank being aware of his clean-cut image laughed, "I can't imagine what Move fans would be saying if I was up there."

It soon became obvious that Rick Price was the incoming bassist. Previously from the group Sight and Sound, Rick was from Rednal. He was part of the snug, almost incestuous at times, Birmingham musical scene and history. *Melody Maker* reported that Rick Price made his debut on bass in Belfast on Friday 9th February. Carl said he didn't know anything about Rick Price coming into the band. "I turned round one day and there he was?"

Rick had joined The Sombreros, who changed their name to Sight & Sound. He managed to get hold of the gear he wanted, a Fender Strat and a Vox AC30. The repertoire of the band was mainly The Beach Boys and Four Seasons. Sight & Sound morphed into a "hippie" flower power group. "We were managed by Mike Carroll for two years. By the beginning of 1969, Sight & Sound had become a harmony / comedy band. At the time, there were lots of groups, doing this type of act in the Midlands. Mike Sheridan was our comedy guru, and the first version of our new act was almost entirely, a crappy copy of Mike's old act. It got us loads of work in social clubs all around the country though, so who cared? My part of the act included an uncanny impersonation of Wayne Fontana. Followed by a very unflattering impression of Roy Wood. This included an impression within an impression, with the impersonated Roy Wood doing his impression of Dusty Springfield in the set!

Roy came to see Sight & Sound at a club one dark January night in 1969. He swept in, wearing a long black cloak looking all very mysterious and offered me a job with The Move. Rick was gobsmacked, he was aware of (the Move)'s pedigree from the word go. "The original line-up was definitely the best. The strong four- and five-part harmonies were virtually unheard, in any British pop music at the time. Added to that. They always seemed to have, a vast supply of obscure American material. Which was the envy of every other band. Before Roy swept in that night, I had never spoken to, or even met, any of the group. I was taken completely by surprise and, of course, said yes! 'Blackberry Way' was in the charts and headed for Number One. There had been rumours for a while, that The Move were looking for a new bass player. But most people expected it to be offered to Richard Tandy or Jeff Lynne. The job would not go to a relatively, inexperienced chap like me. The next day I woke up Mike Carroll to tell him the news. When he saw me on the doorstep so early, he must have thought there had been a death in the family. My usual waking hours at the time were from about three in the afternoon, until four in the morning. As he filled the kettle he said, 'What's up? Don't tell me you're leaving the band.' When I said yes most of the tea things ended up on the floor."

Price continues his tale, "We had just spent five hundred pounds on new band photographs and publicity. And so, all of it would now be out of date. He must have been very angry, but he had the decency to sit me down. He talked to me about the pitfalls of wealth and fame etc. He talked about the way that my life was about to change, beyond all recognition. Eventually we did part on good terms. Although we have rarely spoken since. That's probably down to me. Because supposedly my attitude to people changed completely. I'm told I went through a period, of being an absolute and complete twat. With this in mind, I'm prepared to accept the words, of my alleged friends. When they insist that I was once one of those flash tossers."

"So, I joined Bev Bevan, Carl Wayne and Roy Wood to become part of The Move - Edition Number 3. Even before I had learned half The Move stage show, they were at number one. I appeared on *Lift Off With Ayshea* and *Top Of The Pops*. I was wearing a shirt borrowed from Roy. With a pair of Carl Wayne's trousers and shoes. The first session that I recorded was the next single, 'Curly' and 'This Time Tomorrow'. Little did I know that the Move group was already in its death throes... All I knew was, I was going to be a pop star. To me that meant performing. Nothing else. The machinations of management were a total mystery to me. I didn't realise that Peter Walsh Management was steering The Move towards the respectable side of the business. Underground clubs in Ireland soon turned into cabaret clubs in

Newcastle and Birmingham."

"As the new boy, I was on set wages and had no input into the business side of things (something I'd live to regret in the not very distant future). Not that I would have been any help at all. I knew nothing about the business. 'What business? This is just for fun, isn't it?' We did a lot of cabaret work, much to Carl's delight and Roy's disgust. It wasn't that Carl preferred cabaret work. I think he could see that there was a large untapped market out there. Roy, on the other hand hated the whole concept. I have vivid memories of an adventurous evening at Batley Variety Club involving a flying vodka and orange. Over a six-month period, we did most of the Batley clubs and a few obscure rooms in the Northeast of England. One evening we strolled into the Baileys nightclub in Birmingham to check out the room before we performed there. Lo and behold! Just in front of us was the legendary Roy Orbison, playing on stage!"

Rick thought arriving back home that things would level out. "I thought things couldn't be better. How naïve. I was on great money, appearing in magazines and on TV. My mum could now watch TV in colour, thanks to my new-found wealth. She also filled scrapbooks, as if her very life depended on it. I discovered some newspaper cuttings in her scrapbooks after she died. Some of those magazine articles now make me cringe when I read them now. It seems that I had an opinion on everything. I mean, I voiced an opinion then on stuff that I don't even have an opinion about now. You see, I was a flash tosser. Thanks Mick, and thanks Laurie."

Rick could feel the undercurrent of tension in The Move. "Although Carl and Roy were finding it harder and harder to work together, nobody was letting on. It wouldn't be long before Carl would leave. But I didn't know it at the time. Most of their disagreements, took place in private, and as the management company felt no responsibility toward me, I was the last to know most things."

Rick Price recorded two albums with The Move, *Shazam* and *Looking On* and played on their hits 'Curly' (Rick sings the lead vocal on the single's B-side 'This Time Tomorrow') and 'Brontosaurus.' During this time, the pissed off and feeling edged out, Carl Wayne left the band. The voluble Carl was replaced by Jeff Lynne, with whom Roy Wood made plans to form a new group. This eventually became The Electric Light Orchestra. Rick also was part of the touring and recording band Wizzard formed after Roy bailed out from ELO.

One night, Richard Tandy, Jeff Lynne and Roy Wood, after liberally enjoying conviviality and liquid refreshments all piled back to Jeff's house in Birmingham. They tried hard not to wake up Jeff's parents. In fits of stifled, merry laughter, they tried to demo a new Roy song on Jeff's Revox. Roy had wrapped his head in a pillow, to try and keep the noise down, all leading to further gagging fits of laughter.

Richard Tandy, who later played keyboards with Electric Light Orchestra, played harpsichord on 'Blackberry Way'. Trevor Burton is playing bass. Trevor was put off by his feeling, that the song was both dreary and really light pop. Trevor felt sometimes Bev had a problem playing this particular beat as it was very slow, and could quite easily throw the drummer off, with a potential to drag the beat. Meanwhile, Trevor discovered and was now really digging the 'Three Kings' as he described it. "I was listening to B.B. King, Freddie King and Albert King (all three stellar blues guitarists)."

Despite the success of the single, the style of psychedelia-tinged pop sat uneasily with Trevor Burton. Trevor left the group shortly after! As Bev Bevan remembered with some awe. "Trevor actually left the band, while it was having a number one hit!"

Roger Spencer happened onto the initial recording of this possibly best loved Move song. "Jeff bought a mellotron off a solicitor or a doctor or something. He had it in his front room. Roy had the song 'Blackberry Way' and he wanted to put a mellotron on it. He came around to Jeff's house. I was actually there on the day he did the demo in Jeff's front room at 368 Shard End Crescent. Because of the low-tech microphone that Jeff used, me and a fellow called Garnet Mellon, who was a bit of a character that hung around with the band in Shard End got two cushions off the couch and put it like a horse wears blinkers, one on each side of Roy's head, and put the microphone in there and Roy sang into that. Garnet Mellon is his real name by the way. He was a roadie, stroke friend and lived with Jeff, and went to school with Jeff. Roy took that demo from Jeff's front room with the Mellotron into the studio and said, 'This is the sound I want.' When the record came out, I remembered Bob Reisdorff (the head honcho at Liberty Records) rang up and said, 'Hey, have you heard that record by The Move 'Blackberry Way'? They stole our sound. I'm not saying that it was stolen or any other thing untoward, I remember when the record came out that Bob said, 'Oh my God these guys are so loud!'" Folklore has it that the Mellotron, was sold to Chip Hawkes from The Tremeloes.

****

Dave Morgan's name is threaded throughout Birmingham's rock history. "I think that Carl recognised the tremendous value of songwriting in the industry. He realised that the songwriters, or the writers and publishers make a lot. A lot more than the bands. The amounts that Roy was making, was huge compared to the rest of them. Carl realised the value of it, and he thought, "Well, I'm going to find writers and help them."

The B-side of 'Blackberry Way', 'Something' was specially written for the band (or through Carl) by David Scott-Morgan. Dave Morgan was poised as part of the new Penny Music set up with Carl Wayne and Richard Tandy to encourage Birmingham writers and to influence and widen The Move's catalogue. Thereby increasing Carl's publishing interests, by bringing in new outside song material. "Carl helped me enormously by singing my songs. I've got loads of demos of Carl singing my tunes. I didn't write any more, in the end because Penny Music fell through on the whole publishing thing. I think Carl tried to license Penny Music to another publishing house and that didn't work. Carl ended up signing me directly to the publishing house. Carl signed each song, individually. As far as Richard Tandy and Penny Music, he didn't sign Richard at all. Richard got left out of the process completely. I didn't sign to Penny Music in the end. I signed individual songs to individual publishers. Carl could occasionally be handy. At one of the publishers, Carl was having a disagreement. I turned round and Carl had pulled the guy over the table, almost going into a fist fight."

Dave Morgan adds some background to writing 'Something': "I just came from the point of view of 'How can I write it? How can I craft it?' It's just totally trying to write a pop song. I came up with that tune and I called it 'That Certain Something'. I played it to Carl and straight away he said, 'Yeah, we need to change the title to 'Something'.' He sang it and he sang it so differently, because he put all that blues stuff on it. It just jumped alive when he sung it. He brought the tune to life!"

Dave soon ran into Don Arden. He has a part alarming and part hilarious story: "Later on, I was down in Don Arden's office. Don Arden was managing The Move. I'd gone down with Carl that day and Don said to me, 'Dave, come here, I want a quiet word with you.' Don took me out onto the balcony overlooking Denmark Street *(eerie shades of Robert Stigwood?)*. I'm looking over the balcony and he says to me, 'Dave, you know The Move really need a major hit with this next release... the last one, 'Wild Tiger Woman', didn't make it. They really need the song that's gonna break it for them this time around. I wanna ask you, which do you think is the most commercial track? Is it this one that Roy's done, 'Blackberry Way'? Or do you think it's this one that you've written, 'Something'?' I was thinking, 'Well, what a question to ask.' He's asked me, so I just thought about it for a bit... and I hummed them to myself. I said to Don, I think 'Blackberry Way' is the more commercial. Don looked at me, "Hmmmn! Okay, Dave, thanks for that.' That's all he said to me! And of course, that was the choice, 'Blackberry Way,' It's become an anthem for Birmingham, to be honest. I'm really proud of my song on the B-side of that. At one point it was in the balance, because Carl wanted 'Something' as the A-side. I think Roy definitely wanted his as the A-side. Don Arden was thinking hard, because they're both pretty good songs."

Pauline Evans remembers when she was in Roy's car on the way to a local gig one night. As Carl's fiancé, "he turned to me and said, 'You're too good for Carl', because of the way Carl was treating me. He remarked that it gave him the inspiration for 'Blackberry Way'. Reading the lyrics, they did fit my situation with Carl perfectly. Roy is an amazing musician whom I am lucky to have known. However briefly in the scheme of things I remember walking with Roy up the Birmingham Road in Wylde Green, on one lovely summers day. We were in pursuit of cream cakes, at my favourite café, Hindleys. And to his credit, Roy was totally unaware of his mega status or of the admiring and astonished looks he was getting from motorists and shoppers alike."

Roy adds more detail here, "The reason Carl did not sing on the recording was, I did a demo of the song at home and played it to producer Jimmy Miller. He thought that my voice was more suitable for the song than Carl's. So that's what we did. I recorded my vocals at Air Studios. I never did write songs based on personal experiences. You can take it from me, they were all just stories. For 'Blackberry Way', I had an image in my mind of a soldier who had returned from World War Two. He was walking around the area where he used to live. The soldier was remarking on how things had changed while he had been away, which made him feel sad. Also, the reference to the girl was that she was no longer available. Was it the war that had changed that, or was it something he had said? At the time that the record was released, there weren't really specific videos to promote them. I always had a picture in my mind of the middle section of the song — the *'Oooh La. Oooh Laaah'* parts. I thought it would have looked ideal with the troops leaving the station on a train. Waving handkerchiefs to their girls and families and all that sort of thing. Anyway, so now you know." Thanks for clearing up that story, Roy. I personally feel if the song is autobiographical or indeed just pure fiction — a good song is a good song.

The B-side of 'Blackberry Way' was another beautiful song. In some ways, it could be seen as a wonderful double A-side. Although it wasn't released with that format in mind, it's much less freaky, but similar in ways to The Beatles 'Penny Lane' / 'Strawberry Fields'. Perhaps in the way that 'Blackberry Way' and 'Something' both have a heavy orchestral air. 'Something', with its Tony Visconti string section, and 'Blackberry Way', with its sonorous Mellotron and harpsichord, played by the recently departed and much missed Richard Tandy.

David Morgan had played 'Something' to Carl on his acoustic guitar. Thereupon Carl quickly demoed the song with Trevor Burton playing some initial shuffle style drums. The early demo version of 'Something' is included on the wonderfully expansive 4CD *Anthology 1966-1972*. It was first recorded at Olympic Studios on 16th April 1968. It featured Nicky Hopkins, on three (count them) overdubbed grand pianos! The version with Nicky Hopkins is excellent. Although the piano is very high in the mix. It's also about two minutes longer and it works very well.

As I write, there is a new documentary called *The Session Man* about the fabled Nicky Hopkins. Hopkins played piano on well over 250 albums in a three-year period. At that crazy, busy time in London, before going to America.

Carl's vocals are spot on. The song could have been done in a more restrained or ballad-like manner. Due to the song's implied tone, Carl really uplifts it with a rousing, melodramatic and raw vocal performance. However, Carl never overdoses on the vocal melodrama. Bevan's drum performance is full-on exciting. He executes crisp, kinetic rolls around the kit, starting out from the snare. They are tasteful but still have an unrestrained feel and plenty of the rock aggression that Bev excelled at, both live and in the studio. This could be among one of Bev's best recorded drum sessions. In terms of both tightness and the sense of spontaneous freedom in his playing. A master tape was compiled from Take 15. The new version added orchestration. That was undertaken two months later at Trident Studios. According to Mark Paytress, "Three further takes were produced and mixed to mono at Olympic Studios on 16th September. Including Carl Wayne belting out a version in Italian, entitled 'Il Torrente." All these sessions were produced by Denny Cordell.

As a relevant aside, *Produced by Tony Visconti* is a box set retrospective of Visconti's work. It features two his collaborations with The Move tracks. CD One features 'Mist On A Monday Morning'. CD Two has 'Something'. In total, there are 77 tracks on the 4CD box set, all curated by Visconti himself. Tony says, "This boxset covers five and a half decades of my efforts, in the art of making iconic recordings. Some of it is familiar and some will have a eureka moment! 'I didn't know Visconti produced that one!'"

Visconti added the recorders to 'Something' as well. "I can relate one story that's mainly about the recorders. I played on the song. I wasn't present on most of the recording sessions. Denny Cordell only called me in for the orchestral instrument overdubs when needed. His sessions with The Move really exhausted them, especially Bev Bevan's drum sound. Denny was obsessed with getting the best bass drum sound possible. He had Bev play the kick drum alone for an hour or so, just to get it all sounding good. In 4 or 8 track recording, the drums, bass and maybe a rhythm guitar were all recorded on one track. So, the sub mix was extremely important."

For Visconti the song has a level of importance. "'Something' is one of my favourite songs. Denny paid me extra for writing the arrangements. He was very fair about that, because he realised the skill it took to write those arrangements. The recorder was a big thing in those days. A few pop musicians were using the recorder.[19] They were an instrument British kids learned in school. I had two battered recorders that were about to take their last gasp. Instead of asking for money, I asked Denny to buy me two Moëck recorders from a shop called Musica Rara, right near Carnaby Street. Those were the recorders I played on 'Something'. We must have been using two 8-track machines by then. Because there is a lot is going on in that recording. I wrote for a small string section and two flutes. Those were independent parts to the recorders. I must've driven engineer Gerald Chevin crazy. This is one of the songs I believe that eventually led to the forming of the Electric Light Orchestra."

Noel Gallagher, while he headed up and wrote the hits for Oasis, obviously loved this song. The 1994 single 'Whatever' bears some sonic resemblance to 'Something'. The Oasis track uses similar, evocative string arrangements. A lawsuit at the time granted a co-writing credit to Neil Innes. Innes was famous for being in The Bonzo Dog Doo-Dah Band and also for fronting, the satirical Beatles parody group The Rutles. The plagiarism claim came from the fact that 'Whatever' had a striking similarity to the melody of Innes' 'How Sweet To Be An Idiot'. This song was performed at some of Monty Python's live shows. 'Whatever' is a strong, anthemic song in its own right. It was said 'Whatever' sounds like any number of other songs as a mark of Oasis's confidence in their songwriting. Hmm…

****

By this stage in The Move's career, Dumpy Harris is really feeling the strain, two and a half, nearly three years of constant driving and setting up the band. And going through some of the controversies alongside them. "There was another episode that I've just thought of. We've been all over the country and it was a lot of miles. I was getting concerned about the amount of driving. At the time, we had a doctor in Harley Street. He prescribed me some pills to keep me awake (amphetamines). We were coming back from Wales, and they kept me awake alright." The guys in the back of the van were trying to sleep, but Allen (completely speeding off his box) just wouldn't stop talking!

Harris the all-round good guy had, had enough! He wanted out. "It was mostly because they wouldn't stop overnight anywhere. They always had to get back home and that was a lot of driving. I was in Birmingham city centre one day. I was in Digbeth which is down by the Bullring. I just went into a phone box. I phoned Carl up and said, 'Carl, I'm packing it in mate, I'm finished.' I regretted the way I left really. It was very sudden. I felt I could've done it much better."

Don Arden was now deeper into management. With both feet planted firmly into the industry. He already had problems with the Small Faces. Now he was having problems with another Galaxy Entertainment booked band Amen Corner. He heard again that this band were searching for new management. Amen Corner had been

19 Roy Wood uses them as a particularly piercing introduction to the seventh Move single 'Curly'.

approached by certain characters, around the business.

This time, Arden found himself up against a consortium of wealthy and influential figures. Apparently, these were backed by a powerful pop music entrepreneur. Arden thought these guys saw themselves as a benevolent consortium, with a trade union bent, looking to do better deals for pop artists. He thought the involvement of the unnamed pop mogul was a coup waiting to happen, to pressurise Arden into selling off at a good price, the more important gems in his jewel box.

The trouble began when an intermediary of the consortium phoned Arden. They suggested immediately that he release Amen Corner from their management contract. Arden's reply was characteristically blunt and intimidating; "I warned him that committing suicide might be much better than causing trouble for me." Similar to the supposed threat from Tony Secunda of having Arden gangstered off, "the story was that £3,000 had been put up to get me fixed. I know full well that it is possible to hire someone to maim or kill for a few thousand pounds. But this time, I was actually scared, because there was talk of getting me, through my one weakness — my family."

Arden had always been fiercely protective of his family. So, he acted in sharpish manner. He hired three bodyguards, for a three-figure sum to provide, all round-the-clock protection for Arden's wife and children. This is while a counter-plot was being birthed. Don then hired a further six bodyguards and briefed them of his plans for frightening off this consortium. They now focused on a patsy. Don suspected this guy had connections with the consortium. He also seemed the weakest link in the snaking chain to their financed Mafioso-style vendetta.

Arden's henchmen set out to his mews flat. Fully armed up with sawn-off shotguns and revolvers. The potential victim saw these thugs from his upper window. He started screaming his lungs out. They literally put the shits up this guy. After leaving this mews dweller in a terrified state, the heavies casually returned to their car and drove away. Arden had presented his calling card, with no aggro and no shooting. With this effective ploy, he persuaded the consortium that it would be complete folly, to risk taking this dispute to its logical conclusion.

Arden's intimidatory come back, was itself a dangerous move. It could have backfired on him in various ways. He was contacted shortly afterwards by a senior police officer investigating complaints concerning guns. Don Arden's charisma, cunning and verbal convinced the police their informant was a phone-lying crank. In spite of all this, Arden could not hold onto Amen Corner. They left him for other management shortly afterwards. There was talk about Don taking legal action to retain his interests in the group. Arden later claimed that he had sold Amen Corner's contract, for a cool profit of £50,000.

Don Arden and Wilf Pine had now become more simpatico and comfortable. Don was using Wilf's undoubted skills to manage and promote bands, thus enlarging the Arden management stable. He was also using Wilf to smooth over troubled waters. For example, when things got a bit iffy in dealing with television people. The precious BBC types, who in some cases were neurotic and uptight middle-class wankers. Although 'Blackberry Way' did eventually go all the way to number one, it needed some work to help it along the way. At one stage, it looked like 'Blackberry Way' on entering the bottom rungs of the top twenty was maybe stuck there. Wilf found himself coping again with the manifold problems, of his favourite group. They were staging a comeback after their troubles with Secunda. Plus, the breakdown and departure of Ace Kefford. Plus, the failure of the fifth single, 'Wild Tiger Woman'. Don was particularly anxious for some real re-establishing success, with 'Blackberry Way'.

Arden had been mounting a heavy promotion campaign for the group. He was working up live dates, radio interviews and television appearances, up and down the country. Wilf was also closely involved in all these live appearances. Don Arden was making further concerted efforts to push the single up the charts. It now needed a boost, by a Move TV appearance. Where else, but the game changing, musical flag show *Top Of The Pops*. This usually guaranteed further big record sales. Wilf uncovered there was an unofficial ban on The Move's appearance on the show because of previous "wild behaviour." It also appeared that Don Arden's persistent pleading and reassurances to the BBC were not working at all.

A chance but very opportune meeting between Wilf and BBC producer Colin Charman resulted in Wilf talking him into a change of heart, allowing them to perform 'Blackberry Way' at the studio. Charman's strict condition was that a member of the crew and/or Wilf would be staying with The Move throughout the show to guarantee their good behaviour. Everything turned out well.

However, Wilf was watching behaviour he found suspicious and untoward. Members of the band were going over and talking to a young guy. He was sitting on his own in the studios. Wilf whispered to his factotum Clive "Jinxie" Jenkins, telling him to go over and eavesdrop on their conversation. Bev Bevan and Carl Wayne had spoken to this guy. They were then followed by Roy Wood and Trevor Burton. Wilf spoke to Bev and asked, "Who are you talking to?" Bev replied, it was a guy called Clifford Davis.

He was an associate of Peter Walsh, who ran Starlight Artistes Agency. One of their acts, doing really well chart wise then, were The Tremeloes, with a string of hits. Jinxie returned and said he'd overheard Clifford Davis offering The Move his services as their manager and Peter Walsh's services as their agent. Jinxie also said that Roy and Trevor were polite, saying they would discuss his offer with everybody. Wilf and Jinxie were to meet with Don Arden immediately after this to report back on the *Top Of The Pops* appearance etc. Wilf thought that a chat with Carl Wayne might be in hand, before Don found out about Clifford Davis. The proposed talk with Carl didn't happen. The possibility of some imminent carnage was very high.

Wilf and Jinxie met up with Don. This conflab had Arden immediately sensing that something was up. That something was being left unsaid. So, Wilf and Jinxie related the "real" story, word for word, as they had seen and heard it. Don suddenly jumped to his feet; he was screaming blue murder! He shouted out to his wife to fetch his clothes, as he was going to go and kill Clifford Davis. His wife calmed Don right down. He agreed to sleep and think about it the next morning. This gave rise to an event, that went down in history and musical criminal lore. It was very much misreported. It also probably got mixed up with another hanging-out-the-window folkloric tale. More on that later.

The very next day, Don had the car brought round to the office straight away. "Where are you going?" Wilf enquired. "We are going to see Mr Clifford Davis and

Mr Peter Walsh at Mr Walsh's office," he replied. "Fine by me," said Wilf.

They were in the car and driving through morning traffic in the direction of the Starlight Artistes' office in Southampton Row, Holborn. Wilf gave Don Arden some unaccustomed words of caution. He outlined that after their recent brushes with the law it would be virtual suicide if they became involved in any sort of violence. Particularly at eleven o'clock in the morning in a crowded office.

Don seemed to be the model of sweet reasonableness, as he insisted that the very last thing, he wanted was a show of violence. Perish the thought. All he intended was to confront Mr Walsh and Mr Davis in person, tell them he knew exactly what was going on and point out to them that, as the Move's agent, he had a legally binding contract with them all. "That's what really matters," he explained. "By seeing them both in person I can put an end to all this nonsense straight away."

Don Arden and Wilf Pine entered the reception area of Starlight Artistes, asking to see Peter Walsh and Clifford Davis. Looking understandably startled, the receptionist enquired if they had an appointment. Don replied that they had just been passing and had called in on the off-chance of seeing them. When he told her his name, she said that Peter Walsh was out, but Clifford Davis was in his office. She would enquire if he was free. She took a while to return. Long enough for Don to light a large cigar up. When at last she reappeared, it was to tell them that Mr Davis would see them straight away in Mr Walsh's office.

On entering the office, Wilf came face to face with one of the biggest desks he'd ever seen. Seated behind it in an equally impressive large black-leather chair. Was a diminutive and nervous-looking individual in a smart grey suit, whom Wilf recognised as Clifford Davis. Don didn't waste time on introductions and spoke to him softly and very clearly. "Clifford Davis, I would like to ask you what you're up to, trying to persuade The Move to break their contract with me in favour of yourself and Peter Walsh?"

Instead of answering, the character behind the desk stayed absolutely silent, as if he was rooted to the spot, where he sat in Peter Walsh's large black-leather chair. "I'm waiting for an explanation," said Don Arden, his voice quieter than ever, but even then, he didn't get an answer.

At this point Wilf decided to intervene in this one-sided conversation. He observed that Mr Davis had had a lot to say on the subject the night before when he was talking to members of the group. So, perhaps he should try answering Don's questions now. Then the verbal floodgates opened, and once Davis started there appeared to be no stopping him. He began to ramble on about The Move, being free agents ever since they broke with Tony Secunda. Don listened with surprising patience. "That may be so," he said at last, "but I think you miss the point. I'm not here, because you put yourself forward to manage the band, but because you were inciting them to break the legal contract, which they have with me as their agent. By signing up with Peter Walsh's agency instead."

When Clifford Davis started to deny this, Wilf once more interrupted, this time calling him a liar! At which point Davis, once again fell silent. It was now that Don leaned across the desk. With a faint smile on his face, Don tweaked his cheek. As Wilf describes it, "Rather as you might do with a child, when making a point." As he did this, Don said that he had nothing more to add, except that if anything like this ever happened again. Clifford Davis would not be so lucky. With that, he turned on his heel.

As Arden was just about to reach the office door, Davis opened his mouth again. He uttered the wrong statement, with the wrong emphasis. Davis chose to deliver what proved to be a very dangerous (for him) parting observation. He said that he wasn't "worried by threats and that, anyhow, he knew where Don Arden lived." Wilf Pine immediately struggled to restrain the enraged Arden.

"Within a heartbeat, Don had spun around, and if I hadn't stopped him, he would have dragged Davis, bodily across the desk. What might have happened then, I dread to think."

Davis's comment threw Don into a rage on top of his prior fury. Don looked down at the only weapon he had on his person. He was holding in his hand — his large cigar. In a gesture of total contempt, he stubbed it out, slap bang, on Clifford Davis' forehead. *Ooops!*

Years later Peter Walsh recalled this eventful day: "He didn't hang anybody out of a window in my office. He just came in and beat up a guy that was working with me called Clifford Davis, who was then managing Fleetwood Mac. He beat him up in this chair actually! When I say, "beat him up", I mean he slapped him around the face a little and threatened what he would do if he didn't lay off The Move... I don't know why he came around when he did. I was out at lunch, fortunately, so he got Davis and gave him a good going over. When I came back it had all finished. I got police protection against him... In fact, if anything, Don Arden was my protector because the police warned him, and this came from very high up at Scotland Yard, that if anything happened to me, he would be dragged in immediately and whether it was him or not, he would be charged. We got his accusations and what he was going to do to me on tape. So, he never did anything at all. He was warned off in a big way, a very big way, because I had a lot of muscle at Scotland Yard... He doesn't speak to me anymore, but he's very wealthy now."

Wilf dragged Don out of the office and into the waiting car below. Arden fumed all the way back to Denmark Street. It was only when he saw his wife Paddy and daughter Sharon descending from a taxi, that he remembered he was taking them out to lunch and he began to calm down. "Wilf, not a word to them about what happened," he whispered. "I promised Paddy not to lose my temper."

After greeting them, Don asked if they would wait with David (his son) for a few minutes in the outer office as he had to have an urgent con flab privately with Wilf. Don was getting slightly worried by possible recriminations from Davis and the Starlight Agency scuttling to the police, issuing a claim against Arden, for possible ABH. Particularly from Clifford Davies, over the visible results, in terms of Don's choice of ashtray.

It all ended calmly, and many people ended up being Don's friends. David Arden was amazed: "No, Peter Walsh never wanted to get near to the old man." However, "Clifford Davis became a good pal of the old man. I've come back about 7 o'clock and there's glasses going, there's a couple of people with the old man. There's Clifford Davis with the old man. I'm thinking, Clifford Davis? What the hell is he doing here? The last I knew the old man had stubbed his cigar out on his forehead."

Just before Christmas, Wilf Pine was happy to see 'Blackberry Way' go to number one in the charts. As consolation for the hole he had burned in Peter Walsh's chair, Don duly sold him his agent's contract for The Move, in return for a very large sum of money. Not too long afterwards, Don himself received a double jackpot when the Move, although dispensing with his services as their agent, chose him to be their manager, in preference over the cabaret purveyor, Peter Walsh.

Rob Caiger observed the advance from the free-wheeling 60s into the more bracing 1970 music industry. "This is where Don Arden was good. He had learnt from not being perfect in the 1960s. He was an agent; he was a booker. Don Arden was also clever. ELO did albums and they went to America as soon as they could. And they toured hard but with everything financed and supported so the band could focus on the gigs. Don Arden had seen all the mistakes, that your Secunda's and Oldham's had made. Plus, the mistakes Don himself had made, which is why he became a manager in the 1970s and then set up his own record label. Keep control. He made mistakes later but for a time, he had one of the world's biggest groups and independent record labels. That doesn't happen by accident."

Tony Iommi of Black Sabbath is regarded as innovating a lot of the tunings and approach to the "heavy metal" music genre. Like Ace and Trevor Burton, he grew up in a tough part of Birmingham. Having to defend himself either by fists and boots or the use of a knife. Like other musicians who dealt with Don Arden, in the beginning, Iommi felt the same intimidation. "I think he intimidated everybody. The way they dealt with people then was quite different to now. It's all lawyers now. Back then they'd send someone to beat people up. We saw that a few bloody times. But when Don managed the band again in the 1980s I didn't feel threatened by him at all. I actually felt a bit sorry for him. He used to call me in for meetings — just to have someone to talk to. He was quite a lonely person."

David Arden was brought into the family business: "Well, we became the agents." Don Arden took over Galaxy Entertainment from Ron Kingsnorth. Ron had promptly decamped for New Zealand. Galaxy Entertainments had over a hundred groups in its heyday. As well as The Move, they had the Amen Corner, the Nashville Teens, the Applejacks, The Action, Neil Christian, the Fairytale and The Skatellites. Arden carefully built his roster with whom he felt had the strongest chance of achieving success. His decisions were generally sound, but raw talent and strong potential could not always be translated into stardom. One band that couldn't cross the stardom line was The Attack, featuring David O'List, who later achieved success in The Nice.

While waiting the emergence of a new act to rival the chart-topping feats of the Small Faces, Arden temporarily revived his own singing career. He was probably influenced by the dramatic rise in sales of ballad material in the UK during the first half of 1967. With Tom Jones, Engelbert Humperdinck, Vince Hill, Frank Sinatra and even Harry Secombe, all scoring massive hits. He was now responsible for booking the formidable hit machine which fell into his hands in 1967. When Arden took over the management of Amen Corner from agent Ron King, they had already achieved chart success.

David Arden recalls, "In all honesty, if you were in a group and all of a sudden, you've got a manager, and an agent, which is Tony Burfield at the time as well, but then he goes, 'What the fuck's this name?'

David Arden recalls that, "Andy (Fairweather Low) the singer didn't really like the old man. I think he wasn't his cup of tea. 'Who the fuck are these people? They're coming out of nowhere and they're my manager. I would feel the same. Ron King was supposed to stay on for a few months to gradually introduce me and the old man. King went for the money and disappeared. So, I don't blame Andy or the rest of the group. By the summer of 1968 they had notched up four hits, 'Gin House', 'World Of Broken Hearts', 'Bend Me Shape Me' and 'High In The Sky'. They were regarded by the media, as a well above average group. What the press did not reveal was the intense power struggle, serving as a backdrop to this group's short career."

Don saw David Arden as his A&R presence. An easy-going, young man with a friendly personality. Someone to nurture the artists personally and bridge the gap between him and the acts. An exciting time for the young David Arden. "I took over when I was 17. The Move did a gig at the Royal Albert Hall with The Byrds and The Bonzo Dog Doo-Dah Band and others. This was The Move's second date at the Albert Hall (7th July 1968). Carl invites us there to see them. 'Why don't you come down to the show and have a chat.' My God! I thought it was loud. I think they were the loudest group I had ever heard. Every time I saw them, they were so fucking loud. They were really great at the gig. There was that aggression in them that I liked. And the old man liked it too. The Byrds were also on the bill. That's when Carl said, 'Do you want to be our manager?' Don said, 'If you want me to be of course I can.' That's what Don did. I always thought he had a special love for The Move."

"So, Charlie (Carl) Wayne comes in and he just loves the old man. They were already pissed off with Secunda. Charlie wasn't a druggie type anyway. Whenever I went out with Charlie he was never interested in drugs. No; Bev, Roy and Carl didn't use drugs, but it wasn't the old man or me that took them away from Secunda. They were already disgruntled with him. It just so happened, when the old man and myself got into Galaxy and Charlie met the old man, he said, 'Oh, I like him.' Carl would be in the office every day when they weren't working. By then, I'd been their agent for about four months. One day, Bev and Carl were there, and I think Roy was there. Bev and Charlie came up the office in a hurry. Secunda's office was like three doors down in Denmark Street. All of a sudden, they're not there, they're laughing and acting like kids. They're steaming round to our offices. They've all run down like little boys down the stairs! They have run out the Galaxy office, because Secunda's coming — Boom! They're gone. Secunda's coming up the stairs and he's going, 'These fucking children! My God, where's your gun? Where are they? Where have they gone?' What they'd done was thrown stink bombs into his office. He was really pissed off! I don't think they ever went back to him after that."

Secunda's story could be said to have ended with 'Flowers In The Rain'. He lingered on until the end of their management contract. It was still in place, but he'd gone. David Arden didn't think Tony was a good manager. He said, "What did he do after the Move?"

Rob Caiger: "I know David Arden will assess him as a fellow manager, but I look at Secunda and see someone that shouldn't have tried to do everything under the guise of a manager. I never saw management as his role. He was a brilliant marketing manager but never a business or personal manager. I wouldn't criticise him over contracts. Music business contracts were poor for everyone at the time, but Secunda should have had someone looking after the business and someone hands-on with the band members. Like Andrew Oldham and Tony Calder at Immediate Records. But even their set up didn't end well."

Pauline Evans also left The Move scene around this time. The young, beautiful lady later got married to Barry Pritchard (Barry passed away in January 1999). Barry was the long-time singer and guitarist with The Fortunes. Another popular band from the 60s that did very well in the charts.

Roy Wood said of Carl Wayne's departure, "In late 1969 after 'Blackberry Way' that's when Carl left just after. He got annoyed about not getting songwriting credits and the publisher money and stuff. Carl wanted some of the publishing money. There was another guy called Dave (Scott) Morgan, who went on to join ELO years later. Carl got him to write songs. Carl put the songs on the B-sides, 'cos he needed to get money out of it. I played Carl 'Blackberry Way' and he refused to sing it. I did 'Blackberry Way' and I did 'Fire Brigade' as a lead vocalist. To be honest, I don't think the management really cared who sang on them."

The *numero uno* mistake of Secunda's early management without a doubt was failing to capitalise on the US market. Sadly, the Move's lone US tour, which took place in October of 1969 proved disastrous. Not in any musical sense at all — The Move acquitted themselves very well; but due to a number of factors, which included poor, or utterly no organisation from the US label. A&M Records were clueless, apathetic and distinctly useless — or certainly the employees dealing with The Move were. They hadn't bothered to make any cursory enquiries about The Move: Who the band were? How had they done in the UK? How many records they had sold? How many hits had they had in the UK? This lack of 'day one' work shows a collection of piss-poor employees working in the company on behalf of Herb Alpert and Jerry Moss.

Inner turmoil, meanwhile, was still sabotaging the band. However, this may have been forgotten momentarily, to be placed, quietly bubbling away, on the back shelf for a while with the "one for all and all for one" camaraderie the band experienced on this madcap jaunt into the USA. The band would have had to swing together in a brotherly fashion. To make this road trip work. Of course, these issues have a way of rankling and never being resolved. Unless they get resolved, in frank, open and in broad daylight terms!

Bev Bevan describes the exhilaration and exhaustion of doing the zany, badly organised, first USA tour. "We had to drive right across the United States — nearly 3,000 miles — with only one night's sleep. It was the only way we were going to make our booking on time and as we couldn't afford to fly there was no option. But on this tour, I got the feeling, that I was to enjoy many times again. That feeling of camaraderie, that "boys are back in town" attitude, just devil-may-care, full of jokes and laughs. There was a carefree atmosphere and an underlying feeling that however grotty it became, you were all in it together."

The three-week cross-country tour was a shoestring operation, poorly planned, and with no album to plug, had little real impact. The band flew into New York thinking they were to undertake an East Coast tour, only to discover that there was no one from A&M Records to meet them or organise things, and that the dates were booked for the West Coast. They rented a car and played shows with The Stooges at the legendary Grande Ballroom, before setting off down Route 66 to Los Angeles for five nights at the Whisky a Go Go. A further drive to San Francisco culminated in a series of gigs at the Fillmore West sharing the bill with Joe Cocker and Little Richard.

"Had we gone during the Secunda era, we would have taken America by storm," Carl Wayne insisted. "But with no record to support when we were out there, we were rudderless." The singer found himself doubly out of sorts because The Move had worked up an entirely different set to take across the Atlantic. "We did one Move hit, 'I Can Hear the Grass Grow', which we stretched out for almost 15 minutes. I think we did 'Hello Susie', which Roy had written for The Amen Corner. The rest of the set was West Coast songs such as 'Open My Eyes' by The Nazz." Carl's stated opinion was, "I mean, Roy's a good guitarist, but he's no Hendrix or Jimmy Page. I wasn't impressed and I'm not sure that America was wholly convinced either."

Rick Price never forgot that bonkers and short US tour. "We also toured the USA later that year. It was a tour that should have taken place back in January but put back with Trevor Burton leaving. Then me joining the band meant it had to be put off for eight months. When I say toured the USA, don't run away with the idea that it was all articulated trucks and air-conditioned tour busses — no sir. Five of us, Carl, Roy, Bev, me and Upsy in a car with a U-Haul trailer on the back, full of gear. Exactly like the words of the song, we drove from Chicago to L.A. along Route 66."

Regarding the band's set list, it's true they didn't have an album to promote during the tour. As *Shazam* was to come around four months later. Some tracks on that album obviously impacted the setlist, the group put together on the road in America.

16th October 1969
1. Open My Eyes
2. Hello Susie
3. Under The Ice
4. Open My Eyes (Reprise)
5. Cherry Blossom Clinic Revisited

18th October 1969
1. Open My Eyes
2. Don't Make My Baby Blue
3. Cherry Blossom Clinic Revisited
4. The Last Thing On My Mind
5. I Can Hear the Grass Grow

****

Shazam had drawn some rave reviews. It was acclaimed by *Rolling Stone* as "powerful and intricately structured and flowing! A brutally energetic rock 'n' roll album." However, again, all was still not well in The Move camp. Carl Wayne had a desire to pursue a solo career as a balladeer.

Bev Bevan had often noticed and felt uncomfortable, with at times, agitating feelings. Bev felt that Carl would often (always?) be looking for opportunities. Within, outside and beyond The Move horizon. It could feel like Carl was keeping his options open all the time instead of truly committing to the future development of the group.

This was adding a further layer of inconsistency and anxiety to the puzzled drummer. However, in interviews around that time Bev had mentioned he also had his fingers in some other business ideas, saying, "I'm starting a production company called Dog. I am producing with a guy called Mike Walker, who used to play bass with a Birmingham band called Redcaps. Our first effort is a recorded version of Roy Wood's 'Vote For Me', which was recorded by a Brum group called Stacks, which featured keyboardist Richard Tandy. We have been negotiating with record companies, and it should be out soon."

The general tenor of the interview suggested they wanted to get involved in a lot more production work. Carl Wayne was also feeling that his views and concerns had some obvious merit. He felt his role was diminishing and was being reduced further. From his position, as the once regarded, fearless unique, and standout lead vocalist for The Move.

Again, no management strategy was involved in trying to work out these repeating quandaries. In essence, to find ways to give people what they wanted. There was seemingly little communication from Roy towards Carl to examine what he needed — how to allow him to feel fulfilled with his important and powerful role in the band. Which had been a very large one. As the powerhouse lead singer, interviewee, spokesman, and extrovert showman. Complete with the crowd enthralling, axe destruction and his all-round, charismatic personality. This had helped them solidify their role, with all the adjacent publicity, over the previous four years.

There were ongoing fights and issues, around who was producing what. With this second album, Gerald Chevin was kept on as Advision Studios engineer. As stated before, Roy's songwriting pace was not very fast. 'Beautiful Daughter' was a lovely song, left over from the year before. A classic song, which rightly made the *Shazam* sessions. It could have made a wonderful Move single in between.

Another song, called 'Hello Susie' written by Roy, found both a home and a number four UK chart entry for Amen Corner — fronted by the cherubic, high-register voiced, angelically–faced Mr Andy Fairweather Low. 'Cherry Blossom Clinic' was re-visited, both in song and in added title. These three Roy offerings made up side one of *Shazam*.

On the second side, the three majestic cover versions were chosen and sung by Carl. They were picked with due diligence and were all top choices. Before his stark break away from the band these were good cover choices. Further reinforcing the almost 100% hip choices they made in doing other songs. As validated by their timely catalogue of superb covers. Mostly they covered them with big, fresh strokes. Sometimes making them much "better" than the original versions. *Shazam* has striking cover artwork by Mike Sheridan. On a mid-blue background, Carl, Roy, Bev and Rick are seen illustrated as superheroes. Drawn and coloured in a strong, basic magic marker style.

Roy Wood evokes the *Shazam* period: "As for *Shazam*, the management asked me to take over producing the band. Then Carl and myself had differences and everybody wanted a piece of the cake. We just put it down to a band production because Carl was also involved in the production. He wanted the say on what songs were on the album as well. He chose the cover versions on side two. I don't think the album holds up that well. And I wouldn't play it now — there was something missing. I can't really put my finger on what it is. It's probably down to the fact we weren't together personally as a band. We weren't pulling in the same direction. If you're having a good time in the studio, that actually comes across on the tape. That was a bit of a miserable album for us. It was the move away from pop, into a more underground progressive music. That was more the direction we had wanted to go in, for quite a long time. But then we did the cabaret circuit and that utterly spoiled all that. It ruined the direction of the band. Looking at it from Carl's point of view, I think that was really frustrating. That's probably why he left in the end. He was singing less of the songs. The band was also becoming more directionless at that same time."

Carl also revealed that he was starting to write songs himself and producing things for his own underground group, 'Bertie Bird and the Concrete Biscuit' (surely another colossal wind-up by Mr Wayne?). Who he hoped to launch upon the Americans when The Move arrived there for their first tour in September. "It's a very short tour of only 17 days," said Carl. "But we will be taking our two-track album along to promote and play at places like the Fillmore East. I don't give a fuck about the hippies. I'm just going to sing, and we are playing, what we play."

There was the case of a German guy who made the mistake of throwing things at the group while onstage. This resulted in his face forcibly coming into collision with a chair. "We were banned in Germany," reflected Carl sadly… "But I think the misunderstanding is being sorted out," he added very optimistically. In fact, three future tours of the country were actually cancelled. Promoters were claiming the band were violent on stage and they were slated in the German press.

Carl continues on the German trouble, "We're only human, everybody's got a bit of violence in them — we just bring it into a set, by smashing up television sets and other equipment on stage. The trouble on the last tour started when the audience decided they wanted to join in! And we had to draw the line there. We are still using the "wild" act abroad. The fact is, we would like to let off a bit more steam, if we could! We also plan to use this act when we go to the USA this year. They can't keep us out of Germany. We shall be back there later in the year. Billing is important to us, and we get billed as 'the most evil group in the pop world.'"

The Move's seventh single, 'Curly' appeared in July 1969 on Regal Zonophone. That A-side and the Dave Morgan-penned B-side, 'This Time Tomorrow', were both produced by Mike Hurst. Hurst had also handled early recordings by Cat Stevens ('Matthew And Son') and the Alan Bown Set ('Outward Bown'). 'Curly' was said to be recorded with reference to the roadie of the Brum band Sight and Sound, called Curly Williams.

Bev Bevan simply hated 'Curly'. He hated the lyrics too. *"Where's your girly, where's she gone."* Bev thought, "'Curly' was embarrassing, really sugary and dreadful." He thought it was taking pop music to an extremely saccharine extreme.

Roy Wood didn't like it either, he felt it was incredibly "corny." He stated he was unhappy with the record label's decision to release it as a single over other songs that he preferred. It felt now like they were the "the good old Move" rather than the earlier, dangerous live five–piece that would frighten people live as they were that intimidatingly great.

The song itself took over thirteen takes to achieve a result — to secure a performance everybody was happy with. Mike Hurst originally was brought in to produce *Shazam* but he only ended up producing the one single. There was an annoying, processed tambourine sound going throughout 'Curly' which could give mild headaches to the more treble sensitive listener. I'm talking about the production side of it. The song's coda has nice, backwards, squalling wah-wah guitar effects from Roy. Squeezed through some filtered effect or other.

The sessions started on 8th May 1969 and carried on into June. One standout on 'Curly' was its intensely Beatlesque ending. I asked musical maestro John Altman to explain the engaging, harmony vocal ending to this song. He explained, "It's a major sixth chord. An F major 6th. In addition to the F major triad (F, A and C), you add the 6th of the scale, a D."

In fact, it's the same chord inversion as the end of The Beatles' 'Help!'. The Beatles is an A Major 6th! It's a really cool vocal ending to this strange, listless, sugary Move song. It's a wonderful vocal Move trick. They also used it for the end of their version of Darrell Bank's 'Our Love Is In The Pocket' with the soulful Ace Kefford on lead vocals.

'Curly' too has a rather strange production. The recorders are simply ear-piercing beyond belief. Sounding like they were compressed through the recording console. All the way right into the ground. One could ponder, whether it was a 'Wild Tiger Woman' scenario again — whether the song was recorded very quickly.

The Mike Hurst production certainly stands out. It is said that Hurst was not available for the last mixes. Roy took over and did the final mix for this release while Jimmy Miller was in the next-door studio, recording 'Honky-Tonk Women' with The Rolling Stones. It has a different "sound picture" from the previous six singles. I found it very shrill, in its production, particularly the recorders throughout. There is an interesting effect on Carl Wayne's vocal at the beginning. This pushes him back in the mix. before the song kicks in with its pronounced, compressed production style. It feels like it's all top end and the recorders, are just short of ear rupturing.

In the 19th July 1969 issue of *Melody Maker*, Chris Welch said the song was "an obvious success for The Move." The song peaked at number 12 in the UK singles chart. It was the last single by the band to feature Carl Wayne. It was the first with Rick Price. The instrumentation is mainly acoustic, and Roy Wood was featured on multi-tracked recorders. He also plays acoustic guitar and adds a cappella harmonies, with the sole electric instrument, the mellotron, appearing only briefly.

Released as a single only, it was later included on the remastered versions of *Looking On* in 1998 and *Shazam* in 2007. Roy by then owned a collection of odd instruments (steel guitar, mandolin, cittern, bouzouki, bassoon) that he had bought and collected with his ongoing Move royalties. As he learned each instrument, he was developing material outside the band's creative scope. During downtime from his Move commitments Wood recorded musical demos and pieces over a two-year period at Phonogram and at Abbey Road Studios. The songs from these 1969-1971 sessions were later collected into his 1973 debut solo album *Boulders*.

A short press piece described the next Move record (very optimistically) as being a double album. They said that the first disc would comprise 14 original songs written by Roy Wood. The second disc would be devoted to compositions by

Richard Tandy and David Morgan, who are both contracted to Carl Wayne's new publishing company Penny Music. It was claimed that the 28 tracks were being cut at the Birmingham recording studio, owned by Cal Wayne and Trevor Burton and that it would be the first time the band would record outside London.

The double LP was apparently planned for release by Regal Zonophone. It was also reported that The Move's much delayed tour of America had been finalised. The group was to begin a three-week visit on 14th September with an itinerary including concerts club dates and an appearance on US TVs *Johnny Carson Show*. The final three days of The Move's visit were to be devoted to recording in Los Angeles, where it was hoped that a new single would be cut for release. It was claimed that after the soon-to-be issued 'Wild Tiger Woman', agent Don Arden had begun negotiating a four-week US college tour for The Move for beginning of April.

29.
Lying in wait for the moon to break...

Shazam bears little relation to the first album. There seemed to be unspoken, ongoing predicaments bubbling under the surface. There was something lacking in the progression of the band. Cohesion seemed to have dissipated as they dealt with the sacking of Secunda. And with yet another change in sound and personnel, Roy Wood's song output had slowed.

Rick Price recalled the sessions as, "Great, we were in hysterics, a lot of the time, especially Carl and I."

People describe the album as "heavy progressive rock." But this describes it in a very lumpen way. Limiting its much broader, aural landscape. The Move always had a certain playfulness, a wry sarcasm, that still comes through on *Shazam*.

Shazam was released nearly two years after *Move*, in February 1970, consisting of just six extended tracks, compared to the thirteen cuts on *Move*. The arrangements are more complex, and the instrumental talents of the band members are certainly on display. From the LP's opening track 'Hello Susie', the one new Roy Wood original on the record. 'Hello Suzie' with its attacking beat and gorgeous melodies which continue throughout the album, had already been a sizeable hit for Amen Corner, reaching number four in the UK charts. Roy had a great love of setting up staccato guitar tracked riffs that reverberate and set up the song's structure, before settling into the main song with one of Bev's trademark, double stroke, snare drum rolls. 'Hello Suzie' also leads the way for the grungy, swampier, slowed down rock of 'Brontosaurus' and other songs on *Message From The Country*.

'Beautiful Daughter' with its exquisite Tony Visconti strings (also plays the bass guitar) was recorded earlier. 'Cherry Blossom Clinic Revisited' is a reworked, expanded version of the classic song, which closed the debut album with a naturally funny Carl Wayne introduction. This is spoken in a gloriously dense and really guttural Brummie accent. Both funny and a nod to his home city.

Carl was often known for his funny impersonations and mimicry and his ready sense of humour which endeared him to many people. Roy Wood has fun on this one — his tracked acoustic guitars are featured, gleefully quoting Bach's 'Jesu, Joy Of Man's Desiring', 'The Sorcerer's Apprentice' (aka 'Teddy Bears' Picnic') and Tchaikovsky's The Chinese Dance) from his ballet The Nutcracker. *Shazam* is fun and inventive; it is tongue in cheek in places. Carl's funny asides, outside in central London to taxi drivers and members of the public, are still funny and haven't dated.

The Move certainly sound better here aurally. Lots of space between the instruments and you can hear Bev Bevan's stripped back style very clearly. With more emphasis on punchy, bass drumbeats. Rather than the immense, clattering, frenetic drumrolls, we heard (and loved) on the first record and the first four Move singles.

Shazam comprises an exactly, equal mix of originals on side one and cover tunes on side two: Kicking off with an absolutely brilliant, complex arrangement of Ars Nova's version of Wyatt Day and John Pierson's 'Fields Of People'. This is followed by an extremely heavy version of Frankie Laine's 'Don't Make My Baby Blue' written by Barry Mann and Cynthia Weil. The album closes with a gently percussive rocked-up version of folk singer Tom Paxton's 'The Last Thing On My Mind', sung beautifully by Carl — a fitting tribute to his vocal talent on this his swan song. It shows off Carl's versatile, strong mid to lower tenor. He sings deeply and soulfully. He is unrestrained in places, with some hints of the great, raw feral rasp we heard earlier on the *Something Else From The Move* EP on 'It'll Be Me' and 'Stephanie Knows Who' for example.

With double-tracked, sublime vocal phrasings and some truly wonderful harmonies, this recording features a more 'mediaeval Madrigal' choral type sound. In contrast to the more Beach Boys / US soul type of harmonies the original five-piece band excelled at.

A false start and an interruption from Gerald Chevin from the recording console introduces 'Don't Make My Baby Blue' before Wood's snarling lead guitar shifts the track into overdrive. It has a wonderful feel as if the band are slightly dragging the time. Which adds to the crunching heaviness of the entire track.

All tracks prominently feature Roy Wood's lead guitar(s) and tracked acoustic guitars. Rick Price's detuned bass were certainly different and were put together by him and Roy Wood. It has been said that Trevor and Roy, worked out the bass and guitar parts before Rick came in, but this is difficult to verify. The bass adds another undertow and dimension to the record's dimensions and sound picture.

There is lots to hear on this album, which seems like a long piece of music. 'Fields Of People' inches toward the eleven-minute mark but the album actually runs to just over 39 minutes in total. Carl Wayne's lead vocals introduce 'Fields Of People' which features beautiful harmony vocals and an infectious groove led by Wood's gentle guitar work. There is a long Wood banjar/sitar excursion, while the song's chanted chorus builds, adding to the charm of this ten-minute musical adventure.

Bev Bevan is obviously fond of this record. "Of all The Move's albums, this is my favourite! Mainly due to the fact that this is my favourite drumming on those four LPs."

This album and *Live At The Fillmore 1969* both around this same period show Bev adopting a crisper, more measured style of drumming. Still peppered with thunderous and machine-gun like rolls around the kit, but just a little more restrained in his percussive aggression.

Bev continues, "The album failed to chart, hardly helped by the fact that Carl Wayne had just left the band shortly before it was released!"

American music critic John Mendelsohn reviewed it in *Rolling Stone* (when it was still a hip and readable culture magazine in 1970): "If like me, you're the sort who collapses on the floor, frothing with delight, palpitating obscenely with excitement and glimpsing nirvana in the presence of rock 'n' roll at its most remitting brutal, flashy and devastatingly vulgar manifestations, you simply can't live without The Move's *Shazam* album for another instant." Frothy praise indeed — and it showed that a few choice hipsters in America were already digging out The Move in record bins and getting into their variable and always-changing music.

Gerald Chevin does a wonderful engineering job in his mixing of the thundering rhythm section and driving lead guitar, with Wayne's restrained lead vocals. The album closes with an incredible arrangement of Tom Paxton's 'The Last Thing On My Mind' with Wood's overdubbed guitars at the fore. Wayne's robust but plaintive vocals, are a perfect complement, giving the tune its deceptively heavy sound. Jangling guitar and delicate harmony vocals, set the scene for an incredibly inspired, wah-wah driven guitar solo by Wood. With just the right amount of phasing, added for good measure on this seven-and-a-half-minute gem. It also ends on a glorious Beatlesque harmony finale. With its final vocal lift, which is stunning. Think The Beatles 'Help!', their own single 'Curly' and their Ace sung cover 'Love Is In The Pocket'.

Shazam was released in remastered form, first by Salvo, as a 1CD set, remastered and overseen by Rob Caiger. This features the remastered album; plus, eight bonus tracks. 'Hello Suzie' as a US single edit is included as a bonus track. The Roy Wood original 'Beautiful Daughter' features superb double-tracked lead vocals by Wayne.

After this, a 2CD set was released by Esoteric Recordings in 2016. The new Esoteric edition supplements the album's original six tunes. With an incredible 37 bonus tracks. It contains a total of 43 tracks, containing over two and a half hours of music. Making this the absolutely, definitive edition of *Shazam*. CD one has bonus tracks. The second CD has two *Shazam* outtakes plus 16 tracks of BBC live sessions with two interviews, one with Bev and one with Carl.

The CD bonus material begins with both sides of the album's three related singles, 'Wild Tiger Woman', 'Curly' and the gorgeous 'Blackberry Way'. These tunes sound crisp and are all joined with their B-sides. Disc one closes with an album outtake, a longer, stereo version of 'Wild Tiger Woman'. Plus, an extended version of its B-side 'Omnibus'. An alternate mix of 'Curly' and a demo of that tune's flip 'This Time Tomorrow'.

Disc two on the Esoteric edition contains a total of twenty-five tracks. Seventy-one minutes in all, opening with a demo of a song 'That Certain Something' with Trevor Burton playing a shuffling beat on drums. A 'reduced' mix of 'Beautiful Daughter' is offered. Before the shift to twenty-three cuts recorded at the BBC between May 1968 and November 1969.

As was common, The Move recorded tracks for the BBC that stood alone, as part of their repertoire. As they travelled through the various musical phases in their fast-paced career. Among these are a cover of Neil Diamond's 'Kentucky Woman'. Takes of the classic Byrds' 'Long Black Veil', another favourite Goffin/King's 'Goin' Back', Brian Wilson's 'California Girls', Paul Simon's 'Sound Of Silence' (a slight veering to MOR here) and Nazz's 'Open My Eyes' all performed with The Move's aptitude for top-notch covers.

The only jarring selection for me is 'Going Out Of My Head' sung by Carl. Which veers too closely into middle-of-the-road, cabaret territory. It wasn't quite

Carl's vivid, open-throated version of 'Ave Maria'. But one can imagine Carl pushing, the 'PJ Proby on mushrooms' approach with a little restraint! It doesn't sit squarely with the other great covers.

These are added to selected renditions, of some of the band's best-known songs. Including all the three singles released in conjunction with *Shazam*. This 2CD deluxe edition was compiled by Mark Powell. The 20-page colour booklet contains another excellent essay by Mark Paytress. It includes complete track annotations, with remastering by Ben Wiseman at Broadlake Studios, plus lots of gorgeous photos. Compared to the Move's long-gestating 1968 eponymous debut, their 1970 sophomore effort *Shazam* is more or less unified.

Carl Wayne had the most input he had ever had on this record. He chose all the material on the B-side. Plus, inserting funny Vox-Pop interviews dotted throughout the recording made out and around Gosfield Street where Advision Studio was located. These interviews are a genuine, good laugh, in a unique, uncategorisable manner. It is another Move record, which doesn't fit into any easy classification. None of the six songs here clock in under five minutes. With two tunes sprawling well over seven minutes.

The thunderous opener 'Hello Susie' is the only new Wood song. It's all wildly inventive music and, as in the recording itself, The Move may never have been better than they are here. There are more ideas in each of these long, languid jams, than many bands have in a career. *Shazam* is a recording that rewards repeated spins many times over. An oddity, but a very, very listenable one.

Carl Wayne always felt that Roy Wood's songs were brilliant, "As great as they were! In some respects that was also, a self-inflicted wound."

Over a year and a half, they lost Kefford and Burton. Then Carl Wayne. This was the death knell of The Move as was. Even though they produced some great singles. All the verve, the crazy fire, the wild energy — alas — was all well and truly gone.

At times when the music press dictates a certain thing, I have observed the music media often does this thing where it goes through these brain-dead lemming periods. Where, for example, say, during punk and after punk (dubbed as 'post-punk'), so-called "indulgent" guitar solos weren't allowed or were frowned upon. So, because of these unsaid but unofficially, instigated, so-called "hipster" rulings, very few (guitar breaks) appeared on any record. However, later, during the Madchester "baggy" period, it was okay for The Stone Roses and John Squire to display his guitar virtuosity when needed. Without any recognisable, further censure from the self-styled 'influencers' at (say) *NME*. John Squire is a great player, and the group had a unique, slippery funky feel. But that is one example of a band, that within a generation, gets an "allowance" to do something. Whereas other bands were not allowed to do so. Again, in an unsaid, "unofficial" manner. I can remember the *NME* particularly having a sort of '1984 group think" approach to what was in and what was not. Pervasively around that time and for quite some time.

Roy Wood: "In the beginning, we got a lot of ideas from Danny King's extensive record collection. Much later on when we were doing covers of stuff like 'Sounds Of Silence', that's when Carl and I started having problems. Carl didn't wanna sing my songs anymore. And so, I let him choose songs, that he wanted to sing. I didn't agree with Carl's choices a lot of the time. It was starting to sound much towards cabaret."

I agree with Roy. There were way too many middle-of-the-road choices. 'Going Out Of My Head' for example didn't sit well with The Move's repertoire. It jars on the bonus material on *Shazam*.

****

Don Arden also managed Skip Bifferty, a band that couldn't seem to handle the rigours of the road or the rigours of Don Arden. During their early days they were full of ambition, thinking of themselves that they were going to be huge, like many a band. However, they couldn't handle the road night after night. The stark reality of climbing that mountain to success. Arden was singularly unimpressed. "They weren't tough enough to make it... They wanted to become stars. Just when we got them up from £10 to £100 a night they went to pieces. They forget that nothing comes easy, you've got to work for what you get. They had no staying power, no patience and they wouldn't accept guidance. And artistes have to co-operate with me to make it."

Skip Bifferty also got Arden's goat up. They wanted to end the management agreement. They were scared so they shot off to the suburbs in Greater London. Even going to Beckenham police to report Arden. They were advised to report any future threats. Frightened and emotionally intimidated, they confessed their worst fears as two cars pulled up outside their house and they were confronted by several heavies. Flashing shooters around and threatening some unpleasant consequences. Wisely, they made a phone call and after a lengthy chase one of the cars was stopped in London's Tottenham Court Road. Several offensive weapons were discovered in the vehicle and the heavies were duly charged. It was another astonishing episode in the career of an Arden group who found themselves hopelessly out of depth in their dealings with the all-powerful Al Capone of Pop.

When Arden first entered the lives of The Move, they had created more short-term controversy than any of their contemporaries, bar the Rolling Stones. When the Move elected to appoint Don Arden as their new agent, Secunda was angrily opposed, forcing them to choose between himself and his elder rival. Eventually, they took on Arden, but the decision was far from unanimous and almost split the group. Kefford was already on the way out. With all kinds of ongoing, simmering tensions in the group.

One might have assumed that Don could at least rest easy in the knowledge that no manager would dare attempt to confront him. Just like the Small Faces and Amen Corner before them, the Move had found themselves slap bang in the middle of the entrepreneurial feud involving Arden and Peter Walsh.

After the disastrous spell with Walsh, The Move decamped back to Don Arden. In this next spell with the Move, it looked like Arden had a dying group, but he always retained faith in the band, who struggled on as a trio, with Roy Wood as lead vocalist.

Having flirted with acid rock, pop art, flower power and psychedelia. They now emerged as a quasi-sludgy, heavy metal band with 'Brontosaurus' and 'When Alice Comes Back To The Farm'. Wood even adopted a startling new image and appeared like a tribal warrior with multi-coloured backcombed hair and a painted face. The Move were already changing plans with the arrival of singer-composer-guitarist Jeff

Lynne. This was all part of the planning to launch ELO into the music marketplace. Arden was initially sceptical about such a radical move away from The Move's success.

Arden was an old school style manager. He stayed from the bottom up, treading the boards as a young singer. Paying his dues, he went on to change his name from Harry Levy to Don Arden. He genuinely enjoyed the business from all angles. He honestly liked creative people and got on well with them. Particularly if he thought they were up for some serious graft and had some original ideas. He loved the creative process, and he enjoyed the company of creative people.

He moved down from Manchester to London. The Ardens all moved into a property owned by Winifred Atwell. Miss Atwell was a very popular wartime pianist. Atwell was also a popular recording artist. She was a great favourite for Londoners and throughout all the UK. Don sang and recorded Yiddish songs for the Jewish market. At weekends, he would also entertain them with his impressions of Al Jolson. Arden sang for a budget label called Embassy. Embassy Records were distributed through Woolworths. Which then, was a household department store. Woolworths sold pretty much everything, including its famous, pick 'n mix sweets counter.

Don even sang a version of 'Blue Suede Shoes' put out under the name of The Canadians. He was still recording well up to 1967 and a crackly acetate exists somewhere of Don singing 'Sunrise Sunset'. Don also bought himself shares in the notorious Star Club in Hamburg. Made famous and more notorious, as the venue where The Beatles learnt their trade. The young men under the tutelage of Astrid Kirshner were taking speed pills (Preludin) by the bucket load. This helped with playing and performing umpteen sets a night. As an apprenticeship, it honed their music to a razor-sharp edge. It also allowed John Lennon to wear a selection of toilet seats around his neck and run around the stage bollocks naked when he was frothing at the mouth and was particularly speeding out of his brains. This, in a pre-punk display of amphetamine style stage craft. Until all four were as musically tight and cutting as razor blades — four young men as one!

Reading Steve Jones's *Lonely Boy* book (the fantastic guitar player for The Sex Pistols), Steve learnt to play guitar on amphetamines. I wonder how many players / bands really learn to play and get over some of the initial humps of learning by taking loads of speed and just playing and playing?

Arden then got into music tour management, overseeing the redolent package bills, which were very popular at the time. Further to this, he went on to manage the troubled singer, Gene Vincent. Vincent was a handful — all by and to himself. Gene alone must have taught and honed Don into adopting a few much-needed tricks; in the how-to-psychology school of personal artist management.

Gene's erratic behaviour swiftly brought on the end of their relationship. It was said that Gene pulled a knife on Don Arden. This was in one of his many alcoholic-induced rages. Andrew Loog-Oldham remembered Don warmly: "Here was a Jew that ran London and thank God!"

Oldham was writing press releases for Don Arden. He started out with his sensationalistic, wind-up press releases! These were around Little Richard, who was to be playing in London. In which, as part of his release, Oldham both entreated and cajoled. "Inviting the press to come and see the theatre seats being ripped to shreds."

Cecil Bernstein owned the Granada Theatres chain. Bernstein wasn't at all impressed, by the 17-year-old Oldham's attempts to incite teen violence. Don Arden remembers this momentary stand-off: "Bernstein was such an old idiot! He was prepared to cancel a sold-out tour — which is very unusual for a Jew in business (laughs). So, I had to change Andrew." Andrew Loog Oldham wanted to be right next to the Arden magic. "I wanted to be around the larger-than-life characters like Don Arden."

Arden also developed the Small Faces career. Again, from the ground up. He squeezed them into already existing tour dates in the UK. He was getting them on for 5 to 10 minutes, on each package tour bills. The first Small Faces single flopped. But Arden was not going to let go of his little proteges that easily. He got all round, music biz, singer, actor, hustler and songwriter Kenny Lynch. Señor Lynch had been right there, and right at the beginning. He appeared on the first British tour by The Beatles. Kenny came up with a brilliantly inane song 'Sha La La La Lee'. Inane in the sense that it's as superficial as can be! But it's a great pop single, a right old burrowing ear worm. Mr Lynch managed to write that one in all of 5 minutes. That immediately ran up the UK charts to number 3. No doubt helped by Arden's inimitable style of getting loads of housewives to get themselves out of doors and to go out and buy lots and lots of copies. Sort of a 'domestic white goods, payola system'.

Don Black, who wrote songs for the first Carl Wayne album, differentiated between Brian Epstein and Don Arden. "Brian Epstein was a very quiet, classy, graceful, elegant man. Don was the complete opposite. He was brash, he was loud. I never found him threatening. But he was more rock 'n' roll than Gordon Mills and Brian Epstein. Don would just thunder in where angels feared to tread."

Don Arden remembered Brian Epstein's sense of ethics: "He believed that if you do a deal then you stand by it!"

Some other shady and notorious managers were found in the slipstream of Don Arden. Men like Mike Jefferies, who was initially based out of Newcastle. Jeffries had managed The Animals. Peter Grant, the future superstar manager of Led Zeppelin learnt some of the rock 'n' roll ground rules back then when he worked for the Arden company. Don Arden had no compunction about threatening people. Particularly those who tried to encroach on his management territory. There is the oft repeated story (now legend) about Robert Stigwood, when he tried to poach the Small Faces, by then a very hot property. Robert Stigwood saw the world from an entirely different angle. When he was dangled headfirst, out of his office by Don and his posse.

This Robert Stigwood story has to be commented on. As it has reached the stage of folkloric legend. Certainly, a music business legend, like Clifford Davis, an approach was made to entice or poach the Small Faces. They were a hot property. They reached a collision with Don Arden, and they wanted out. They were concerned about monies that couldn't be trace and / or owed. In fact, one of Robert Stigwood's associates was making noises about interest in the group. Don became extremely angry on hearing this news. He contacted two well-muscled friends and had two more equally huge, tough guys involved.

Don Arden remarked in one interview that he'd rehearsed an outline to put the shits up Stigwood. "We went along and met the impresario at his office. There was a large ornate ashtray on his desk. I picked it up and smashed it down with such force that it actually cracked open the desk. This gave a good impression of a man, who was wild with rage. We had all rehearsed the next move. I pretended to go berserk, lifting the impresario bodily from his chair. We dragged him over to the office balcony and held him. So, he's now looking down to the pavement. Which is four floors below. I asked my friends whether I should 'drop him or forgive him.' In unison they all shouted, 'Drop him!' Stigwood was by now, rigid with fear and shock. I thought he might just have a heart attack. Immediately I dragged him back into the room and told him never to interfere with any of my groups again."

The ashen, deathly drained Stigwood, who actually never even contacted The Small Faces, promptly took Arden's advice, as did so many other people in the pop music business. One such person was a member of a band called The Nashville Teens, the pianist John Hawken. He enquired about what he thought were missing monies to Don Arden. His response to this was threatening the musician with defenestration. This ties in nicely with the Stigwood story.

"No-one got killed! Drugs killed; terrorism killed but Don Arden never killed." Further stated Andrew Loog Oldham.

Don had put his son David Arden in charge of liaising with Tony Secunda. This was at first, towards building up relations with The Move. David Arden immediately thought The Move were an albums act. He did not see them, as just a pop singles novelty act.

Carl Wayne had a very cool and practical idea. "They told me that they were going to finish up with The Move and do ELO. I said, 'Let me keep The Move and you guys go into ELO. If you've decided that's where you're all going to go. Go now but let me keep The Move.' My plan was to bring Ace and Trevor back (the fire of the band) let Roy write the records. We would have taken it into another area. Which may have been more interesting. But they said, 'No, we're gonna keep it going, till it suits us to drop it.' I remember saying how I felt that it was really fucking selfish and despicable. So, I said, 'Fuck you! I sack you all!' Well, I knew I couldn't really do that! That was the last throw of the dice — so I walked."

In purely practical terms, if Roy and Bev and Jeff Lynne, who wasn't interested in The Move anyway, were going to harpoon the band, why not give it to Carl and let him mould it with Trevor and Ace?

Dave Morgan and Carl had some other Move related talks, "After and between 'Something' and 'This Time Tomorrow' Trevor left. When Carl told me that he'd left, Carl said to me, 'Hold on to your attitude because you might be getting a call from me to join The Move'. For now, he said Roy wants Jeff Lynne to join, so he's asked him. So, we've got to hang on and see what comes after that. So, Roy had wanted Jeff, but Jeff said, 'No, I'm going to stay with the Idle Race'. Carl phones me up and asked me, 'Do you want to join on bass in place of Trevor?' I said, 'Thanks, Carl', and I really thought about it. I was with Steve Gibbons, and we were doing really good stuff together and doing songs together. So, I said, 'I'm going to stay with Steve Gibbons.' Carl didn't like that at all. He really didn't like me doing that. He wanted me to join. It soured our friendship. Yeah. he wanted me to join The Move. I think he was going to use my songs as a wedge to do what he wanted within the group. Carl wanted me to have half the songs through Roy and blah blah. I could see it all becoming a big fight like that. It was something to do with the smell of it that I didn't like! It wasn't the opportunity — the opportunity itself was great."

Certainly, from a business management point of view, there would be two opportunities to book bands and put out records and make money for both. In a way, it really doesn't make sense. They could have given Carl the opportunity to bring in Dave Morgan and Richard Tandy and develop other songwriters for Penny Music. If Ace was up to it — to enlarge and expand upon his already reasonable pool of songs. Perhaps Trevor also, who could have brought in rawer, more R&B and blues styled, penned material. Guided with some well-chosen Roy Wood material, it could've been absolutely brilliant.

I cannot see any downside here at all. In fact, when The Move thing completely finished and ELO was up and running and then Roy Wood and Wizzard appeared, I don't know why Don Arden didn't get Carl Wayne to seriously revisit this idea of a revamped Move, rather than Carl's desultory trip into Las Vegas territory. Apart from Ace keeping it together and Carl was a steadying influence here. Trevor could and would, pull out of his encroaching problems later on with harder drugs.

Bev mentions this openly, "Frankly I'm amazed that Trevor really made it through that. He really was getting into some real trouble back then. Which did happen with Trevor, during and after the Balls period. There had been talk of The Move going to America since 1967, but for various reasons it had not panned out." Bev Bevan assessed, "Secunda found various reasons for us not to go. Which was a shame because I think we could have done well in the States. Particularly, with that early incarnation of The Move. The original line-up for definite. It was October 1969 when we finally, after more delays with Visa problems, boarded a plane and flew from London Heathrow to New York. The four guys in the band, Carl Wayne, Roy Wood, Rick Price, myself, plus our one-man crew, that were called 'roadies' in those days. Upsy Downing was a legend as a crew guy. Because he'd done many tours with Jimi Hendrix."

"It was the silliest American tour that anyone has ever been on. We had a record deal over there, but no-one met us on our arrival in New York. It was as if they rather hoped we would never turn up." The band flew into New York thinking they were going to undertake an East Coast tour, only to discover that there was no one from A&M Records to meet them or organise things. Also, that the dates were booked for the West Coast.

"Upsy knew his way around and hired a truck and a Dodge Sedan and on the back, we hitched it all up to a U-Haul trailer. We put all our equipment in there, the hired amps and the guitars, the stuff that we bought from England. We took off along the freeways for Detroit and did two nights at the Grandee Ballroom with Iggy and The Stooges. But our next date was Los Angeles. Whoever had organised this tour had not been studying a map at the time. So, we drove from New York, we drove to Detroit and arrived at the Grandee Ballroom in Detroit in the afternoon. That was before our first gig and that was the first time, we stepped on stage in America, and we opened for Iggy and the Stooges. We got a good reception as I recall. It was all so new to us this whole American experience."

"I remember landing in New York and naively I'd left my camera in my suitcase and that had disappeared during the flights. I was pretty peeved about that. We got to New York and got a place to stay. So, we're all in the same room. And we went out sightseeing as tourists do. I remember us all just walking around looking up at all the skyscrapers! We've never seen anything like it and again Upsy knew people and he took us to Manny's which was *the* music store in New York. I bought myself a Slingerland drum kit which was fantastic and about a quarter the price, it would have been back in England."

"And then we did the most extraordinary thing. We just got on Route 66 and we drove. We just drove and drove and drove. We only stopped, as I remember, one night at a Holiday Inn somewhere in New Mexico. And again, all of us I think, in one or two rooms. That was our one night in a bed. We just drove that best part of 3,000 miles across to the West Coast of America. Along the way I remember stopping for gas somewhere and in the middle of redneck country in the States. These cowboys couldn't believe the state of Roy Wood in particular and Rick Price, who had really, really long hair. You know, they were just, 'Hey pretty boys — what are you doing over here?' Then we just got into this enormous fight, it was a proper Western brawl. Upsy who was probably the toughest of the five of us, waded in. I thought to myself, 'Great. This is Hollywood. This is living.' Woody had his hair to his shoulders and this Redneck about eight feet tall began tugging at it: 'Hey are you a boy or a girl?' 'We want no trouble,' we said. 'We're English.' We assumed that would end all conversation immediately. But no! We started walking back to the car when other Rednecks began shouting: 'Fucking sissies!'"

"Upsy then made his appearance: 'What's the trouble?' he asked. 'These guys are in a band and they're with me.' Upsy fancied himself as a bit of a hard case, but one of the Rednecks — about half the size of an eight-foot-tall baboon — he was the smallest of these cowboys, but built like a brick shithouse. He gave Upsy one on the jaw. We dragged him back into the car. He went straight over the bonnet of the car, turning, and twisting. He was knocked out like a light. He landed in the dust on the other side, half unconscious. Me and Carl Wayne dragged him into the car and drove off, with the Redneck yobs yelling and shrieking, 'Come back here and fight, you Limey faggots!'"

"Carl was at the wheel, and we just roared out of this service station, this old filling station, dust flying everywhere and the old cactuses in the background, with all these cowboys chasing us down the street. It was something out of a movie, it was brilliant."

Rick Price interjects, "Two days off in L.A. and then, after playing The Whisky on Sunset Strip, another long drive up to San Francisco. Upsy and Carl shared the driving. Our prize at the end. Was that we shared a stage and a dressing room with Little Richard and Joe Cocker."

Bev further described the road trip "So we just drove, and we drove, and we eventually arrived in Los Angeles. Again; because of Upsy's experience. He knew the manager at what was fondly known as the 'legendary' Riot House, the Hyatt House Hotel on Sunset Strip. They gave us a great deal and again there was five of us in the same room."

Rick Price: "We checked in to The Hyatt House on Sunset Strip. All the visiting bands stayed there. It was known locally as the riot house. This is the place where TVs first went out of bedroom windows. Where things were thrown off the roof etc. It sounds like a dump, but it wasn't. After two weeks of sharing a room with the other four, it was sheer luxury to have my own loo at last. The tour was mostly a disaster, done on a shoestring budget."

Bev continues. "We were all there for about a week and the first night there, we went to see, the gig where we were going to play. That was the Whiskey A Go Go on Sunset Strip. Chaka Khan and Rufus were playing. They had just finished their stint — they were a great band! Really great! We loved the place as soon as we saw it. Either it was the following night or the night after that. That we set up and we then did five nights at The Whisky."

Rick Price remembers they contacted the US record company. "Because we had a day or so to spare, we visited the offices of A&M Records in Hollywood. Imagine the blow to our egos when we arrived, and nobody knew who we were? Eventually we were invited into one of the pluggers' offices. He waited until we were all present. Before he pulled our record from the bottom of an extremely dusty pile. Was he trying to make a point, d'ya think? Am I making one now by not remembering his name?"

"People came to see us; some A&M Records people came to see us. I think some of the guys from Procol Harum came to see us. I particularly remember The Doors coming to see us and the legend that was Jim Morrison. He walked in, a really great looking guy with his entourage. We were actually onstage playing and we just saw him being carried out. Four people, two legs, two arms, carried out completely unconscious. I don't know what he was on. But it was obviously a sign of things to come. So, we did these five nights at The Whisky. I just loved it. I really got into that. This was 1969 and we were these naive kids from England. Just thrown into this hippy scene in LA. A few days later, we were wearing caftans and saying peace maaan! Love, man, any brown rice? We were just captivated by the whole scene and the girls, the food, everything. It was just the drinks, the lifestyle, the drugs, everything. It was all very, very new to us really. Next up was the Fillmore. The fabled Fillmore West in San Francisco. We were to play four nights at this fantastic venue. It was an absolute privilege; we were way up in the bill. We thought Little Richard was going to top the bill. Because when we started out, Little Richard, along with Elvis, was a complete rock 'n' roll idol, but he was actually second on the bill. It was Joe Cocker and the Grease Band topping the bill. I remember we met Little Richard backstage. He was sitting like he had a throne made. He was even wearing a crown. He was just the epitome of a rock 'n' roll star. He was a great guy to work with, but he just was such a superstar."

Rick Price recalls this gloriously mad phrase: "The whole Route 66 journey had been a hideous nightmare. We had been booked into a series of Motels along the route, all sharing one family room. These rooms usually housed one double, two singles and a camp bed — cosy. We had been chased out of a roadside diner/bar by rednecks looking to pick a fight with these longhaired English faggots. When we got to Los Angeles, the hotel that we were booked into refused to admit us. As we walked into the lobby — a local looked us up and down slowly and recited those immortal words: 'Well, I'll be dipped in shit'. It was the first time I'd heard that phrase. I've used it myself many times since, but never to such good effect."

"Joe Cocker, we'd known him for years. Joe, we'd met him at various gigs and on *Top Of The Pops* and stuff. He was just a regular guy, along with the rest of the guys from Sheffield in his band. Just great guys to work with."

Reflecting on the 2012 release *Live At The Fillmore 1969*, Bev comments: "It's just there is so much energy in The Move's performance. And great songs. I'm amazed at how well we played. The harmonies are terrific. My drumming sounds really good. It all sounds very, very powerful. It must have come as a bit of a shock to the audience there. Because Little Richard's drummer and Joe Cocker's drummer were quite laid back, compared to my standards. I was giving my drum kit a real thumping and the tracks are great. Woody had written 'Hello Susie' for Amen Corner. We really made that much heavier. Plus, another Nazz song, called 'Under The Ice'. They sound so good and obviously have been cleaned up very well. I'm really proud to hear these songs again and delighted that they finally, after all this time, have come to light."

In my opinion these soundboard quality tapes were given a good boost by the record label in the remastering, with reasonable bottom end and bass. Well worth a listen — some very good vocal parts, Roy's guitar stuff works, even though it's not double or treble tracked, and Carl's vocals are strong as always, good three-part harmonies and some great drumming. On these dates, Bev uses more 'staggered' drum fills than usual. By that I mean, he slows down the drum rolls on some songs to aid the dynamic impression.

"We finished that set of nights at The Fillmore West, somebody spiked poor old Rick Price's drink. They dropped some LSD in his Coca-Cola and he was completely out of it. We got all these Move promotional postcards and Rick was throwing them up in the air going, 'Woo, Woo! Look at this!' I was sharing a room with him, and I had to actually, eventually give him a slap, to put him to sleep, because he would not have gone to bed."

Rick shudders at the acid trip: "It's bad enough taking that muck when you do it on purpose, but quite another thing when you've got no idea why you are feeling so weird! After the concert I was suddenly feeling unwell. Not sick, not dizzy but out of it. At the risk of sounding like Phoebe Buffay (from the TV series *Friends*) — I was "strangely hovery." Upsy kindly offered to run me back to the hotel and return later for the others. When the rest of the lads got back, they found me semi-conscious in the middle of what appeared to be a burgled room. We hadn't been burgled, I had ransacked it and was in the process of unwinding all of Bev's exposed film. He was not a happy drummer boy, and when it became obvious that I was not about to calm down and let them sleep, he very kindly offered to knock me out. Thankfully, Roy and Carl decided a better course of action would be to take me for a long midnight walk. We walked to a coffee shop where they sat with me most of the night. It was the last night of the tour, and we were flying home next day. In the morning, still no better, the others bundled me onto the plane where I slept all the way back to Heathrow. Thank God!"

Bev said they beat a retreat from the US: "We were going home the next day, but Bill Graham thought we were going back to the Fillmore East! To play some shows there. We were like, 'Yeah, yeah, see you next week, Bill.' We got on another Pan Am jumbo jet and flew back to London and from there back onto Birmingham. Back to our beloved hometown of Birmingham. Because three weeks in America for The Move was, well, just quite enough for us."

****

John 'Upsy' Downing was born on 25th November 1944 in Birmingham. He is known for 'The Last Experience'. He was married to Marina Davies. Upsy was Jimi Hendrix's tour manager in the USA. He also tour managed the extremely, unpredictable Ozzy Osbourne. Upsy had a very colourful career, touring with some great bands, ELO, Barclay James Harvest, Jimi Hendrix. He was long-time best friends with drummer Keith Smart. He worked with Hendrix, right up to the day that the guitarist passed away in London. He wouldn't take any shit from bands or crew members. On a couple of occasions, it turned ugly and resulted in a fist fight. On one occasion, some guy insulted The Move. Upsy retaliated and hit the guy so hard he was knocked out sparko with just one punch. He ruled his crew with his own list of rules, and it was nicknamed 'Upsy's Law'. You worked to his strict rules of management.

Tony Ware knew Upsy well. "I loved Upsy when ELO went on the road, you know, you actually have Upsy and he was their solid tour manager. There was Upsy, and there was another guy, Roy Lemon, He was another one. Well, Upsy was well ready for The Move. You listen to this for a combination: Upsy was the roadie for Cliff Richard and then for Jimi Hendrix. (Laughs). It was a tough game. I think it was just the surroundings too. I mean, the dodgy managers and the dodgy agents and all the gangsters involved. It was quite the game, to be mixed up in in those days."

Allen Harris remembered Upsy as easy to work with. "He had a strong work ethic, and we were a solid road management team." Allen thought that sometimes Upsy was a bit heavy-handed in the way he treated the girls trying to get to the band through the stage doors.

In 1987 while on tour with Barclay James Harvest, Upsy and the band all boarded a ferry in the port of Dover. But Upsy never disembarked — and his body was later found washed up on a beach at Zeebrugge, the port and seaside town in Belgium. His official date of death is 29th April 1987 in the North Sea, Belgian Territorial Sea.

Allen Harris said: "I heard that Upsy might have been in a fracas/confrontation with some Hells Angels on that journey and he ended up overboard. I can't clarify it, but I did definitely hear that. I only found out about this later when I went to see the Steve Gibbons Band in concert."

John 'Upsy' Downing's death is a mystery. It was recorded as an 'accidental death'. Did he fall over the side or was he met by one of the Hells Angels guys? Did he piss someone off on a prior tour? Was it foul play, due to some bad drug deal? Did someone owe someone some money? We will never know, and it was registered as an open verdict. The loss of Upsy was a big blow to many people in that immediate scene who held him in the highest respect and regard. RIP John 'Upsy' Downing. The UK producer Martin Smith's debut album *Bitter Sun After Dark* features a song 'Bitter Sun', written in Downing's memory.

****

To prove the ongoing Move unpredictability, on their return to the UK, The Move went, like many West Midlands bands before them, onto the lucrative cabaret circuit. By this time, they were under the new management of Peter Walsh who had bought the group's contract from Don Arden and specialised in cabaret acts.

Bev grimaces, "We immediately were put on the cabaret circuit. And me and Roy hated that. But Carl was in his element and Rick Price, he also quite liked it because, he'd got a cabaret upbringing as well."

By this time the Baileys Club circuit was well and truly pleased to have The Move perform. 'Curly' had just hit the number 12 spot in the UK charts.

Laurie Hornsby remembered Upsy setting up The Move's gear at The Cavendish Club. "Upsy was accompanied by the Brian Ford Trio. Who were tinkling out 'The Girl From Ipanema'. The cheesy, manky compere saw a long-haired, moustachioed man in the audience. He then asked him, 'If his moustache was in reality, his eyebrows, that had popped down for a drink.' The plum compere received a swift threat, verbally telling him to fuck right off. The burbling host moved on pretty sharply. He proudly announced, 'Here they are, The Move, and don't forget Bob Monkhouse is here next week!' My, how the mighty had fallen!"

"Peter Walsh Management were specialists on the cabaret circuit, so we followed groups like The Tremeloes into the clubs. But we should have gone to America when Cream and Hendrix did," claimed Carl.

More Move hits followed ('Chinatown', 'Brontosaurus' and 'California Man'), but Wood's pioneering dream of a rock band with strings eventually won out in 1971. Roy Wood stated, "I had the idea for ELO as early as the time of The Move's first album... Although people thought I was mad. EMI were interested as long as we carried on with The Move."

It was said that primitive technology scuppered early shows. During which Wood and Lynne were undergoing more clashes of ego but Wood blamed the split on the management. David Arden would disagree.

Peter Walsh was their third management change in just over the space of a year. The cabaret shows caused increasing friction between Carl Wayne and Roy Wood, whose increasingly wild appearance on stage would often draw ridicule from the generally square, scampi-in-a-basket, booze guzzling older audiences. But the money was really, really good.

Bevan: "Me and Roy were both about to get married. Suddenly, we were earning a couple of grand a week. It was like, wow. So, it was six nights a week, two shows a night. And I couldn't really play my drums — I was a loud drummer. I'd just not hit the drums, like I liked hitting them. We've just done this really heavy tour in America. Playing with Joe Cocker and Little Richard. Then, the next thing we know — we're at the bloody Sunderland Fiesta Club, with Carl singing 'Ave Maria' for God's sake!"

Roy would often sit with his back to the audience. Sitting and playing on Bev's drum riser. He really hated doing these crapola cabaret shows. Roy probably just thought of the coffers going into his bank account. Bev Bevan has mentioned in interviews that the money came in handy.

In the winter of 1969, a nasty incident involving an audience member happened. During one of these cabaret performances. Some ignorant clown, who was probably very pissed up insulted Roy Wood directly to his face due to Roy's dress, attire and hair. Bev remembers it as, "You get off stage, you fucking poof". Roy immediately responded by hurling a full glass of vodka (and tonic) at the idiot. Apparently, it hit the guy full on, splintering and splitting open his head.

Bev witnessed the incident: "Roy looked totally out of place, more than the rest of us did. This guy also tried to throw a pint of beer over Woody. Woody had this vodka and tonic in the glass. I mean, Woody can't throw a dart! He is not an athletic guy at all. It was just pure chance he hit the guy. I mean, the odds of hitting him! The guy tried to throw his pint of beer at Woody. That's when the bouncers came and hauled this guy out." However, The Move's cabaret gig went on that night, as if nothing had happened.

"Whenever Carl did interviews, I think he went out of his way to be outspoken and say outrageous things. Just to get the headlines and stuff. I don't think he meant half the stuff he said really. I think that was the decider for Roy. He said, 'I don't wanna do this anymore'."

Carl Wayne threw an involuntary strop. "The truth of me leaving, was that Roy tired of cabaret and I don't blame him. He was tired of all those variety clubs and similar places. I think it was unfair of the group to blame me for that! They wanted to be away from Don Arden. And to then go with Peter Walsh, the ultimate cabaret specialist. So, it wasn't me that decided to play those cabaret venues... It was the management and the agency. They were the ones who put us in there. The final blow was when Roy threw a glass at somebody in the audience. This was in Sheffield, I think. He almost took the bloke's eye out. I said, 'I'm sorry but that's the end of it. I can't be doing with that. I'll go and smack someone, but I ain't going to throw glasses at somebody!'"

And so, the further dismantling of this great band continued slowly but surely. Carl Wayne quit the group and went solo. After recording an (unreleased) album. He amassed some success as a cabaret singer and TV actor. It was a far cry from smashing televisions on stage in those earlier, publicity-drenched, heady days with The Move just four years before!

By the end of 1970, The Move had stopped touring and that left an out-of-work Rick Price with plenty of time for other musical projects, including an album with Mike Sheridan. Plus, another album, with a new, fresh line-up called Mongrel, who had initially been formed around backing Carl Wayne in his new solo performing career.

Despite more recording with The Move and appearances on TV shows like *Top Of The Pops*, the group came to an end. Followed by the launch of ELO. Rick Price was edged out in favour of Richard Tandy. Carl said he didn't know anything about Rick Price coming into The Move at first. Almost as suddenly as it started, Rick's place in the spotlight seemed to be over.

"I left The Move in February 1971. Or at least The Move had left me. By then Jeff Lynne had replaced Carl Wayne. Although, we did half a dozen live performances, it was clear that everyone else in the band was now concentrating on the formation of ELO. The first ELO album started out as a Move project. I played bass on all the original tracks. But I have it on good authority that Roy re-recorded all my parts. Hmmm, I was now consigned to the bassist digital heaven."

Suddenly Rick's money flow fell over the edge. "Having such a big change in our financial circumstances when I joined The Move had allowed Jo and me to put a deposit on a house and get married. Here we were, two and a half years later and despite The Move having further hits without Carl, it was suddenly all over. And we were struggling, to pay the mortgage. I was doing the occasional gig. But not taking a proper job, in case the phone should ring! Jo had to work shifts to pay some of the bills. Both our families chipped in and helped us out. This, from time to time and somehow, with the help of a brilliant solicitor named Aiden Cotter, we managed to hold on to our house. At one point the TV shop even tried to repossess our telly. The bloody cheek!"

Rick Price had already experienced the hard life of a struggling band on the road. In 1966 The Sombreros were sent over to Dortmund in Germany, where they performed for a month. Rick said, "We would work fifty minutes every hour from seven in the evening until two in the morning. We could only finish early if the club was empty. Even one punter meant that you had to keep going. Because we weren't paid until the end of the second week, we had to live on tinned food that we had taken out with us from the UK."

During this time The Move put out a single, another rocker definitely in the vein of Little Richard. Roy Wood was enamoured by Little Richard and loved his singles and his larger catalogue. Jerry Lee Lewis was Jeff Lynne's fave rock and roll musician. So, all combined, they came up with a hot, rocking single. It contained 'Do Ya' on its B-side. Plus 'Ella James'. Ingenuously, they called this a double B-side. 'California Man' coasted quickly. All the way up to number 7 in the UK charts. It was only about a month later when ELO released their debut single called '10538 Overture'. At this stage, The Move were signed to Harvest Records (a subsidiary of EMI and referenced as an "underground" and "prog rock" label). Harvest also released The Move album *Message From The Country* in 1971. As well as Roy Wood's first solo album 'Boulders' and the Wizzard releases.

Nick Mobbs was the Harvest label manager when the single was released. Apparently, Harvest's office was located somewhere in a dark corner in the bowels of the EMI building in London's Manchester Square. Mobbs got involved in some verbal ructions with Don Arden. Arden, for some strong reason, hated the 'California Man' single. Don Arden just didn't think it was very commercial.

Nick Mobbs recalled, "Arden thought, that between Roy and us, it was a bit of a disaster really. Arden said to me 'Please go round and convince Roy that this is not a good song for a single release.' But when I heard it, I thought, 'it sounds pretty commercial to me.' Don said to me, 'Look, can't you just tell him, it's absolute rubbish!' So, we released it and it is doing okay. At the time, Roy (much more than Jeff) was thinking about ELO and of course in the end Jeff developed it — but it started with Roy. We had hired the Royal Academy of Music to have an ELO press launch etc. Just before they did their first gig, Don called up and said, 'Jeff will do it, but Roy won't.' Don said, 'Drive up there with David Arden and see what Roy is feeling about all this.'"

Mobbs described the Arden family and business scene: "The Arden organisation was very interesting. You had his son David there. Also, there was Sharon, (now famously known as Sharon Osbourne, wife of Ozzy Osbourne). Sharon at that point was the office secretary and she was a liaison point. Particularly regarding sales figures. She would be phoning up every day. She wanted the sales figures. She sounded like a little girl in the office, and she was very cute. The change in her then to now is absolutely extraordinary, and good luck to her. Of course you heard all the stories about Don, but he was an absolute pussycat with me. On one occasion, I got wind that they were trying to take Roy Wood away from EMI and Harvest. I'd been away on a winter holiday. When I came back, it got to the point that 'I Wish It Could Be Christmas Every Day', was coming out imminently. And also, the Wizzard phase was happening. I actually found out that the release was being printed up with Warner Brothers label stickers on the singles."

Mobbs was initially confounded when he found out what had been going on while he took his break: "I was going, 'What's going on here? They're signed to Harvest and EMI and not to Warner Brothers!' EMI's legal department was going, 'Don't worry about it. Don has gone crazy — they can't release it!' In fact, they didn't release it. Although Don had several thousand copies printed up with Warner Brothers stickers on them. He wanted to get them away from us to Warner Brothers and as soon as, by the looks."

Mobbs thought a direct meeting with Don, a man-to-man approach was the correct way to try and solve this dilemma. "I went to see Don one night. He was sitting in his office, very low lighting and a lovely smell of leather. Leather desks and a leather recliner. A kind of 'Godfather' type scenario. I went there with the express mission of saving the deal and holding the act with Harvest / EMI. I believe I spent about a good forty minutes making this unbelievably persuasive case. They should stick with EMI and what we could do for them etc, etc. Don sat there, immensely polite, and afterwards he said, 'Nick, I really appreciate you coming here today and explaining all this to me. But Warner Brothers will be ringing you tomorrow with a very attractive job offer'."

A small independent label, Gemini released *This Is To Certify That...* in 1970. An album initially composed of Mike Sheridan/Rick Price co-writes. This was followed by an album by Rick Price in 1971, called *Talking To The Flowers*. Although their Gemini label career was short-lived, these two Price/Sheridan recordings are considered to be an important part within the Brumrock tapestry. The songs blend some Move influences, Baroque pop, more rockier vibes and freakier "poppy" musical shades. It has to be said, however, that both original album covers are just short of being totally horrific. *Talking To The Flowers* looks like Indian restaurant wallpaper after Linda Blair snarfed a quick vindaloo and violently spewed up, rendering the flock paper an unearthly demonic green. What mankind-hating bastard, designed that cover? It also has 'Rick Price' in large, horridly black letters on the front. I cannot stress enough. That it is a truly and remarkably horrible cover. *This Is To Certify That...* is moderately better, looking like one of those desktop published certificates. The type that people used to get for attending a one-day course. Like some form of local council bullshit.

A definitive 2 CD set was released in 2004 through President Records. Firstly, it rectifies the eye-assailing artworks from before. It repackages those with a reasonably designed cover. Masochists and complete lovers of ocular pain can still view the original covers within. Be warned: continued exposure may damage your mental health. Disc one features the *This Is To Certify That...* album, complete with tracks, 'Davey Has No Dad', 'Tomorrow's Child', and the much admired song, 'Sometimes I Wonder' (a taste of LA via Birmingham) and 'Lamp Lighter Man', together with Mike Sheridan's solo 45's, 'Follow Me, Follow' (with searing strings arranged and performed at Morgan Studios by Roger Day) and the sarcastic, edgy, novelty single 'Top Ten Record'.

Disc two collects the Rick Price solo recordings, pairing the aforementioned *Talking To The Flowers* with twelve previously unreleased tracks from August 1971. This was to be a second Rick Price solo record. This side contains Price's songs, like the standout 'I Can Get Found'. The varied material takes in Barry Mann and Cynthia Weil, through to the cult songwriter Jerry Jeff Walker. Appreciated by "psych" lovers and Brum Beat aficionados completists alike, this is highly recommended listening. It has a sturdy version of 'Lighting Never Strikes Twice'. The superb B-side that showed up backing The Move's 'Brontosaurus' single on Regal Zonophone. For a trio of unknown, niche albums, Gemini have done a great job of packaging the CD. With extensive liner notes, cool photos and an overall nice graphics job. Thank God!

For a while during 1971, Rick Price joined up with Carl Wayne and toured along with the West Midlands group Light Fantastic, who had an exciting, theatrical live act going on. While Carl and Rick's performance of various ballads together were well received by the cabaret audience, it was always support band, Light Fantastic who stole the show in Rick's opinion. Despite Light Fantastic also acting as Carl and Rick's backing band their support act made the headliner's set something of an anti-climax. However, Light Fantastic couldn't sustain their career momentum or translate their work into good recordings.

They dissolved after a few months of false starts. Then Carl Wayne proposed another new venture to Rick Price in 1972.

Carl came aboard, and the band members began rehearsing. After a few weeks, all concerned realised that they were missing something. It was the singer Carl Wayne himself. He never actually participated as a musician, although he did send in some songs. He also never appeared at any rehearsals. The members eventually decided to forget about Wayne and go out on their own.

They chose the name Mongrel. A recognition of the fact, that all of the members had come from different bands. The line-up was Rick Price (bass), Roger Hill (guitar), Stuart Scott (guitar), Keith Smart (drums) and Charlie Grima (drums and percussion, (Grima had joined from another Brum band called The Ghost), with keyboard player Robert 'Bob' Brady taking most of the vocals.

Mongrel were one of the stranger, more enigmatic offshoots within The Move's overall tapestry. Mostly because their existence was brought to a sudden, jarring halt! Virtually in mid-stride, just as they were starting to establish themselves and halfway through finishing their first (and only) album, the group vanished into thin air and out again, this time into the realm of Roy Wood.

Keith Smart was a solid, fiery drummer. He became best known as one of the two-man drumming battering ram in Wizzard. Keith has also played for legendary Brum Beat band, Danny King & the Mayfair Set. He played with cult freak-beat band, The Lemon Tree and was drummer with The Ugly's, best known for the hit 'Wake Up My Mind'. He was also in The Rockin' Berries and recorded with Clifford T. Ward. Keith was one of three revolving drummers in Balls, who were mooted as a supergroup. He also was attached to Velvet Underground legend John Cale. Along with his close childhood friend Trevor Burton (who was playing bass) Keith appeared on a Cale retrospective compilation *Guts*, released in 1977.

Mongrel went out playing live, building their sound from the ground up! They had no recording contract but between them had enough recognition from prior bands to make some noise in the UK press. They got signed to Polydor for one album, released the following year (1973) with the title *Get Your Teeth Into This*. It is a strong debut record with catchy, distinct tunes. Mostly composed and sung by Bob Brady. There are some great songs on the record, strong harmonies, catchy hooks, and stylish supple drumming from Keith Smart. There were some excellent piano-led songs. From the opening chords of the first tracks, 'Lost' and 'What A Day', Brady's vocals, the massed unison vocals and his rippling piano solo (hinting at jazz influences, with its diminished chords) is a confident opening. Giving off the patina of a very assured band. 'Last Night' has that British sixties Beatles-like piano plonking one note intro with a relaxed Brady vocal — another very commercial cut. Other tracks such as, 'Sing A Little Song', 'Nobody Loves You', 'Get Your Teeth Into This' and 'Lonely Street' add up to a bravura, commercial record that all hint at Mongrel's potential as a recording band.

Mongrel could have lasted. They finished the debut album as a cohesive, functioning band. Had it not been for the intervention of Roy Wood. According to Rick Price, Wood showed up at a gig where Mongrel were still working out the live sound and their album. They were supporting Heads Hands & Feet (featuring Albert Lee and Chas Hodges). After the show, Wood simply hired them to become Roy Wood's Wizzard. He was putting together a new group and he wanted Mongrel to be that new band. All but Bob Brady and Stuart Scott agreed. The keyboardist and guitarist declined and kept some semblance of the group going long enough to complete the album. Smart, Grima, Hill and Price all went over to Wood, and all but Hill, became members of Wizzard. Mongrel were gone before their only album was even released.

Ron Dickson of the Light Fantastic supplies some backstory to those confusing times: "That year we did a tour of cabaret venues, backing and supporting Carl Wayne. We were trying hard to get a recording contract and did a fair amount of recording with Roy Wood at Lee Sound Studios in Pelsall, near Walsall. Finally, we clinched a deal with MAM Records and released our first single 'Love Is Everything' written by our guitarist Keith Locke. It was produced by Johnny Worth, who had great success with 60's artist Adam Faith. 1978 saw the end of Light Fantastic, a great live act and a great decade. We had run our course for ten years, always chasing that one lucky break. During which time we had seen fellow local bands rise to fame, but it had unfairly passed us by."

Rick Price lucked in again when Mongrel morphed into Wizzard. So began a new chapter in Rick's life that made him a "glam rock" star, playing on two UK number one hit records 'See My Baby Jive' and 'Angel Fingers', plus the perennial holiday classic 'I Wish It Could Be Christmas Everyday'. Wizzard's memorable and colourful appearances on *Top Of The Pops* saw Rick wearing a variety of glittery and outrageous outfits. Including angel wings, roller skates, and Monty Python's Mr Gumby styles.

It appears for many years, no one knew why Roy bailed from ELO, especially from a situation he had wanted to create for some years. Ever since Tony Visconti did the strings on 'Flowers In The Rain' and 'Cherry Blossom Clinic' prompting Roy to imagine his songs surrounded by strings, both in the studio and on stage. When Roy Wood walked out on the Electric Light Orchestra in June 1972, leaving the band in the hands of Jeff Lynne, it was chalked up to "musical differences." Even Bev Bevan has professed he hasn't ever fully known the reasons. Headlines spoke of artistic tension and personal grievances. Eventually, Lynne's ELO became a huge success. And while Wood's Wizzard had their own taste of success along the way, after two years of riding on a sumptuous run of singles, Wizzard disbanded due to in-house mutinies about money, touring pay, recording costs and more.

Roy Wood maintains Wizzard had its many high points: "It was the best band socially too. You'd find us in the bus on the motorway, all the lights on. We were all doing the hokey cokey with a crate of Newcastle Ale." Even so and in spite of all the camaraderie, the eight-piece ensemble folded in 1976. "People were browned off with not getting paid, so they started playing elsewhere."

As regards ELO, Jeff Lynne had stated flatly, "We couldn't work together; it was like having two bosses," Roy Wood always maintained there was a different story to be heard behind the scenes. Manager Don Arden was to blame for Wood's decision to depart. This, soon after the launch of ELO's self-titled debut album. ELO was built in 1970 on the foundations of Wood's psychedelic pop. Jeff Lynne was brought in as Roy admired his work. They had a good relationship. It was an ambitious attempt to explore a large, new sound picture. A new approach was being offered up with classical instruments and a rocking backline. Taking in theatrical, larger-than-life stage personas. This is what they felt they had by the time ELO's debut single '10538 Overture' was released. Wood described it like this, "We wanted to produce a widely based jazz and classically influenced free-form music." One reviewer described the first LP as "sonic terrorism." By the time '10538 Overture' was enjoying chart success at the end of June 1972, Roy Wood was gone.

Don Arden wasn't the type of character you crossed easily. Infamous for his treatment of Robert Stigwood. And for any number of violent and aggressive outbursts, at those he didn't like (even if only temporarily). Don had his own vision of how his bands should operate. And even though The Move eventually escaped his clutches they wound up back with him again. He later managed Carl Wayne at various times. The Move had two stints with "the Don" after their disastrous and short management by Peter Walsh Artists, and the cabaret circuit. Making good money but angering Roy Wood and causing even further rifts between him and Carl Wayne. Wood wanted to build on the embers of The Move and he still wanted to be very successful. Wood maintains that Arden, wasn't interested in his visions and plans at all.

Roy ran into problems, which he assessed as "Unfortunately we had political disagreements, mainly to do with the management," and that he left "with true regret." Don Arden "was the man that ruined my career," Wood told the Birmingham Mail in 2009. "His business dealings all came out in the end. At the time it was reported that I'd had a huge row with Jeff Lynne. That simply wasn't true. We've never had a real row, and we're still mates now."

David Arden, the son of Don Arden, firmly rebuts Roy Wood's claims regarding his father. "For the avoidance of doubt, Roy Wood's decision to leave ELO was his and his alone. In fact, he had already formed Wizzard and recorded 'Ball Park Incident' in secret before informing my father and myself of his decision. We had to inform Bev and Jeff that Roy had also taken ELO members Bill Hunt and Hugh McDowell with him! I can only assume that the demise of Wizzard and the failure of Roy to produce a successful album, together with ELO's meteoric global rise to success, made it hard for Roy to own up, even to himself, his error. However, it is my informed opinion that his error contributed to ELO's success. Which I believe would not have happened, had he remained with ELO. Roy was undoubtedly a huge musical talent. His recordings are a testament to that. However, with the exception of his participation in The Move, sadly, most, if not all of his live appearances, fell well short of what was required. And this is not just my memory of events."

David Arden says Roy was being very paranoid. "Well, everybody tried to help him, and everybody that tried to help him, he thought was ripping him off. And that started with the old man. Yes, even saying that it was Dad's idea for him to leave ELO and form Wizzard. Which is the biggest sort of bullshit ever in the world! Roy is fabulous, but he did an interview in the *NME*. Must have been around 1975. The headline was 'I'm a secret big head'. You can understand, I'm not talking about Rembrandt and all those kinds of people, but they're fucking mad. Great, my dad always knew, this talent of Roy's and Trevor's he called insanity. Dad liked Trevor very much, he thought he had a very wicked sense of humour. He's very uncompromising, Trevor, isn't he?"

Wood had taken a potshot at Arden two years earlier, soon after the impresario's death. "The bloke ruined my career," he told the *Daily Telegraph*. "He enjoyed the image of being some sort of mafioso. But all he was, was a crooked manager who couldn't keep his fingers out of the till. I had as much chance of becoming Lord Mayor of London as getting my money back from Don Arden. But there was a lot of that around in those days." Asked whether he felt any warmth for the businessman in the light of his death, Wood added, "Unfortunately, I seem to have mislaid the number for Interflora."

It has been proposed that Arden wanted Wood and Lynne to fall out. He could make more money if they split, and both ran their own bands. Two bands with one stone. If that's true, Arden was right! While the Electric Light Orchestra are regarded as having soared much higher than Wizzard, it was Wizzard that brought home the bacon butties — certainly initially! In terms of record sales and they were never off the TV.

Wood might prefer to be remembered for his haunting Move track 'Blackberry Way' or Wizzard's 'Angel Fingers'. Roy laughed warmly in 2012 at being described as having "owned Christmas" for a number of years, with the eternal anthem 'I Wish It Could Be Christmas Every Day'.

Lynne and Wood have met over the years on occasions since the split. But it appeared any kind of musical collaboration isn't going to happen. They also shared the stage together in 2017. When ELO were inducted into The Rock & Roll Hall of Fame. The Americans present may not have picked up on the humour when Roy said, "I thank Jeff for his dedication in writing the songs. Otherwise, we wouldn't have been invited here tonight."

But those sentiments echo comments he made about the Electric Light Orchestra in 1974: "Even though I'm not part of it anymore, I am glad it came to light. It would have been frustrating if it hadn't. It's a good band, and Jeff is still a good friend of mine." In 2012, Wood added, "The upside is that we did get two very different, but equally off-the-wall and awe-inspiring bands, out of the split."

On one hand Roy appears to applaud the fact that two bands made what is generally considered to be worthwhile music. On the other hand, he says that Arden ripped him off. Which is not an unusual thing to hear in the record business.

Since the start of 1968, the Move had begun to slowly (if not deliberately) fragment as a result of personal and musical differences. According to Wood, the management were indifferent to who sang leads. When the management decided that Wood would be the producer for *Shazam*, Wayne pushed right back! He became the co-producer and Rick Price also received a producer credit along with Gerald Chevin for Straight Ahead Productions. Those pesky and eternal musical differences would lead to the foundation of the Electric Light Orchestra. Carl Wayne left The Move shortly after the band's sole tour of the United States in January 1970.

Carl Wayne went solo and made several singles and albums, some including songs written and produced by Roy Wood. Among his singles were 'Way Back In The Fifties' and 'Hi Summer' backed with 'My Girl And Me', both written and produced by Lynsey de Paul. This was the theme song to an ITV variety series he co-hosted, *Maybe God's Got Something Up His Sleeve*, which received ribald panning from Annie Nightingale and others. He issued a version of John Lennon's 'Imagine'. He also tackled a cover version of Cliff Richard's hit 'Miss You Nights', Roy Wood's 'Aerial Pictures' was another. He was originally offered the chance to record 'Sugar Baby Love' but rejected it as "rubbish". It was given to a new band, The Rubettes and it launched their career with a Number One hit. Oooops!

As well as 'Hi Summer', his work on television included singing the theme songs to the talent show *New Faces*, one of which, 'You're A Star!', became a minor hit for him in 1973. In 1977, Wayne took part in the *Song For Europe* contest, hoping to represent the UK in the Eurovision Song Contest. His song 'A Little Give, A Little Take' finished up in 11th place out of twelve songs. Wayne also made a few recordings with the Electric Light Orchestra as guest vocalist. Although these remained unreleased, until they appeared as bonus tracks on a remastered re-issue of the group's second album *ELO 2* in 2003.

He never again made the charts after leaving The Move. But he still enjoyed a steady career in cabaret and on television, recording versions of songs from the shows of Andrew Lloyd Webber and Tim Rice. As well as a lucrative career doing voice overs and jingles. He sang backing vocals on Mike Oldfield's *Earth Moving*, released in 1989. In 2006 an album of his performances, remastered with the involvement of Wood and some previously unreleased cuts, was issued under the title *Songs From The Wood And Beyond 1973–2003*. Two tracks by Wayne and Choral Union appear on the 2 CD set *Electric Light Orchestra – Friends And Relatives*, a compilation of tracks by Electric Light Orchestra and associated acts. In his acting career he had a small role in the Birmingham-based soap opera *Crossroads*, and in 1974 married Susan Hanson, another member of the cast. His most acclaimed stage role was as the narrator in Willy Russell's *Blood Brothers* between 1990 and 1996. Later he became a presenter on BBC Radio WM, in the course of which he interviewed several of his former colleagues from The Move, among other guests. He was also a fund raiser for leukaemia research and ran several London marathons for charity. He also made an appearance on *The Benny Hill Show* in 1985, in which he played 'The Face' character in a parody of *The A-Team*.

Laurie Hornsby was incredibly helpful in filling many cracks in my knowledge of the earlier and broader Birmingham musical scene. Laurie has written two excellent books. The first was *Brum Rocked* published in 1999. The second publication was *Brum Rocked On*, following in 2003. Both were published in large format paperback, with tons of photographs. Both books are a treasure trove of information about the never-ending, ever-evolving feast of bands and musical scenes that went on in Birmingham. These books went onto form the basis of some live events in Birmingham. These featured Bev as well as Trevor Burton and Danny King.

With his two excellent books, Laurie Hornsby tied in a lot of detail. On the many aspects of the Birmingham musical history. Both feature incisive and funny writing from Laurie himself and they both come highly recommended. Moving forward, the books were encapsulated and presented as a live show. It was Carl's idea to do that show, *Brum Rocks*.

"Yeah, it was Carl's idea. What happened was he phoned me up. He said, 'What we've got to do is a theatrical show.' Carl and myself would narrate it and he would also be singing in with a band and I would be playing a bit of rhythm guitar. The original idea that Carl had was to put The Move together. Wow! He said the only missing link would be if Roy wanted to do it. He said Bev would do it and Trevor would do it. He said the only thing that Bev and Trevor would throw at me was that Ace would maybe play up." Carl said, 'I can handle Ace.' He said, 'We're perfect.' He says, 'There's no problem there.' So, Carl was fine about it. It was going to be according to Carl, his original idea was Carl, me, Bev, Trevor and Ace. He said I'll invite Roy Wood, but Roy won't come. Carl said it doesn't matter because we've got the songs. Roy plays up, he said if any mention of The Move comes up. Brian Yates had been in touch with Bev."

Emu's World was a popular children's, eighties TV show featuring Rod Hull and his arm-length Emu puppet. Carl helped out on this show. He used to dress up as a Knight of the Round Table and do all these silly little sketches.

In 2000 on the retirement of lead vocalist Allan Clarke, he joined the Hollies, touring Europe and Australasia. Around this time Carl met with Trevor, inviting him for dinner. Carl realised The Move could go out live too. He said, "I did approach Trevor with the idea some months back and he didn't go for the idea. But he's since come round a little bit."

Carl took him to a nice, swanky restaurant in the middle of Birmingham and allowed Trevor to pick off the menu and whatever? Because Carl was picking up the bill. At the end of it, Carl says, "Well, I've got an offer to put to you. We should put The Move back together."

Trevor says, "Well, Roy wouldn't want to know."

Carl, "That's okay. We can still do the songs."

Bev has come along. Carl continues, "I can get Ace. I can handle Ace. And Ace would have done it. I'm presuming I've got you Trevor? Are you okay with that?"

Trevor suddenly stood up facing Carl across the table: "No I'm not okay with that!"

Carl looks up, puzzled. "What's the matter?"

Trevor's retort was priceless… "Why don't you just fuck off back to Emu Land!"

With that Trevor left the table and walked out of the restaurant. Trevor did eventually come round, so Carl said. Those wonderful, combustible personalities were still in place.

"I put it in Carl's mind, because Carl was very experienced in theatre. I got a phone call from Brian Yates. He got Carl's number. Carl phoned me back. He says, 'Oh, it would be good to see Brian again. He was a good old mate of mine.'" Laurie adds.

"Because Brian used to sing under the name of Mark Stewart and the Cresters with John Lodge, the Moody Blues."

Regarding the Brum Rocks live shows, Laurie says the gigs were tremendous. "What was coming off the stage was incredible. With Bev, Trevor, Steve Gibbons, Danny King. They were fantastic. We took the roof off The Hippodrome. In 2008 we also did another five or six gigs, more or less the same theatres, but they opened Birmingham Town Hall after they spent millions on a refurb, and we opened it. We did the Friday night, with the Brum Rock show. We had Jasper Carrot with us and Robert Plant was a guest. We did three years of exactly the same show. It was getting too repetitive though, as Jasper will tell you that. And then Steve Gibbons said to me halfway through 2009 that he wasn't enjoying it at all, because Steve's very switched on. He looks for new things all the time. If you could bottle Steve, you would be a millionaire. He said, 'I'm leaving, this is the end of this run.' Yeah, so they did another season without myself and Steve, where they bought in Raymond Froggatt. Then the following year, Jasper Carrot joined. I was wondering what was going on, because I thought, how can I make it all Jasper Carrot now? Yeah, I had three years. Brian phoned me up and he said, 'Are you leaving the show?' They were just trooping on playing songs and it was a disaster really. That's when Jasper came along."

These further shows were introduced by Jasper Carrot. He introduced various artists from the Birmingham area. There is an interestingly, clannish and fierce pride from Brummie residents, in relation to their musical history. The Bev Bevan band underpinned the entire performance. The band featured, Tony Kelsey, Phil Tree and Abby Brant. There was a large screen at the back of the stage where photographs were projected of the guest stars (from years ago to the current day). There were also scenes from Birmingham in years gone by, which evoked memories for the audiences. Trevor Burton who needs no further introduction, went down really well, with one reviewer saying, "Burton astounded me with his guitar skills, and he has an extremely, versatile singing voice.

Geoff Turton, who still performs with The Rockin' Berries, gave a witty performance, coupled with crowd pleasing numbers such as 'Pretty Woman'. Danny King has been described as 'Birmingham's first pop star.' He demonstrated amazing vocal ability while singing favourites 'Move It' by Cliff Richard and 'True Love Ways' by Buddy Holly. Topping off the line-up was Joy Strachan-Brain from the locally-based band 'Quill'. Joy on this night opted for more slamming R&B songs. She took songs like 'Nutbush City Limits', the massively popular Ike and Tina Turner number. 'Going Back' by Dusty Springfield was also a stunning vocal performance. Jasper Carrott kept things buzzing, even picking up a guitar himself in the second act, exclaiming, "are you ready to rock 'n' roll?" before bursting into a folk song! The tapestry of talent to come from Birmingham is deep and wide. For me, as author of this long - overdue book. The Move represented a jewel firmly planted, in the middle of the Brum crown. The show ended on a jubilant note, with the popular 'Blackberry Way' lifting people's spirits.

30.
Is there something that you've wanted? More than anything?

Dave Scott-Morgan joined one of the other happening Birmingham bands. A band that had never really broken out of the regional scene. But they produced very cool records. "My mum was horrified when I told her I was going to join a group called The Uglys. Singer Steve Gibbons had called up out of the blue one day. He asked if I'd be interested in joining The Uglys. I saw them play at the Hen and Chickens in Langley. They were great and not the slightest bit 'ugly'. Steve was great on stage, with lots of pomp and circumstance and aplomb. And he had a lot of very cool, prescribed stage moves. He was a great Birmingham performer. Steve only made one incursion in the British charts in the late 1970s with a cool, punchy cover of Chuck Berry's song 'Tulane'. Such was the world of rock 'n' roll." The Uglys have had a very interesting collection released since their heyday. It's called *The Quiet Explosion* released some years back — it is well worth a listen.

Dave Morgan often worked with an influential and future band mate who sadly passed away, at the time of writing towards the end of this book. "Richard Tandy and I go all the way back to The Chantelles. Richard was a dedicated musician, sitting at home, day after day. He endlessly practised the piano, practising scales and learning songs. He was in another league to me, in terms of his musical dedication."

The incredibly interlocked and almost incestuous Birmingham scene is frequently illustrated by the links, these musicians have enjoyed over the years. Morgan was with Steve Gibbons in The Uglys between 1967 and 1969. At this juncture he was the bassist and vocalist. Morgan was part of the spin-off Balls, so-called planned "supergroup" with Steve Gibbons and Trevor Burton. Until, under the crafty engineering of Tony Secunda he was replaced by Denny Laine. Dave Morgan subsequently became the bassist and vocalist with Magnum. He departed before their debut album. Dave was also the guitarist with ELO from 1981 to 1986. He is credited with performing background vocals on the 1983 ELO album *Secret Messages* and Jeff Lynne's *Armchair Theatre*.

Morgan formed the Tandy-Morgan Band with Richard Tandy in 1985. Together they recorded the concept album *Earthrise*. The album contained fourteen tracks, which were all written by Morgan, featuring Tandy's keyboard arrangements. *Earthrise* was produced with Steve Lipson and eventually released on vinyl in 1986 on the FM Revolver label. In 1992 Morgan released the album on CD. In 2011, a revised and updated version, titled *Earthrise Special Edition* was released on the Rock Legacy label.

In 1969, the final Uglys line-up recorded a Dave Morgan composition titled 'I've Seen The Light' at Advision Studios for a proposed single. The powerful descending guitar intro by Will Hammond, repeated throughout the song, provided the extremely, catchy 'hook.' Dave Morgan also composed the single's B-side titled 'Mary Colinto'. The song was inspired by Jimmy O'Neil's sister Kathy. At the time The Uglys were still managed by John Singer who negotiated a contract with MGM Records, to release and promote the record. Unfortunately, things did not go according to plan. Tony Secunda had an idea to form a new Birmingham group to be fronted up by the former Move guitarist/vocalist Trevor Burton. To this end, Secunda proposed a deal with Steve Gibbons. This deal was for control of The Uglys (excluding their name and the guitarist Will Hammond) and Secunda agreed to finance them.

Will Hammond got the news. "A few months after we recorded the single at Advision. Steve Gibbons and Dave Morgan turned up on my doorstep. They told me that they were all leaving. They were joining up with Trevor Burton to form a new band."

With The Uglys now effectively dissolved. MGM cancelled the release of their 'I've Seen The Light' single. This resulting in only a small number of demo copies being pressed. Only two of these are known to actually survive today. With one owned by Will Hammond and the other one being sold recently for £1,200 pounds. Surely, this could be one of the rarest and collectible UK psychedelic 45's from the 1960s!

Other songs written by Dave Morgan were the singularly wonderful 'Something', written for The Move. Morgan also wrote 'This Time Tomorrow' for The Move.

"The late, great Carl Wayne sang many of my song demos, during the late 1960s. These were usually at my mum's house. He sang them into a Bang and Olafsen, Sound-on Sound tape recorder."

Dave Morgan also recorded an album in 1970, issued on the now defunct US Ampex label as *Morgan*. It was released later on the Global label in Germany. It wasn't ever released in the UK and has not been reissued. After 1987 Morgan continued releasing solo albums on his privately owned label. Some of which are inspired by his Christian faith.

Richard Tandy was born on 26th March 1948 in Birmingham and educated at Moseley School, where he first met his future bandmate, Bev Bevan. Richard Tandy would also later be reunited with Bevan in 1968 when he played the sonorous harpsichord, on 'Blackberry Way' and briefly joined them live, playing keyboards. He switched to bass while Trevor Burton was momentarily sidelined due to a shoulder injury. When Burton was able to play again, Tandy left to join The Uglys.

In 1972, Tandy served as the bassist, in the first live line-up of Electric Light Orchestra. He then became the band's full-time keyboardist. He has collaborated musically with ELO frontman Jeff Lynne on many projects. Among them songs for the *Electric Dreams* soundtrack, Lynne's solo album *Armchair Theatre* and the Lynne-produced Dave Edmunds album *Information*. Richard Tandy passed away at the age of 76 on 1st May 2024. A much loved and much regarded musician who

Is there something that you've wanted? More than anything?

added so much to the sound of ELO and any other projects he was involved with.

Willie Hammond The Uglys guitarist had been shunted sideways and moved quickly out of the picture by Secunda in favour of Trevor Burton. Again, Secunda needed the name changed.

The name of the band should be as "in-your-face" as possible. To attract, maximum attention by being direct and also very provocative. The final name reflects Secunda's and Trevor's up-yours attitudes. Therefore, Trevor Burton's suggestion was followed, to initially call the group 'The Balls'. This name should allegedly reflect the powerful (ballsy) guitar playing of Trevor Burton. Burton had originally come up with the 'spherical' name, they were all thrown into a bag or on the floor to select the best name.

Keith Smart remembered, "We all met up Steve Gibbons' house. After loads of suggestions we went with the one that accurately described the style and feel of Trevor's guitar playing. Well, that's one version. Following in the trend notably set by Traffic, Secunda arranged for his new band to 'get it together in the country'."

They rented a country house in Fordingbridge, Hampshire in April 1969. Fordingbridge offered seclusion and also a pub nearby. The pub was often (over) used. But the rehearsals didn't quite work out. One of the reasons for this was that the musicians got up at different times. They then spent the time they were awake together mainly in the pub. In fact, Keith Smart recalls clearly. "The first thing that we did to help out the creative flow was open an account at the village off-licence."

The juices started flowing, just not really in the all-important musical sphere. What was achieved during these rehearsal times, didn't seem to sparkle with creativity either. Dave Scott-Morgan remembers that the rehearsals were mainly "undisciplined and loud." Morgan then continues, "The music was almost exclusively, interminable twelve bar blasts. These went on for hours ad-nauseam — the archetypal rock 'n' roll groove."

Secunda also hired Traffic's producer Jimmy Miller to oversee the recording sessions. Secunda had arranged a large cash advance from the record company. The group eventually started to compose and record new material, while playing a few local gigs. Dave Morgan left during the summer of 1969. It was said he wasn't considered "balls" enough by Mr Secunda. And so he had to hit the tarmac.

Secunda talked up the band big time to Warner Brothers telling them it was a terrific business plan. Secunda glommed them twice, getting two advances on the same band. The second advance when Denny Laine joined. Secunda informed the agog Warner Brothers Balls had both the vital spark of The Move but they now, also have the voice of 'Go Now', Mr Denny Laine — an utterly unbeatable combination. Nice work Tony!

This plan is going to yield a great new band with great new songs. Dave Morgan, "I didn't like the Tony Secunda thing and all the power things that went on. I got pretty killed in all that. Later in Balls I got embroiled in it myself and I didn't like that."

Dave Morgan was ousted in the reshuffling. "Denny Laine joined them, and then it was really… With Denny coming along, that Richard (Tandy) and I got turfed out, and Keithy Smart got kicked out as well. So eventually it all ended up being Denny Laine, Trevor Burton and Steve Gibbons. I think that is what Tony Secunda always wanted. He wanted those three in a kind of supergroup. Anyway, that is the history."

Keith Smart also rejoinders, "Tony Secunda worshipped the ground that Trevor Burton worked on. He firmly believed that the switch from (The Move) to new ground with the reborn Uglys was a terrific business plan for all of us."

Morgan was summarily replaced, and / or pushed, after Denny Laine, the ex-singer/guitarist of The Moody Blues and his own outfits had slotted in. But Balls had split at the end of 1969. With Richard Tandy going on to join The Move (for live gigs only) and then Electric Light Orchestra.

Keith Smart was in Balls for a while too. Secunda and possibly Denny Lane, preferring that his face didn't fit. Smart thought there was a lot of manoeuvring and machinations going on behind the scenes. Keith Smart eventually joined with Roy Wood and Wizzard on drums, along with second drummer and conga player Charlie Grima. Balls reconvened as a quartet the following summer. This time with Burton, former Plastic Ono Band drummer Alan White and a new vocalist Jackie Lomax. Lomax was soon replaced by the returning Steve Gibbons. Ex-Spooky Tooth drummer, Mike Kellie was to replace White in January 1971. Talk about moving the goalposts and the musicians!

In the very beginning of the Balls saga, it was probably this initial openness and free flowing variation in the line-up that led to some fake news in connection with this group's formation with Brian Jones from the Rolling Stones part of the group. But the actual player was purely a namesake saxophone player, who had been in The Undertakers with Steve Gibbons, Trevor Burton and others, here and there. Anyway, Brian Jones had already died on the 3rd July 1969! The idea to form a new band was born, during various nightly jam sessions.

Burton had become known for his bass playing, a most strong, agile and inventive sound. But he now saw himself, as the main guitar-slinger in this new band. Later, Trevor's determination to develop as a six-string player led to problems with Mr Denny Laine. We have already seen how Denny Laine's incipient ego had caused lots of troubles and trembles in The Diplomats.

Trevor is now reminded of the edginess inherent in yet another, inner-band, power struggle. "Denny got a bit bent out of shape. Because I wanted to play the guitar. But Denny wanted me to play bass. Denny really wanted to play guitar. But I thought, I was a better guitar player (laughs)!"

The word around town had been that Trevor Burton was rumoured, to be forming a new group with Noel Redding, who, like Burton, was a guitarist who had switched to bass for The Experience. Roy Wood suspected the prospect of forming a band with Redding had further encouraged Burton in his decision to leave The Move. However, nothing came of this band. Personally, I think a band between Redding and Burton would not have been any great, big shakes. As Redding's Fat Mattress group were no big noise at all. A sort of mediocre rock band that released a couple of records. Trevor in his stoned state may have mistaken Redding's association with Jimi Hendrix to be gilding him with a charisma I don't think he had.

Burton had also jammed with members of Traffic and became a friend of Steve Winwood. Trevor almost got to join Blind Faith in 1969. Trevor later said that he had, "Nearly got the job on bass, Steve Winwood wanted me, I think, but Ginger Baker wanted Ric Grech instead." I don't know why, as Trevor is a much funkier and

Is there something that you've wanted? More than anything?

stronger player, in my over-inflated estimation.

Interesting decision, as Trevor had quite a pronounced, undercurrent of grit and funkiness in his bass style. Whereas, in many ways, Ginger Baker, was a clodhopper of a drummer. He could make thunder; he could make tom-toms attack. But I always felt he didn't have much groove. Although loud, confident, with a big, brash sweep and with his Phil Seaman, jazz training providing him with solid technique. A base that underpinned his playing. Many UK drummers didn't have that type of schooling back then. Baker never had a particularly 'groovacious' drum feel. An old friend of mine who played with Bill Laswell (the bassist and legendary New York producer) on a Ginger Baker recording recalled, Laswell felt that "Baker could be difficult, not only in personal terms. His bad tempered and arrogant mien, hung like a cloud around him. But also, in terms of trying to get a groove out of him."

In February 1969, Denny Laine participates in an early Blind Faith session. He is aware that Balls is being put together. At this point, he decides not to join the outfit. Laine later joined Ginger Baker with his large personnel, Ginger Bakers Airforce group. In the spring of the following year on a no strings basis. When he returned to Britain, Laine jammed with the ad-hoc outfit Balls. The band purportedly recorded a song titled 'Go To The Mountains' for Apple Records. But it was never released, or indeed heard of ever again.

As writer Dave Thompson kindly let me know, "It was Secunda who blagged enough cash, out from sundry record labels! To keep a band called Balls in luxury for life! Without them ever having to do anything so tiresome as make a record." Money, that was initially invested towards their extensive stay in the country.

Mick Clifford was working for *Beat Instrumental* as a features writer. He did one piece with Ace Kefford in April 1968 called "Move Music" — the subheading was "It doesn't educate anybody," says Ace. Mick was busy doing various industry jobs. "I'd been head hunted by Tony Secunda, to work with his new band Balls, Denny Laine and Trevor Burton. I worked initially with MGM, then I subsequently went to A&M. I moved onto a freelance contract. My time with Secunda was very brief, just around three or four months. I think it was obviously Secunda's accountant's office and Tony was using the office, grace and favour. For a while, when I was at the Trevor and Denny house every day. I would describe it, as very 'smoke-filled.' I got along much better with Trevor, than I did with Denny Laine. When I was communicating with Tony, they were living in the suburbs in London. I think it was Clapham — they hadn't as yet, gone down to the country retreat. The flat had four record players, going on at all times. They liked to throw all-night parties. With washing up left in huge piles for fortnights at a time. Apparently, the landlord wanted to see them urgently. One can only imagine what the landlord's next move would be."

During the time that followed, some musicians left the group. There are different versions about the reasons. The hoary old cliche of 'musical differences' being one. Of course, it was only a short time before loads of problems arose within the Balls line-up. Morgan and Tandy fired as incompatible… Keith Smart also left (or he was probably pushed) to be replaced by Spooky Tooth drummer Mike Kellie. Steve Gibbons, who was among the fracas, blamed Secunda who was ruthlessly sifting out, and sorting out, all the musicians. Those who in Secunda's opinion did not fit in with the image of a successful band "or as having balls". There was lot of quarrelling in the band. They couldn't agree on a steady drummer either. This must have been to do with all the dope being smoked. Not a drug that generally leads to much logical reasoning and clarity of rational opinion.

Steve Gibbons remembers, "We could never settle on a drummer, and we did auditions with lots of different guys. I mean, just look at the three they had already. Keith Smart was a good player and had a solid pedigree, Mike Kellie was a unflashy player but again, a solid timekeeping ethos. And of course, Alan White, who went on to have a long and illustrious drumming career. What was the big deal with all of these players?"

Keith Smart wryly remembers, "Then Denny Laine came on the scene…Tony Secunda brought Denny Laine in, and Denny stayed and then Denny didn't like Dave Morgan or Richard Tandy, so they had to be gotten rid of. Then it came to a stage with isolating, Trevor away from me and Steve Gibbons, especially from me. And then it was my turn to leave. There was a great talent of musicians there, it was fantastic. I gotta say, Denny wasn't the easiest guy to work with or to get on with!"

It appears Denny just couldn't be in a band situation without manipulating and playing ego games and pitting people against each other. Although he was a talented musician and songwriter. He couldn't seem to leave his personality defects aside, long enough in order to nurture these musical situations.

Denny Laine remembered his link to joining up with Balls: "Ginger Baker came to my house one night and asked me to join a big band he was putting together called Airforce… It was an utter shambles — too many players! All trying to out-do one another and not enough discipline."

As writer Alan Clayson nicely put it, "Airforce was particularly overloaded with under-employed Brummies — Trevor Burton and Traffic's Steve Winwood and Chris Wood. As well as Denny, and Birmingham Town Hall was a fitting debut performance. Most of the musos, stuck it out for just one more engagement — at the Royal Albert Hall — where a rambling and unrepentantly loud set was captured on tape. From this cacophony, they salvaged a single, Bob Dylan's 'Man Of Constant Sorrow' sung in Denny Laine's fully-developed "hurting" style."

Steve Gibbons says about this in the TV documentary *Untold Stories*, "I am pretty sure that Tony Secunda had this agenda going on. He looked at the individuals and he thought 'He'll do, he'll do or he won't do.' He was looking for who is bill-suitable (or balls-suitable). To be honest, I was a part of this too. But he did not consider, the rest of The Ugly's to be part of it. One by one he gave them all the sack!"

It's not absolutely sure how hands on (or off) Tony Secunda was with this project. Possibly preferring to let them get on with it. Or leaving them to their own devices. But Secunda lost (or eventually developed very little) interest in the group. After the advance came through, perhaps he felt his role was over.

He took over some other management reigns rapidly. Feeling he had a very hot property with the up-and-coming Marc Bolan. While his then first wife Chelita was very involved in the visual look of the rising up and "rebranded" Bolan. This separated him from the earlier Tolkein-wreathed, hippie-dippy, dope-smoking feel of the Tyrannosaurus Rex duo with his bongo playing cohort, Steve Peregrin Took who had been given the big elbow.

Took was briefly managed by Secunda trying to record stoned out music which

Is there something that you've wanted? More than anything?

was released posthumously with the bloody awful name of Shagrat. Secunda managing Took was very possibly some kind of revenge tactic due to Bolan's subsequent, very underhanded tactics towards Secunda. This, after Secunda renegotiated Bolan's contracts, with more money and a brand-new label. Getting him out from under the grip of David Platz' Essex Music. Tony was rewarded with the usual, and could be said inevitable, Bolan tactics and betrayal. Marc Bolan went from writing spaced-out, Tolkienesque, twee, twerpish poems, to cocaine addled arrogance pieces and superstardom.

Marc jumped quickly from Tyrannosaurus Rex to T. Rex and the music dramatically changed. Like the ode to his new manager Tony Secunda, called 'Telegram Sam'. (A re-run of the huge hit 'Get It On'). *"You're my main man."* The tune also names road manager and Secunda's main factotum. "He also referenced, 'Jungle Face Jake'. 'Jungle Face' was a cat called Sid Walker. It is said the term 'main man' was popularised from Marc's use in this tune.

On the 5th and 6th August, having contributed to Ginger Baker's Airforce album and spending 18 months rehearsing material with Trevor Burton and ex-Plastic Ono drummer Alan White, Balls were scheduled to make their live debut at the Popanalia festival in Nice, France. The group missed the concert. Although their lone single, Burton's written 'Fight For My Country' backed by Laine and Alan White's 'Janie Slow Down' was rush released in France by Byg Records. 'Fight For My Country' was also released by Wizard Records, Tony Secunda's then latest label imprint, but it failed to chart.

'Fight For My Country' was a spirited anti-war anthem, featuring a raw, impassioned Trevor vocal and including backing vocals from Steve Gibbons and Denny Laine. The up-tempo B-side 'Janie Slow Down' has a rousing Burton vocal (which to my ears) is the stronger song. When this rare Balls single was issued in France, it had a longer version of 'Fight For My Country' coupled with a different Trevor Burton composition titled 'Hound Dog Howling' on the B-side. 'Fight For My Country' has also appeared on compilations and as a Trevor Burton solo track. No other Balls recordings have been issued since. Trevor once remarked, "The tapes are in the vaults of the record company somewhere. God knows what they sound like now, after all these years."

The group is rumoured to have recorded around 12 tracks for an album. The sessions included contributions from ex-Family and ex-Blind Faith member bassist Ric Grech. Another gig planned for 18th October and supposedly to be Balls' debut UK live performance at London's Lyceum also never happened. The group planned to record the show for a live album, but further internal problems resulted in the cancellation. Alan White subsequently left after this feeble meandering. The third sticks man in a revolving door of very good drummers.

Laine and Burton performed an acoustic set at their next show, held at Trent Polytechnic, Nottingham. They vowed to undertake a UK tour in January 1971 but by then the group had broken up.

Steve Gibbons remembers, "We could never settle on a drummer, and we did auditions with lots of different guys. We used to rehearse in a barn. We always chose to rehearse about three o'clock in the morning. We would get complaints from the local constabulary. As the raucous racket would carry for miles at that time of night."

Secunda had hoped to create a new group along the same lines as Steve Winwood's highly successful Traffic. He had hired Traffic's producer Jimmy Miller for the group's recording sessions. Secunda did not lose his inherent hustle. However, with Denny Laine, the dysfunctional situation didn't necessarily ease up. In fact, it worsened. According to Denny, "The idea was that we were going to swap instruments around and bring different people in for different things." Head speak for being so stoned it didn't matter what or who, or when or where were playing.

A stoned overcast, torpor settled over the project. Problems soon arose including the use of "certain substances" at the farm. The state of confusion increased. Very little musical rigour appeared to be involved in terms of planning and moving the band forward. The usual excuses were proffered — the cliqued and boring, musical differences. Of which there were plenty. Long drinking sessions were held at the very convenient local pub. Cutting into many hours of playing and recording time.

After the two cash advances they were being requested (or pressed) by Warner Brothers to show some recorded evidence and come up with some damn good material. They had brought a completely new frontman on board, Jackie Lomax. Lomax had been signed to The Beatles new Apple Records label, and released his George Harrison-produced album *Is This What You Want?*

However, Lomax didn't fulfil any of the band expectations. Or maybe any expectations at all. Trevor Burton told me, "Jackie Lomax was more of a solo artist, and it became obvious he didn't really enjoy the collaborative group thing."

Lomax left and a familiar Birmingham face returned, namely Steve Gibbons. At least, they had gotten rid of the tendentious Denny Laine. He had caused too much trouble and now was looking to find a place to rest with Paul McCartney's Wings. Perhaps one man that Denny Laine would have to defer to, whether he liked it or not! The old routine of jamming and visiting pubs continued. Despite rumours of a finished album, it has never seen the light of day.

According to Denny Laine, "Tony Secunda and Jimmy Miller fell out over money and that was the end of that! Balls finally disintegrated shortly after!" Balls had a lot of potential but after all the smoking, toking and drinking and possibly snorting. All they had to show for it, after a good year or so, was that solitary 45rpm single release. The single did not get released until September 1971. By this time Balls had long since ceased to exist.

It was re-issued under Burton's name in June 1972. Trevor Burton went on to do sessions. He guested on bass guitar with a little-known band Crushed Butler in 1970. He cut twelve studio recordings with the group. Again, these were intended for release on Secunda's Wizard label that operated between 1971 and 1973 and distributed by EMI. Initially Secunda wanted to develop a multi-media empire. He had earlier interests within Radio Geronimo. One thing would feed another, radio stations playing his records across the airwaves. Secunda wanted to exert that cross-platform control.

31.
"Go home to Birmingham and get yourself sorted out - or else you're going to die!"

Shortly thereafter, Burton guested on rhythm guitar with the Pink Fairies between August 1971 to July 1972. He was with them long enough to appear on a BBC live session. He also played on two songs from their second album entitled *What a Bunch of Sweeties*. "I just wanted to do my own thing really," said Trevor, "so I became a session musician for Island Records."

During this time Trevor enjoyed jamming and recording with several high-profile musicians, notably his friend Paul Kossoff, who had been the minimalist and unique lead guitarist in the mighty Free. "Of all the albums I have been on. Probably about 15 or 16 albums with different people. The *Backstreet Crawler* one I did with Paul is my favourite. I played bass on the whole of the B-side which was all recorded, totally spontaneously. It was a jam lasting for about 22 minutes. We just recorded it, and Paul said, 'that's it' and that was to be the whole side. It was one of the last things I did with Paul before he died. It was very special."

Trevor became ensconced around Island Records. He was particularly rooted at their Basing Recording Studios scene for a while. He was coming into contact with heavy 'class A' drug users, around that scene. It's here he has said he started to develop a serious heroin problem. With all the attendant health, money and life problems that "smack" brings in its wake. Burton maintained that American musicians were bringing the gear over. "I was getting turned onto it that way."

Trevor gives some reasons why Paul Kossoff, Chris Wood (Traffic) and others were now really feeling the pinch. "It was a dreary period; it was all very stoned. A lot of it had to do with loneliness. Nobody was looking after Kossoff. Like today, there were no teams of people, you had to look out for yourself. I think Chris (Wood) of Traffic was lonely and I think Paul Kossoff was lonely. They just sank deeper into the dark pit with all the drugs and booze. And then they couldn't get out."

Burton was realising he didn't want to go all the way down either. He was becoming trapped in a situation, to a large degree of his own making. He remembers not so long afterwards, hearing that Paul Kossoff had overdosed on a plane at the age of 25. Kossoff was on a redeye flight to New York.

Tony Secunda came back around good for Trevor. Secunda went round to his pad one night, he put his foot in the door. Secunda told him in no uncertain terms: "To get back to Birmingham and clean up. Or I was going to die. We were all doing heroin, Mandrax and all that shit."

Trevor remembers the unique manager, with whom he had a strong bond. "He gave me a hundred quid, told me to clear off! I took his advice. I left London and I went back home to me mothers. I went cold turkey and cleaned myself up." Not the easiest thing to do but Trevor Burton did it. That steely rebelliousness and inner drive that Trevor had demonstrated onstage now came up trumps to allow him to fight his deadly and fatal drug addiction.

After some re-orientation, Burton also worked with Birmingham vocalist Raymond Froggatt until 1975. After Balls, Steve Gibbons joined The Idle Race. This became the Steve Gibbons Band. Burton joined in April 1975 on bass and vocals and the group enjoyed a healthy live career. Charting in 1975 with 'Tulane', their reworking of the Chuck Berry song. Steve Gibbons also returned to Birmingham, and he also faced a big re-orientation.

The 1970s were changing, pubs were no longer putting on so much live music. Music was becoming more corporate. After the freewheeling, making-it-up-as-we-go 1960s the music industry was more controlled by bean counters and people wanting immediate return on their investment. Careers for these boys, that had blazed along for some years now had to be re-looked at. To be re-charted, replanned, to see if there was any longevity, in the front view mirror.

There had also been changes in groups, with a local sphere of influence. In the not-too-distant past, Birmingham used to have performance opportunities on every street corner and venue. Now, during the mid-1970s onwards, the disco era began and the pub owners, preferred to hire disc jockeys rather than full bands. Not a great vantage point from whence to make a new emergence into the live scene. It was yet another starting point for Steve Gibbons, who describes it thus. "It was a big struggle to re-establish yourself, but which was exactly, what I had to do. Eventually Steve and Trevor's paths would cross again.

32.
Let the wind blow you out of my memory, Let the rain wash you out of my eyes

One instance that brought The Move back into focus again was Carl Wayne deciding enough was enough on paying away The Move's royalties for almost 40 years for something the band had not done. He knew challenging trust law would be a long, convoluted and expensive process but what he had not reckoned on was how little appetite his fellow band members would have for that fight. While all were supportive, it was left to Carl to swing his axe once more to demolish the establishment's wall of silence.

He contacted reissue producer Rob Caiger to run through his ideas, having known Caiger from his work with ELO and The Move's later EMI Harvest catalogue. Carl had met Caiger on and off over the years and had been impressed with his in-depth knowledge of Birmingham bands, especially The Move. Always meeting in London's Soho district, including Joe & Co Studios in Dean Street where Carl had recorded many TV and film commercials, and which had been previously owned by Tony Visconti as Good Earth Studios.

Carl and Caiger spent almost a year researching the real facts behind the case and why The Move were hung out to dry for the sake of Wilson's Labour government. Despite Simon Platz of Bucks Music (The Move's catalogue owner and publisher of their songs and son of Essex Music's David Platz) providing financial assistance to engage renowned and respected music-industry solicitor James Wyllie, gathering information and witness testimonies to help mount a challenge to the ruling proved difficult. Caiger recommended to Platz and Carl that reissuing The Move's long-neglected back catalogue could only help with the case by bringing the band back into the public eye, especially as the 40th anniversary of 'Flowers In The Rain' was fast approaching in 2007.

Caiger prepared a strategy to bring The Move's catalogue back into print after 40 years. He started by shocking the band members when he revealed none of their albums had been available in the UK since their original release.

The Move's catalogue had merely been licensed to record labels in the UK and around the world for release as Move compilations or as part of various artist compilations. Only during the nineties in Germany and early noughties in Japan were the original albums released on CD. In each case, CDs were produced from audio sources of varying quality, some of which included vinyl disc dubs.

Earlier, during the eighties and nineties, Bucks Music had put what they considered to be the best sound for all their artists onto DAT (Digital Audio Tape) to be used as masters, as many record companies did during this period. Unfortunately, Bucks Music were music publishers and no longer had their own record company, Fly Records. They had long lost the technical expertise to identify their best sound sources, and the experience needed, to know which were the correct single mixes and album versions, to build an archive of production master recordings suitable for CD.

As was common practice, Bucks Music would send DAT copies to record labels licensing material and from these labels would produce their own CD compilations to cash in on the boom in CD sales. Unfortunately, DAT had limitations meaning sound copied from it to CD was nowhere near the quality of the original vinyl LPs released in the sixties and seventies.

The Move's beautifully produced and arranged songs, expertly recorded and engineered by Chevin and Offord had been reduced to shiny, thin-sounding echoes of the band's huge and powerful "magnetic wave of sound" for the sake of digital convenience.

Caiger took Carl into Abbey Road Studios while he was working on ELO reissues for Jeff Lynne and played the singer The Move's original singles and LPs against recent CD versions. Horrified at what he was hearing — and not hearing, "where's the fucking bass?" Carl immediately called a meeting with Simon Platz. The meeting soon became heated during which Caiger had to restrain a white-hot angry Carl from dragging a visibly shaken Platz across his desk. Once the blood had returned to Platz's face, the publisher did stand up and faced Carl. He acknowledged his company could have done more for The Move over the years, especially over 'Flowers In The Rain'.

The meeting ended on a handshake, with a relieved Platz promising Bucks Music would license The Move catalogue as deluxe remastered CD editions with bonus tracks, with Caiger appointed reissue producer and given full access to their archives, to identify rare and previously unreleased material from which to compile a career-spanning boxset. Carl also insisted the contracted members of The Move (himself, Roy, and Bev) would have full approval before anything was released and as a courtesy, Ace, Trevor, Rick Price and Jeff Lynne would also be kept informed of the reissues. This commitment was music to fans' ears who had longed for a decent airing of The Move's catalogue. Just as importantly it would present first-time listeners with a scrumptious motherlode of largely forgotten songs plus some great unreleased material.

Caiger was diligent in his research and was able to track down missing and misfiled tapes that over the years had been spread across many separate archives in London: "I found all the master tapes. I found many of the Advision Studios session multi-tracks that hadn't been reused and taped over. I found just about everything. This is when Carl started talking to Roy and Bev about the bigger Move picture. They're not silly boys and knew that if you have a catalogue of hit and iconic songs it has to be out there working for you, not only bringing in money but promoting the band and giving it a long-overdue platform to do things. In this case, with the 40th anniversary of 'Flowers In The Rain' approaching, the re-promotion of the catalogue would give the band an opportunity to highlight the injustice they'd suffered as a result of the court case with Harold Wilson."

Caiger also explained how some early Move demos recorded in early 1966 were found. He didn't have to look far but for a year, an acetate of four previously unreleased songs had sat in the window of The Record and Tape Exchange in Notting Hill Gate, just round the corner and a short walk from the offices of Bucks Music: "Yeah, for a whole year, myself and Simon and the staff had walked past the store. Not seeing a priceless Move acetate just sitting there, in a white sleeve with a Johnny Haines studio label. The store manager heard about what we were doing and contacted me and said they'd had no interest from anyone buying it for about a year, so the store owner told her to put it on eBay. So, with the auction coming up the next day, we struck a deal to get it. No matter what anyone else bid, we would bid more and then invite them to attend the restoration and mastering session at Abbey Road Studios. In the end, we didn't pay anywhere near what we bid but what really swung it in our favour was for them to spend an evening with us in Abbey Road."

Caiger makes the point that if The Move had a more experienced manager focused on business and less on publicity stunts, the group would have been in a more advantageous relationship with its record label: "As successful as the singles were, a strong manager would have focused them on establishing an album catalogue, as their contemporaries were busy doing. Or bought in other writers or looked for covers which may have inspired Roy Wood to write more songs more quickly. Look at the first Move LP. It was based around their early stage set but took far too long to come out and by the time it did, their sound and line-up had moved on. If Secunda was a stronger, more confident manager, he would have listened to Roy saying, 'I can't write all the material' and recognised it was too much for such a young man at the start of his career. A strong manager would have suggested using some of Ace's songs, encouraged the other band members to write or got an outside writer like Dave Morgan to help Roy with the workload."

"Part of the problem was Tony Secunda was trying to control everything while creating stunts and drumming up publicity. While what he did was inspired and brilliant at times. He also needed someone watching the business, so the band got the full financial and artistic rewards from Secunda's publicity. A wiser head may have reigned Secunda in, before he distributed the Wilson postcard. A more experienced partner would have insisted The Move work with an American promoter to tour the US and clean up, as The Beatles, The Stones, The Yardbirds and The Who were doing. Secunda had enough contacts and offers to make this happen but feared losing control once the band were outside the UK."

"Another problem is Secunda is dealing with a music publisher that also has the rights to the recordings. Not unusual for the time but not to the band's advantage as all their musical eggs are in one basket. It's also the music publisher dealing directly with the record company. The publisher is looking at The Move through a publisher's eyes and what they want is songs. Profitable songs which at the time meant 45rpm hit singles. If Secunda had insisted on dealing with Deram and Regal Zonophone directly he would have been under no illusion they wanted songs for singles but also albums. And he would have been under pressure from the labels to produce probably two a year, plus non-album A and B side singles and 4-song EPs to sell to the fans. That's where the record company profit is. So, there's a different perspective from the music publisher who earns from radio plays, covers, sheet music and also physical sales. Had Secunda been a strong, business-focused manager, The Move would have had a healthy singles and album catalogue, not a series of stunts and fantastic stories, that filled space in long-forgotten music papers."

"The only time The Move started to happen and organise was towards the end of their career when Don Arden took over. The music world had changed because it became geared towards albums. Albums and tours, especially in America, were where the real money was. And Don Arden with his long experience and hard-nosed attitude was perfectly placed to take The Move away from Essex Music and Fly Records and negotiate a new deal with EMI's Harvest Records that paid enough to The Move but also funded Roy and Jeff's new Electric Light Orchestra project."

33.
Lightning never strikes twice in the same place...

The Move fell through the cracks in the space of three to four years. A tempestuous three- or so-year reign, with a lightning ascent to the top. Considered to be the best live band in the UK. Along with a bunch of well-regarded, top five hit singles and then they were gone.

What happened to the original mighty five? Rumours surfaced occasionally - over the years that there was to be a reunion, here or there. But it never happened. Sometimes the greatest of bands should leave it and simply not reunite. As in the case of The Beatles. Aaah but hold on — the recent AI evolved 'Here and Now' although dividing opinion, has kept the name, the credibility (in some quarters) and the longevity intact.

You would hear the odd mention from someone, on the fringes of the rock business. Probably most memorably was Mark. E. Smith from The Fall. The Fall covered 'I Can Hear the Grass Grow' (2005). Mark loved The Move and preferred them to The Beatles or The Rolling Stones. He saw The Move as a "proper psychedelic group." A report had Mark holding up a dog-eared vinyl copy of *The Best Of The Move*. Mark slurred on, "This is the third and fourth sides of a double best of collection. I don't know where it's from. It's got tracks I've never seen before on it, and the amazing The Move Live EP. It's got 'So You Want To Be A Rock 'n' Roll Star' on it, and a Love cover, 'Dear Stephanie'. The second side is all cover versions, apart from 'Night Of Fear' and 'I Can Hear The Grass Grow'. I like The Move, they sound English — I like The Kinks as well. But there was no one great LP. The Move sound real Brummie! Especially when they had Carl Wayne, they were great! I think the song structures were really fascinating. Roy Wood was just a genius; he always has been for me. I grew up with them, I saw the original ELO with Roy Wood in it. And I saw The Move — 'Night Of Fear' was superb with that bit of Tchaikovsky in it. 'I Can Hear The Grass Grow' I didn't hear that until about 1974. I remember taking acid to it. My sister gave me the record, she'd got it from a second-hand shop. I couldn't believe people had made records like that. It makes all this psychedelic rubbish now look a bit sick. I mean, 'I Can Hear The Grass Grow' — what the hell is going on in that? Apparently, Carl Wayne didn't know what the lyrics he was singing were about either. That's why he left The Move — he found out what he was singing about! He went on to record 'You're A Star, Superstar' and marry Diane out of *Crossroads*. I'm really trivial about stuff like that!"

There is a kind of glorification of rockstars etc. as they destroy themselves through drugs and drink. I'm thinking of Mark E. Smith, with his constant "fuck you" attitude, but also his ongoing, constant alcoholism. Which would've brought him to his knees. I can remember once being at the Phoenix Festival somewhere. I remember seeing Smith backstage — he just looked really wrecked. I don't mean he was falling about or anything. Just his face was etched with disease… with the relentless grind and destruction of the demon drink. I got a flash of just "sheer alcoholism" in operation. An insight ripple ran down my spine and gave me the momentary jeebie cold shivers.

The Move Anthology 1966-1972, is (so far) the ultimate, remastered 4 CD box set. The music, much of it previously unreleased, added a whole new dimension to the groups' albums and hit singles. Most serious music listeners in the USA, missed out on the riotous Move story. As they only did that smattering of live dates in 1969. Thank God, that Carl Wayne had held on to the soundboard tapes of the Live Fillmore shows. For years before his death, he made it his personal project to try and get them released, to no avail. Carl passed everything to Rob Caiger to make sure it got released and he secured a 2009 release of their historical Fillmore West 1969 live concerts. One US music lover gushed, "Listen to the fantastic music of The Move via state of the art reissues. They were without a doubt one of the most fab bands during the golden days of UK British pop, creating rock music for the ages - Play it LOUD!"

34.
Bound together by a legend - to protect us and defend...

Come the 1970s, The Move were struggling for direction and eventually the mutual admiration society, coupled together the stellar talents of Roy Wood and Jeff Lynne. They finally hooked up. It looked as if they would re-ignite The Move (at least momentarily) and bridge the gap, towards their ultimate, cherished dream. Solidifying the long nurtured, ambition of Wood, towards solidifying the emerging ELO. Incorporating both men's sizable, songwriting talents and ambitions. Bev Bevan seamlessly joined ELO on the drums. Rick Price said he played on the sessions but alas, his bass parts are over-dubbed by Roy. Videos from the time, show Richard Tandy playing bass. The pairing of Roy and Jeff had happened. And then — in a seemingly, abrupt manner — Roy Wood had bailed out! He suddenly left, amazing both Bev and Jeff Lynne!

By upping his bagpipes and leaving to form the Phil Spector*esque*, wall-of-sound, tongue-in-cheek, rock 'n' roll revue, called Wizzard. Watching all this at first hand was Bevan who had known Wood since the very beginning. To this day, Bev is flummoxed as to why the Wood/Lynne axis did not flourish. There was no big row between Roy and Jeff, who have remained friendly to this day.

Jeff Lynne remembered the interim period as The Move became ELO. "The Move weren't as famous as they used to be when I joined. It was okay, but we didn't really do anything good or play anywhere other than little clubs. We joined up to make ELO. That's what Roy and I were attempting to do. But it didn't work out and Roy left after less than a year after we'd started ELO. The gigs were a real mess; you couldn't hear the cellos, because they only had microphones for the string instruments at that time, rather than pick-ups. I don't know what it sounded like for people in the audience, but it didn't sound particularly good from where I was standing."

ELO, initially signed to Harvest (EMI) and were managed by Arden from the band's inception. With son David handling tour management. During 1973 and 1974, ELO and Wizzard moved from Harvest to Warner Bros. Records in the UK. In 1975, the two bands and Wood's solo releases moved again in the UK to Jet, with their recent Warners releases becoming part of Jet's catalogue. Wood left Jet Records and disbanded Wizzard in 1976, after Jet refused to release Wizzard's third album *Wizzo*, because it was not deemed commercial enough. His final single on the Jet label was 'Any Old Time Will Do'.

Flowers In The Rain - The Untold Story of The Move

Jet Records was started by Don Arden in 1974 and would go on to include Lynsey de Paul, Gary Moore, Alan Price, Riot, Adrian Gurvitz and Magnum.

The first release on Jet Records was the single 'No, Honestly' which hit the UK top 10 for its singer and writer Lynsey de Paul in November 1974.

Black Sabbath were also managed by Don Arden, but not signed to Jet Records. When Ozzy Osbourne left the band, he was signed to Jet. Two studio albums and one live album by Osbourne were released on Jet. Arden's daughter Sharon, who was working for Don and Jet, started dating Osbourne and eventually married him.

ELO's '10538 Overture', written by Jeff Lynne, was first recorded as an intended B-side for a single by The Move. Both Roy Wood and Lynne sang on it, as happened later with The Move's 'California Man'. The song is about an escaped prisoner, Lynne wanted to give the character in the song a number, as opposed to a name. He chanced upon the number 1053, while looking at the mixing console. Wood suggested adding a number '8' to fit the melody better. This song is said to derive some influence, from Patrick (*Danger Man*) McGoohan's influential and extremely offbeat TV series *The Prisoner*.

Although it was first intended for The Move after the many cello parts were added, it became the Electric Light Orchestra's first single release. Roy Wood was practising cello furiously. He was transposing Jimi Hendrix riffs onto the (usually) classical instrument. He felt that this tune needed cello in a big way. So, about fifteen cellos were overdubbed onto the piece. Also featured is a big dramatic, multi-dubbed, arpeggiated Beatles style guitar intro.

In spite of his optimistic description of the song, it was during the singles' chart run that Roy Wood left ELO. 'Classic Rock History' critic Brian Kachejian rated it as ELO's 8th best song, calling it a "sentimental grooving ballad." Stereogum contributor Ryan Reed rated it as ELO's 9th best song, saying that "The late-'60s Beatles influence, was never more apparent. From the metallic, descending electric guitar riff (Echoing shades of 'I Want You (She's So Heavy)' to the Indian-tinted cello lines and disjointed stereo panning."

'10538 Overture' was an idea that Jeff (Lynne) brought along to the studio. Roy details the recording session, "After recording the basic backing track the other guys went home, leaving Jeff and myself to run riot with the overdubs. At the time, I was very keen on collecting instruments. I had just acquired a cheap Chinese cello. After we had finished overdubbing the guitars. I sat in the control room trying out this cello and sort of messing around with Jimi Hendrix type riffs. Jeff said, 'That sounds great, why don't we throw it onto the track'. I ended up recording around fifteen of these cello parts. Then as all the instrumentation built up. It really was beginning to sound like some monster heavy metal orchestra. In fact, it sounded just bloody marvellous."

Jeff Lynne, in a 28th March 2006 'No Answer' interview adds, "I had this guitar track, like a real big riff on a guitar. I laid it down in the studio and Roy Wood got his Chinese cello and he overdubbed about fifteen cello riffs. He was double tracking all the time and it sounded fantastic. We thought, it was like 'Wow!' and we just sat round playing it for days."

35.
In this sad position where I lie - callous friends just pass me by...

During the prior sessions for the second album *Shazam*, tensions had escalated between Wayne and Roy primarily. Their interpersonal issues were further exacerbated by an ill-advised venture into cabaret country. The money was good, but the experience rotten. Carl Wayne exited in January 1970, just weeks before the album's release. Wood now made a second proposition to Lynne. He had now joined The Move on the condition that they would soon retire the 'Move' name, then pursue Wood's Electric Light Orchestra (ELO) concept.

In March 1970, The Move released their first, Lynne-era single, 'Brontosaurus'. Another Wood composition, backed with 'Lightnin' Never Strikes Twice,' which was co-written by Price and Mike Sheridan (here credited as Mike Tyler). Wood produced both sides of the single, which reached a reasonable number 7 on the UK singles chart.

The single was a sluggish, dragging grind through Roy doing a "humorous" number, about dancing the Brontosaurus, '*She could really do the Brontosaurus, And she can scream the heebie-jeebies for us.*' The song itself goes into a double time rock out. Providing some relief from the pre-grungy torpor of the main piece.

Considering Roy's very shy and retiring manner at the earlier Move gigs, here Wood debuted the beginnings, of his startling Wizzard image! Replete with huge, back combed hair, huge, platted beard. And with his new facial "star" makeup. Roy wouldn't get run over very easily at night wearing this remarkable and outrageous attire!

'Lightnin' Never Strikes Twice' is a beautiful song by Rick Price and featuring tight double tracked harmony vocals from Rick. I thought this song was almost on an A-side level. It also features superb drumming from Bev Bevan, with some tasty double/rolls. Roy rearranged the song somewhat, from the original version that had appeared on the Sheridan/Price album. The Move plugged this with a performance on *Top of the Pops*.

On 16th May The Move played Joint Meeting 1970, a three-day event at the Eisstadion in Düsseldorf, Germany, with sets by Abacus, Brainbox, Chicken Shack, Colosseum, Edgar Broughton Band, Ekseption, Free, Humble Pie, Octopus, Rare Bird, Steamhammer, Taste and Wallace Collection.

On 23rd August The Move headlined the Knighton Rock Festival at the

Wesley House in Knighton. The noon-to-midnight event also featured sets by Clark Hutchinson, Forever More, Killing Floor, Paper Bubble, Pete Brown and Piblokto!, Roger Bunn's Enjin, and James Litherland Brotherhood (the prototype for Mogul Thrash).

That July sessions commenced for the first Electric Light Orchestra album, involving Wood, Lynne, and Bevan. The process was painstakingly slow, due to the arrangements requiring lots of overdubbing. Plus, Roy's getting to grips with numerous string and wind instruments (cello, double bass, oboe, bassoon, clarinet, recorder, crumhorn). Roy was attempting, to master all these for the sessions. The album would take eleven months to finally complete. Aside from the Knighton appearance the band had effectively retired their live act.

They were still under contract to produce another Move album with their publisher, Essex International, which had just set up a new independent label, Fly Records. Its second release was The Move's ninth single, 'When Alice Comes Back To The Farm,' a Wood penned track. This was backed up by Jeff Lynne's 'What'. The single was their first co-production.

The Move released their third album, *Looking On* in December 1970 on Fly (UK) and through Capitol (USA). It contains the last two A-sides and Lynne's recent B-side. It also had three new songs from Wood ('Feel Too Good', 'Turkish Tram Conductor Blues', plus the title track) and one from Lynne ('Open Up Said The World At The Door'). There was the hidden, miniature co-write 'The Duke Of Edinburgh's Lettuce'. Four of the seven proper tracks all tip the six-to-eight-minute timings.

Roy wanted this to be the final Move record, to disband and get on with the ELO project. In spite of Roy Wood's later condemnations, Don Arden negotiated a higher royalty rate for them. They also needed an infusion of some upfront cash. Arden also cut a deal for a nice £25,000 advance (as Bev says, £8,333 pounds each!). That was part of the process which allowed them to develop the ongoing ELO concept further.

Looking On was co-produced by Wood and Lynne at Advision Studios and also at Philips Studios between May and September 1970. In addition to vocals, guitar, and occasional bass, Roy Wood plays oboe, sitar, banjo, slide guitar, cello, and saxophone on assorted songs. Wood and Lynne play bass and drums, respectively, on 'Feel Too Good', which also features P.P. Arnold and Doris Troy on backup vocals (these two had also provided backing vocals on the Ace Kefford Stand 'For Your Love' single). Wood sings lead on everything, except the two Jeff Lynne numbers.

The engineer on *Looking On*, Roger Wake was very busy in that period. He had worked on numerous 1969–71 Philips recordings, including albums by Ambrose Slade, Cochise, Czar, Gracious, Harsh Reality, Linda Hoyle, and Nucleus. The *Looking On* artwork features a brown, sepia tinged overhead shot. Nameless bald men, standing and crammed closely together. If it is supposed to represent conformity, stability and squareness. It does but with the added effect of being an incredibly dull album cover.

Looking On is not a record I like to listen to. My preference was for Roy's writing earlier on in The Move. There is a kind of sludginess in this music, I don't find particularly attractive. The album met with various reviews — lukewarm in tenor mostly. However, the collected Esoteric remastered release on CD does contain 'Lightnin' Never Strikes Twice'.

In this sad position where I lie - callous friends just pass me by...

'Turkish Tram Conductor Blues' also appeared on the 1971 Ariola compilation *Think – Pop Progress 1971*, a two-LP set with tracks by Elton John, Gary Wright, Humble Pie, Lee Michaels, Man, Paul Brett's Sage, Procol Harum, Strawbs, Supertramp, and Titus Groan.

Rick Price, who was never even told about the ELO sessions summarily left (well - he had to really) The Move when he found out, the other members, were all working on a project without him.

Looking On was released on 11th December 1970. It didn't receive a chart placing. The singles 'Brontosaurus' and 'When Alice Comes Back To The Farm' are both included. 'Brontosaurus' was released on Regal Zonophone and 'Alice' on Fly Records. 'Brontosaurus' spent a good 10 weeks on the chart. 'Alice' received no chart position.

One review of *Looking On* went onto critique, "Fickle, erratic. The Move have always been whatever the times required — gangster soul men, strobe-lit hatchet men, professional flower children, rock revivalists, honest-to-goodness hit paraders and now, eclectic heavies. They have changed direction so often and so drastically that nobody has ever had a chance to relate to them. Just when their gigs at UFO were beginning to give them "head approval" — during a period when "head approval" really meant something. They moved to the safer pastures of the charts and have commuted uncomfortably between the two ever since. Around the time of 'Blackberry Way' with Jimmy Miller producing them and reports of a new album which would confirm Roy Wood as the fine and much underestimated songwriter he is. I thought it might get better for them. But it didn't happen that way. This album sounds a little like the last gasps of this Move, just as *Shazam* marked the end of the previous Move and the departures of Ace Kefford and Trevor Burton."

Message From The Country was the fourth and final Move album. Again, it featured Jeff Lynne, Bev Bevan and Roy Wood. It was released on Harvest on 4th June 1971. They recorded 'Do Ya' and 'California Man' both with that kind of rock 'n' roll vibe that both songwriters Wood and Lynne favoured by that point. 'California Man' was the second last single from The Move. It hit the top ten charts at number 7. 'Do Ya' was released in September 1974. But it failed to chart.

The Move was pretty much over. They only really existed in 'marquee value' and in name terms. They played their final concert as a testimonial for Birmingham City football legend Ray Martin. This was held at the Swan Lake suite in the huge Swan pub. The band headlined over The Idle Race and Raymond Froggatt. For some reason The Move were very late arriving on stage. They took the stage to a chorus of loud booing! At that gig the Move comprised Roy, Jeff, Bev and Richard Tandy on rhythm guitar. They played 'Down On The Bay', 'Tonight', 'Fire Brigade' and covered The Beatles' 'She Came In Through The Bathroom Window' from 'Abbey Road'.

36.
Why don't you turn around and look at me, I often wish I knew you...

Apart from plays on legacy radio and magazine features and mentions, here and there in the heritage monthlies. Publications like *Uncut*, *Mojo*, *Record Collector* etc. The Move basically just completely disappeared out of the history of British bands. Following on are some detailed "what happened to…" explanations about these five unique musicians.

Christopher 'Ace' Kefford

Kefford has at various times suffered immensely. In the late 1980s and into the 1990s, he suffered lapses into mental health issues through trying to deal with these and further addiction issues. Ace maybe the one who probably realises the greater extent of "What ifs" and the "If only I have not done this, or drunk that fated phial of LSD, one dark night in Birmingham".

Allowing forces that capsized his mental abilities and took him over the edge into severe mental illness, over the years, Ace has composed many, many songs. Some are basic demo recordings, showing his variety of abilities in unfinished form. The song frameworks could be adorned further and arranged in many ways. To bring out both the soul and simplicity of some of his writing. For a while, after the rapid ride through The Move. Kefford had put some ensembles together and tried again for success. Which mostly has eluded him. By that I mean, on a commercial level. Which can happen extremely often — in an extremely, high-risk music business.

Ace mentioned in an interview in 2014, "I had come out of hospital, I had six electric shock treatments. And I had a dirty trick played on me! I'm not gonna say anymore in this interview. Subsequently, I've haven't seen a single penny in the way of The Move albums! In the way of any royalties, over the last 50 years in relation to The Move."

He's talked about putting it all in a book and telling the truth. As yet that book from Ace has not materialised. I hope I have covered some of it, in this book. But you can only get as far with what you get. The multifarious machinations of Tony

Secunda and Denny Cordell and their various companies, after all this time? You would be lucky, to get dribs and drabs, here and there, about what really happened. With many of the main players dead. I remember being told once, when digging around in the past, that monetary issues are the crux of the music business. Could be a dangerous occupation. Certainly, the money made from advances etc. didn't go to The Move. How much of it did Tony Secunda and Denny Cordell put away? How much got paid for recording sessions, offices, business overheads? It would require a detective of Rob Caiger's pedigree, legally, to chase a paper trail. If indeed any such paper trails would exist! With other nefarious possibilities happening in and among the late 1960s, who really knows?

After he left The Move, Ace attempted the solo recording, finally released in 2003 as *Ace The Face*. From the over surfeit of LSD and the subsequent paranoia and flashbacks that he had experienced. Secunda was pushing Ace way before he was ready. There had been various other ensembles. The Ace Kefford Stand had morphed into Kefford / Bonham — no not with John Bonham but with Bill Bonham, a young and very talented multi-instrumentalist. Bill looked somewhat like Ace then with his cool, long blond locks and a musician attitude.

Ace had another outfit but apparently, this didn't last very long. They were called Spread Eagle. This grew out of the Kefford/Bonham duo. They had now added a drummer, which I believe may have been Sean Toal from Northern Ireland. Before Kefford/Bonham of course there was the Ace Kefford Stand covered earlier in this book.

Bill Bonham was an up and coming and versatile musician. One of Bill Bonham's regular bands in the 1960s was The Answer with whom he toured in Europe and the Mediterranean. This band was re-named Obs-Tweedle and was fronted by a dynamic young vocalist called Robert Plant. Plant joined after his previous group, Band Of Joy had disbanded.

Bill Bonham remembered, "At a gig we played at Walsall College, Jimmy Page and his manager Peter Grant, came to see us. He offered Robert Plant a job, as singer for the 'New' Yardbirds, who then became Led Zeppelin." Bill Bonham remembers the family connection: "My father who ran the Three Men In A Boat Pub in Walsall suggested Obs-Tweedle. I joined up with cult singer Terry Reid and that was from 1967 into 1968. When I left Reid, Ace Kefford had just abandoned The Stand. Although Ace and myself did play as the Ace Kefford Stand. We also went out as Kefford-Bonham and when we got a drummer, we then changed our name to Spread Eagle."

Spread Eagle did one advertised gig at Rebeca's in Birmingham on 10th June 1970. They supported the popular and charting group The Foundations. The gig was compered by Radio One DJ Dave Cash. Spread Eagle also supported Charlie and Inez Fox on a couple of gigs. As far as I know this band did not record any music. Bill Bonham fills in more detail, "We broke up around 1970. I wish I could remember more. I eventually emigrated to the USA and worked for many years at Disney World in California as an audio-visual expert. I continued to play keyboards in local line-ups and write songs expressing my Christian faith." Sadly, Bill Bonham passed away in 2015. Laurie Hornsby said, "Bill Bonham committed suicide. He was living in Los Angeles."

Why don't you turn around and look at me, I often wish I knew you…

In a slight but related aside, a Birmingham group dubbed the greatest "lost" band of the rock's psychedelic era is back in the studio, after the discovery of their missing masterpiece. In a story that has echoes of the Beach Boys' mysterious, unpublished album. The industry has long swirled with rumours about Fairfield Ski's 1973 debut LP. This line-up and band featured the young Bill Bonham. Critics described the eponymous album, recorded at such top London studios as Abbey Road, Apple and Trident, as one of the "important missing pieces in the jigsaw of prog rock's story." The band members Bill Bonham (keyboards), Dave Hynds (drums), Nigel Wright (guitar and lead vocals) and Matt Bridger (bass) thought it was the piece of work that would propel them to stardom. But the high costs of the polished production, finally took its toll and it was sidelined by financial problems. For all you cool completist cats, it's now available to listen to on Spotify under Fairfield Ski.

A bassist known to Ace from around Birmingham, called Terry Biddulph, auditioned and started working with Ace. Terry was in the early pre-Rockstar formation of the next Ace vehicle. At the time, they were simply known as The Stand. They all drove down to the furthest southwest part of England to play a bunch of live gigs around Devon and Cornwall. This pre-Rockstar band did record some demos.

Terry remembers co-writing with Ace on at least two or three tunes. John Grimley was another young guitarist living in Corby. "Bob Grimley, my brother, was in a band called Scene Stealer. They released one album called *First Offence* and they did have a little success. This was through a label Rebel Records. They were the label that Ace was hoping to promote us, but that didn't happen. Scene Stealer were doing well, and my brother says to me, 'Do you remember Ace Kefford from The Move?' He says, 'Well, they're looking for a guitarist and it's come through Rebel we're working for. I put your name forward.' So, the next thing, I got an audition down at Chris's cottage in Inkberrow in Worcestershire. It was a fixed old cottage, and it was very small."

Ace clears up some confusion about the Atlantic advance, for the Ace Kefford Stand. "We were living in a cottage, called 'Interberga', a beautiful Grade 2 listed building. Earlier, Cozy Powell thought that I had said. 'I'd ripped off Atlantic Records, for about £70,000 grand.'"

And that's how Cozy and others assumed Ace could afford this lifestyle. The funky cottage, plus the Ragbag boutique that Ace and his wife Jenny ran, located at the top of Evesham Street in Redditch. But apparently, it was Jenny who had come from a family with lots of money. They were based on Jersey and the family were not short of a few cruzeiros. Ace rebuts this assumption by Cozy Powell. "That story from Cozy, about me ripping off Atlantic Records. That's a load of old bollocks. I never took a penny off any musician ever! But in fact, I put a lot of my own money into bands."

Ace recalled moving into the quaint Inkberrow village. After the council re-routed roads in Redditch, it was impossible for local businesses to make any money. With a low passing footfall their Ragbag business went bust. An unknown commentator says, "They sold really way-out stuff, coloured flares, flowered cheese cloth dresses, beads, feathers and Sgt Pepper-style stuff. I used to go with my friend on Saturday afternoon. Then to the Unicorn on Saturday night and the Chinese restaurant in Evesham Street for a curry. We got invited to a party at Chris's cottage.

Had a great jam session in there one night. A song 'Don't Let Your Deal Go Down' was jammed that night."

Jenny Kefford was nothing if extremely resourceful. She also brought in income, working as a hairdresser. The Kefford's by now had two sons, Gary and Darryl, and appeared to be living a life of domestic stability.

Inkberrow lies near the towns of Stratford on Avon, Great Malvern and it's around a 25-mile drive away from Birmingham. This compact village has been often quoted as the inspiration for the fictional town Ambridge in *The Archers*, the long-running and immensely popular BBC Radio drama.

Towards the mid and later 1970s, Ace still had the impetus to form one last attempt at a band. To record his original songs and further co-writes. Even, if they did not hit the live boards full on. This was an endeavour called Rockstar. Or, on one gig poster, which advertised them, as Ace Kefford and His Rockstar (sic). Enter another shady but also well-loved character. Wilf Pine was a handy enforcer, he was also, a well-known underground villain. Ace, in an interview from about 10 years ago says, "Yeah! Wilf arranged all this, and he managed to get this released through MCA records. "I really didn't like the name — it was shite."

I can remember years ago, reading (literally) just one paragraph somewhere about Rockstar. I remember thinking 'This is a strange choice for a name!' The name could invite various comments or even snide remarks. A possible inference about, or presumption of stardom in the name.

According to USA–based music writer Dave Thompson, who went on to manage Melanie (Melanie Anne Safka Schekeryk, 3rd February 1947 – 23rd January 2024), "I was working my first ever job at the National Rock Star music paper, which started out at that exact same time. I was buying it throughout its (short) lifespan and the whole Ace thing just stuck with me all these years. Because it was so, I dunno, desperate! They did a tie-in, with the short-lived music paper 'National Rock Star'. The first issue came out with a sew-on patch saying, 'I'm a Rock Star'. That kind of summed it up! It was the worst name for a mag and a worst name for a band… I never heard the group, but I remember thinking they deserved one another."

Rockstar only managed two gigs, one being The Boat Club in Nottingham on Saturday 21st May 1977. The Nottingham Boat Club is indeed the stuff of legend. Everybody who was anybody played the intimate 250-capacity venue back in the day, which closed in 1982. The other Ace / Rockstar gig was at The Corn Exchange in Faringdon on Friday 16th September 1977. The poster informed the public that the first Rockstar single was to be called 'Too Late To Cry' and it was to be released before Christmas 1976. Unfortunately, the single was never ever heard of again.

Rockstar, after demoing and rehearsing solidly for months in Inkberrow, went down to London under the umbrella management of Wilf Pine. There they recorded an album's worth of music with the producer Steve Rowland at IBC Studios at London's Portland Place. Rockstar was said to have signed a three-year, worldwide recording contract with MCA Records.

However, the single mentioned in this particular article did get released. The A-side was 'Mummy' and the B-side was called 'Over The Hill'. Both sides were written by Kefford. 'Mummy' was a poignant tune and dealt with the break-up of parents as seen through the hurting eyes of a confused younger child. Ace's vocals

Why don't you turn around and look at me, I often wish I knew you…

are caressed by filtered, chorused guitars.

Tony Ware cast his memory back to the last song he recorded with Ace. For Ware (who got a little emotional during our interview), it was "a very poignant moment". "Ace was lying on the floor in the studio with me. He suddenly started strumming out the chords and he just came out with the song 'Mummy'. It was a very different song to all the others. He was playing the song on acoustic. I played a couple of chords in there. I'm going to tell you — do you know I mentioned Quick Riches? Well, Rockstar have lastly written that song 'Mummy', and that features the Quick Riches backing orchestra. Steve Rowland said, we could put strings on it. I don't think we were involved with the string arrangement. It was just dumb, you know, without us. What we found out was, that it was Cliff Richard's fucking orchestra." Hence the "Quick Riches" joke.

I can't understand why Rockstar didn't catch on somehow. 'Over The Hill' is a solid rocker with buzzing guitars and a simple strong chorus. This song is forceful and has (particularly around the choruses) a distinct David Bowie flavour. Was Ace remembering, his and Trevor Burton's initial meeting with Bowie at the Cedar Club, those years before? The event which fuelled the impetus, to form, what became The Move.

"'Only 17' was a really great song and we really loved it. It was very Birmingham, very The Move, very ELO. With all this 'ding, ding, ding' and we played it to death. Like a bunch of 12-year-old kids. We were really excited with the finished product. Steve Rowland looked at us all and he looked at Chris. He said, 'Who wrote this?' And of course, Chris said, 'Oh I did' and Steve Rowland says, 'It sounds, like the fucking Beatles?' Really? We couldn't wait to play it to Wilf Pine. Wilf Pine walked in the mixing room. We played it at full whack and Wilf hated it. He said the same as Steve Rowland. 'It sounds like the fucking Beatles.' 'Mummy' was recorded just before that Christmas. There was a lot of very good material. A good 17 songs in all… We had finished the album recordings and then came 'Mummy,' which was the last song recorded. Steve Rowland had the string arrangements put on. Roy Featherstone (the head of A&R at MCA Records) came to the studio, to listen to all the recorded tracks. He picked out 'Mummy' straight away. The problem with 'Mummy' is… it wasn't the band. That wasn't the song. It was just a completely different song to all the other songs we recorded."

Tony also examines the relationships at the time. "I was very close to Ace then — you've got to be when you're working with somebody. And when you are writing with people. His personality then? Ace was great. I can't find any bad news about Ace at all. When I worked with him, he was absolutely fine. I remember one night; we went back to the Lancaster Gate Hotel at 4:00am… when we just couldn't sleep. Ace and me, we walked up to Euston Station. We were trying to find the tea wagon. You could smell the rain, the trains and seeing all the down and outs. It was evocative, walking around London at that early time of morning. Experiencing the thrill of recording our music."

"Tony Noble, he was our main roadie guy. He was a great road manager — Tony exemplified what being a roadie was all about. We went back to IBC studios and recorded all that. Steve Rowlands who recorded Rockstar. Was already an established producer, having worked with The Herd, The Pretty Things, The Real Thing; plus, controversial singer P.J. Proby and many others. A current 'Look Out' news feature, excitedly talks of acetates being prepared from demo tapes. Pine had shopped the band, and he favoured the deal, that MCA came up with. Apparently, he had secured a publishing deal with Heathside Music. David Apps of Evolution was appointed as Rockstar's agent.

Of course, Tony Ware felt comfortable around Pine. "Wilf Pine was our manager, and I really loved him. Well, he would do everything for us and our families. Our wives and boyfriends and girlfriends and whatever. But when you say to people, Charlie Kray (The eldest of the three the eldest of the Kray brothers) is one of the nicest people. He was the loveliest gentlemen I've ever met in my whole life... Charlie had just come out of gaol. The next day he came to London to IBC Studios. To see Wilf and to also meet Rockstar. Next thing we know that same night, he took us all out for a meal to a Mexican restaurant. It cost a fortune, and it was all just incredible."

Wilf Pine was industrious. He had also started organising a tour. It looked like all the Rockstar ducks were being set up, firmly in a row. Other songs mentioned, that had been recorded, were titled as follows: 'Only 17', Wild Rose', 'You Are Your Own Best Friend', 'Lily' and "Too Late To Cry'. And of course, 'Mummy' and 'Over The Hill'.

However, soon John Grimley realised things were not progressing. But he didn't know why. Was the deal called off by MCA, after the 'Mummy' single's release? Did Wilf Pine and Ace fall out? It's hard to say. Grimley certainly didn't know what happened. It ended quietly — it just petered out and that was it. Tony Ware said, "Ace had everything, and it was very difficult, and I don't really want to comment too much on that".

IBC Recording Studios become internationally famous after being used by recording artists like The Kinks, The Who, Bee Gees, Cream and tons of others. IBC enjoyed a good name as a top recording studio. Due to the success, and the large number of hits garnered by its clients, like the Who in the late 1960s. Chas Chandler renamed the place Portland Studios and bought it in June 1978. However, Don Arden bought the facility and used it for recording for his Jet Records label. The studio was run by David Arden.

Seven Ace Kefford demos were found in a reel box entitled 'Interberga'. These feature Ace and his Gibson Jumbo. Probably recorded around the mid 1970's. These are posted to YouTube by Nicola and Melvin Hancox. Songs with possibility, simple, strong and showing further evidence of his writing talent. Preceding Rockstar, Ace had attempted various ensembles. One prior to this was named Gritt. This ensemble included his two cousins Chris and Reg Jones, (also Terry Biddulph and Clive Robson). The Jones's were both considered very solid musicians. Both brothers had a long pedigree, and both were very much a big part of the Brum Beat scene for a long time. They were playing all original material according to posters. They were managed by Roy Graham, a local promoter and put on a lot of gigs in the Birmingham and Midlands area.

In July 1975, a newspaper feature reported that they had signed a deal. "Gritt formed by ex-Move guitarist Ace Kefford and brothers Reg and Chris Jones. Have signed a contract with Roy Graham and Associates, guaranteeing them one million

Why don't you turn around and look at me, I often wish I knew you…

pounds, over a five-year period." Terry Biddulph and Chris Robson were the other musicians. Gritt lasted for just over a year. They did some local gigs. Probably at The Railway in Curzon Street — a small but very popular pub venue in Birmingham.

Also, a version of Ace Kefford's Band was advertised as playing the Watchfield Free Festival. This festival was held from the 23rd through to 31st August in 1975. Alan Clayson sent me a poster for this event, outlining the bands on the bill, including his own Argonauts group. Ace Kefford's Band is on the Thursday afternoon bill. It was advertised in the *International Times* as the People's Free festival. The former military site at Watchfield, became the location of the People's Free Festival which had been held during the previous three years, despite opposition, in Windsor Great Park.

The Windsor Free Festivals had been violently terminated by the police in 1974. This new site was offered as a venue due to the government's embarrassment at previous police actions and was attended by several thousand people. Musicians who performed there also included Hawkwind and Vivian Stanshall. Watchfield Free Festival was the only free festival to be government sponsored (with assistance by then-Home Secretary Roy Jenkins) or be given official recognition.

Terry Biddulph also remembered some details about Gritt. "Roy Graham was a promoter who lived in Yardley. He also went under the name of Graham Bodman — his real name. (Bodman's father was killed, in the Birmingham Pub Bombings in 1974). Gritt played all original material. It was written exclusively by Chris Jones, Ace's uncle. The material was heavy rock: a blend between prog rock and pop. Quite melodic and of its time.

Chris Jones apparently had an opportunity, to join The Moody Blues prior to Justin Hayward and just after Denny Laine left. He was a very good, lead guitarist and songwriter. Reg Jones was also a good front man, with an excellent voice. There was another iteration of Gritt before I joined. But my understanding is that they were not together very long. Sean Toal joined the band (which was by then called Rockstar) around April 1976. I left to join a group called Sorahan in September 1976. Principally because I didn't think the band was going anywhere and Sorahan had gotten a recording deal."

Tony Ware, who was in Rockstar remembers details on Gritt. "I used to hang around The Railway in Curson Street quite a lot. Ozzy used to come down there and Robert Plant. Plant was also in a band with Ace's uncles, The Way of Life with the Jones brothers (Plant was also in a Mod covers band called Seasons before this). They used to regularly play at The Railway Club. They were okay, I would say Gritt because Terry Biddulph was with them. Yeah, they were very talented. They never really went any further. They never broke out. What we all realised was, you have to leave the city — and it was called London."

Terry Biddulph remembers answering an advert, "I think the band was called Spread Eagle before this. Gritt advertised for a bass player and a drummer. It was me and I think a guy called Chris Robson on drums. I auditioned and it was Reggie Jones's brother, Chris Jones. Some of the stuff was really good. It's of its time if you listen to it now. I would estimate, I was in Gritt for a year. We didn't get a deal, but a good few people came to see us perform. It was a funny time then. Chris Kefford was the draw, because he was the one that had fame. I think Chris was quite disillusioned around that time. I don't know if it's what he really wanted to do. So, at the time, I did enjoy Gritt a lot, but there was a lot of personal aggro in the band. I thought they were much better musically than Rockstar. There was a degree of aggro between them basically and we fell out over money. Really it was between Ace's uncles, and they didn't speak after that as far as I know. It's an unusual story."

Terry resumes his connection with Ace: "After Gritt, we had a pre-Rockstar band. We did a few tours of Cornwall, and we stayed down there for a bit. After I left, Wilf Pine came in and they had more serious management. They signed an international deal with MCA. The single came out and then nothing happened. I left and joined Sorahan. Sorahan released a T. Sorahan written (and Zella Studios recorded) single, 'With His Siller In His Hand'. (Siller meaning money or silver). Sorahan were signed to the Bronze label at the time, but briefly."

Nicola Hancox gave me some further information on Chris and Reg: "Reg Jones is my dad; Chris Jones was my uncle and Chris Kefford is my cousin. Ace is the son of Reg and Chris' eldest sister Lilian. Ace's father was also named Chris. He was known by the family as 'Big Chris', he was a tall and well-built man. Ace's siblings are Janet, Lynne, Paul and Karen who are twins. Reg Jones passed away in 2004, Chris Jones passed away in 2009."

Chris and Reg Jones also headed up an important (certainly within the interlocking Birmingham music history) group named The Way Of Life. This ensemble featured both future Led Zeppelin drummer John Bonham and bass player Dave Pegg. Pegg went onto Fairport Convention among others. The Way of Life also featured musicians, that went onto other Midlands outfits, like the Lemon Tree, Idle Race, The World of Oz, Locomotive, Cathedral and Quartz. Hilariously, at one stage John Bonham was sacked for playing too loudly. No such problems for John later on when he thundered on international world stages and arenas!

The Jones brothers rebuilt the group by bringing in Mac Poole, then Barry Smith (Baz St Leger) who'd worked with them previously in The Chucks during 1965. Another drummer called Barry Spencer Scrannage also played with them. Although I'm not sure of the entire chronology of the drummers. The final incarnation recorded some material for Polydor Records, before splitting up in late 1968. The Jones brothers continued to play live on the local scene.

Laurie Hornsby recalled that after Reggie's funeral, "We went back to the Odd Fellows pub, just outside of Redditch. Chris had set all the gear up and everything. We played all the old rock 'n' roll songs that we used to play in The Chantelles, down at the Warstock pub, where they used to play. Jeff Lynne was in the Chantelles."

After The Chantelles, Chris Jones had been part of The Chucks who, like The Rockin' Berries, The Hellions (featuring a young Jim Capaldi) and Shades Five, had all served a professional apprenticeship in Germany. On their return to Birmingham, they decided to reform The Way Of Life. Bringing in guitarist "Sprike" Hopkins (from Gerry Levene's Avengers) and on bass, Tony Clarkson, who'd once backed Nicky James. James was also willing to join The Way Of Life too (as their second vocalist). Barry Smith was the drummer.

In the afternoon before their first gig, at Club Cedar on Constitution Hill, they tried out various drummers in the darkened venue. With its various smells of disinfectant and echoes of the previous night's intake of alcohol and tobacco. "John

Why don't you turn around and look at me, I often wish I knew you...

Bonham showed up and he literally demanded the job," exclaimed Reg Jones. "He told all the other hopefuls to go home." They were all impressed by his confidence and arrogance. They complied, and John was in the band. They began to get booked regularly at Club Cedar. Alan Clayson noted, "Even though one member's bar tab, one night, swallowed up the entire band's agreed fee."

Tony Clarkson was soon replaced by the versatile Danny King. After this, The Way Of Life were taken on by manager Rik Gunnell. Gunnell was much less provincial in outlook. He managed the chart-topping Georgie Fame. He also had fingers up various pie charts! Rik Gunnell booked the amazed lads, into the Bag O' Nail's Club in Soho, London. They attracted a good audience, with luminaries such as, Manitas De Plata, Paul McCartney and Tom Jones, amongst the audience.

This is where provincial attitudes and the big city meet. In the form of Danny King who in Birmingham was considered just to the right side of Jesus, as a singer and player. Plus, as described earlier in the book, the owner of an amazing R&B soul collection that The Move had first dibs on.

Danny King may have been thinking he was sauntering around on the *Coronation Street* set. Danny pulls out a packet of Park Drive cigarettes and a box of England's Glory matches. Danny then proceeds to light up onstage. Under the glare of both the spotlights and the West End, London audience. A well-aimed, drumstick, bounces, thwacking right off the top of his head. Ouch! From further back on the stage, John Bonham was bellowing for all he was worth. "This is the fucking Bag O' Nails, you know Danny!" Bonham was screaming his throat out! Danny King rubbed his head, remembering, "I loved Bonzo. Beneath all the big front, was a warm and gentle man."

As well as having a projectile voice, John Bonham also (and in the same decibel register as Bev Bevan) was insanely loud behind the drum kit. Many promoters were complaining, as the mixing desk lights are all going way into the red. And that was just Bonzo's drums and high velocity playing. The Way Of Life were asked at many venues, could they somehow, please turn down the volume? Bonham had a better idea. He thought The Way Of Life needed much louder equipment. So, the volume level went up!

There was yet another Ace-evolved band called Prima Donna. It was reported that they had a Monday residency at the Birmingham Railway Inn on Curzon Street. Laurie Hornsby remembered the popular pub venue, "where The Railway used to be is called Millennium Point now."

It was further revealed that Ace had been lumbered with contractual difficulties for two years which meant, he couldn't really do any work. Prima Donna was a three-piece band. Ace was on bass and lead vocals. The line-up was Chris Jones on lead guitars and vocals Sean Toal on drums.

Ace recalled, "Prima Donna also went down to London and played a few pub gigs. It wasn't gonna work. I got tired of it all. The rehearsals at the cottage for months. I would write a whole lotta new songs, a lot of new material. I'd get publicity photographs done of the band. We would go to the studio then we would do demos. You would send them out with little response. I just thought, 'I can't do this anymore'. I don't know whether mentioning The Move, at those times, was a good thing at all."

Chris Jones had a poignant memory. "The last time I saw John Bonham, was when he came to The Bromsgrove Baths, two months before he died. We had gotten a band together called Prima Donna with a guy called Sean (Toal) on the drums and Ace and myself. We invited John on stage, and he played with us. That was the last time I ever saw him."

During a break in rehearsals, John Bonham had gone to see Reg and Chrissie Jones' new band, which also featured Ace on bass, play at Shenstone College. Also in the audience was John's old mate, Johnny Hill. They both got up on stage, to back the Jones' boys.

Ace was experiencing the effects of heavy drinking around this period. Possibly to relieve the pressure of the continuing attempts to bring a band through to success. He was going down the local pub all the time, often in the company of John Bonham and / or Ozzy Osbourne. "I had woken up with a very blank mind and no real memory."

The blank out in Ace's memory was from December 10th, which is my birthday all through to January 12th, which is my son Daryl's birthday. "I could not remember a thing." This sounds very much like an alcohol-induced blackout or a series of alcohol induced blackouts. Apparently, Ace was extremely disinhibited during this period. He was doing a lot of drinking in his local. Although he didn't get barred from the pub. He was probably spending too much money in there. One night, he ripped both sleeves off a bemused guy who had just entered the pub. This chap was happily wearing his brand-new overcoat. Just that now he was spontaneously setting a new trend in sleeveless, heavy winter overcoats.

In terms of further Ace Kefford activity or reported news and media and bands, after this resourceful, continuously, hard-working period... It all went completely quiet... I did find out in the latter stages of writing this book that in 1998, Reg Jones (vocals) and Melvin Hancox, his son-in-law (guitar) had reactivated The Way Of Life with Ace on bass and vocals and Mick Bonham (John Bonham's brother) on drums. They did play a few festivals together. One festival was called 'The Gathering' and that was a successful gig. One of the songs in the set, at the time was a new Ace Kefford rock 'n' roll number called 'Red Leather Shoes'. Two other songs by Ace were 'You're A Failure' and 'Dancing On Air'.

In another little-known fact, Nicki Hancox, the wife of Melvin Hancox, reveals some further information. "At that time Ace said he was chatting to Carl "Charlie" Wayne about reactivating The Move. So, Ace's presence became irregular, and the band continued on without him."

This journey travelled on until Reg Jones's passing (in 2004) which directly led to The Melvin Hancox Band, as it stands today. Melvin recalls that Ace is really quite a character and he is lots of fun to be around. Nikki Hancox expands upon Melvin's beginnings, "Trevor Burton was also very helpful to Melvin, in his beginning years as starting out as a musician. Trevor used to run a venue in the back room at the Hen and Chickens in Langley in the 1980s. This is where Melvin first saw Chicken Shack and Stevie Marriott. Trevor gave Melvin some support slots when he was still at school."

In a jokey way Melvin and Trevor were thought of as 'rivals,' on the Birmingham music scene. Melvin remembers Trevor saying, "This will get them talking, we're taking it to the Gonosphere!"

Nothing was heard of, or from Ace Kefford for years. Filling in some back story now, Barry Smith remembers, "We met up again through John Bonham's funeral and wake." Bonzo was remembered on 10th October 1980 in a small service,

Why don't you turn around and look at me, I often wish I knew you...

having died suddenly on September 25th. He was cremated, then memorialised at the small church in Rushock, Worcestershire. "I was working on my studio in Worcestershire. Ace wanted some work and then we both worked on it together. I would pull into where the cottage (Interberga) was, just on the main road. Ace was there on the step. Always dead-on time, with his sandwich box and flat cap. He was always ready to work." Both men did a lot of work in those days. Away from the direct music business. Working every day, up to sixteen hours, putting in some hard graft.

Many years later, seemingly out of nowhere, The *Bradford Telegraph and Argus*, dated 16th February 1994 ran a feature called 'Next Move For Ace'. It was one entire page, with a picture of Ace, looking happy and relaxed. Smiling, he is wearing glasses with long hair. There was a number attached to the feature. This informed readers, that he was looking for a "good rock 'n' roll manager". The feature basically described the history of The Move, in some very broad strokes and Ace's move to Bradford. It described him successfully completing The Bridge House program in Bradford. Here he was stabilising himself and he was living in the city for a while. During that time, after rehab Ace recorded a good few songs direct onto cassette, just him and acoustic guitar.

As I was finishing this book, Ace's acoustic demos were posted to Facebook by Martin Kinch. These include some other unheard songs. The six songs are, 'No More Running For Cover', 'Shank's Pony', 'Rock And Rolling' (For Peace)', Hold On Tight', 'Another Victim Of The Game' and 'We've Gotta Save The World'.

During his stay in Bradford, Kefford recorded three last tantalising demos with Dave Pegg of Fairport Convention. They were posted on YouTube approximately ten years ago. Ace agreed to put them out, from a reasonable, sounding cassette copy. They are very good. All have sterling vocals by Ace. They have a 'Born Again' alternative, country rock feel. The opening cut is a rousing, clarion call to 'Love And Peace'. The second song features prominent violin and is called 'Dancing In The Light', another sunny song of redemption. The lyrics are hopeful and energising. *"The past no longer haunts me, the future's looking bright."* This song denotes coming through immense difficulties and making it through to the other side.

The third cut is very expansive and named 'The Calling'. *"You have to play by the rules, you sinners and fools. When I turn out the light, that's when I hear the calling."* I had heard this song once before as, when he lived in Bradford, I had visited Ace with my then fiancé Andrea. We were staying in York, and I'd read that newspaper article. Then we both drove over the Pennines to Bradford. We actually met with him at his apartment. Ace played songs for us on acoustic guitar. It's a long time ago, but I remember 'The Calling' being one of those played. That is another story too. One song was also 'Love And Peace'.

All three demoed songs, communicate the elevated (and poignant) feelings of a man who has come through an enormous life struggle. Who has accepted certain facts, about his life and glaring issues. About choices or behaviours, which unknowingly, involved him in his own downfall. The songs are autobiographical, honest, but also very positive. Apart from Dave Pegg on bass, who also produced. It features other members of Fairport Convention. Ace was then living in Bradford, after a successful stint in rehab.

Dave Pegg remembers the sessions, which took place at his Woodworm Studios. All three songs were recorded on 4th November 1994. "It was a favour to an old mate. I knew Ace from The Move... who were always one of my favourite bands. The session was mixed at the same time and Ace took away the masters and the mixes. We tried to find one when I compiled the 'Box Of Peggs' retrospective but with no success."

Ace in an interview from 2004 remembers one thing about Bradford. "I met up with a drummer who had been in the band Smokie. A guy called Pete Spencer. He took me back to where he lived. Smokie were alright — they had some pop hits, but they didn't have the image of The Move or anything. He had a recording studio in a massive looking mansion house. I'm thinking 'I'm just coming out of a fucking rehab and I'm totally skint.'"

I remember in a phone call with Dave Ball that Ace had gone to London with the said new 1994 demo recordings. He took some meetings, to play the tape to some music people, (Possibly his old mucker Muff Winwood was one?) which must've taken some guts after such a long time out of the business.

I hope Ace will put it out there one day — just to let people enjoy it. A collected CD from Ace on that level (Similar to Trevor Burton's recent *Long Play* CD release) may not sell much these days (as nothing really does), but as a statement of his artistry, it would be really wonderful. Gather up the Spread Eagle, Gritt, Kefford Bonham, Prima Donna, Rockstar material. Put it out there for people to listen too. If the quality is good enough, why not?

John Grimley (who had played guitar in Rockstar) had driven Ace, and Grimley's friend and music lover Richard Jackson to The Locarno in West Bromwich. This was on 28th April 1981. This was the nearest anyone ever came to seeing any sort of Move reunion, in that Bev Bevan, Roy Wood, with guitarist Mike Hopkins and Ace came up on stage, to thrash out 'I Can Hear The Grass Grow' and 'California Man'. The Move (on that day) also cranked out 'Watch Your Step' (with Ace singing) and 'Shake Rattle And Roll'.

"Well, me, Chris and my mate Richard, we walked in and Roy Wood was about 20 feet away and Chris stopped and Roy Wood went, 'Chris!'. They ended up putting their arms out and giving each other a big hug. Chris was nervous about meeting Roy and Bev again," recalls Grimley.

There was no rehearsal, probably just a couple of minutes of remembering chords backstage. But yet — even through that raw, unrehearsed noisy get together the vibes and the chemistry was still evident. All it needed was Mr Wayne and Mr Burton to arrive and to ramp up that bands unequalled, elemental power.

The charity gig also featured Gerry Levene & The Avengers (with Gerry Levene, Jim Onslow, Mike Hopkins, Roy Wood and Bev Bevan), Mike Sheridan & The Nightriders, Willie and The Poorboys, Pat Wayne and the Beachcomers, Jimmy Powell & The Five Dimensions.

Ace felt some old animosities were still there and he noticed it at Heartbeat '86, another charity gig. Bev Bevan helped to organise the star-studded charity concert at Birmingham's NEC Arena. The charity would go on to make over £1million for Birmingham Children's Hospital. Ace thought about a second very momentary, loose 'Move' reunion of sorts. "Roy had Rick Price on bass." Ace feels Roy might have fallen off the stage, if he had the mighty Kefford jumping around. "All I did in the end, was bang a tambourine, in the finale with Robert Plant, George Harrison Jeff Lynne, you name them."

Ace's mental health issues, combined with his addictive processes saw him entering and working through therapy programs (and no doubt the 12 Step Programme). He attended rehabs in the 1990s and further recovery programs. Ace also spent time in sheltered accommodation. This being a typical route for an individual coming through the rehab system. In both the UK and the USA rehabilitation traditions. Ace never spoke about The Move or subsequent musical endeavours. He kept a low profile, but as he got older, his attitudes began to change. He began to feel, a very deserved pride in The Move. The initial flame of which, he and Trevor Burton had instigated.

Funnily enough Ace and Trevor Burton did play again, as part of a tribute fundraiser for Terry Wallace, aged 66, a founding member of Carl Wayne and The Vikings, who died in 2008. A post said, "Self-taught Mr Wallace's last performance came at his own benefit gig in Witton's Barn Social Club last year (2007). The gig included performances from other top names from the Birmingham music scene of the 1960s, including Mike Sheridan, Danny King, Trevor Burton and Ace Kefford. Laurie Hornsby was up at the bar with Steve Gibbons, Steve said, "Have a look at Ace. He hasn't lost it at all. He was fantastic."

Ace leads a balanced life these days. Ace was finally diagnosed with the debilitating mental / bodily illness of bipolar disorder. He was prescribed Lithium, which is used to balance out the incredibly, see-sawing, mental swings, caused by this acute condition. Unfortunately, he also suffered an accident causing some spinal injuries and a subsequent stroke in 2014. Ace was left unnoticed for a long 23 hours. Apart from the damage done to his vocal chords, his personality and his mental health are in good, orderly balance. Ace is not able to write and sing, after the accident and stroke. He is close to and in touch with both of his sons, Gary and Darryl and to the larger Kefford family.

Martin Kinch from the Cherry Blossom Clinic website and related Facebook page puts out welcome and regular information from Ace to the many people interested, in his ongoing well-being (me included).

At Christmas 2023, Ace and Martin did a charming and warm "Christmas Message from Ace" which was funny and heartwarming to watch.

Ace has a really funny sense of humour, and an impish remembrance of days past and an incredibly detailed memory. In one interview, he talks about Bev accidentally ripping down a toilet receptacle off the wall in some dump on the road somewhere. Bev didn't know his own strength It's just such a hilarious, small moment but very, very funny. This must be a deep and great relief for Ace.

That after so many years of inner torment of trying to self-medicate with drugs and alcohol. Striving for any answer, to that which had constantly ailed him. That which had afflicted him so badly and for so long. Leading to some very destructive life choices and dangerous blind alleys.

In many ways, Ace is a living miracle, after suffering so much. Now, he can enjoy his latter days, with some balance and some peace of mind. Many people don't realise addiction to alcohol and / or drugs can be a way of coping with immense and overpowering fears, anxieties and often also, reactions to out of balance chemical reactions within the sufferers' body. As Ace himself says, "I live in the day." As people in successful recovery will know, 'It's just one day at a time.'

Carl Wayne

Bev Bevan saw the gradual eroding of Roy and Carl's relationship, musically and therefore in friendship. "Basically, Roy and Carl became distant as that last year went on. Carl became pissed off because he felt he was being rowed out as the lead singer guy. I think Carl could see how much money Roy was making, writing all the songs. Roy and I, even though we did the cabaret thing, we didn't wanna do it anymore. Roy became wary of Carl, because he always had these prospective, business things going on."

After The Move, Carl looked back at his first, initial recording project. "Even though we carried on for a while, for me, The Move with the departures of Ace Kefford and Trevor Burton was already finished. I recorded an album with Heads, Hands and Feet (a band that apparently signed, for a colossal advance at the time, a reported £500,000) this was a band perhaps best known for their gunslinging guitarist. A versatile, fluid player called Albert Lee. "We recorded an album for Polydor, which was never released. Chas Hodges, Albert Lee and Pete Gavin (drummer) did the kind of stuff, that I should've been doing after The Move. I had been castigated, for what I did when I left The Move. Don Arden, always wanted Tom Jones in Vegas and in 1969 when I left The Move, the biggest thing in the world then was Elvis Presley, Tom Jones and Engelbert Humperdinck. Don Arden saw me in that role, so we put me together with Don Black. We recorded a single which embarrasses me to this day. It was called 'Maybe God's Got Something Up His Sleeve'. I remember Annie Nightingale, who was a good friend of mine reviewed it and said, 'I think Carl has done this one for a joke'. It was really bad, and I should not have done that — that was a definite wrong move. Don Arden fixed me up with a major deal with RCA, quite a bit of advance money involved. I went for the money, but I made the wrong choice. The RCA album was available in Japan but has long been deleted generally. It featured a variety of material and a son of MOR / AOR audience. It includes cuts like I did the album with Heads, Hands and Feet four years later. We did 'Respect Yourself' and 'Song For You'. I think they were pretty good, those ones."

Carl often thought about The Move and in one line he says The Move "were destined to succeed but they were equally destined to fail…" Did it goad the band towards any form of reunion? Only Carl Wayne, who was always the personal glue that held them together, had made (several) attempts to reform them. He was the ongoing instigator. Personality-wise, he got on with them all. He was a diplomat and essentially a charming individual. Deep down, his first and deepest love, was the first five-piece Move. He has often been quoted as saying The Move were at their best, before the first singles did any chart business in early 1967.

Carl Wayne recorded three tracks with ELO in February 1973 at AIR Studio Two. The sessions consisted of the following cuts, 'Your World' (Take Two), 'Get A Hold Of Myself' (Take Two), 'Mama' (Take One). All songs were composed by Jeff Lynne. These three recordings featured the 'electric' part of ELO but minus the strings section. Carl Wayne was searching for a new song(s) to record as a single.

Why don't you turn around and look at me, I often wish I knew you…

Something with a heavier more soulful approach. David Arden reflected that Carl could be quite magpie-like at times, in his many changes of mood and direction towards his music and career. He wanted to move away from the earlier lighter pop he had been directed in under the earlier management.

He had signed with Don Arden, who suggested a recording session with ELO. Lynne wrote two brand new songs and they did a re-interpret of 'Mama'. Personally I thought 'Your World' had a really nice edge to it. It was good to hear that Wayne, raw vocalising again, outside of The Move. Carl would've liked to expand this further, "I would've liked to have done a dozen of Jeff songs from scratch, sit down with some great players and see what we can come up with. Not that Jeff needs it — but I'd love it."

The sleeve notes mention "Carl was joined for the sessions by Jeff Lynne, Richard Tandy, Bev Bevan and Mike D. Albuquerque. Carl was pretty much into a Lovelace Watkins type scene. He didn't like it very much. I think he was misguided by his old managers. Carl arrived at AIR Studios in the evening, in 'high spirits' and 'happy as a summer morning". He loved working with some old pals again and handed out a good number of bottles of white wine. Sadly, the tracks were never finished and the session multitracks remained lost, until discovered again this year (2002)." This second CD with the three songs was called *The Lost Planet*. The entire digitally remastered double CD was released in 2003. Again, under the helm of Rob Caiger and Rob Keyloch's remix and production values. The sessions were digitally remastered by Peter Mew at Abbey Road Studios.

Not everyone was impressed by Carl's immense professionalism and his choice of career direction. David Arden and his father Don were in the audience when Carl gave one of his first, cabaret type shows, in Birmingham at The Cedar. "We heard a voice behind us saying 'I always thought he was a fucking cunt. And now I know why." We turned around to see Trevor Burton behind us, casting his verbal opinion on the show. Trevor — a true rebel to the last.

Dave Arden remembers Carl's return. "Carl Wayne has now come back to the old man and said, "I want to go solo, Don! Don got him a big deal at RCA as a solo artist. It was a real 'fuck off deal' in those days with, funnily enough, David Jacobs, the DJ, who was then actually in A&R at RCA. He was the one that did the deal with the old man, for Charlie Wayne."

Immediately after leaving The Move, Carl wanted some forward career advice. He called Olav Wyper at RCA Records who knew him well. "He said to me, 'I've just left Don Arden's office, and will you buy me some lunch?' So Charlie Wayne came to the office and we went across the road to eat. He said to me, 'I've gotta get away from The Move and get away from Don. I'm the lead singer but I've got no money, I got a house, but I got nothing else. I wanna go solo, what do you think?'" Carl asked me, 'If I went out as a solo act, would you want to sign me?' And I said, 'Well, yes, of course. Why wouldn't I? You can go on your own. You've got a good enough voice; you've got a good enough reputation. Everybody likes you. You can go it on your own.'"

"I did introduce him to the theatrical producer Bill Kenwright. Bill and I were lifelong friends and in fact produced a number of shows, in the West End together. Bill was casting the classic *West Side Story* and had a problem with one of the roles. I said to him, you know, you should think of Charlie Wayne? He thought, 'what a good idea.' So, he interviewed him."

"I don't know how long Charlie did *West Side Story*. I saw him in it, but I can't remember for how long. Interesting thing was that Bill later hired him to do *Blood Brothers*. He was in that for six years, playing the narrator. And he was brilliant at that. I said, 'Well, you're the lead singer! I'm sure you could go solo, but it depends on your contract with Don Arden. Charlie said, 'what do you suggest?' I told him, 'Go and see a lawyer — see how watertight the contract is. Then go and talk to Don or get the lawyer to talk to Don. Don't get me involved in this though, okay!'"

"The very next day, I get a phone call from Don Arden, screaming at me, 'You fucking Norwegian cunt.' I said, 'Don what's the problem?' He roared, 'You're the fucking problem, filling Charlie Wayne's head with all this nonsense! Telling him to go and see a lawyer, how fucking dare you! I will come down there and throw you through your fucking window, out into fucking Curzon Street.'"

Olav did not appear to be too phased! 'Don! For God's sake... Tell you what, if you really wanna do that come down here! I'll tell reception to let you up, when you get here! Come up to my office, it's on the third floor and then throw me out the window... If you can. I had remembered the many stories of Robert Stigwood being hung out the office window, after committing a band poaching 'gaffe'. Arden roared, 'Don't you talk to me like that! Fuck off! You're the one talking to me like that!'

"Don never did show up and throw me out the window. Arden traded on fear and there was his alarming reputation. But sometimes if you stand up to them - you can usually get them to back down? Usually! Eventually Don and I became friends and laughed about it years later. And Don said to the group of people we were in, 'Olav Wyper is the only one, that ever stood up to me and gave me back what I gave them.'"

Olav adds this PS, "Although, I have to confess, I did take the trouble to go downstairs to the commissionaire and the secretary on the front desk at RCA at 50 Curzon Street and said, 'For God's sake, if Don Arden comes round do not let him upstairs to see me!'

Olav added, "I really believe if The Move had really, really good management they would've been absolutely world-class — a world beating band! I also believe that Carl achieved probably a third of what he could have achieved. Had he been better organised and had better people around him."

In 1982 Carl Wayne appeared with the band Magnum and re-visited The Move in a short, strong live set. Carl Wayne & Magnum perform Move songs at the Heroes & Villains concert to celebrate fifteen years of Radio One. This raised funds for the Nordoff-Robbins Music Therapy Centre. It was recorded at The Odeon, Hammersmith, London on 21st September 1982. The Magnum members were Tony Clarkin, Kex Gorin, Wally Lowe, Bob Catley and Mark Stanway. They ran through a gusty, energetic showcase of 'Flowers In The Rain', 'Blackberry Way', 'Fire Brigade' and 'I Can Hear The Grass Grow'. Carl dedicated the tight set to Roy Wood.

Carl Wayne had tried over the years for a Move reunion. He really wanted this to happen. Rob Caiger remembers that one last "private" show happened in London. Carl joined Roy Wood and his Big Band onstage and apparently the show went very well. There was talk of taking it forward. Carl although keeping himself very fit, by running marathons and looking very good for his age. Suddenly became very ill,

Why don't you turn around and look at me, I often wish I knew you...

oesophageal cancer was diagnosed and Carl sadly died young at the age of 61. On Tuesday 31st August at 2:00am in the morning, Carl Wayne passed away peacefully in his sleep. During The Hollies European shows in July, Carl was his usual enthusiastic and energetic self. Dominating the stage and dazzling the audience with his superb performance and vocal skills. A few weeks after his last concert with the band, Carl went into hospital for a routine check-up. Without warning, his condition suddenly deteriorated and within a few short days with his family at his bedside, Carl died.

After leaving The Move in 1970, Carl had worked extensively in theatre, television, film and cabaret. He married Sue Hanson in 1974, and the couple had one son, Jack. Jack has inherited his father's musical talent. Previously, he has been a slamming drummer in various bands, with a hard-hitting technique. He has also been a chef. From a very young age and coming from an athletic background, Jack threw himself into gymnastics, both at school and competitively. At 13 he discovered Wakeboarding, it took Jack just five years to become British National Champion, European Champion and fourth place in the Wakeboard Cable World Championships in 2000. Jack Wayne now runs a successful weight training and body reforming programme. The resemblance to his father in terms of his eyes and facial features is striking.

Carl was one of the UK's most in-demand singers and recorded countless sessions for the music and advertising industries worldwide. A great campaigner for Leukaemia Research, Carl regularly ran marathons in support of the charity. His last being the London Marathon which he completed in just over 3 hours, 30 minutes.

"I miss him so much," sighs Sue who lives comfortably in Surrey and Spain; Carl left her £1.4 million in his will. "We were joined at the hip. He was very charismatic and made me laugh so much. He was a rock musician, but he was my rock. He did absolutely everything for me, so I found it really, really hard by myself. He was ill for two-and-a-half years before he died and he was hugely courageous. He never moaned and did concerts with The Hollies right up to his death. He went onstage with a chemotherapy drip hidden round his waist and pumping the drugs in. Very few people knew just how ill he was."

Carl was a major vocal talent, hugely underrated and in many ways unheard - gone way too young. Laurie Hornsby attested to the fact that Carl's tenure with The Hollies was superb. Hornsby said he couldn't believe how much Carl elevated the band sonically. That is not taking anything away from Allan Clarke's long tenure as their superlative lead vocalist. Three Move songs were slotted into The Hollies' set, along with their own hits-heavy back catalogue. 'I Can Hear The Grass Grow', 'Blackberry Way' and 'Fire Brigade' were three live favourites.

Helen Macdonald thought The Hollies gig came at just the right time for Carl. "In many ways it got him back up on stage in a high-profile capacity and touring around the country (and overseas). It gave him the chance to see and catch up with many old friends and fans (as well as make new ones). The shows were great and in classic Carl style, he didn't try and copy Allan Clarke but put his own stamp on everything. His vocal performances were amazing. People say he breathed new life into the band and helped it through a rough time. The fans absolutely loved him."

This is echoed by The Hollies' drummer Bobby Elliot: "We are shocked by it (Carl's death) because we didn't expect it to be so sudden. The Hollies and the world of music have lost a shining star, a true professional. It is a very sad day for the band. Our thoughts and prayers go out to his wife Susan, son Jack and all of his family. Carl was one of the music business's great characters. He was a fearless performer and a powerhouse singer. It has been an honour to work with him."

Due to poor sales, none of Wayne's solo releases remained on catalogue for long during his lifetime. In 2006, an album of his performances, remastered with the involvement of Roy Wood and some previously unreleased tracks, was issued under the title *Songs From The Wood And Beyond 1973–2003*. The aspects that mar some of this as a listening experience are the electronic drums and programming, prevalent in the 1980s. Which, in many ways hasn't always dated well.

Blood Brothers had a run at the Phoenix Theatre in London's West End for 24 years. Many people will remember Carl for this, a most acclaimed stage role. He played the narrator between 1990 and 1996. Helen MacDonald casts her memory back, "I met him whilst he was playing the role of the narrator in the West End production of *Blood Brothers*. I was 16 and on a school trip in July 1992. His performance completely blew me away. His looks, the voice, everything. I didn't meet him until a little after this first experience. The first time I met him, was October 1993 at the stage door, after a Saturday matinee performance of *Blood Brothers*. Once he left the show, I went to see him in various other things including cabaret at The Cockney Empire. We lost touch for a while, but then I found him again in cabaret at The Talk Of London. I was in a relationship with Rob Caiger at the time. All three of us became very firm friends. Rob took on a managerial role for Carl and I developed Carl's website and an email list for news and chat amongst his fans. We socialised a lot and I participated in a lot of interesting events, some of which Rob arranged. Carl became a very close friend of mine. I think Carl's friendship with me and Rob gave him a renewed vigour for his career, towards the end of his life."

"I saw Carl in the role over 20 times. The show was fantastic, and he really made the role of the narrator his own. It was like, it was written for him and was the best thing I ever saw him do. I always dreamed he'd return one day after leaving the show in 1996, but it sadly was not to be."

Helen remembers Carl's big personality. "He was friendly, kind, warm, funny, outgoing. He could be grumpy and awkward at times also! He was also not very punctual — I don't recall a single occasion when he was ever on time to meet me. He had lots of energy, a passion for life and what he did. Singing and performing was everything to him. Like most performers, he sometimes lacked confidence in himself, he wasn't at all conceited."

Carl used to participate on both the website and the mailing list. There is also an 'In Memory of Carl Wayne' Facebook page. Helen talks with respect, "The perception was that it was a 'fast' illness for Carl, but it wasn't particularly. Carl passed away a couple of years, following his initial diagnosis and operation and never gave up, still performing until a couple of months before he died."

Macdonald's lasting memories of Carl are etched deeply. "He was an incredible talent, a huge part of my young life, who left me many legacies and taught me a lot. He always encouraged me and helped me to believe in myself. I loved him and always will. He was really kind. He genuinely liked people and enjoyed meeting and talking to fans. I never saw him be rude to or ignore anyone that waited for him after

Why don't you turn around and look at me, I often wish I knew you…

a show."

John Altman could be described as a renaissance musician. He has been around the music business forever in various capacities. Over the Covid pandemic, myself and Elliott Goldstein in America were involved in many podcasts. Including multi podcasts, with various music industry people and John was one of the regular guests. It was then I got to realise the broad sweep of John's career. Everybody from Quincy Jones to Peter Green all the way to Amy Winehouse.

John shines a light on Carl Wayne's later career. Away from the Move stages and axes and controversy. And into a little-known area of the music arena. "People think, you know, that is quite demeaning come down, for the guy. A rock star and now, he's a jingles and cabaret person. But if you think about the people who work vocally for me. You had Paul Carrack, you had Chris Thompson, you had Carl Wayne. You had all kinds of people who had very successful solo careers. It wasn't a come down at all. It was secure, well compensated and they didn't have to struggle by going out on tour. They don't need that when they're getting older too and the old bones are starting to ache a bit."

This world is a supplementary world within music and John fleshes out what Carl did within it. "That's a tricky one to remember, because Carl was always there on the scene. I suspect there were a list of singers. Another one on that list would be Chris Amoo of The Real Thing. They're all studio singers, who you hired to do lead vocals, backing vocals, imitate someone else, or not imitate someone else! Just be good singers, whatever the commercial or the record called for. So, Carl showed up among that bunch of singers… I would think in the late 70s, early 80s. But he was incredibly reliable. He had an amazing ear. He was very, very funny! Well, people were just happy to see him on the session, because he would do funny voices, he'd crack jokes. Not over the top in the sense, that you think, 'Oh, God, why don't that guy shut up?' It wasn't a nervous thing. He was one of the guys. Everyone was glad to see him. There was a whole pool that we all used to use, and they welcomed him in with open arms."

John develops this insider info, "So there was a bunch of male singers, Tony Burroughs, as I say, Bob Saker who's still one of the go-to voices (He is the Honey Monster). Martin Jay who was 5,000 Volts, who has a really good poppy voice. Paul Da Vinci who was in The Rubettes. Nick Curtis who unfortunately died young, David Langer, Ken Barrie who was the voice of Postman Pat. Then the females who were most visible, if you like, who would be working with David Bowie, The Stones and people like that. So Clare Torry, who sang on *Dark Side of the Moon*. Stephanie DeSykes, who had a big pop career herself. I had Elaine Page do one thing. Miriam Stockley, Tessa Niles, who sang backing for David Bowie and Mick Jagger and Sting, Katie Kissoon. They all were all '20 Feet from Stardom.'"

He explains Carl's singing styles, "Carl had more of a tenor voice, didn't he. Very strong voice, very in tune and very recognisable but not over the top recognisable. I certainly could easily say, 'Oh, that's Carl Wayne singing.' But it wouldn't be in the sense that, 'Oh, you know, why is he impinging his personality on this?' He did a wonderful ad for Martini… Chris Cumming wrote that. Cumming also wrote the music for Poirot. But there were basically only about five or six of us who did everything! Because it was such a tight, narrow discipline. You had to make it work in 28 seconds and make your point and get out! A lot of people couldn't do that, from Michael Tippitt right down to Mike Oldfield. They couldn't write something in 28 seconds and make it exactly 28 seconds and make it work?"

"I even had Carl singing lead. I did a tribute to Rodgers and Hart at the Pizza Express. Gemma Craven the actress, was the female singer. So, he was singing all 'Lady and the Tramp', 'Where and When', 'Manhattan', 'There's A Small Hotel' and 'Blue Moon', all of that. I did see him at the Talk of London doing his cabaret act. He would sing things like 'My Way' — you would expect somebody to sing that in cabaret. He also sang things that had soul. It was a mixture. He had a particularly good voice, for going out and all that."

John also remembered another major Brummie talent. "I did a gig with Denny Laine a few years ago in Los Angeles where he did *Band On The Run* live and then did a whole set of all The Moody Blues' hits that he was on, like 'Go Now' he played harmonica as well."

"When I was doing commercials, particularly in the 80s and 90s, the directors were Ridley Scott, Hugh Hudson John Frankenheimer, David Bailey, Terence Donovan, Brian Duffy, Adrian Lynne, David Mallet — they were the directors! My copywriter would be Salman Rushdie, he was my lyricist — Bloody hell! Chis Hardy, whose son is Tom Hardy would be the copywriter on some of them. The accounts guy would be Guy Ritchie's father. The creative director of the agency would be Nick Welsh, whose daughter is Florence of — and the Machine. The quality of what you were doing was amazing, because you were working with Ridley Scott. You were doing a Midland Bank commercial, but the director was Ridley Scott or the product commercial. It wasn't somebody holding up a product and saying, 'Buy this.' It was clever, well-written. David Putnam, they all went into moviemaking, Alan Parker, Jonathan Fraser. It was high, high-level creativity. There were hundreds of studios, we would be in the studios which were in Bryanston Street. We would be in Pye Studios, Phillips Studios, CTS in Wembley, CBS, in sort of Scud Street way, Warren Street. All huge studios, chapels, I mean, there are hundreds and hundreds. All the big publishing houses would all have their own domains. I think there were a couple of studios in Denmark Street that we used. Regent Sound — but we rarely used those because they were demo studios. Let's say we want to do XYZ. I would then phone up say, Bill Griffiths who's now the big film booker. He was my advertising producer and booker. Then there was Christine Poundsford whose sister is married to Robert Lindsay. They were the only three bookers, that I ever used in advertising. I would say I need a guitar, and they knew who I booked! Mitch Stoltz on guitar, this one on bass, that one on drums, Charlie Morgan or Ralph Stalmann. I'd say I need four male singers; I think a good blend would be Bob Saker, Tony Burroughs, Carl Wayne and Martin Jay. Always it was, get me these specific people. If there was only one singer, I might say, Chris Amou would be good for this! Or Jimmy Helms would be good for this! The sessions are very much of a muchness. You had a one-hour session for the band and that was it. So, you went to the next one. They'd nail it in a couple of times. Two, three rehearsals, take it. Thank you very much!" And so, Carl Wayne inhabited that world, behind the scenes and stayed busy.

An American band called The Shazam were formed by guitarist, vocalist and songwriter Hans Rotenberry. The band hailed from Nashville, Tennessee, earning a

Why don't you turn around and look at me, I often wish I knew you...

loyal following among power pop obsessives for their big pop sound, with a pronounced British influence. The Shazam were formed in 1997 when Rotenberry teamed up with bassist Mick Wilson and drummer Scott Ballew. The group released their self-titled debut album in 1997. During this writing they have released a new album called *Meteor* in 2024. The band's name suggests a big Move influence. The Shazam joined in the cafeteria at Abbey Road in 2000 with Carl and Bev, who added lead and backing vocals to the Shazam band's renditions of 'I Can Hear The Grass Grow' and 'Beautiful Daughter'. The Shazam even had a light-haired bass player, with a passing resemblance to Ace the Face. "You're thinking of Jeremy, our guitar player who just happened to look like Ace. Absolutely unintentional. But Carl and Bev did point it out!" The Shazam also opened for Paul Weller at his Earls Court gig that year.

Hans recalls some treasured moments in 2000. "I met Carl through Rob Caiger, who contacted me and introduced himself after reading some UK press we had received, which compared us favourably to The Move. We were touring over there, and he asked if we would be interested in meeting Carl. We met them at a pub in Leicester Square, London. Carl was instantly like an old friend. He was youthful, extremely charming, funny, confident. They had scrapbooks of old memorabilia, prints of photo session outtakes, live recordings I had never heard, lots of stories, an amazing night."

"We had been invited to spend the day at Abbey Road on May 25th, 2000, to play live TV with other artists. After many beers, I said to our new, old friend Carl Wayne, 'Wouldn't it be cool if you got Bev and Roy and used The Shazam to fill in the rest and have The Move play that day?' The next day, Rob had it set up — not only were we playing, but we were gonna do 'I Can Hear The Grass Grow' with Carl and Bev in the garden at Abbey Road. When we returned that May, Carl had a studio set up where we could rehearse. What a day…we ran through every Move tune we could think of with him. I really wanted to do 'Beautiful Daughter'. Carl was at first doubtful, but it turned out so good we were like "'maybe we should do this instead?' So, Rob Caiger arranged it, where we got extra time in our broadcast set that evening to do 'Beautiful Daughter' as well."

"The day of the Abbey Road broadcast, we had the penthouse studio as our dressing room. Bev was there, we spent hours hanging out, running through Move tunes. The familiarity between Carl and Bev was hilarious, jokes and name calling. They called Roy but he didn't want to be involved. I asked someone to ask Roy about one chord in 'Beautiful Daughter' and was told that he said 'No, it's a secret chord — no one will be able to figure it out.' It rained, so no garden set at Abbey Road. We then moved the lunchtime 'Grass Grow' inside to the cafeteria. Great fun, with Bev standing there with a tambourine, singing his incredible deep bass vocal parts. I wish I hadn't looked into the camera when I sang my parts though. I guess I was thinking Macca on the 'Hey Jude' film. When we were done, the cafeteria cleared out. People approached them and getting Move stuff signed. One of them was Paul Weller. So, my introduction to him, was him approaching and shaking my hand. Later that night after 'Beautiful Daughter', Weller came back, and we chatted. He asked about 'those chords' on 'Beautiful Daughter' and I told him the story and how I played it. I have a great photo of that moment. He later invited The Shazam to open his November show at Earls Court, which I am happy to say we did. Weller treated us like royalty, and I will never forget that. He's the real thing."

"Carl came up on stage with us afterwards at The Garage. Another time I was wandering around London and bumped into him in Chinatown! Interesting person to just randomly encounter a thousand miles from home and old friends already. Carl was so cool. We didn't do much UK touring after that. We had problems with the label, getting another UK label didn't work out. But Carl and I stayed in touch until his untimely passing. I had grown up listening to ELO, loved 'Do Ya' but didn't realise it was a Move song. I had never heard of them but noticed 'California Man', having been a big Cheap Trick fan. The rock magazines said the 'R. Wood' credit was Ron Wood. When I was 12 I found a compilation cassette in a discount bin. My introduction to The Move was 'Hello Susie' and 'Brontosaurus'". Good god! Everything I loved about dynamic 60's rock in one place — Byrds jangle, Beatle harmonies, Who power, Zeppelin drums, great acoustic guitars, incredibly interesting, near whimsical tunes and that heavy bass! I always thought of them as a garage ELO. Years later I actually did name my band Shazam because that was the combination of sounds, I wanted to have…"

In a poignant, timely and sweet epitaph to Carl and The Move, in 2003 Carl Wayne joined Roy Wood and his band on stage at Covent Garden's Roadhouse. They played 'I Can Hear The Grass Grow', 'Flowers In The Rain, 'Fire Brigade', and Blackberry Way. Carl said, "Woody had been asking me to sing with him for 12 years, but I always avoided it. These two hadn't played these Move songs together in public, for more than 30 years. This time, he had decided to go and see Roy's band. But at the last minute decided to stay at home with his wife. He got a call from Roy Wood on the road saying they were lost on the tour bus. Carl was giving them directions, over the phone. "I was giving him directions to the venue. That's when I decided to make an effort — I got out there and joined him on stage and it went down a storm."

This was just two months after Carl had his major throat surgery. He was then on to some other gigs with The Hollies, on their 40th Anniversary outing.

Barry Miles opines on another release, *The Move - The BBC Sessions*. "Their colourful manager, the late Tony Secunda, wanted them known as an underground band, then flavour of the month, and to this end they recorded 'I Can Hear The Grass Grow'. Secunda pressured Joe Boyd to put them on at UFO. UFO was the hippest underground club of all, but they performed their standard act. Smashing a bank of televisions with axes and chopping up their specially built stage. The hippies were 'horrified.' They moved back from the stage and there were a few boos. At the end of the set there was no applause. Destruction was terribly unhip, unless it was done by The Who because they got it from Gustav Metzger, the inventor of auto-destructive art. The Move received lots of publicity from Secunda's crazy antics. But it was all froth and hype. They never really established their own image. In 1967, bands needed a well-defined image: acid heads, pot heads, rock rebels, whacked-out Mods, mystical, satanic, etc… The band themselves were divided about their image — Burton and Kefford (and Bevan) were rock 'n' rollers. Carl Wayne aspired to be a cabaret singer and Roy Wood veered towards pomp-rock."

Barry Miles continues, "John Peel saw their worth. Through the hipster DJ recommendations, the first record played on the new BBC Radio One was 'Flowers

Why don't you turn around and look at me, I often wish I knew you...

In The Rain'. This was followed the next day by a live session on Peel's first *Top Gear* show. Three tracks from that session are here, including 'Cherry Blossom Clinic', planned as a single about a mental institution but withdrawn before release. Though not as interesting as the studio recordings. These BBC sessions show the essential power of the group playing live. Recorded. over a two-year period beginning January 1967. Their sonorous sound textures and increasingly complex arrangements prefigure ELO."

Thus spake Barry Miles with a good amount of combined insight and brevity. Barry Miles under his other author's name of Miles, was responsible for the Paul McCartney book *Many Years From Now* and many others.

Roy Wood

After Roy's abrupt departure from ELO, leaving both Jeff Lynne and Bev Bevan mystified. he already had eyes and ears to do something else. A large line-up, Wizzard was a very expensive band to keep going on the road. Studio time was an even bigger drain on the band's finances. The costs of running the band were far higher than the income being earned by the band members. Bill Hunt had a mighty obsession with obliterating the pianos at various venues. Roy's massive obsession with overdubs and Phil Spector-like walls of sound pumped the hourly studio budgets way, way high. Rick Price alleged in a radio interview, "When we finished recording 'Angel Fingers' it was surmised that we had probably spent more time in the studio, than even Paul McCartney had with the entire recording of the *Band On The Run* album." Yikes![20]

If Rick Price's estimate is true or not, record company advance money was spent on long, long hours of studio time. Increasingly, the members of Wizzard had to rely on live touring work for their income.

Wizzard made their live debut in August 1972 at Wembley as part of The London Rock & Roll Show. Colin Bell saw them the following year. "I saw them live for the first time, months later when they played Hastings Pier Ballroom on 9th February 1973, and I must be scrupulously honest. They were a shambles, much to my disappointment. The band were clearly under rehearsed and all over the place, in stark contrast, to when Roy appeared there several years earlier with The Move. I was expecting a great night, including listening to them perform their debut hit 'Ball Park Incident', it was not to be! It was pretty obvious to all of us that he loved The Ronettes, The Crystals etc, that Roy's vision of the sound of Wizzard owed a lot to Phil Spector's famous 'Wall Of Sound', all of this reaching its apex with my personal favourite 'Angel Fingers'."

Wizzard's first single was the explosive 'Ballpark Incident' combining the Move's harder rock edge with the Phil Spector-influenced production. This helped the single to Number Six on the UK charts. The B-side is the strangely named instrumental 'The Carlsberg Special (Piano's Demolished Phone 021 373 4472)' composed by keyboard player Bill Hunt. including his real phone number!

In April 1973 Wizzard hit it out of the ballpark again, reaching Number One with 'See My Baby Jive' written by bassist Rick Price. Another smash successfully duplicated, by its follow-up, 'Angel Fingers'.

[20] Tony Visconti had a hand in the *Band On The Run* recording. All the orchestral arrangements for the album were taped at AIR Studios in a single day. These were conducted by Tony Visconti. He was given just three days to write the arrangements, including for the 60-piece orchestra on the title track. He was not properly credited for his work, until the 25th Anniversary reissue of the album in early 2024.

Unfortunately, the band's first album *Wizzard Brew* didn't sell anything like those three. It was more experimental, not quite in line with Wood's solo records *Mustard* or *Boulders* but inhabiting some of that area. The group's inexorable rise started to wobble after this. Roy Wood's career at this time may have confused the public. By continuing to record and release solo records under his own name. At the same time, he was running a parallel release schedule with Wizzard.

The (now, evergreen) Phil Spector style, full on, 'I Wish It Could Be Christmas Everyday' reached number 4 in 1973. Another catchy single, 'Forever' made it to number 8 that same year. Another forgotten now winter release, 'Rock 'n' Roll Winter' featured Roy's then girlfriend, the wonderful Lynsey De Paul on backing vocals.

'This Is The Story Of My Love' only reached a relatively lowly number 34. It's sad for a classic Wizzard cut, deserving to do much better. But such is the fickle hand of releasing records and the public response.

The two Wizzard albums *See My Baby Jive* and *Eddie & The Falcons* both failed, critically and commercially.

There was critical disappointment (maybe even some ennui?) around the release of *Eddie & The Falcons*. This appeared to signal the end of Wizzard as a unit. Meanwhile, *Boulders* (1973) and *Mustard* (1975) were again considered too idiosyncratic to achieve any major sales as the music business began its rapid cycle to becoming more corporate. And in so many ways, more staid and format bound as the 1970s lengthened. Taking all the 1960s experimentation and starting to subdivide it up, into formats, divisions, genres, charts and styles. The free-form, freewheeling, experimentalism found between 1965 to 1970, had now begun to change somewhat. As usual the bean counters had won!

A couple of tours in the UK and one tour of the US. But even this was not going to be enough to ensure regular wages for the band. One by one the band members found other more lucrative things to occupy their time. By the latter stages of 1975, another band had bitten rock 'n' roll dust.

Roy wasn't living on the streets though. By this time, he was the proud owner of a country pile called Gothersley Hall. Sitting in around 6 acres of private gardens and grounds. Parked outside was his own Jensen Interceptor with the number plate, ROY 1. Roy has moved many times since then, but this was an impressive pile of bricks and mortar, which could probably be described as mock Tudor-Gothic.

It was reported in 2020 that the £1.5 million house where Roy wrote, 'I Wish It Could Be Christmas Everyday' was up for sale, described as having six bedrooms and surrounded by a good variety of tall trees and open countryside. Of that famous Christmas song, Roy said, "It's May 1973 and I'm sitting in the kitchen of my house in Worcestershire. In the corner of the room in this stately pile, Gothersley Hall in Stourton, stands a jukebox that's rarely played. It's full of old original label rock 'n' roll records I've collected over the years. Very rock 'n' roll. Even in the merry month of May I hadn't deliberately sat down to write a Christmas song. The more I think about it I reflect that over the years, there have only been novelty records out at Christmas."

One obscurity I came across, involving Roy's output, was a track called 'Jeepster Rap (Home Demo)' which features Roy and Marc Bolan blabbing together. They

Why don't you turn around and look at me, I often wish I knew you...

are "rapping" in the kitchen or somewhere. It's on a 3CD box called *A Wizard, A True Star - Marc Bolan & T.Rex 1972-77*, released in 1996 with sleeve notes from Mark Paytress. It was later available on an Edsel CD called *Interstellar Soul* in 2007, basically a re-issue. It's not entirely worth tracking down, but it's a curio for any rabid completist.

A specific, romantic episode took place in Easter 1975. When Renaissance had a few days off, Dick Plant, the engineer at De Lane Lea studios where they had recorded *Turn Of The Cards*, called Renaissance's angelic vocalist supreme Annie Haslam. "He said, 'Why don't you come down to the studio? Roy Wood is going to be here, and I think you two are going to hit it off. I thought, 'Hmmm... green hair?' So, I went down, and it was love at first sight. His sense of humour was the first thing. But he was a handsome man underneath all that hair."

Wood asked her to dinner at Trader Vic's in the Hilton on Park Lane, and they went there with Robert Plant and his wife. Haslam recalled, "I lived in Hampstead at the time, and I said, 'There is a fair at Hampstead Heath, let's go up there. As promised the next morning I called my friend Betty Thatcher about my date with Roy. From that conversation she was inspired to write a song, and she came up with 'Trip To The Fair'. It's a wonderful song telling the story of that first interesting and eventful night. She did that with a few songs. 'Ocean Gypsy', also on the album, was about me and [the band's manager] Miles Copeland. He was my boyfriend for two years from 1972."

1977 found Annie Haslam and Roy Wood putting their talents together, recording the progressive rock masterpiece *Annie In Wonderland*, her first solo album. It was produced by Roy, who wrote three of the songs. He arranged all the songs, played nearly all of the instruments, including a lead vocal on 'I Never Believed In Love'. Roy illustrated the cover. The album features a range of musical styles enabling Haslam to experiment with other vocal styles. The five-octave range for which Haslam is well-known, is still evident in the showcase number. 'Rockalise'.

The album peaked at number 167 on the Billboard chart. Roy Wood had compositions, like 'I Never Believed In Love' and 'Hunioco' as well as Renaissance's Jon Camp inspiring album opener 'If I Were Made Of Music'. *Annie In Wonderland* is appreciated as a piece of musical artistry that stands the test of time. There was an interpretation of classics like Rogers and Hammersmith's 'If I Loved You'. A special edition CD was later released, using the original Sire Records tapes. It was remastered for the audiophile medium. There was also a reunion of Annie Haslam and Roy Wood who teamed up for a new bonus track of 'Flowers In The Rain'.

It took five years for Roy to escape his contract with Arden. During which time Wood recorded under pseudonyms ("I'm not saying who"). He produced local acts and an album for chart toppers Darts. Then formed the jazz/rock-inclined Wizzo Band. But only released the second of two albums. He released another solo album *On The Road Again* and formed Helicopters, "It got difficult as we were using people who were all playing with other groups."

Since releasing the self-played *Starting Up* in 1986, Wood spent five years setting up a studio at his Shropshire home where he recorded theme and incidental music for Central TV. "I like something with a bit of meat to it. The stuff I did for a documentary on murder was a challenge."

During 1992 Wood was reported as having written two songs for Cheap Trick vocalist Robin Zander's new album. Wood is currently working on his own. "I've got more into the computer side. I'm playing everything myself! So, I can make samples of myself playing the cello, and then play real ones over the top."

Two songs were co-written with Jeff Lynne. Roy was (then) currently looking for a record deal. "Which hasn't been easy. The market has been saturated with rap for a while. And real songs, haven't been that much to the forefront. It really wouldn't make any difference to me, not to have another hit. But it's frustrating when my songs are not heard by the general public who only hear all the re-issued stuff. They probably think I've run out of ideas and just want to cash in." Wood denies that he's become something of a recluse, since the hits dried up: "I live well out in the sticks, but I'm not hiding out — not purposely anyway."

Rob Caiger reflected on the trajectory of Roy Wood's career. "Boy! Wizzard were worked to death. Roy had to do a solo career. He had a Wizzard career, he had to write, not only for himself and his group but for other artists, record, engineer, produce, do interviews, do loads of TV appearances. Because TV loved him and tour relentlessly. He was responsible for it all, what he wrote had to be hit material. Because he was providing a living and wages for the band. And he was doing all that! But you can only do that for so long and at that level. He was incredibly creative and productive during the early to mid-seventies. But I feel he drove himself too much, with much encouragement from his management. But what do you do? Management is there to support a successful career and make money for themselves and their artist. Roy is on a creative roll, writing incredible and varied material (including a huge amount of work still unreleased). So does Don Arden put that all on hold, space out the releases and tour dates, so the band aren't earning as much as they did before? Does Arden risk his artist resenting him, for putting his career on hold for a period of time? Or do they all plough on regardless to make money while they can? In the end, the workload made Roy seriously ill, and he was forced to retreat away from it all."

"After Roy had recovered from his illness, his next project was to surround himself with the Wizzo Band, a large jazz-fusion band playing the music he wants to play. But with much less of the spotlight on him. Ultimately, it's too large and uneconomical to be successful. But with a regular income from his Move hits and 'I Wish It Could Be Christmas Everyday', Roy is able to slim down what he does to a one-man operation, recording in his home studio. In his opinion (and with some justification) everyone he's worked with has ripped him off at some point? So — why not do everything himself?"

David Arden opines, "Roy says that about everybody. David said that they were always there for him. Like the time when he did a ridiculous John Barry cover single. We said, 'This is great, Roy, but it's just a fucking minute long.' Sometimes they did things to humour him. But it was made it into a three- or four-minute single."

Rob Caiger also found missing components. "Yeah, I found the tape for '1,2,3'. I found all the versions that Roy recorded for that. There were different takes with the guitar solos and no fully completed single. David Arden told me that Don had a fearsome reputation, but he also said that Don generally was very good to the guys he managed. He had an awful lot of love, and he loved Roy and apparently Roy got on well with him. But Roy told me he felt he'd been ripped off by Don and should have

Why don't you turn around and look at me, I often wish I knew you...

been more protected than he was before he got ill. The truth is probably somewhere in the middle."

David Arden also dealt with Carl, "One minute he wanted to be a solo singer. Then he wanted to be in The Move in another minute? We would often do things for Carl. But we didn't think they were ever gonna make any money out of them. We did them, because they loved Carl. He was a great guy, and he was a great performer."

Rob Caiger interjects: "What David Arden is saying about Carl is David's perspective and from a management perspective paying the bills, absolutely right. But his and Don Arden's focus is on the company and making money. For Roy Wood, what they needed to do was say: 'Roy, we need to take some time off.' They — and everyone else involved — never recognised how important time away to recharge the creative batteries was. You keep working the golden goose while you can, especially in a young, still developing industry. The Ardens originally had The Move, which became ELO. Then by accident or managerial design, they had two groups, ELO and Roy Wood's Wizzard. And then a strong solo artist in Roy himself. That's quite a roster of talent and a lot of the workload and publicity fell on Roy because without exception, everybody loved Roy. They were working many golden geese but in ELO there was a partnership. Bev watched the business and promotion, took on more of the interviews while Jeff focused on writing and recording. Jeff also had a second in command on the creative side in Richard Tandy. There was a support structure there which Roy didn't appear to have. He had Rick Price helping him and Dick Plant in the studio but that was it."

"What Roy probably needed was a disciplined producer. It would never have happened unless it was Brian Wilson! But a very strong record company or management should have laid down the rules, saying, 'This is what the album needs, and this is what we need you to do.' *Wizzard Brew* needed some of the hits on it which would have helped chart it higher and kept it on catalogue instead of being deleted soon after release. His solo album *Mustard* was brilliant but was let down by poor promotion and its cover. One of the photos of Roy surrounded by all the instruments he played on the album would have been a much better and effective LP cover."

Even though he was doing well-received gigs and writing, Roy was not releasing material. Later, Roy did some recording with Jeff Lynne to see if record companies were interested. But while 'Me and You' was superb, no labels offered a deal. *The Singles Collection*, a recent Wizzard 2 CD set from 7T's Records (Cherry Red Records) was released in December 2023. This gathered up the A and B sides of Wizzard's catalogue of hits.

The first disc moves towards its conclusion with the gentle instrumental 'Dream Of Unwin'. A piece I've often used as a "bed" in my radio programmes. Disc 2 starts with the excellent invitation of 'Are You Ready To Rock', a glorious confection of big band, swing, jazz and best of all some zany bagpipes! Love it. It would be the bands last top ten hit reaching number 8. 'Marathon Man', an unremarkable instrumental, although featuring some fetching guitar, and written by drummer Keith Smart follows, before Roy treats us to another homage to more early rock 'n' roll shenanigans with 'Rattlesnake Roll'. 'Indiana Rainbow' and 'The Stroll' credited respectively to Roy Wood's Wizzard & Roy Wood's Wizzo Band see the band take a more jazz orientated approach. But it is apparent they are running out of steam.

The penultimate track 'Dancing At The Rainbows End' sees Roy retreat to a more commercial production. But it was too little, too late. With little airplay and a planned tour cancelled — the glory days were over. During their heyday in the early to mid-70s, Wizzard provided us with some classic "glam/retro" hits that will no doubt still be playing on the radio, long after this presenter has left this earthly building & quite right too.

The Roy Wood Story on Harvest Records which was released in 1976, recapped his career with EMI Records and performed well as a 'best-of Roy.' His subsequent records, *On The Road* (1979) and *Starting Up* (1987), failed to achieve the sales or success of the earlier 1970s work. Had the worm turned? Was the dye cast? Maybe the natural order of an artist's career was delineated here. Perhaps, a deep dig by management and then label would need to be performed to ascertain what way Roy could operate into the future. A very tricky transition for any artist.

Message From The Country was the fourth and final studio album by The Move and the group's only album on EMI's Harvest label. Recorded in 1970–71 at the same time that the Move was also laying down tracks for the eponymous first Electric Light Orchestra album, which was called *No Answer* in the USA. A contractual obligation, *Message From The Country* also signalled the end of The Move and allowed them to continue as the Electric Light Orchestra. The Move record has some similarities in style to the new band's debut album, especially in the use of overdubbing to capture all of the instruments being played by Roy Wood and Jeff Lynne. Nevertheless, Wood and Lynne were determined to maintain some differentiation between the sound of their two groups. For example, by using Wood's saxophones on *Message From The Country* and the cellos only on the Electric Light Orchestra debut. During The Move sessions they recorded '10538 Overture', a Lynne composition that was originally intended to be a Move B-side. Wood overdubbed a cello riff over the basic track fifteen times over. But Wood and Lynne decided the song was better suited to The Electric Light Orchestra.

The lengthy sessions for ELO, involved only Wood and Lynne, because of all the overdubbing. During the sessions, bassist Rick Price bailed out from The Move. He realised he was no longer needed, but he wasn't told in ready terms. They didn't replace him. Roy Wood simply added bass guitar duties to his other roles. He erased Rick Price's tracks on the existing songs and then re-recorded the bass parts! Why Wood re-did Price's parts is unclear. Wood has confirmed that Price played on the original take of '10538 Overture'.

Bevan, in the liner notes for the remastered 2005 reissue of *Message From The Country*, is quoted saying that "it is his least favourite Move album." In true contrarian fashion, Wood has said, "It was probably the best one we ever did." All previous Move singles had been solo Roy Wood compositions. Recent singles had also featured Wood singing the lead. For this album, Wood is credited to composing only four songs. With four songs from Lynne, one Lynne-Wood joint credit and one Bevan song. Lead vocals on the album were ostensibly split between Wood and Lynne depending upon the writer.

In addition to all of which, he's second to absolutely no one, as a producer. In so far as your actual technical know-how is concerned. "Their ain't the producer alive, who records and mixes rock and roll drums, quite so breathtakingly as Roy Wood, for

Why don't you turn around and look at me, I often wish I knew you...

instance." So gushed, one reviewer at the time.

Of the last two Move albums get *Message From The Country* first. When it came time to cut this last album for Regal Zonophone/Fly Records, Wood either didn't have just a couple of new tunes ready for recording, or he wasn't overexcited to relinquish them, for the presumably small songwriter's royalty Fly's publishing company, had him contracted for. Seven tracks on the album (including a funny, country style debut by Bevan, two previously released singles, two Jeff Lynne tunes, and only two new Wood tunes) and everything save the singles is quite obviously padded with effect-laden guitar, sitar, and what-have-you solos that generally ask more of the listener than they give back. Ultimately as boring as they are impressively arranged and played, they resemble only in quantity the ridiculously orgasmic sitar/banjo rampage that polished off *Shazam's* 'Fields Of People'.

Padding aside, *Looking On* also contains two decidedly sub-standard examples of Wood's (usually) composing genius. The plodding 'Feel Too Good', one of the least distinguished songs he's ever done, and the very unpleasant, flopped single, 'When Alice Comes Back To The Farm', is trebly, raunch rock and is simply hard to listen to.

Some of this early Lynne / Wood stuff was very jarring, with very trebly vocals. It was troubling to my lugholes anyway. I thought the changing sound, concepts etc, were nowhere near the original Move material. But don't get me wrong — *Looking On* certainly does have its moments. Both of Lynne's contributions, 'What?' a stately, almost symphonic, sci-fi affair with several beautiful melodic themes running through, and 'Open Up Said The World At The Door', a delightfully corny, 1940s-ish jazzy vehicle. This closes with sensational harmonies over a guitar-led bolero. Those are more brightly listenable. Who could ever forget 'Brontosaurus', the absurdly heavy, speaker-shattering, favourite of the Quaaludes / barbiturates generation? Sludge-arama of the very highest order.

The Move had hightailed it away from Fly Records over to Harvest/Capitol. As detailed elsewhere, they wasted no time in getting into the studio. Cutting the uniformly better sounding *Message From The Country*. The Move, sound more relaxed (and "silly", as Jeff Lynne says in the CD sleeve notes) on firmer ground on this record, than with the preceding *Looking On*.

'Ben Crawley Steel Company', which concerns the story of a simple steel-driving man who turns into a bomb-brandishing revolutionary is a humorous pastiche of a truck driver's country music choices. Featuring a funny, voluble, treble tracked, lead vocal (in a register so low, you probably forgot it existed) by super-drummer Bev Bevan. At times Bev drops into the 'Zing Went The Strings' register. Just to remind us, who is the bass-boss around here. It's completed with phased, falsetto background vocals. 'No Time' is a prettier acoustic number, featuring Wood blowing his redoubtable recorders. That's a nice guitar picking clearly recorded. It's attributed to a P. Copestake to whom composition of this is attributed. He was also credited with "refreshments" on *Looking On*.

'Don't Mess Me Up' was indistinguishable from a real Sun-period Elvis recording. Except for the glimmering newer production styles in evidence and Bev's slightly too playful lead vocal. The guitar solo sounds just like Scotty Moore in a further reach to authenticity. Bev's 'The Minister' resembles The Beatles vocally; 'Paperback Writer' and is particularly melodic, and Redbone vaguely in its arrangement and use of Leslie-amplified guitar.

A superb rocker, as is the brutish 'Ella James', which slightly reminds of McCartney's 'Ooh You' complete with those big slightly arpeggiated double guitars from Lynne and Wood. The Eddie Cochran styled 'Until Your Mama's Gone' has a bone-crushing bassline, lasering fuzz-guitars, and the ruff-tuff vocal by Roy. 'My Marge' mixes 'When I'm 64' instrumentation with a Bonzo Dog / The New Vaudeville Band vocal. The Monty Python-esque vibe. 'The Words Of Aaron' and the title cut (the latter being Lynne's only composition on the album) are both classic, latter day Move. Deep grunting bass from Roy Wood, mostly densely produced with nice use of effects, phasing and flanging etc. As featured strongly on the title track, towards its coda. With delicate backing, ingeniously and intricately assembled.

Some gorgeous vocal harmonies, overlaid strange and intriguing lyrics, carried by noteworthy tunes on 'It Wasn't My Idea To Dance', reveals Wood singing lines like, "Now it's too late to want your freedom / It wasn't my idea to dance." The song has a handsome refrain repeated at the intro. The grunting bass pumps along in a more treble, sinister low register. Could the oboes be described as dissonant Near Eastern woodwind? It also sounds like Bev is playing cardboard box and jawbones in the background. Later this would probably be done on a sampler. Here he is hitting, some dampened, sounding percussive accents around his sturdy drumming. The recording bears repeated listening. The remastered 2005 released CD includes 'Tonight', the charting single, plus 'Chinatown', 'Down On The Bay', 'Do Ya' and 'California Man', that are not on the original Harvest record. There are four alternate mixes/takes of 'Don't Mess Me Up', 'The Words of Aaron', 'Do Ya' and 'My Marge'.

This was overseen by Rob Caiger. The tape transfers for analogue were done by Jonathan Allen and Alex Scannell at Abbey Road Penthouse Studio, Paul Hicks and Rob Caiger at Abbey Road Studio 2 and Rob Keyloch and Rob Caiger at Church Walk Studios.

****

Roy also played bass for Bo Diddley. He wrote Britain's Eurovision Song contest entry for the MOR combo the New Seekers and thanks to Wood's extravagant appearance, Wizzard managed to glom on to the glam-rock movement (Glom rock anyone?) without sounding anything like any other glam-rock band. Indeed, Wizzard occasionally sounded absolutely nothing like anything else.

EMI had launched its new subsidiary music label to compete, with the demand for the new style of progressive rock music. The first release in July 1969 was a UK issue of Deep Purple's *Book Of Taliesyn* which had originally been released in the US on the Tetragrammaton label at the end of 1968. Deep Purple had originally been on EMI's Parlophone label for their debut *Shades Of Deep Purple* LP so it made a logical sense both artistically and commercially, to launch Harvest with a moderately well-known act. Despite having been known as EMI (Electric & Musical Industries Ltd) since the merger in 1931 between The Gramophone Company and Columbia Gramophone Company, no mention of EMI appeared on the Harvest labels or sleeves until mid-1971. When the EMI 'boxed' logo was printed above Harvest on the label,

Why don't you turn around and look at me, I often wish I knew you...

the legal entity that appeared on labels and sleeves was The Gramophone Company Ltd, it was finally renamed EMI Records Ltd. in 1973.

Harvest featured some highly successful acts, notably Deep Purple, Edgar Broughton Band, The Move, ELO and Pink Floyd, but would also release some very obscure artists that would fail to achieve any commercial success. Many original UK releases are now extremely collectable and whilst not quite achieving the stellar values of some other labels' rarities (e.g. Vertigo Swirl). They are still highly prized by collectors.

Roy Wood has become one of the more elusive, if sometimes active musicians of his generation. He continued to record into the 1990s. It must be frustrating for an artist as creative as Roy Wood, with his versatility and ability to play many instruments to a reasonable degree, to accept his diminution out of the public eye. He appears over the years, to have become very reclusive. In one recent interview he spoke of, "About not seeing a person for about five days in a row." There is nothing wrong with leading a solitary existence — or indeed a solitary life. It can speak to a certain kind of intelligence, where solitude is swapped for the banalities of current life.

It appears to me, every musician's life, commercially speaking, has a peak. In Roy's case, we are talking about an artist, who wrote and has had an astonishing run of hits, numbering twenty-two in all. In nearly all cases, unless you break up, at a peak there is the possible or indeed inevitable decline. Ageing, health etc, which is part of everyone's life and part of every musician's life.

As accrued money comes into the picture, so does the question of how to invest it and how to hang onto it. In many earlier cases, how quickly to spend it. Domesticity and marriage and maybe the arrival of children. Plus, the potential for problems with record labels, issues with management, inner creativity, problems and reactions to fame and success. The very real worries about keeping and maintaining success and of losing it. It can all add up to musicians losing their 'freedom mojo.' Creativity isn't guaranteed and everyone has a learning curve. A creative plateau and as many artists would hope — some more further pinnacles. Different people respond differently to an intense time within the public spotlight. And how they enjoy this elusive thing called fame.

Of Roy's bands after Wizzard, The Wizzo Band music is quite heavily arranged. It is quite intense with dense Bonhamesque styles of drumming. If indeed Wizzo, could in any way be called 'jazz,' It is more jazz, in a big-band arrangements sense. It has aspects of fusion and some different time signatures — 7/8 and 3/4 tempos. But the music seems too tightly sprung to allow for incredibly spontaneous solo work, as is usual in jazz performances, live or in the studio. This of course could've been an aspect of their life performance. The Wizzo Band cancelled a nationwide tour, splitting up early in the spring of 1978. Funnily enough, the overall "jazz fusion" era, almost ended up as excruciatingly over the top as the progressive rock era did. Two tracks on the Wizzo album were over the eleven-minute mark. Critics appeared to dislike the music. But nothing Wizzo cut troubled the charts at all. With the added ignominy of radio, ignoring their album entirely. They released two singles 'The Stroll' preceding the album, and 'Dancin' At The Rainbow's End'.

The Helicopters comprised Roy Wood (vocals, guitar), Robin George (backing vocals, guitar), Jon Camp (bass), Terry Rowley (keys) and Tom Farnell (drums). In 1978, following Wood's work with Annie Haslam, Renaissance bassist Jon Camp asked Roy to form a part-time band. And so it was that Helicopters came to be. The band played live gigs (performing some Move classics and '10538 Overture'). They signed to Cheapskate Records (the M.D of the label being one Chas Chandler — ex-Animals bassist / singer and Jimi Hendrix and Slade management pedigree.

The first single put out was 'Rock City', which funnily enough, sounded very much like Jeff Lynne and ELO. It's a glorious, anthemic song. It's further coupled with another wonderful song on the B-side, called 'Giving Your Heart Away'. Personally, I prefer the B-side, but in their own ways, they are both wonderful songs. Helicopters lasted until 1983, when they appeared on Jim Davidson's TV show. 'Giving Your Heart Away' was a very good song, perhaps suffering with a mismatched production.

Carl Wayne covered this song (and it does sound, like it was made for Carl's voice) on *Songs From The Wood And Beyond 1973-2003*. I personally preferred Roy's version.[21] Roy was doing songs around then in the vein of 'Lionheart' and 'Boadicea' which I couldn't really understand. They had a somewhat 1980s hangover to them. They felt somehow dated and forced. Roy tours annually with his band at Christmas time to promote 'I Wish It Could Be Christmas Every Day'. This brings Roy a healthy royalty statement every year. It is a very nice earner and helps keeps his name out there. It is the fate of some musicians to become legends. Remotely remembered for a few hits. People didn't want to hear Roy's "jazz music" even if it was really interesting and wasn't perhaps what you could call jazz. I guess it comes down to making music for yourself, at the very end of it all.

Rob Caiger reflects on things that would not be apparent to fans and critics that have unfairly criticised Roy's career over the years: "Ultimately, Roy needed strong, stable management that not only looked after his career, the business side and his catalogues but also personal management that could have protected him as a person. I sometimes think that Carl Wayne would have had this role nailed down. But being so close to Roy since they were kids, the nailing down, might have used real nails!"

"Criminally there's no Roy Wood or Wizzard album still in print. There's sometimes a burst of activity when an independent label requests to licence material from Warner (also the owner of EMI and Harvest) and a limited pressing of an album or compilation appears on CD for the UK and Europe, which then become harder to find after a year or two. Not one of his Wizzard or solo albums are respected and referred to as an album like ELO's *Out Of The Blue*. In my opinion, his best work was *Mustard* but Roy is really only thought of as a singles artist, one of the best UK songwriters who wrote brilliant songs and founded incredible bands such as The Move and ELO and wrote a mega-hit and classic, immortal song in 'I Wish It Could Be Christmas Everyday'. Not a bad CV but whenever the press writes about him, they usually include the word 'underrated' and refer to him in the past tense."

"Roy should be thought of more. He has made his mark in life through his talent and hard work. His songs didn't just appear — let alone hit songs and timeless classics praised by everyone from the milkman to his songwriting peers, including his hero, Brian Wilson. His music and songs have contributed greatly to musical culture and

---

21 In a real-life Roy Wood interchange, I managed a band for a couple of years when I was based in London. We did a week's worth of gigs supporting Roy Wood and His Big Band. We played at Preston Guild Hall, Nottingham Road Menders, Worthing Assembly Hall, Folkestone Leas Cliff Hall and one other, around 1995.

Why don't you turn around and look at me, I often wish I knew you...

has enriched the lives for millions of people over the years and also inspired many to pick up an instrument, to write, to find the courage to get up on stage and sing and perform. Or go into the business, like I did. That's an incredible legacy to have and worthy of huge respect. And we should never forget people that have given us all that, a huge part of themselves and always not without some personal cost. And Roy Wood has given so many so much."

Back in the 1990's; The Fortunes band came to Roy, wanting to record some demos. This, with a view to developing possible singles and album material. The Fortunes had covered 'Fire Brigade' which was released in the States. It wasn't a patch on The Move's version, or even a definable re-interpretation. But The Fortunes had a strong sound and had done well.

Roy had written and presented The Fortunes with five songs. One of which The Move / Wood fans will be familiar as it was recorded with Carl Wayne. The songs demoed were 'Red Cars', 'Blame It On The Rain', 'Starting Up', 'Raining In The City' and 'Aerial Pictures' — which is completely similar (if slightly faster) to the Carl Wayne version. All have a driving 1980s feel to them. Complete with that clattering, 1980s electronic drum machine production. There were other songs written by Wood for other people, something Roy professed earlier in his career as what he wanted. To be more of a backroom man, writing the hits for other people to perform.

He wrote a quirky song called 'Caroline' recorded by The Casuals in 1969. 'Farewell' was a song written, produced and played by Roy, written especially for Ayshea Brough.

Roy could be seen on the arms of some very attractive women at this time. As his status and popularity grew, apparently so did his confidence. Nothing like some chart success, plenty of TV appearances and a cool run of hit singles to put a spring in a young man's bouncing step.

Ayshea Brough was a British singer, model and actress who presented *Lift Off With Ayshea* an ITV show running from 1969 to 1974. The two had become friends when Wizzard had appeared on the show. The single, a really considered and pretty song, did not perform very well chart wise. But it is a good example, of Roy Woods style at the time. *Lift Off With Ayshea* also featured many up and coming glam acts during its heyday. Ayshea did become briefly engaged to Roy before she got involved in a tempestuous but brief marriage, to the heart-throb actor Steven Alder.

'Dance Around The Maypole' was another rarity, and a collectible written by Roy for The Acid Gallery. 'Hazel Eyes' was recorded by young star Neil Reid and also by Carl Wayne. In my opinion, that song suffered from an overblown production. It sounds like Roy was playing paper and comb and overdubbed them about a million times. It is a pretty song, pared down to its basics. But the production seems to fight the song or to overpower it. The songs themselves, mostly give credence to Carl Wayne's assertion that it was difficult for him to plant his vocal personality on a Roy Wood song.

This is evidenced here in that so many of the songs sound like Roy or The Move combined. His imprint or DNA is obviously very strong in the song structures and sound. Roy managed a good bit of production work, notably for Darts who enjoyed a lengthy period of popularity. Roy produced one of their best hits, the old chestnut, the incredibly infectious 'Duke Of Earl' which managed to climb to number 6 in the UK in the summer of 1979. The Jackie Wilson classic from 1957, 'Reet Petite' was also covered by Darts. This was produced by Wood, but unfortunately this one stalled at number 51.

In May 1974 The Move had a compilation release called, would you believe, *The Best Of The Move*. Greg Shaw reviewed the album and gave a brief overview of their career as such. "True, of all the British bands whose American breakthrough has been stifled by unfortunate circumstances, The Move were among the most deserving of greater fame. That recognition, however, has at least come their way posthumously, by means of increasingly fervent fan activity for both splinter groups (Wizzard and The Electric Light Orchestra) and two fine anthology albums. The 1973 collection *Split Ends* brought together selections from their short-lived Capitol album *Message From The Country*, and the several dazzling singles that had appeared subsequently, including 'Do Ya', 'Chinatown', and 'Tonight'. A good start, but it remained for the people at A&M to fill the remaining gaps. This album, in the works for over a year, does just that. Sides One and Two comprise in its entirety the Move's first album, never issued in America. It's brash, youthful, aggressive, lacking in direction but full of drive. Written entirely by Roy Wood, with the exception of two oldies (Eddie Cochran's 'Weekend' and The Coasters' 'Zing Went the Strings Of My Heart') and an energetic version of Moby Grape's 'Hey Grandma', the album catches young Wood in 1967 as a songwriter of brilliant promise but without the sure discipline evident in his later work."

Over the years Move compilations, appeared here and there. One notable release, and before all the most recent remastering work, was a 3CD box called *Movements 30th Anniversary Anthology*. The booklet notes mention that the CDs, offer up every track The Move ever recorded before signing with Harvest Records in 1971. Rob Caiger was involved with this release, which had pretty good sound for its time and was notable for some good sleeve notes by John Platt. It was the first time I had ever heard the previously unreleased 'Vote For Me'; the Italian language version of 'Something'; an alternate mix of 'Curly'; an un-dubbed mix of 'Wild Tiger Woman', plus the demo of 'Second Class (She's Too Good For Me)', a Roy Wood song which stayed as a backing track as no vocals had been applied.

After a hiatus following the release of the album *Starting Up* in 1987, Roy also put out a version of the Len Barry hit '1–2–3' on Jet Records, released July 1987. It featured some tasty backing vocals, some cool bass playing, with a nice 'phat' sound. But an absolutely horrendous, jackhammering, slamming drum sample which tends to date the piece dramatically. Wood did a guest vocal appearance on a track on Rick Wakeman's *The Time Machine*, then went on the road with his band, billed as Roy Wood's Army.

In 1989, Jeff Lynne and Roy Wood came together to record two tracks: 'Me And You' and 'Get What You Want'. Roy Wood relayed some info about these cuts in August 1994. "At the time I was staying at Jeff's house socially and we were just messing around. I played him this idea for a song that I'd had which eventually ended up as a song called 'Me And You'. I played him the tune for the verse and all that. He said, 'Well, I'll throw a few bits in'. We ended up writing it together and recording it. It turned out well. He also had a guy staying with him named Richard Dodd who had

Why don't you turn around and look at me, I often wish I knew you...

recorded The Traveling Wilburys and he's a great engineer. It turned out well and we stayed up one night. We wrote another song, that we thought we could do as a single and stick it on the B-side. It was called 'Get What You Want'. 'Me And You' is an out-and-out pop song and 'Get What You Want' sounds like an old skiffle number."

Both numbers had immediacy and felt fresh and spontaneous. 'Get What You Want' would've fitted nicely onto a Wilbury's EP or whatever. Roy was also quoted in December 2009 as intending to release the song. "I'm hoping to include it on a new compilation, I'd like to put together next year." The song(s) never made it onto the compilation, which was released as *Music Book* in 2011.

Robert Sandall in the *Daily Telegraph* in 2008 did a review of *Anthology 1966-1972*. He wrote, "It's a mystery, how The Move have missed out on the fame and reputation enjoyed by contemporaries such as The Kinks, The Who and The Small Faces. For an all-too-brief lifespan of four years, they were a tremendous force. Their suited singer Carl Wayne, was an icon of gangster cool, guitarist Roy Wood was a songwriter of rare inventiveness, and drummer Bev Bevan was a gifted "pyrotechnician." *(And let's not forget the two 'gone wrong' Mods, giving the band even more wild energy and street attitude, Ace Kefford and Trevor Burton).*

"Ambitiously taking on most of British rock's growing repertoire of innovations, The Move threw their cap at everything from the Mod theatrics of the Who — smashing television sets with axes and detonating explosives on stage — to the chamber pop experiments of The Beatles. Their talent for creating catchy three-minute singles, made them regular chart fixtures and led to their psychedelic ditty 'Flowers in the Rain' being chosen as the first single played on BBC's Radio One in 1967. Band morale started to crumble after their manager, Tony Secunda an ex-wrestler from Streatham *(Ahem! An ex - wrestler? Not quite Robert?)* used a libellous image of the then PM Harold Wilson on the sleeve of one of their singles *(Actually a post card)* which resulted in a costly lawsuit. Eventually their musical brain, Wood left to form Wizzard. The story is well told on this long-overdue four-CD set which contains all the big hits — 'Night Of Fear', 'Fire Brigade', 'I Can Hear the Grass Grow' and, sounding lovelier than ever, 'Blackberry Way' — while 'Mist On A Monday Morning' contains Wood's most affectingly lyrical string arrangements. Those wanting a shot of something more visceral can head straight to CD2. A rare live recording of the Move at the Marquee in London. Proof, if any is needed — that nobody rocked harder in 1968 than this stroppy Brummie quintet."

Roy Wood toured with Status Quo in late 2009. They did a Winter tour, taking in most of the large stadiums in the UK. Roy made the curious statement that, "their version of 'I Can Hear The Grass Grow', is better than ours."

Roy has also launched his second gin, brewed at an East Staffordshire distillery. He teamed up with a Uttoxeter distiller, Nelson's Distillery & School. To produce his latest seasonal spirit. Roy appears to be busy, accepting a doctorate for his contributions to popular music. He was awarded an Honorary Doctorate of Music at the University of Derby in 2008. Roy was seen on a 2014 BBC Midlands TV interview. He said to the TV reporter, "I've lived on my own now for about twenty years. I can go four or five days without seeing anyone." This is not a criticism in any way of Roy. If this suits your lifestyle — to live in a manner, being one of solitude and not necessarily of loneliness. You have merely chosen one preferred way to live.

His constant love of The Beach Boys hasn't abated at all. "It was so good, meeting The Beach Boys in New York. They learned one of my songs 'Fire Brigade'. Singing one of my songs, with all those harmonies on it, was just fantastic."

Roy was at one stage working on a recording called, 'Roy Wood's American Jukebox', covering much loved songs from USA bands, at the time of this TV broadcast. However, with the current state of CD releasing, where even The Stones or say the hugely successful AOR band Journey, would think carefully about releasing a CD, Roy's 'American Jukebox', as far as I can see, has not been released.

In 2015, his long and eclectic career was recognised with the Outer Limits award at the Progressive Music Awards in London. Wood was inducted into the Rock and Roll Hall of Fame in 2017 as a member of Electric Light Orchestra. Recently Roy's appearances on the live stage have involved him working with Alfie Boe. They seem to enjoy playing together very much.

Trevor Burton

Trevor Burton can quite happily be called one of the wild young men of rock. Trevor had returned to Birmingham on Tony Secunda's advice. He cleaned up his act at his mother's place and got off the heroin turnaround. Which can only end up in certain places. Either gaol, mental institutions or death. Thankfully, Trevor chose life and has had a long musical career.

His next notable step on his musical journey was to hook back up with Steve Gibbons. He ended up as part of the Steve Gibbons Band, touring the world for eight years. A particular highlight during this time was when they supported The Who, sometimes in stadiums with around 80,000 in attendance. A time which Trevor describes as "scary and fun." He also had a stint with the Raymond Froggatt Band - another unsung Birmingham talent.

Trevor played a blond Fender Precision bass with Steve Gibbons. The bulky, long necked bass suited and became part of Trevor's stroppy, extrovert and rebellious personality. Prowling around the stage, adding backing vocals, lead vocals, as well as playing well primed bass. Trevor left the Birmingham scene for a while in the spring of 1998. Here he played the role of guitarist, with The Big Town Playboys. No recordings exist, as far as I know.

Since 1983 he has led the Trevor Burton Band. You could say Trevor was born to play. It's what he has stuck to his entire life. Despite at one point several years back, becoming gravely ill with Legionnaires Disease. He took nearly a year to recover from it and to be able to sing again. His lungs were so damaged, but as soon as he did, he got back down to business. "Well, it's what I know and I still feel like I've got loads more to do," he said in his relaxed Brummie tones, when I asked after 50 years in the business, if he ever felt like hanging up his guitar. "I very rarely feel like stopping, very rarely. What else would I do now anyway? Become a milkman?"

Trevor Burton released the impressive album *Double Zero* in 1985 on Bluesbar Records (BARLP1, 1985). Not a blues album but a warm mixture of sounds in the vein of Eric Clapton, Dire Straits or Rockin' Jimmy & the Brothers of the Night — even some reggae stuff. It features Trevor on guitar and vocals, Stuart Ford on slide guitar, Crumpy on bass and Tony Baylis on drums (Baylis had played in a Stourbridge band called Parker's Alibi). *Double Zero* is now quite difficult to find.

Why don't you turn around and look at me, I often wish I knew you...

Another recommended blues-based release by Trevor is *Blue Moons* (MASC 003, 1999)

These days he may be less wild but Trevor, still living in Birmingham, doesn't show any signs of stopping. "I'm planning to do another album this summer," he said. "Usually, I only take about three days to record an album. Because I think if you can't get it within three takes, then forget it. But this time I want to go into the studio for a month to record it and be a lot more experimental. I've got some ideas buzzing around in my mind. But I want to try it all out, once we are in the studio," he said.

Long Play features eleven tracks, including two songs penned by Trevor. As well as interpretations of nine modern classics. Plus, classics yet to be discovered: tunes from contemporary songwriters like Vic Chesnutt, John Vanderslice, Jeff Mangum of Neutral Milk Hotel, John Darnielle of the Mountain Goats and more. The album is carefully curated and arranged by Trevor to reflect his current tastes. Stripped down to its bare essence, *Long Play* is a painfully honest album, that transcends generational divides. *Long Play* was released as part of Record Store Day UK, on 21st April 2018 in both the UK and US as a limited-edition of 1,000 blood-red 180-gram vinyl and a small run of cassettes. Each vinyl album came with a limited-edition bonus CD, including three songs Trevor plays with a full electric band; fiery renditions of tunes from Phish, The White Stripes and The Weakerthans. Reminding us Trevor is still, in every way, a Brummie rocker.

Trevor also made a live in-store appearance on Record Store Day UK at The Diskery Store in Birmingham.

"This album is different than anything else I've played before. In that it's acoustic — almost all just my voice and guitar, with some keys and backing vocals by Abby Brant, a great Birmingham musician. I wanted a challenge, and I thought trying something new and raw would be a trip and it has been. Michael (Hession) from Gray Sky Records came to a Trevor Burton Band gig, afterwards we chatted for a bit. He said he wanted to record my voice, and I said okay. Simple as that. We went through how we wanted the record to sound. We immediately agreed that it should be fresh and stripped down. That it should focus on songs that were new to me. And different from what I'm used to, that I could approach in my own style. I also put in a couple of my own songs, that fit the theme of the album. And it just kind of took on a life of its own."

As Trevor gigged constantly before his current illness. People would've gotten a chance to hear songs from the record live in intimate gig situations in Birmingham. "I'm playing an acoustic set on Record Store Day with songs from this album, maybe some of these songs will show up on the road this year. We'll see."

Trevor Burton received further respect and props. He got a 'star' on the Kings Heath's Walk of Fame in Birmingham. Trevor said: "To have been chosen to be given a star on the King's Heath Walk Of Fame is fantastic. I would like to thank all involved for making it happen. It's great that it's being remembered, as it will bring back lots of memories for people who rocked there, back in the sixties."

Oscar and Ollie Ireson, Trevor's two sons, also have a band. A country punk mash-up outfit, called The Temple Street Resistance.

In June 2019, the Birmingham press reported that a party fundraiser had been launched for Trevor, who was now suffering with a serious illness: "A major benefit concert took place on June 23rd 2019 for Move founding member Trevor Burton whose health declined suddenly last year. Forcing him to retire from performing live music — a profession he has enjoyed for more than 50 years! Trevor had to give up playing last year, when serious illness affected his ability to play and has now confined him to a wheelchair. Funds raised from the benefit will help towards making Trevor's house more accessible for him to cope with his now limited mobility."

The Trevor Burton Benefit Show was on Sunday 23rd June 2019 at The Robin 2 in Bilston. A great night was had at the sold-out event, largely organised by Trevor's long-time musician friend Maz Mitrenko who was also the MC. It started off with a performance by Andy Fairweather Low, the acclaimed songwriter, record producer, session musician, and sideman, to some of the biggest names in the business.

His rousing rendition of Amen Corner's big hit 'Paradise Is Half As Nice' had the audience singing along at full pelt. The legendary Raymond Froggatt along with his long-time guitarist Hartley Caine, performed a laid-back set in his own unique style. Other well-known local performers playing at the benefit were Emma Jonson, The Climax Blues Band, and The Trevorless Burton Band who all gave wonderful performances, clapped on by the enthusiastic audience. A big highlight of the evening was The Roy Wood Rock & Roll Band. Following Roy's performance of his well-known Wizzard hits, it was a real treat for those attending to see Roy play some early Move hits, with plenty of opportunity for the audience to join in. In addition, a rare appearance was made by Ace, who was back-stage with Trevor. Ace lent his support for the duration of the show. Trevor, Ace, and Roy together signed an electric guitar. The main prize in a raffle held at the event. In my two interviews with Trevor, he was funny, engaging and very warm to talk to. In spite of present handicaps, he was funny and we had a good laugh.

Rick Price

Richard Price was born in Birmingham on 10th June 1944. Rick played with various Birmingham-based rock bands before The Move (1969–1971) and Wizzard (1972–1975). His first band The Cimarrons, were inspired by The Shadows. He then moved on to The Sombreros, who later changed their name to Sight & Sound, moving into a more psychedelic direction, collaborating with Mike Sheridan as a songwriting partnership.

After leaving The Move he signed a contract with Gemini Records. He recorded an album (with Mike Sheridan) the album *This Is To Certify That...* released in 1970, followed by a solo album, *Talking To The Flowers*, in 1971. He then joined Carl Wayne in Light Fantastic before forming Mongrel with future Wizzard drummers Charlie Grima and Keith Smart. With Wizzard he had two British Number One hit singles, 'See My Baby Jive' and 'Angel Fingers', as well as the number four Christmas classic 'I Wish It Could Be Christmas Everyday'. All of these were hits in 1973. After Wizzard split, he joined the Wizzo Band on pedal steel guitar in 1975, but they broke up in 1978. Price was also a member of The Rockin' Berries from 1990 until his death. Price was married to Dianne Littlehales, (professionally known as Dianne Lee of the successful 1970s duo Peters and Lee).

Rick Price: "Almost from the day Wizzard was formed, we were never off the TV. We had outrageous costumes, we had road managers dressed as gorillas and even

Why don't you turn around and look at me, I often wish I knew you…

Mike Sheridan made an appearance as a second Roy Wood. Every time we got a *Top Of The Pops* we felt obliged to come up with even more outrageous outfits. Well, we did have Sweet and Mud to contend with."

Wizzard had half a dozen UK hit singles with a total of 76 weeks in the record charts. However, while Wizzard's success in Britain was initially greater than that of ELO. They couldn't break the North American market.

Rick said: "A second tour of the USA had fallen through because the band members, including myself, wanted more money. We felt we'd done the first tour on the cheap and that, along with the big spending on the studio recordings, made us believe that someone was taking advantage. I'd say we could have negotiated a better deal, but tempers were frayed and it all got a bit silly."

Wizzard continued into the mid-1970s before disbanding, mainly due to disagreements with record company management, over finances and promotion. Rick Price needed work and so through business connections. He was offered the job of tour manager for the famous UK pop duo 'Peters & Lee'. When Lennie Peters and Dianne Lee parted ways in 1980. Rick and Dianne eventually married and performed on-stage together, as a duo around the UK club circuit.

Rick died unexpectedly on 17th May 2022. He was held in a lot of love and affection by his colleagues.

Steve Gibbons

Trevor Burton's long time compadre Steve Gibbons also received a Star on the Kings Heath's Walk of Fame — on Sunday 6th November, at the weekly live music event Birmingham Rocks, held at Velvet Music Rooms on Broad Street. The presentation was made by The Lord Mayor of Birmingham, Councillor Maureen Cornish. The presentation was followed by a live performance of Steve Gibbons on stage, accompanied by the Steve Gibbons Band with Johnny Caswell on guitar, Simon Smith on bass and Howard Smith on drums. Mike Olley, general manager of Westside Business Improvement District, which organises the Walk of Stars, said, "Steve Gibbons truly deserves this recognition, and we are proud to be making him the 48th Star on our Broad Street Walk of Stars. He is not only a giant in the world of music, but he has never forgotten his Birmingham roots. Devoting himself to fundraising for many local causes, such as Birmingham Children's Hospital."

Steve Gibbons was born and raised in Harborne and started his professional life as a plumber's apprentice, but he was a big Elvis Presley fan and joined a band called The Dominettes in 1958. Their first performance was at The California pub near Weoley Castle, with other regular venues including the Grotto Club on Bromsgrove Street, The Sicilia Coffee Bar in Edgbaston and the Firebird Jazz Club on Carrs Lane.

By 1963, The Dominettes were renamed The Uglys, whose hits included 'Wake Up My Mind', 'It's Alright' and 'Something'. Gibbons then teamed up with Trevor Burton to form Balls, before he left to join The Idle Race which quickly evolved into the Steve Gibbons Band.

As well as his music career, Gibbons — now aged 82 — also devoted time and energy fundraising for the Birmingham Children's Hospital and other charities. The 'Star' was the result of local campaigner Jim the Hat, along with his friends, who collected thousands of signatures on a petition, handed in to Westside Business

Improvement District, which organises the Stars. The nomination was carefully considered by the Walk of Stars committee, chaired by Birmingham comedian Jasper Carrott. Jim Simpson, the former Black Sabbath manager and one of Birmingham's greatest music impresarios via Big Bear Music organised the presentation.

To be the focus of the latest Birmingham Rocks event on 6th November. Jim Simpson said, "Steve Gibbons has been at the heart of rock music in this city, almost since the very beginning, and this 'Star' is a much-deserved tribute to his life and work."

Steve's further input and memories are also included in the appendix piece dedicated to the enigmatic and dynamic Tony Secunda.

Jeff Lynne

Jeff Lynne, born in Erdington, Birmingham, grew up in the nearby Shard End area. He began his musical career in 1963 as a member of the Andicaps, leaving that group in 1964 to join The Chads. From 1966 to 1970, he became a founding member and the principal songwriter of The Idle Race. Although the band secured a deal with Liberty Records and were admired as a cult favourite for their creative and distinctive songs, they didn't manage to break into the charts.

In 1970, Lynne accepted Roy Wood's invitation to join The Move. However, this was soon followed by the formation of the Electric Light Orchestra (ELO), a project that aimed to blend rock with classical music, something both Lynne and Wood were passionate about. Shortly after ELO's formation, Wood unexpectedly left the band, leaving Lynne to take control of the group, with Bev Bevan staying on as the drummer.

Under the management of Don Arden, and with road managerial support from David Arden, ELO toured extensively across the United States, building a massive fan base. Their commercial success was immense, with the band selling around 50 million records worldwide. ELO's 'first era' ended in 1986 when Lynne decided to put the group on hiatus after a hugely successful run of albums and singles.

Lynne's earlier encounter with The Beatles in 1968, while he was still with The Idle Race, was a pivotal moment in his life. He and the band were invited to Abbey Road Studios during the recording of 'The White Album'. Watching all four Beatles work together left an indelible impression on him, and he later admitted, "Being in the same room caused me not to sleep for, like, three days." This formative experience grew into a much larger reality later in his career, as Lynne became a highly regarded producer, working with several members of The Beatles.

In the mid-1990s, Lynne was brought in to co-produce alongside George Martin on newly rediscovered Beatles tracks for their *Anthology* project. He worked on the singles 'Free As A Bird' (1995), 'Real Love' (1996), and most recently 'Now And Then' (2023). These songs were based on basic cassette demos recorded by John Lennon, and the remaining Beatles, with Lynne, added overdubs, new instrumentation, and harmonies. Lynne played a crucial role in shaping the final versions of these songs, which were a significant part of the Beatles' legacy.

Lynne also formed the supergroup The Travelling Wilburys in the late 1980s, featuring an all-star lineup including George Harrison, Bob Dylan, Tom Petty, and Roy Orbison. They released two critically acclaimed albums, blending Lynne's signature

Why don't you turn around and look at me, I often wish I knew you…

production style with the unique talents of each member. Lynne's production work didn't stop there. He also produced George Harrison's highly successful *Cloud Nine* album in 1987, which was widely considered to be Harrison's best work in years.

Throughout his career, some critics have remarked on Lynne's distinctive production style, noting its 'Beatlesque' sound. While some have criticised this aspect, it has become a defining feature of his work, and his productions are instantly recognisable. His talent for fusing orchestral elements with rock, and his meticulous approach in the studio, has left a lasting imprint on popular music.

After ELO disbanded in 1986, Lynne became one of the most sought-after producers in the music industry, collaborating with a number of music's biggest names, including Paul McCartney, Tom Petty, and Roy Orbison. Despite this, his connection with ELO remained strong, and in the early 2000s, Lynne revived the band with the album *Zoom* (2001), though it was originally intended as a solo project.

In recent years, Lynne has experienced a resurgence in popularity. In 2014, Jeff Lynne's ELO performed to a massive crowd at Hyde Park in London, which led to the release of *Alone In The Universe* in 2015. This album, their first in over a decade, was followed by another, *From Out Of Nowhere* (2019).

Both albums were well received, demonstrating that Lynne's blend of symphonic pop-rock still resonated with audiences. In 2024, at the time of writing, Lynne is currently touring the United States, billing this as a farewell tour for ELO. He remains the only original member, continuing to bring the music of ELO to fans across the world.

Bev Bevan, reflecting on his career, once said, "I know that I was born with a God-given gift to play drums and percussion, for which I am eternally grateful. I am also thankful to have worked in my career with three total geniuses of rock and pop music — Roy Wood in The Move during the late sixties and early 70s, Tony Iommi in Black Sabbath during the mid-80s, and of course Jeff Lynne in ELO during the 70s and early 80s. Thank you, thank you, thank you!"

Bev Bevan

Over the years Bev Bevan refined his style of playing but he is still a loud drummer. In many ways if you listen to music these days. Drummers are more back beat players (or programmed) in many ways. The different time tempos, the savage attack of the Keith Moon, Aynsley Dunbar, Kenny Jones and Bev Bevan style are still out there in the hard rock arena. In 1976, Bev recorded a solo single, 'Let There Be Drums', his version of the old Sandy Nelson classic.

Bev has enjoyed a solid and long-lasting, touring and album career. Since the ELO days he has gone onto front his own bands; A version of ELO, a version of The Move (including Trevor Burton for a while). He has run the Bev Bevan Band and now is playing full time with Quill. Which includes his now wife, singer Joy Strachan-Brain.

Bevan also owned and ran a record store in Sparkhill in Birmingham. It opened in early 1971 named Heavy Head Records at 803 Stratford Road. One benighted chap remembers, "I used to work as a rep for Polydor Records. I called on all the record stores in the Birmingham area. One day I called in on Heavy Head and a guy sitting at the counter, eating his sandwiches said, 'I almost signed for your label.' I said, 'Who are you?' He said, 'Jasper Carrott.' I said 'with a name like that you have no chance!' What do I know?" The Heavy Head store finally closed its doors in 1976. The store also had its own football team, Heavy Head Records Eleven, which included Bev Bevan, Rick Price and Carl Wayne.

In autumn 1980 Bev released his book *The Electric Light Orchestra Story*. It is good read, and a must for every ELO fan. It gives good insights into the life of a rock musician. In the same year, his then wife Valerie gave birth to his first son Adrian. On ELO's 'Time' tour, Bev had to be replaced on drums by Pete King, the drummer of their support act, After The Fire, for some fourteen gigs in February/March 1982. Bev had been flown to a British hospital, with a case of kidney stones.

During 1988 Bev could be seen as part of the backing band for Beverly Craven and Bobby Womack on a BBC TV show. In 1988 The OrKestra featuring former ELO members Kelly Groucutt with Hugh McDowell and Mik Kaminski were Bev's inspiration when he witnessed their fascinating live set. It inspired Bev to continue with the by then defunct Electric Light Orchestra. He started looking for musicians who would be suitable to play in the group.

He had to obtain rights from Jeff Lynne, for the permission to use the name ELO. Both he and Jeff owned the rights to the band's name. Each would come to own 50% of the company. This was solidified legally after Roy had left ELO back in 1972. When they decided to re-form the band. "Jeff didn't feel that way, and I couldn't persuade him to keep ELO going. So, the only way around it was to form a new band and to call it ELO Part II. This we did, following an agreement between my lawyers and Jeff's lawyers. Which took over a year and several tons of paperwork. Jeff gets a cut of the action (50% of the money from the new group's first two albums) and everyone knows, it's a band that doesn't include Jeff in its line-up."

In the summer of 1990 Bev spent his time getting the band together and recording the debut album. From the members of the old ELO, Louis Clark, Mik Kaminski, Hugh McDowell and Kelly Groucutt all agreed to join. Although most of them did not play on ELO Part II's debut album, joining the live band later. This new band also saw Bev as a songwriter (mainly as a lyricist), giving him the freedom to have more creative input and control than ever before.

Following the success of Heartbeat '86, Bev Bevan organised another charity concert at the NEC in Birmingham. This was to raise money for a national charity organisation. This very successful event called "Barnardos Bandwagon" took place on October 8th 1992. It featured acts like Edwin Starr, Ian Gillan, The Roy Wood Band and, of course, ELO Part II who headlined the gig. At the end of that year Bev could also be seen making several TV appearances supporting other artists and performing with his spare time group Belch (featuring Jasper Carrot and Tony Iommi).

Bev joined Black Sabbath to help them out on one European and two further American tours in 1983/1984. Sabbath drummer Bill Ward had become seriously ill. Bev was an old mate of Tony Iommi and Geezer Butler. He did not have to think very long about the offer. He was asked to join until Bill could return. Bevan was again known for his heavy style of drumming during this tour. He also appeared in the Black Sabbath videos 'Trashed' and 'Zero The Hero'.

A headlining appearance at the 1983 Reading Festival — extracts of which have

Why don't you turn around and look at me, I often wish I knew you...

appeared on a reissue of the *Born Again* album was only Bevan's second gig with the band. "It was just all over the shop," recalls guitarist Tony Iommi. "Bev didn't know any of the songs at all. But he did try. As we went on with the tour, he got a lot better. We went to America, and he did really good. As to that particular stage, doing the Reading Festival was a definite wrong one for us."

Bevan rejoined Black Sabbath briefly in 1987. Here he recorded percussion overdubs for the album *The Eternal Idol*. He was eventually replaced by Terry Chimes after Bev refused to play shows in South Africa, at the time under apartheid rule. (Good on you Bev!) Bev showed some ethical and moral allegiance to more than just the making of ready money.

Bev had quit ELO Part II by 2000. Selling his 50 percent share of the Electric Light Orchestra name. As well as the rights to the ELO Part II name to Jeff Lynne. Lynne thereby became the full owner of the ELO name. He took legal action to prevent Mik Kaminski, Louis Clark, Parthenon Huxley, Eric Troyer and Kelly Groucutt, from continuing to call themselves ELO Part II. They initially tried to alter their name to ELO2. They could not use that name either, so they changed their name to The Orchestra. Possibly chosen due to its similarity to the band Kelly Groucutt ran in the late 1980s with Hugh McDowell and Mid Kaminski, called OrKestra.

After Carl Wayne's tragic early passing Bev formed in 2004, Bev Bevan's Move with Phil Tree and former ELO Part II colleagues, Phil Bates and Neil Lockwood. They did some short tours, playing a set containing a good chunk of the early Move classics. Bates left in July 2007 to re-join ELO Part II. Which by then was renamed as The Orchestra. Bevan was then joined by former Move guitarist Trevor Burton. Bevan and Burton had buried the hatchet a long time before. Roy Wood was not pleased with this 'moving' incursion. Bev Bevan always maintains that Roy was asked to come and join them. It seemed Roy was typically recalcitrant about this invitation. Was this just a 'storm in a teacup' rather than a full-on disturbance?

However, as evinced on 23rd August 2007, Birmingham rock legend Roy Wood vowed never to work with Bevan again. Wood was reported to be furious at Bev's decision to call his new group The Move. He wanted no part of a revival of the famed Brum band.

Roy said: "I don't want people turning up to these shows, expecting me to be on stage, because they're going to be disappointed." When The Move disbanded in 1972, we were at number 10 in the charts with 'California Man' and I thought that was a good place to leave it. This version of The Move has not got my blessing! To me they will never be more than a tribute band. I will never work with Bev Bevan again!"

Bev said he had asked Roy to join the revival tour to mark the 40th anniversary of the release of 'Flowers In The Rain'. Bevan told the *Mail*. "It's a difficult one. I do not know why he is so upset. Because Trevor and myself, are both original members of the Move. If he had taken the time to look at a poster, he would see we are calling ourselves The Move featuring Trevor Burton and Bev Bevan. "I did ask him to be part of it, but he didn't want to do it. That's his decision. It has the 100 per cent backing of Carl Wayne's widow Sue and if Ace Kefford had been fit, he would have been part of it too. I am genuinely disappointed, that he is not happy with the situation."

This was also tying in with the remastered Move catalogue being released. There

Flowers In The Rain - The Untold Story of The Move

was a tasty, remastered 'Flowers In The Rain' CD maxi single. There were numerous entreaties from Carl Wayne over time, to see what it would be like if The Move, could at least get back together and attempt a rehearsal. This of course fell on deaf ears where Roy Wood was concerned. His feelings obviously trumped those of Carl for instance. One does wonder about Roy Wood's ambivalent feelings about The Move.

For example, his flippant and throw away comments in interviews could possibly be engendered because, The Move is the one project in which it wasn't all about Roy or indeed led by him? The Move were a five-piece dynamo and Roy's songwriting, vocals and guitar playing, was undoubtedly an incredibly important part. But in terms of the overall success, there is no ambiguity. The band itself was a force of nature. As revealed by Carl, Trevor, Bev and Ace (Tony Visconti, Tony Secunda, Joe Boyd, Will Birch) and just about everybody else. The band were a fabled live unit. Some of the old 'Move' would flash up occasionally when Trevor Burton joined up with Bev making it two original members of The Move. In this 'Move', Trevor still had flashes of the old fire and the old rebelliousness.

Bev chuckled as he recalled a couple of events. "He has always been that sort of character, you know. He is volatile and very definitely so, God, yeah. We did a show only a few years ago and it was just me and Trevor. We were doing Butlins then. We do the sound check and the guys at Butlins, who are very good actually, they do know what good sound is! And the sound guy says, 'Oh, the guy in the blue shirt, (that being Trevor). Could you turn down please?' Trevor immediately replies to the guy, 'Really! How does fuck off sound?'"

Bev has presented a well-received radio show on BBC Radio West Midlands on Sunday afternoons. He also reviews records for the Midlands newspaper *Sunday Mercury* and has a blog on its website.

The Best of Broad Street Awards announced Bev's inclusion on 17th January 2011. Bev would be honoured with a star on the Birmingham Walk of Stars. Rockers and fans joined together to pay tribute to the Brummie music. Bev was presented with a prestigious Walk of Stars plaque at a special charity night. He was joined on stage by Tony Iommi, Jasper Carrott, Trevor Burton and Raymond Froggatt. They all rocked the city's Gatecrasher nightclub to celebrate the award. Iommi and Carrott having already been honoured with a Star. These, funded by traders' group the Broad Street Business Improvement District. The all-star line-up played a memorable gig with a punchy set featuring songs from Bev's career such as 'Fire Brigade,' 'Flowers In the Rain' and 'California Man'. They also belted out classics like 'Summertime Blues' and 'Go Now'. The Star was presented by the Lord Mayor of Birmingham Len Gregory, who said: "The line-up for this celebration is amazing. We are all here to honour a legend worthy of a place on the Walk of Stars."

An emotional Bev wiped away a tear as he spoke about the award. "I never thought it would come to this when I started playing drums as a young schoolboy in Sparkhill. To think the star will be set into the pavement for ever is unbelievable," added Bev. He paid tribute to wife Val and son Adrian. "They have stood by me through all the ups and downs. "His good buddy Jasper Carrott, joined in the tributes. He said: "Bev is one of my greatest friends and one of the top three rock drummers in the world. He thoroughly deserves the honour."

Bevan is also a patron of The Dorridge Music School (Knowle). In 2012, Bevan narrated the audiobook version of Tony Iommi's biography *Iron Man: My Journey Through Heaven and Hell with Black Sabbath*. Bevan's 2014 personal calendar contained no fewer than 102 gigs in eleven months. Some of which were the final gigs for The Move. Before Bevan and Trevor Burton went their separate ways again.

In 2014 Bevan joined Quill, a Birmingham-based band (not to be confused with an earlier Woodstock era Quill band from the USA. Who released just one self-titled album). The Bev Bevan Band has played gigs with Jasper Carrott under the name 'Stand Up And Rock' since 2017. As somebody who could've retired years ago Bev is one of the truly hard-working guys in rock music. He constantly does interviews; he has been very helpful in the research for this book. There is something more that keeps people going… The pure love of music and sharing it with other people and it is very inspirational. The need to play, is in your blood. It is what musicians do.

Bev was asked to play drums on Paul Weller's *Wake Up The Nation* album. Paul Weller is (as the foreword to this book makes absolutely clear) a massive Move fan. He is also a big lover of Bev Bevan's drumming. Weller made one proviso when Bev came onboard to record. Bev laughed as he recalled Paul's reasoning, "Paul said to me, 'You're not my first choice you know'. I thought 'What?' He said, 'My first choice was Keith Moon but he's dead.'"

Bev played on two cuts on the record. 'Moonshine' the opener, is a raucous, piano tinkling rocker, with solid heavy drums from Bevan. Bev hits the skins hard on the title track 'Wake Up the Nation' another mid-tempo pulser, with a nice bounce from Bev on the drums. This song, in terms of Paul's vocals, has a slight Johnny (Rotten) Lydon inflection. As well as a raw, buzzy punk vibe.

Bev Bevan enjoys a stable life and in 2023 Quill released a CD/stream called *Celebrates Midland Beat*, which includes a new version of 'Blackberry Way' by The Move. The CD also covers other versions of Birmingham bands that charted, some well-known and some less so. Such as 'Ordinary World' by Duran Duran, 'The Day We Caught The Train' by Ocean Colour Scene, 'Can't Find My Way Home' from Blind Faith with Steve Winwood's plaintive vocals and 'Say It Ain't So' by Murray Head. Quill have a Volume Two recording on the way. Bev is a happy, contented and stable rocker. For a man who could sit back on his laurels, I don't know anybody else, that probably does as many interviews as Bev does.

Whether it be on ELO, Don Arden, the original Move, or more recently, his charming tribute to the deceased Richard Tandy, Bev gives out his knowledge, enthusiastically, so others can enjoy his vibrant and lengthy history. From the age of 19 when he joined Denny and The Diplomats in 1963, to the current date. That is an astonishing 61 years. Bev Bevan has never stopped working. And considering he has led the life of a rock 'n' roll musician, throughout many USA tours and has been a road traveller and a seasoned drummer for years, he has come through it all with a smile. Maybe, even a wry detachment about it all? Bev Bevan is always doing gigs, rehearsing, involved in Birmingham music interests. Even though he is very busy he has been incredibly helpful during the writing of this book. There's an adage, "If you want to get something done ask a busy man".

Quill is Bev Bevan's main project now, as a drummer, songwriter and partner to the main singer Joy. Bev commented further, "Over the years I have always been an admirer of Quill. I was particularly a fan of Joy, who I considered to be the best female singer around the Midlands area. When I was asked to put a band together, for a national tour called 'Stand Up And Rock' and found that the show needed a female lead vocalist, I immediately asked Joy to be part of it and she agreed. Since then, 'Stand Up And Rock' has become one of the most successful shows around with sell out tours around Great Britain. About a year ago I joined Quill as percussionist (being a drummer, I have always also liked playing percussion instruments too and have done so in the studio with The Move, ELO, Black Sabbath and Jose Feliciano). It's great to be doing it live on stage now and playing drums on some songs too. The line-up has changed since I joined. The band now has a more folk and country rockier edge to it. The band is also now concentrating on just theatre shows and festivals and I'm very proud to be part of it. I am delighted to be on this current, newly released album *Brush With The Moon*, which was released in 2015."

This effort wistfully marked a turning point for the group. Especially for singer Joy. Her bass player-writer husband Ben passed away before the recording began. "One of Ben's passions was writing songs," she notes on the album's back cover. "With the help of Quill, ex-members, family and friends, we have completed ten tracks, using Ben's vocals from his demos… The album has truly been a labour of love."

"Joy and I are writing songs together and we are looking forward to recording tracks. For another album, to be released later this year," said Bev.

Bev got involved with Slade drummer Don Powell, in the 'Let There Be Drums' project. This featured over twenty drummers. They are all recorded on the Sandy Nelson's 1960s classic 'Let There Be Drums'. The project was designed to raise funds for out of work musicians and road crew, affected by the COVID pandemic and lockdowns, of interest to me as an author and with my deep interest in drums and drumming.

Bev has also played percussion with Bobby Womack and Jose Feliciano. A very little-known aspect of his drumming history. "My future is very much with my band called Quill." Bev Bevan told, Noise11.com. "We have nearly finished a new album and we've got some good guests on it. (We have) Andy Fairweather-Low, Chris Norman of Smokie, doing a duet with the lead singer Joy. We've got John Lodge from The Moody Blues playing bass on it. The son of the old string arranger, Lou Clark, who did all of the arrangements for ELO is on it. Lou sadly died earlier this year. His son Lou Clark Jr has taken over the mantle. And he has a few string arrangements on this album as well."

There is an introduction to Bev Bevan's website by Raymond Froggatt. Although it is basically light-hearted and funny it devotes its basic intent to describing the nature and primal mystery of playing the drums and the universal, rhythmic urge. "Drums are like people, if you hit them, they scream. If you stroke them, they will sing and sigh. If you don't know how to use them, you will confuse them, and if you play them out of time, they will simply leave you forever. Bev Bevan has hit, stroked, used and played drums all his life. He can play anything with the hands of an angel or the arms of fury. It's plain to see that the drums love Bev, as much as Bev loves the drums. When the last Brum Beat is heard…Bev Bevan will have left town." Raymond Froggatt. Amen to that!

Bevan during the writing of this book, could be heard paying a sad honourable

Why don't you turn around and look at me, I often wish I knew you...

tribute. In an interview on BBC West Midlands Radio, recorded on 2nd May 2024, Bev celebrated, remembered and mourned, his long-time running buddy in ELO, Mr Richard Tandy who died a few days before, aged 76. Richard Tandy, the keyboardist in Electric Light Orchestra, had shaped much of the British rock band's sound, died. "We had lost touch, and I hadn't seen him for about eight or so years. We went back a long, long way. I first came across Richard when he played on a couple of The Move tracks actually." (Bevan had recruited Tandy to play harpsichord on the number one hit 'Blackberry Way').

Richard went all the way back in Brum Beat circles and history. To an early version of The Chantelles. He also played in an edition of legendary band The Uglys. He also popped up in an early version of Balls. He probably, due to his gentle nature and looks, got declassified by Tony Secunda. As probably not being ballsy enough for the required Balls line-up. He then skedaddled back to Birmingham, with Keith Smart and Dave Morgan in tow. Richard went onto many more, future musical adventures. To show he was nothing if versatile, Richard also backed Jasper Carrott on his hit 'Funky Moped' with Jeff Lynne and Bev Bevan playing on the sessions. Bev continues the interview "And of course Richard, was a founding member of ELO."

Bev recalls clearly. "We played on every album together from 1970, all the way through to 1986. Right through to the last ELO album, (*Balance Of Power*) it was just the three of us. Jeff, Richard and me. I spent a lot of time with Richard. Who first and foremost was an absolutely wonderful musician. He was a great bass player. Early on, he began to master and subsequently became a great keyboard player. He also learned every kind of Moog synth going. He knew how to play all the new, electronic keyboard stuff and synthesisers."

His death was announced, by the ELO leader Jeff Lynne, who wrote on social media: "He was a remarkable musician and friend, and I will cherish the lifetime of memories, we had together." A cause of death was not given.

Here is an encapsulated slice of ELO detail. In the years that ELO recorded and toured. They sold more than 50 million records worldwide. They had 27 songs that reached the top 40 in the UK singles chart. They had 15 hits in the top 20 on the US Billboard Hot 100 chart. ELO held the record, for the most Hot 100 hits without hitting the number one position.

Post Script

Bev recently ran into Ace Kefford at a Quill gig. I wonder what thoughts ran, through each of these now older and wiser heads as they pondered, thinking back to all those days and years ago? To being very young, hungry men on fire with a musical mission. To burst out of the confines of Birmingham. To take the British music scene head on — which they did. To play some of the best music heard on these Albion shores — which they did. To be one of the best, vocal and musical live proponents in these shores — which they did!

They could never have foreseen what would happen when Tony Secunda; through a crazy, pre-planned set of equally spontaneous and careless actions had a publicity postcard printed up for 'Flowers In The Rain'. One of which in its limited print run, got deliberately posted through the letterbox of Number Ten Downing

Street. The seat and address in London of British political power, the official home and HQ of the British Prime Minister. Then the presiding Harold Wilson. The furore even during those times of immense cultural changes in that year of 1967, was simply mind-melting.

In these days of intense, super-saturated social media, someone reading this may think, what's all the big deal? But remember back then news did not travel very fast. News was pretty slow. Not as slow as a carrier pigeon. Or stagecoach. Or by omnibus or even shipped by boat. But much, much slower than now. If you were beckoned to The High Court of England by the highest in the land. By the British Prime Minister and his cohorts. It could be likened to being thrust into the eye of a searing inferno. Into the hottest, encroaching shitstorm — from the depths of Hades.

These were young working-class men. Caught up in a news, media and legal circus, beyond their own making. And way, way beyond their understanding. They must have mentally plunged down a lift shaft. Leaving their stomachs figuratively hanging, hundreds of feet above in space. The tough, hardened and relatively unshakeable Tony Secunda was now given to experience the hyperborean fears of hidden, possibly unnamed forces. Way beyond his wily, business control which rustled icily around him. A whispering susurrus of threat, in unspoken undertones. Letting him know clearly… via an unrecorded appointment and a subsequent, stark visit by two unknown gentlemen that he too; could be summarily dealt with and also very easily. Yes! Secunda was a tough man in the brutal arena of the music business. But way beyond him and the music scene was another silent and very secret business. That could do away with him, in so many ways. With any or all of these methods… Presenting themselves as just banal, every day, natural causes. Or maybe, as a sudden freak accident. Or indeed, whatever else was wanted, needed or required. Like simply snuffing out a candle…

Bev Bevan understands the truth about the original five-piece Move. He knows they were *the* band. As the bits fell off — it all got much safer. Robbing the band of the innate sense of thrilling, musical danger. This developed as an edgy extension from within their natural personalities. From here, it all progressed to the eventual point of birthing ELO. ELO were a gigantic, international success story. That is another story. But for me, nothing I have heard, and nowhere have I found a band bearing this unique elemental fire, fury and the charismatic 'X' Factor that The Move had in spades. I'm not just talking musical chops or the fact they had four great vocalists. It was a wild and unfettered edge. A fantastic visual look, teamed with their ferocious attitude to live performance. An unsaid urge, to be standing at the very top while at the top — to work their way up. They truly were a force of nature.

I wrote this book to place The Move at the pinnacle of British recorded and live music. In terms of rock book literature, the market is now utterly saturated. With many same bands, being way over and over-analysed. Endless tomes on Led Zeppelin, The Stones, The Beatles have had release. Until this book's publication — absolutely nothing on The Move. They are not immediately slotted into the hard rock or pop genres. Possible big reasons, they fell through the cracks. There were lots of mistakes made. It was a unique time — freewheeling, full of spirit, energy and innovation. Apart from the immediately scary, dividing fissure line incurred through the 'Flowers In The Rain' debacle. Derailing their steady inexorable, upward ascent.

Why don't you turn around and look at me, I often wish I knew you...

There was too much emphasis on Roy Wood's (brilliantly unique) singles. They sold so well — bringing in even more publicity and brand recognition to the band. But, in many ways, they capsized the band. Pushing them away from being the lethal, live musical troupe they were. With utmost respect to the talent of The Beatles and all the other best bands there has never been a band with the animalistic force, before The Move or since. Of course, multitudes of music lovers will disagree.

I'll leave the last words to Bev Bevan. "I regret that we didn't stay together, as a five-piece band. I regret that the first line-up didn't go to America. That would be the main regret for me! It's a shame that Roy was the lone songwriter then. Roy wrote great songs, but he didn't write enough. In hindsight, we should have tried to help. I've realised in recent years, that I can actually write lyrics. I started out with Denny Laine and The Diplomats and Denny was a real powerhouse. Then after that The Move I was with every version of ELO with Jeff Lynne. I was in Black Sabbath for a couple of years. I've been with Quill now for a few years. These are all great players and great bands. But the original, five-piece Move was without doubt the greatest band that I've ever been in.!"

With much respect, any further writing, detailing ELO and Jeff Lynne etc. is a book for somebody else to write... Do it soon — before everybody has left the birthday party.

Isn't it amazing?

Afterword

I just love The Move. I got chatting to Roy Wood in my local once. 'No Future', which became 'God Save The Queen', was my riff and I said to him, "The 'Fire Brigade' chords sort of ended up in 'God Save The Queen'." Roy said, "I had noticed." Roy was fine about it.

Roy told me the story about being locked in at The Madison Hotel room all night. The Move had come down from Birmingham. Later that night, Tony Secunda said, "Go away and write a hit single for tomorrow morning. They had a recording session the next day." Roy didn't have a song. All the guys wanted to go out clubbing. They effectively locked him in the hotel room. Roy was left with a bottle of whisky and a pen and a guitar. He said, "I didn't have one idea and he said that next minute — I heard a fire engine going by, with the sirens."

I was about ten when they were on *Top Of The Pops*. I thought these guys are fucking amazing. They looked kind of cool. There was that anarchic side to them. I actually had to stay off school, because I had a bad cold. I heard the first track on Radio One being played which was 'Flowers In The Rain'. I mainly knew the singles. I followed them for a bit up to 'Brontosaurus' and then up to 'When Alice Comes Back To The Farm'. From a songwriter's point of view, they were really well-constructed songs. I mean, he is a proper songwriter!

I liked the fact that they all sang! That was also really brilliant! Four great vocalists in the frontline. The way they used the English language to express themselves. I thought it was quite something. What it was, I got it from their accents. It's like bands from Manchester, they have an edge to their voices that came from the accents. I think the Brummie thing gave it a bit of that edge as well. It made it sound quite different. I was just getting into them, as they were breaking up. Then there was all this talk about the Electric Light Orchestra. Then ELO made that one record, when Roy was still in the band. It was called '10538 Overture'. I thought it was fantastic. Then Roy split from the band…

Glen Matlock,

February 2024

Appendices

The cancelled US tours

1968

5th July   Carousel Ballroom, San Francisco, CA – Jimi Hendrix, BB King, The Move
(show cancelled due to closure of the Carousel – a Rick Shubb poster was created but never printed for this show – but when printed many years later had the incorrect date on it)

6th July   Carousel Ballroom, San Francisco, CA – Jimi Hendrix, BB King, The Move
(show cancelled due to closure of the Carousel – a Rick Shubb poster was created but never printed for this show – but when printed many years later had the incorrect date on it)

7th July   Carousel Ballroom, San Francisco, CA – Jimi Hendrix, BB King, The Move
(show cancelled due to closure of the Carousel – a Rick Shubb poster was created but never printed for this show – but when printed many years later had the incorrect date on it)

2nd November   Fillmore East, New York City, NY – Richie Havens, Quicksilver Messenger Service, The Move *[The Move cancelled]*

8th November   Fillmore East, New York City, NY – Steppenwolf, Buddy Rich, The Move
[Replaced by Children of God]

9th November   Fillmore East, New York City, NY – Steppenwolf, Buddy Rich, The Move
[Replaced by Children of God]

15th November   Grande Ballroom, Detroit, MI – The March Brothers, The Move
[Replaced by Steve Miller]

16th November   Grande Ballroom, Detroit, MI – Steve Miller, The Muzzies, The Move
[Replaced by The Third Power]

17th November   Grande Ballroom, Detroit, MI – Moody Blues, The Move
[Replaced by The Frost]

1969

31st January   Fillmore East, New York City, NY – Iron Butterfly, Led Zeppelin, The Move
[Replaced by Porter's Popular Preachers]

1st February   Fillmore East, New York City, NY – Iron Butterfly, Led Zeppelin, The Move
[Replaced by Porter's Popular Preachers]

20th February   Fillmore West, San Francisco, CA – Sons of Champlin, Cold Blood, The Move
[Replaced by Albert King]

21st February   Fillmore West, San Francisco, CA – Sons of Champlin, Cold Blood, The Move
[Replaced by Albert King]

22nd February   Fillmore West, San Francisco, CA – Sons of Champlin, Cold Blood, The Move
[Replaced by Albert King]

23rd February   Fillmore West, San Francisco, CA – Sons of Champlin, Cold Blood, The Move
[Replaced by Albert King]

21st September   Unganos', New York City, NY – The Move
22nd September   Unganos', New York City, NY – The Move
23rd September   Unganos', New York City, NY – The Move
24th September   Unganos', New York City, NY – The Move
25th September   Boston Tea Party, Boston, MA – J Geils Band, Lonnie Mack, The Move
26th September   Boston Tea Party, Boston, MA – J Geils Band, Lonnie Mack, The Move
27th September   Boston Tea Party, 15 Lansdown Street, Boston, MA – J Geils Band, Lonnie Mack, The Move
3rd October   Grande Ballroom, Detroit, MI – The Move, Teegarden & Van Winkle, The Stooges
3rd October   Grande Ballroom, Detroit, MI – The Move, Teegarden & Van Winkle, The Stooges
8th October   Whisky A Go-Go, West Hollywood, CA – The Move, Gypsy
16th October   Fillmore West, San Francisco, CA – Joe Cocker & The Grease Band, Little Richard, The Move

Flowers In The Rain - The Untold Story of The Move

17th October   Fillmore West, San Francisco, CA – Joe Cocker & The Grease Band, Little Richard, The Move
18th October   Fillmore West, San Francisco, CA – Joe Cocker & The Grease Band, Little Richard, The Move
[The Move cancelled and left the US – there is a suggestion that the two nights they actually played were October 17th and 18th) but recordings exist of October 16th and 17th]
31st October   Fillmore East, New York City, NY – Mountain, Steve Miller Blues Band, The Move *[meant to be replacing the Steve Baron Quartet]*
1st November   Fillmore East, New York City, NY – Mountain, Steve Miller Blues Band, The Move *[meant to be replacing the Steve Baron Quartet]*

Chelita Secunda (Salvatori)

First wife of Tony Secunda and scenester extraordinaire.

Chelita Salvatori was born on 1st January 1945, into a wealthy, white Trinidadian family. Her mother, Connie was English, and her father's family were from Corsican origin. As a girl, Chelita was sketched by Picasso and was educated at the Lycee in South Kensington, London, and in Paris, from where she ran away because, as her childhood friend Barry Powell recalls, "she hated the nuns." When she was 18 her father died from burns after his yacht had blown up.

Chelita brought chic and art and cultural aspects into Tony Secunda's life. This is reflected in aspects of The Move's career. Their ongoing sartorial excellence, the groovy artsy posters, in a resplendent Op-Art style, designed by Nigel Waymouth for a Marquee gig for one example. A comic book running for months in *RAVE* magazine; designed and drawn by Michael English. There were many exciting areas, in which the fine art, graphic arts and UK art college scene, was overlapping into the music scene.

Returning to London in 1963, Chelita Salvatori was taken up by the photographer Norman Parkinson, a family friend whose introductions helped launch her into the fluid 1960s society. "It was all like... 'Have you met John Lennon? And this is Princess Margaret,' recalls the artist, Kevin Whitney. Parkinson also introduced her to *Harper's Bazaar*, beginning a career in journalism during which she worked for IPC (as features editor for *Woman*), and as fashion editor of *Nova*. She also met and married the pop manager Tony Secunda. In 1966, when the designer Ossie Clark's collection combined blue and green, "a radical breakthrough" according to Henrietta Rous, Secunda "dyed her hair blue to celebrate and became his PR".

She joined Ossie Clark and Alice Pollock's venture, Quorum, as promoter of Clark's designs, and would work with Sir Mark Palmer in his model agency, English Boy.

Robert 'Bobby' Davidson looks back at the complex, exciting and inevitably betraying relationship, he had with Tony Secunda. "Tony married Chelita Salvatori in 1963. She was the daughter of a wealthy white Trinidadian family, who became very influential in many of his projects. She was one of the most dynamic women, I have met. She was always experimenting with new make-up ideas and hair colouring on herself. Which she later used to great effect on Marc Bolan. She pre-empted the 'glam rock' thing, with her mad green and orange eye make-up. Her cheeks highlighted in pink and over that, reflective diamonds and sequins."

Tony Visconti recalled, "Chelita saw that Marc Bolan was very pretty. It was her idea to take Marc around town and hit the women's shops. Getting him into the feather boas and the beautifully embroidered jackets he wore. She was the first person to really use make up on Marc. She didn't just put some make-up on him, she threw glitter on his cheeks."

Chelita and Tony had a tempestuous relationship, which ended after about five or so years.

Chelita was on phone number terms with The Beatles and The Stones and was responsible for hiring such models as Kari-Ann Jagger and Amanda Lear. They later became cover girls for Roxy Music. A band whose style owed something to Chelita's own glamorous image. Emerging as they did, towards the end of the Glam Rock period.

In 1970 Chelita was engaged by Marc Bolan's wife June, as PR for Bolan's group T. Rex. In 1972 Chelita made a cameo appearance in Bolan's film, *Born To Boogie*, dressed as a nun. Chelita advised Bolan on fashion and style. But she also was his coke dealer. Between them, Chelita and Tony must have accounted for one quarter of all the cocaine in London.

Duggie Fields, the London based artist was part of that scene. In 1968, Fields went to live in Earl's Court Square and shared a flat with Syd Barrett, who had just left Pink Floyd. Fields continued to rent the flat and work in Barrett's former room, using it as his painting studio and remodelling the visual appearance in his personal style. Chelita was Mickey Finn's lover during the heyday of T. Rex. Like Mickey, Chelita had battled serious addiction to heroin for many years. In 1979 Chelita left London for Trinidad with the intention of "escaping the smack stigma and setting up a small hotel." Chelita did recover, attending Narcotics Anonymous meetings.

In 1988 she went to the Wiltshire clinic Clouds and kicked the heroin habit. Like her friends Anita Pallenberg and Marianne Faithfull, "they all made their journeys in recovery in the same way," recalled Field, "Anita was a big inspiration to Chelita."

Nigel Waymouth was a very good friend of Chelita. He was one of the three young hipsters, that started out running Granny Takes A Trip, the famed 1960s shop at the end of Kings Road, Chelsea, London, selling wonderfully ornate jackets, trousers and clothes for men and women. Particularly known for their brocaded Liberty style William Morris jackets.

Waymouth and Michael English also were part of Hasphash and the Coloured Coat producing a zany album called *Featuring The Human Host And The Heavy Metal Kids*, released in 1967. With a follow-up *Western Flyer* in 1969 featuring a prevalent use of the bagpipes.

After leaving the fashion arena, Waymouth became a dedicated painter, mostly in portraits. "I knew Chelita better, than my wife and the next wife. We went away together to Trinidad, just as sort of holiday. Sadly, she'd need to come to heroin, it was in the early '70s. Yeah, but she gave it up, I think the damage was done, because she died of a heart attack or something, but not until much later. Mickey was one of my best friends, yes, she was, involved with Mickey, she fancied him, yes. But I don't think he was reciprocating quite as much as she had wanted it to be. Because Mickey was also involved with somebody else. They were different characters, and Chelita had an independent streak in her. I cannot say any more than that, because I don't really know why they parted."

"I found her very enthusiastic. She was quite determined to get things done. She was a very young editor, of *Harper's Bazaar*. She was incredibly young when she got that job. That tells you just how determined and focused she was. As a person, she was great fun, she was a good company to be with. She was intelligent and you could converse about a lot of things. That's why we had a friendship. We struck up a friendship. It wasn't a romance, it was a friendship. But it went quite deep. She was always looking out for me. When I got involved with ladies and certain marriages and things. She was always at hand. She was my best friend."

In the mid-1980s, she became the London correspondent for the Parisian magazine *City*. She later performed the same role for the influential, Japanese magazine *Hanatsubaki*. Derek Jarman gave her a part in his 1986 film *Caravaggio*. Chelita organised the Alternative Miss World competitions for Andrew Logan. Logan had known her since the early days. Logan's 1987 portrait shows her clad in a bright yellow turban with a heart containing a portrait of her daughter Tallulah. Chelita had only recently moved to Marrakesh, where she had been working single-handedly to open a hotel. An effort which may have brought on the heart attack that killed her. "Chelita was one of the most dynamic people I've ever met," said Logan. Chelita was already assuming legendary status among her friends.

Piers Secunda, "It's not unusual, my mother (Patricia McRoberts and Tony Secunda's second wife) worked in the fashion world in the 1970s. So, she would know Chelita because Chelita was a stylist and was extremely close friends with Manolo Blanek — a legendary shoe designer, in the fashion world."

A young art aspirant, Ray Gange was studying at Chelsea School of Art. He got to know Chelita and had the benefit of her connections, her intellect and information about painting and financing and galleries in London etc.

"She was an 'it' girl for a while. She had been photographed by Norman Parkinson. Long before I met her, she was a proper London fixture, a mover and shaker. She was fashion consulting, for magazines like *Vogue* when I met her. Around that time, I remember she was responsible for helping launch Julia McDonald's career, a fashion designer. I don't know that she had a salaried job but she did freelance work and she was very highly regarded. I met her at Chelsea art college and it was just round the corner from my house. So, I'd pop round and have a cup of tea and a chitchat. She lived off the Fulham Road, right next to Chelsea football ground. In a place called Italian village. It was like a secret garden — probably about 15 or 20 places there."

Gange continues his train of thought. "Chelita was very witty, very intelligent, very sophisticated. With a good line in sarcasm. She was great, very entertaining and very educational. If you hung around with her you would learn about different aspects of life and culture."

Even though Gange was in his early 30s, he didn't know much about the art world. "She wasn't with the guy from T. Rex, Mickey Finn, that had long ago finished. When I met her, she had just split with her daughter's father. She sold her house in Fulham; she bought a building in Morocco (in 1987) and she was going to turn that into a hotel. Unfortunately, she had a heart attack on the staircase. They reckon it was from the stress of trying to get this hotel built. But it also might have been that her heart might have been weakened by her 1970s /80s lifestyle. She knew everybody and she was a very inspiring person to be around."

Dougie Fields did a fantastic image of her for her London funeral. When we went to the funeral. On all the seats there was a little postcard size reproduction, of the painting that Dougie Fields had done. Tony Visconti said that he quite liked her! "Yeah, she had a lot to say, and she was very into the scene and the art scene."

Alas; just like her first husband, the exciting and intensely volatile Tony Secunda. Chelita was to die at a relatively early age. Chelita passed away on the 7th of March 2000 in Marrakesh, Morocco. She had packed a lifetime's worth, or maybe even two into the time she resided on this planet.

Flowers In The Rain - The Untold Story of The Move

Tony Secunda

"It's easier to apologise than to ask permission."

The recondite enigma that was
Anthony Michael Secunda
(24th August 1940–12th February 1995)

I am especially indebted to both Piers Secunda (Tony's son through his second marriage to Patricia McRoberts) and to writer Dave Thompson who worked closely with Tony. Secunda acted as Dave Thompson's literary agent for the last four or five years of his life.

Tony Secunda was once described by the extremely portly, writer and jazz singer George Melly as follows: "Secunda was the most perfect specimen of all those ex-public-school layabouts, who had been sitting on their arses, up and down the Kings Road for almost a decade, wondering what to do with the only talent most of them had, an instinct for style."

Johnny Rogan aptly described him as "One of the great sensationalists of the sixties."

Tony Secunda was one of an elite corps of pop group managers who galvanised the 'Swinging Sixties' and helped shape the course of popular music. Among them were astute publicists and wheelers dealers like Andrew Loog Oldham and Kit Lambert and Chris Stamp. The men behind the Rolling Stones and the Who respectively. But Secunda was perhaps the wildest and toughest of them all. He was the driving force behind some of the biggest hit-makers of the era. Including the Moody Blues, The Move, Marc Bolan, John Cale and Steeleye Span.

Secunda was the grandson of Israel Secunda, an ethnic Russian emigrant who had arrived to London from Daugavpils in modern day Latvia. At that time, Latvia was still considered part of the greater U.S.S.R. Tony was born in Epsom in 1940. His father Hyman Secunda had worked with his grandfather Israel in the textiles trade in Whitechapel, East London until World War One. Hyman was packed off to France to fight. Hyman came back, very damaged from the monstrously debilitating World War and struggled through life from then on. Daniel Secunda (who was Tony's cousin) ran a market stall on Petticoat Lane. He sold fabric when he was younger. Before he got into the music business.

Daniel Secunda was also active in the music business in London and New York over the same period. Daniel worked with artists such as Judy Garland, Joe Cocker, Heads Hands and Feet and The Heartbreakers, amongst many others. He was very close friends with Jimi Hendrix. He was a director of the latter-day Track Records and subsequently gained rights to some Track recordings. Releasing Shakin' Stevens, Marc Bolan and Jimi Hendrix albums on his own Media Motion label.

Tony Secunda was educated at Epsom Public College. After leaving he obtained a job in London, working for the magazine publishers Fleetway Press. Secunda was a frequent visitor to the 2i's Coffee Bar. He was intrigued by the new rock 'n' roll movement. It has been recorded he spent time in the Navy, employed as a Merchant Seaman. His first role in the music industry that got him noticed was becoming the manager for The Moody Blues. They were his first Birmingham based band. It's common knowledge that they had a massive UK and international hit with 'Go Now.' But financial bickering quickly ensued. The details are not exactly clear and Secunda parted ways with the group amid significant acrimony. He departed with vocalist Denny Laine as his most exclusive supporter.

Denny Laine went on to have a long-time relationship with Secunda. Certainly, all through his sojourn, as one third of Paul McCartney's Wings. Secunda had stayed on as his personal manager.

When Secunda took over the management of another very promising Midlands group The Move they brazenly set out to rival The Who with a wild stage act involving their own brand of chaotic "auto destruction".

Encouraged by Secunda, the band adopted a violent gangster image, complete with Savile Row tailored Chicago-style suits. Secunda worked in partnership with the producer, the late Denny Cordell. The two men stayed in touch until the end of each other's lives. For me, The Move and Secunda were the most successful marriage of insane publicity, hit making and performative controversy and strength. I wish they could've gone onto bigger and crazier things.

Tony Secunda was working in partnership with Harold Pendleton (who was running The Marquee) as part of Marquee Management. He discovered The Move and he knew this was *the band* to create money and success and furthermore, controversy. A band who could fire up his weird, roiling anti- establishment ideas and arouse plenty of outrage, trickery and renegade publicity. This dovetailed nicely with The Move enjoying a red-hot Thursday night residency at the London Marquee Club. A prime spot to impress movers and shakers; plus, the A & R bodies from London record companies, and also their growing public. They took over from The Who on Thursday nights. Making heads turn, by playing two 45-minute sets and taking The Marquee apart. There was another band called The Action who had been compared with The Move. Tony Secunda was said to have failed to pull off a coup to overthrow The Action's management.

Then turning his attention to the fledging Move who, initially, according to Mike Evans, "He created in our image (ever noticed how Carl Wayne nicked Reggie King's hand-over-the-ear singing technique?). They were happy to do whatever it took, and it paid off commercially."

This boils The Move down to being a hollow act and also sounds like sour grapes. Evans is forgetting they were the best band to come out of Birmingham. Boasting four first class vocalists and initially pumping out a great set of obscure R&B and USA soul sides allied to a dynamite stage act. These are things that Tony Secunda couldn't teach them. Also, a lot of people did the 'hand over the ear' thing. It wasn't an unusual thing to do in recording studios by vocalists. By the time Secunda had come across Carl and the guys they were gig hardened and seasoned vocalists. Like all good managers he wanted to put them on the map and Secunda certainly succeeded. The string of hit singles by Roy Wood didn't hurt either.

Dave Thompson encapsulates Secunda's qualities and innate, dark charisma. "Marc Bolan called him 'Telegram Sam'. Macca called him 'Sailor Sam', and Linda McCartney once said he looked like a rat. So he sent her one through the post. Secunda promptly visited the nearest pet store, picked out the meanest, ugliest rat they had and had it delivered, gift wrapped (of course) to Mrs M. He was the greatest agent, I ever had. It's twenty years since he died — the daft bugger. Tony Secunda was the man who put the 'mad' in management and took the old age out of it..."

Tony Secunda was one of the most controversial and influential and also unknown managers in the 1960s rock business. Secunda is the one (possibly due to dying relatively early at the age of 55) that has undoubtedly disappeared. He has vanished out of the chronicles of rock history. So fascinating is Tony Secunda; I thought, without disrupting the flow of The Move book, to add this appendix on Mister Secunda alone. To try to make some sense of his character, his personality, wind-ups, stunts, pranks and management style. During his initial 'hot' or 'high' years of management, which ran from 1965 through to around the latter 1970s. He then had a second period in the USA, which ran up to his unfortunate early demise in 1995.

Secunda later became ensconced on the West Coast of America. He was located outside San Francisco in the larger Bay Area. Living in the Belvedere, Tiburon area. About a half an hour's drive over the Golden Gate Bridge. Out from San Francisco city and into Marin County. A lot of the rockstars, managers and drug dealers etc had all moved out of the city and got property there. Amongst the massively tall dark green pines and lushly forested areas, the air is good, clean and bracing. After they all made some massive cash during the big musical and cultural splurge that had blown through the city like gold dust.

Secunda joined the community, that had grown filthy rich from this first great talent explosion. Erupting from San Francisco and the larger Bay Area. He had branched out with an interest in conservation and in tree work. Tony had set up a literary management agency. I only discovered recently that he was still in management, as a literary agent. He worked with Dave Thompson, a well-known British music author, with over two hundred published titles. That part of Secunda's life certainly wasn't covered in the UK. Possibly by then he had been forgotten, he had fallen through the cracks.

Secunda was a mesmerising individual — hated by some, feared by quite a few others. Dismissed by a good few industry insiders but with a feeling of fealty, respect and a certain amount of awe by others, including me, from a far off distance. Secunda's history is convoluted, weird and pretty fabulous. Some years later on 22nd February 1995, an obituary for Tony Secunda appeared in *The Independent* newspaper based in London.

Chris Welch, a longtime music journalist, described Secunda as follows: "Tony Secunda was a dark, brooding and somewhat menacing figure. He thrived on taking risks, and he was not afraid to indulge in the most basic scams and publicity stunts. But he achieved results for his artists and took the ethics of the underground hippie scene, into the boardrooms of the music industry."

Tony Secunda has melted into the hazier rock music background, unlike other managers of the time. In fact, he inhabited a unique space. Due to his eccentricity and his defined use of *sui generis* publicity stunts. The Move were definitely Secunda's plaything. Much more so than his previous act, the relatively controllable and benign Moody Blues. The Moodies were nowhere near as untrammelled, as wild and dysfunctional as The Move. Secunda didn't just suddenly appear fully formed — he had to pay his dues. Which he did in other areas of the entertainment and music business. His mercenary attitude to business and to some people was rooted in his ruthless personality. With a pronounced tinge of threatened (and at times actual) violence.

The spoils in the music industry — after the unheard of sensation caused by the emergence of The Beatles and of singles, EPs and albums as colossal sellers — heralded the music business was about to break big, big, big! And in an entirely new manner. It would've made him realise, that music made for an easier life, so to speak. In terms of being able to make, large amounts of money relatively easily. With less of the physical graft he had experienced before. Who wants to break their backs making money when you can do it without recourse to damaging your spine?

Secunda himself said in an early interview, "I opened up a club in Leytonstone in East London with Chris Andrews."

He discusses his earlier achievements, "After we'd opened the club in Leytonstone with a big publicity campaign, we found the place was becoming packed, every time we opened the doors. By the time I was 18, I was earning £150 a week. I met Stanley Dale who managed Tony Hancock, Spike Milligan, Eric Sykes and we all shared an office. Then we went into partnership and opened a string of ballrooms."

For reasons not exactly clear and regrettably for Secunda maybe as a temporary setback. His partner Stanley Dale, ousted him from his managerial post. Secunda elaborates further. "I ran into a guy called Johnny Kidd — he'd had a minor hit record but as all the national newspapers were on strike he'd received no exposure at all. Kidd was complaining about having no work. Clem Cattini, Brian Greg and Alan Caddy were his backing group, and they were only getting about 30 shillings a night, five nights a week. I took over and I upped their money — and they started happening. At the time, I was also running about eight venues. 'Shaking All Over' then hit the charts. A stupendous classic piece of psyche rock 'n' roll, with that succulent guitar solo. We became the first people, to quote £100 and £150 fees for just one night. People said you will never get that sort of money for a number one record."

After this Secunda changed gears for a while. He decided to go into wrestling and became a wrestling promoter. This is where Secunda first really began to learn what it was all about. "I had to zoom around five nights a week. I'd go to a drill hall. I'd set up 1,000 chairs, number them, set the lights up — run the whole show myself. In fact, after the show was over, I'd pack it all up, go out and put about 150 posters around. Then leap into the next town and do it all again. I did that for about a year."

Paul Lincoln was his partner, and he was the guy who really turned Secunda on to what he learnt about show business and showmanship. Secunda remembers, "I made so much money, I went a bit crazy for a while. After that, I went AWOL and nuts for a while. I met a guy called Alex Murray and he said, 'Let's go to South Africa', so I looned off there with him, all within 48 hours of him making the suggestion. Over there, we sang and produced records with Mickey Most. Mickey Most had about ten number one records out there. Then I went out to the Congo (Africa) for a month and then I returned to London in 1964."

Back in the smoke, he started doing the music administration for Lesley Duncan. The first, big break came when he began exploring the Birmingham Beat scene. "It was then I found The Moody Blues." Later on in that first year back in the UK, Secunda's luck transformed when The Moody Blues struck number one, with the gigantic international hit 'Go Now'.

According to Don Arden, who replaced Secunda as The Move's manager, Secunda was furious when The Move dispensed with his services. Secunda took it personally and told everyone how he was going to "do" Arden. Don Arden claimed that Secunda was "totally wrecked on drugs the whole time" and ultimately died by his own hand. The first part of Arden's statement is partially true in some aspects, but not the second.

Although his memoirs appear to be the only source for this last statement, this does not tally with the facts. Plus, through several remarks Dave Thompson has made to me one startling point was made, although it can't be accurately verified. That Secunda wanted to take a "hit" out on Don Arden and have Arden shot.

His path also crossed with Procol Harum who had the massive seller with 'A Whiter Shade Of Pale' produced by his good pal producer Denny Cordell. These two men's lives were linked throughout — they were an unofficial music scene duo for a while in London. Sharing an office and cross platforming The Move, Procol Harum etc.

Secunda was trying to offload Procol Harum and sell off the contract. "My asking price is £75,000," said Secunda, "and there are four years left to go on the contract. My reasons for selling Procol Harum, boils down to the fact that our personalities clash. It's like a divorce — it's better for future happiness that we should part. Let's be frank," he said, "for one thing, Procol no longer agreed with me on their future music style. They became terribly introvert and incommunicative [sic]. They refused to accept my guidance and adopted a prima donna manner. They turned down £100,000 worth of engagements I had arranged for them and that's an awful lot of bread. Because of this, I decided I could not negotiate for them any longer." So endeth the Procol Harum / Tony Secunda episode in his ongoing management history.

One young chiselled, handsome man whose path crossed with Secunda on at least two endeavours was Steve Gibbons of The Ugly's who secured a recording contract with Pye Records. The first release from the group in 1965 was an original song entitled 'Wake Up My Mind' composed by Burnet, Holden and Gibbons. The single was advanced for its time and featured some socially conscious lyrics — very unique and boasting. It did not sell well in the United Kingdom but reached number 14 on the national Australian chart. A second Ugly's single released the same year was 'It's Alright'. This one featured very catchy underpinning using a harpsichord. The band appeared on *Ready Steady Go!* but unfortunately this wonderful song didn't chart.

Steve remembers the choices for many. "There was a huge factory in Birmingham on the main road towards the Lickey Hills. It's a lovely spot, one of the greenest parts of Birmingham. When I started out there was a huge printing works on one of the main roads called Kalamazoo. Lots of kids from our school went to these various places. There were so many factories, office blocks where the kids would go. There was a place called Chad Valley, which made toys."

But music was strong in Gibbons, he was building up a name in Birmingham with the musically fertile Uglys. "When The Move happened, their harmonies were brilliant. That was down to Roy, he showed them how to do it. I thought they were going to be big, because they practiced so very hard. All these bands were

Appendices

mushrooming all over Birmingham. The Move really opened the door, particularly with their harmonies. I mean, if you're in a band you're in the frame, aren't you? The triumph of The Move (albeit they rid themselves of Secunda) impelled Steve and others toward a further stab at superstardom with Balls. "That's when Tony Secunda latched onto us and took us out to this place in Fordingbridge and then he went back to London. I remember I had a lovely old MGT3 and I drove down from Birmingham there in that. He left us there to come up with some hit records. The hope was Denny Laine, if he could do it once, then he could do it again. Maybe Denny lost his mojo? Denny didn't actually come up with any great songs, I mean maybe a bit. He got us down in the country, got us completely stoned and we were to make an album and that's how it was… That one song came out as 'Fight For My Country,' which Trevor wrote. That wasn't very much for all that advance and for all the people hanging around."

Steve Gibbons went on to be managed by Secunda as a solo act. This included the release of his first solo record *Short Stories*. Again, it is said Secunda got a considerable cash advance for Steve. Some of which was ploughed into the ornate record production. The production was overseen by Jimmy Miller, who made his name with The Rolling Stones, and this was a successful liaison.

On Steve's debut solo record, the musicians were the cream of London's finest, Albert Lee the guitarist's guitarist. On drums from Balls (and going on to future stints with Lennon, Harrison and Yes) was Alan White. Mike Kellie was also on some tracks. Beatles pal Klaus Voormann was one of the bassists featured, along with Greg Ridley. Also on bass was his long-time running buddy with the Steve Gibbons Band, the funky, extremely talented Trevor Burton. A large US American choir featured Madeline Bell, an American living in London and another famous solo and backing singer Doris Troy, who rounded off the package.

The album was a lively confection of country and pop with harder rock songs. Some would credit the album with "a Rolling Stones tinge" to the sound. Inevitably, it was released on Tony Secunda's new record label Wizard. Although the record garnered critical applause, Secunda's discovery of Marc Bolan as a major star talent at this time overshadowed the usual amount of dedication Secunda would put into marketing Steve Gibbons new project.

Gibbons had already spent a two-year period under Secunda's management. It was only a short time before problems arose within Balls. Dave Morgan and Richard Tandy were fired as incompatible, with the new group's musical direction… Keith Smart also left to be replaced by Spooky Tooth drummer Mike Kellie. Steve Gibbons blamed Secunda for being ruthless. In sifting and in sorting out all the musicians who, in his opinion, did not fit the image of a successful band or as "having balls." Gibbons talked about it in the TV documentary, Untold Stories, "I am pretty sure Tony Secunda had this agenda going. So, one by one he gave them the boot. We would have nightly rehearsals in the barn, after visiting the pub. Not only did the constant change of musicians prevent progress. The way of life of the band, did not exactly encourage very concentrated work."

During his time leading The Steve Gibbons Band, Steve penned a composition called 'Chelita'. It is a beautiful song, big and expansive with a big open Bruce Springsteen vibe. It was produced by Tony Visconti as was the entire *Down In The*

Bunker album. It was directed at Chelita Secunda and the destructive lifestyle she was involved in, namely the excessive use of cocaine. "In Denmark Street, he had the second floor. Tony was a moving target; I mean he went around to various offices around London. There was one occasion which I'll never forget. One of my wisdom teeth was really playing me up. I was living out in Stanmore. I drove into London in my little Riley Elf. I had got an appointment or interview, something like that. When I got to the office, my tooth was really painful. Tony said, 'Go round the corner, man'. Round the corner was Harley Street. 'There's a dentist on the corner,' he said, 'He'll put you right — Terry Downs the middleweight champion has already gone in there. I advised him to go'. And I said, 'Oh really?' And he said, 'Yeah, the guy's brilliant'. But this guy wasn't brilliant at all. It was a wisdom tooth, and he said, 'That's going to have to come out'. When I had my wisdom tooth out, this dentist was an Australian... Secunda had recommended all these people to him, big posh offices, velvet etc... Anyway, it absolutely raised the pain, I was in bloody agony. What the fuck in hell? I said to Secunda, 'The guy was terrible'. He goes, 'Well, what do you expect, man? He is a dentist he always hurts people'. It hurt me, I never got to sleep until about 7 o'clock the following day."

Steve Gibbons met his significant partner at the same time as Bev Bevan met his (Val) at the Cedar Club. Steve met a very attractive young woman called Patti Bell. She gets several mentions in Eddie Fewtrell's book *King Of Clubs*. "Yeah, Patti was wonderful." It is lovely to hear somebody talk about their ex-partner as being wonderful. "I did find Tony to be a nasty piece of work. But 'hatred' is not the right word, Tony was an aggressive man. He knew how to handle young guys and how to get them to sign contracts."

Gibbons said that Secunda would introduce him to people. Steve didn't fully understand who these people were and why he was being introduced. "I had moved to London eventually to work; I was under Tony's wing. He was living in the heart of London, there was some guy that he approached — he may have been gay, I don't know. He was a bit longer in the tooth than I think he imagined. Tony took me see to this older guy — he was like a major or some old army guy. I was thinking 'What a weird place to bring me to.' It was a very nice place, a very big posh house. Tony said, 'He's an interesting guy, you will get some good ideas from him — really bizarre'. He would try all kinds of things out to see whether this guy would take a liking to me or vice versa. I don't know who this guy was, he seemed a well-to-do bloke. Could have been a doctor or something like that. That was just one episode. It was like Tony wanted this other guy to size me up. It's like he wanted a second opinion maybe. He would introduce me to people, their reaction was 'Oh right, that's a big star. He is going to be a big star'. That's my supposing. I mean, why did he introduce me to these people? It was bizarre. He got me to *Vogue*. He made an appointment at *Vogue* to take photographs of me. Who are these people who saw me as a potential face?"

Gibbons was a good-looking young man with chiselled features. He looked the business; he looked like a rock star. "But I felt a bit like a fish out of water whilst I was there. I thought, 'What the bloody hell am I doing here?' He had this horrible thing which he did. He wanted to do something with my eyes. These lenses type things were about the size of a half a crown. You just slid them under your eyelids and these lenses were chrome on the surface. If someone looked at you, they would see their reflection. Was it for the stage or for *Vogue* magazine? The whole thing was about outrage, to get in the papers. I was on the front page. It was *The Sketch* or *The Mirror* newspapers. So that was his pathway to fame. I think he was strange in the way he went to bat, because he used to promote wrestling matches and all that."

Steve Gibbons' relationship ended with Tony Secunda selling his contract to Bill Curbishley, the manager of The Who. "When Bill Curbishley confronted Secunda, because we had this meeting about me leaving and getting out of the contract. Tony gave Bill Curbishley a quote of how much he wanted to release me. It was one-wheeler dealer against another. Bill was a big figure. I remember with Bill and his final words when this meeting came to an end. He turns to Secunda and says, 'Right, there's your fucking money, now just piss off!'"

I asked Piers Secunda, whether he was aware of The Move and the relationship with his dad. Piers began to unravel parts of the riddle surrounding this tale and filled in some important biographical gaps about his distant father. "Let me explain a little bit about the nature of my relationship with Tony: I didn't hear Tony's name spoken until I was 13 years old. When I did, I was completely stunned. Because my mum was on the phone, talking to somebody and I was in the same room. And she mentioned his name. She had never ever spoken to me about him and a couple of her close friends had told me, 'Don't talk to your mother about him'. Of course, I had no idea what that meant. Or why she had a very acrimonious divorce from him. Why did she consider him to be such a very dangerous liability? So, when I asked her about him, what she said was, 'Don't ever get in touch with that guy! He will show up to wherever you are! He'll demand to see you and he will kick doors in to get near you. And he will damage your life!'"

After being given the thorough fright of his young life, Piers' naturally rebellious personality started to assert itself. Piers could have been, understandably, scared off into keeping a million miles away from the father he knew next to nothing about. A father that his mother had tarred with the darkest of brushes. "Well; that never happened but retrospectively, I can understand that. It gave me a kind of terrifying insight into what she had experienced. There are lots of different reasons why. But also, she also was an exceptionally difficult person and unbelievably selfish... I mean, actually on the register of people who I have known throughout my life, she is by the widest margin the most selfish person I have ever encountered!"

Piers continued the story which has a peculiar and eerie tinge: "I think that her behaviours had a lot to do with his behaviour as well. She was a very provocative person. She provoked people in ways which are (or were) not always positive. And I can see how the two of them would have severely clashed... I was in touch with Tony for two years and we spoke on the phone, twice a week and we talked a lot about all the stuff because we'd never physically met. I'd been growing up in London and in Sussex, which was where my mum and my stepfather were. It was then I got in touch with Tony. My mother only found out after he died. She was shocked and horrified, but it was the best thing I ever did. Because for a very brief time, I knew him, and I had that experience, and it meant a hell of a lot to me! We talked about a lot of different things, and he taught me a lot. He taught me about the management of people and all sorts of stuff. We would speak for like two hours at a time. Every phone conversation was like a dam had broken."

When Piers asked why he had never heard from his father before, Secunda said, "Did you not get my letters?" Patricia kept Secunda's letters away from Piers: "My mother realised it was his handwriting when he wrote, and she freaked out. We just talked and talked. When he met my mum, he was living in Fulham. He had converted an abandoned church. More of a chapel than a church. He converted it into a flat so when he bought that, he was still with Annie Lowey. Then they split up. My mum was involved with helping him finish it up. She put literature into it. In her paperwork after she died and her photo albums, there were photos of the place. I recognised it instantly. It was in Fulham, and they then moved into a house in Holland Park. That's the address where Tony got the restraining order against him."

Did Robert Davidson have any impact into your life back then? Piers knew that answer: "No, I missed that stuff because I was born in 1976. Robert's relationship with Tony was business until Tony married his ex-girlfriend, which was my mother."

Robert Davidson had also mentioned another woman. This woman was not (Shell heiress) Patricia McRoberts (Secunda's second wife). She was another very beautiful woman. Robert said that he first met Tony at the flat of a woman, called Annie Lowey, who was a fashion model. Piers remembers her, "Tony and Annie had a son called Phineas, now called Hannah. Annie died in 2023.

Piers expands, "Shirley Ann Scott was Tony's sister. Tony's sister lived in Cornwall, and she was a ceramicist. Her work is in the Victoria and Albert Museum. She was quite beautiful, wasn't she? There's a picture of her in the bath with her husband. They had a daughter called Anna Scott."

The stormy and controversial relationship between Secunda and The Move is outlined in great detail in this book. After The Move period, observers talked of Tony's venture into the realms of dealing cocaine. Also, he hadn't left the arena of rock management, he was still very involved. In 1971 Secunda became the manager of Marc Bolan and T. Rex. He helped Marc Bolan to set up his own record label, the T. Rex Wax Company through Electric and Music Industries (EMI).

Marc Bolan desperately wanted to move on. It was time for the ambitious pixie to reinvent himself. To uproot his folksy but ambitious music from the clutches of David Platz. At that time, allegedly ranked among the biggest sharks in the industry. Bolan turned to the one fish (the species as known as piranha) who could have eaten Señor Platz and all his pals for breakfast. Secunda had then taken the management of T. Rex away from Mark Fenwick. Bolan and Tony also parted company in a very abrupt and snide manner. Through the ongoing ego driven and unpleasant machinations of Bolan.

Tony was becoming notorious for the amount of cocaine he was now consuming. He was also famous for supplying cocaine to the artists he managed. Whether this was a control mechanism on Tony's part, which sounds probably likely, there's nothing like a drug addled and drug dependent client, to whom you can supply the necessary medicine, to enable a full blown, dysfunctional manager and artist relationship to develop.

Tony certainly made an impact on Marc, or certainly (Tony and) cocaine did. Marc wrote a song for Tony Secunda. The clue is in the initial letters of Tony's name (TS) and the initial letters of the song 'Telegram Sam'. Tony Secunda even signed himself 'Telegram Sam' on the liner notes on the Steve Took album that was released posthumously. 'Telegram Sam' was Bolan's affectionate nickname for Secunda. Other people who show up in the song: 'Jungle-Face Jake' was Sid Walker, Secunda's black assistant and 'Bobby' is Bob Dylan. Bolan also referred to Secunda as his 'Main Man' which entered the lexicon of daily speak around then. 'Golden Nose Slim - I know's where you've bin'. 'Nose' was snorting coke through the nose, one method of taking cocaine. 'Knowing where he's been' was code for the white powder residue around the nostrils, which can be often seen in coke users.

In 1972 Marc achieved two Number One hits. 'Telegram Sam' in January, followed by 'Metal Guru' in March. Marc performed his biggest ever gigs when he played two shows at the Wembley Empire Pool (Wembley Arena). By the time the Wembley gigs had rolled around Tony Secunda had gotten Marc a brand new US record deal. Secunda was summarily fired by the sneaky, coked out Bolan just before the two Wembley gigs. Photographer Keith Morris had asked where Tony was, he was told "Shhhhhh — He's been sacked and Marc has banned him not only from back stage but from the entire building." Secunda was not a man to take such a thing lying down. He sought revenge and found it in the form of Steve Peregrin Took.

It's been said that the last good T. Rex single was 'The Groover', released in June 1973. Bolan's use of cocaine was at an all-time 'high'! He was totally snow blind by this time. He was not heeding any good advice about moving his career forward in a typical, 'I know better' coked up arrogant fashion. He certainly wasn't listening to his steady and influential producer Tony Visconti. He was mostly totally out of his head. The music deteriorated badly. "He would never develop beyond the three-minute single," says Tony Visconti. "With Bowie, the glam rock smoothly segued into a kind of art rock."

Joe Boyd had a definite point of view on cocaine. "Chelita Secunda was a fascinating person. I never really got to know her well, but I used to see her at parties. We got along; she was very friendly. But I was not a coke user. I never used coke, I always felt coke was a big mistake. I think a lot of bands would say that now. It destroyed so many groups, didn't it? I went off it very quickly because I would hear it through the microphones. You know, you would be sitting in the studio listening to a group. They would be getting somewhere with a track. The white lines would come out and the quality of music would just go down, down and down."

While he was Bolan's manager Tony had discovered that the royalties owing to Steve Peregrine Took for the reissued Tyrannosaurus Rex material were being withheld. Tony was managing Took. He first started to castigate Marc by getting Took and him the money which was rightfully his. The back royalties were enough to buy Took, a small house in London. Secunda realised Steve had some talent and signed him up to Warner Bros.

It was reported, "For the first time since he left T. Rex in 1969, he's found a manager he trusts. His old management troubles, started after T. Rex's first tour of the States. Took was presented with a bill for £2,000 and from that day onwards, he fought shy of managers". However, the cocaine supplied to Steve Took, just as Secunda had with Marc, was having a much different effect on Took. It made him very paranoid. Initially Steve didn't even know Secunda had managed Bolan. When he found out, he became paranoid that it was all a big 'Bolan plot' and he ceased trusting Tony. Steve missed a big opportunity. And in true loser, stoner fashion, he refused to produce any finished work for Tony. The material Tony did get were simply notated, as he wrote on the box "Took ramblings". Secunda also reported that Took received visits from Syd Barrett, who at the time was living in Cambridge, but would relocate back to London. Secunda said it was likely that Barrett is on the recordings done in the flat by Took and company.

Piers Secunda felt his father appeared to deal well with rejection and could walk away although bearing resentment. "I remember him telling me that he was not sentimental about most things. However, a person who collects things is sentimental in some respects. He told me that the first really nice car he had was a Jaguar. He was driving this Jag, and it broke down on Hyde Park Corner. He rolled over to the side of the road and got it onto the curb. He just got out and walked away and he abandoned it. At one stage he was living in Warwick Square with Eric Clapton."

Justin Villeneuve was a suave handsome and debonair man about London. He was managing the UK's top model Twiggy. Secunda asked Justin to involve himself in the management of Motörhead, the band led by ex-Hawkwind mentalist and amphetamine sulphate enthusiast, bass player Lemmy Kilmister. Tony told Justin to come down to Brighton and to meet him at one of the piers. There was going to be a Motörhead concert. He wanted Justin to see the band and get involved in some promo work.

Justin told Piers Secunda. "It was bikers and guys in leather — all looking very scary! Justin was a bouncy guy and a flamboyant character. He probably had a carnation in his buttonhole. You can imagine the juxtaposition. The music and beer start and they all started pogoing. The pier started rocking and shifting and bouncing. Very quickly, a load of police appeared. Motörhead fans and the bikers were not having any of the police nonsense. They started picking them up and throwing them into the ocean, right off the pier. Justin realised this is actually not for me — he left immediately, and he never looked back."

Secunda called Lemmy and they met for lunch and a management deal was proffered by Secunda. Lemmy thought it was great, after hearing some of Tony's outrageous ideas. He took them off the road for a year, he wanted them to write a hit single. But they couldn't seem to come up with anything. Secunda had two big Motörhead murals painted in London. Highly visible and a constant reminder to passers-by of the band. Under Secunda's direction they recorded 'Louie Louie' the old rock 'n' roll favourite. Tony was actually going through his divorce with Piers' mother at the time. He was going through an extremely distracted period of his life. It is also alleged that Secunda declared himself bankrupt during this period.

Secunda remained steadily active and further managed the folk group Steeleye Span. Who had a surprise Top Ten hit with 'All Around My Hat' in November 1975. After a hiatus, Secunda resurfaced in the early Eighties, when he became briefly involved in the management of Marianne Faithfull. His aggression in dealing with record companies was not at all to Faithfull's taste and the relationship ended after a short period. It is said that her record producer Simon Miller-Mundy was apparently instructed by Faithfull to hand a bag over with £3,000 in cash to Secunda at a central London bank. They both walked out into Trafalgar Square, where Secunda suddenly announced, "The funny thing about people, is they don't like money." He proceeded to demonstrate this by offering passing students bundles of notes saying, "Here, take it." They refused, looking mightily suspicious and Secunda strolled on, having made his point (Secunda really loved engineering this confrontational thing with bundles of cash!).

Denny Laine, during his time with Wings, had his solo album *Ahh Laine* released on the Wizard label. As was stated, Denny leaves all his problems to Tony — which leaves him free to be a true musician. Denny says, "You can't have ulcers and then play music." Wizard was distributed by EMI. The releases are collectibles now. The sleeve designs were designed and illustrated by Malcolm Neal who had also illustrated William Burroughs books. Stylish and possibly comparable as a precursor to Barney Bubbles' super work.

A bit later, Marianne Faithfull's and Tony's paths coincided again more smoothly. "David Dalton came to Ireland for two weeks. He's a very shy person. Tony Secunda had become a literary agent, he was working with Dalton. Tony came to Ireland first to talk to me. I needed that. He really made me realise that it was very serious to get an offer from Little Brown Publishing and Michael Joseph. This was not the moment that I could do my flouncy "Oh no" sort of thing. Tony had managed me for a little while just after *Broken English*. I was very fond of Tony. Tony was making amends, and he negotiated for me a book deal you could not believe. To Dalton's fury, who insisted that the deal favoured me. We had, had this history, and he was making up for that. Tony came out of this very honourably and he suggested David, who I've ended up very close friends with. By then I realised that Tony was on the level. He picked David Dalton who was a big Rolling Stones fan."

Some guy Chrissie Hynde knew had been painting a ceiling for Secunda. He had told Tony about this chick who could sing and play guitar. Tony wanted to break into the new punk thing. Chrissie Hynde had been in an outfit called The Frenchies with the redoubtable Chris Spedding. She returned to America but then came back, rehearsing with Mick Jones, before he formed The Clash. She also tried to do something with Malcolm McLaren. She had worked in McLaren's clothes shop in London in 1974. She had been in McLaren's Masters of the Backside with Dave Vanian, Rat Scabies and Captain Sensible, who all became The Damned, circa 1975 and The Berk Brothers (before they ousted her and got in Johnny Moped as the lead singer). Chrissie had already led a colourful life of sex, drugs and rock 'n' roll and been involved with the Hells Angels at home in the States and in London. She desperately wanted to be in a band.

Around mid-1977 she had been contacted out of the blue by Tony Secunda. "At this point the punk rock ideology had rubbed off on me, I remember going into his office the first time with a big sneer on my face. I put my feet on his desk and started badmouthing everything in sight. He was very cool about the whole thing, he just said, 'How can I hear you?' So, I told him I had a guitar and an amp, and he said he'd get a car to come and pick me up the following morning and bring me over to do some songs. I thought, 'Wow, someone's going to pick me up in a car, the big time at last! I got there and knocked out a couple of chords from 'The Phone Call' and I was still being pretty offhand and obstinate about the whole thing. I was glaring at him when I was playing and stuff. But he said, 'Yeah, great!' and I went 'Wow!' 'cause he wanted to do something for me right from the start. And the fact that he'd been involved in all these projects like The Move and Marc Bolan, gave me a great boost to my confidence."

Secunda had faith in the emerging Chrissie Hynde song catalogue. He promised to arrange some studio time and to procure session musicians. So, she could cut some demos. "I really wanted was to get my own band together. Eventually though, I figured that Tony really did need something (some good demos), he could get people to hear. He was being very good to me, paying me a small wage and helping me with the rent."

Secunda placed her on a retainer, so she could leave her day job and concentrate on writing music. Hynde went into a studio with Nigel Pegrum from Steeleye Span and Fred Berk from Johnny Moped's band and recorded a version of 'The Phone Call.' Secunda appeared to lose interest in backing them at a crucial time — just before they broke through. Tony had taken demos to some record companies and things were looking up. "Then, one day I was talking to Tony on the phone and he just hung up on me! I'd said something he didn't like. In those days, if someone hung up on me, I'd never talk to them again." She never did talk to Secunda again!

The Sex Pistols were right up Tony Secunda's street. In a little known but extremely interesting piece of information, Tony approached the infamous group with a management pitch. He focused on Jamie Reid, famous for producing that great punk, blackmail lettering style that became the iconic artwork for the Pistols. He bounced one idea that promised the group and Reid big cash bonuses, for every piece of artwork or print that Jamie Reid would produce. I think Secunda would have made the Pistols even more outrageous and controversial than they were. Like The Move, The Pistols and Secunda could've been another marriage made in hell. When I spoke to Glenn Matlock, he had no idea about this.

There was not a deal that Secunda could not break. Not a handshake he couldn't transform into thumbscrews. Even the artists whom Secunda admired and whose careers were invariably bettered by his attentions had to acknowledge he'd screwed them somewhere down the line. Those whom he didn't embrace were in deeper trouble still... John Cale (of the much talked about but much less sold Velvet Underground) was lucky then. He had merely earned the promise that Secunda was going to kick in his teeth. Instead, the pair became close companions. "A very rabid friendship," as Cale put it... "for much of the next three years" with "Tony's promotion of paranoia resulting in some harrowing escapades, not all of them at all amusing."

It was Secunda who led the midnight raiding party on an Island publicist's apartment. Suspecting he was the person who had hidden Brian Eno's house keys. The suspicion was proven correct too. But only after Secunda kicked in the practical joker's front door. Then, practically and very believably, Tony threatened to remove his testicles, slice by slice. It was after that, that Secunda said that Cale hired him on as his manager. Nothing like a bit of bollock slicing to seal a deal. Although their relationship was never ratified by anything as pedestrian as a contract. Tony was more of a pit-bull than a PA. Secunda busied himself spreading the rumours and encouraging the confessions, which led to the *NME*'s Chris Salewicz mourning that Cale "is a little too aware of his legend (I, for one, am not sure of the relevance of knowing, whether or not he beats up his wife)."

It was Secunda too who suggested that Cale take the stage wearing a gas mask. Or, most notoriously of all, appearing in concert in Cambridge in a disguise, proclaiming him to be the Cambridge Rapist. At precisely the same time that the university city was living in fear of just such a character. It was Secunda who would nudge the artistic muse on those occasions. Especially when he felt Cale's lyrics were growing too languid. "John loved writing ballads and Beach Boys songs and sometimes in the studio we would have to gang up on him a little, remind him of who he was!" "We" presumably meant the extra inclusion of Chris Spedding, the mercurial axe slinger and even in that company, the coolest dude alive. But Cale would respond, clipping a line in this song, extending a syllable in that one. If the resultant performance had not been reduced to rabid shreds by the end of the session. There would always be time for another take. "John in the studio was no different to John onstage," Secunda marvelled. "When the madness hit, it hit hard."

According to John Cale, the first time he met Tony Secunda, early on in the *Fear* recording sessions, "I reprimanded him for having the worst reputation in the music industry." Tony commenced to take a stranglehold on this particular music scene. With the emphasis, (even he acknowledged) on the strangling. Dave Thompson states, "It was Secunda who blagged enough cash from sundry record labels to keep a band called Balls in luxury for life without them ever having to do anything, so tiresome as make a record."

Secunda was primarily involved with one recording by John Cale featuring two Move alumni: Trevor Burton on bass and Keith Smart on drums. Dave Thompson corrects one sleeve note. 'Heartbreak Hotel' (from the *Slow Dazzle* album) is credited to an A. Secunda as producer. Tony said that was actually his cousin, presumably Danny. The recording appears on the 1977 compilation *Guts*.

Dave Thompson reviewed it: "Released in spring 1977 with John Cale back on the road and revelling in the controversy, he had created by the chicken-beheading incident! In which Cale separated the head from the fated fowl's body with a meat cleaver onstage (this, at The Greyhound in Croydon). Terrifying and revolting the audience. Apparently two members of his band walked off stage, as they were developing into pre-vegans. *Guts* distinguished itself further by extracting the *Slow Dazzle* outtake 'Mary Lou' from the archives. *Guts* emerged as a best-of that actually lived up to its billing."

Chris Salewicz, features editor and writer at *NME*, "I had a really bad experience with Cale, he was a fucking piece of shit! Just from my experience of him, 'cause he just, and I think he was well known for this… I went on a press junket to Amsterdam with Vivian Goldman. Cale is playing with Chris Spedding and Chris Thomas is in the group, both of whom I knew. After the gig, I'm talking to them both. For some reason, Cale suddenly turns against me, it was just fucking vile. I can't remember exactly what happened, but it shocked me to the very core! I remember that. Cale was just horrible."

The music photographer Adrian Boot also knew Secunda. After university Boot was living in Jamaican as a physics teacher at The University of the West Indies. "I ended up as a photographer, but that's a whole different story. Tony was always a little bit dodgy, I guess. One person that was very close to him was Michael Thomas. Thomas wrote for *Rolling Stone*. He wrote a book with me called *Jamaica: Babylon on a Thin Wire* many, many moons ago. The only reason I mention it, is because Michael Thomas and Secunda went to Jamaica. In fact, they went via Venezuela. Tony

Secunda went out there to do a cocaine run. An undertaking much less dangerous to do in those days, than it would be today! They did the deal, they got back to Port Antonio, Jamaica. With suitcases full of coke, which was to be flown on to Heathrow. The reason Tony was doing this and why he went over to Venezuela in the first place was because his company was in financial trouble. It was on its uppers. They got back to Jamaica and ended up lodging in Port Antonio. Tony Secunda was perpetually coked out during this period. Michael Thomas and Secunda ended up in a bar in Port Antonio. Secunda was a little guy, but he was as high as a coked-up kite. He starts threatening everybody and throwing a major wobbly in this bar. Michael Thomas remembers this as being hugely traumatic. "We're in this place! Man, this was really fucking scary. I thought it was the most traumatic thing, I ever got to experience in my life. Meanwhile, God knows how many kilos of cocaine, are up in the hotel rooms?"

Piers remembers this or another similar story from other angles, "The time when he jumped into a bathtub full of cocaine. Basically, he travelled from South America up to the United States with a suitcase that had a couple of bags of cocaine, kilos of cocaine in it. The reason he did this was, he needed the money to start up either a record label or a music publishing company or something. It was to pay for a business thing that he needed to establish. There were no X-ray machines in the 70s. So, he just put them in his suitcase, and he got to Miami, and he went from the airport to the hotel. He suspected that a taxi was following him. He was suspicious, he got to his room, and he unpacked a bit of his suitcase, and he saw what he believed was a peephole in the wall. He believed that somebody was watching, and he put tissue paper into the hole. When he was first checking in, there was something he had said how the manager of the hotel had taken over his check-in process, from the person behind the counter. He pushed the person out the way and said, 'I'll deal with this one.' Tony said that the guy was very, very nervous and his hands were a bit shaky. So, he checked Tony in and put him in a room. When he went to the bathroom to run a bath and came back into the room the piece of paper had been pushed out of the hole. He knew then, he was in a room, which was being watched and it meant he had been rumbled. He immediately took the suitcase into the bathroom where he'd been running a bath and took the two bags of coke and emptied them into the bath. He then flushed the bags down the loo. He then ran back into the room and put the tissue back in the wall. Went back to the bath and swilled the bath water around, to dissolve the coke. Then came back into the bedroom and the tissue paper had come out of the wall yet again! They started breaking the door open and he jumped into the bath. When they came through the door, the bags had gone down the loo, the coke had dissolved in the bath. They came bursting in through the door and Tony was lying in the bath pretending to take a bath, very chilled out. You know, like, 'what on earth are you people doing?' He ended the story when he said to me, 'A lot of people think you know, a line of cocaine, is a pretty big deal. Try getting into a bathtub with two kilos of it. The hot water opens all the pores in your skin. They took him down to the police station. They interviewed him. They had smashed the door open with a battering ram. Somehow, they knew whether a dog had detected the suitcase. They followed him and they tried to bust him. But he had moved just a little bit faster than them, and he got away with it."

Adrian Boot got on well with him. "I have a good nose for people, but he was not somebody I would trust necessarily. Then again back in those days, band managers generally you could rarely trust. Maybe Brian Epstein was the exception. Don Taylor, Bob Marley's manager for a while, even he was shaving. Famously, he arranged a free concert in Africa for Marley. Don Taylor was doing deals with African promoters in the background and collecting the money. Bob found out and I think Bob beat Don Taylor up."

Piers had heard stories about Tony using drugs to set up a couple of companies. "I understand that had happened. Other people around him told me that was the case. When he had money, he was buying coke and having a good time. I also know from friends of my mum's that he just disappeared, sometimes for several days. The flat which he lived in with Annie Lowey, which was on Basil Street, was very close to Harrods. Tony liked the finer things in life. Annie showed me Tony's Harrods loyalty card. He had a credit card account there. He loved being able to go there and buy expensive things and nice food. When I did finally appear, albeit on the phone he trod very gently and very carefully because he was obviously very anxious, that I would disappear into the world again. He was very careful about what he was willing to say, and I was young and impressionable, and he knew that. He did tell me a few things about people that he knew in the past and whatever that would impress me. I asked him on one occasion if he ever met Jim Morrison and he said 'yes! I did actually and I went to a concert that they did in Los Angeles, and I was very unimpressed by their performance.' Another time he was on a plane coming back from the United States. He had a briefcase with a lot of cash in it. It was Pan Am. The top decks of Pan Am 747 used to have a bar. Tony was in the bar. The story was told to me by a family friend, who actually dated my mother before Tony took my mother away from him and ultimately married my mum. This guy basically told me that Tony was drinking a brandy, then he started drinking and chatting with another person. They stayed up through the night, sitting at the bar, chatting and drinking. Somebody came along and said, 'I'm sorry, gentlemen, you have to go and sit down because we're approaching London now. You have to take a seat'. Tony said, 'I haven't finished my drink, so I'm not going to sit down yet'. Then the steward said, 'Sir, no, you don't understand. You have to sit down. We're going to land soon. You have to sit down'. Tony: 'No, I haven't finished my drink'. He refused, and in due course, they actually got somebody out of the cockpit to announce, 'We're now circling because Mr Secunda is not in his seat, and we can't land'. Tony very reluctantly went down the stairs and went to sit down. But when he got to the bottom of the stairs, instead of going to his seat, he opened his briefcase up on the floor, taking out a thick brick of cash and he doubled back into the economy part of the airplane. Took the paper band off the money and waved it and said, 'Look, everybody' to the people sitting in their seats ready to land. 'Look, everybody, here's cash money, real money!' And he threw it across the airplane. It went flying everywhere and people went nuts trying to get it. When they landed and as they were all getting off the aeroplane, the captain was standing by the door. Tony was approaching. My family friend was standing outside the door on the jetway, so he watched all this happen. The stewardess pointed to Tony and said to the captain, 'That's him, that's him right there'. Tony stopped and looked around and this guy said, he lent forward and said to him, 'Mr. Secunda, you will never ever fly on

Pan Am again'. It was like saying 'You'll never be allowed to play in the park on the swings again'. It was an empty, totally empty statement. It meant nothing. Tony just leant forward into the guy's face and said, 'fuck off!' Then he got off."

London may have seemed all altogether too small for Tony Secunda as the punk scene fizzled out. Management of these rock artists was not bringing him, anywhere near the exhilaration he had experienced with The Move.

Mick Farren once eulogised Secunda aptly with the observation, "He never met a bag of cocaine, he didn't like."

Towards the end of his life, Secunda was indeed sketching out an autobiography that he insisted would be titled 'The Cocaine Chronicles'. This would be written by friend and author/ally Dave Thompson. He reluctantly realised that he would have to wait until everybody was dead before he could publish it (Piers remembers clearly, drawing some detailed illustrations for the proposed cover).

Dave Thompson enjoyed a close relationship with Secunda. Dave sums up Tony Secunda perfectly. "The key to Tony was he knew how to get attention! He knew how to shock people and his "management technique" was based around a combination of the two. Drink and drugs, as I said, just allowed him to step beyond what even he might have considered the far boundaries. If you look back over music history there were very few true "personality" managers… Yes, we've all heard of Larry Parnes, Peter Grant, Colonel Tom Parker etc. But what we actually know about them beyond their artists would barely fill a postcard. But then you have people like Andrew Oldham, Tony DeFries and Tony who in a way, were the artist! The musicians were simply the vehicle that brought them to attention — and that's no disrespect to The Stones, Bowie, The Move etc. But those three would have made that initial impact regardless of who they were managing. They wanted to be noticed, and they succeeded."

Appendices

Dave Thompson interview with the author

Where was Secunda was living — Tiburon or San Anselmo?
"Tiburon. A very nice house, although I was a little surprised to find a shotgun behind the front door. He told me they had trouble with carol singers, but he was probably joking."

You say Tony understood books and understood authors can you flesh that out a little bit Dave please?
In as much as… he's the only agent I ever worked with who I took seriously. You've probably worked with those people; just think of all the things you hate about them and then imagine an agent who didn't do any of them. No stupid ideas that he knew I'd not be interested in. No interest in me ghostwriting for washed up 80s metal singers: no chasing the buck with a Spice Girls picture book.

Can you tell us a little bit more about the Bobby Womack thing? He has passed now and another interesting character gone.
Bobby was out of his head most of the time. Obnoxious, demanding, contradictory! He'd tell the same story three times in one night and then he denied half the things he'd said, when I asked questions about them…Or, despite being on his own in a motel, miles from anywhere, in a city where he (allegedly) didn't know anyone. He spent an awful time going out with friends — whenever I asked if he was up for talking. In the end I told Tony I gave up… Tony flew up to try and sort things out. And he also gave up halfway through. But we held to ransom the tapes I had made… Bobby's people wanted them back and Tony made them pay for the work I had put into it.

How did you and Tony see the book on his life?
Did you have a publisher interested? Had Tony set up a publishing arm?
Ah, 'The Cocaine Chronicles'. A heavily dramatised version of the desert trip. But with Roy Rogers and/or Trigger as a sort of guru like character. Who would lead Tony through various steps of remembrance… the Navy, the music, the drugs… different characters from his life slipping in and out via the intended interviews. That one or other of us would do… *(Interspersed with talking saguaro…like weird scenes in the Joshua Tree National Park… and aliens of course).*

Key to all this was, Tony was a heavy drinker. I barely touched the stuff. So quite early on in the trip, we stopped at this ramshackle liquor store, in the middle of nowhere. He stocked up on more spirits than I've ever seen in my life. I bought a case of Jolt, which was a high-caffeine soda. So, we were both kinda manic, but I was sober, and we were both just sparking off one another. There was a publisher interested… St Martin's Press, but they were concerned about a lot of legal which Tony dismissed as them being wannabe star-fuckers. I'm not sure I was ever convinced the book would happen because his ideas were constantly changing. But they were the basics of what we were setting out to achieve.

You mentioned a label called Cleopatra. Did it release anything or was it a holding label, you had set up to release stuff in the future? I know you've already kind of answered that but to flesh that out that is quite interesting.
Cleopatra is one of the biggest indie labels in the US — kind of the American Cherry Red. This was back in their younger days of course. But they were already ambitious and had a fairly large catalogue. With Hawkwind and various other US space rock bands. So, the Steve Took and Motörhead stuff fell straight in. The label was looking to expand, and Tony's tape chests were exactly what they were looking for — readily licensable material. Purchased direct from its owner (he still had all the contracts too). And I still work with Cleopatra — I was Melanie's manager until her death. The last deal we made was signing her up to Cleopatra. Now I'm overseeing reissues of great swathes of her catalogue. Probably much as I would have been doing, if they'd gotten hold of Tony's stash.

Did Tony also talk about his short-lived, so-called supergroup Balls? Was his Wizard record label deliberately named as Roy Wood had Wizzard as well? Did he say anything else about Ace? Did he say anything else about Trevor? I know he loved those two. Did he say anything about Roy Wood?
You're going to hate me for this but again, those were the kind of things I was saving for when we sat down seriously with the book. He would be rude about Roy Wood but there was definitely a lot of affection and respect there. I got the feeling that he thought Ace was the star in the band. Trevor Burton was a good friend, Steve Gibbons, too. I think Tony was genuinely surprised (and disappointed) that Balls turned out like it did. He played me tapes one night of one of their rehearsals and they sounded so good."

Dave you must be the only person in the world apart from the people involved, who has heard those tapes. Who did Tony say The Move blew off stage and how did he think they would've been a huge success?
Everyone! They only had to take the stage and in Tony's eyes — everyone else was an also ran. Hendrix, Floyd... Who did they open for at the Paris Olympia? They blew them off stage as well.
The Rolling Stones

As for what he saw in them — great songs, amazing stage presence, good ideas, not bad looking... he saw The Move as the bridge between pop superstars and "serious" rock! But without the complications of being better known, for one or the other. They were also very hard working, which Tony always looked for in people, because that's how he was. They were the classic example of his basic philosophy! The artist made the magic (wherever the ideas came from) and he made sure people knew about it.

Why didn't Tony get them out to the Monterey Pop and to the USA with the early magical five piece? Joe Boyd said that's where his management really fell over in particular with The Move.
Joe Boyd is right. I don't think Tony appreciated the importance of the American market. As much as he should have... he could be very provincial in his outlook.

Also, he was kind of risk-averse and that didn't change. For example, one of his big fallouts with Bolan was about America. Marc wanted to focus on that market, Tony wanted to make sure that the UK and Europe wouldn't lose interest while he did so. Marc then sacked him, focussed on America and look how quickly the hits dried up. It was then over.

How did he get the knack, or did he ever speak about his undoubted knack of doing deals? Would you say he was good at doing them? Apparently Tony did two deals with Balls. One first and then a second, when Denny Laine came in. That was another deal set up, because Denny was now in the band as I heard it?
I mentioned his drunken blow-up in a restaurant one night. That is exactly the line of questioning I was pursuing. He seriously didn't understand what I was talking about. As far as he was concerned, he was simply doing what a manager (and later a literary agent) should do. Make sure he got the best deal possible for his artist. It wasn't a knack — it was common sense.

Why did Marc Bolan fuck him over? Tony did so much work for him and got him out of the clutches of David Platz and Essex Music. As you've told me, a new record label, all that stuff. Loads more money, tons of cocaine, no doubt the 'Telegram Sam' business, but why did Bolan fuck him? Did Tony ever talk about Visconti?
Visconti didn't seem to like him at all. Go figure. He probably was too much business for Visconti — and not enough art. Again, I can't say, but let's just say there are some people, who have worked very hard to build up an image. The ultimate hippy, the ultimate cool dude, the ultimate producer — without whom their best-known artists would have remained in the gutter? Hitless and shitless, until they died of bitterness (laughs). Tony was very good at seeing through such disguises and calling people out on them.

Did he say anything about going to Epsom or being born in Epsom and going to a private college?
Not really... I was also a boarding schoolboy, so we swapped anecdotes. But I don't think he was especially scarred by the experience. It was better than going to state school...

Aaah! I tried to trace Neil Smith the artist who drew the 'Flowers In The Rain' postcard, but I couldn't find him. Do you know anything about him — is he still alive?
I haven't got a clue. I just remember his name because Tony loved his work. He had some original drawings of his.... Not sure if the postcard was among them though! *(Piers Secunda along with Bev Bevan is one of the few people who have a copy of the notorious printed card.)*

Any bits about Andrew Loog Oldham to fold into this as he was one of the other great movers and shakers?
Not really, beyond the fact they were both amazing people, and seeing the two of them together was even more so... I've often found the same thing with other writers but learned to ignore them. I remember Barry McIlhenny used to really annoy me! I

was at *Melody Maker* for a while, at the same time as him. I found him completely bound up in his own self. Chris Welch I really got on with, Carol Clerk too! Mick Farren was another good friend, but they were kind of the exceptions. And Chris Charlesworth of course... I worked with him so much at Omnibus, before I moved to the States. Even if he did turn down my John's Children book.

Dave reflects on information I sent him from the main body of this Move book.
Interesting, while reading your Tony Secunda biog... It doesn't mention that alleged Seltaeb connection either. I think that's Visconti being mischievous. I am a little unsure about bits of your chronology though. I thought the merchant navy was direct from school and then came Fleetway The 2i's and so on. Edna Savage would have been around the 2i's period and he was definitely off the boats by then. *(Edna Savage was a Warrington born singer entertainer, who achieved a run of success in the 1950s. She was a sweetly voiced songbird and achieved considerable success. Known for her trademark choker - a velvet ribbon around her neck, tied with a brooch. After a run of well received singles, her career slipped away during the mid-60s.)*

Didn't the Regal Zonophone period coincide with The Move directly... in fact, wasn't the label reactivated specifically for Denny and Tony's work?

Yes it was set up for Cordell to operate that stable of artists. In lieu of giving him his own actual label. EMI reactivated Regal Zonophone for him.
Which also brought Procol Harum, Joe Cocker, T. Rex, etc into their world. That's where Tony first crossed swords with Tony Visconti, then came Radio Geronimo followed by T. Rex and then he got involved with Wings. He was still active in the Wings camp well into 1974. He then started managing Steeleye Span in early 1975 after their manager Jo Lustig was ousted. The band felt they had made very little money in 73/74 especially on the US Tours. They were unhappy with the management and revenue. Given what Tony Secunda managed to achieve within six months of starting with Span, he began to turn things right around.

Secunda started putting the band on the map. Employing some of his madcap publicity styles to get them on the front pages. On their Australian tour, he caused a 'front page scandal' with one of his PR stunts. In a radio interview, he offered a competition in which a "night of love" was promised with any male member of the band to the winner. The Australian National press went ape shit. There was a "hysterical furore" involving the Church, state and the police force. One editorial barked, "It was disgusting, degrading and it advised the band to abandon their plan to degrade Australian Womanhood! Or to get out of the country, as soon as possible. The church strongly urged parents not to allow their children to the concert. At the end all embarrassment was avoided. The winner, a 22-year-old librarian called Linda chose Bob as her surprise date! All the outrage turned out to be a champagne dinner at a Sydney nightclub. Steeleye Span invited Linda's boyfriend along as well. And a splendid time was guaranteed for all.

Secunda also brought in Mike Batt (of Wombling fame) into the scene, with the attendant hit singles and of course there was the Hammersmith Odeon thing! Single, 'All Around My Hat' and its B-side 'Black Jack Davy' sold a healthy 300,000 copies, a huge amount for a 'traditional' song. The single that made the band famous was chosen by Mike Batt as their first single, who worked on it to make it more commercial. It also became the name of the album. It stayed for seven weeks in the top 20 for a total chart run of 9 weeks. On 24th November at Hammersmith Odeon.

Secunda concocted another very funny publicity stunt with one of his fetishes, 'the free money, giveaway trick.' At the Hammersmith gig Tony Secunda decided as a publicity stunt to take the entire nights takings, £8,000 and stuffed it down through the ceiling during the encore tune 'The Mason's Apron' into the hands of the startled audience. Adrian Hopkins, who was part of the Chrysalis promotional team was now working with the band on a regular basis. He went up to the ceiling to drop the money down. Tony made damn sure that Adrian wasn't ripping off any of the money himself. In his paranoid state, he made Adrian strip off to check he hadn't kept any other cash. The stunt made headlines in the newspapers including the *Daily Mirror* on page 3. They were going to repeat it the next night, but Hammersmith Council refused. It also turned out to be an accountant approved tax dodge. Which also was a great publicity stunt as well or vice versa. By that Christmas of 1975, the band were a household name and nestling wonderfully in the UK top five.

For example, when T. Rex did a show in New York, Mark Bolan stood on the stage and said, "I want to invite you," and he said to the audience, "I want to invite you all to my hotel for a party. He invited thousands of people to the hotel. It was a genius move because it stopped all the NY traffic. There was a mob of thousands of people. He appeared on the balcony and waved, and everybody went crazy. Tony had a very, very shrewd idea to get the press taking photos. To get the crowd into a kind of euphoric state! He arranged for a large volume of the night's takings at the concert, to be brought to him in a black rubbish bag. He took it to the hotel, and he said, "Marc, throw this off the balcony! This he did and the crowd went utterly ballistic! You can imagine you know, as it started to rain money down on them.

He parted company with Steeleye then next up picked up with Lemmy and Motörhead. He was with them until mid-1978 I think when Gerry Bron started sniffing around. Then came the brief Chrissie Hyde period. Which I think went as far as introducing her to Dave Hill at Real Records and then Tony moved over here (to the USA). I think you'll also find that his Dwight Twilley flirtation, came around then in the USA.

Dave reminded me of one email:
Frankie was his third wife of course. Frankie was the one who Rock Scully led into a bad place. Followed, not too long afterwards by Mr Scully himself. It was very sad — she was a lovely woman. Always laughing, jollying Tony out of his foul moods. She was very much Tony's "sane" side when he'd been over-indulging. In fact, it was only thanks to Frankie, that he was to stop a lot of the "fun stuff." Which makes it even sadder how he went — he'd given up smoking, stopped drinking, no drugs, was going out running… and pop!

You're a little harsh on Tony's bands… I think he exaggerated a little when he laid claim to Johnny Kidd and The Moody Blues, but he was on the team. There was some kind of relationship (a working one) with Edna Savage too! Although that was right after he came out of the merchant seaman stint. So, I'm not entirely sure how big a role he played. After The Move of course, there was Marc Bolan!

As for the the London cocaine story... Tony and Chelita dealing most of the coke around at the time. Tony made a similar claim; whether it's true or not it's hard to say. One of the working titles for our book was 'The Coke Chronicles', so you're probably right! So many of the people involved in his tales, have passed on since then.

The framing device was brilliant too — a parody of *Fear & Loathing* (the famed Hunter. S. Thompson book). All about the time, he and I drove out into the California desert to meet Roy Rogers. With him telling me his stories the entire way. Apart from when the rental car had a blow-out. Right after we decided the guys in the car in front of us were probably alien invaders Because they certainly didn't drive, like they'd spent any time on this planet!

****

After Dave's welcome detail on his relationship with Tony. It's best to wrap up this appendix on Tony, through the eyes of Piers: "After he was married to my mum, he moved to California in the 80s and he married Frankie Papai. She was a San Franciscan and her father was a cartoonist and he invented Mr Magoo. She wrote cookbooks and she had an amazing singing voice. For a little while, she wanted to be a singer but got commercial success by writing cookbooks. One of them is called *The Turkey Cookbook*. Tony used to joke that they'd eaten so much turkey for about two years, that they reverted to eating anything except turkey for Christmas. They ate venison for Christmas, because he wanted to have 'Bambi' for lunch. If you want to know what Tony was like, watch the film *Austin Powers*. He sounded like the title character Mike Myers plays."

"He was also an art collector. He was a collector as opposed to a hoarder. Because a hoarder never gets rid of anything. He collected things and when I saw his house I was astonished, because there were things in there which he had very clearly gathered over the course of time. Frankie showed me there was a sort of Chinese daybed set into a recess, in the wall underneath. It was a huge box, and she pulled it out and opened it, saying take a look at this... because I was really interested in psychedelic music posters. She opened it and there was a block, a stack, about four inches high of 1960s psychedelic music posters. There were sheets of tissue paper in between each poster, which is really the way that an art conservator would take care of stuff... I was learning all about the 60s and Tony and the whole thing and he was telling me stories on the phone. Again, I had to hide all the drawings so that my mum would never see them, and she'd only see the respectable looking drawings, you know. I leafed through them all, and Frankie said, "I'd like you to have one." "I was quite emotional about that when she said that. Anyway, I never got it because she ended up in a relationship with Rock Scully (Grateful Dead manager) who was definitely dangerous — a real piece of shit."

"Tony collected graphic art from the 60s — not just related to the music posters. There were early designs for Pink Floyd logos and The Move logo and the drawings and sketches He called Move, the 'Pacman' logo. The one with the wedges, cut out of the circles. I really liked that logo. He loved the work of Stanley Mouse, a well-known psychedelic illustrator artist. He cherished those things and his awards discs, which were displayed on one wall in his house. A whole field of them across one wall. He got into The Band a lot and liked that kind of Americana Folk thing that they may have been responsible for reviving. That's partly why he was so enraptured with the folk band Steeleye Span, that he ended up managing in the 70s."

"My father did have grudges. Oh yeah! Marc Bolan had fucked him after he had made him a shitload of money. He had a real problem with it. It was 20 years later, he basically told me that Marc Bolan, (Actually, he told me a bit of a fib) he told me Bolan fell over on stage on tour in the USA — he was wasted — which is true! Tony said, 'this guy's out of control, I can't manage him anymore.' He got an airplane and went to Rio. He did get on a plane and go to Rio but the reason was, because Bolan had fired him! He didn't want to tell me he was upset and very pissed off about it. He had a problem with this right up until the very end — because he had made Bolan a very significant fortune. Then other people came in and took over the corporate side of the management. They set up trusts in the Bahamas and hid all the money. Then it was all stolen!"

And of course, the amazing and fated Move. "We talked about the whole 'Flowers In The Rain' thing. He really loved the whole experience of working with them and when the Harold Wilson thing happened it upset him a lot when they said, 'We can't work with you anymore.' I'm sure it angered him as well but retrospectively. He felt that although some things had gone badly, and they got sued. He also said the spotlight of the entire world was on The Move and that was the big opportunity for them. To become probably the biggest band that there was! A lot of people have said that to me! Justin De Villeneuve (who managed and was in a relationship with Twiggy) told me it was the dumbest thing — they ever did to dump Tony at that moment. If they had stuck with Tony, they would have gone on. The next stage would have been something else... They would have gone on a world tour you know..."

There is a sad coda to the Tony and Frankie story - at first it is very up lifting. After Tony's sudden, young death it becomes deeply overcast. Bringing the bad weather was the emergence of Rock Scully. An individual hustling, living and part of the Grateful Dead set up for some time. I insert Pier's observations of this sketchy sounding individual here rather than the end of Tony's story. "What happened to Frankie Secunda at the end? Rock Scully made her into an alcoholic and then a heroin addict and she died of an embolism. I don't say those words lightly but he did and she wasn't an alcoholic or a drug addict before he came into her life. Right!"

"Tony died in February 1995. Within four- or five-years Frankie was dead. Poor Frankie. After she encountered Rock Scully she developed extreme drug dependency. She married Rock on whom she became utterly dependent at that stage and then she became Frankie Scully and then she died. Fuck! I would be very happy for you to publish that. I think it's quite important actually that what Scully did to Frankie is known. I don't have a problem with it going in there. Rock Scully was an absolute piece of scum, a piece of shit."

"The last years of Tony's life were very quiet. Secunda spent his time connecting publishers with music musicians and music stories. Instead of managing musicians he managed writers. Striking deals with a publishing company for a writer, who he liked and respected. At the time there was a Red Hot Chilli Peppers book and I recall seeing a letter from Tony complaining about the royalties. One book had sold something incredible, like 160,000 copies that week. Tony wanted to create the very best deals, advances and royalty rates for his authors. He lived the last few years in Tiburon, outside San Francisco. Frankie and he used to walk about a mile and a half into Tiburon to go shopping. Then carry the shopping back for exercise. He had gotten away from the drugs in the 80s. He had an adrenaline injection into his heart, and he had an out-of-body experience. Which he described to me in incredible detail."

"He had a heart attack in a recording studio in San Francisco in the 80s, and a paramedic unit gave him an adrenaline injection straight into his heart, like in *Pulp Fiction*. He had been in the studio over the weekend and had brought in a load of coke. It was his own personal stash, and he was enjoying it over the course of the weekend. He went out and then came back into the recording studio. He stumbled in through the door and fell over on his face. Frankie was there. This was actually in the sound room. Some of the band were playing, I guess maybe one of the band members thought it was like a prank or something. They were all laughing. Then somebody said, 'Oh, he's not moving.' A couple threw their instruments down and ran forward. Frankie ran forwards as well. Tony was having a heart attack. Frankie had done a paramedic course a number of years ago. She was breathing into his mouth to give his brain oxygen. She screamed - telling people to call an ambulance. Somebody ran down the hallway there was a phone, they called an ambulance. The paramedic unit was a roaming vehicle. They have those in the States. The ambulance was literally a couple of blocks away. So, it was there, super, super fast. Frankie had been breathing into his mouth and trying to do cardiac massage. The paramedics chucked all their gear down and started talking and asking questions. Someone said, 'He's taken a whole load of cocaine over the weekend.' Out came a syringe and they gave him an adrenaline injection. The moment the adrenaline injection went in, he sat bolt upright taking in a huge deep breath and clawed at his chest and realised there was a sting sticking out of him. The paramedics kind of grabbed him and held on to him. 'Stay still, stay still.' They got him into the ambulance and got him to the hospital."

"A couple of days later, they said, 'We're confident you're okay to leave.' Frankie was there. They put him into a coma because I remember her very clearly saying that she was there when Tony woke up. She used to call him TS and she said, 'Is there anything you want?' He said, 'Yeah, I'd really love a Mars Bar.' Frankie got him a treasured Mars bar and before they went home, he said there's something I need to do. Frankie was bemused but said 'okay.' Tony said I need to go back to the recording studio. I went back to the studio and Tony waited for a band to finish rehearsing. Tony came in and Frankie said that he just very calmly and very casually walked across the other side of the room at the recording studio and looked up at the ceiling and then stood there for about three seconds and then he turned around and walked back and said, 'Frankie, we can go now.' She didn't understand what had happened. For God's sake, let's just get home. When they pulled up outside the house, there was a tree they used to park under. Frankie said, 'So, about the recording studio? What was that all about?' Tony said. 'Frankie, when you were pounding on my chest and breathing into my mouth, I had an out-of-body experience. I was up on the ceiling looking down at you. I felt something very cold against my shoulder' and he thought initially he was thinking that maybe when you die it's very cold. He had this thought in his head when he had woken up in the hospital. So, he wanted to go back to the studio to look at the ceiling. Lo and behold, there's an air conditioning vent in the ceiling. Tony said the right-hand side of his body was up against the air conditioning vent. The curious thing about all this, is when I first came into contact with Phineas (Tony's son with Annie who is now called Hannah), literally eighteen years later — because I took the Rolodex (a desktop rotary card index) at Rock's house. I took three quarters of the Rolodex and put it all into another Rolodex I had. There were five Rolodex's and I took it all with me. Because I was like — 'Fuck you, Rock Scully!' Scully was just a pathological liar, who stole all of my father's possessions when Frankie died. He didn't even tell me that Frankie passed away, just emptied Tony's house. I didn't know she had died for several months. Anyway, those Rolodexes, I went through them all later. To my incredible disappointment, Phineas, who I wanted to meet, his name was not in any of the Rolodexes."

"Many years later I met Phineas and we had a conversation on the phone. I asked him if he'd ever met Tony. And he said, 'yes, I did. I was very young and we all shared rooms in a hotel near Earl's Court. Tony was passing through town, and Annie was there. Annie and I stayed in one bed and Tony stayed in the other bed. Tony told me a story, like telling a kid a bedtime story, He said, 'Oh, that's amazing.' What was the story Phineas says, 'Well, it was pretty weird, to be honest. It was about having an out-of-body experience.' So, my story about my dad is not at all weird for you, because you've heard it from your dad. I'm not religious in the traditional sense, But I have an understanding of my own mortality, and I do believe in reincarnation. I don't doubt for a millisecond that what Tony said was absolute truth.'"

"Frankie said there was a bag permanently located in the kitchen drawer. Inside the bag was coke, some weed etc. When Tony got back from the hospital, he said, 'I'm just going to lie down and have a snooze and, you know, someone wake me up in half an hour.' Then she brought him a cup of tea. I remember Tony telling me that when he woke up, they were chatting and he said, 'Come on, I'm going to get up. I've been on liquid in the hospital for a couple of days. While she was cooking the meal, Tony was in the kitchen, he walked over to the drawer and picked up the bag and emptied it down the sink. And that was it. After all those years of really doing loads of coke from say the mid-60s all the way up to 1985...'"

Not quite in the Sly Stone league. But it was a long twenty years of doing cocaine. Apart from burning a hole in your pockets and through your nasal septum, it is way long enough for anybody.

Joe Boyd remembered Tony (and Denny) well. "I did speak to Gerald Chevin before he died, Denny Cordell told Gerald Chevin about the Procol Harum thing. He said, 'I made five big ones Gerald.' Gerald said, 'What do you mean, Denny?' "He said, 'I mean five million Gerald.'"

After Denny Cordell went to the States he started Shelter Records, made a bundle, then he left the rock 'n' roll business. Joe Boyd states that Cordell developed a different and unique way of running his new business. "Well, Denny had enough money, and he went back to Ireland and started a horse farm. That's it and somebody told me, who knew him more from the landed gentry side, rather than the music business side, told me, it was intriguing. Denny broke all the rules of trainers. Of how you're supposed to feed and train horses. And they said, 'Yes, that's right.' He had a completely original theory about nourishment and exercise for racehorses. He carried it out and did really well. And it wasn't just some crackpot thing. He actually did quite well. But then he was struck down by cancer at such a young age. He died just two months after, oh shit, Tony Secunda (it was actually six days). The two of them who had completely different trajectories… died just a little while apart. My God if you'd ever predicted where Tony Secunda would end up, nobody would ever believe you. From wrestling to rock manager to printing maps of US National parks and living in Marin County."

Dave Thompson looked back wistfully. "Denny Cordell died just six days later. Andrew Loog Oldham told me, "That was typical of Tony — he always went ahead to smooth Denny's way."

****

Discography

Rob Caiger was responsible for producing The Move reissues and boxset, overseeing everything from the audio to photos, artwork and sleeve notes, completing a large amount of the work with Carl Wayne until his untimely death. Caiger recovered original acetates, multitrack session reels, outtakes and master tapes from archives in the UK and America. With mix engineer Rob Keyloch, every audio source was assessed for the best sound, restored where needed while multitrack reels containing recording sessions and previously unreleased material were newly mixed for Roy Wood and Bev Bevan to hear. Sound engineer Nick Robbins, working closely with Keyloch, was responsible for remastering the sound which Caiger then checked and approved for Bucks Music's A&R head Ronen Guha to circulate to the band members for final approval.

The Move catalogue and recordings were at last being treated with due respect and care for the very first time and here Caiger, inputs his feelings about why this was so important: "We tried to stay faithful to the original recordings and work with what was on the master tapes. But we were very aware there was more that had been buried during the manufacturing process for the original mono and stereo pressings which was now being revealed by remastering. Obviously, we knew that these songs were not going to be listened to via the medium, they were originally produced for, as an LP or 7-inch single heard on a transistor radio or through a Dansette or first-generation sixties hi-fi system."

There was much more on the tapes which Nick Robbins excellent remastering was able to reveal, especially on 'Move' CD 1. "When it came to creating new mixes from the session multitracks with Rob Keyloch, we were mostly dealing with the sound as it was heard live in the studio, before any processing or effects. The best-preserved tapes were the 4-track multitrack reels from Advision Studios which had been brilliantly recorded by Gerald Chevin, an absolute genius engineer. I was so pleased I was able to talk to him over the last few years and thank him for all his excellent and pioneering work. For each new mix, Rob Keyloch was able to separate 12 or 16 individual channels of music and vocals from each take on the original 4-track multitrack tapes. Sometimes we couldn't separate out all the individual instruments or there were vocals missing. There were instances when instruments had been mixed together on one track or were recorded together in the studio — drums, bass and a rhythm guitar — as one rhythm track. We also recognised when individual instruments couldn't be mixed together by us as good as or better than the original mixed "bounces" or there was an effect applied to instruments and vocals that we couldn't match. We then left the original bounced mix, for say drums, bass, rhythm guitar on one track (or a section of vocal harmonies) and mix the remaining tracks around that. Or we would try something else... All I can say is that I'm glad and in awe of the incredible sonic wizardry of Rob Keyloch for conjuring up all of the brilliant mixes! All I can say is that I'm glad for - and in awe of - the incredible sonic wizardry of Church Walk Studios engineer and producer Rob Keyloch. For conjuring up, all his brilliant mixes!"

Flowers In The Rain - The Untold Story of The Move

To ready myself to research and examine The Move's unique history I have collected all the recent Salvo/Fly and Esoteric CD remasters. It's been a joy to hear the songs in their newly remastered and clear condition. To be able to hear the strings by Tony Visconti on the first 'Move' record and on the 'Flowers' single, very clearly. And with much more attack, was what the Move guys wanted! The Move always felt they were recorded 'too thin' by Denny Cordell.

Of course, this was the time of transistor radio listening. Thinner, lots of top end, brittle and trebly. But still managing to convey, the glorious, joyous choruses of the newly minted pop and rock. I have assembled, the necessary listening material to engage, remind and push me into the crucial 'Move' mindset.

These include...
Move first Salvo album 2 x CD remaster.
Move Esoteric first 3 x CD remaster.
Shazam One x CD remaster.
Shazam Two x CD remaster.
Something Else: Live at the Marquee CD.
The 4 x CD Move Anthology.
Flowers In The Rain CD single with bonus tracks.
The Best of The Move - Salvo remastered CD version.
Ace The Face - Ace Kefford Lost album CD.
Carl Wayne and Roy Wood: Beyond The Move CD. Something More From The Move (Bootleg CD of cover versions - the Sweden live material mostly).
Magnetic Waves of Sound; Essentially a greatest hits /singles best of CD and DVD pack.
Best of Roy Wood; Through The Years CD. (an older EMI Gold release).
Message From The Country CD with bonus tracks, an EMI release.
The Best of The Move - an early release from Repertoire Records.
The Move Singles Collection and More. (The enclosed booklet contains an interesting Carl Wayne interview from Rob Caiger). Crimson Records.
Black Country Rock; A bootleg CD - containing BBC Radio sessions between 1967 and 1968.
The Move Collection: Castle Communications CD.
ELO 2 remastered x CD - featuring 3 x great outtakes with Carl Wayne. *Your World, Take 2, Mama, Take 1, Get A Hold Of Myself, Take 2.*

Single releases
Night of Fear c/w Disturbance: Released 9th December 1966. Deram Records. Chart - Number 2.
I Can Hear The Grass Grow c/w Wave The Flag and Stop The Train: Released 31st March 1967. Deram Records. Chart - Number 5.
Flowers In The Rain c/w Here We Go Round The Lemon Tree: Released 25th August 1967. Regal Zonophone. Chart - Number 2.
Fire Brigade c/w Walk On The Water: Released 26th January 1968. Regal Zonophone. Chart Number 3.
Wild Tiger Woman c/w Omnibus: Released 30 August 1968. Regal Zonophone. No chart entry.
Blackberry Way c/w Something: Released 29 November 1968. Regal Zonophone. Chart - Number 1.
Curly c/w This Time Tomorrow: Released 18 July 1969. Regal Zonophone. Chart - Number 12.
Brontosaurus c/w Lightning Never Strikes Twice: Released 6th March 1970. Regal Zonophone. Chart - Number 7.
When Alex Comes Back To The Farm c/w What ? Released 9th October 1970. Fly Records. No chart entry.
Ella James c/w No Time: Released 7th May 1971. Harvest Records. (Single withdrawn).
Tonight c/w Don't Mess Me Up: Released 21 May 1971. Harvest Records. Chart - Number 11.
Chinatown c/w Down On The Bay: Released 23 October 1971. Harvest Records. Chart - Number 23.
California Man c/w Do Ya – Ella James: Released 14 April 1972. Harvest Records. Chart - Number 7.
Do Ya c/w No Time: Released 13 September 1974. Harvest Records. No chart entry.

EP
Something Else From The Move: Released 21 June 1968. Regal Zonophone. No chart entry.

Appendices

Albums
Move: Released April 1968. Regal Zonophone. Charted at Number 15.
Shazam: Released 27th February 1970. Regal Zonophone. No chart entry.
Looking On: Released 11th December 1970. Fly, Capitol. No chart entry.
Message From The Country: Released: June 1971. Harvest, Capitol. No chart entry.

Compilation albums
Flyback Three: Best of The Move: Released March 1971.
Fly Records. (Also as 'Fire Brigade' on Music for Pleasure).
Split Ends: Released December 1972. United Artists. Chart - Number 172.
The Best of The Move: Released May 1974. Harvest Records.
California Man: Released October 1974. Harvest Records.
Greatest Hits Volume One: Released May 1978. Pickwick Records.
The Move Collection: Castle Communications. 1986. CD.
Best Of The Move: Released 1997. Repertoire Records.CD
Shines On. Released September 1979. Harvest Records.
The Early Years: Released November 1992. Dojo. CD.
Great Move! The Best of The Move: Released 20 April 1998. EMI / United Artists CD.
Looking Back, Best of The Move: Released 20 April 1998. Music Club CD.
The BBC Sessions: Released 1995. Band of Joy. CD.
Movements: 30th Anniversary Anthology: Released March 1998. 3 x CD.
Omnibus: 60s Singles, A's and B's: Released August 1999. Edsel / Repertoire CD.
The Complete Singles Collection: Released 2000. Crimson CD.

Remastered album releases
The Move: Message From The Country: Released 2005. Remastered with bonus singles. Harvest EMI. CD.
Move: Released 2007. Salvo. Deluxe 2CD.
Shazam: Released 2007. Salvo. Deluxe expanded CD.
Flowers In The Rain EP: 2007. 4 x track. Salvo/Fly CD.
The Move Anthology: 1966–1972. Box set with book.
Released October 2008. Salvo. 4CD.
The Very Best of The Move: Released 27 January 2017. Salvo. CD.
Move: 2016. Esoteric expanded. 3CD.
Shazam. The Move: 2016. Esoteric. 2CD.
Something Else from The Move: 2016. Esoteric. Expanded edition.
Move: Remastered from mono: 2016. Esoteric w bonus.
Shazam: Remastered. 2016. Esoteric with bonus.
The Move: Magnetic Waves of Sound: 2017. Esoteric. 2 discs. CD/DVD.
The Move: Live at The Fillmore 1969: 2012. Right Recordings. 2CD.
The Move: Live at The Fillmore 1969: 2015. Right Recordings. 2 x LP.

Bootlegs
When the 60s Come Back to The 80s.
Luxembourg bootleg CD.1989.
Something More from The Move
Black Country Rock: 1993. The Move. Live BBC sessions.
Looking In: 1996. The Move. Third Eye.
Omnibus. The Move: Melvin Records. 1997. LP.
Family Tree. The Move: 1997.
Colour Me Rare: 1998.
The Move: Live at The Fillmore 1969: 2023.
London Calling. 10" mini album. EP.

Other Move / Brum Beat listening.
Brum Beat: Motorcity Music: Released 1993. Sequel Records. Remastered CD.
Brum Beat: The Story of the 60s Midlands Sound: Released in 2006. 2 CD, Sanctuary/Castle Music

Flowers In The Rain - The Untold Story of The Move

Ace Kefford
Ace the Face: Released 2003. Sanctuary/Castle Music CD.
Ace Kefford: The Lost 1968 Tapes: Released 2018. Fly Records.
Ace Kefford Stand: For Your Love c/w Gravy Booby Jamm:
    Released in 1969. Atlantic Records single.
Big Bertha featuring Ace Kefford: This World's An Apple c/w Gravy Booby Jamm.
    Released in 1969. Atlantic Records single.
Rockstar: Mummy c/w Over The Hill. Released 1976. MCA Records single.
The Lemon Tree: William Chalkers Time Machine. Released 1968. Parlophone Records.
Ace's great song writing debut. Would have fit well on the original Move album.

Trevor Burton
Fight for My Country / Janie Slow Down (Balls - Wizard Records) Single. 1972.
Double Zero: Released in 1985.
Trevor Burton: Live at the Adam and Eve: Released in 1995.
Trevor Burton: Blue Moons: Released 1999.
Pink Fairies: Featuring Trevor Burton. Mandy's and Mescaline Round Uncle Harry's: Released 2016. (Originally recorded 1971).
Pink Fairies: What a Bunch of Sweeties: Reissued 2020 1CD. 2023 on LP.
Pink Fairies: Neverneverland: Originally recorded 1971. Reissue on CD 2003.
Jim Capaldi: Oh How We Danced / We'll Meet Again: Featuring Trevor Burton.
    Released 2009. Raven Records.
Jim Capaldi: Short Cut Draw Blood: Featuring Trevor Burton. Island Records.1975.
Crushed Butler: Reissued RPM Records. Digipak. CD. 2005.
Crushed Butler: Reissue Radiation Reissues. Italy. CD. 2017.
Paul Kossoff: Backstreet Crawler: Featuring Trevor Burton.
    Island: LP. 1973. Deluxe Edition. CD. 2008.
Steve Gibbons: Any Road Up: 1976, Polydor
Steve Gibbons: Rollin' On: 1977, Polydor
Steve Gibbons: Down in the Bunker: 1978, Polydor)
Steve Gibbons: Street Parade: 1980, Polydor
Steve Gibbons: Saints & Sinners: 1981, RCA 6017)
Steve Gibbons: Caught In The Act-Live: Polydor. 1977.
Repertoire Reissue. CD. 1990.
Steve Gibbons Band: In Concert - 166. BBC Vinyl.1978
Live at Rockpalast: Steve Gibbons Band. DVD. CD. 2011.
Steve Gibbons: Rollin' - The Albums: 1976-1978 Extended Box Set) 5 x CD: Esoteric: 2023.
Trevor Burton: Long Play: Gray Sky Records. Released: LP. CD. 2018

Carl Wayne
Carl Wayne: Re-mastered. Released by BMG Japan. July 2001. (Debut solo record).
Carl Wayne with Roy Wood: Songs From The Wood And Beyond. 1973-2003.
    Castle Music. 2006. CD.
Carl Wayne with Roy Wood: Beyond The Move 1973-2003.
    Castle Music. 2006. CD. (The cover does not feature Roy Wood?).
ELO: The Lost Planet. Three Carl Wayne vocal cuts with ELO.
    Released 2003. Harvest / EMI Records.
ELO: Friends and Relatives. Released in the UK. 1999.
Carl with Et Cetera: Soldier's Song/White Christmas (English Language).
    Major Oak Records. 2003. Maxi Single. CD. 2003:
Carl with Et Cetera: White Christmas (German Language) Major Oak Records. 2003.
Carl with Et Cetera: Blackberry Way. (English Language) / Blackberry Way (German Language).
    Major Oak Records: 2003.
Carl with Et Cetera: Sorry Suzanne. The Bootleg Mixes. Acasa Records. CD maxi single. 2006.
Carl and The Vikings: What's The Matter Baby c/w Your Loving Ways.

Pye Records. September 1964.
Carl and The Vikings: This Is Love c/w You Could Be Fun At The End Of a Party.
Pye Records. April 1965.
Carl and The Vikings: My Girl c/w Shimmy Shammy Jingle. ABC / Paramount. October 1965.

Bev Bevan
ELO
(Bevan played on all ELO records up to 1986.)
ELO: Live At The BBC. Released 1999. Eagle Records. 2CD
ELO: Live San Francisco.1976. World Records. (Unofficial).
ELO: Live At Winterland.'76. Released in 1998. Eagle Records. CD. LP.
ELO: The BBC Sessions: (deleted). BBC / Eagle.
ELO: The Night The Light Went On In Long Beach: Released 1974: reissued 1998. Epic CD.
ELO: Joyride Movie Soundtrack: Released in 1977. United Artists Records. LP.
ELO: Live At Wembley 1978. Reissue Blu-ray. 2015.

Black Sabbath
Eternal Idol: Released in 1987. Vertigo – Warner Brothers. CD.
Black Sabbath: Paranoid at Reading Festival. Released in 1988.
Deep Black: The Massachusetts Broadcast 1983: Released in 2022: CD (Unofficial).
Blackest Sabbath: Released 1989.
Black Sabbath: Between Heaven And Hell: Released in 1995.
　　Raw Power/Castle Communications. CD.
Black Sabbath: Live in Stockholm 1983: Released in 1992. Barcelona Records: 2 x CD.

Bev Bevan narrates the audiobook:
Tony Iommi: Iron Man: My Journey Through Heaven And Hell With Black Sabbath. 2011. (UK)
　　Simon & Schuster (U.S.) Da Capo Press/Perseus Books.

ELO 2
ELO Part 2: Released 1973. Harvest / United Artists. LP. CD. Re-issued in 1991.
　　Renaissance Records. Telstar Records. Scotti Records (USA)
ELO 2: Moment Of Truth: Released in 1994: Curb / Edsel Records. Reissue 2021: CD. Also 2 x LP.
ELO 2: One Night - Live In Australia: Released in 1995. Reissue in 2007.

Quill
Brush With The Moon: Released in 2018. CD. Digital download.
The Cropredy EP: Released in 2017. CD. Digital download.
Ghosts Of Christmas: Released in 2019. CD. Digital download.
Riding Rainbows: Released in 2022. CD. Digital download.
Celebrates Midland Beat: Released in 2023. CD. Digital download.

Others
Kelly Groucutt: 'Kelly' solo album. Released in 1882.
L'il Jenny Records. 2001. Remastered CD.
Jasper Carrott: Funky Moped. Released in 1975. single.
Bev Bevan: Let There Be Drums: Released in 1976. Jet Records. single.
Red Shoes: All The Good Friends. Released in 2012. Cedarwood Records. CD.
Animals & Friends: Instinct. Released in 2004. Organic Mountain Records. CD.
Tony Iommi Band: Wonderful Land. TWANG: A Tribute to Hank Marvin.
　　Released in 1996.
Pangea Records. CD.
Del Shannon: Cheap Love: Released in 1983. Instant Records. single.
Distant Ghost: from Drop Down and Get Me. Released in 1990. CD.
　　(Bev on Distant Ghost and Cheap Love)
Bev playing percussion: Emerald Sabbath: Ninth Star: Sabbath tribute. 2018. Digital download.

Flowers In The Rain - The Untold Story of The Move

Paul Weller: Wake Up The Nation. With Bev Bevan. Released in 2009. Island Records: CD.

Bev Bevan with Don Powell Band: Let There Be Drums. Released in 2021. Streamed track.

Bev Bevan / The Don Powell Band: I Am the Beat: Released in 2024.

Bev Bevan / The Don Powell Band: I Am the Beat: Cinematic version. Released in 2024.

Roy Wood Solo, Wizzard, compilations etc
Roy Wood Wizzard: Wizzard Brew. Released 1973 Harvest / EMI. Reissued remastered 2015 CD.
Roy Wood Wizzard: Introducing Eddy And The Falcons. Released 1974. Warner Brothers.
    Reissued (remastered expanded) Esoteric 2020 CD.
Roy Wood Boulders: Released 1973. Re-released Harvest / EMI Records. 2015. CD.
Roy Wood Mustard: Released 1975. Jet Records. Re-released Esoteric remaster. 2019. CD.
Roy Wood, Through The Years: EMI Gold. 1999. CD.
Roy Wood: Look Thru' The Eyes Of (Hits & Rarities Brilliance & Charm... 1974-1987).
    Released 2007. Castle Music. 2CDs.
Roy Wood's Helicopters: Rock City. 45 rpm single. Released 1980. Cheapskate Records.
Roy Wood's Helicopters: Green Glass Windows. 45 rpm single. Released 1981. EMI Records.
Roy Wood: On The Road Again: Released 2007 Wounded Bird CD. Reissued 2015.
Roy Wood: Starting Up: BMG / Castle Communications.1987.
    Remastered with bonus tracks 2006. Universal.
Roy Wood & Wizzard: Main Street. Released 2000. Edsel CD.
    Esoteric Reissue (expanded and remastered) 2020 CD.
Roy Wood, Wizzard: Main Street.
Roy Wood Music Book: Released 2011. Harvest EMI. 2CD
Roy Wood Wizzo Band. Super Active Wizzo. Rhino – Warner Brothers. 1977. Reissued CD 2015 Rockers:
Roy Wood, Phil Lynott, Chas Hodges, John Coghlan. We Are The Boys!
    CBS single. Rock 'n' Roll medley.1983.
Roy Wood with Doctor & The Medics: Waterloo. Single CD. Released 1986. I.R.S. Records.
Roy Wood: Raining in The City. Legacy Records.1986. CD single.
1-2-3. Released in 1987. Jet Records.
1-2-3: 12-inch mix. Released in 1987. Jet Records.
Roy Wood & the Wombles. Wish It Could Be a Wombling Merry Christmas Every Day!
    Released in 2000. Dramatico.
The Best of Roy Wood (1970 to 1974) Music For Pleasure LP. 1985.
Roy Wood and Wizzard: The Best Of and The Rest Of. Released 1989. Action Replay Records.
Roy Wood - Singles: release 1993. Connoisseur Collection.
Roy Wood and Wizzard: The Best Of... Released in 1996. Diskey Records.
Through The Years: EMI Gold. Released 1996. CD
Roy Wood: Exotic Mixture: Best of Singles A's and B's. Released 1999. Repertoire records CD.
Outstanding Performer: Released 2003. Castle Music CD.
Roy Wood with Carl Wayne: Beyond the Move. (1973–2003) Released in 2006. Castle Music CD.
The Wizzard! (Greatest Hits and more – the EMI years). Released in 2006. Harvest Records. CD.

Unofficial
The Genius of Roy Wood. CD compilation.
Songs of Praise. Roy Wood - The Move. 2 x CDR, CDROM

Appendices

The Move bibliography

Kings Of Clubs: The Eddie Fewtrell Story: Brewin Books. 2007.
Starmakers and Svengalis: Johnny Rogan: Futura Paperback. 1998.
Tony Visconti. Bowie, Bolan and The Brooklyn Boy: Harpers. 2007.
The Englishman and The Mafia: Johnny Pearson. Arrow Books. 2003.
White Bicycles: Joe Boyd. Serpents Tail. 2005.
Shindig Annual: Number One. Andy Morten, Jon "Mojo" Wills.
Brum Rocks: Laurie Hornsby. TGM Books.1999.
Brum Rocked On: Laurie Hornsby. TGM Books. 2003.
Record Collector: Number 179: July 1994.
Record Collector: Number 180: August 1994.
The ELO Story: Bev Bevan. Mushroom Books.1980.
Record Collector: 100 x Greatest Psychedelic Records: Diamond Publishing. 2005.
Trevor Burton: Sent papers and photocopied articles:
Move press cuttings and clippings - from Jim McCarthy personal collection.
Martin Kinch: Use of online interviews and articles.
Denmark Street. Peter Watts: 2023.
The Marquee Club. Robert Sellers: 2023.
All the Madmen: Barrett, Bowie, Drake, the Floyd, The Kinks, The Who and the Journey to the Dark Side of English Rock: Clinton Heylin. Constable: 2012.
Two Riders Were Approaching: The Life & Death of Jimi Hendrix: Mick Wall. Trapeze: 2019.
'N Between Times: An Oral History of the Wolverhampton Group Scene of the 1960's. Keith Farley
Alan Clayson: Ace Kefford - Emailed Word document. 2024.
Ugly Things: Number 22. 2004.
2Stoned: Andrew Loog Oldham. Vintage Books. 2003.
Pop Goes To Court: Brian Southall. Omnibus Press. 2008.
Alan Clayson: Led Zeppelin: How, Why and Where it All Began. Book Two. Kindle. 2019
I Shot Frank Zappa: Robert Davidson. Aureas: 2022.
Hidden Man: John Altman. Equinox Books: 2022.
Happy Trails: Andrew Lauder. White Rabbit. 2023
Sleeve notes - From The Move remastered CDs.
The Move: Anthology. 4 x CD: Remastered. 2007.
The Move: First record - first release. Fly/Salvo. 2007.
The Move: Shazam: Remastered 2 x CD. Fly/Salvo. 2007.
The Move: Debut. 3 x CD release: Esoteric. 2017.
The Move: Shazam. 2 x CD: Esoteric. 2017

DVD / TV documentaries etc:
Pete Frame: The Birmingham Beat: Rock Family Trees. BBC TV.
Pink Floyd London 1966–1967. a.k.a. Tonight Lets All Make Love in London… plus. DVD. Peter Whitehead
Martin Kinch - Ace Kefford interview: Part One. YouTube
Martin Kinch - Ace Kefford interview: Part Two. YouTube
Martin Kinch - Keith Smart interview: YouTube
Des Tong - Big Albert interviews x 2
Martin Kinch – Ace Kefford interview: Part One. 2024 (YouTube)
Martin Kinch – Ace Kefford interview: Part Two. 2024 (YouTube)

Cover versions 1966 to 1970 (original lead vocalist in brackets)
1. Tired of Being Lonely (Ace). The Sharpees.
2. You Better Believe It Baby (Carl). Joe Tex.
3. Stop and Get a Hold Of Myself (Trevor). Gladys Knight.
4. Don't Hang Up (Carl, Bev). The Orlons.
5. Why (Carl, Trevor). The Byrds.
6. Is It True? (Carl). The Isley Brothers

7. Eight Miles High (Carl). The Byrds.
8. Respectable (Ace). The Isley Brothers.
9. Cherry Cherry (Roy). Neil Diamond.
10. We Go Together (Pretty Baby) (Carl). The Olympics.
11. Our Love Is in The Pocket (Ace). Darryl Banks, JJ Barnes
12. Morning Dew (Ace). Tim Rose.
13. So You Wanna be a Rock 'n' Roll Star (Carl). The Byrds.
14. Too Many Fish in the Sea (Roy). The Marvelettes.
15. Hey Grandma (Carl). Moby Grape.
16. Stephanie Knows Who (Carl). Love.
17. Zing Went The Strings of My Heart. (Bev, Ace). The Coasters.
18. It'll Be Me (Carl). Cliff Richard & The Shadows.
19. Sunshine Help Me (Carl). Spooky Tooth
20. Weekend (Trevor). Eddie Cochran.
21. Everybody Needs Somebody to Love (Trevor). Solomon Burke.
22. Something Else (Trevor) Eddie Cochran.
23. Abraham Martin and John (Carl). Dion, Marvin Gaye
24. Fields of People (Carl). Ars Nova.
25. Don't Make My Baby Blue (Carl). Frankie Laine.
26. Under The Ice (Carl). The Nazz.
27. Open My Eyes (Carl). The Nazz.
28. Higher and Higher (Carl). Jackie Wilson.
29. Long Black Veil (Roy). Johnny Cash. Lefty Frizzell
30. Piece of My Heart (Carl). Erma Franklin
31. Goin' Back (Trevor). The Byrds.
32. The Christian Life (Trevor). The Byrds.
33. California Girls (Roy). The Beach Boys.
34. Going Out Of My Head (Carl). Little Anthony and the Imperials.
35. Evil Woman (Carl). Guy Darrell, Spooky Tooth.
36. Sounds of Silence (Carl). Simon & Garfunkel.
37. Walk Right Back (Carl). The Everly Brothers.
38. The Last Thing On My Mind. (Carl). Tom Paxton.
39. Kentucky Woman (Roy). Neil Diamond.
40. We Go Together (Pretty Baby) (Carl). The Imperials.
41. Open The Door To your Heart (Ace). Darrel Banks.
42. Too Much in Love (Carl). Denny Laine.
43. The Price of Love (Carl?). Everly Brothers.
44. Hold On (Ace). Sharon Tandy.
45. Stop Her on Sight (Carl, Trevor). Edwin Starr.
46. Baby I Need Your Loving (Carl). The Four Tops.
47. My Girl (Carl). The Temptations.
48. Your' Cheating Heart (Carl). Hank Williams. Elvis.
49. She's A Woman (Roy, Jeff). The Beatles.
50. Walking The Dog (Carl). Rufus Thomas.
51. She Came In Through The Bathroom Window (Roy, Jeff). The Beatles.
52. Ave Maria (Carl).
53. One Night. Elvis Presley. (Carl).

Appendices

TV and radio appearances performances: 1966 —1971

*All performances are from the BBC Light Programme &
Radio One sessions that exist in archives - unless stated.*

5th December 1966	*Ready Steady Go!* Redifusion TV
12th January 1967	*Top of the Pops*, BBC1 Television 'Night of Fear' *(wiped)*
19th January 1967	*Top of the Pops*, BBC1 Television 'Night of Fear' *(wiped)*
26th January 1967	*Top of the Pops*, BBC1 Television 'Night of Fear' *(wiped)* (Repeat)
4th February 1967	*Saturday Club*, BBC Radio 1
	'You'd Better Believe Me' / 'Our Love Is (In the Pocket)'* /
	'Night of Fear' / 'Stop Get a Hold of Myself' / 'Cherry Cherry'* /
	'Tired of Being Lonely'
	Recorded 31st January 1967 (*off air recordings)
9th February 1967	*Pop North* (Tracks unknown) *(wiped)*
6th March 1967	*Tetes De Bois et Tendres Annees*, French Television
	'Night of Fear' / 'I Can Hear the Grass Grow'
6th March 1967	*The Rave*, Granada Television 'Night of Fear' / Unknown Track *(wiped)*
21st March 1967	*Top of the Pops*, BBC1 Television 'I Can Hear the Grass Grow' *(wiped)*
12th April 67	*The Rave*, Granada Television
	'I Can Hear the Grass Grow' / Unknown Track *(wiped)*
13th April 67	*Top of the Pops*, BBC1 Television
	'I Can Hear the Grass Grow' *(Appearance cancelled)*
15th April 1967	*Saturday Club*, BBC Radio 1
	'I Can Hear the Grass Grow' / 'Kilroy Was Here' (v1) /
	'Walk Upon the Water' (v1) *(Recorded 10th April 1967)*
20th April 1967	*Top of the Pops*, BBC1 Television 'I Can Hear the Grass Grow' *(wiped)*
20th April 1967	*Pop North* (Tracks unknown) *(wiped)*
23rd April 1967	*Easybeat* (Tracks unknown) *(wiped)*
4th May 1967	*Top of the Pops*, BBC1 Television 'I Can Hear the Grass Grow' *(wiped)*
4th May 1967	*Dee Time*, BBC1 Television 'I Can Hear the Grass Grow' *(wiped)*
11th May 1967	*Dee Time*, BBC1 Television
	'I Can Hear the Grass Grow' Possibly repeat *(wiped)*
20th May 1967	*Top Pop*, Danish Television
	'Night of Fear' / 'Kilroy Was Here' /
	'Walk Upon the Water' / 'I Can Hear the Grass Grow'
23rd May 1967	*As You Like It*, Southern Television
	(Tracks unknown) *(wiped)*
26th June 1967	*Beat! Beat! Beat!*, German Television
	'Night of Fear' / 'Walk Upon the Water' /
	'I Can Hear the Grass Grow'
6th September 1967	*Basil Brush Show*, BBC1 Television 'Flowers in the Rain' *(wiped)*
7th September 1967	*Top of the Pops*, BBC1 Television 'Flowers in the Rain' *(wiped)*
7th September 1967	*Pop North* (Tracks unknown) *(wiped)*
15th September 1967	*As You Like It*, Southern Television 'Flowers in the Rain' *(wiped)*
17th September 1967	*Easybeat*
	'Flowers in the Rain' / 'Morning Dew' /
	'So You Wanna Be a Rock 'n' Roll Star
1st October 1967	*Top Gear*, BBC Radio 1
	'Cherry Blossom Clinic' (v1) / 'Hey Grandma' (v1) /
	'Stephanie Knows Who' / 'Kilroy Was Here' (v2)
7th October 1967	*Pete's People*, BBC Radio 1
	'Hey Grandma' / 'Eight Miles High' / Tracks Unknown *(wiped)*
20th October 1967	*The Joe Loss Show*, BBC Light Programme
	Tracks unknown, broadcast live not recorded
23rd November 1967	*Top of the Pops*, BBC1 Television
	'Flowers in the Rain' *(wiped)*

Flowers In The Rain - The Untold Story of The Move

15th December 1967	*Live from The Concert House, Stockholm*, Swedish Radio 'Something Else?' / 'Flowers in the Rain' / 'Why?' / 'Hey Grandma' / 'So You Wanna Be a Rock 'n' Roll Star' / 'I Can Hear the Grass Grow'
21st December 1967	*Pop North* (Tracks unknown) *(wiped)*
1st-5th January 1968	*Pete Brady Show* (one track played per day, likely repeats.)
28th January 1968	*Top Gear*, BBC Radio 1 'Cherry Blossom Clinic' (v2)* / 'Weekend' / 'Fire Brigade' (v1) / 'It'll Be Me' *(*wiped) Recorded 22nd January 68.*
3rd February 1968	*Saturday Club*, BBC Radio 1 (Tracks unknown) *(wiped)*
5th-9th February 1968	*Jimmy Young Show* One track per day 'Useless Information' / Unknown tracks *(wiped) Recorded 04.02.68*
08th February 1968	*Pop North* (Tracks unknown) *(wiped)*
12th February 1968	*Pop North* (Tracks unknown) *(wiped)*
17th February 1968	*David Symonds*, BBC Radio 1 'Fire Brigade' (v2) / 'Walk Upon the Water' (v2) / unknown wiped tracks.
24th February 1968	*Pete's People*, BBC Radio 1(Tracks unknown) *(wiped)*
3rd March 1968	*Top Gear*, BBC Radio 1
8th March 1968	*The Joe Loss Show* Tracks unknown, broadcast live not recorded.
25th-29th March 1968	*Pete Brady Show* One track per day, possibly repeats.
15th-19th April 1968	*Jimmy Young Show* One track per day, unknown.
29th April-3rd May 1968	*Jimmy Young Show* One track per day, likely repeat of above.
10th May 1968	Saturday Club Tracks unknown *(wiped)*
13th-17th May 1968	*Pete Brady Show* One track per day 'Kentucky Woman' / 'Higher and Higher' / 'Piece of my Heart' (v1) U*nknown (wiped) Recorded 02.05.68.*
20th-24th May 1968	*Jimmy Young Show* One track per day, unknown.
3rd-7th June 1968	*Pete Brady Show* One track per day, likely repeat of 13-17.05.68
17th-21st June 1968	*Jimmy Young Show* One track per day, likely repeat of 20-24.05.68
21st June 1968	*The Joe Loss Show* Tracks unknown, broadcast live not recorded.
1st-5th July 1968	*David Symonds* Tracks unknown *(wiped)*
15th August 1968	*Pop North* Tacks unknown *(wiped)*
5th September 1968	*Pop North* Tracks unknown *(wiped)*
16th-20th September 1968	*Jimmy Young Show* One track per day. 'Piece of My Heart' (v2) / 'Long Black Veil' / 'Wild Tiger Woman' / Unknown (recorded 04.09.68)
20th September 1968	*The Joe Loss Show* Tracks unknown, broadcast live not recorded.
5th October 1968	*Saturday Club*, BBC Radio 1 (Tracks repeated on 'Pop Session' World service) 'Goin Back' (v1) / 'Flowers in the Rain' (v?) / 'Wild Tiger Woman' (v?)
7th-11th October 1968	*David Symonds* One track per day, unknown.
14th November 1968	*Radio 1 Club* 'Wild Tiger Woman' (v?) / 'Goin' Back' / 'Blackberry Way'* (*studio version) *Recorded 06.11.68.*
9th-13th December 1968	*David Symonds* Tracks unknown *(wiped)*
25th December 1968	*It's Englebert Humperdinck* 'The Last Thing On My Mind' / 'Blackberry Way'

All performances from here on BBC Radio 1 sessions & exist in archives unless stated.

4th January 1969	*Colour Me Pop* 'I Can Hear the Grass Grow' / 'Beautiful Daughter' / 'The Christian Life' / 'Flowers in the Rain' / 'Last Thing on my Mind' / * 'Wild Tiger Woman'* / 'Goin' Back' / 'Fire Brigade' / 'Something'* / 'Blackberry Way' (*studio versions) – BBC TV, recorded 28.12.68.

394

Appendices

5th January 1969	*Pete's Sunday People*
	'Blackberry Way'* / 'California Girls' / 'The Christian Life'
	Rec 18.12.68 (*Released version)
6th-10th January 1969	*David Hamilton* one track played per day, likely repeats.
9th January 1969	*Top of the Pops*, BBC1 Television 'Blackberry Way' *(wiped)*.
16th January 1969	*Top of the Pops*, BBC1 Television 'Blackberry Way' *(wiped)*.
20th-24th January 1969	*Dave Cash Show* one track played per day, likely repeats.
23rd January 1969	*Crackerjack*, BBC1 Television 'Blackberry Way' *(wiped)*.
25th January 1969	*Beat Club*, German Television 'Blackberry Way'.
30th January 1969	*Top of the Pops*, BBC1 Television 'Blackberry Way' *(repeat)*.
3rd-7th February 1969	*Jimmy Young Show* one track played per day, likely repeats.
12th February 1969	*Cilla*, BBC1 Television Blackberry Way *(wiped)*.
12th February 1969	*Discotheque*, Granada Television 'Blackberry Way' *(wiped)*.
17th February 1969	*Calendar*, Yorkshire Television
	'Blackberry Way' / 'Beautiful Daughter' *(wiped)*.
24th-28th February 1969	*The Keith Skues Show* one track played per day, likely repeats.
6th March 1969	*Radio 1 Club* Tracks unknown *(wiped)*.
6th March 1969	*Symonds on Sunday*
	'Rock 'n' Roll Woman' / 'Good Times' / 'Blackberry Way'*
	(*Released version) (Off air recording exists).
April 1969	*Pop Session*, BBC World Service radio
	'Blackberry Way' / 'The Birthday' / 'Last Thing on My Mind'
	(Off air recording exists).
27th April 1969	*Symonds on Sunday* 'Beautiful Daughter' / 'Going Out of My Head'
	(Rec 22.04.69)
2nd-6th June 1969	*Tommy Vance* one track played per day, likely repeats.
15th June 1969	*Symonds on Sunday* 'Curly'* / 'Evil Woman' / 'Sounds of Silence' /
	'Abraham, Martin & John' Recorded 09.06.69 (*Released version).
16th-20th June 1969	*Tommy Vance* one track played per day, likely repeats.
4th-8th August 1969	*Tony Brandon* one track played per day, likely repeats.
18th-22nd August 1969	*Tony Brandon* one track played per day, likely repeats.
25th-29th August 1969	*Chris Grant* one track played per day
	'Hello Suzie' (v1) / 'Open My Eyes' / Unknown tracks
	(wiped) Rec 18.08.69.
15th-19th September 1969	*Chris Grant* One track played per day, likely repeat of 25 -29.08.69
5th October 1969	*Annie Nightingale* unknown tracks *(wiped)*.
24th-28th November 1969	*Dave Cash* one track played per day
	'Fields of People' / 'Walk Right Back' /
	Other tracks unknown *(wiped)* Recorded 13.11.69.
8th-12th December 1969	*Dave Cash* one track played per day, likely repeat of above.
29th March 1970	*DLT* 'Falling Forever' / 'She's a Woman' (v1) Rec 23.03.70.
9th April 1970	*Top of the Pops*, BBC1 Television 'Brontosaurus' *(wiped)*.
14th April 1970	*Beat Club*, German Television 'Brontosaurus'.
20th April 1970	*Sounds of the Seventies* (with Andy Ferris)
	'Brontosaurus' / 'Lightening Never Strikes Twice' / 'What?' *(wiped)*.
	Rec 18.03.70.
14th May 1970	*Top of the Pops*, BBC1 Television 'Brontosaurus' *(wiped)* (repeat).
18th May 1970	*Sounds of the Seventies* (with David Symonds)
	'Looking On' (v1) Rec 18.03.70.
26th June 1970	*Pop Scotch 70*, Grampian TV 'Brontosaurus' (unconfirmed) *(wiped)*.
27th-31st July 1970	*Johnnie Walker* unknown tracks one per day *(wiped)*.
4th August 1970	*Sounds of the Seventies* (with Mike Harding)
	'When Alice Comes Back to the Farm' / 'She's a Woman' (v2) /
	'Looking On' *(wiped)* Rec 28.07.70.
10th-14th August 1970	*Johnnie Walker* unknown tracks one per day, probably repeat.
15th September 1970	*Sounds of the Seventies* (with Mike Harding), probably repeat.

Flowers In The Rain - The Untold Story of The Move

31st October 1970	*Disco 2*, BBC2 Television 'When Alice Comes Back to the Farm' *(wiped)*.
21st November 1970	*Lift Off with Ayshea*, Granada Television 'When Alice Comes Back to the Farm' *(wiped)*.
31st December 1970	*Beat Club*, German Television 'When Alice Comes Back to the Farm'.
29th May 1971	*Whitakers World of Music*, London Weekend Television 'Tonight'.
24th June 1971	*Top of the Pops*, BBC1 Television 'Tonight' *(wiped)*.
8th July 1971	*Top of the Pops*, BBC1 Television 'Tonight' *(wiped)*.
24th August 1971	*Lift Off with Ayshea*, Granada Television 'Tonight' (ITV) *(wiped)*.
14th October 1971	*Top of the Pops*, BBC1 Television Chinatown *(wiped)*.
18th-22nd October 1971	DLT One track played per day 'Chinatown'* / unknown tracks (**studio version*)
4th November 1971	*Top of the Pops*, BBC1 Television 'Chinatown' *(wiped)*.
11th November 1971	*Top of the Pops*, BBC1 Television 'Chinatown' *(wiped)* (repeat).
20th November 1971	*Old Grey Whistle Test*, BBC2 Television 'Words of Aaron' / '*Ella James*'* (**not broadcast*).
24th November 1971	*Lift Off with Ayshea*, Granada Television Chinatown *(wiped)*
23rd December 1971	*Sounds of the Seventies* (with Pete Drummond) 'Message From The Country' / 'Words of Aaron' / 'Ella James' / 'Ben Crawley Steel Company'* (*wiped) (All studio versions) Recorded 15.12.71.
3rd February 1972	*Sounds of the Seventies* (with Pete Drummond) Likely repeat of 23.12.71.
13th-17th March 1972	*Johnnie Walker* unknown tracks one per day *(wiped)*.
15th-19th March 1972	*Alan Freeman* unknown tracks one per day *(wiped)*.
25th May 1972	*Top of the Pops*, BBC1 Television 'California Man' (*wiped*).
26th May 1972	*Johnnie Walker* unknown tracks *(wiped)*.
8th June 1972	*Top of the Pops*, BBC1 Television 'California Man' (*wiped*).
12th-16th June 1972	DLT One track played per day. 'Do Ya' / 'California Man'* (**studio version*) / *Unknown tracks*.
22nd June 1972	*Top of the Pops*, BBC1 Television 'California Man' (*wiped*).
3rd-7th July 1972	DLT One track played per day, likely repeat.
8th December 1972	*2 G's & the Pop People*, Granada Television 'California Man' (ITV).
25th December 1972	*Top of the Pops*, BBC1 Television 'California Man' (*wiped*).

Acknowledgements

Thank you to all these wonderful people, that gave their precious time to talk to me. It was a privilege to enter into their lives. To hear these wonderful memories and experiences, in relation to this largely unknown, vibrant musical history.

Bev Bevan was ultra helpful with details and with four interviews. Bev is now essentially, the spokesperson for The Move, since Carl Wayne passed away.

Special thanks to Keith Smart for getting me Trevor Burton and David Arden and his own interviews, (Keith knows everybody it seems?) David Arden for the longer interviews, Piers Secunda for four interviews, plus the extra insights into his father Tony Secunda, Martin Kinch for invaluable information and online resources. Plus, his online interviews with Keith Smart and Ace Kefford, Carl Wayne, Trevor Burton for two funny interviews and permission for his 'Hit and Run' lyrics, Debbie Burton (Ireson), Roy Wood (for questions and answers which were emailed), Paul Weller for his heartfelt Foreword, Rob Caiger for repeated interviews and invaluable help and detail (we got there in the end Rob! Thank you!), Tony Visconti for succinct answers on the recording of 'Flowers In The Rain' Denny Cordell and more, Robert Davidson for repeated interviews and his wonderful original photos, Ace Kefford for being 'Ace the Face' - the coolest of them all, Glen Matlock for his cool Afterword, Nicola Hancox for additional info and photos, Melvin Hancox of The Melvin Hancox Band, Ray Gange for Chelita Secunda info, 'Big Al' Chapman, Bob Sawyer, John Davies, Jan Davis, Robert Sandall, Dave Pegg, Helen McDonald for Carl Wayne interview and info, Gerald Chevin RIP, Andrew Lauder (Liberty Records), Dave Scott-Morgan, Mandy Morgan, The Movement Facebook page, Gregg Wetherby, Chris Dolmetsch, Mark Petrus, Steve Gibbons for a couple of tasty interviews, Dylan Gibbons for help with The Uglys material and interview, Baz St Leger for two interviews and advice (a.k.a. Barry Smith of The Chantelles), Will Birch for a great interview, Allen 'Dumpy' Harris (the original Move roadie) for his long interview and meeting me on the road, Allen's partner Chris Pitman, Brum drummer Barry Spencer Scrannage, Alan Clayson for kindly sending Ace / Move documents, Olav Wyper, Carolynne Wyper @ SMA Talent, Rikki Farr, Barry Miles, Jez Collins at The Birmingham Music Archive, Dave Ball for his funny phone interviews and chat about the Ace Kefford Stand, Joe Boyd for his great insightful interviews, Malcolm Toft, Robert Keyloch, Laurie Hornsby for interviews (and for his excellent 'Brum Rocked On'), John Woodhouse of Brum Beat, David Stark, Leslie Ann Jones, David Courtney, John Altman for latter-day Carl Wayne, Ronin Gutha from Bucks / Essex Music, Nigel Waymouth, John Pearse, Des Tong/YouTube videos on Brum music and 'Big' Albert Chapman, David Barraclough at Omnibus Press, Chris Charlesworth, Bob Leftsetz podcast, Raconteurs podcast, Andrew Hickey podcast, Joel Selvin, Denis McNally, Shindig's Jon Mills, Shindig's Andrew Morton, Pauline Pritchard (aka Pauline Evans), Nick Pritchard for getting me to Pauline and for added help, Shaun Pritchard for his extra help with Pauline interviews, June Woods (Move Fan Club), John Kirkby in Las Vegas - interviews, Terry Biddulph (pre- Rockstar and Gritt etc), John Grimley for Rockstar information, Tony Ware for two later excellent interviews, Dave Thompson for added Tony Secunda info, Keith Farley (RIP), Paul Olsen, Chris

Saleswicz on Secunda, Adrian Boot for the Secunda nuggets, Mike Smitham of The Fortunes, Shauna Osborne - Doyle; regarding her father David Lloyd-Doyle, Val Weedon (MBE), Robert Sellers author, Peter Watts author, Hans Rotenberry of The Shazam, Lynn Hoskins from Useless Information, Ron King, Xavier Guenther (Australia), Roger Spencer (Idle Race), Dave Pritchard (Idle Race), Derek Arnold (Lemon Tree, Quartz) Max Bell, Mark Paytress, Wilf Pine, Mike Clifford interview, Ollie Cherer and Del Querns @ Musics Not Dead in Bexhill, Tony Bacon, Colin Bell for Hastings Pier, DJ Jeff Dexter, Bernie Fallon, Charlie Harper, Ron Eve, DG Torrens and Martin Tracey of Contrary Trees Productions for their support, Peter 'Rocky' Morley, Andy Fairweather Lowe, Paul Reeves, John Cooper - Clarke for that fabulously moving "Quote"…

Plus - some others who wished to remain incognito…

About The Author

Jim McCarthy is a UK based writer, graphic novelist and illustrator/comic book artist / concept artist. I have produced illustration and comic strip art for many publishing houses in London. Amongst them 2000AD - for whom I co - created comic characters; Bad Company, Bix Barton, The GrudgeFather, Kid Cyborg and worked on the popular Judge Dredd etc.

I have immersed myself in American music and culture. Resulting in my first researched book, which was published in the USA. Through Hal Leonard, this debut book was titled 'Voices Of Latin Rock,' It was the first book to examine in-depth - Santana, Latin Rock culture and the Mission District in San Francisco. From where this exciting, political and musical art form emerged. It features a Foreword by Carlos Santana. This innovative book resulted, in a ten - year series, of sizzling live shows in San Francisco, promoting Autism Awareness. These were given further credence, by appearances by Carlos Santana, the original Santana band, Booker 'T' Jones, The Doobie Brothers, Taj Mahal, Los Lobos, The Gregg Rolie Band, Sheila E, the political activist Dolores Huerta, Azteca, War, Sly Stone, George Clinton and many others.

I have produced a series of insightful, contemporary graphic novels, all linked to music subjects. The most recent published is 'Wake Up and Live,' Bob Marley. The others have examined cultural hot points - across the musical spectrum. Books; such as, 'Gabba Gabba Hey' The Ramones, 'Neverland' The Life And Death of Michael Jackson, 'Restless Lives': Guns N' Roses, 'Nothing Else Matters': Metallica, 'Godspeed': Kurt Cobain, 'Death Rap' Tupac Shakur, 'In My Skin': Eminem: The Sex Pistols Graphic, 'Who Are You': Keith Moon. Kurt Cobain Manga Edition, Sex Pistols, Manga Edition. Plus an Omnibus Press first - An original music story - the first published by Omnibus Press, 'Living For Kicks' A Mods Graphic Novel.'

My first book on Santana and Latin rock culture 'Voices of Latin Rock sold well. I followed it up, with a self-published Kindle Edition on Macasso Books, named 'Voices of Latin Rock: The E-Mix.' All new, an entirely separate book on this musical phenomena.

My books have published in the UK and the USA.
They have been translated and published, in the following foreign rights territories. Russia, Czechoslovakia, Spain, Norway, Italy, Poland, France, Croatia, Germany, Japan and Argentina. I have garnered much press and publicity in national and international newspapers, magazine articles and reviews about my published works. This includes a full-page feature in The New York Times recently. I am currently completing 'Flowers In The Rain.' A long overdue book about the "first punks" The Move.

Jim McCarthy Bibliography

Music Biographical Books / Graphic Novels
Voices of Latin Rock: The People and Events That Created This Sound. Hal Leonard. 2005,
Godspeed: The Kurt Cobain Graphic. 2005 and 2011.
Eminem: In My Skin Graphic, Omnibus Press, 2004,
Death Rap: Tupac Shakur – A Life. Omnibus Press, 2005,
Sex Pistols: The Graphic Novel: Omnibus Press, 2008,
Neverland: The Life and Death of Michael Jackson: Omnibus Press. 2012
Sex Pistols: The Graphic Novel, Manga edition. 2012.
Godspeed: The Kurt Cobain Graphic - Manga Edition: Omnibus Press. 2012.
Gabba Gabba Hey: The Ramones Graphic Novel. Omnibus Press. 2013.
Metallica: Nothing Else Matters. Omnibus Press. 2014.
Reckless Life: Guns And Roses. Omnibus Press. 2015.
Living For Kicks: A Mods Graphic Novel. Original story. Omnibus Press. 2016.
Who Are You? The Keith Moon Graphic. Omnibus. 2016.
Voices Of Latin Rock. The E-Mix Edition. 2017. (Macasso eBooks 1)
Wake Up And Live: The Bob Marley Graphic. Omnibus 2017.
Flowers In The Rain: The Untold Story of The Move: Wymer Publishing. 2024.

2000AD - Comic / Graphic collections
Bad Company: Goodbye Krool World. Rebellion. 2007.
Bad Company: Kano: Rebellion. 2007.
How To Draw Monsters For Kids (Search Press) 2012.
How To Draw Fantasy Creatures (Search Press) 2015.
The Complete Bad Company: Rebellion. 2011.
First Casualties; Bad Company trade paperback. 2016.
Bad Company -The Ultimate Collection.Volume One (Hardback) Rebellion. 2018.
Bad Company - The Ultimate Collection.Volume Two (Hardback) Rebellion. 2019.
2000AD Creator Interviews. (2000AD ebooks) 2015.
Bad Company -The Ultimate Collection.Volume One (Hardback) Rebellion. 2018.
Bad Company - The Ultimate Collection.Volume Two (Hardback) Rebellion. 2019.
2000 A.D. The Ultimate Collection: Hachette 2023.
2000 A.D. The Ultimate Collection: Hachette 2023.

Foreign Rights Editions
Godspeed: Une vie de Kurt Cobain.
Flammarion Books, (French) 2004.
Godspeed: The Kurt Cobain Graphic: Andante: Robinbook Editiones. (Italy) 2004.
Eminem - In My Skin. Andante: Robinbook Editiones. (Italy) 2004.
Eminem - En Mi Piel (Biografías De Las Estrellas Del Rock) (Spanish) Paperback. 2005.
Godspeed: The Kurt Cobain Graphic: Swarskopf & Swarskopf. (Hardback edition - Germany) 2005.
Eminem: Dans Ma Peau. City Editions. (French) Paperback. 2005.
2PAC Shakur - Death Rap: Sein Leben als Comic (German) Hardcover. 2006.
Kurt Cobain El Angel Erraco / Rock Star Biographies:(Spanish) Paperback. 2006.
Guns N' Roses / Tutta La Storia - A Fumetti! (Edition BD - Italy - Hardback) 2015.
Como disegnare Mostri. Il Castillo (Italian Edicione). 2014.
Como dibujar Monstrous. Edicione DRAC - (Madrid - Pain) 2018.
Metallica: Novela Grafica. Redbook Ediciones (Barcelona: Spain) 2017.
Ramones. Novela Grafica. Redbook Ediciones (Barcelona Spain) 2018.
Guns N' Roses Novela Grafica. Redbook Ediciones (Barcelona Spain) 2018.
Ramones. Graphic Novel. E/P/A Editiones. (France) 2018.
Bob Marley. Wake Up and Live. E/P/A Editiones. (France) 2018.
Bob Marley. Wake Up and Live. Redbook Ediciones. (Barcelona.Spain) 2018.
Sex Pistols. La Novela Grafica. Redbook Ediciones. (Barcelona. Spain) 2019
Keith Moon. La Novela Grafica. Redbook Ediciones. (Barcelona.Spain) 2019.
Godspeed. The Kurt Cobain Graphic. Redbook Ediciones (Barcelona Spain) 2020.
Novelas Gráficas del Rock: Metallica - Guns N' Roses - The Ramones. Non Troppo: Spain. 2021.

Appendices

Macasso Books: eBook imprint from Jim McCarthy
Voices Of Latin Rock. The E-Mix. (Macasso eBook 1) 2017.
iPhone Images - Volume One (Macasso eBook 2) 2019.
iPhone Images - Volume Two (Macasso eBook 3) 2019.
Digital Heart (Macasso eBook 4) 2019.
Sketch One. (Macasso eBook 5) 2019.
Sketch Two (Macasso eBook 6) 2019.
Lenny Wirral: Deptford Cowboys. (Macasso eBook 7) 2019.
Ditko: Volume One: Dark Triad.(Macasso eBook 8) 2020.
Ditko: Volume Two: The Psychomantheum. (Macasso eBooks 9) 2020.
Ditko: Volume Three: Red Rains Leviathan. (Macasso eBooks 10) 2020.
Trapped in Roseland: - An Aortic Romance. (Macasso eBooks 11) 2023.
ADHD: Addiction and Me. (Macasso eBook 12) 2024.
HEERO. Graphella One. (Macasso eBook 13) 2025.
HEERO. Graphella Two. (Macasso eBook 14) 2025.
HEERO. Graphella Three. (Macasso eBook 15) 2025.
Book of Revelation: (Macasso eBook 16). 2025.
PO- ET- REE: Selected works. (Macasso eBook 17). 2025

Social Media pages, resources and links

Robert Davidson Online: I Shot The Move.
Robert's webpage with his original photographs. As the main in-house photographer for the original Move band. On the payroll of the notorious manager Tony Secunda. Great photos on The Moody Blues, The Stones, The Action and the famous iconic shot of Frank Zappa and others.
https://davidsononline.co.uk/

Brum Beat:
Wonderful web page and resource run by John Woodhouse who is now domiciled in Canada. This has a great index of the major groups and acts, relating to Birmingham bands.
It also has relevant articles and features about the scene. Reviews of albums, books and news. Overall, it's a fresh looking, informative, deep dive for people who want a broad spectrum of information. On the ever-fascinating Birmingham music scene.
http://brumbeat.net/

Cherry Blossom Clinic: Facebook page.
Martin Kinch's long established Facebook page.
Full of rare info and interesting information (no pun intended). Interviews with all members of The Move, ELO and other veterans from the Birmingham scene. Highly recommended.
https://www.facebook.com/profile.php?id=100026982232389

Cherry Blossom Clinic Website.
Martin Kinch's website with tons of archived interviews with Carl Wayne, Roy Wood and members of ELO etc. The entire shebang — take a look around. Martin has been around The Move / ELO scene for absolutely eons.
https://www.cherryblossomclinic.x10.mx/

The Movement: Facebook page. Run by Greg Wetherby.
A more recent Facebook page with a healthy turnaround of rare and interesting pictures of The Move and other related items. Again, another recommended Facebook resource.
https://www.facebook.com/groups/1768121623552108

Useless Information: Move information.
This was a Move – ELO information page. An archive which still exists online.
Link unavailable at present.

Yesterdays Papers
Tightly edited and excellent set of YouTube videos. Including some great stuff on The Move, whom Yesterday Papers really loves. One Move video included is top notch and is called *'The Band That Got Sued by Prime Minister Harold Wilson.'* Other stuff on The Move, The Action and the overall 'psychedelic' scene in 1966 / 67 / 68 / 69 etc. Well worth a visit and your subscription.
https://www.youtube.com/@YesterdaysPapers/videos

Flowers In The Rain - The Untold Story of The Move

Garage Hangover – The Move gigs.
For those of you who need a good comprehensive Move gig list overview. This appears to be the very best place - I have seen on the internet.
https://garagehangover.com/the-move-gigs-1966-1970/

Man In The Clinic.
Martin Kinch *(Also see above at Cherry Blossom Clinic)* YouTube channel with tons of Move stuff. Move related videos and ELO videos and rarities. Plus; two recent and very welcome Ace Kefford interviews from 2024. Plus, a nice Ace Christmas message.
https://www.youtube.com/@manintheclinic

Psych Road Vaults:
A nice selection of Ace Kefford rough demos.
Actually seven in total with Ace on vocals and his Gibson Jumbo acoustic. Showing some rough gems
that could have surfaced as finished songs. Recorded at 'Interberga', the cottage in the village of Inkberrow where Ace lived with his wife Jenny, throughout the 1970s and into the 1980s. Put together by Nicola and Melvin Hancox.
https://www.youtube.com/@psychrdvaults5367

The Melvin Hancox Band
Cooking music trio, led by guitarist Melvin Hancox. Managed by his wife Nicola Hancox, the daughter of Reg Jones. One of the two Jones brothers, the other being Chris. They were both Ace Kefford's uncles. The celebrated Birmingham brothers, who led The Way Of Life and more for years. Including The Band of Joy, Prima Donna, Gritt and other bands.
https://www.themelvinhancoxband.co.uk

ELO-Devi
Another mostly ELO and Jeff Lynne centred YouTube platform. With some nice rarities. Like The Move, Roy, Bev and Ace (and guitarist Mike Hopkins). The Move get together at the Locarno Ballroom in 1981.
https://www.youtube.com/@elodevi

The Official Carl Wayne website.
Run by Helen Macdonald. Both a tribute and some interesting interviews photos, lots of information on the much-missed Carl.
http://www.carlwayne.co.uk/

In Memory of Carl Wayne.
Memorial to the fabulous vocalist and the original and much missed lead singer of The Move. Another resource run by Helen MacDonald.
https://www.facebook.com/people/In-Memory-of-Carl-Wayne/100027716421705/

Streets of Birmingham.
Des Tong drives Bev Bevan around the streets of Birmingham. They informally discuss the history, the musicians, the places (The Move). A fun, absorbing and info - packed drive. Here is a link to the first part. There are three parts in total. All well worth watching.
https://www.youtube.com/watch?v=n1zZaV6RyIg&t=5s

Birmingham: A City Rooted in Talent
The Move's musical and cultural contribution to Birmingham and the UK is recognised in this documentary. Produced by Contrary Trees Productions Ltd. This includes filmed interviews with Bev Bevan.
https:www.youtube.com@ContraryTreesProductions-tq2tp)

The Bev Bevan Official Website.
The official webpage of celebrated drummer Bev Bevan. His impressive career encompasses Denny Laine and The Diplomats, The Move, all incarnations of ELO, Black Sabbath, Paul Weller and more. Bev is currently the drummer with Quill.
https://www.bevbevanofficial.com/

Bev Bevan Facebook Page.
Quite simply - the Bev Bevan page on Facebook. Go and check it out.
https://www.facebook.com/bevbevannews

Quill - with Bev Bevan.
Quill is a six - piece group, from Birmingham UK. They play a blend of Rock, Folk and Americana. 2023 saw the band celebrate a 50 year long career. Coinciding with the launch of a brand new line-up. Including legendary Brum drummer Bev Bevan. Known all over the world, as a member of ELO, The Move and Black Sabbath.
https://www.quilluk.com/

Appendices

The Roy Wood Official Website
The official website of Dr Roy Wood himself.
The writer of a mighty twenty-two hit records.
A truly unique music original, never to be replicated.
https://www.roywood.co.uk/

Roy Wood: Facebook Page.
Roy Wood's dedicated Facebook page.
https://www.facebook.com/DrRoyWood/

Countdown of Roy Wood's 20 biggest hits.
Just like it says on the video.
https://www.youtube.com/watch?v=BHK3-rJ-PDs

The Shazam:
The Shazam are an American band, led by Hans Rotenberry and directly influenced by The Move. They are based in Nashville, Tennessee. They performed with Carl Wayne and Bev Bevan at Abbey Road Studios in 2000. Performing 'Beautiful Daughter' and 'Grass Grow.'
https://theshazam.com/

Des Tong: Life Stories with Des Tong.
Web page featuring interviews with Trevor Burton,
Bev Bevan, 'Big Albert' Chapman and more Birmingham related videos.
https://www.youtube.com/@destongTV

Jim McCarthy: Writer, Artist and Conceptualist.
I always knew that The Move biography, had my name on it. So, it came to pass. It was written, before it was too late. I am reinventing myself, after this historic book's completion. It has been a labour of love and a real blessing. Thanks for the opportunity to tell this unique, fated story. I hope it intrigues, educates and inspires you… As the original Move did for me.
https://www.jimmccarthy.co.uk/

Flowers In The Rain - The Untold Story of The Move